BiG SNEAKY BARBARiAN

BOOK 3

Big Sneaky Barbarian
Book 3

Seth McDuffee

Podium

To the single constant in my life,
my twin flame, the one who raised me,
and who I hope to one day share a plate of pancakes with:
Weird Al Yankovic

All rights reserved. No part of this publication may be reproduced, stored in a retrieval system, or transmitted in any form or by any means electronic, mechanical, photocopying, recording, or otherwise without prior written permission from Podium Publishing.

This is a work of fiction. Names, characters, places, and incidents are either products of the author's imagination or used fictitiously. Any resemblance to actual events, locales, or persons, living, dead, or undead, is entirely coincidental.

Copyright © 2023 by Seth McDuffee

Cover design by Leah Kochevar

ISBN: 978-1-0394-4081-4

Published in 2023 by Podium Publishing
www.podiumaudio.com

Big Sneaky Barbarian
Book 3

FIRST OVERTURE

Once deemed regal and fierce, the tiger lay in perpetual boredom and fear within the walls of the dilapidated zoo. Its days were spent in a cage that felt—though it had no word for it—like a prison, as it paced back and forth in a ritual of despair, longing for a life that it had never truly known.

The tiger did not understand the concept of captivity, but it knew it was not free. The humans that brought it food were faceless feeders. The strange shiny animals that cleaned its enclosure were a source of constant noise and disruption. The tiger had tried to bat at them before, but the thin, impervious vines it was forced to remain behind had seen to it that it could not reach. It had labored instead to growl and act very intimidating so that the creatures would know it did not appreciate their presence.

There was one human that the tiger had grown to love. A simple caretaker who brought it toys and treats and talked to it in a voice that was gentle and kind. The tiger longed for freedom, but it also longed for the caretaker's company. Each day of his arrival, for it was not every day, was a joyful one. His existence was a comfort, and the tiger liked that the human was furry at its muzzle and sported a tail from the rear of his head. Sometimes, he would be gone for many days at a time, though the tiger did not mind—for when he returned, he'd always bring extra food. The tiger only minded on days when there were not many anxious visiting humans because the man would bring the angled-shape object that made the loud noises. He'd mewl, growl, and roar along with it, speaking to the tiger as though offering explanations. Though the creature thought that perhaps this activity brought the human joy, so it resigned itself to being tolerant.

Some days, the human was visited himself, and the tiger did not have the capability to understand what some might consider irony. His guest was always the same: a woman. She had the same faint smell of the man on her, and the tiger reasoned that perhaps they were a part of the same streak. The familiar scent made the creature agreeable to the woman. However, she always seemed frightened of the tiger and never entered the enclosure despite the man's coaxing. The tiger thought that was likely for the best—the fear confused it, and it did not know what it might do were the woman to get too close. Despite this, the visits were infrequent and always brief. That was fine for the tiger; it much preferred to be undisturbed.

However, all joyous things must come to an end.

The tiger did not know that the day the human brought it many treats and stayed long after the sun had disappeared and night had blanketed them that it would be the last time it would see him. It sensed pain in the man. This frightened the tiger, and it snarled at him, the only time it had ever done so. After his visit, the tiger never saw the man again. The tiger knew this had to be because it had reacted the way it had, and the sense of loneliness closed in on it.

The visitors to the zoo had dwindled, and the tiger was left alone for hours on end, dreaming of the days when there were other tigers in the enclosure. It remembered the sounds of their growls and the feeling of their fur against its own. It dreamed of the kind man and his treats and his toys. It dreamed of being free. With each passing day, his scent faded further until, at times, the tiger wasn't sure it could smell him at all. All of these things it wished for and none of those things would it have. Now it was alone, with only the incessant hum of the shiny creatures to keep it company.

The tiger grew hungrier. It was fed less and less frequently, and when it was given food, the portions were meager. The tiger did not like this much at all, and it resolved to leave.

One day, during a torrential rainstorm, as one of the faceless caretakers abandoned it to escape the downpour, the tiger noticed that the gates to the enclosure were left ajar. This had never happened before, and it filled the creature with a confusing sensation. Hope. The tiger sensed its chance, and with a sudden burst of energy, it leaped out of its prison and ran as fast as it could. The rain lashed at its fur, and the wind whipped through the trees, but the tiger was free and felt more alive than it ever had before. The rain brought out the man's scent, and the tiger thought it might follow the smell and find him. Though, were it too far gone, the creature would instead make its home somewhere outside the zoo, where it could roam, hunt, and *live*.

The tiger escaped.

It ran through the streets, dodging animals and humans, reveling in the sensation of the wind in its face and the pounding of its paws on the pavement. But the world outside the zoo was busier than it had ever imagined, and copious were the large metal predators that prowled the passages of this larger world. The tiger became frightened. Despite its hunger and loneliness, it was a proud beast, a creature of vast intellect and strength. It knew it could make its way to the jungles beyond this chaos if only it could navigate the screams and jeers and smells and dangers. However, some of the screeching, caterwauling monsters beyond were as large as the big gray beasts with trumpeting faces near its enclosure. And they moved faster than even the tiger was capable of.

One of these colossal creatures struck the tiger, its body tumbling through the air until it crashed to the ground.

When the tiger opened its eyes, it found itself in a strange and wondrous place.

As the tiger stirred, it discovered that it had departed from the tumultuous bustle of the human settlement and arrived in a luscious, flourishing forest. The atmosphere was thick with the aroma of greenery, and the ground beneath was plush and damp. The tiger could hear the sweet symphony of birds tweeting, insects buzzing, and water flowing nearby. As the tiger stood up, it realized its hunger had vanished, and its wounds were inexplicably mended.

The tiger slunk through the forest, investigating its newfound liberty and delighting in the joy of this new natural realm. It no longer needed to fret about being locked in a cramped cage or suffering from too little food. Rather, this place was teeming with abundant sources of nourishment and water, and the tiger was free to explore wherever it pleased.

The tiger remembered its old life almost as if waking from a terrible nightmare. The one it would no longer be a victim to. It knew that it would never go back to the zoo. It was free and happy, and nothing would ever change that.

But, of course, that changed suddenly with the arrival of the creature. Like a large, burbling bubble of water it had appeared, swimming with oceanic depths and clouds—all very confusing to the tiger. But the tiger was proud and brave, endeavoring to be unafraid of this new beast.

When the thing spoke to the tiger . . . the tiger was made to *understand*.

Pathways unlocked in its cognizance, furrowed by the beast's words. For the first time in all of its life, the tiger understood another being fully. From this new breakthrough, the tiger learned of the beast's purpose, and what its own trials would be. As the tiger listened intently to the shimmering creature, it came to understand that there was much about the world it had not known. The creature told the tiger that it had the opportunity to choose its own existence, to be as it wanted to truly be. For the first time in its life, the tiger felt a sense of hope and wonder that stretched beyond its limited experience. It was a dizzying sensation, and the tiger was both overwhelmed and fascinated by the possibilities laid out before it.

The shimmering creature asked the tiger if it wished to remain in its current form—a powerful, beautiful, and regal beast—or if it desired to become something different, something that could perceive the world in a new way and experience a variety of sensations, movements, and functions. The tiger pondered the question, and for a moment, its mind drifted to a form other than its own, something it had never considered before.

The form the tiger envisioned was one grown of love. Taught to it through kindness and compassion, even when it was trapped within the den of the zoo. It wanted more than anything to embrace this form and delight in its presence. The tiger thought about how this form might help it forge connections with others, to befriend them, and to learn from their perspectives. Perhaps, in this new form, it could find the understanding it craved and be free from the loneliness that had plagued it for so long.

With a sense of resolution and excitement, the tiger decided to embrace this new form. It felt as if it were stepping out of its skin, shedding its old self, and emerging anew. The shimmering creature seemed to understand the tiger's choice and prompted it further, asking what path it would like to follow in this new existence.

The tiger could not comprehend the physical words the creature spoke, but it felt the intent behind them. As the connection between the two deepened, the tiger grasped the notion of choosing its own destiny. It began to understand that it could choose which aspects of its new form to enhance, which qualities to refine and develop.

The tiger knew that it was already cunning, more so than others of its kind. Yet it yearned for more flexibility in its mental behaviors, to learn how to form connections and bonds with others so that it would never be abandoned again. It wanted to be more than just a powerful predator; it sought the ability to navigate the complexities of a world it had never known.

The shimmering creature acknowledged the tiger's desires and guided it through the process of selecting and strengthening the traits it wished to cultivate. The tiger felt its mind grow sharper, nimbler, and more capable of understanding the nuances of the world around it. Its heart swelled with the promise of new experiences and relationships as it embraced this potential.

As the metamorphosis transpired, the tiger found themselves enveloped in a world replete with nuance and richness, as if the veil of their previous life had been lifted to reveal a vibrant tapestry of existence. Their senses, once geared towards the primal instincts of a predator, were now attuned to the subtle intricacies of the world that had been obscured from them. The sights, sounds, and scents that once served as mere indicators of prey or danger now carried layers of meaning and beauty beyond their previous comprehension.

The transformation had granted them not only a new form but also an expanded consciousness. They came to understand that the choices they had made were in the crafting of a body and the selection of a path—a Class, as it were. The development of their Intelligence, Wisdom, and Charisma had imbued them with a heightened understanding of their surroundings and a capacity for empathy and connection that had been beyond their grasp as a mere beast.

Yet with this enlightenment came a new understanding: shame. The simplicity of their origins now appeared to them as a limitation, a hindrance that had held them back from the true exaltation of their being. They could not help but mourn the decisions made from ignorance and the life they had led as a captive creature, devoid of the complexity and depth they now experienced.

In their new form, they stood upright, nearly bereft of fur, and for the first time, they began to perceive the world with a clarity that both enthralled and daunted them. They possessed the ability to understand, yet they did not *know*—for their life had been that of a beast. The knowledge of stalking prey and stretching claws held little relevance to them now, as they were no longer a creature of stealth and predation. Instead, they bore hands capable of creation rather than solely destruction, appendages that could shape the world around them in ways they had never before imagined.

This ascent to a higher plane of understanding felt akin to walking in the footsteps of a deity, only to discover that the god they had once revered was, in truth, diminutive and inconsequential. The magnitude of this realization weighed heavily upon them, yet it also imbued them with a sense of purpose and determination to forge a new path—one that embraced the depth and complexity of the world they now inhabited.

Thus, they embarked on a journey of discovery and self-realization, seeking to learn, to grow, and to truly understand the realm of wonders they had been granted access to. And with each step, they left the shadow of their former life further behind, embracing that which lay before them.

In their new form, they soon discovered that the world beyond was unkind to those such as themselves. They encountered others like them, and others who were not quite like them but bore a close-enough resemblance to cause confusion. These beings were not kind; they turned against them, cheated them, lied to them, and even resorted to physical violence. It seemed as if some even *enjoyed* the suffering they gifted to them, languishing the act with peals of joy.

So, the once-tiger fretted.

The transition from a powerful predator to a vulnerable, conscientious being had left them ill equipped for the harsh realities of this new world. But not for long.

Eventually, they realized the true potential of their intellect, designed for absorbing information at an astonishing rate. They learned—anything and everything, and with remarkable speed. They honed their mind and sharpened their cunning, growing stronger in their mental prowess.

In time, the knowledge of their old world, once deemed useless, was pertinent once again and began to inform their actions and elevate them above their circumstances. They learned not only how to survive but also how to thrive, excelling beyond the ordinary means. For what were the most successful of this new kind if not predators? And this one had *been* a predator.

Over time, they gathered others under their wing, forming a community of like-minded individuals who looked up to them for guidance and wisdom.

Just when it seemed as though things could not be any more perfect in this new world, after years of honing their skills and doing what they did best . . . they encountered something else. Something that sent their understanding of what it was like to be the top of the pile in this new world crashing to the earth and buried beneath the silt. A being that changed the once-forlorn concept formulated in their changing mind—and again they were following in the footpaths behind a god.

The Drifter.

This figure changed them—the course of their life; setting them on a path they could not have foreseen.

The Drifter challenged them, tested their mettle, and pushed them to confront the limits of their abilities. In the process, they came to understand the true nature of the world they inhabited and the potential for both good and evil that lay within themselves and those around them. This avaricious domain within which the Drifter taught them was wholly unwell, but it was a purifying fire—and by the might of the gods, was it a thrilling discovery to temper oneself in that all-consuming flame and emerge from the other side.

Faced with these revelations, they were forced to question all at its most fundamental core, to grapple with the dichotomy of existence—once a beast, then a creature of intellect and empathy, now on the path to their own ascension beyond the understanding they had ever known. The Drifter's influence cast all in a barren light of transparency, unearthing the truth behind every atom in the shifting shawl of certainty. Compelling them, urging them to navigate the complexities of their identity and the ever-shifting landscape of the world they inhabited. Lo, they were mighty.

With each step forward, they left an indelible mark on the world and on those who crossed their path, transforming not only themselves but also the very fabric of the reality they inhabited. They became something much more, and further still, they burned with a *purpose*. They would know *truth* and they would know what the Drifter sought, and they would glean the most precious treasure this world had to offer. It might only take but time. However, time, for them, was a most plentiful creature indeed.

And so, they began to plan.

PROLOGUE

A TILT OVER TITLES

"Grab the banner!" the woman screamed, her voice raw from doing so for hours.

She ducked under a sword swing and returned one of her own, the blade of her steel biting hard into the leather-clad shoulder of the elf—or was he half?—that had tried to separate her bones from her spirit. He cried out as blood sprayed up in a gout, drenching the both of them. The woman yanked on the handle of her weapon, ripping the edge from its fleshy sheath and leveling a kick to the man's hip that sent him crumbling to the ground. She flipped the blade, bringing it down in a grievous, life-ending thrust before peering back at her legion.

Sweat and blood streamed down her forehead and into her eyes, but she'd long grown used to the sensation enough to ignore it for the din of battle. She was submerged in a sea of writhing, gnashing, clamoring bodies, each existing as a commingling of fear and blood lust as they battered and cut and broke and bashed against one another in the slop of combat. Every gabion, every parapet, every buttress and other structure in the sprawling acre-sized courtyard of the fortification was confessedly *lousy* with fighting folk. As their commander, she had caused it. Then the volley began.

She moved like lightning, a blur of silver and steel, dodging and weaving between streams of magic. The air around her crackled with energy as bolts of lightning and blasts of fire surged toward her. But she was too quick, her blade a shimmering arc that easily deflected each attack.

It was harrowing. But she was not afraid. She was a warrior, forged in the heat of battle, honed by years of conflict. And she would not be defeated by a handful of mages. Instead of fear, she felt . . . exhilaration. A natural sensation of belonging. Ever since she first stepped forth into the dirt and muck of this strange earth, she'd felt more at home than she ever had. And never more than when there was fighting to be had.

She darted forward, her sword leading the way. The mages recoiled, their spells faltering as they realized her attack's sheer speed and ferocity. She struck with unerring precision, her blade flashing like silver fire as she cut them down one by one.

Their magic was no match for her skill, and as the last of them fell, she took a moment to catch her breath, her chest heaving as she surveyed the battlefield. The mages were gone, but there were more enemies to face and more immediate battles to be won.

She squinted. She spotted the standard on a hill high overhead, tattered and torn but still clinging to the goddamned pole.

"Grab the *fucking* banner!" she screamed again, drawing another several eyes to her location. Men and women bent in the crook of vengeance, goats all, hungry to take down the wolf that had invaded their buck shed. The woman sneered and lifted her sword—a golden-hilted beauty with a perfect, silvery sheen to the blade—even now, caked with blood.

"As you will, then, cretins," she barked at them. "But you'd best kill me from afar. I'm a menace up close."

There was no smirk, growl, or returning of words from the four who faced her, only unvarnished, grim advancement. The woman took quick stock of them. A dwarf, haggard, tired, favoring one leg over the other, his knuckles curled around the handle of a sword with a chipped edge. A half-elf, lightly armored, no helmet or gorget, a slim spear held firm in the right hand but wedged tight between the elbow and her flank on her left. A human, a sword in either grip, her armor dented and covered in viscera, her eyes hard beneath her conical helm, a scar crossing her grimacing lips. Lastly, a large young man hardly older than a boy, his kingdom tabard still crisp green and unblemished by blood or grime—likely fresh to the assault—his only weapon a pair of iron clasps and a long coil of chain.

They mean to take me prisoner, then? the woman thought. *That's unfortunate for them.*

Having taken their accounts, she stole one step back to allow her Ability to work its magic. She'd used it recently, though she wasn't sure if it would be too soon. The cooldown was ten minutes. That could have been mere moments or hours before; one could never know for certain in the midst of fighting—and she had no time to check her menu. The woman in the abused armor with two swords was the most dangerous, then the dwarf, then the spear-wielder. The child wasn't a worry. They drew themselves into the area she affected, and when they did, she pounced. Her Ability caused a flash to go off around her feet as she sprang into the air. The hardened woman with scarred lips was unimpressed, but the other three's eyes grew wide. But it was too late for them. The scar-faced fighter brought one blade up in a slashing arc, going for the commander's legs while her off-hand weapon remained close to defend her body. But the commander had reckoned two-swords was seasoned in battle and would perform thusly. The raw-voiced woman brought her own sword down to counter the swipe, and the metals rang loudly as they met. But her gold-and-silver sword shoved scarface's aside toward her swing, and she stumbled.

She landed hard in the churned-up earth next to her foe, abandoning her momentarily and flashing toward the dwarf, who had no time to bring his own weapon up as she feinted a jab at his face. He stepped back on his stronger leg, and she pivoted her sword to crash against his weakened knee, and he went down with a scream in a tangle of his limbs. Then she slid forward on her own knees under the waiting strike of a spear point and hacked the end off it before jamming her mailed fist into the half-elf woman's solar plexus. The half-elf doubled over, and the commander chopped into her unprotected trapezius and jugular. She heard heavy movement and spun, keeping her sword diagonal across her body and blocking the unseen slice of the other warrior woman who'd recovered from her unbalancing. The commander pressed the other fighter's blade down and swiped to the right to catch her second blade with a heavy blow, forcing it to spring back and opening the woman up to an attack. Her torso was protected, so instead, she chopped at the wrist holding the first blade, hearing a tremendous *crack* as the bones broke within the armored gauntlet.

The warrior cried out through clenched teeth, striking again with her healthy arm. But it was too slow and the other woman too strong. She ducked, the swipe passing harmlessly overhead as she slammed her pauldron into the woman's rib cage with all the might and ferocity she could muster with her shoulder. The warrior fell, and the woman quickly arrested her ascent by slamming a boot down on her neck. Soon, all that remained was the boy. He was big but untested, and the woman knew it. Her Ability faded, but so had his spirits. He backed away, seeing his protectors killed or otherwise maimed. The women let him flee. She did not kill children.

Unassailed momentarily, the woman glared at the arrogantly fluttering ensign still atop the hill. Spotting her subordinate, she roared in his direction with a voice nearly empty of sound.

"Voder! You son of a fucker—tear down that banner!"

The man paused mid-murder of a soldier and looked in her indicated direction before returning to her with a nod.

"Yes, Commander!" he barked back.

She sighed.

The captain led several men to do as she bid, and she continued fighting.

Less than twenty minutes afterward, the fight was finished. The woman breathed heavily, adrenaline still pulsing through her veins, her sword arm raised as if ready to strike again. She looked around and saw her bloodied but barely battered legion, triumphant in their victory. They looked at her with reverence and awe as if they had just witnessed a miracle.

But this was no miracle. This was pure, unadulterated strength. Voder and his men returned, the banner in their grasp flailing against the wind as they offered it to her. She lowered her sword and approached the standard, taking it in her hands. Then she raised it above her head, letting the torn cloth flutter in the wind again, symbolizing their dominion over the body-strewn battlefield.

The legion gathered around her, cheering and shouting, their voices hoarse from the hours of fighting. But as she looked upon their faces, she saw joy and pride in their prowess. They had fought and persevered, and at a cost so stunningly small, it was almost negligible.

She let the banner drop to the ground, a token tribute to the few fallen. The legion fell silent, their cheers dying away as they, too, remembered the cost of their victory, but only for a moment. This was a time for celebration, to revel in their strength and bask in the glory of their success.

"Speech!" her men shouted. "Give us a speech!"

The woman smirked. Then she turned to her legion and spoke with iron and pleasure. "We are the destruction of these oppressors. The victors. The just. The enemy may have fallen, but their mewling cries will forever linger as a reminder of our creed. We lost few, but their sacrifices will be remembered and celebrated. We stand here, our swords raised, our annexed banner waving, a symbol of our small triumph over death and destruction. His Majesty's mightiest—the king's backwash, more like—will tremble at the mention of our name, for we are the conquerors, the masters of this battlefield. Corpse-makers. Remember this day, for it is a day of victory, a day of glory, a day of our rebuke. Redmark!"

The legion nodded, their faces alight with pride, and they returned the call of *Redmark* with vigor. There was no mourning there, only domination's afterbirth. And so, with heads held high, they made their way into the broken gates of the inner halls of the fortification, the banner trailing behind them, their feet crunching over the broken stone and splintered wood.

The walls were stained with the blood of the fallen, a beautiful ode to the brutal nature of their battle. The woman felt a rush of excitement as she surveyed her new domain, the fruits of her victory laid out before her.

Her men fanned out, plundering the place of anything of value. They tore down the banners of the Royal Army, defacing their emblem, and claimed their spoils as their own. All the while, the woman looked on with the same satisfied contentment crawling across her face. She moved through the halls, nearly numb with joy, stepping over rubble as she made her way to the small room outfitted as their enemy's command center.

It's hardly larger than a bedroom, she thought. *No wonder they lost so soundly; you couldn't fit half a strategy in here.*

Some of her men followed in behind her. Though she didn't think it was necessarily wise, she didn't stop them as they ransacked the room, dumping the contents of shelves and cabinets onto the floor in search of anything of value. They'd earned it. Their commander stood in the center, surveying the chaos with a smile. They had won. *She* had won, and nothing would stop her from claiming what was rightfully hers.

And then she saw it, a box with the royal crest emblazoned upon its top. Her heart racing, she approached the box, her hand shaking as she reached for the latch. The lid fell open with a snap, and she cackled triumphantly before closing it again.

"Is this what victory looks like?" she wondered, her voice ringing out over the room.

"Commander Fawn," said a voice, and she turned to see Lieutenant Sir Penheart slipping into the chamber. She raised an eyebrow.

"Yes?"

"Chessit is back, Commander," the man said dourly. She'd have been more concerned by his tone, but he was always dolorous when he wasn't the most crucial topic of concern.

"So soon?" she wondered aloud, not particularly to Penheart, but he seemed to think it wise to respond.

"He has zun Gara in tow," Penheart said stiffly.

Fawn bristled.

"*Sir* Penheart," she said carefully, "I am surprised to hear someone of your stature forgetting themselves so easily. Really? Shall we try that again?"

This lack of respect had been hashed and rehashed ad nauseum for the last few months. The commander was tired of each smarmy, cavalier, nearly offhanded approach to this former trusted knight of the realm's omissions. They built up over time, feeling as though they were completely disregarding her own station and causing her no end of frustration. Each piling on top of one another until she felt her bandwidth for tolerance was truly frayed to the final hairs. She thought she remembered a term bubbling into her mind—*microaggression*. That was a term the younger generation had used . . . well, *before*. Perhaps she had it wrong, but she thought that maybe that was what this was, but she'd never been particularly mindful of whatever hot buzzword people used.

Now she silently wished she'd paid more attention to diffusion methods of such a tactic rather than just waving away the term whole cloth.

"With all due respect, Commander," Penheart said, "I do not ascribe to those . . . designations. We are not fighting for the sake of titles and rank but for the greater good. As you well know, I am of the belief that using articles of gentry only serves to reinforce the oppressive system we are trying to overthrow. Perhaps, as rebels, we would be better off without them?"

He gave her a smug smile.

"You forget yourself *again*, Sir Penheart!" Fawn snapped suddenly, and the man instantly clammed up. "How *dare* you speak to me in that fashion? As if I've somehow forgotten the fucking point of our endeavors. The use of titles isn't just about formality. It's about honor. About respect and that which drives us forward. We are not just a group of *rebels—Sir Penheart*—we are a noble brotherhood fighting for the right to live in a just society. And by using the proper address, we honor that fraternity and the cause we serve."

She glared at him silently for a moment to watch him squirm under her gaze. Then, quietly, she continued.

"Despite your claims of . . . whatever it is you think might be a virtuous cause, I suspect you simply do not want to give acquiescence to his established rank because of his origins."

Now it was Penheart's turn to bristle.

"Commander," he said icily. "I care little as to his being a *matau*; I am only—"

"You know precisely what I refer to, Sir Penheart," Fawn interrupted.

"I only postulate that—"

"You do a *lot* of fucking postulating, it seems, Sir Penheart—I wonder if you can even spell the word?"

Penheart stared at her for a long moment.

"Well, there you have it," she said. "You should spend less time on your irrelevant contention and instead preoccupy your bother with being a bountiful member of this retinue. Your singular requirement in our ranks is that you *do your duty* . . . *and* one of those gainful commissions is in referring to your fellows with propriety. If that is something *trying* to your silky sentiments, then I shall be more than agreeable to see you are relieved of your posts, and you can fuck off and be a *sir* in someone else's periphery. Now. Will that be too burdensome for your delicate disposition, or are you done being a curmudgeonly bitch?"

There was a long, awkward void between the two, a yawning chasm. The moment of tension continued building between them until finally, with a heavy *ahem*, Penheart spoke.

"As you will, Commander," he said, his voice laced with resignation. "I will address the rest of this lot with their proper godsdamned titles."

Fawn smirked, her eyes glittering with victory, but quickly turned her attention to the matter at hand.

"What did Chessit discover?" she demanded impatiently.

The fact that Akiva zun Gara was there was . . . interesting, but she'd need to hold off on that for the moment. Chessit had been on a mission. Returning with the matau was unusual but wasn't outside the realm of possibility. She'd need to speak with zun Gara about his whereabouts and what he'd been up to in the previous weeks. Until Penheart had entered the room grimly, the matau was presumed dead, but they'd not found his body anywhere.

One mystery solved, she thought.

Penheart hesitated momentarily as if weighing whether he should continue the argument before relenting.

"Scouts have uncovered a new supply route used by those bastards," he growled. "It is fortified like damnable hell, but Chessit believes we can lie in ambush and enact fabulous fucking chaos."

Fawn's eyes lit up with a fierce intensity, the thrill of potential battle coursing through her.

"Lovely," she said. "We will need to plan properly, but if Chessit thinks there is a way, there are probably seven others he plans to keep to himself. In either case, it is a solid opportunity."

Sir Penheart nodded, his determination unwavering. "Assuming you are not too cross with me over the title nonsense . . . I will lead this mission if you allow it, Commander. We will drop on them like rain and kick those assholes in the teeth."

Fawn smirked, a hint of admiration in her expression. "Do not be too . . . bold, Lieutenant. This cannot be a haphazard affair, or we will all end up as fucking martyrs."

Penheart grinned back, a glint of mischief in his eyes. "Worry not, Commander. I am not that damned stupid."

Fawn rolled her eyes. "Do not forget your place, Sir Penheart."

Penheart chuckled, his voice light and carefree. "I will try, Commander. But I promise naught."

He raised a brow.

". . . and zun Gara?"

Catching the hard flints of her eyes, he sighed again.

"Apologies, Commander," he said, and then more slowly, "what would you like me to do with *Margrave* zun Gara?"

"Send him in, of course—Chessit first, however," she said with a smirk, her subordinate finally falling in line. "I am sure he has much to report."

Sir Penheart simply grumbled and looked as though he might protest again, but she waved her mailed hand at him. At that, he turned and strode out of the room. Fawn watched him go, a confusing mix of exasperation and pride twisting inside her. She knew that Penheart was a valuable ally—even if he was an egregious little shit. Despite their clashes, she was grateful to have him by her side in battle.

A minute's worth of heartbeats later, a big, stocky frame scuffled into the commandeered command center, a crescent of teeth splitting weather-beaten features.

"An' here ye sit in ye magnanimous resplendence," Chessit said. "Didn't take ye long, seems, t'wrest the illustrious Shalewinter from sun-bleached kingdom cleavage."

"Welcome back, Chessit," Fawn said, rolling her eyes at his words. "I'd a cold longing for your crudely suggestive allegory. The word is that you bring good tidings?"

Chessit looked surprised that she already knew, then snorted.

"Seems Penheart's still the camp gossip," he returned.

Fawn chuckled.

"He hasn't an inch of willpower in that regard," she said. "But, please, allow him his small indulgences."

Chessit came to a lean next to where she stood, his shoulder pressed against the wall's fresh paint the others had used to mark out one of the kingdom banners on the wall. It smudged, but that didn't matter—this bastion had been liberated and would soon fly their colors anyway.

"Like what ye've done with this hovel," he said. "Pretty—mayhap, were me proclivities wont to suggest such a notion."

"Newly christened from conquest, and without a stitch of proper paper to plaster the wall with," said Fawn. "Now . . . the tidings?"

"*Tidings* bein' an unusually auspicious term in this instance," he continued. "Definitely got a mind to pour some gravy over a few o' the less-usual accounts the matau's servin' up—but, aye, good tidings all the same."

"Why does it always return to food with you, Chessit?" Fawn asked, tucking the discovered box away into her pack. "I have never met anyone so obsessed with the concept."

"Ah," Chessit said, some of his warm humor returning. "Because it's the only thing in me whole life that's never led me astray—save that time we stumbled afoul of them purple berries 'twere north of that lake in Hathburia. Ye remember?"

"Oh, goodness, Chessit! How tired you must find my recollections. Of course I recall. It may have been nearly ten years ago, but one never misplaces the memory of the first time a friend projectile-vomits on them from the branches of a tree twenty feet above."

Chessit winked.

"Just me way of flirtin', lass."

Fawn tittered like tinkling bells before realization settled on her. Her face went stony with the business necessary to discuss

"We can discuss previous adventures at length another time, perhaps. You've found the Margrave?"

"Aye," Chessit said, removing a knife from his belt and casually chipping at the dirt beneath his fingernails with the point. "Got a mighty oak of a tale under his helmet, as well."

"Oh?"

"More like 'Oh, *shit*,' truth be the tellin'."

"Well, will you be gifting me a preview, or will it require needling our esteemed guest with interrogation?"

"I'll cede him to do the dirty justice of his yarn, but, aye—I'll spoil a bit for ye. It concerns the orc that ran you through the armpit with that coat hook."

Fawn's furious gaze could have melted granite.

"See him in," she hissed.

"Yes, marm."

As she waited, a notification popped up in her vision. It was a System message.

Fawn's eyes scanned the contents of the prompt, and she raised an eyebrow.

"A Quest?"

However, when she reached the end, her brows had knitted themselves into a furrow.

This isn't good, she thought to herself.

CHAPTER ONE

CAMP NOWHERE

Boy, oh boy.

Let me tell you something, homies. It absolutely sucks to think you've finally made it to a place of respite only to have everything turn upside down the moment you make it. Like swimming up for air and when you reach the surface inhaling a gallon of snot, instead. That's what it was like arriving in this encampment.

I'd been looking forward to seeing the gang—you know, the crew who'd been haphazardly jettisoned from good ol' Earth and into . . . whatever the hell this world was. I mean, sure, I know it's called Regaia, but like . . . what *is* it? It wasn't a normal world. It was fantasy and junk. But, like, *bad.* I mean—in my esteemed and venerable opinion, *all* fantasy is bad; but this was worse. It had *math.*

To get you up to speed, I'd just survived a night of horrors in a city under siege by giant centipede creatures and fought off death—*again*—just to catch a glimmer of hope in the idea that I could meet up with the others from my world. Only when we got here, we saw the whole place was a smoking ruin.

So, yeah, a big, hot mouthful o' mucus.

Fuckin' best of times, worst of times, am I right?

Oh, but get this, to make matters worse: the minute we stepped inside the radius of the camp, a group of deranged psychopaths came shrieking out of the woodwork, seemingly hell-bent on showing us their best idiot impressions.

"What the fuck is going on?!" I shouted as the stampede of humanoids came rushing out at us.

We'd been here all of, what, ten minutes? And now we were gettin' the whole-ass belt strap—buckle and all—from whatever needling nasties had decided to lay waste to this particular stretch of forest.

Rua, transformed now into a red-haired elf lady, brandished her weapon—an absolute unit of a motherfuckin' monster known as the Behemoth Blade. Edwig, meanwhile, lifted one of the wands I'd lent him in his jiggly, amorphous appendage, preparing to rain down magical oblivion. Jumpy, Clucky, Slappy, and Mortimer—my ride-or-die, pinkish-pearl egg-monster bad boys, took defensive positions around us, while Rexen, the once-powerful wizard—now insane fluorescent specter—cackled with the unhinged glee I'd learned to associate him with.

I, being the voice of reason, removed my haladie from my waistband and screamed, "Fuck it all. Let's do this, you bitch-sucks!"

As we prepared to unleash a hot load of death and dismemberment on these indeterminate individuals, I could suddenly make out a little more as to what was happening.

They're not running at us with malicious intent. They're . . . running at us in fear?

I saw quite a variety of different races heading our way, weapons or magically charged hands raised, prepared to take us all out or die trying. It wasn't until Rua dropped her sword slightly and the folks leading the charge began to slow with realization that I understood. This wasn't a group of camp-destroying terrorists. These were the survivors. Which meant that these also happened to be the people I'd been on the train with.

"Rua?" asked a man with sandy-brown hair and a poised sickle. He was wearing pretty shabby clothes, and no armor that I could see. Really, he just looked like a medieval peasant, especially compared to the others in the group—who, by the way, in case anyone was wondering, wore a myriad of metal, leather, and expressions of confused anger.

Rua held up her hands.

"Hey!" she called, straining to lift her voice louder than the din of the chaos. The rest of the group began to slow or stop, muttering in bafflement.

"It's Rua," someone said.

"Oh, thank god it's not another one of those—"

"—couldn't have been a second attack, you idiot. That would—"

"—the fuck is she hanging out with? A globby—"

"—the ugliest creature I've seen so far."

Man, I hated this level of pandemonium.

"Alright, everybody shut up!" I yelled.

There was a momentary lull of silence before everyone piped up again.

"—the hell does he think *he* is? Probably a—"

"—what is with those spots? I —"

"—kill him *and* the slime creature over there if—"

"—working with those monsters. Not safe at all."

"I *said*—" I shouted, taking in a huge intake of breath before releasing Blackout Warchant. "SHUUUUUUT! UUUUUUUP!"

The sound erupted from me like a feral roar, and I was quite pleased that it was easily the best death metal scream I'd yet been able to produce. Furthermore, it quieted the group up real fast-like when the colorless blast hit them, ruffling their hair, fur, and clothing. I took another breath, raised an eyebrow, and smirked.

"Alright, *all y'all* need to calm the fuck down right now and tell us what the holy piss is going on. We're not your enemies—at least, not yet—and I—"

"Loon!" Rua snapped, and I paused, looking over at her.

She was hitting me with the most withering glare imaginable and gestured to the group.

"They're obviously rattled. You can't say things like"—she dropped her voice and sounded suspiciously dumb and scathing—"'We're not your enemies *yet*, hee hee.' They've just been attacked, man. Don't give them a reason to kill you."

I released a noise of pure contempt and slumped my shoulders before urging her with my hand to continue. She turned to the group.

"What happened? Was it those gold things again?"

A tall, handsome human in a leather chest piece stepped forward. In his dark hands rested the haft of a huge hammer, and he made sure to keep a concentrated gaze on me before turning back to Rua.

"No," he said. "It wasn't the things from before. These were new. They were kind of like . . . I don't know, fire . . . spiders? Anyway, they hit us in the middle of the night, and we barely had a chance to defend ourselves. *But we did.*"

The last line was delivered with a sense of finality so severe, I felt an involuntary goosebump or two rise to the occasion. But it wasn't just *what* he said. It was the way he said it. I knew his voice. Of *course* I would know his voice, I'd heard it every day for years, and pretty regularly for the last few. It was a little different due to, I guess, the change of form . . . but it was still mostly the same. This tall, dark, muscular paragon of humanity was my former childhood best friend, Nick Harmon.

"Any casualties?" Rua asked, all business now.

"Hard to say," Nick said, rubbing his chin in thought. "We can't seem to find Alpha or some of the others. I mean, I doubt they're dead, but it's weird that they weren't around at all for the attack."

"Hopefully, he's inside the belly of a flaming spider right about now," said another individual—a very tall dog . . . person?

"Even if he is, he'll probably be trying to blame the flames for being too hot or *woke* or something," said the serf-looking guy.

"It doesn't matter," Nick said. "Whether or not he's survived, we've got work to do. So, we should probably get started as soon as possible. Rua, great timing on your arrival. Did you run into anything we should know about out there? You were gone for a while."

"Yeah . . ." Rua said hesitantly.

Nick, seemingly sensing something was off, raised an eyebrow.

"You good?" he asked seriously.

"Yeah!" Rua said, realizing she'd unintentionally cast some suspicion on herself. "Just exhausted—and I definitely didn't anticipate coming back to a smoke-choked hole in the woods."

"Don't worry about it," Nick said, clapping her on the shoulder. "As long as there's nothing pressing we need to be watching out for. I'm sure there's going to be plenty of time to chat about your adventure. Now—"

He cast a glance out at the rest of us.

"Who're your friends?"

At that moment, Edwig decided to slither on over and produce a jiggly appendage for shaking.

"Pah! How rude of me! I'm Quintham—Edwig Quintham, Undermagister Researcher of the august and venerable Mages' Order at Yosper Hall in Tallrock."

The rest of the group—about twenty people or so it looked like—regarded Edwig with the usual amount of skeeved-out suspicion you'd expect to have for a creature that looked like a walking, talking, anthropomorphized sinus infection. Nick, though, was all class. He grasped the offered arm and gave it a solid pump before introducing himself with a grin.

"It's a pleasure to meet you, Edwig Quintham," Nick said politely. "I'm Saban."

Instantly, Edwig turned to me with a look of smug satisfaction.

"You see, Loon! *This* is how you properly greet someone new!"

"Hey, Edwig," I said. "How about you go find a bucket of bleach to crawl into?"

"Pah!" he exclaimed. "Not on your life, Loon. I'm too busy fraternizing."

"Yeah, well, you're talkin' a lotta shit for somebody who still owes me money."

"Pah! Not this again!" Edwig groaned.

"*Yes*, this again," I shot back. "You owe it, so pay it. Don't try to deadbeat-dad me, you ass. I got eggs to feed, so gimme my motherfuckin' *blood money*."

I realized suddenly that I hadn't really even given Nick his due hello. So, noticing how baffled he seemed by me and Edwig's exchange, I thought I'd offer a few more servings of chaos and confusion into his daily pyramid. I cleared my throat, smiled, and took a step forward to spill the beans on who I was. But, before I could greet him, he wheeled specifically on me with a severe expression plastered onto his features.

"And who are you?" he demanded.

I cocked my head to the side. Man, if I hadn't known who he was, I might've been a little intimidated by that. However, because I, in fact, *did* know who he was, I was marginally less impressed.

"I could ask you the same thing, Hammertime," I said. Then I immediately realized my mistake.

"... Gabe?" Nick ... um, *Saban*, now, suddenly asked, his eyes widening as he took me in.

Fuck! I forgot I can't be dropping homeworld references to other people *from the old country if I want to be mysterious.*

"No!" I exclaimed, then caught myself again. "I mean ... uh, who's Gabe?"

Nailed it.

Rather than respond to me, he looked to Rua, who nodded and shrugged. Then Saban dropped his hammer and did something very strange: he raced over and wrapped his arms around me in a hug.

"Ah!" I squealed, trying to push him off of me. "What the fuck is with this whole crew and *hugging*! I do not consent! I do not consent!"

A small flash of pinkish-purplish-blue appeared next to my face as, suddenly, Rexen was floating there, his own arms wrapped around my head to mimic Saban's action.

"Everybody back off—I'm in *fighter flight* mode, and I'm not going to apologize if you get hurt!"

"It's fight *or* flight, Loon," Rua said.

"Not the way I do it," I said. "I'm going to get away in the most painful, combative style possible—now. Let. Go. Of. Me!"

I successfully removed Saban's strong grasp and stared down in a huff, but he was just grinning in that familiar way.

"Jesus, man," I breathed. "What's your fuckin' Strength score, five hundred?"

"You're alive" was all he said in response.

"Not without many, *many* glorious attempts by countless people to correct that fact," I said. "But, yeah. I'm here. Looks like you're not doing too bad for yourself, Mister ... *Saban*."

Of all the things to name yourself after, this goofy bastard goes and chooses a fuckin' production company?

"Huh?" he asked, raising an eyebrow at me. "You think I chose a weird name?"

"Well ..." I said, pausing. "I did. But, based on your reaction ... now I'm not so sure. Saban, like ... the company that adapted our *favorite TV show when we were kids*?"

"Oh!" He chuckled. "No, but that's not a bad guess. I actually got my inspiration from Nick Saban."

I blinked at him.

"Uh . . . who?"

"Nick Saban?" he said. "Miami Dolphins Nick Saban? University of Alabama Nick Saban? Greatest coach of all time?"

I scowled.

"Okay, first of all—that is patently false. Coach Eric motherfuckin' Taylor from *Friday Night Lights* is the best that ever was, and you know it," I said. "Second: how the hell would you expect me to guess that? You know I don't know nothin' 'bout no damn sport ball."

I huffed dramatically, but then I caught his shit-eating grin and I screwed my face up petulantly.

"I'm just fucking with you, my guy," Saban said. "I absolutely chose the name because of the Mighty Morphin' implications."

I gaped.

"You. Fucking. Dick."

Saban laughed, and for the briefest of moments, I saw my old friend there.

"Yeah, sorry," he said. "Couldn't help myself. Just wanted to see your reaction."

"Hey," I started, grinning like an idiot. "I'm just happy to know that *Power Rangers* is still as much of a core memory for you as it is for me."

"Ah, shut up," he laughed.

"No, I'm serious," I said. "I have like five strong recollections from my life, and that's one of them. The other four are just me trying new Pop-Tart flavors."

"What can I say?" he asked. "That shit was kind of lame, but . . . still kind of slapped."

"Yeah, we turned up pretty hard for it. Except you'd never let me be the Gold Samurai Ranger—I always had to be *Jayden*."

"Still with this?" Saban said, still smiling and shaking his head. "It's been *years*, my dude."

"You never forget the first time you're betrayed," I said. "Making me be Samurai Fire . . . I'm mad all over again."

"Dude," he said. "What's wrong with Jayden? He's the *leader*."

"First of all: Jayden's a bitch, and you know it," I said. "Second, you can never trust an adult man with blond hair. Also—yeah, I'm going to talk about it: we're just supposed to believe that some *white guy* and his Aryan sister are descended from an ancient Japanese samurai clan? Hard pass. Antonio was the real GOAT and his Ranger suit looked way cooler."

"Speaking of looks . . ." Saban started, grinning.

Oh, don't you dare, you dick.

"What *are* you?" he continued. "You sort of resemble, like, I dunno, a big . . . goblin, or something? But then you have those shiny pink speckles on your skin. And your hair is . . . well, it's *unique*."

"Wow," I said. "Really? You know this is my body now, right? No takesies-backsies. So—rude. Also, you need to go to the optometrist and up your bifocal prescription, Mr. Magoo, because I'm clearly an orc. And I'll have you know that I *earned* these spots. It's a feature I picked up after being *exploded*—so, show some damn respect: I fought and died for this country. And don't even get me started on these luminous locks . . ."

I gave Rexen—the culprit of my follicle monstrosity—the stink eye, but he just smiled back at me.

"Exploded?" Saban asked, a disbelieving grin on his face.

"Yeah, exploded," I said, shrugging. "Or, like, whatever you call it when you get crushed so hard, your body parts pop like a spoiled grape."

He shivered.

"Yeah, let's go with *exploded*."

Then he shook his head, looking me up and down in amazement.

"You've changed a lot, Gabe. Or it sounds like I should call you Loon now, right?"

I shrugged.

"*Loon* is fine. But yeah, a lot's different."

I glanced around at the other survivors, trying to gauge their reactions to the revelation of my identity.

Most of them seemed surprised but not hostile. Some were whispering among themselves, probably trying to remember who I was. Others were eyeing me warily, as if they didn't quite trust a big-ass spotty monster with electric hair.

"So, I know you guys are having a moment right now, but . . . we should head back to the central part of the camp," Rua suggested. "We can catch up on the way and figure out what to do about these new threats."

Saban nodded in agreement.

"Yeah, let's get moving. We don't want to stay out here and risk another attack."

New friends! Buddies! Rest! Finally, relax! came the mental messages from my foursome of possessed roe. They bounced happily next to me, earning some concerned looks from the others.

Maybe, I returned through our weird telepathic link. *Keep your glowing red eyes peeled, though, m'babies. We don't know what to expect.*

Which was true; I just didn't realize how annoying that foreshadowing would be.

CHAPTER TWO

THE CLICK BEFORE THE STRIKE

As we began to walk, I fell into step beside Saban, and we exchanged stories of our time in this world. He told me about how he and the others had banded together, learning the game-like rules and seemingly only barely surviving all the while. Their trip so far had been one hilarious misfortune after the other, where twice now they'd had to defend themselves from large-scale threats.

I shared my own badass origin story, explaining how I'd been separated from everyone else and had to survive on my own. Which I did expertly because I'm a fuckin' *champion*. You'd be proud of me, because I only bragged like twenty-five times. Then I told him about the companions I'd met along the way—Stinky, Edwig, my egg posse, Jes and Frida's crew, and, of course, Rexen—and how we'd formed our own odd little team.

I found it a teensy bit fucked-up how normal it seemed now to drop casual references to things like Spells and magical weapons and all that noise, while still being perfectly understandable and relatable to all parties.

During our stroll, we finally came upon the guts of the train wreckage, a vision of wrenched steel and shattered glass that looked like some pretentious artist's version of a post-apocalyptic sculpture. It was a monstrous, gnarled mass of charred railcars, strewn around like a child's discarded toys, crumpled and crushed beyond recognition.

Surprisingly, it had taken some auxiliary pieces along for the ride; skewed tracks clawed their way from the ground, glistening in the twilight like the skeletal remains of some prehistoric beast. Here and there, the torn entrails of luggage spilled open, their contents a memento mori of the lives that had been forever altered on that ill-fated journey. It was clearly stuff that was obliterated too badly to be of use, because I couldn't imagine any other reason they weren't using every part of this particular buffalo.

And amidst the wreckage, the telltale signs of violent disruption were all too evident—shredded seats, splintered wood, shattered windowpanes that lay around like a thousand glittering teardrops. I was impressed that the homies had just allowed it to lay around messy like that—grab a broom or something, ya sloppies.

It was one thing to hear about it, another to see the remnants of the chaos from afar, but to stand in the heart of it, to breathe it in, to see the haunting remnants of life as it once was, was fucking surreal. It felt like I was standing in the mouth of hell, staring at the twisted teeth of the beast that had tried to chew me up and spit me out. The real kicker? They'd walked away from it—crawled out of this mechanical monstrosity's belly, survived its fiery wrath, and lived to tell the tale. Damn, if that didn't make your balls shrink, I don't know what would.

But we continued on. Presumably to the "central area" or whatever Rua had mentioned. I couldn't be assed to tell what anything really was, because it was, as I mentioned multiple times, destroyed. However, I kept jabberin' on, like I be doin' sometimes. In fact, I was smack-dab in the middle of my incredibly professional retelling of my encounter with Pontivex when we were interrupted.

"—and this fuckin' dude was all like, 'Gimme tasty meats,'" I said in a squeaky voice reminiscent of Beaker from the Muppets, "and I was all like, 'You want *meat*? Like, *raw*?' This asshole didn't even want it cooked or nothin'! Just regular ol' still-on-the-bone shanks of—"

"What the fuck happened?!" an annoying voice interjected. Whoever it was, they sounded like they *sucked*.

"Hey!" I shouted into the direction I thought it had come from. "I'm *trying* to tell a fuckin' story here, guy, so—"

"Who the fuck said that? That's insubordination. I promise you don't want *any* of this—not after the night I've had."

I scowled. Who was *this* now? He had a really suck-ass tone and I didn't appreciate it at all. *I* was the sassy sourpuss around these parts and I wasn't about to let some random dude . . . give me grief, or whatever.

"How 'bout ya show yourself?" I shot back, glancing around for whoever had been getting shitty in their hiding spot. "I've got a big-ass foot lookin' for a butt to call home, so if you're trying to catch an attitude, you're going to get more than you bargained for!"

I kept looking around, not quite able to spot where in the immediate surrounds this little dick-touch was wagging his chompers from. I saw Saban tense next to me and Rua's intake of breath. The crowd we'd been sorta orbiting slowed, and a dread settled among them.

"What the fuck?" I said, shooting glances in every direction. "What's goin' on—is there going to be another attack?"

"Ooh! I hope so—it would be a delight to see how my valiant disciple would fare in a forest!" Rexen said.

"Arjee," I said, "shut up. I'm serious, why's everybody got their funeral faces on?"

"So!" the voice came again, dangerously close to me. I jumped.

"Gah!"

I craned my neck over my own shoulder to see the shape emerging from the trees not ten feet away. A stumpy figure began shambling into view from the shadows of the canopy, and he wasn't alone. A . . . dwarf—at least, that's what it seemed like—appeared, flanked by others. They were an every-flavored assortment of fantasy-inspired races, not all of which I recognized. The dwarf gave me the impression that he'd been the one who'd been trying to rattle my cage, and let me tell you, he looked dumb. Pale skin, paler hair and beard plaited into cute braids that screamed that he was compensating for something. He wore a vibrant technicolor dreamcloak that barely concealed the leather chest piece he wore beneath, and his hands were clad in silly cut-off leather gloves. He probably thought he was super edgy, but he just looked like he'd gotten kicked out of a medieval motorcycle club.

The hodgepodge of equally unimpressive LARPers that made up his entourage consisted of some sorta gray-skinned . . . devil . . . woman? I dunno. Anyway, next to her was a *boring* human who looked like he wanted to be anywhere else. Rounding out their ragtag team was a haughty, smug-as-fuck-looking elf-man.

I wasn't bothered by this anemic lumberjack and his cronies. But it was clear by the tension-temperature of the group around me that there was something more to this.

"Sorry," the dwarf announced—definitely not sounding sorry in the slightest. "Did I startle you?"

"Yeah, I'm not used to garden gnomes coming to life," I said. "Did a witch cast a spell on you or something?"

"Hilarious, *Spot*. Did you get full-body herpes from that blob creature?" the dwarf shot back, pointing at my illisinaf companion.

Okay . . . I thought to myself. Go after me all you want, but why you gotta drag Edwig into this, he's— Oh, Jesus Christ, he's heading over to introduce himself.

Sure enough, Edwig was slopping his way on over, appendage outstretched in the perfect picture of politeness.

"Pleased to meet you," he said with a smile. "Quintham—Edwig Quintham, Undermag—"

"Eww!" the dwarf exclaimed, leaping backward as if he'd seen a particularly hairy spider. Edwig seemed taken aback. Almost . . . hurt. I remembered my teasing of him, saw his expression now, and felt a jolt of guilt in my guts. However, the dwarf, like all bullies, seemed to recover quickly from his temporary grossed-outness. He straightened up, bolting a vicious smirk back in place and let out a scoff.

"I'm Alpha," said the dwarf. "And just who the fuck are all o' you stomping around on my property?"

"Property?" Rexen asked. "Who's got property?"

The little covetous apparition seemed to tingle with the promise of treasures, but I stepped forward to cut off his line of thought, drawing a clear barrier between my group and the dwarf's. I already knew who this guy was, since I'd been traveling with Rua for the last few days.

"You're that asshole from the train," I said, glowering.

"You could be talking about anyone," he mused. "There were a *lot* of assholes on th—"

"Mr. No Bitches with the shitty friends," I clarified. He'd been appropriately nicknamed Steroid Steve during the scuffle, and I actually didn't know what his real name was. Now, apparently, it was Alpha. What a joke.

"And you're . . . *who*, exactly?" He wondered, looking at Rua as if expecting her to provide additional context.

"I'm *Loon*," I said, crossing my—now—substantial arms over my barrel chest and raising an eyebrow. "Maybe you didn't notice, but your whole camp got attacked while you were apparently off doing . . . friendship . . . practice, or something."

I grinned, satisfied that I'd salvaged that.

Alpha's smirk disappeared and was instead replaced by a grimace. He marched over to Saban to stand directly in front of him.

"Is that true? We were attacked?"

Saban nodded grimly.

"Some kind of fire spiders," he said. "I'm not entirely sure what they were, but—"

"Did they destroy our stuff?" Alpha interrupted.

"Hey, fuckface," I said, getting pretty miffed at this dude's attitude. "Maybe take a look around for a half-second. Obviously they destroyed your stuff. What, were you hiding?"

Alpha snapped his head to me with a scowl.

"I swear to fucking god if you don't shut your fucking mouth, I'm going to melt you from the inside out."

I bristled.

"Oh, really?" I asked warningly, straightening my back and putting a hand on my haladie. "You think you can back that up, you chapped—"

"Loon," Rua said.

I turned to look back at her.

"Eh?"

She just shook her head as if to tell me I didn't know what I was getting into. Curiously, in the back of my brain, there was an itch. Something telling me I should maybe take her opinion into consideration.

However.

I thought that maybe, right then and there, it would make sense for her to take the fact that I was clearly the strongest person here into consideration. Well, at least, I thought I might be. I was Level Twelve, and she'd just recently ranked up to Level Four—and she'd been battling shit with me while the rest of these jabronis were just hanging around playing *Little House on the Prairie*. There's no way I wasn't the strongest person here, right? I could take him.

"Anyway, don't write checks your shitty combat abilities can't cash, buttdick," I said. "You're rude as fuck, and someone needs to show you you're not—"

"Duellum," Alpha said simply, cutting me off. There were audible gasps of horror around me, and I craned my neck to look at everyone's faces.

"What's *due* ... what's that?" I wondered. "An insult?"

I turned back to Alpha.

"If you're going to say something snarky, at least make sure the person *knows* you're talking shit. That's, like, the first rule of insults, or something."

However, he just sneered.

"It's not an insult," he said. "You look like a chunky piece of shit. There, *that's* an insult."

"Yeah, well, *you* look like someone whose hometown smells like dog food," I said. "Now, that's a real—"

"Loon," Saban said with a groan. "Alpha just *challenged* you. If you accept, you will be obligated to fight him. I'd recommend—"

"A *Kumite*?!" I roared triumphantly. "Oh, hell, yeah. Sign me all the way fucking *up*! I'm gonna throttle this dirty dickhead, and beat him all over the ... You know what? I hear it. Yeah ... the phrasing was bad. Anyways, how do I accept? Do I just have to say *Due*—"

"*Don't*," Saban said seriously. "You don't know what you're getting into, man. It's not a good idea."

"Oh, this monster knows exactly how smart he *isn't*," Alpha said, shucking off his robe in preparation for a rumble. "Let him make his decision and find out firsthand who the top dog is around here."

"You can't be serious," Rua said, and her sentiments were echoed from the crowd of people forming. "We don't have time for this. The camp was just *attacked*. Don't we have *stuff* to do?"

"Yeah, we should probably—" someone else began, but was cut off.

"Nah," Alpha said. "Nothing's more important than busting down some annoying little beta who thinks he can just waltz into my home and start acting like he's hot shit. So, maybe everyone who disagrees should just shut the fuck up or face a similar consequence."

Rua had told me all about this guy. He'd been quick on the draw in saving everyone when they'd first arrived, and now he was something like their leader, having used some . . . I dunno, magic stone or some bullshit to make them his hostages.

Man, why don't these people just overthrow this bitch? He can't be that strong, can he?

I looked over at Rexen, who had been strangely silent. He had adopted that uncharacteristically dour expression he'd had when we'd been in the stomach of the oomukade queen back at the town.

Well, you're fucking useless, I thought. *Jumpy, Clucky, Slappy, Mortimer?*

I heard a chorus of responses in my mind and smiled.

You guys feel like showing off?

I got a very strong impression of affirmation from them—which was how they communicated sometimes. I nodded.

"Right, so, we gonna do this thing or what?" I demanded. I had a hankerin' to put this guy's dick in the dirt. He'd been such a fucking toolbag on the train in our previous world, and apparently, he'd only gotten to be more of a pest in the last couple weeks here.

"Say the words, bitch," Alpha spat, cracking his knuckles.

"Oh, right," I said, sidling closer and adopting a confused expression. "Uh . . . what were those words again?"

Alpha's laugh was full of mockery.

"You dumb motherfucker," he began. "I just told you it's—"

"DUELLUM!" I roared as I kicked him in the chest.

CHAPTER THREE

300

Alpha flew backward as my dope-as-tits Spartan kick landed perfectly in the center of his torso. He hit the ground hard with an angry groan. I wasn't sure if that surprise move was going to go well, considering I'd abandoned my boots earlier and was still barefoot. Apparently, I was a fucking savant when it came to this sort of thing, though, and naked tootsie or not... Loon gon' kick.

I laughed, yanking my haladie out of my waistband—I, uh, still hadn't picked up a utility belt—and aimed the blade at him.

"Do you yield?" I demanded, trying my best to imitate a mighty knight of old.

Alpha held his hand up, struggling to breathe.

"Ha!" I said, shooting a look at the assembly with a wide grin. "Did you guys see that?! He yielded!"

"I'm... not... yielding... you... fuck," Alpha wheezed, finally gaining the ability to stand but still doing so very poorly. "That's... not... how the fucking Duellum... works."

"Fuck off," I said disbelievingly. "You said to *say the words*, so I *say* the damn *words*."

"As much as I enjoyed viewing the immediate and utterly embarrassing tyrannical toppling of such a wretchedly pathetic man as him," said the gray-skinned devil woman from nearby, "unfortunately, he is correct. It is not how the Duellum is conducted."

I scowled at the group.

"The fuck?" I huffed. "I figured you guys would be more than happy to see me take him down a peg. Even if that's not how it works, I still *whipped his ass*. Ain't there, like, points for style?"

"There are *rules*, you fucking *cuck*," Alpha continued, apparently having found his oxygen once more. "We've gotta go to the spot."

"What spot?" I said.

Alpha gestured to an indeterminate place to my right. I craned my neck to look and noticed a clearing near the . . . central area of the camp. Around the edges of the flat, otherwise-featureless ground were symbols that seemed like, if this wasn't Incantation Town, they would have been airbrushed on.

"You can't fight me unless it's inside your *clearly booby-trapped* Thunderdome? No dice, junior. I'm *stupid* but not stupid enough to think that you don't have some sort of magical bullshit to spring on me the moment I enter that bitch. Let's do it right here."

"You fuckin'—" Alpha started, but Saban interrupted him, placing a calming hand on my shoulder.

"There's a process," he said with a smile. "You *accept* the duel by saying the words, but then you have to set peramaters, and go through the formal steps."

"Aw, man—formalities?!" I demanded. "This is dopey. Ain't no codes of conduct in a real fight! I use the laws of the street!"

"Do you, now?" Edwig wondered.

"Shut up, Edwig," I said.

"Yes, let him use the street!" Rexen commanded. "Each cobblestone shall be an emphatic grave marker as my pupil pummels his foe into paste! What a delight!"

"That's not what 'laws of the street' means," Rua said.

"Yes, it does!" Rexen returned.

Rua just shook her head, taking the intelligent path of not arguing with insanity.

"Gah!" I moaned. "Fine! What're the rules, then?"

"You—" Alpha started, but Edwig interrupted him.

"As the contested," the illisinaf explained, "you are able to choose the time, place, and type of duel that it will be, so you should be able to—"

"Nope!" Alpha interrupted him in return, sidling forward. Edwig seemed taken aback, and incredibly offended by being corrected.

"Pah! I'm confident in how the rules are—"

"Shut up, snot monster," Alpha said. "Whatever you think you know, you're wrong. *My* Duellum is different."

"Of course it is," I groaned. "Lemme guess, no matter the outcome, you win? I have to have one hand tied behind my back and you get a *gun?* Listen, I ain't letting you . . ."

I paused, unable to find the proper idiom. Goddammit, it was on the tip of my tongue, too.

". . . have your cake and eat it too?" Rua offered.

"Yeah! That one!" I exclaimed.

"I thought so," Alpha sneered, insinuating something I wasn't privy to.

"*Thought*, nothin'!" I returned. "Just tell me your dipshit-ass rules, Alf. It won't matter anyway, because I'm gonna beat your ass so bad, you're gonna cry every time you even *think* about putting pants on."

"The rule is . . ." Alpha said, suddenly dramatic in his reveal. "We fight. In the ring. To the death."

"Is that all?" I asked, chuckling. "Son, in case you didn't know, that ain't much of a concern for our kind."

I was met with a wall of silence. I cocked an eyebrow, glancing at the somber assembly before me. No one wanted to meet my eyeline, like I'd just made a weirdly insensitive joke. Which was weird, because I usually knew *exactly* what I'd said to make someone uncomfortable.

". . . Unless there's something about the Duellum that *makes* that a serious consequence?" I wondered to the masses.

"For incomprehensible reasons," the devil-woman said, "a Duellum arrests the typical reaction. Anyone who expires within its confines . . . is gone forever."

Edwig shook his head.

"That's not—"

"Wait, *what*?!" I exclaimed.

I snapped my head to Alpha, who was still smirking.

"You're out here *murdering* people? Oh, that does it, you dwarf *bitch*. Bring it on."

Alpha shook his head, laughing.

"It's your *literal* funeral, fucker."

"Yeah . . ." I said darkly, "we'll see about that."

I twisted my neck, wrenching it to and fro to get the kinks out. Then I made a show of windmilling my arms in circles. I was gonna warm up like a motherfucker, if for no other reason than to show I meant business.

I was standing on one side of the magical circle and Alpha was on the other, doing his own stretches. He seemed far too confident for the severe ramifications that he could potentially be on the losing side of—which actually made me a bit uncomfortable. Bravado was one thing, but in a life-or-death situation, you'd think there'd be even a teeny-weeny kernel of visible anxiousness on his part. But there wasn't any. If permadeath was on the table, I'd bet biscuits to ball hairs that this incorrigible son of a skid mark had something up his sleeve he thought gave him the upper hand. That meant I had to find out what that was.

"Rua," I said, gesturing for her to approach. The red-haired elf woman trotted over with a grim expression on her face but quickly fixed a very transparently unconfident grin on her features as she got close.

"Hey, uh, what's up?" she asked in forced casualness.

"Alright, this seems fucky," I said. "Don't put on a brave face, dammit; you're bad at it. It's making me itchy. Just shoot it to me straight: how bad is this gonna be?"

"Well . . ." Rua trailed off, seeming to try and find the right words to not give me an emotional gut punch. "Not . . . super . . . swell?"

"Fuck," I hissed. "What am I missing? Does he have, like, a magic rocket launcher or something?"

"He's got some kind of corrosive magic," Saban said, suddenly joining us. "Like an acid, or something."

I glanced at the man who was now shorter than me—the opposite of what he had been in our old world. Man, just when I was able to appreciate some of the things about this fresh existence, I was about to die forever.

"Acid?" I asked. "Like, he sprays it?"

"It's got a few forms," Saban continued. "Sometimes it's liquid, sometimes gas—like a cloud. That one is nasty."

"Jesus," I said. "How many times has he done this?"

Rua shrugged.

"Just once, but—"

"Three times," Saban interrupted soberly.

"Huh?" Rua asked. "He did it twice while I was gone?"

Saban nodded, his eyes on Alpha at the far end of the circle.

"Weren't you only gone for a few days?" I gasped. "He's a fucking psychopath!"

"Loon, listen," Saban said. "This is really, really bad, alright?"

"No fucking duh," I agreed.

"Every single time Alpha does this, the duel is over quick. He tries to win right away. Fortunately, I've seen how he fights," my old friend continued. "Both in a Duellum and against the things that have attacked us. He always starts off with a distracting blast of the stuff, then he hits them wherever they move to. Most of his attacks are mid-to-long-range, so staying back is not a great option—though it *does* give you more reaction time."

I sighed.

"But even if you were to get up close, that's when he's going to use the cloud version of his attack. It's only got a range directly around him and is more a defensive measure—but it's still going to eat through your flesh like a buzzsaw."

"My flesh?" I asked. "But I'm *mostly* flesh!"

I glanced down at my lack of anything resembling protective gear. I'd ditched the Sojourner threads back in Tallrock for a blue shirt and a leather jerkin, as well as a pair of buckskin pants. I still had my Trespasser's Veil, which allowed me to be oh so stealthy, but I didn't think that a blank clearing was the best location for hide-and-seek. I'd donned my Grenalyn's Gussying Gauntlets, for that bit of extra *oomf*, but other than my pack, I didn't have much. I had *almost* equipped the Guardian's Buckler, but I thought I might need both hands for bustin' some chops. I sorta wished I still had Berg's helmet to protect my dome a little better or do some plus-one punchin'—but I'd lost it in the fight with one of the oomukade days back.

"Anyone hiding a HAZMAT suit under their hat?" I asked.

"I've got knowledge—and secrets—under mine," Rexen said, appearing next to us suddenly and miming removing a cap that was not there from his head. He looked up where his handless appendage was, confused.

"Arjee," I intoned, "I think you went and found yourself some more senility."

"What happened to my hat?" the specter wondered.

"You never had one!" Edwig said, suddenly arriving as well.

Rexen scowled darkly at the amorphous illisinaf.

"I've had one this whole time," he corrected. "I just don't know where it is right now. Did one of these creatures burgle it?"

His swirly eyes narrowed further as he perused the group of Sojourners in the camp.

"So, what're the rules to this thing exactly?" I asked, ignoring the creature that I was technically the property of.

"Well, in a typical Duellum," Edwig began, gesturing toward the circle. "You can essentially do whatever you need to to win—since this one's a fight to the death and all."

"Ugh," I groaned. "Don't remind me. But *anything goes* actually gives me a very optimistic outlook on the whole—"

"Well, not *anything*," the blob-man clarified.

"Goddammit," I exclaimed. "So, what, then?"

"You're not allowed to have outside help," Rua said. "So, none of us can step in. Neither can . . ."

She gestured to Jumpy, Clucky, Slappy, and Mortimer. The eggs looked up at me happily as if expecting a compliment.

"Aw, man, really?" I whined.

I turned to face the possessed roe and shook my head.

"Sorry, boys," I said. "Looks like Daddy's gotta do it all on his own—single-parent style."

"But you can use any weapons or items you bring in," Edwig offered. "Since there were no exceptions made when the Duellum was accepted."

"Alright," I said, feeling a bit better. "This is good—see, this is the kind of information I need. So, he's got acid and junk—any weapons?"

"He's got a hatchet that he doesn't really utilize much," Saban said. "Tends to stick to his Spells, but I'd still watch out for it. He's also got some potions on his belt."

I turned to look at Alpha, who was—was he doing the fucking splits? What a show-off. I squinted, noticing an array of colorful bottles hanging above his waist.

"He's got a utility belt?" I asked. "Whoa, where'd he get something like that? And where did those potions come from? Did he find 'em?"

I couldn't imagine this crew—least of all the domineering dwarf—had been able to procure any means of magical manufacturing for potions.

"Not sure," Saban admitted. "It *might* be part of his Class, but . . . yeah, I dunno."

"Any idea what they do?"

"Only one of them," Saban said. "Something called an *Eagerness Dram*."

"What's that do?" I asked. "Sounds like a euphemism for boner pills."

"It's—"

"It boosts Stamina and Defense," Edwig interrupted him. "Low Tier—probably Common or below. It's not a true potion, either—almost exclusively appears as part of Class Ability. If I had to bet on it, I'd say the effect would last only about ten seconds—fifteen at most."

Edwig squinted at the others hanging from Alpha's belt.

"Let's see. Looks like . . . a Potion of Speed, a couple of health tinctures . . . Not sure what that purple one is— Wait, is he a Blight Brewer?"

"How'd you know?" Rua asked, surprised.

"Pah! Rua, I'm a *researcher*. Arcana's my chips and jam. It's a fairly common Class—at least in the circles I orbit—not particularly sophisticated in combat, but focused around potion production with a lighter emphasis on corrosive defense."

Edwig paused to look in the dwarf's direction, raising an eyebrow.

"It's not a great dueling Class—or, at least, I wouldn't think it would be . . ."

"Well, regardless," I said, clapping , "that's what he's using it for. So, guess you need to get back to the . . . Bunsen burner on that theory."

"The what?" Edwig asked.

"Nothing—never mind!" I said. "Maybe I can wrestle some of those away from him."

"Pah! Not on your life, orc," Edwig said. "If they're Class-based, they've got an arcane seal on them."

"A what?"

"It keeps what is his *his*," Rexen added helpfully. "Or what is his *mine*."

"Now you're talking. Take notes, gang. Arjee here is going to be devising a way to steal his gooey gumdrop buttons."

"Yes!" Rexen said. "You kill him, disciple, and I will help you reap the benefits."

"Okay, see, now that's *less* helpful, Arjee—"

"I don't think you have time to be messing around and arguing," Rua said. "The Duellum is about to start."

I sighed.

"You're right, we're outta time. Anyone have any final words of wisdom or nuggets of advice?"

Everyone just stared back at me blankly.

"Alright, cool," I declared, picking up my haladie. I felt the weight in my hands, finding some comfort in its familiarity. "Let's do this thing."

Alpha was now standing, hatchet in hand, a cocky grin plastered on his face like a jack-o'-lantern. I found myself suddenly wishing that I had a pumpkin-carving knife.

"You're a goner, fuckhead," Alpha jeered. "You've bitten off more than you can chew."

"Yeah? Well, I've got a big mouth, asshole," I shot back. "I can fit a whole *buncha* shit in it."

Ignoring the snickers from the crowd, Alpha stepped into the ring, standing at the very edge. He held up his hand, giving me a douchey come-hither gesture.

"Get your ass in here, bitch," he barked.

I grimaced, glancing at Rua. She was attempting to muster a reassuring smile, but it came off as more of a painful grimace. Not the morale boost I was hoping for.

"I'm not too thrilled about the death thing, but you should know, Stumpy," I called out, pointing my haladie in Alpha's direction, "I fight dirty."

"Yeah, I'm fucking trembling," he said.

I took a deep breath, then stepped into the ring. It was eerily quiet, the only sound the crunching of pebbles under my bare feet. There was a tension in the air so palpable that you could carve through it with a knife—but I didn't have a knife. I had a haladie, and I barely knew how to use it. I looked across the circle, locking eyes with Alpha. His pupils danced with an unsettling excitement.

Well, time to fight for my life. Classic Loon.

"Alright," I called out. "Let's get this party started, chump."

CHAPTER FOUR

BLOODSPORT

Suddenly, like some sort of dramatic villain, Alpha lifted his hands. Our battle ring lit up, the symbols around the edge tossing out a strobe-light display, and if I hadn't been so angry, I might have suggested he take that act to a Daft Punk concert. I whipped my head around to my mateys on the sidelines, hoping for a quick rundown on what the hell was happening, but their faces were just question marks.

I swiveled back to Alpha, who was wearing a predatory grin.

"Ah, did no one mention this little perk during your powwow?" he quipped, voice oily. "As the leader of this place, I've got a little defense protocol set up."

I heard a mental whisper from Rexen, who was, surprisingly, keeping a respectful distance. This came in the form of Commune, a Spell that sorta stopped time for a perceivable minute for him to talk to me.

Ah, pupil! He's using Citizen Surge, the little spirit said.

And that is? I responded, impatiently.

A marvelous Settlement Ability that lets him soak up all the shiny, juicy energy of everyone under his command. Then he gets stronger! *I hypothesize it will last for around one hour.*

God. Dammit, I thought. *He's using fucking cheat codes? Figures. Only the most disgusting people try to pull them kinda stunts. Makes me sick to my stomach.*

But, my beautiful pupil—you have also utilized advantages such as this in fights. Remember when we fought Koobumpup?

Who the fuck is Koobumpup?

In the beastie's belly. My disciple's memory is poor at times. I helped you break down all that information—which you used to whittle him to a whining little babe.

Oh. He was referring to when he used a sweet Hack-the-Planet Jailbreak Spell, or Ability, or Skill, or whatever-the-fuck you call it on that butt-turd

Tides flunkie Rafe Crowmoon. One that was absolutely past the gray area of what would be considered legal conduct and definitely allowed me to grab the upper hand in the fight.

That's not his name, Arjee, I corrected. *And yeah, so I bent the rules a tad—it was different. I'm the good guy.*

So you continue to profess, Rexen said.

Okay, do you know any additional information about this Citywide Purge—Citizen Surge.

I know, Arjee. I was just having some fun with it, because it sounds like it's going to be a pain in my cheeky crack and I wanted to take away some of its power.

I see, pupil! Very interesting. What I assumed was a malapropism was actually intentional. That is funny.

Yes, I said. *Jokes are notoriously much funnier when you explain them. Anyway, anything else I should know about this Ability? Does he get other people's powers or like summon a blue shell?*

Iunno. Each iteration has the potential to be much, much different from any others, silly! But . . . probably not. His Level was low before, and now it is higher but still not much better.

What's his Level?

Thirteen. A paltry sum.

Fuck! I groaned. *I'm only Level Twelve!*

Oh, is that all?

I scoffed.

Anyway, was that all there was? Kinda gotta hop to it if I'm going to beat this dude's britches inside out before sundown.

Nope— Oh, wait! Yes.

And what would that be?

I read the glyphs. I read them real good.

What the fuck does that mean? That dumb Scooby-Doo *Halloween script around the edges?*

Such a smart pupil!

Arjee . . .

Yes?

What did the fucking runes say?!

Oh. Hm. Lemme see . . .

I think it happened. I think I could actually feel a section of my brain burst open.

Sorry! he said after a long moment and an additional cast of Commune. *Had to peep them again! I'm quite old, you see, and—*

Please, seriously, Arjee, I pleaded. *I am fucking begging you to get to the point.*

Impatient disciple. Adding it to my list.

I almost demanded to know what list he was mouthing about, but then realized—rare for me—that I was potentially being baited into a tangent. Instead, I just waited.

Fine, fine, pupil. The glyphs said to me that while Spells, items, and Skills will be active . . . Abilities will not be available for the first minute of the Duellum.

Okay, I said with a chuckle. *So what? This whole fight is going to be dunked the minute I hit him with Blackout— FUCK! That's an Ability isn't it?*

Indeed, Rexen said sadly. *For being my pupil, you have a decidedly inadequate amount of Spells in your arcane inventory. Sad.*

Well, shit. So, this wing-clipping motherbitch is trying to ensure that I don't have anything available to me? How is he even able to do that? I thought we agreed on terms.

Yep! But the circle was part of the terms. It is set up this way for that specific purpose.

Wait! I thought it was required!

Nothing is ever required, pupil, Rexen said. *Except perhaps the adoration of a very fine hat.*

Jesus fuck, again with the hat thing. I swear to god I never heard a single thing about hats the whole time we were in Tallrock. Now, suddenly it's the goddamn Hat Chat Podcast. And— Wait, never mind. Shit, I'm getting off topic. I've gotta do this Duellum—and at a handicap.

Good luck! Rexen exclaimed.

Yeah, thanks for lifting my spirits, Gravytrain.

What is that?

What is what?

Gravytrain. Is that similar to a gravy boat?

Sure. It's just a play on your last name—you know, Gravetongue?

Ah, yes! I see. Gravytrain is indeed a wonderful title from my esteemed and darling pupil-baby. I am glad I could ensure your path remained unclouded.

This is really it, though? Nothing else to share?

That was all, Rexen said. *I just did not want you to approach from a place of ignorance.*

I chuckled.

See, that's the thing about me, Arjee: I'm always—

Commune ended, and the world spun back to life. I was left holding the bag on my own stolen quip.

"Well, shit," I said.

Then I turned to the dwarf, who was still doing his Super Saiyan power-up. When he finished, I just shook my head.

"Beautiful," I said, slow-clapping. "So, you've got some ultra unfair landlord powers? Just as I suspected: you can't fight your own battles."

Alpha raised a finger.

"Shut up," he ordered. As if he'd had any right—I mean, *I* didn't live there.

"Just do whatever it is you're gonna do, butt-noggin," I said.

"Duellum! Commence!"

Man, from the way he declared that, it really seemed like he thought he was announcing a heavyweight boxing match. However, before I could even utter a smart-assed rebuttal, he acted. Which . . . was precisely what I was waiting for. The moment he lunged, I moved.

A cut-off gloved hand extended toward me, and in an instant, a torrent of viscous, acidic nonsense surged in my direction, streaking across the air. It was a shimmering, smoky gray and looked like something Godzilla might projectile-vomit. I reacted, leaping to the side with a roll. The acid splashed onto the ground where I had stood, eating away at the earth and leaving a smoking pit in its wake. Then, without even looking at the dwarf, I immediately pushed myself off the ground and into a backward roll to the *other* side of where I'd started the fight, carefully hopping over the spot where the acid was doin' its *thang*.

"That all you got, ya thumb-sized anal fissure?!" I yelled.

Man, without my Blackout Warchant, fighting someone who mostly uses acid magic is going to be a real fucking pain in the dick. Anyway, here goes nothin'!

Springing to my feet, I grabbed my haladie and hurled it at Alpha, the double blades spinning end over end. He narrowly avoided the attack, but the pass nicked his shoulder.

"Ha!" I cheered.

"That's right, orc!" Edwig cheered. "First blood!"

"Bleeeeeeeed!" Rexen cackled menacingly. Dude was super messed-up sometimes.

There were other indistinct hoots and hollers from those gathered to watch, and I played to it, raising my hands in the air like a proper entertainer.

"Not bad, shithead!" Alpha retorted, looking at his arm. He smiled smugly at me before casting another wave of acid in my direction.

That was when the haladie returned, and I saw a look of surprise cross his features as I caught it like I was on the front of a Marvel poster. But I wasn't about to give him time to be impressed. I sidestepped his acid and threw my haladie again, clipping him in the thigh this time. He winced but must've decided he'd had enough, because he raised a fist, and more corrosive goo ejaculated toward me.

Damn, this fucker really is a one-trick pony! He's worse than me!

"Aww, whassamatter, Alf?" I cooed after strafing past this Spell as well. "Did somebody not anticipate I'd know what the fuck I was doing? I told you, I'm not—"

BAM!

I reeled backward as something hard hit me right in the forehead. Stumbling, I blinked stars out of my vision and looked up to see Alpha smirking. Next to me on the ground was a fist-sized stone.

"Really?!" I spluttered, clutching at my forehead. "You're throwing rocks now, you four-foot fucknut? Was your fancy acid not cutting it?"

"Pupil!" Rexen shouted from the sidelines. "He tricked you!"

"Goddammit, Arjee, I know that!"

I felt a trickle of blood slide down my brow and wiped it away. The sight of crimson on my fingers sparked a fury in me hotter than a rural school radiator. I'd gotten distracted and underestimated him, I guess. Not anymore.

"Oh, it's on, Dingleberry Shortcake," I snarled, twirling my haladie with renewed vigor. "Imma show you what a real acid trip looks like."

"Bring it!" Alpha taunted, hunkering down into a defensive stance.

With a howl worthy of a cuckolded banshee, I flung my haladie again, the blades spinning in a deadly arc. This time, he wasn't quick enough. One blade bit into his arm and he howled, spewing more of his acid shit in my direction. But I was already well beyond where he expected me to be. I had backed all the way up and gotten a nice, powerful throw in from my blades. They spun slightly to the right, but then, I'm not sure what happened, they wobbled in midair and darted left. Alpha, who was already moving that way, only had time to bring a hand up to block. But the haladie arced just past his raised fist and hit him right in the teeth with the handle. It rebounded into the air with a resounding *crack* and came spiraling back in my direction.

The entire crowd of people released a wincing groan all at once. The sound was nostalgic and made me feel like a character in a sitcom who'd just broken his boss's priceless vase.

Alpha had also made a very precious noise when the weapon had popped his pearlies, and now he was spitting blood out of his mouth.

As my haladie returned, I gripped it tight and shot him a feral grin.

"I can do this all day, jagoff. So, if you wanna keep onesie-twosying this bitch, I think you're going to end up at the bottom of this bracket."

Alpha grunted and wiped blood from his bearded chin. He glanced at his wounded arm, then at me, his eyes glowing with rage. He was about to say something—no doubt another *super* clever, gut-bustingly hilarious comment— when my haladie whirled in for another attack. The sharp blades nicked him again, drawing more blood. I mean, that was on *him*. Why was he just standing there? We were fighting. I mean, I wasn't moving either, but I'm more of a reactive-type guy, ya know?

With a surge of effort, he thrust his arm forward and a stream of acid erupted from his hand. The caustic goo gushed toward me, but I was already moving. As I vaulted into a backflip, I flung my haladie, the double blades finding their mark on Alpha's leg.

"Argh, you prick!" he screamed.

"Holy shit!" I said, turning to my friends in the crowd. "Did you see that?! I did a fucking backflip-attack! That was dope as fuck! I—Ulp—Hold on a second."

I caught the haladie and raised it menacingly at Alpha, but he rolled his eyes. Then he did something I didn't expect—just kidding, he totally just globbed acid at me like we were in a turn-based JRPG.

This next attack, though, hit a little too close for comfort. I'd had to roll as his acid spray splattered the ground where I'd just been standing. Steam hissed from the spot, a grim reminder of what could happen if I wasn't quick enough.

"Watch yourself, orc!" Edwig commanded from the sidelines.

"I'm *watchin'*, I'm *watchin'!*" I returned.

"Time's up!" Rexen shouted.

I smirked at the dwarf.

"Just one slip-up," Alpha spat, his voice a toxic growl. "That's all it'll take."

"Talk less, Alf," I replied with a crooked grin. "You're blasting your diarrhea all over the damn hell."

I feinted to the left, then swung to the right, flinging my haladie . . . yet again. It connected with his forearm. Alpha cursed, and in his distraction, I sprinted in, caught the blades on the rebound, going for a close-range attack. I slashed at him, but that was when he managed to summon a defensive cloud of acidic gas around him. I instinctively held my breath and pulled back, feeling the edges of the noxious cloud nibbling at my skin.

But I had just the thing. I figured Alpha thought Rexen's shout had been encouragement for me to whip his ass—but couldn't be sure. So, I tried something. I hit him with the full force of my Blackout Warchant. I released my nullification roar point-blank, and for a moment, the cloud was dispersed. Then I switched tactics. I stuffed the haladie in my teeth and then spun, removing my wands from my waistband.

Bet you didn't know I could use Fire and Lightning, bitch.

I took a step back for safety and flicked the wand of flames at him. With a muffled roar from my occupied mandible, I sent a blazing sphere hurtling toward the smug little sock sniffer. But Alpha was faster than I gave him credit for, his corrosive magic dousing the fireball mid-flight, reducing it to a pitiful sizzle.

"Tha'ssa new'un," I muttered from behind the haladie in my jaws, switching to the wand of lightning ball. I pointed it at Alpha, launching a crackling arc of electricity. He was ready this time, too, and he threw a glob of his magic directly at the electrifying attack. The two energies collided, resulting in a bright flash and a loud bang that left my ears ringing.

"Stop ushink y'magic to canshel o't mine, y'fuck!" I screamed, my frustration mounting.

My fingers twitched towards the Wand of Supreme Unlocking, then paused. What was I going to unlock, his death? It was a ludicrous idea, but so was everything else that happened today.

"Co' clo'er!" I taunted, trying to coax him into my range.

"No, you come here!" Alpha retorted, stumbling as he dodged another fire attack. That was when the effects of the Warchant faded, and he was able to summon his cloud again. I stuffed the Lightning Ball wand into my waistband and yanked the haladie out of my mouth.

"Have you only got three moves?" I accused.

In response, Alpha reached a hand out and I watched as one of the glittering bottles around his belt loop disconnected and flipped right up into his hand as if pulled along on a magic fishing line. Without even touching the stopper, it came uncorked, and he glugged down the green liquid inside before wiping his mouth and exclaiming, "Ahhhh!"

I stared at his Jedi maneuver with barely concealed jealousy.

Okay, that was actually pretty fucking cool. Dammit!

"Orc!" shouted Edwig. "That was very neat!"

"No, it wasn't!" I shouted back.

"Pah!" he returned. "You'll change your mind when you find out it's a Speed Potion!"

"Hey!" Alpha growled. "Tell your monster to stop cheating."

"Shut up!" I yelled back. "You cheated first! Besides—that's just information, turd boy. You think just 'cuz you got buff potions and junk, you're a real fuckin' stud?"

"I got more than buffs in here!" Alpha bragged. "A whole lot of shit that will mess you up, fucker."

So, he's got some bad-guy syrup in there, too, eh? Well, that's fine, 'cuz I'm . . .

I paused, feeling an itch in my brain . . . a symptom of what I now knew was my eleven brain cells suddenly hatching an idea.

"Fine, then! My turn!"

I darted forward, surprising Alpha so much that he hurriedly threw the empty potion bottle at me. But, because I'm apparently *great* under pressure, I simply caught it, barreling forward. As I closed the distance, I unleashed

Blackout Warchant again, bellowing with all the force I could muster. The sound wave raced forward, an invisible bulldozer aimed directly at Alpha. He tried to counter, but the corrosive magic fizzled and dissipated in the face of my nullification. His cloud of hurty dispersed, opening another aperture of opportunity as his confused and stupid expression fixed itself to his dumb dwarf face.

Seizing the moment, I blasted him with flames, and while he was busy being distracted by that, I stuffed it into my waistband, along with the bottle, and swapped it for another.

I pig-squealed, and a wave of pink magical flashes burst from the tip of the wand of unlocking. However, instead of directing it at Alpha, I aimed it at his belt, where he stored his vials. Instantly, a few of the vessels sprang open, the contents spilling onto his legs and feet. His screams filled the air as he jumped around, trying to brush off what I was hoping was dwarf-devouring liquid.

"Holy shit, it worked!" I said, shocked at the effectiveness of my harebrained strategy. There was an odd, joyous triumph in watching Alpha hop and skip, flailing his legs around. I had to admit I'd never seen a dance quite like that.

"Pah! This fight is terrible!" Edwig shouted.

"My pupil is boring!" Rexen agreed.

"Yeah, this fight sucks," said some other opinionated double-suck.

"Boo!" came a low voice from somewhere deep in the thicket of people.

In his desperation, Alpha removed a different potion from beneath his leather chest piece—a sickly yellow one—presumably to neutralize the effects, but it only served to fuel the chaos. The combination of liquids pooled around his feet, making the ground slippery. He tried to steady himself, but his foot slid and he face-planted into the bubbling ground.

I doubled over, clutching my stomach, my laughter echoing through the field. I reached out and touched the ground to keep myself from falling. I noticed a wave of chuckles emerged from the spectators, and I knew I'd found my moment.

"Oh, man," I wheezed, "you look like a certified idiot right now. Licensed and bonded."

Alpha rose from the ground, a furious gleam in his eyes. Now visibly annoyed, the dwarf made a final, desperate move. He jerked his hand into the air, and a gout of gross gray goo sprang up from the earth right in front of me.

"Gyah!" I roared, leaping backward, and that was when I felt a sharp lance of pain blossom from my chest. I looked down and saw a hatchet—Alpha's hatchet—sticking out of my left pec. I paused, staring at it, and then turned sharply, realizing what he'd done.

"You mother—"

SPLASH!

I felt an insane amount of burning agony splatter against my left shoulder. He'd got me—but not as bad as it could have been. Still, it stung like a bitch and seared my skin. Fortunately, I'd guessed the hatchet was a distraction and had pivoted quickly enough to avoid the worst of the attack. I fought the primal urge to throw my hands to the wound, to do anything that would stop the burning. I didn't need this gobbling up my digits. But goddamn, the fucking nerve of this guy—this stuff was no joke. It felt like it was burrowing its way into my flesh—and then I remembered it was acid and probably *was* doing just that. However, it seemed to hit some sort of barrier, because a message sprang up.

Condition: Acidic Burns I
Will continue to lose 1 Health per 10 seconds
Acidic Burns I's effects have been dampened due to resistances.

Ha-HA! Take that, you stupid chode weasel!
"Gotcha this time, didn't I?" Alpha declared, his voice jubilant. I could smell the acid in the air, and it was terrible, mixed with the smell of corroding flesh.
"Yeah," I said. "You did."
Then I activated Pernicious Volley and threw the rock I'd been holding.

Pernicious Volley
Trading accuracy for sheer, raw power, you can increase the damage you output with all manner of projectiles. For [8] seconds, Pernicious Volley allows you to target multiple foes and unleash untold aerial hell upon them with the chance to cultivate exponential damage with each successful strike. However, trier beware: this caterwaul bombardment packs a doozy of a punch to your Stamina and will exhaust [10] points per [1] second. The outcome for efficiency is Strength quotient + Throwing Weapons Skill.
Caveat:
If the user chooses a nontraditional weapon, then the Throwing Weapons Skill will be substituted with the Improvised Weapons Skill. This is the perfect Ability for those who value a less-measured approach or just want to see what happens when you decide to sow a little chaos.

So, my little *laughing so hard, I can barely stand* routine from a moment ago had been dual-purpose. First and foremost: self-esteem assassination. I'd wanted to make sure he knew I found him to be a literal dunce unworthy of any respect. Second, and most importantly, I'd taken advantage of the discord and palmed the rock he'd hit me in the fucking head with.

That very same stone fired from my hand with the speed of a fucking comet, blasting Alpha right in his chest and knocking him onto his back. He howled in pain from the ground. Not wanting to waste my efforts, I yanked the empty potion bottle out of my pants and tossed that, too. It whipped his way, smashing into his face and, I'm pretty sure, cutting it up *super* bad in the process.

Then I lifted my haladie and aimed at his prostrate form on the ground. I felt something familiar bubble up in my brain. A seething, rich anger that was not as explosive as my usual sort. This fury was cold and quiet.

This was a duel to the death, and he'd already made a bunch of attempts on my life. Sure, this motherfucker was a pain in my ass. Yeah, he was a stinky, fuck-faced clown. But those weren't reasons to kill him. The reason to kill him was because he was an imminent threat to my life, and I didn't have to feel bad about that. He'd killed others already—people who hadn't come back. I had a feeling there was something about this little crack circle that was responsible. But not nearly as much as he was. This was about survival—and there wasn't room for mercy in survival. There was only room for winners and losers, and I wasn't about to be a loser.

My haladie felt alive in my hands as I aimed for the sprawled dwarf on the ground. My pulse thrummed with the anticipation of victory. It was one of those moments that begged for contemplation, for a noble monologue about restraint and heroism. Perhaps a dialogue where I wrestled with the inner turmoil of ending another life.

You know how, in the movies, the big heroic hunk usually pauses, giving the villain a chance for a redemption arc? The audience expects that, right? Some grand gesture of kindness, proving that the main character is above it all—that he isn't a fuckin' giganto knob rash like his enemy. The protagonist usually hesitates, maybe even offering the villain a chance to surrender or join the right side. The crowd sighs in relief, comforted by the triumph of human goodness.

I could almost hear the imaginary audience in my head, urging me to show mercy. To let Alpha live, to walk away and teach him a lesson about humility and respect. The typical hero wouldn't take a life; they would rise above, offer lenience, and even a second chance.

But I wasn't that kind of hero.

I released the haladie right at the numpty sumbitch with all the pent-up, Ability-fueled frustration I had in my angry orc body.

And that's when a flaming creature landed on my back.

The haladie went wide, missing Alpha entirely, and I stumbled forward. A sharp, piercing pain sliced through me and I howled. The crowd, which had been cheering until now, fell silent.

Then the screams started.

I grabbed the only thing I could—one of the legs—and executed what I like to imagine was a judo-perfect shoulder throw, slamming the beast onto the ground. That was when I actually got a good look at it. And wouldn't you know it, it was, for lack of a better word, a fire spider.

The damned thing was not only flaming but also bigger than a pit bull and a whole lot meaner. Its flaming body lashed out, its spidery legs scrabbling for purchase again.

"Nice try, you punk bi—"

It flexed its legs backward, pushed off the ground, and shot right at me, burrowing its legs into the *front* of my torso this time. Then it bit me again.

"Fuck! Fuck!" I roared.

I flailed, panicking, desperate to get it off. It was a whirl of arms and legs and fire and pain and shrieking. I rolled on the ground, trying to extinguish the flames. The stench of burning hair and flesh filled the air.

The spider hissed, a chilling sound, and bit down harder. Something incredibly gross flowed from its fangs, seeping into the bite and sending fresh waves of agony coursing through me.

Alpha, the prick, was just staring like a moon-eyed piss flap at what was happening. But I couldn't deal with him right now. All I could focus on was the flaming arachnid latched on to my chest, the venom coursing through my veins, and the heat of the fire cooking me alive.

But I wasn't going to die there. I wasn't going to let a damn oversized, candle-mimicking *bug* or a tiny, acid-spewing dwarf beat me.

So what? I thought. *This isn't the fight you expected, but it's the fight you're going to win. Fuck 'em up Loon style.*

My body screamed in protest as I pushed through the pain, rolling and pounding the spider with my fist. The flames flickered, sputtered, and then died down. With a final, brutal slam, I smashed the spider off. But I wasn't done. I grabbed it by the legs, pinning them in hog-tie fashion, and spun in a circle before chucking that motherfucker with all my strength, sending it bottle rocketing away. I staggered, panting heavily.

My back *and* my front felt like they'd been fried, poison was wreaking havoc in my capillaries, and I had probably lost a fair amount of blood. Still, I looked around at the scene. The entire camp was in disarray. The whole camp—and I mean all of them—scrambled about in fear and confusion. The organized chaos of a minute before was now just plain original-recipe chaos.

I turned to Alpha, a smirk pulling at my lips.

"Well, I bet you didn't see that one co—" I started, but my words were drowned out by a sinister sound.

A high-pitched, almost ultrasonic chittering filled the air, cutting through the pandemonium like a noise-canceling lightsaber. We all froze in our tracks, heads whipping around to locate the source of the sound. Then the ground began to move. Or at least that's what it looked like.

From the edge of the encampment, a wave of creatures flooded in. They were spiders. Dozens of them. Hundreds of them. Each one bigger than the last, their bodies glowing with an eerie, unnatural light. A sea of flaming arachnids charging toward us.

The eerie silence that had fallen over the camp shattered like glass. Screams filled the air as everyone realized what was happening. Some people tried to grab their weapons, others started muttering Spells, and the rest just seemed to be tearing off to escape the inevitable death. It was a fucking scene, that's for sure.

Somewhere amidst the chaos, the elf that had arrived with Alpha suddenly stood on a tree stump and shrieked.

"FIRE SPIDERS! RUN!"

CHAPTER FIVE

THEY KILL . . .
IN SUFFICIENT NUMBERS

I was in the fucking forest, and I was running my hot little ass off.

I was up to my eyeballs in incandescent eight-legged horrors, their bodies clicking and clacking as they bore down on me, flame-kissed fangs glistening. My skin singed and sputtered under the onslaught, each graze of their fiery bodies carving a searing reminder of my predicament.

My haladie sang its deadly aria, spinning and slicing through the air with an elegance that stood at odds with the grim reality of my situation. Every cut into a bug body offered a fleeting moment of satisfaction—until the inevitable hiss of my flesh meeting their fiery death throes brought me back down to earth. I was being slow-roasted to high hell.

But it was like trying to hold back a torrent of fire with a twirling toothpick. One step forward, two steps back into a pit of glowing hellspawn. Worse yet was that most of the trees were dense but too low to the ground to be of much use in getting some clearance from these fucking things.

"Arjee, I need an up 'n out!" I yelled, my voice drowned in the screeching chaos of spider cries and the unending chitter of their bodies.

"Ahead, pupil! Ahead!" Rexen shouted jubilantly.

I peered through the wave of inferno death and saw it: a gnarled tree, older than sin and twice as twisted, beckoned. I sprung toward it, hoisting myself up the rough bark, heart pounding a manic drumline against my ribs.

But the fiery brigade was undeterred. They swarmed the base of the tree, an ever-rising tide of dancing flames and snapping mandibles. Their glowing bodies painted a horrifying canvas of light and shadows against the tree trunks, a performance of my impending doom.

Into the shadows of thick branches I danced. I slithered among the flickering silhouettes, a whisper against the noise. But they were adapting, getting smarter. The creeping heat grew ever more intense, their fiery bodies inching closer.

With acrobatic deftness, I launched from branch to branch, a silhouette specter, dropping shards of metal fury with each leap. The haladie moved as an extension of me, gleaming arcs slicing through the air, meeting scuttling bodies in a deadly embrace.

But they were many, and I was one. One doughy orc against a sea of arachnid fire, each wave washing over me, dragging me further into the depths of this flaming nightmare. I leaped down and started hoofing it hard. The world distorted around me, everything fading into an unending tide of fighting and fire.

My Health bar flickered in my vision, and I cursed. This was a fucking ticking time bomb. Every hiss of sizzling skin, each searing bite was a cruel reminder of the precipice I pranced on.

And as I teetered on the brink, Rexen floated above the chaos, a spirit amidst the storm, his voice slipping through the cracks of reality with all the charm of a manic mad hatter.

"Running, running, running. Always running, my pupil," he mused, a grin in his voice, "But never getting any faster."

"Not the fucking time!"

But the show, as they say, must go on. Especially when you're rolling deep in some flame spiders. Only the fight mattered. Only survival.

Even as I was slicing and dicing the pint-sized pyros into barbecue bits, my brain kept a subconscious tally of the Experience flooding my vision. It was like watching the digits on a gas pump—simultaneously satisfying and terrifying in the reality of what it represented.

Beside me, Rexen seemed to think this was the perfect time for a float down memory lane.

"I remember when I battled the Slavering. Vile, oozing, gross creatures they were, but oh, they had the tastiest little organs inside them. Burst in the mouth like a candied fig."

"What?!"

Rexen smiled, his eyes on the middle distance as if recalling a beloved Christmas memory.

"Ah, my pupil. Just an enemy of yore. The Slavering. Known for their paralyzing neurotoxins and insatiable appetite for brain matter."

Rexen's casual remembrance was less than comforting.

"Can you *not*, Arjee?" I grumbled, "I'm trying to keep my tender inside meats from becoming the day-olds at the delicatessen—and also pull off some money-ass kills!"

But the phantom was too caught up in his own narrative to pay me any heed.

"Flayed them like fish, I did. Squish, squish, squish, they went. Oh, it was so therapeutic!" he crooned.

Yeah, because that's just what I needed right now—a tale of a massacre set to lullaby rhythm.

In the middle of my internal rant, I failed to notice the drop in the terrain ahead. One second, I was running like a goddamn stallion; the next, the ground disappeared beneath my feet.

Suddenly, I was tumbling down a steep embankment, an avalanche of limbs and expletives.

I rolled like a demonic tumbleweed, trees and rocks and forest parts flashing by in a dizzying blur. I was a pinball in the world's worst arcade game. I was Thunderbirds. Every bump and thud sent shockwaves of pain through me.

"GyaaaUwaaaahYuuuaaaahUwaaah!" I shouted in rotational agony.

When the world finally stopped spinning, I sprawled face-first on the forest floor, swallowing a mouthful of dirty earth. Dazed and disoriented, I looked up, ready to take on the world again.

"I . . . did . . . didn't . . . hear . . . hear . . . no bell," I groaned quietly and pathetically.

And then I saw it: a cavernous depression in the earth, teeming with flame-bodied spiders, their eyes glowing like embers in the dark. Behind them all loomed a huge, ugly motherfucker of a spider, sporting a body flame so large it could cook a marshmallow from my pocket. It was like staring into a very specific, spider-infested corner of hell.

"Oh," Rexen commented with morbid cheerfulness. "We've stumbled upon their nest! Isn't that nice?"

"It is . . . *not* nice, Arjee!" I hissed, still dizzied. "In fact, it's—"

"But now we have brought their doom onto them! Go, my pupil! Rend their bodies, break their spirits. Kill them all."

Sure. What's life without a few spiders? Or a few thousand.

"Grahhhh!" I shouted, spinning my haladie and taking down another spider as I ran. To be clear, I was not running *toward* the nest of highly dangerous, insanely volatile, excessively burny arachnids—I was running away.

"You are traveling in the wrong direction, pupil!" Rexen proclaimed, grabbing my shoulders as if attempting to steer me back on track.

"Stop that, you lunatic!" I roared, slashing as another of the beasts leaped out at me.

"The true path to valor is behind you!"

"If I die right fucking now," I started, dodging out of the way of a flaming body, "I'm going to make sure my first order of business—"

CHOP!

"—as a ghost is tracking you down and beating the absolute fuckin'—"

SLICE! SLICE!

"—bejesus out of your astral ass!"

"Ah, the pupil overtaking the master," Rexen lamented. "A tale as old as time. But I should warn you: I bite."

"What else—"

I hit a group of spiders with a couple of sick body blows.

"—is new?"

Ping. Ping. Ping.

"Hold up!" I said, stabbing down into a spider and watching as it erupted into flaming death. I flicked it off my haladie and kept going. "Arjee! Do you hear that?!"

The sound had been distant but noticeable.

Rexen mimed placing a nonexistent hand to a nonexistent ear.

"Indeed, pupil," he sang. "Victory is but a whisper away."

Ping. Ping.

My boys! I internally hollered. *About damn time! Where are y—*

That's when a monstrous figure burst from the forest. A gargantuan flaming spider landed right in front of me, clearly the big boss of these unholy arachnids.

"HOLY SHIT!" I yelled, digging my heels into the dirt to halt my momentum. I windmilled my arms to maintain balance, sliding toward the behemoth of a bug.

The monstrosity chittered ominously, and thanks to my stellar, uh, language arts degree, I was able to comprehend its meaning.

Mmm . . . meal on the run. Meal is fleeing. I eat fleeing meal.

"Oh, you've got to be fucking kidding me," I groaned, backing away with my haladie at the ready. "He's huge, nasty, and dumber than a box of hair!"

"Some would argue that's an accurate description of my pupil!"

Ignoring the incorporeal burn from Rexen, I opted instead to communicate with Spidey in fluent Arachno—uh, Ancient Chitinus.

"Not food!" I yelled back, then paused.

Damn.

I was at a loss for insect words.

". . . still not food!"

You food, the spider corrected. *Running food. Big, tasty, escaping meal.*

A message popped up, revealing a congratulatory message. Or so I thought at first.

So cool! You can speak to . . . spiders, or whatever. Now you're Leveling Up? Guess you can speak to them even better now! Think you're a real hot shot, eh?

Well, whoop-de-fuckin'-do! Feast your eyes, folks! Our brave "hero" here is a cunning linguist! Except instead of anything useful, he's gossiping with smoky, elephant-sized spiders—or whatever these fire monstrosities are. Congratulations; you must be so proud!

I mean, before, you were merely squeaking out basic sentences like "Me not food"—which, by the way, *super* persuasive argument, good job on that—but now, well, now the world's your oyster. Who knows what articulate, profound discussions you'll have next with these overgrown bugs? Maybe you'll wax philosophical about the meaning of life, or discuss the nuances of early arachnid poetry.

Really, though, friend-o, the sheer scale of your accomplishment is staggering. It's right up there with other great milestones like inventing the wheel, discovering fire, or figuring out how to open childproof treasure chests. Truly, you stand among the giants.

I bet you're puffing up your chest right now, aren't you? Strutting around, flexing those wimpy muscles, and beaming with the kind of pride that only comes from such an extraordinary boon. "Look at me; I can speak Spider!" Oh, bravo, Sir Chitter-chatter! Take a bow, you fucking genius.

Remember this moment, bask in your glory, for you have ascended to new heights. You, my friend, are an official spider-speaker of Regaia. Now go, dazzle us with your newfound conversational skills. Can't wait to see how this turns out.

"Uh . . ." I wondered, looking at my wannabe spectral mentor. "What the fuck was that?"

That was not the usual type of message. It's usually snarky, but . . . I mean, wow. That was a little overkill. And did it just imply I Leveled Up my Ancient Chitinus?

Since we were connected by some kind of weird sugar baby, sugar daddy situation, Rexen could see what I saw, and at the moment, he was staring directly at the message. Or he was until it unsummoned itself and left me face-to-face with the huge monster in my path.

". . . I don't *know*," Rexen breathed, seemingly shocked.

"Forget it," I said. "We can figure it out later!"

I made to turn, but that was when the spider struck, smacking me hard with one of its legs. I flew, smashing hard into the roots of a tree, the air ejecting from my lungs. I rolled over, planning to make a swift exodus, but my bare foot was suddenly tugged and I found myself dragged harshly across the ground before being yanked upside-down into the air.

"Fuck you-fuck you-fuck you!" I shouted, slashing around my body to try to make contact with the flaming, grabby leg.

The spider, holding me about five feet from the ground, shook me. Hard. I heard my back crack and my head started spinning.

"A little help!" I yelled to Rexen.

"You're doing great, pupil!" he called back.

"What the—" I screamed. "No, I'm not! Summon me to you, you fucking dick!"

Rexen sighed.

"Being a savior is rough stuff—sometimes, *I* want to be the one to be rescued. As a treat."

The spider dangled me over its open mouth.

"Ar*JEE*!"

"Yes, yes, pupil," Rexen dismissed. "Your life is very valuable and worth saving—can we get beer after this?"

"Arjee!" I barked. "How would that even— Fuck it— Yes! Now fuckin' . . . do the thing!"

As the spider released its hold and gravity dropped me toward its considerable maw, I felt the wrenching, free-floating feeling of Rexen's Ability take hold. I sideways jackknifed in midair, jerked around the waist by magic or whatever and down toward the ground. I turned it into an adorable little somersault and was up again in a jiff, running.

"Les'go!" I said and hopped to the right, juking out of the way of a huge grasping leg and around two of the—and I can't believe I was referring to them as this—*small* spiders. I saw more barreling toward me as I ducked beneath another of the big one's strikes.

"Jumpy! Clucky! Slappy! Mortimer!" I yelled into the chaotic din. "To me!"

I wasn't sure where they were, but I'd definitely heard their bouncy ricochet sound a moment before—I thought.

"Arjee!" I yelled, seeing the telltale flash of pinks and purples next to me. "Can you tell where they are?!"

"The roe?"

"So, you *can* tell," I confirmed. "Lead us to them!"

Rexen sighed again.

"My pupil's never going to grow big and engorged with power if he keeps turning down perfect opportunities to— Oh, they're to the left."

I pivoted on a dime and dashed left, not caring if it was a straight shot, just wanting to get in the general vicinity. Thankfully, it seemed like most of the army of pyronids—as I'd decided they were called—were at my back and not in my ill-conceived path.

It only took about another minute of weaving through tangled branches and roots before I burst out into a clearing. I saw the camp across the stretch, the last vestiges of sunset making the whole spot look quite pretty—you know, if there hadn't been a bunch of people screaming and fighting for their lives against the pyronid onslaught. Apparently, I'd run in a gigantic circle, and just beyond the clear path to the makeshift settlement, the battle was still in full swing. Most importantly, however, was that right as I emerged, I found my egg bois.

The four of them were bouncing in their concentric-death-sphere pattern, staving off some of the flaming beasts that had decided it was a good idea to engage. Dozens of spider legs lay in a kind of detritus halo around their attack circumference. It looked like the baddies were starting to understand the tempo of this conflict, too, as they were beginning to back away.

"Holy balls!" I cheered. "Boys! It's time for a fucking reunion!"

At the sound of my voice, the eggs turned in unison to see me charging toward them, looking like a one hundred percent belligerent, barefooted blunder. My haladie was a blur in the air, gleaming in the sunlight, and I barreled through a few straggling spiders as I drew near. The eggs, as if in response to my enthusiasm, took the fight up a notch. Their spin-cycle kicked into overdrive, alternating between weaponized dodgeballs and slashing through spiders with the fervor of a vengeance-seeking Sawzall.

With a shout, I leapt into their midst, the haladie whirling and humming as I hacked away at anything that didn't resemble a bouncing, homicidal egg. I quickly fell into rhythm with them, our movements synchronizing until we were a seamless massacre unit that left no quarter for the pyronids in our path. The roe whirled around with me at their epicenter, letting the occasional monster inside their dome of death before I'd cut it down with a slice of my double blades. I was actually starting to kind of enjoy myself as we almost literally mowed a path back toward the camp.

"Arjee," I shouted over the clatter of combat and the hissing of flaming spider bits, "check this shit out! Tell me you're fucking seein' this."

"I am, yes," he said, sounding a bit distracted. "And even more enticing: there's something quite large and extremely upset coming this way!"

A shadow fell over me as the huge spider I'd been evading crashed through the trees behind me, its maw gaping wide as if to devour everything in its path. It collided with the orbital death machine my possessed roe had forged, and they blasted apart from one another in a springy explosion. They flew away from me, leaving one large, objectively handsome orc completely exposed.

Shit.

My pulse shot up to a hundred miles a minute, adrenaline lighting up every nerve in my body. I bolted, sprinting back toward the camp with the massive spider in hot pursuit. My legs burned from exertion and the air felt as though it was on fire in my lungs, but I had to make it.

I raced through the camp, weaving between tents and makeshift fire pits, narrowly avoiding brawls and skirmishes left and right. A human woman screamed as she smashed a pyronid with a frying pan, the heat from the spider's body sizzling the meaty grease within. A pair of grizzled dwarves were back-to-back, hacking and slashing at anything that came their way with an ax and a mace respectively. Their braided beards were dusted with ash and grime, but they whooped and hollered like it was the best time they'd had in ages. The dog man I'd seen before turned out to be a . . . well, an *okay* archer. He fired ice arrows? He missed almost every shot, but I thought I saw one actually hit a target—his face impassive even as the world burned around him.

It was a fucking wild, madhouse rumpus.

But amidst all this, I felt an odd sort of calm. This was the world I knew now, a world where I fought side by side with my murder eggs against flaming spiders, where I was chased by a monstrous queen spider while a floating sugar skull narrated the chaos.

The large spider was gaining on me—leg-quantity advantage, I think—and I was starting to feel the incredible exhaustion of prolonged athleticism on a body designed for short bursts—or, more likely, zero bursts. My Stamina bar was in the red. My throat was a desert of dehydration. My stomach hurt. I knew that at any second, I'd be out and then I'd truly be fu— I barreled over a tent, coming to an enormously painful sliding halt.

"Ugggh!" I groaned, trying to turn over to at least *see* my own demise. The massive flaming beast bore down on me, mouth chittering a war cry of hunger and glee.

There was a flash of movement and a thunderous roar. A blur of color swept across my vision and met the colossal spider with a slam that reverberated through the ground beneath me. The ground shook, and the spider was thrown off balance, its eight legs flailing in a frenzy of confusion.

My heart lurched in my chest. I knew that silhouette.

". . . Saban?" I croaked, my voice barely a whisper as I craned my neck to look.

There he was, my former best buddy, a man who, before, was the envy of my whole school, but now would make an Olympian blush. His muscles strained under his leathers as he crashed against the beast again with the enormous hammer. In the fading light, his dark skin shimmered with sweat and the dust of battle, his face twisted into a feral grin that was both terrifying and awe-inspiring.

He growled, swinging his hammer with all his might against the suburban tool shed-sized monster. Each strike connected with a bone-shattering crunch.

My mouth gaped open, half in disbelief, half in relief. But the shock was short-lived as another flash of movement caught my eye. This time it was a cascade of red hair and a shimmer of metal—a sight I'd recognize anywhere.

Rua, her hair like a sunset and a sword bigger than she was, dashed forward. Her gigantic sword was held in a two-handed grip, and the strange symbols etched into the metal of the blade glowed a blazing blue, ready to amplify any power thrown at it. She leapt toward the spider, her sword slicing through the air with a grace that was chillingly beautiful.

"I owe you one!" I yelled over to Saban and Rua, my voice ragged.

They ignored me, their attention solely focused on the mammoth spider that was regaining its composure.

Huh. How 'bout that?

"Let's cut him down," Saban said, his eyes never leaving the spider.

"Already ahead of you, man," she replied, a devilish smirk playing on her lips.

With a battle cry that echoed through the camp, they charged at the spider. The arachnid reared up, hissing menacingly. I could only watch, stunned and exhausted, as they attacked the beast. It gave me fuckin' goosebumps.

The spider reacted . . . poorly to this ambush—having just had its sweet, juicy meal denied. It stood its ground, and I felt the heat suddenly wicking off of its body as the flames billowing out of its various orifices suddenly flared, increasing in size. They coalesced around it, forming a sort of protective barrier before expanding out even farther, forcing Saban and Rua to leap back a few feet to keep themselves from being french-fried.

That was when a rich timbre of bug noises reached me. From all around, the sound was like an overwhelmingly nasty choir, except the singers all happened to be creepy-crawlies from Planet Pain-In-My-Ass. Dozens upon dozens of flaming figures scurried into view, backlining the big boy spider as they assembled around the camp.

The next wave of spiders was there.

CHAPTER SIX

YOU CAN'T BENCH-PRESS YOUR WAY OUT OF THIS ONE

My blood ran cold as I realized the magnitude of the battle we were embroiled in. I was spent, the energy sapped from my body—which was stupid. I was way higher Level than the rest of these schmucks, and I was laying around on the ground like an old grandpa. Rexen was quiet, possibly conserving energy. Saban and Rua were now locked in a duel with the spider, their chances of victory looking slim in the face of the approaching onslaught.

I stood.

"Alright," I said. "Let's fuckin' do this!"

I lifted my haladie and charged.

Then I paused, because I saw one of Alpha's potions on the ground. It was greenish with swirls of red and blue, and I couldn't tell if it was the helping or the hurting kind of elixir.

I tried to use Eye of the Saboteur on it, but all I got were question marks.

I picked it up, looking over my shoulder at Rexen.

"Can I drink this?"

Rexen studied it for a second before shrugging his shoulders.

"Iunno."

I yanked out the Wand of Supreme Unlocking and hit the potion with the Spell, the arcane lock dissolving and the cork pushing itself out and onto the ground.

"Screw it," I said, and tipped it upside down into my mouth.

I felt warmth fill my muscles and watched as my Health and Stamina bars nudged upward to about a quarter more than they were previously at. Apparently, this *was* the drinkable kind. I noticed my Arcana bar flashed but didn't move at all because it was already full, but had to assume if I'd been in need, it would have refreshed that as well.

"Al*right*!" I cheered. "Time for some patented tomfoolery!"

The fire was all around us now. Well, it wasn't just fire—it was a swirling vortex of flaming spiders, an arachnid apocalypse right out of the shittiest B-movie disaster-flick playbook possible. Despite the fact that I was in a different, much more magical world, it was still surreal. The scope of the conflict, the frantic energy, the screams, roars, and the terrifying chorus of skittering arachnids, staring at all of it with my two sorta-actually eyes. It was a scene of absolute, terrifying chaos. And I was right at the heart of it all.

I was about to yell for the eggs when I heard their familiar pinging. I glanced over my shoulder, seeing them bouncing in one direction, their mirthful ricochets slicing into the swarm of spiders. Their whirling became more erratic, deadlier, as they continued their ferocious onslaught.

Ducking under an incoming stream of fire that spurted out from where webs were on normie spiders, I noticed frightfully how—in this bonkers burning bedlam—these creatures' movements were almost imperceptible. Then I realized something else. Because of the insanity of the situation, I was far from defenseless. If it would work for them . . .

Oh, hell, yes! Moment-of-truth time, bitches!

Suddenly, I wasn't just fumbling through the battle anymore—I was *carving my merry way through it*. The massacre around me was goddamn intense, but with the confusion and masses of bodies, my Sneaking Skill was coming in *clutch*. The spiders could sense me, sure, but in the midst of the havoc, they struggled to keep track of my movements.

I found myself slipping in and out of the spider's sightlines, slicing into their carapaces before vanishing again in the fray. My B-Rank Level-Whatever-the-fuck Sneaking was making a difference, keeping me from being overwhelmed, allowing me to navigate the battlefield without drawing the ire of the entire horde.

The real game-changer, however, was the chance to utilize a new Ability that had been lying dormant in my skill set—Nightfall Strike. The power of the attack depended on the victim being unaware, a state of obliviousness I was suddenly very fucking adept at inducing. It was like the sweetest, deadliest surprise, and I imagined it might take the form of a shadowy fire bursting forth from my weapons whenever I struck from stealth.

With my newfound confidence, I decided to test it out on the next unsuspecting spider. Slipping into sneaks, I closed the distance between myself and one of the smaller pyronids. As I neared, a cool shiver ran down my spine, an indistinct pulse radiated from my haladie—apparently, Nightfall Strike was ready.

Leaping out of the shadows, I struck. The blades bit into its back, rending through it like a spoon through oatmeal. The spider screeched, then was cut off by not having a fucking screecher anymore, its flaming form convulsing as it collapsed in a heap. What was left of it, anyway. The attack was potent, amplified by the damage boost from my Ability. The Nightfall Strike left nothing in its wake but scorched and shredded spider remains. It hadn't had a dope visual effect or anything, but it was hard to argue with the results.

"Did you see that, Arjee?!" I whoop-whispered, trying to keep my joy contained while dancing away from another spider. "Tell me you fucking saw that!"

"Yes, yes, pupil," he replied, his tone barely masking the gleeful thrill in his voice. "You've certainly mastered the art of lurking. And bringing death to spiders. As expected of one of my select few apprentices."

As I continued my kung fu chaos waltz, clearing a path towards the biggest spider, I felt a sense of exhilaration I hadn't felt since starting this adventure. I almost lost my shit laughing as I took in the tumult unfolding before me. I could see now that the homies were whaling on the ginormous lead spider like he'd just tried to steal an old lady's purse.

There was Saban, smashing his hammer around like a kid high on Pixy Sticks. Every swing sent tremors through the ground like it was made of pudding. His idea of fighting a giant spider was evidently demolition derby-style, and all I could do was gawk.

Rua, sword the size of a surfboard, was working that Behemoth Blade like she was cutting up a goddamn holiday ham instead of a living Halloween hell decoration. There was magic pumping into it from somewhere, and the runes along the edge lit up the place, sparking off the blade and frying the spider's shell, stinking up the place like bad seafood barbeque.

And Edwig, fucking Edwig. The blob-shaped, sweater-vest-wearing, nerdy magic researcher was playing puppeteer with his Unseen Hand spell. That poor spider was getting pushed around more than a freshman on senior prank day. I noticed that he'd pause every so often and cast a Spell of some kind on Rua's sword, which was where the amplification was coming from. I didn't know what it was but trusted that between the two of them, they probably knew what they were doing.

The rest of the campers? The brave, dumb fucks were trying to play hero, flinging themselves at the spider with the grace of a bunch of monkeys at a banana festival. Me, though? I was about to charge in there, 'cuz y'all *know* I can't be left out of a jam-packed injury jamboree. But this was when I smacked right into the most annoying obstacle of them all—Alpha.

The smug, pasty dwarf—fresh from his near-loss in duel before we'd been rudely interrupted—had just popped up out of the blue. Just my luck, caught in a monstrous mosh pit with a grudge to settle.

I instantly held up one of my wands—you know, I wasn't even really sure which one at the moment—but Alpha just looked past me and sprayed three whole spiders with his acid shit. They chittered in hilarious pain before dissolving into flaming nothing, and Alpha spun, blasting another few into similar straits.

"He is still strong," Rexen said, and he almost sounded impressed. "Still has time on his Citizen Surge."

"Well . . ." I started, not quite sure what to say to that. It appeared that he was actually *helping* rather than doing the big-bad-guy move of choosing an inconvenient time to have our one-on-one.

I slashed another monster that got too close to me, and found myself standing next to Alpha as I rolled out of the way of another attack.

Just fucking great. We're surrounded together.

"Get the fuck out of here," Alpha said to me as I cut down a spider that leaped in our direction. He punctuated his statement with the defensive cloud of his hydrochloric hate shield. I sidestepped, not wanting to get chemically cremated, and just snorted at him.

"Why?! Afraid I'm going to—" I ducked from beneath a leaping spider's attack but wasn't able to dodge as another latched on to my forearm. I shrieked and began shaking it off frantically. But it stayed lodged, so I started stabbing it like a madman until it stopped moving and I was able to pry it off. Meanwhile, Alpha was still at it with his Spells.

"Yeet!" he shouted, hitting two at once with a blast of acid. "Yeet! Yeet! Yeet!" Each douchey exclamation was delivered with all the cocky seriousness of someone who has never once in their life stopped to consider how stupid they looked. Still . . . it didn't stop him from utterly demolishing anything that came within range. The acid splattered, too—so, any spiders hanging out next to their best friend often received a healthy dose of residual damage, which greatly dissuaded them from trying to get closer.

However, as we slashed and splashed, the horde kept coming, and I was really starting to tire out. My Stamina was getting low—dangerously so—and I wasn't sure how much longer I could keep this up. To make matters worse, I noticed that every bite added a bit more of a gunky green tint to my Health bar, and that seemed . . . not super good. A poison effect of some kind, I'm sure, but it was weird that I didn't get a notification for it. Oh, well, fuck it.

I was breathing like an out-of-shape racehorse, my attacks were getting slower, and my patience was wearing thin. I shot a look at Alpha, who seemed to be as energetic as he was stupid—which meant he still had Stamina in reserves. Fucking Citizen Surge.

"Hey!" I shouted at him.

He looked back, just having finished doing his little wall-of-acid maneuver. "What?"

"Gimme one of your Stamina potions or whatever—I'm fucking fading here."
"Fuck off," he said, and turned back to the fight at hand.
"Ooh, you little shithead," I hissed. "I know you've fucking got some, and—"
I was interrupted as two spiders glomped on to my torso at once.
"Fuck this!"
Rather than fight them at their advantage, I belly-flopped onto the ground, suplexing them into the dirt and then stabbing their idiot brains in half with the haladie. Then, seeing as how trying to use Sneaking was useless at the moment, I hauled off with the wand in my hand and blasted more of the buggy bitches to bits with crackling electricity magic. It wasn't until I'd killed about five that I realized how lucky I'd been to have been holding the Wand of Lightning Ball. I hadn't checked, and it would have been super embarrassing to hit them with a firebolt or, worse, unlocking.

But they didn't stop. Wave after wave surrounded us and, as a result, drew me farther and farther away from the battle I *actually* wanted to be having with the big one. I could see from my vantage that several more of the crew from the camp had joined Saban, Rua, and Edwig, and were enjoying the just desserts of lookin' fly as a motherfucker as they assisted in ruining that huge bastard's day.

"Those are my cookies!" I bellowed, and tried to fire over the writhing mass of personal space invaders to get a cheap shot in on the big boy. But one of the smaller ones leaped at one of the non-spidey combatants and I accidentally hit it by mistake. It dropped out of the air, and the elf—I think—that had almost been murdered gave me a salute before continuing to fight.

"Goddammit! I wasn't trying to save someone; I was trying to look *cool*!"

But I was interrupted by being clocked in the chin by a spider, and it reset me to being pissed off in the opposite direction again as I killed it for its insolence.

And on it went. I couldn't even keep track of how many spiders fell before me as I convulsed in the swarming sea of them. However, my Stamina being almost depleted eventually caused my movements to become sluggish, and more and more of the monsters were getting solid digs in. Blood flowed from about a thousand different wounds, and my muscles screamed. I'd already been exhausted, and now I was fuckin' *beat*. But because occasionally the fates saw fit to reward me for being a motherfuckin' ultra stud, I got a notification.

Condition: Fatigued
Fatigue I
- *Abilities and Skills suffer -5% efficiency while under the Fatigue I condition effect.*

Another message populated then, and I grinned from ear to ear.

Because of Fatigue I, Loon's Bombastic Beatdown Aegis has temporarily reached Tier I effects.
- Strength Attribute increase [+4 multiplied by 100%]!
- Dexterity Attribute increase [+4 multiplied by 100%]!
- Constitution Attribute increase [+4 multiplied by 100%]!

Strength: 38 (Fatigue I)
Dexterity: 38 (Fatigue I)
Constitution: 88 (Fatigue I)

"Arjee," I said seriously, despite my smug grin.

"Pupil," Rexen responded, nearly matching the sincerity of my severity—though I couldn't tell if he was being genuine or simply adopting a tone for funsies.

"I'm going to need you to warn anyone without eight legs that they should get as far away from me as possible. It's gonna get fucked-up."

Rexen surprised me by merely saluting and flitting away—presumably to heed the caution I'd tasked him with.

Alpha was still standing by me, handling the spiders. He laughed.

"What—you a fucking werewolf now?"

I shook my head.

"Fuck you," I said. "I don't care if you live or die—so do whatever you want. But you heard me, dipshit—get the fuck outta here if you care about yourself at all."

He just laughed again and didn't make a move other than to keep fighting.

Well, no one could say I didn't try to warn him.

I focused. The feeling. Simmering just below the surface. I'd been holding it back for nearly the entire insect insurrection, but now I didn't have to. Every fang and every stab, every bruise, just making me angrier and angrier. I couldn't even consider the idea of how cool it was to uncork the dick-punching of a lifetime on people like the Hulk—because that would set me back too much. Instead, I married the sensation with the furiousness of how I still felt about the world I was trapped in. The system. The bullshit rotting diapers who had pulled me there. My losses. I channeled my trauma and pain and sadness to a razor's edge, and then I released it.

Primal Rage.

CHAPTER SEVEN

NOBODY PUTS GABE-Y IN A CORNER

And that's when it fucking happened. The familiarity was like a floodgate had been flung open in my mind, and I felt it hard. Primal Rage. The taste of it was like molten copper on my tongue, the scent of it, pure adrenaline. A bestial roar clawed its way out of my chest, echoing out through the chaos like the fanfare of the damned.

I felt my very essence surge. Every fiber in my being screamed with a raw, savage delight that was both terrifying and intoxicating. I could feel the adrenaline coiling in my gut, ready to explode into action, a wildfire raging beneath my skin.

I was going to kill everything. Everything. It would die. I would destroy. Destroy. *Destroy.* Fucking murder them all and drag them into hell on my back.

In my haze, the screams around me faded into the background, drowned out by the throbbing pulse of my own heartbeat—war drums. My muscles vibrated, twitched, alive with an intensity that made the rest of my life seem like a muted, watercolor dream.

I could hear the hissing of the spiders, could taste the stench of their venom on the back of my tongue, could see the intricate patterns on their burning carapaces. Everything was magnified, distilled to its purest, rawest form. I was no longer just Loon. I was a force of nature, a hurricane made flesh.

I was fucking alive.

My body moved without my command, cleaving a bloody path through the swarm of fiery spiders. Each slash, each thrust of my blade was met with a gush of arachnid innards, their chitinous bodies parting before my scorn. Blood—mine, theirs, who the fuck cared—spattered across my skin, a macabre masterpiece in crimson. But each wound, each prick of pain only spurred me on, fueling the inferno inside me. I was a goddamned phoenix, born anew in blood and fire.

The pain? Oh, it was there, a myriad of tiny mouths gnawing at my flesh. But it was distant, muffled beneath the uncaged animal that roared in my veins. Each bite, each scratch was simply proof of my existence, a beautiful ode to my indomitable will. Pain was nothing and everything. My life force also seemed unerring, unmoving, even as my enemies drove their might into me. Mine was a strength that would not be cowed.

Fuck, it felt good.

With each spider that fell before me, I moved closer and closer to the big one, the twisted beast that commanded this horde of spawn. It was a mountain, a god amongst these insects, but to me, it was just another target. What good is a candle flame against the infernos of hell? The war drums were pounding. Pounding. Pounding. A wild, visceral beat that matched the rhythm of my onslaught. Pounding.

I was coming for it, the symphony of my wrath growing ever louder, the world painted in shades of red and fire. And I was grinning like a madman, lusting for the taste of victory, for the heady rush of the kill.

I was on the war path, and I was loving every goddamn second of it.

I didn't know how long I lived in the din. Dwelled in the mire of the mayhem—beautiful fucking mayhem. It was only a moment. It was infinity. I devoured the space keeping me from the big one, dashing the flock of its believers. I stabbed. I struck. A spider leaped into my path, intent on a feast of my flesh, but I caught its flaming body in my hands—hands built for murder. I yanked the monster forward and crashed my skull against its head.

SLAM.

SLAM.

SLAM.

SLAM.

Again and again I cudgeled it against my crown and left it a demolished husk when I was done, hurling its body into the tide rising against me and continuing forward. I stabbed a beast through the abdomen, wrenching upward, ripping its bowels out. Then I stuffed my hand inside, seizing the guts and tangling them around my fist as I broke another pyronid with pure pummeling anger. The creatures continued, but so did I. I saw the edge, my quarry in my sights, not far. Battling. Warming up to its death by my hands.

With a final, savage bellow, I hurled myself toward the big fucker, my blade gleaming like a comet's tail in the fiery glow. The world tilted on its axis as I left the ground, the raging force in me detonating like a supernova.

I hit it like a goddamn cannonball. There was a screech of surprise as I plowed into its massive body, and for a brief, glorious moment, I was the eye of the storm. I was a whirlwind of violence, a maelstrom of destruction. My blade cut into the spider's body, black ichor erupting from its wounds and splattering across my arms.

I was a tempest, a typhoon of raw, unfiltered power. My fists, hardened by the feeling coursing through me, slammed into the spider's face. Each strike was a promise of pain, each kick a declaration of dominance. I was the embodiment of fury, the avatar of wrath.

I laughed. A savage, throaty chuckle that teetered at the brink of a mindless abyss. The joy of it, the thrill was like a drug, and I was fucking high.

I howled.

Rua's mind grappled with the enormity of the arachnid onslaught. It was a seething, frenzied sea of fiery bodies that surged toward them in endless waves. The sheer volume of these horrors was mind-boggling—they were an inexhaustible tide of destruction that battered against them, crashing in ceaseless, relentless waves. While she posited they must not be high-Level, they were so numerous that it hardly mattered. She'd already seen several of the members of the settlement fall to their combined strength, their desperate cries for help swallowed by the roaring tumult of battle, and that was not even considering what would happen if they didn't kill the gargantuan spider soon. The monster towered above the rest, a monument to their impending doom. Its rugged, flaming armor seemed impervious to the combined attacks of Saban, Edwig, and herself. Despite their unyielding assault, the creature persisted, seemingly undeterred, the flames in its eyes undiminished.

Edwig had been calling upon his Copy Spell, which was currently mimicking attacks from Dalton—Alpha's second-in-command. The elf was nearby, though he was using his abilities to fend off the encroaching horde. Rua didn't fully understand the mechanics, but she knew Edwig's actions reinforced her own attacks as he cast the mirrored effects on the Behemoth Blade. She thought it might be some kind of non-elemental Spell, as it lacked the distinct characteristics of fire, water, lightning—common elements she had come to associate with much of the world's Arcana. Her knowledge of Regaia's arcane intricacies remained limited, a lamentable fact that bothered her more than she cared to admit. She hoped that would change eventually—the prospect of delving into the logistics of Regaia was pretty enticing. But she'd have to survive first. Which meant putting down this current threat.

Amid the chaos, she moved with coryphée grace, wielding the Behemoth Blade with surprising ease. Its curious lightness belied its enormous size, and its perfect balance gave her the illusion of fighting with a much-smaller weapon. In her grip, the ancient steel felt like an extension of herself—a lethal dance partner that moved with her in a butcher's ballet.

She reveled in the surge of adrenaline that made her senses sharp, her movements quick. But beneath the exhilaration, a persistent question gnawed at her mind: how were they to overcome such overwhelming odds? The thought was like an insistent whisper in the back of her mind, a quiet voice drowned by the battle but not entirely silenced.

Even as she attacked, her mind raced. Strategies, tactics, desperate plans, all whirled in a frenzied vortex of thought. She knew they needed a breakthrough, a decisive strike to turn the tide. But what? And how?

As she cleaved through another wave of arachnids, Rua felt a grimness settle within her. One way or another, they would find a way.

Rua's gaze was pulled from the monstrous spider she was battling when a bloodcurdling roar cut through the frenzy of the fight. It was like the baying of a wolf, a savage call to arms that made her blood chill and her heart pound.

Her eyes fell on Loon wading through the last of the fiery arachnids, a grim smile tugging at the corners of his mouth. He was covered in blood and soot, his eyes ablaze with an unholy light. She had seen him fight before but never with such animalistic intensity.

There was an odd thrill that tugged at her, a morbid fascination as she watched him. Her fingers tightened around the hilt of her sword, her breath hitching in her chest. She was struck with a sudden realization: this was a man who not only embraced the chaos but thrived in it.

And then, with the finality of a guillotine, Loon howled and launched himself at the monstrous beast.

He crashed into the titanic spider, a guttural screech escaping the monster as it bucked beneath his impact. For a single, suspended heartbeat, there was quiet. But then Loon had transformed into pure rage. His blade bit into the spider, spewing its lifeblood.

He continued. His fists pummeled the spider's hideous face. And he laughed. A sound as wild and unhinged as the scene unfolding around them, teetering dangerously on the edge of madness. The sheer ecstasy of battle, the intoxicating thrill of the kill danced in his eyes, fuel mainlined in his blood-soaked euphoria.

But all of that dissolved in an instant just as the Primal Rage seemed to leave his body. His eyes softened, his body relaxed, and despite the severity of the situation, he seemed to return to a more-confused state. Of course, that was also when the spider connected with a powerful blow that caught Loon off guard and sent him soaring over the battlefield, landing right in the thick of the writhing mass of spiders.

"Oh, Loon . . ." she groaned.

* * *

"WUHHHHHHHH?!" I choke-screamed confusedly as I was fucking punted straight outta the fight and into . . . another, more annoying fight. I landed in the swarm of spiders with a crunch, and I screamed again reflexively—prepared to find out I'd broken my neck. But I realized from the cries beneath me that I'd *actually* broken something else: a spider.

I rolled off quickly and inspected my kill. I'd been wrong: it was four spiders.

"Ha! Take that, ya varmints!" I cheered.

But man, these motherfuckers were not at all interested in letting up. Like British soldiers in a Revolutionary War movie, they simply filled in the gaps where their comrades had fallen and swarmed me. That was when several loud *thwack*s thundered from somewhere beyond the scope of my immediate fight. Spiders fell dead around me, crossbow bolts in their bodies. I glanced up from the direction they looked like they'd come and saw the human who'd arrived with Alpha, posted atop the train wreck, one eye closed, the other staring down the sight of the crossbow like a sniper. I gave him a wave of thanks and he nodded, then sent a few more bolts over the course of as many seconds, and I realized he was clearing a path for me.

Well, far be it from me to look a gift horse in the—

"Ah! Bitch!" I screamed. I'd fucking stepped on one of the dead spider's fangs in its stupid open mouth, and that was when my Health bar went full booger green and I suddenly got hit with a chubby case of the woozy-wobblies.

You are Confused!

Hey, hey, you've got a . . . Is it a bee? A leetle baby beeee. Beebee. No! It's a case of venom in your veins! . . . Or was it gravy in your socks? Eh, who's counting? Six. No! Shelven! I'm confused, you're confused, we're ALL confused—but I'm confused too!

Minus: a lot of stuff, man.

Intelligence: woof.

Wisdom: Double woof.

How did you get that hand towel? Give it back water! Give it back—water! WATER!

How long's this party going for? Oh, let's say sixty . . . somethings. Could be minutes. Could be days. Could be really, really short years. Wait, are you going to die? Heheheheh! Ha! Oh . . . what're we laughing four times eight? SIXTEEN!

Confusion! Confusion! Confusion! Saying it makes it go to jail. You're under arrest.

I'm going to break this down for you. At the time, immediately following this oh-so-delightful prompt, this was roughly the way I was perceiving the world around me:

Land spinning. Whoa. Whoaaaa. I don't feel so good in my head parts. Bad-style. I wanna make puking happen, but I dunno which way is up, down, or up. Swaying. Uh-oh. Oh, I'm fine— No, I'm not! Am I . . . drunk? Am I super drunk? Do I want a sandwich? I should get a sandwich. Meat. Ballll.

Other stuff is biting me. Swat. Swat. Swat their silly-billy heads—why are they still biting? Little buggers. Ignore! There we go. Going to the . . . place. The big spider place. This bitey stuff keeps dying because the long wood things are biting them back. My helpful friend is being helpful. What a good guy. He's gettin' a Christmas card! Why does everything smell like pain? Oh, right. It's Saturday. LIVE FROM NEW YORK, IT'S— Ow. I fell.

Where is that sandwich I asked for? Never mind, I'll just get it myself. Dammit, getting more bites. Why? Because I asked for a sandwich?

MORE CONFUSION
You.
Blug. This ain't good.

Muscles: Ham's shake.
Thinkity-Winkity: Sharp as a pair of curtains.
Dex . . . dextorily: Flamingo playin' maracas!
Ham's shake 2: Midichlorians are the powder hutch of the smell.

I'm going to tell you right now—I don't really know what happened for most of the rest of that, but at some point I came to, mid-step into a particularly nasty little patch of flaming grass. I paused, the entire world suddenly roaring to life with pain.

"AHHHHHHHHHHHHHH!" I screamed.

Christ fuck! Everything hurt so fucking bad! Fuck!

I zeroed in on my Health bar and almost screamed again.

3/550 Health remaining!

I was gonna die! Thankfully, as I looked around, covered in burns, punctures—and something purple on my crotch that I was absolutely not going to ask questions about—I could see a trail of dead spider bodies marking my passage. Worse was, I'd meandered off course and was now near the outskirts of the skirmish. The number of spiders had dwindled considerably but not enough to make them give up and go home, apparently. There were still easily a hundred of the fuckers moving around, attacking people. I was now well out of sprinting distance of the big spider. At least I could get my bearings and— *Ah, shit, the spiders are still coming for me.*

"Rip in peace," I muttered.

CHAPTER EIGHT

OGRES ARE LIKE ONIONS

However, it was precisely at that moment that several homies tore their way through the ranks to join me in the outfield.

First, Rexen—useless, but it's the thought that counts.

Second, third, fourth, and fifth—Jumpy, Cluck, Slappy, and Mortimer. Not useless.

Sixth was . . . somebody I'd never seen before.

He was a rail-thin . . . person who looked mostly like a human wearing some standard-fare fantasy drip. What changed his Race category, though, was that he had bright green hair and a beard to match. Oh. And a pair of deer antlers jutting out of the top of his fucking head. He seemed a bit twitchy, his eyes shifting around like he was being forced to be there under the threat of some horrible punishment.

"Um . . . hi," I said to the newcomer. ". . . How's it going?"

"It's . . . okay," he said, his voice dripping with anxiety. He kept looking over his shoulder at the approaching horde. "Could be better, actually."

"You, uh, alright there, bud?"

"Yeah . . ." he said, his face screwing up in a nervous wince as there was a loud explosion beyond. "Just . . . trying to keep from pissing myself."

"Oh—yeah, that'll happen," I said. "Just gotta let 'er rip and clean yourself off later. I mean, I assume so—I've never done it, but, hey—what else can you do?"

The man scowled at that thought and looked like he was going to be sick.

"Okay, well, there's not much time for chatting here—I'm Loon. That's Arjee—and these are Jumpy, Clucky, Slappy, and Mortimer. If you can't fight, just stay behind us and—"

"Tanner," he said. "And . . . I can fight; I'm just bad at it. It's not really my best feature . . ."

"Okay... *Tanner*," I said. "Well, shit. This changes my plans..."

I'd been planning to bounce my way over the first wave and dash apart the middle section, then activate my flight power. But now that there was someone else here... And like... why *was* he here? Did he show up to help and then get cold feet? Was he already out there hiding? I supposed it didn't matter, but goddamn, this shit was going to make matters more difficult.

"... Still—stick behind us while we drop nasty nonsense on these fucks," I continued, "and if you can get a hit in, fuckin' do it—but maybe don't do it while we are—"

"I'm... mostly a healer..." he said hesitantly.

"Oh—shit! Never mind! This is some motherfuckin' serendipity! You're a medic, and I'm basically at death's door right now. Suppose it's—"

"Yeah..." Tanner interrupted softly. "I saw. My interface lets me see all the injured people... and junk. That's why I... made my way over here."

He huffed out a big, loud sigh, like he was extremely overwhelmed, and then, with his head slightly down, bent his elbow—not even fully extending his arm—and pointed a single digit directly above him.

"Lifeblood Invigorate..." he muttered.

There was a flash, and some kind of magical symbol appeared in the air, rippling with green light. The dazzling show was about ten thousand times more intense than the... negative gusto the antlered man had displayed. In seconds, I was wrapped up in a veritable blanket of healies, impressed as I watched my Health suddenly top itself off.

"Whoa!" I exclaimed, examining my body as the wounds and bruises suddenly evaporated from my flesh. "Fuckin'... *damn*, dude. This is some dope magic you got! I think I'm gonna keep you around for a wh—"

"Time to fight, pupil!" Rexen interrupted.

"Awriiight—never mind, we'll take it as it comes!" I said, trying to sound more excited than I actually felt, and clapped. "Let's get back in there, boys!"

Tanner shifted, slipping back behind our ranks as the spiders scuttled up to bat. The roe projected their thoughts into my mind.

Fight. Crush. Obliterate them fully! Boo!

I snorted. Some of them were a little more advanced than others. Clucky's progress had been interesting to witness as he was developing into... something more. Already he seemed able to understand nuance a bit better than the others, and to follow and execute more sophisticated instructions.

"Clucky, I want y'all to fall back behind me while I clear a path, then when it looks like there's a good opportunity—death globe centered on me."

Will. Do, came Clucky's response in his oddly lower roe voice.

"Arjee—scout ahead, let me know where the best path to push is to get us right up in the action."

Rexen nodded and released a delighted sound, then shot forward to hover over the chittering sea of spiders perhaps only fifty feet from us.

"Tanner . . ." I said. "Keep us alive, I guess—whatever you can do. I'll try to make your job boring, though."

With that, I charged, the Wand of Lightning Ball in one hand and my haladie in the other.

With a surge of energy, I charged into the fray, a roiling storm cloud of spider bodies and slicing blades. Sparks of electricity danced across my wand, casting an eerie blue glow in the gloaming. The roe followed in my wake, bouncing through the air like lethal ping-pong balls.

"To your left, disciple!" Rexen's voice rang in my ear, directing me where to go.

I wheeled around, haladie flashing as I cleaved through a spider the size of a mini-fridge. It let out an unholy squeal as its body burst apart, ichor splattering over my clothes.

"Ha!" I exclaimed, slinging the goop off my blade.

Just as quickly, I pivoted to meet another spider. Rexen's shouts guided my every step, driving me into the thick of the chaos. I *Chainsaw Man*'d through the swarm, each strike ripping through exoskeletons with the efficiency of a well-oiled machine.

And then I saw it. The death globe. A swirling maelstrom of spinning roe encircling me in a dome of shimmering teeth. Each one of them was a spinning top, biting and gnashing at anything that tried to break through. Rexen had guided me into the eye of the storm.

I glanced over to see Tanner trapped in there with me. The look on his face was . . . I dunno, strange. Like if someone could be both apathetic and also terrified.

"Um . . . Loon, right?" he breathed, "I . . . uh, didn't sign up for this."

"Bruh, none of us did," I grunted, slashing through another spider. "But we're fuckin' here now, duder. Just keep us alive, alright?"

Turning back to the fight, I lifted my wand, electricity crackling down its length. I pointed it at the swarm of spiders and let loose a blast of lightning. The air sparked as electrical energy arced from my wand to the spiders. They convulsed and twitched as the raw power surged through them, lighting up their bodies like fucked-up fairy lights. The smell of burnt bug bodies filled the air, making me gag. But I kept going, lightning pouring out of me in a continuous stream.

Rexen's voice echoed in my head, a calm oasis in the storm.

To your right! Ten paces! There's a large group clustered there.

I swiveled, adjusting my aim, and let the lightning crackle through the ranks. They shrieked, their bodies jerking in the agonized throes of death. With each strike, I could feel the numbers around us dwindling, and did I dare to hope? Perhaps the tide of the battle was shifting.

I glanced over at Tanner, his face pale covered in a sheen of sweat in the unnatural light. But he was standing firm, casting out waves of healing energy that washed over me, healing the injuries as I sustained them.

"Attaboy, Tanner!" I shouted over the din of the fight. "Fuck it up with them good vibes!"

Almost there, disciple mine! Rexen said mentally.

Hell fuckin' yeah, I returned.

The air was thick with smoke and the stench of electrocuted flesh. My heart pounded in my ears, the adrenaline slowly receding as the reality of our victory began to sink in. Around me, the battlefield was a carpet of charred spider bodies, their formerly glowing eyes dull and lifeless.

As the last of the spiders around us fell, I glanced around, expecting to see the grotesque body of the giant spider. Instead, all I saw were more of the smaller ones, their numbers thinning but still large enough to be of concern.

"Rexen!" I barked, spinning to face the little fucker. "I thought you said you were guiding us towards the big one!"

His hovering form bobbed in the air, his eyes twinkling with a kind of manic glee.

"Oh, I was!" he trilled. "But then I saw all these little ones and thought they would be fun to fight!"

I groaned, rubbing a hand over my face.

"That was not the plan, Arjee."

"Plans, shmans!" he said, grinning even wider. "This is the true path to mastery, pupil! Relish in it!"

I was about to retort when more spiders rolled in.

"Fucking . . . *goddammit!*"

I noticed the roe lagging, their once-bright luminescence dimming. They were still fighting, but the relentless wave of spiders was taking a toll.

"Tanner!" I called, pointing to the roe. "You got anything that can . . . Stamina . . . boost them?"

He blinked at me, his eyes wide.

"I have something like that, but . . . I've never healed a . . . a *monster* before," he admitted. "I don't know if I can."

"Will you . . . jus— Just fucking try!" I shouted, slicing through another spider that had gotten too close.

Taking a deep breath, he gestured lazily and muttered a Spell. A soft green glow enveloped the roe, and their energy seemed to return full force.

"Shit, yeah, Tanner!" I cheered. "You're getting a promotion!"

"Promotion . . ." he wondered.

Just then, a ground-shaking roar echoed across the battlefield, silencing the chitters and screams of the spiders. I whipped around, scanning the field, and saw a tidal wave of spiders suddenly erupt into the air, their bodies sent flying like shrapnel. In their wake stood a monstrous creature, a terrifying beast that dwarfed even the largest spider on the field. It was massive, standing at least fifteen feet tall, with a hulking, half-doughy, half-muscular form that spoke of incredible strength. Its skin was rough and dark, with patches of moss and dirt matted into its long gray hair. Its face was brutish, with a broad nose, deep-set eyes, and a mouth full of broken, yellow teeth.

"Double-fuck me sideways," I hissed, my eyes wide as I took in the sight of the creature. "What in the holy dick is that?"

"Oh . . . that's Tartarus," Tanner whispered beside me, eyes wide and fixed on the giant creature.

I blinked at him, incredulous.

"What? Don't tell me . . . he's one of *ours*?!"

Tanner nodded, swallowing hard.

"Yeah . . . he's a . . . um . . . He's . . . from before. A teacher, or something."

What were the odds there was more than one teacher onboard the train at the time of our rehoming? Probably pretty nil. Because of that, I made an assumption.

"Mr. Eldon?!" I shouted. "Seriously?! He named himself after fish-stick sauce?"

Now, if it was him, *that* was a fucking surprise. My painfully dull and mundane history teacher—and let's not forget: field-trip chaperone—had rolled himself a fucking *monster* Race?

"Where the hell was he hiding?!" I demanded. "He's a bit big to have gone unnoticed before."

Tanner shrugged.

"He . . . mostly keeps to himself out in the woods. At least . . . I think so. I haven't seen him since we got attacked on our first day."

As if on cue, the former instructor let out another bone-rattling roar and yanked a fucking tree trunk outta the ground like it was a baseball bat. He began to barrel through the sea of pyronids, each furious swipe of his makeshift cudgel sending spiders flying and clearing a wide path.

With each bellow, the earth-shaking sounds caused an echo of . . . anxiety to ripple through my body. It was an instinctual, deep-rooted terror, and every fiber of my being screamed at me to run.

I took a step back, my mind reeling.

Why am I feeling like this? Why would I be scared of an ally?

As I hesitated, struggling with the impulse to bolt, Rexen must've noticed . . . or possibly *felt* my emotion and piped up. His voice was gleeful, almost pining.

"Do you *sense* that, pupil!? *That's* the ogre's Racial ability. It's not just loud; it's scary! It casts a fear effect on all who hear it. Pretty neat, huh?"

"Neat?" I shouted, my voice trembling slightly. "Why the fuck is he just blastin' that shit off all friendly-fire style? I feel like I'm about to shart myself!"

It took me a second for something to make sense. Had Rexen just said he was an *ogre*? Goddamn. I really got short-changed in the species offerings when I showed up. I'd had the choice between this . . . and human. Fuck this system.

"Do not be an envious disciple," Rexen said.

"I'm not!" I said indignantly. "This isn't what envy looks like, you fuckin' bimbo! I just think it's fuckin' rude to spray-and-pray *phobia* beams in mixed company, that's all! Somebody's gonna get hurt."

As . . . Tartarus kept charging, I realized he was beelining toward the massive spider. My hackles rose. What the fuck? That was *my* kill. I'd already made a good dent in it, softened it up with my angry antics, but it seemed like Tartarus was gonna steal the final shot. The motherfucking *hell* if I was going to let that happen.

"I've got an idea!" I said, turning to my roe. "Protect, uh, this Tanner fellow. Arjee, you're with me!"

"Let's *murder them*," Rexen hissed jubilantly, rubbing the ends of his arms together.

"Wait . . . where are you going?!" Tanner called out, panic edging his voice. The spiders were closing in again and he looked terrified, his eyes darting from me to the roe to the oncoming horde.

"Be right back!" I called, not bothering to explain.

I stepped out of the rotating homicide sphere and reached up, tapping the choker around my neck: Bahlgus's Enchanted Gorget of Flight. Instantly, the ground beneath my feet disappeared as I shot up into the sky. A colorful tail of light trailed behind me, the result of the cosmetic add-on baked into the extra features of the item.

As I climbed higher, the battlefield below began to shrink, turning into a chaotic patchwork of fighting figures. Tartarus was easy to spot, the giant ploughing his way through the spider hordes. And just ahead of him was my target, the massive spider that I'd staked my claim on.

I had no idea if my plan would work, but if it did, it would be fucking *tite*. At the very least, I wasn't going to let Tartarus get the glory of taking down the giant spider. I'd sat through far too many of his boring-ass lectures in my life to let that happen. Up, up, *up* I went, flying forward a bit to ensure I'd be right over the top of the big beast when I hit my max distance. Then, with a final look at the battlefield below, I turned my gaze toward my target and prepared to dive.

"Outta the way!" I screamed, though I doubted anyone could hear me over the noise of battle below. I angled my body downward, pointing myself like a missile.

"GRAWWWR!" I bellowed, in a low, menacing death growl as I fired a blast of lightning from the wand.

"GRAWWWR! GRAWWR! GRAWWR!"

Each Spell flashed down in quick succession. Then I followed it up with my finisher. A surge of adrenaline rushed through me as I activated the Gorget again.

The Gorget hummed and pulsed against my skin, a beacon of arcane power that was now propelling me toward the ground at breakneck speed. The wind whipped around me, tearing at my clothes and hair, as I sped toward the ground faster than an adulterous cannonball that left his phone unlocked at home. I could see Tartarus below, still swinging his massive tree trunk with wild abandon, crushing and tossing aside spiders like they were toys.

The ground rushed up at me, the enormous spider coming into focus. I tightened my grip on my haladie, preparing for the moment of impact, and didn't even bother bracing for the collision. Then I activated my favorite aspect of Calden's Hang Time.

It felt like the world held its breath in the moment before I hit. The ground and the spider were right there in front of me. There was a moment of surreal calm, and then . . .

Rua, positioned precariously on top of the big beast, had the unfortunate distinction of possessing a ringside seat to the madness that unfolded beneath her. She watched with bated breath as Loon did what he always did—something *extra*, streaking through the sky like an ecstatic comet clearly late for an appointment with ground zero.

She noted that the trajectory of Loon's reckless descent seemed to line him up for an extremely intimate meeting with the monolithic spider she had only just successfully hit with a gruesome slice. This particular brand of extreme bullheadedness seemed perfectly on-brand for Loon, she reflected, having seen him do things before that would make a stuntman consider a career in accounting.

As Loon neared his target, Rua instinctively leaped away, hoping she could somehow avoid the inevitable shockwave of his strike from her close proximity.

She wasn't an expert on gravity—though she was probably the most knowledgeable among those present—however, she did know that things falling from great heights tended to make quite a mess on impact. Especially if they were aiming to turn a colossal arachnid into a contemporary art installation.

And then it happened. Loon hit the spider with a force like a prepubescent hydrogen bomb. The spider exploded in a riot of chitinous fragments and alien gore, a spectacle that would surely inspire generations of grindhouse directors. Rua, despite her relative horror, couldn't help but feel a tiny bit impressed.

What followed was rather extraordinary. One might imagine that seeing their gigantic brother obliterated in such a spectacular manner would rally the remaining spiders into a vengeful frenzy. Instead, they did what any sensible organism would do in the face of such an overwhelmingly terrifying display of power—they ran for their many, many lives.

A cheer rose up from the camp, the relief and triumph ringing clear in the aftermath of the explosion. Rua watched in bemused silence as celebrations broke out around her, shaking her head in incredulous wonder.

After a moment, there was a shift, and from the mass of giant fire spider gore Loon exploded outward, his double-bladed weapon high in the air as he roared in triumph.

"Fuuuuuuck yeaaaah!" he bellowed, his body entirely coated in the ichor and viscera of the beast he'd just . . . well, completely obliterated.

"Fuck! Yeah! Fuck! Yeah! Fuck! Yeah!" he chanted, stabbing the air to punctuate each syllable. Then he suddenly froze, doubling over and coughing, until a large gob of goo shot out of his mouth.

"Loon?" Rua cried out, thinking he'd just ruptured something. But he stood up, his face ghostly, his eyes wide.

"Fuck!" he shouted, spitting at the ground. "It got in my fucking mouth!"

CHAPTER NINE

BRING IT ON

So, that was fun—right?

I'll say, while it was pretty death-defying, there were some silver nuggets of goodness to be gleaned in the immediate aftermath of the fight. For one: I Leveled Up, baby!

More than that, though, because I'd accrued enough Experience during the battle royale to Level Up *twice*—and qualify for Level Fourteen. Which meant taking a nice, long glance at my character sheet and grabbing a gander at all my glorious gifts.

You know the drill, right?

Loon
Race: Orc*
Class: Barbarian (Frenzied Saboteur Path)
Level: 14
Profession: Unassigned
Health: 550/550
Arcana: 115/115
Max Stamina: 233
Reputation: Untested

Sodality
Assignment: Cult of the Capricious
Cult Rank: Initiate
Pacts
- Rexen Gravetongue

Attributes
Remaining Points to Allocate: 6
- Strength: 15
- Constitution: 41 (+3 Ring of Redoubt)
- Dexterity: 15
- Wisdom: 11
- Intelligence: 12
- Charisma: 11
- Luck: 3*

Skills
- Acrobat (E-Rank Level 6)
- Camp (F-Rank Level 1)
- Deception (F-Rank Level 1)
- Hunting (F-Rank Level 1)
- Improvised Weapon (E-Rank Level 3)
- Improvised Shield (F-Rank Level 3)
- Insight (E-Rank Level 5)
- Intimidate (F-Rank Level 2)
- Knowledge [Nature] (F-Rank Level 1)
- Knowledge [Infiltration] (F-Rank Level 1)
- Knowledge [Ignition] (F-Rank Level 1)
- Knowledge [Sabotage] (F-Rank Level 1)
- Leadership (F-Rank Level 4)
- One-Handed Weapons (E-Rank Level 2)
- Perception (F-Rank Level 4)
- Simple Weapon Proficiency (F-Rank Level 6)
- Simple Armor Proficiency (F-Rank Level 1)
- Sneaking (B-Rank Level 4)
- Survival (F-Rank Level 1)
- Two-Handed Weapons (F-Rank Level 6)
- Throwing Weapons (E-Rank Level 3)
- Unarmed Fighting (E-Rank Level 5)

Active Abilities
- Armorless Defense (D-Rank Level 6)
- Battle Born I
- Darkvision I
- Enduring Perch II
- Eye of the Saboteur I

- Primal Rage (E-Rank Level 5)
- Pernicious Volley I
- Natural Resilience (F-Rank Level 2)
- Nightfall Strike I
- Super Berserking I
- Uncommon Consumption (F-Rank Level 1)
- Wanderlust II
- Warchant II
- Blackout Warchant

Passive Abilities
- Friendship Strategy
- Inciter
- Outsider
- Unfaltering
- Wildling

Perks
- Adventurous Tastes (First Perk Bonus)
- Aegis Synthesis
- Old Ironsides

Aegis
- Calden's Hang Time
- Loon's Bombastic Beatdown

Boons
- Bone Warrior
- Imprint

Esper Nodes
- Emerald: 3
- Sapphire: 3
- Topaz: 1

I found that now, by whatever fucked-up alchemy, it seemed like my ability to reason out which of my traits had improved was easier to pick out—maybe I was getting used to the information, or maybe something in my internal advancement was helping with that. Either way, my ballin'-outta-control-barometer was steering my eyes right into the spots where I'd done the best upgrading.

During the fight, I'd utilized a ton of zany maneuvers to outlive and outlast the spiders, especially *up in them* trees as I did. Apparently, it was to great effect—cuz ya boi's Acrobat Skill was now at a solid E-Rank Level 6! One-Handed Weapons had—to no one's surprise—shot up as well: E-Rank Level 2. Throwing Weapons was now at E-Rank Level 3, and *more* surprisingly, I'd raised my Leadership Skill to F-Rank Level 4. I checked back through my notifications to see when that had happened, and the best I could tell . . . was that it was right around the time I was dolin' out delicious directions before we launched back into the fray from the outskirts of the camp.

At this rate, I'm gonna be king of this joint in no time.

Wanderlust I had grown as well, advancing to Wanderlust II. According to the display, this allowed me to do fuckin' . . . more damage, while gaining additional uses per charge in a veritable BOGO bonanza. That meant that now, as long as I was rapid-firing the sons o' bitches, I could essentially double-cast whatever was inside them for the price of a single slot of Spell sauce. I was torn about this development, because it seemed stupid to rely on magic when I could just be carving fools up or punching their brains into particles. However, the other side of the coin was . . . well, it was really fucking easy to just pop an enemy right in their stupid fucking face with a well-timed blast from one o' my handy-dandy witchcraft pistols. I mean, they weren't *actually* guns—they were wands—but my point stood.

And *on* that note, that was a fucking dope idea. I had to image it would actually be pretty fucking *choice* to have a pair of magic six-shooters or something strapped to my ample hips while surviving in this world. You know, trawling around, gettin' into seventeen kinds of dirty, devil-may-care diablerie, being cool . . . and stuff. If something like that existed there, I'd be willing to bet you'd have to pretty wealthy to afford it.

Hm. Maybe it's a possibility? I'll ask Arjee—or, actually, on second thought . . . maybe Edwig's the better call.

Eh, regardless, I was more of a beat-'em-up brawler type, and arcane firearms would just bring the world down around me. Way too OP, most likely. In the meantime, I had these damn wands. Which weren't bad at all, as previously established—other than bringing me closer and closer to an eventuality where I played Quidditch. Lame. The wands *were* good, though, seeing as how they could also create some distance or utilize said space when I couldn't get up close. I could definitely see the benefits, but it was really starting to become a downer how often I relied on them.

I looked over at the rest of my shit, noticing that Primal Rage had unsurprisingly gone up. Distantly, I recalled how, during my aggressive tapping of that particular powder keg, I'd been *way* more effective. Even considering

Loon's Bombastic Beatdown—which harnessed the *power of insomnia* to yank my physical abilities into the stratosphere—I'd completely spaced that I had that *extra* Ability granted to me by Rexen's social engineering and utter disregard for the system. Super Berserking—hilariously and *appropriately* named—pushed me even further into "no, fuck *you*" territory, and I'd been healing the whole time as well. Which was probably good, because I was a magnet for pain and misery—and it wasn't always my fault. Man, some of this shit was really starting to . . . as I'd heard Rua refer to it, "come online." I was always a bit of a slow learner—surprise, surprise—but the more time I spent exercising these magic muscles, the better I began to grasp it. So, I wasn't a complete lost cause. That gave me hope.

Another sick-nasty, fuck-around feature was something I hadn't really thought about much: Armorless Defense. Really, I'd kind of been running around assuming that my luck was protecting me, when I hadn't stopped to consider the fact that there was a fat, gnarly Ability sitting on deck, assisting me in absorbing some of the worst damage. Now, it seemed, Armorless Defense had come back from summer camp with a girlfriend who conveniently lived in another town. It had rocketed up to D-Rank Level 6, which, alone, would have been pretty impressive. However, gaining that altitude had also blessed me with a bonus. A Perk, actually.

Congratulations! You have gained a new Perk!
Perk: Old Ironsides
Due to reaching D-Rank in Armorless Defense, you now bear a 25% resistance to piercing! Blows that typically puncture flesh now have more difficulty getting through your rough-and-tumble exterior into your soft, moist, and mushy interior! Additionally, this increases your Natural Resilience:
+15% Resistance to Insects
+8% Resistance to Weather Conditions [Cold]
+5% Resistance to Weather Conditions [Heat]

Aces, my friends—aces all around.

Finally, as if I could even *fit* any more double-chocolate sprinkles on this confetti cake, I'd finally gained another Rank to Warchant, bringing it to Warchant II. Which meant that I was allowed to choose another hot-button battle scream.

Rallying Warchant
The user, in an incredibly heartfelt and genuine display of encouragement, unleashes a mighty roar that inspires up to [1] of their allies to reach new

heights in an area of [Intimidate + Charisma quotient] feet for [Intimidate + Charisma quotient multiplied by 200 %] minutes. All nearby allies, caught up in the awe-inspiring sound waves of the Warchant, experience a surge of adrenaline that enhances their combat prowess. They tap in to their inner warrior spirit, boosting their attack power, defense, and resistance to fear effects over duration.

Select Rallying Warchant?
[Yes/No]

Serpent's Warchant
The user releases a viscous, deadly bellow that has a chance to poison all targets within an area of [Intelligence + Wisdom quotient], causing deleterious effects for [8] Health over the course of [Intelligence + Wisdom quotient] minutes. All enemies suffering from the effects of Serpent's Warchant will surely wish themselves to be anywhere else, oftentimes crying for their mothers and purging violently at the same time.

Cost: 50 Arcana
Caveat: This Warchant requires the use of Arcana.
Select Serpent's Warchant?
[Yes/No]

Warchant of the Void
With a haunting chant, the user brings the chill of the void into their vicinity. It's like a cool, refreshing breeze for the soul, but instead of relaxing goodness, it serves up a cold emptiness that saps the energy from enemies and makes them reevaluate their lives. Those within an area of [Intelligence + Wisdom quotient] feet may start to question the life choices that led them to this point, experiencing a drop in attack power and speed for a disconcerting [Intelligence + Wisdom quotient] seconds.

Cost: 60 Arcana
Caveat: This Warchant requires the use of Arcana.
Select Warchant of the Void?
[Yes/No]

Titan's Warchant
Channeling their inner Troubadour, the user's voice booms out like a particularly angry mountain, echoing with the power and pent-up resentment of the earth. It's not so much singing as it is geological upheaval put to sound. The very ground takes offense at this blatant impersonation, shaking in indignant response within a radius of [Constitution + Strength quotient] feet. This

might throw enemies off their rhythm, possibly knocking them on their tails for an undignified [Constitution + Strength quotient divided by 2] seconds.
Select Titan's Warchant?
[Yes/No]

Well, huh. This was a real noggin-scratcher.

Rallying Warchant? I mean, it had its merits. It sounded like it was basically screaming at your pals so hard that they went into overdrive. Like the head coach of a doomed . . . *sports team* in the final . . . quarter? Anyway, I was already a well-established hell-raiser, but with that, I could really get their blood pumping—but instead of the usual way, I'd use my powers for good, I guess. I pictured myself, smack in the middle of some world-ending monster scrum, letting out a bestial holler that could shatter eardrums. Suddenly, my crew . . . well, they're tearing shit up like they're goddamn possessed. Feral and shit. Just . . . wreckin' fuckin' kneecaps and bashin' skulls inside out—straight-up riot mode, ya know? I'm not gonna lie, it was kind of a cool thought, having that much sway on the battlefield. Not to mention if I timed it right, I could probably drown out Rexen's godawful singing.

Serpent's Warchant, though . . . that thing seemed nasty in a whole new way. Apparently, if I swiped that pretty little poppy, I'd be bellowing so damn loud and venomous that enemies would start puking their fuckin' guts out. That would goddamn rule, and no one could tell me otherwise. Although . . . as appealing as that image was, the cost was a sticking point. It would burn through fifty Arcana like it was nothing. And I didn't exactly have Arcana to burn. Plus, I was trying to move *away* from going full Merlin, not exacerbate it.

Next in line for my discerning perusal was the Warchant of the Void. Now, *that* was a name that would make a grown man question his underwear choices. It had this terrifying ring to it, like the eerie silence just before a violent storm, or the quiet seconds after you tell a wonderfully crude joke during a job interview.

Just thinking about the sound of it, I could practically taste the fear it would spread. Some shit-scared spider-thing hearing my call, looking into my eyes, and seeing not just your everyday, bloodthirsty, wild-eyed wall of all-that-is-unfuckwithable but the embodiment of cold, endless nothingness. A real soul-shriveling terror.

That thought almost had me grinning ear to ear. Almost.

Point was, once again, it relied on Arcana. Fuck that—hocus-pocus weren't my strong suit. In fact, to call it a weak suit would be overstating its place in my wardrobe. More like that embarrassing pair of socks your grandma knitted for you. Yeah, they're warm and all, but you wouldn't be caught dead wearing them in public.

The last contender in this bellow-off was the Titan's Warchant. Right off the bat, the name had my full attention. It sounded like something I'd want to yell while swinging from a chandelier. You know, if I ever found myself in a chandelier-swingin' situation. Which, come to think of it, wasn't that unlikely, based on my track record. However, this was like an apocalyptic temper tantrum—you know, pitchin' a fit that could kick-start an earthquake. I smiled. And who better than yours truly—the original-recipe, hot-headed, hate machine—to put that kind of power to use?

I could already see it: I'm standing in the middle of the battlefield, looking suave as fuck, dressed to the nines in my finest carnage costume. All eyes on me, the tension thick enough to cover in whipped cream. And then I'd let loose, my voice ripping through the air and causing every complaint-wielding dipswitch to take a slapstick tumble.

Eh, but then what? Seemed like the ROI on such a feat was relatively low. I'd have to then run over and, what? *Lean down* to stab them to pieces? I'm a man on the move; I can't be stopping every few feet to get in a ground grapple. Plus, I didn't want to be remembered as the guy who made the *ground dance*.

So, what to choose?

I chewed over the options, my brain wheezing like a worn-out inner tube. Not its usual state, I gotta say. Typically, I had a pretty good gut feeling about what I wanted. But this wasn't choosing between types of waffle toppings or deciding which unfortunate monster's head to knock off next. This was about picking a feature that'd shape how I fought. I looked at them all again and, with the most analytical fortitude I think I'd ever displayed in my entire existence, made a selection.

Rallying Warchant. The name alone had a pretty kickass ring to it. It suggested a kind of strength, a "bonding in the middle of the chaos that I was usually in the thick of" kinda vibe. It wasn't as terrifying as the Warchant of the Void or as gruesome as the Serpent's Warchant. It wouldn't make me feel like a god, like the Titan's Warchant probably would. But as I ruminated over it, I realized I didn't *need* to scare the shit out of my enemies or make them physically ill—although, don't get me wrong, both sounded absolutely fuckin' delightful. I already did shit that would take care of that.

No, I realized quite suddenly, what I really wanted was to be that central, unifying figure—the beacon in the shitstorm, if you will. Someone you look at tearing off into certain terrible odds and think, "If that dopey motherfucker can keep going, so can I." Plus, the idea of supercharging anyone squadded up with me with a ferocious roar had a certain appeal. It was a step up from headbutting the enemy and swaying around dizzied for several seconds; that was for sure.

And maybe, just maybe, people might start thinking of me as more than the dumbass who charges headfirst into danger, laughing maniacally all the while. Sure, I *was* that guy, but perhaps I could also be the guy who pulled everyone else up with him. That crazy, *fearless* dumbass who, when the chips were down, you'd still follow into the bowels of hell. Because he was going anyway, and at least it'd be a fucking *story*.

I mean, who was I kidding? I still wanted to enact total domination over my enemies. But if I could do all that and make my crew fight harder, well, that was a win-win situation in my book. So, with a nod to no one in particular, I made my choice.

Rallying Warchant joined my hedonistic harem of howls.

Then there was just the matter of Points. Well, wasn't this a fucking conundrum? I was stuck with a choice that was about as palatable as choosing between a kick to the balls or a punch to the throat. These damn Attribute points were pesky so-and-sos, but I wasn't about to make the mistake I'd made before in delaying the gratification. No, sirree, these babies were burning a hole in my metaphorical pocket. Six points to spend, and not a fucking clue where to put 'em.

Especially considering I still had reservations from the last time I'd allocated them and I'd hit Milestones. Which—I didn't think was going to happen with any of them this time, but I really wasn't sure. Still, it sticks with you, that memory, even if it fades immediately. They hurt like a motherfucker. I mean, who thought it was a good idea to "reward" progress with something that felt like getting run over by the entire Tour de France? Hell, if I knew reaching a Milestone was gonna feel like that, I would've slowed my roll and settled for a leisurely jog. But no. Apparently, achievement in this world was measured by how much pain you could endure. Well, I was all about underachieving on that front.

So, where to put these li'l tokens of torment? I chewed on my lower lip, mulling it over. On one hand, I could keep the dice rollin' on my original preference and put them all into one stat—really jack up that Con, ya know? On the other hand, spreading the love seemed like a smarter move right now. Constitution was a fucking phenomenal characteristic to massage . . . but I'd been led to believe recently that I *should* be a little more discerning in my overall build.

But I'm not a complete balance-seeking fucker.

Flicking through my stats, I finally settled on the decision. It was time to buff the beefcake. I put two points into Strength, feeling the familiar jolt as my muscle mass got a tiny boost. Seventeen. Not too shabby.

Next up, Dexterity. Two more points. Another buzz, another notch on the stat ladder. Seventeen also.

Lastly, I dumped the final two points into Constitution for a total of forty-three. This was a *hell* of a figure I was cutting.

And the best part? Next time I popped the Loon's Bombastic Beatdown Aegis, these babies were gonna pump up the jam even further. I couldn't wait to see the look on ol' Curly and her goons' faces when I went all double-donkey-punch on their asses. Yeah, these points were well fucking spent.

Then, because I'd already used up all available brain space for the day on that hot little endeavor . . . I decided to take a load off. The whole fucking place was a mess, and I wanted a chance to chill before inevitably diving into duty.

But of course, just as I was sitting down into a comfortable position, my attention was wrangled as someone approached the tree I was relaxin' under. Saban.

"*Noooo*," I whined, before he even had a chance to say anything.

"Come on, Loon," he said with a grin. "We've won the day, but now we gotta do some work to make this place habitable. Comes with the territory. You were awesome out there, and I don't think anyone is going to forget you . . . completely destroying the hell out of that monster—but, unfortunately, we can't rest just yet."

"This is bullshit," I sulked. "This is like spitting in the face of a war hero."

"We both know it's not, man," Saban said, shaking his head but still grinning. "Plus, it'll give you the opportunity to meet more of the gang."

I stood slowly, grunting with exaggerated effort.

"Alright . . ." I said. "But if anyone makes a spider pun, I get carte blanche to sweep-kick the crispy Christ outta them."

"Sure," Saban. "Now, come on. The carnage isn't going to clean *itself* up."

"Cleaning? Aw, piss."

CHAPTER TEN

THE HISTORY BOYS

Surveying the camp was like gazing at the aftermath of a tornado's high school rave. Shit was scattered everywhere, the previously . . . sorta neat camp looking like a toddler's playroom. Dead spiders were strewn about like fucked-up decorations, and the smell . . . goddamn, the smell was like someone had taken a giant dump on a pile of rotting fish and then set it on fire.

"Lovely," I muttered.

On the brighter side of things, the big fucking spider was dead. Bully for me. Its gargantuan, lifeless body now served as a badass trophy of my victory. I wondered briefly if we could keep it as a statue—kind of a "don't fuck with us" lawn ornament, you know? A message to the others. Though, based on how utterly fucking stupid the battle had been, I didn't think that would work. Still, though—heavy intimidation tactic for the right audience.

Saban led me to a section that wasn't currently occupied by a toiling body and slapped me on the back.

"I just wanted to say . . . great work, Ga—uh, Loon," he said. "You really saved our butts back there."

He paused, seeming to consider me for a moment, and I had to tamp down the sudden anger that gave me. I fucking *hated* someone judging me. Even an old friend casting a curious, discerning gaze on me was enough to pinch the metaphorical back-of-my-arm fat and push me toward a tizzy. But, being a calm, rational, *practical* individual, I acted appropriately.

"What the fuck are you staring at?"

Saban just laughed.

"Man, you never change, do you?"

"The fuck I don't! I change *plenty*— Do I look like the same fucking guy I was when—"

"It's a *good* thing, Loon—Jesus," Saban chuckled. "I'm saying that despite everything we've all been through, it's good to know that you're still you."

His tone grew a little morose and his tone more somber.

"Not everyone has retained their sense of self like that," he continued, staring out in the distance at . . . something. I wasn't sure who he was talking about, but I guess I also didn't really care that much. Most of the kids from before were pretty insufferable, so any modifications to their personal brand of *them* was—in my mind—a fuckin' boon.

"Yeah, well . . ." I said, shrugging. "This dumbass world has another thing coming if it's trying to change the way I interact with it. I've become ungovernable."

"Ain't that the truth," Saban laughed. "Hey, do you remember that time we snuck out and saw *Joker?*"

"You're fuckin' yankin' my chain, hombre," I said. "I based like ninety percent of my personality on that movie for the next three months—of course I remember it."

I didn't mention the fact that I also specifically remembered it because it was the last time he and I had ever hung out. We'd been inseparable since we were seven, but something had changed during that summer—probably the fact that I'd started staying with Aunt Ella and Uncle Luke semi-permanently after my mom went to live "away" for a little while—AKA the . . . mental health facility. I'd bopped around with them for months at a time before, but it had seemed that this time it was going to stick. Because of that, I'd been a little preoccupied—obviously. Me and my former best friend had started to grow apart during that rough transitional period, and it fucking sucked, but I didn't realize at the time how much of an *extra special* type of asshole I had been.

However, Saban had shot me a message seeing if I'd wanted to go to the movie—and he knew I was precisely the sort of edgelord shit-for-brains that thought he *needed* to see it, and so we'd gone. After that, though, it was like we'd never been friends at all. Thinking about that actually started to make me a little angry. Why would he—

Saban beamed.

"Man, I miss those days," he said, shaking his head. ". . . That was also the night your pant leg got stuck in your bike chain."

He gave me a knowing look.

"Oh, fuck you!" I shot, offended that he'd brought up such a painful and hilarious memory.

"You were screaming so loud," he laughed, hardly able to control himself. "I kept telling you to backpedal and you kept making it worse."

"Excuse me," I said. "I thought I was going to *die*."

"Then you . . . you h-h-h-h-had to walk all . . . *bow-legged* back to your house so we could . . . c-cut your jeans out of the chain!"

He was full-on hysterical now.

"Yeah . . ." I said, laughing. "Good times."

"I'm sorry," he said suddenly, amusement still in his voice but much more muted.

"For laughing? Well . . . good, ya fuckin' dick," I said.

"No . . ." he said, his lopsided grin fading. "For . . . you know, kinda . . . ghostin' you. It wasn't cool."

"Oh?" I said, pretending I didn't have the foggiest recollection and doing a terrible job of it. "I don't even know what you're talking about. Saban *who*?"

"But seriously," he said, resting a hand on the haft of the warhammer hanging by his hip. "I wasn't around when . . ."

He was, probably for the first time in a long time, unable to find the words to speak his mind.

"It's *fine*," I protested, perhaps *too* strongly. "You couldn't have done anything anyway; it's not like—"

"I wouldn't have been able to change anything, you're right," he said. "But I could have at least been there for you. That couldn't have been easy, man."

I didn't say anything, just simply trying to will myself not to think about it. Lately, I'd been using it as fuel to unlock my ultimate weapon—and while I didn't know if that was a healthy medium for dealing with this sort of thing, I definitely didn't want to have to experience it without my own express, written sayso. However, despite how I thought it might make me feel, I was surprised to find that Saban's words . . . actually lifted my spirits a little. It was weird. Normally, *anyone* bringing that to my brain's attention would have sent me spiraling into a dark plane of no return. But in this case . . . I was mildly comforted. Huh. Weird.

"I said it's fine," I continued. "Listen, I appreciate you saying that, but I'm alright. I've been dealing with things in my own way. Don't worry about it . . ."

I adopted a smirk.

". . . just glad to know you're aware of how much of a fucking asshole you are."

Saban laughed.

"Yeah . . ." he said. "I'm sorry about that, too."

"Well, well, well," I said, waving my hand around at the wreck surrounding us. "Glad to know you're apologizing for everything *except* for forcing me into hard, back-breaking labor."

"Yeah, I'm not sorry about that," he mused dismissively. "You break it, you buy it."

"I'll remember this the next time you guys need help with . . . I dunno, a giant frost cockroach infestation or something. You'll be all like, 'Loon! Please, lend us your mighty strength! You're the only one who can save us!' And I'll be like, 'Quiet, peasant! I have no time for the likes of your douchey Stardew Valley shenanigans. I'm too busy with hero shit.'"

"Wow," he said in mock offense. "I take it back. Power *has* changed you."

"And don't you forget it, bub," I said, smiling. "Now, let's get to cleanin' up this crack-house crime scene. It looks like it's going to take for-fuckin'-ever, but I'm sure that between the two of us—"

"Unfortunately," Saban began, slapping me on the shoulder in apology. "I leave that to you. I've got some other *peasant* matters to deal with."

"Oh, you *bitch*," I grumbled.

"Sorry, m'lord," he said. "I'll leave the hero shit to the heroes."

"Yeah . . ." I said, nodding glumly. "I deserve that."

The rest of the camp was picking through the wreckage, salvaging anything that might be of use. I spotted Edwig off to one side, gingerly lifting a boot from beneath a squashed spider, his face somehow wrinkling in disgust. I let out a short laugh, shaking my head as I moved to join him.

"How's the pickin's, Viggo?" I called out, kicking a dead spider out of the way. It skidded across the ground with a crunch, leaving a trail of charred goo in its wake. Edwig looked up like he'd just been sucking on a lemon.

"It's . . . it's . . . interesting," he muttered.

I raised a brow, grinning at his clear discomfort.

"Aw, come on, baby. Don't tell me you're gettin' the squeamies from a little guts and gore?" I teased, nudging a piece of mangled armor with my toe.

Edwig shot me a glare that could have curdled milk.

"Pah! As *if* I'd be so easily disgusted, orc! I look at your face all the time! I'm just looking for valuable materials."

"Easy, there," I said. "What kind of *materials* are you searching for?"

"Anything that could be classified as ingredients," he said matter-of-factly. "I'm a—"

"A researcher, yeah, I know," I said. "We *all* know. You've told the whole damn neighborhood. Wait, is that why you wanted false goblin ears?"

Edwig looked suddenly like he wanted to crawl away into a hole, but I held up my hands.

"Listen. Considering the, uh . . ." I paused, gesturing around at the carnage. ". . . circumstances, I'll offer a truce on my demands for you to pay me the money you still owe. It doesn't seem right to twist the knife at the moment—especially after all this bullshit. But I'm going to be annoying as fuck about it again tomorrow. Deal?"

Edwig sighed.

"Deal," he said.

"So . . . what did you want those ears for? I feel like there's a story there. What, do they turn you back into whatever you were before you were horribly maimed in that freak *personality* accident?"

"Has anyone ever told you you're a rude orc?" Edwig asked.

"Oh, all the time," I said. "It's, like, one of my ten best features. So, what was the dealio?"

"Well—"

"Goblin jam," Rexen said, suddenly appearing next to us.

I swatted at him.

"You're showing up crazier than usual," I said. "Making no sense. Nobody's out here eatin' monster jelly, Arjee, you dimbus. And if they are—well, then, fuck—I dunno. They're probably already on God's hitlist, so we should just leave 'em be."

"Yeah . . . goblin jam," Edwig agreed.

"Wait, what?!" I exclaimed, wheeling on Edwig. "For real? You *eat* that stuff?"

"Pah! It's not what you think, orc," he said.

"Bullshit," I said. "That's exactly what everybody says when they get caught . . . doin' the thing they say they aren't doin'."

Edwig blinked at me.

"What?"

Rexen floated over to me.

"Yes, I too am confused, pupil."

"Never mind!" I said. "It would take too long to explain—speaking of explaining: what's this lip noise about monster preserves?"

"Goblin jam," Edwig and Rexen both said simultaneously.

"Yeah," I said. "That's, uh, what I meant."

Edwig cleared his throat.

"Goblin jam—a natural process that false goblins are able to produce. Something to do with frequencies."

"So . . . it's more like a *music* kind o' jam, then?" I said, envisioning a bunch of little fairy tale creatures playing banjos and line-dancing. "Hm. A good ol' fashioned hoedown, eh? I can get behind that."

"What?" Edwig asked.

Rexen appeared next to my fucking face, his eyes lighting up like a giddy child.

"Yes, pupil—except *no*, pupil! It's a hum of misaligned Arcana frequencies! As much a symphony—but if all were tone-deaf and the instruments off key!"

I stared at him blankly.

"Well, that's just about the worst hoedown I've ever heard of."

"Exactly!" Rexen continued, unabashed by my mockery, "False goblins! Wonderful!"

"*Not* exactly," Edwig said, taking over. "This guy's confusing the point with his usual nonsense."

"I am not," Rexen declared, suddenly glaring. "I refuse to recognize the badge of 'nonsense' from a beer-hating hat thief!"

"Pah!" Edwig exclaimed, then seemed to think better of arguing with an actual lunatic and turned back to me. "Where was I? Ah, yeah. False goblins—they've got this ability. Some strange... byproduct of their existence where they can 'jam' resonance. And it's believed to be tied to their ears."

"That sounds like something from my world," I said, "But non-magi—uh, arcane. So, you're saying it ain't a spreadable muck of some kind—but messing with Spells and junk?"

"Yeah," Edwig breathed, clearly relieved. "It's a term coined by us—researchers, that is. They don't actually *make* jam, and it's not even real goblins who do this; it's false goblins."

"Wait, so, what's the difference?" I asked.

"Night and day," Rexen nodded.

"Yeah, that technically isn't how you respond to that question," I said. "Gra... gr-grammaric... ly..."

"Actually..." Edwig said, shrugging. "He's weird, but it sort of does make a bit of sense. Your standard goblins typically only dwell in the night. Skulking about. Real nefarious sorts, you know?"

He shivered.

"Gods, I hate goblins," he continued. "But I judge not in the pursuit of knowledge. Conversely, false goblins do their dirt in the day. Still, they don't belong to the same category of creature, not really. They just look similar."

"So..." I said. "What's the *big* difference, then?"

"False goblins are copycats!" Rexen announced, gleefully.

"They're a type of mimic," Edwig clarified helpfully. "Except rather than turning into a whole fat lot of other stuff, they *just* latched on to goblin culture and mirror that."

This was reminding me a lot of a certain horror-sci-fi movie I'd seen as a kid.

I held up a hand.

"Hold up. So, we're dealing with *doppelgangers*? So, you wanted ears from goddamn goblin body-snatchers?"

"Pah! You're not listening, orc," Edwig corrected. "They're not doppelgangers—that's a whole different Fels game. They're goblin-like... just... different.

But yes, essentially. The ears could potentially help us understand how this 'jamming' works. Only one person—Bahlgus—has managed to crack this riddle, but the bastard keeps his secrets tighter than a dwarf's cask."

"That guy again . . ." I mused, touching the little bit of throat jewelry that had assured my ultimate cool fucking victory during the battle. "But what if Bahlgus just had some bad goblin jam and lost his mind?"

Rexen's eyes lit up.

"That's . . . an interesting theory. Unproven but intriguing! We should explore—"

"Pah! You numpty," Edwig interjected. "He was joking, ghost."

"Joke? Ah. Yes. Humor. Ha-ha-ha," Rexen laughed—quite believably. "That's my apprentice—so clever with his on-the-nose commentary."

I groaned, rubbing my temples.

"By fuck, you two are a pair. You're going to drive me to drink—"

"Beer!" Rexen exclaimed.

I scowled.

"You wish, Arjee. No—fuckin', I dunno . . . turpentine or a cup of glass or something less painful than listening to you."

Edwig shook his head sadly, looking at Rexen.

"Somebody buy this guy a beer . . ."

"I want it hot!" Rexen demanded.

I smirked at them, then turned back toward the settlement, placing a hand on Edwig's . . . shoulder? . . . as I passed.

"Well, keep hunting for your ear jam, boys. Just don't invite me for toast when you figure it out. Now, if you'll excuse me: I gotta see a man about a horse."

As I walked away I heard Edwig mutter, ". . . what's a horse?"

"Iunno."

I spent the next couple of hours sifting through the wreckage, helping where I could. It was time to roll up my sleeves and dive in, though thankfully not into any arachnid viscera. Everyone got to work with their separately assigned duties. Even the poor schmucks who reincarnated after being murderized had to help. Well, after they recovered from their pesky resurrection hangover.

I caught sight of Rua in the corner of the camp, elbows-deep in bandages and vials. She had convinced Edwig and anyone with skills resembling healing or alchemy-ing to put their heads together, fixing up the injured. They worked with assembly-line precision—well, as much as a bunch of non-medics could. I shot her a thumbs-up. In return, she gave me a thumbs-up, then immediately turned back to scold Edwig for trying to steal a Health potion from a bird guy with a broken ankle.

Meanwhile, Saban was overseeing the fighter types in fortifying the camp. As always, the guy with the *Kiss me, I'm the hero* tattoo was keeping people calm, and had somehow managed to talk Alpha into being useful. The dwarf—with a face only a mother could love if she were blind and heavily sedated—was smarmily screaming at people to "secure the perimeter" like he thought he was some kinda soldier-king. But they listened.

Man, that guy fucking sucks.

Me? I got stuck helping the laborers.

"Time to put my secret weapon to use," I muttered to myself... every single time I used Eye of the Saboteur.

One good thing about being me—of which there are many—was that Ability. With it, I could see the hidden potential in just about anything—like spotting a glint of gold in a puddle of piss. Which meant it worked equally well for removing puddles of piss from gold. I summoned it and immediately felt the world shift, seeing everything through a blueprint-like lens. The wreckage was still there, but I could easily spot what did and did not spark joy.

I got to work, pulling out materials that still had some life in them, dodging Rexen's excited jabbering and the weird demon lady's methodical inventory count. Veruca—a woman I came to realize was the gun-toting badass on the train—was an oddball. She spoke in a monotone and her sharp gaze didn't miss a fucking thing. She apparently had an Ability called Catalog, which allowed her perfect recall of a range of items. It seemed like it could be useful in a lot of situations, until I learned that it only counted for physical objects and not obscure pro-wrestling stats. *Boring.* Rexen was *way* more interested in it than I was, and I had to imagine he was cultivating some insane scheme to get her to figure out which thingamabobs were most deserving of his covetous, creepily loving gaze.

However, as far as the camp was concerned—net positive, I guess. Between Veruca's doodad Dewey decimal talent and my Eye of Saboteur, we sorted through the wreckage pretty fuckin' handily, pulling out anything that could be reused or restored.

But there was a *lot* of busted shit. Like, deal-breakingly destroyed. Really, though, it's not like there was a lot to work with at the outset. I mean, the camp was formed around a literal train wreck, so... not a huge loss. Still, I begrudgingly did my due diligence to help, even recruiting Edwig to use his Unseen Hand for the greater good and rescue some of my own belongings from within a monstrous pile of carcasses.

Hours passed and we continued to work into the evening. Someone made a pot of some kind of stew, and while it tasted like bat blood, I didn't care. My back ached, my muscles screamed, and my nose was constantly assaulted by the smell of burnt spider corpses. However, as I sat and . . . enjoyed the meal, I cast a glance at the bits of the place I could see in the shadows and nodded approvingly. While still a fucking shit sty, the camp was already starting to look less like the aftermath of a particularly wild after-hours Benihana employee potluck and more like a place where people could live.

After dinner, while strolling around and making a mental note to never go into manual labor, I spotted a towering figure hunched in the distance—the hulking silhouette making even the wreckage look small. Sighing, I decided to abandon my current venture of trying to do nothing and lumbered toward the familiar figure.

"What adventure are we off to now?" Rexen, floating beside me, asked excitedly.

"Wellness check," I said, pointing at the huge individual ahead.

"Yes," Rexen whispered nefariously. "We must decide if he is weak enough to vanquish in one go. Oh, but he's quite big. It might take *two* goes."

Tartarus, the guy who'd spent his past life trying to teach me the ins and outs of American history, had somehow managed to smuggle a copy of the same book in this cancerous urinal cake of a world that we'd been reading in class right before we left on our ill-fated field trip. He was sitting on his oversized ogre ass next to a small campfire, his gargantuan finger tracing over the tiny letters on the page. How a beast like him managed to hold the book without crushing it, I'll never know.

"Didn't take you for the nostalgic type, teach," I said, eyeing him skeptically.

Tartarus looked up from his book, eyes glinting with what I could only assume was annoyance. But then again, the guy always looked annoyed, like he was perpetually on the brink of a sneeze he couldn't quite get out.

"Hm," he grumbled. "You seem eager to distract me."

I shrugged, planting my hands on my hips.

"Just trying to understand why you're burying your snout in a book when we're knee-deep in . . . whatever this is."

I motioned to the wreckage around us.

"Besides, I wanted to say what you did during that battle was *baller* as *fuck*. You're like the John Petrucci of beating spider ass. Didn't know you had it in you. You can probably ditch the books forever now—let sleeping dogs die or whatever."

I paused.

"Which, now that I'm thinking about it, is a super fucked-up thing to let a dog do. How you just gonna stand by while a dog is *dying*? Shouldn't you try to perform CPR or something? Wait—can you *give* a dog mouth-to-mouth? That seems unwise, actually. They could, I dunno, bite the fuck out of your face if they came to in a panic—or worse, if someone didn't know what you were doing, they'd probably think you were trying to get your jollies. Then you get labeled the pooch smoocher, or . . . dog snogger, and that's not a nickname anybody wants. Although . . . I guess if they've gotta go, it's really the most peaceful way. This kid I went to middle school with left his dog outside during a heatwave for fifteen hours while he was inside playing *Call of Duty*. That's a fucking terrible way to go. Anyway . . ."

I snapped my fingers a few times, trying to jog my own memory.

"Where was I? Oh, right. History is stupid and you pummeling the brick-iron bejesus outta those monsters is the coolest thing you've ever done."

The ogre barely acknowledged my presence, merely letting out a distracted grunt. When he finally spoke, his deep voice tumbleweeded out, lazy and unhurried.

"Well," he began, "understanding the past, that's a crucial piece of the puzzle, isn't it? An essential cog in the workings of our existence. Even here."

With the sort of absent-minded look that I'd seen on him countless times in our previous life, back in the classrooms full of bored teenagers struggling to stay awake, he fucking began. I could already sense that this was going to be one of those rambling rants that he'd been infamous for. His penchant for verbosity had a way of turning simple statements into sprawling dissertations that made even the most patient student's eyes glaze over or hopeful for an asteroid strike. It was almost comforting, in a weird, fucked-up way, to see him stay true to his character despite the dramatic shift in our realities.

"Now, you might wonder, why do I care about the past, especially one that seems to have slipped through our fingers, vanishing into a realm that we might never have access to again?"

"Not really," I said. "I was always more of a—"

"The answer," he continued, "is simple."

He paused, his gaze lost somewhere in the pages of his book, a peculiar expression of reverence on his monstrous, inexplicably mustachioed face.

"You see, the past, even if it's irretrievable, even if it's locked away in the vaults of time and space, separated from us by an insurmountable chasm, is still integral to our existence."

He set his book aside for a moment, turning his massive head towards me.

"History," he said, his words hanging in the air like a heavy cloud of fog, "is a mirror. A mirror reflecting who we were, who we could've been, and most importantly, who we are today. It's like a beacon guiding us, an invaluable manual to decipher our present."

With a sigh, he turned back to his book.

"So, understanding the past, even an irretrievable one, can help shape the present."

I was left standing there, confused. Man, was this guy for real? Even stuck in an alternate world, he wouldn't let go of his long-windedness. If this was a strategy to get me to walk away, it was working.

"This guy is kooky," Rexen muttered to me. "The past is not to learn from; it is to *be* from. Strike him down now, pupil, before his insanity infects us."

I ignored the spectral deviant and instead waved at my former teacher.

"Fine, Professor Ogre, you have fun with your dusty ol' history kink. I'm going back to my glamorous life of junk-sorting and corpse-exploring."

"It's quite interesting, actually," he continued, completely ignoring me. "The histories of our world and this one share a surprising amount of similarities."

"Yeah?" I wondered. "You learnin' a lot about Regaia, sitting on your duff in a forest for the last two weeks?"

"Yes," he said, matter-of-factly. Then he paused, seeming to realize I was there for the first time. "I'm sorry, were you one of my students, or are you one of the others?"

I shrugged.

"Yeah, actually . . ." I said with a smirk. "Cluedo McScrabble. Remember me? I was the kid that always brought his, uh, lizard to class? We used to let it ride around on the shop vac wearing sunglasses."

He frowned.

"No?" I wondered, continuing to lie. "You came to my birthday party, ate most of my cake, and then had to leave early because you said your 'mustache hurt.' Not ringin' any bells?"

"No, I can't say that it does—which is strange, I'm usually fairly good with names."

Well, that was a fucking fib. He spent the entirety of the last year calling both of the Ward twins Paul, despite that not being either of their names.

"And you?" he said to Rexen.

"I am but a simple student of the world . . ." the ghost said wistfully. "A world that I have since bent before my mighty—"

"In any case," Tartarus said, "good to see you made it through to the other side, Cluedo."

"Yeah, right back atcha, Tartar Sauce," I said. "But . . . now, I might regret asking this—actually, scratch that, I'm *definitely* gonna regret it . . . but how do you know about Regaia's history?"

"What do you mean?"

"Well, you said the histories of both places have a lot in common—or, I guess, was that all just you being fas . . . fasee—faseeshul? F-frivolishious? F—"

"Ferocious!" Rexen offered.

"Nice assist, but no. I don't think so. Never mind," I groaned. "Tell me what you meant by that."

"Oh," Tartarus said. "My Class."

"Like, what you chose when you got here? Or are you talking about some kind of continuing education course?"

"My chosen Class," he said. "I'm an Archivist."

"You design buildings? Well, gee whiz, brother, you got your work cut out for you here, huh? I mean, have you *seen* this fucking place?"

"No," he said simply. "What I chose has to do with understanding the accounts of this world. It seemed like something I was well suited for."

"Can you translate?" I asked Rexen.

"An Archivist uses Arcana to divine and retain the details of the world around them—by looking at its origins," he said . . . suspiciously helpfully.

"Kind of like how I use Eye of the Saboteur to learn the makeup of stuff so I can better hit people with it?"

"Iunno," Rexen shrugged, suddenly unhelpful again. "The illisinaf would know more than I. He's a researcher. They are likely similar."

"It lets me know the history of a lot of different things," Tartarus agreed. "The knowledge has been largely acquired through inspection of documents and snippets of conversation—though I imagine it will give me more information once I get stronger. I already picked up a few new Abilities after that fight prompted me to Level Up. Which begs the question of the merits of a world that would reward me more for participating in combat than in the actual execution of what my Class is designed to do."

"That's what *I'm* saying!" I exclaimed. "The System is fucking stupid, right? Get this—it said my *Intelligence* was low! Which, as anyone who has met me can attest to, my highly cunning nature and world-famous wit are—"

"So, I've mostly been reading and cataloging the information I've received from my initial codex."

I thought about that.

"Codex, eh? Like . . . a manual?"

"Sure," Tartarus said with a nod. "Though, at this stage, it's more of an instructional pamphlet than a primer. But, I'll be honest, the features seemed like they would be more robust when I selected them."

"Oh . . ." I said. "So . . . you came to a new world, and your first thought was to become, what? A librarian? Jesus, man, and I thought Rua was nerdy. If that's the case, though, how did you get so fucking *strong*? You were kicking the *shit* out of those things."

Tartarus shrugged.

"Ogres have an inborn trait of incredible Strength but lower Intelligence, it seems," he continued. "Reminded me a bit of when I used to play tabletop games. I saw a lot of similarities and wanted to be well-rounded. So, I picked something more physically vigorous for the Race, and bolstered my mental capabilities by choosing a Class with more acumen."

Christ, does everyone know more about how this shit worked than I do? Seems unfair to offload me into this world with a train full of geeks.

"He chose better than you did, pupil," Rexen said gleefully. "My disciple is . . . learning as he goes. But poorly."

I scowled.

"Hey, Tartarus," I said. "Did you know Arjee, here, is actually *super* fucking old? He's practically prehistoric. He's seen a whole mess of shit in this world. I'll bet he'd be more than happy to allow you to pick his brain on every little detail you'd want to know."

"Pupil . . ." Rexen began, suddenly sounding serious. "What do you think—"

"Ah, that would be a fine treat indeed," Tartarus said, looking delighted for the first time in . . . well, I didn't think I'd ever seen him elated in either life.

"Disciple mine," Rexen continued, "do not leave me with—"

"Great!" I interrupted, flashing every tooth I had at the both of them. "You guys can start right now. And don't worry, Arjee . . ."

I winked at him.

"I'll stay close enough that you don't suddenly drift away. Can't have Tartarus missing out on anything."

With that, I chose a spot about fifty feet from them—still within the one-hundred-foot radius he was required to keep with me—and sat down. Then I removed the indestructible orb and began tossing it in the air to myself, chuckling.

Over the next while, I was able to identify a lot of my old school chums, all spruced up like some freaky avant-garde performance piece that took a detour through a *Pathfinder* handbook. The camp, in the ass-crack of dawn, was a surreal soup of sleepy-eyed bedheads and hardy early birds. Made your typical morning commute look like a Walt-fucking-Disney parade.

The peasant-looking guy from when we first arrived turned out to be Matt Marshall. He'd been one of Saban's close homies for the last couple of years and was quite the popular Polly in our school. I was surprised that he'd decided to keep his name, and had also, strangely, chosen the Merchant Class. He'd apparently taken to the idea of what he called "classic isekai" when we'd been sent there, and thought he'd make a sweep if he focused on something built around gaining money as quickly as possible. Which, I'll admit, was a pretty good plan. However, Matt hadn't expected to get plopped down in a fuckin' forest, days away from the nearest town—and, by default, the closest iota of mercantile mischief. As such, he'd felt largely useless since his arrival, save for his "Auditing" Skill, which he explained allowed him to track all of the coins of anyone he was linked with. He'd begrudgingly partied up with Alpha, simply because, as settlement leader, Alpha would amplify the effect, and Matt's Skill would spread to the whole of the camp. This made knowing what the unofficially treasury tallies were much easier. It was still, apparently, a paltry sum, but, like, knowledge is power—or whatever.

Moving through the throng of folks, I caught a glimpse of something in my periphery that made me do a double take. A peachy, tail-wagging hurricane of furry gusto that was unmistakably the same dog-person who'd been firing *terribly* into the fray during the kerfuffle with the pyronids. However, I couldn't hold it against him, because as I learned, it was also Mason Peterson. Scratch that, just "Mase" now. In a bout of *savant-like* inventiveness, he'd ditched the end cap on his original name along with his opposable thumbs.

The dude had gone the canine route, having chosen something called a k'niss, which looked like if the Teen Wolf and Rin Tin Tin hooked up and their lovechild became really fucking sassy. The transformation was wild, but undeniably rad.

So, there he was, wrangling with some wayward lumber like it had personally insulted his mama, and after speaking with him, I learned that for some inexplicable reason, he'd chosen a Class called "Builder." Super boring, but I couldn't *not* chuckle at the irony of someone originally named *Mason* becoming a guy who did construction. Though, now that I thought about it—in the old world, Mase's dad had owned a pretty well-known contracting and masonry company. Had he . . . been named after his dad's line of work? I'd never thought about that until that moment, and I could not believe I'd never before connected the dots. Or maybe it was just a coincidence? Either way, it didn't matter, and it seemed like Mase was taking to his new career with endless enthusiasm. Every wag of that furry appendage, every eager twitch of his ears was loaded with the same high-octane flamboyance that used to make our old high school feel less like a prison and more like a goddamn improv class.

I hung back, taking in the sight of him wrestling with his slab of wood, a grin tugging at my lips. Same ol' Mase, just sporting a new, hairy look. He was still stirring up smiles, still turning the mundane into a stand-up routine as he loudly complained about the quality of trees in this stretch of woodland, one stubborn timber at a time. His flair for aggressive, hilarious oversimplification still shone through, proof that no matter how wild the world around us got, some things never changed.

Nestled between a scatter of makeshift dwellings, half-hewn from the alien wilderness and half-engineered from scavenged materials, I found a small gathering around a sputtering fire pit. It was there, in this communal heart of our camp, where I stumbled upon Jando—formerly Alejandro Guerrera—who'd decided to use his nickname full-time as his moniker there in Regaia.

The guy had seriously embraced his new life, trading in his skateboard for the arcane strings of an otherworldly lute. He had chosen the path of an entwick Bard, which honestly was as surprising as finding out that water was wet. Jando had always had that chill vibe, the kind that rode the rhythm of life without breaking a sweat, so it seemed fitting.

Jando's new form was the same as Tanner's, the overly anxious mope I'd met during the climactic battle, though Jando's version was a lot more . . . floral. Gone was the short, scrawny stoner of our past, replaced now by a tall and slender figure adorned in plant-like flesh. His skin was a rich earthy brown, traced with delicate veins of vibrant green. It seemed that his body was a living, growing part of nature. His face was chiseled and noble, a pair of antler-like horns extending upwards from his forehead. His fingers, now long and nimble, danced effortlessly on the lute's strings, teasing out notes that filled the air with a hauntingly beautiful melody.

The music he coaxed from that enchanted lute wound its way through the camp, carrying with it a palpable sense of melancholy. It was a tune that echoed the collective longing in all our hearts—a yearning for home, for the mundane simplicity of our old lives. I couldn't help but pause, drawn in by the familiar figure lost in the throes of his new-found art.

His eyes were shut tight, a serene expression painted across his face, so much so that it seemed almost sacrilegious to interrupt him. There was a focus, a depth to Jando that I'd never noticed before. Back in the old world, the guy was a stoner legend—half-pipe shenanigans, epic pranks, and blazing it up in the deserted corners of every available scratch of scholastic property. "Pipe and a pipe," they used to say, but now the dude was playing a whole different tune.

A fleeting image flashed before my eyes, of sun-soaked afternoons watching Jando and Molly dominating the pavement with their skateboards. Their infectious laughter, their seamless companionship, two rebels carving joy into the gray concrete. They were the embodiment of freedom, untouched by the mundanity we all felt trapped in.

Now there we were, in an unfamiliar world filled with fucked-up horrors beyond any reasonable necessity. Yet they still stood by each other's side, their bond unbroken, even if their forms had drastically changed.

Just a stone's throw away, Tallulah—formerly Molly—lounged by the fire. Her new form was as different from Jando's as chalk from cheese, yet just as striking. Instead of choosing a more usual form, she'd gone the way of the . . . skylaiths, which, at best, could be described as a group of . . . celestial . . . birds? Feathered wings sprawled lazily at her back, their opalescent sheen catching the firelight. Her face held the delicate features of a bird of prey, eyes as bright and sharp as the turquoise sky, framed by a short crop of silvery feathers that passed for hair in her new Race. As different as she looked, there was an undeniable hint of her old self in her nonchalant posture, the way she watched Jando with a familiar, companionable smirk.

Jando's melody gently receded, the last note hanging in the air like a wisp of smoke. His eyes slowly fluttered open, meeting mine with a slight upward twitch of his leaf-green eyebrows—a silent *hey*. I offered him a small nod of acknowledgment, the corners of my lips curling up in a half-hearted smile. It was a small exchange, but it held a certain comfort, a thread of familiarity in this tangle of fresh, bizarre hell.

Tallulah, catching the subtle exchange between us, cocked her bird-like head to the side and let out a low, melodic whistle, a sound that sounded eerily like a laugh. Our eyes met, and for a brief second, I saw the skater chick I'd known, her smoky eyes crinkled at the corners in mischief. Then the moment was gone, her gaze shifting back to Jando as he began another soft melody.

I lingered for a while longer, the atmosphere around the fire pit offering a strange sense of nostalgia for . . . I dunno. A time and place I'd never experienced. Jando's fingers moved with a fluid grace over the lute's strings, the soft tones pulling at something deep within me. Beside him, Tallulah seemed to sway slightly, her hawkish form elegant, feathers shimmering with every movement. It reminded me of the way Jes had performed for our group in the Crypt, and I suddenly got a little sad. Man, I really wish I'd had some fuckin' brutal-ass beats to pump into my ears right now and drown out . . . whatever I was feeling.

The morning grew older, the mist dissipating as the sun continued its ascent, and I found myself meandering over to the . . . uh, food . . . area. Chowing down on some sort of gruel that was reminiscent of oatmeal—except for its slight violet hue—I watched as the others trickled in, gathering their own early sustenance.

Among the new arrivals was Hannah Rentz—or rather, Pricipita, as she was known now. Swapping her sunny disposition and bouncing blonde curls for an aloof aura, hair as black as night, and a bone-white skeleton that shone in the light of dawn, she was now a something called a bone elf. As far as her Class—I wasn't sure. It seemed to be something particularly inclined for sneaking, but... well, that was fuckin' cool, I supposed. Twinsies. She moved with an ethereal grace, every step seeming planned, practiced. Gone was the girl who giggled in the back row of chemistry, replaced by this creature of terrifying mystery. She was still her, I knew that, but she also *wasn't*. It was a strange dichotomy.

Sitting next to her was Alexis Weber—or just Lex now. Like Pricipita, she was a bone elf—though the two could not have been more dissimilar in their presentation. Where Pricipita was delicate and ethereal, Lex was an imposing figure, a stark contrast. While she shared the porcelain skin and long, pointed ears, her form bore markings in deep red, running in intricate patterns along her arms and legs, crossing over her chest, and adorning her bare skull in a dazzlingly intricate design. These were no random tattoos, but signs of her chosen Class—the metal-as-fuck-ly named Blood Knight. That was the path she'd chosen in this world, which was, what I'd learned, only available to her Race. What a fucking jackpot that had turned out to be for her.

In likely the most surprising transformation of anyone so far, Lex had traded her former "social influencer" persona for a warrior's might, her days of being the most subscribed and coveted Snap and Insta Queen in town a distant memory. Now she held a double-bladed blood-red-ax, its crimson edge gleaming. If you squinted, you could still see the traces of that sparkling smile, but it was now a grin that promised death to anyone foolish enough to cross her. She looked goddamn awesome.

Madison Edwards, still Madison, apparently—look, I'm noticing a strong pattern here amongst my former classmates, and that was one of severe deficiencies in the imagination department concerning naming conventions. Anyway, Madison was one of those folks who seemed to have changed the least, as far as on the outside. She'd kept a human form and had apparently been successful enough in selecting an exterior that matched her original one pretty closely—though she'd adopted the Class of Brawler. Even from across the makeshift dining area, I could see the lean muscle she'd developed, her body now a temple of punishing power.

Madison had always been athletic, but now she seemed . . . more. More focused, more fierce, more formidable. I watched as she engaged in friendly banter with Pricipita and Lex, her laughter ringing out and her fists playfully landing on the shoulder of Mase, who'd taken a break to join them. The girl was making the best out of this shitshow, adapting in a way that I couldn't help but admire.

And then there was Starlily, formerly Abbie Carlson, the girl who haunted the edges of my high school dreams, with her cascade of fiery red hair and that infectious laughter that could brighten even the darkest of days. Her name, while unsurprisingly hippie-ish, was at least a modicum more interesting than just keeping your one from before—but hey, different strokes, or whatever. She'd chosen to become an aetherling Mystic. The transformation had given her an ethereal quality—soft, luminescent skin, eyes glowing with a mystical energy, and ears that seemed to have a mind of their own, expressive in their movements. More, she seemed almost formed of some unfathomable element, with vague intimations of mist trailing off of her body wherever she went.

I found my gaze lingering on her a bit longer than necessary, drawn by a mixture of "the good ol' days" and curiosity. She was mesmerizing, her new form only enhancing her natural charisma. Seeing her now, I couldn't help but wonder what that high school boy I used to be would think. Hell, I wasn't sure what the man I was now thought.

One thing was for sure: I didn't know shit about women, because—as Frida had said it best—"Not all lasses yearn for frills and sparkles. Sometimes, they fancy bein', to use a technical term, utterly fuckin' terrifying."

CHAPTER ELEVEN

THEY'RE COMING TO GET YOU, BARBARIAN!

With a step as light as a falling feather, Rua slipped through the underbrush. Her eyes carefully scanned the forest for signs of her quarry, a peculiar creature, a result of Regaia's eccentricity. The hybrid beast, they'd learned was called a wolp, was a curious blend of rabbit and hawk, boasting an oversized hare's body with the feathered wings of a raptor.

Beside her, with steps not quite as delicate but equally quiet, moved León.

León, despite his compact frame and rough exterior, moved with a finesse that betrayed his profession. In his thick, gnarled hands, he held a self-crafted bow, made from the resilient wood of the yewheart tree, an essential part of his chosen build. A build, it turned out, that was perfect for hunting, tracking, and for being a right pain in the hindquarters during their brief but vehement disagreements. He'd been one of Alpha's pals in the previous world, one of the aggravating men who had hassled some of Rua's schoolmates, previously called Chris. She thought she'd remembered him as the "quiet one," just hanging back in the cut while the others acted like bastards. Still, he'd been one of the ones assaulting Loon on the train, and though she thought painting people with the broad brushstrokes of "the company you keep," in this particular instance, it might have been on the nose. Yet . . . it was a fresh start for most of them, and he hadn't really done much to show he was the same lackey . . . other than still orbiting Alpha and seemingly having a chip on his shoulder. It was an interesting dichotomy.

Aside from his questionable allegiances to Alpha's "inner circle," León was a competent partner on the hunting trail. His sharp eyes and instinctive understanding of the forest played well against Rua's agility, martial fortitude, and expert navigation in wilderness terrain. Their effectiveness as a pair was, begrudgingly, indisputable, even though their conversations were usually peppered with biting remarks and enough sass that, if you'd added a bit of *afras*, you'd end up with quite a handsome bottle of root beer.

The past few weeks had seen many changes sweep through the camp. People found their footing in this bizarre world, learning to wield powers they'd only dreamt of, and forming bonds that felt stronger than anything they'd known in the real world. But with the turning of the seasons, a chill had crept into the air, making the nights longer and the days harsher.

The cold wasn't the biting kind they'd known back home. No, this was a deep, penetrating cold, the type that seeped into the bone and lingered there, making every movement feel like wading through knee-deep snow.

Rua found herself reflecting on this turn of weather, her thoughts meandering through the myriad of changes and challenges they'd faced since their arrival. Life was different, harder in many ways, yet filled with a richness that made the struggle . . . well, not *worth it*, but interesting at the very least. But as the winter approached, bringing with it an ominous air of uncertainty, the fires of nostalgia grew stronger, warming the heart while chilling the soul with longing for the familiar, no matter how mundane that might have been.

But as much as she missed some of the simple comforts of her past life, Rua knew there was no going back. This was their reality now, and they had to face it with as much courage and conviction as they could muster, even if it meant sharing a hunting trail with a dwarf whose loyalty was bent toward the authoritarian lean.

As they moved deeper into the woodland, Rua's eyes picked up a strange anomaly amidst the sea of green and brown—a flash of fur and feather. It was the wolp, nibbling on an errant patch of what looked like juniper berries, its long ears pricked, alert to the smallest noise. A look of silent acknowledgment passed between Rua and León. The game was on.

León was the first to move, slipping into the brush with a grace that seemed at odds with his chunky, stone-like exterior. Meanwhile, Rua opted for a direct approach, drawing the blade Loon had liberated for her in Tallrock, a dull sliver of lethal iron blending with the muted tones of the forest. Not the gargantuan Behemoth Blade she used for conflicts. No, that weapon was, despite its magically reduced weight, much too unwieldy in such thick foliage.

The wolp, however, seemed to have a sixth sense for looming catastrophe, because just as they were about to pounce, it sprang into the air, its hawk-like wings unfurling, and flew off into the forest.

"Shit!" León grumbled. "You spooked it!"

"No, I didn't," Rua said. "It's just good at sensing danger. Don't blame me for something outside both of our control."

"It probably smelled your perfume," the dwarf grumbled.

"I'm not wearing—ugh, it's getting away!"

The chase was on, and they followed the flying hare through the woodland.

León tried to shoot an arrow from his bow, but the dart merely whizzed past the wolp, lodging itself instead in an innocent tree. Rua, in her pursuit, attempted to scale a rugged slope, only to be betrayed by a rogue stone, sending her sliding back down on her bottom with an undignified yelp.

They raced along, tracking the flight of the creature while dodging low-hanging branches, leaping over gurgling brooks, and at one point, they'd been narrowly swallowed by a muddy ravine. After a particularly grueling sprint, León's foot found a concealed rabbit hole—presumably not the wolp's, as best they understood, the creatures roosted in the trunks of trees. The ensuing sight of the dwarf flailing and squawking as he tumbled down a mossy embankment was something Rua would tease him about for weeks, provided they survived the humiliation of their current quest.

On and on they went, their relentless pursuit punctuated by the laughter of the wind and the forest's amused silence. But alas, as the day grew colder, the wolp, with a final triumphant caw, disappeared into the thicket, leaving a disgruntled dwarf and an exhausted elf in its wake.

León grumbled something indeterminate, and Rua merely sheathed her sword, shaking her head. There was a kind of humor in it—perhaps something they would razz one another about in the days to come. But it would not be this day. So, with bruised bodies and egos, they made their way back toward the camp.

It wasn't much later that, even as Rua and León were recounting the almost-ridiculous nature of their day's endeavor, they heard a rustling from the undergrowth. They both prepared their weapons and froze, ready to battle or possibly luck into some grub to bring back. Slithering through the ferns, with a grace that belonged more to a dancer than a creature of her kind, was Zylithia. Previously one of the non-field-tripping commuters on the train, now she was a naga, her body a sinuous combination of woman and serpent, scales glittering like polished jade in the sunlight.

Her tongue darted out, tasting the air, her golden eyes landing on Rua and León.

"Sss-k'h-sssheha," she hissed, her voice echoing the sibilant whispers of the forest. Unfortunately, due to her Race restrictions, she spoke only Nagassh'k, the naga language, a collection of hisses and clicks that had proven quite a challenge for Rua. But she was getting the hang of it, one hiss at a time.

Problem.

"Sss-k'h-sssheha?" Rua repeated, her brows furrowing as she struggled to decipher the meaning. Zylithia nodded vigorously, her forked tongue flicking out in agitation.

After a few moments of racking her brain, it finally clicked.

". . . at camp?" she asked, the realization breaking over her like a wave. She repeated the question in Nagassh'k.

Zylithia nodded once more, repeating the hissing phrase but adding two names that sent a surge of both exasperation and concern through Rua.

"Loon . . . Al . . . pha."

"Of course it's Loon and Alpha," Rua muttered, rolling her eyes. The feud between the two was a constant undercurrent in the camp, each clash building up to what was likely going to be a very explosive fight eventually.

She gave Zylithia an appreciative nod, acknowledging the message before turning to León, who was still trying to get the bramble out of his beard.

"We'd better head back. It sounds like our problem children are at it again," she said.

With a last, lingering look at the serene forest, they departed, each step taking them closer to the brewing storm. As they walked, the forest's peaceful whispers were replaced by the distant hum of discontent, a reminder of the annoyance that awaited their return. After all, when it came to Loon and Alpha, a day without a squabble was a day wasted.

Rua entered the camp to the sight of a large crowd. There was shouting—lots of chaos, really. She nodded hurriedly at Dragoon as she got within the perimeter—the human nodding back as he kept his eyes trained outward, unbothered by the commotion.

As she drew close to the squabble, she spotted Loon, taller than a lot of the others and pointing at the diminutive form of Alpha. The two were clearly in some kind of heated fight, which didn't surprise her at all. They'd been building to this since their unresolved Duellum weeks before. Now, it seemed, it was about to come to a head.

Saban was shaking his head, standing at the back of the group, looking displeased. The elf sidled up next to him, peering over some of the other Sojourners before turning to him.

"What's it about now?" She wondered.

Saban shrugged.

"Alpha mentioned the . . . barrier he wants to build. Again. Loon laughed. Made a few comments. Alpha got shitty about it."

"That's not new," Rua said. "Why am I sensing this is different?"

"Alpha tried to kick one of the roe—Slappy, I think."

"Ah . . . shit," Rua said. "You said *tried*, though. So, he wasn't successful?"

"Nah," Saban said, a smile forming. "The egg bit him and then bounced away. But Loon's still pissed."

"I would be too," she said. "I'm actually surprised it hasn't come to blows yet, though."

"Alpha was able to get the conversation back to the wall by saying Loon *didn't understand it*."

"A smart tactic," Rua said.

"Smart but slimy," Saban agreed, shaking his head. "And that's where we're at now."

Rua peered at the brewing showdown, a battle of wills between the two profanity-spewing titans. She could see the fury in Loon's eyes, the unyielding stubbornness in Alpha's stance. It was a toxic brew, a tinderbox waiting for a spark.

Loon was vehemently making his case, his arms flailing about, looking like a half-drunk maestro attempting to conduct a philharmonic orchestra.

"A fucking *wall*!" she heard him yell, his voice full of incredulity and anger. "We're surrounded by fucking trees, you dumb shit. What are we walling in? Mosquitoes?"

Alpha was, as always, unmoved by the criticism. His arms were crossed over his chest, his expression full of that frustrating, self-righteous confidence that made Rua want to punch something. Preferably him.

"It's about security, *sport*," he shot back, his tone heavy with the patience of a parent explaining basic math to a slow child. "If we've got a wall, we've got control. But I wouldn't expect someone like you to understand *control*."

Rua sighed.

"Two tigers, one mountain," she murmured, shaking her head. This was going to end badly, and she was beginning to regret coming back early. "Well, one of them is about to die for sure, huh?"

"For sure," Saban agreed.

"Look at Mr. High and fuckin' Mighty over here," I drawled, pointing a thumb at the dwarf standing rigid in the center of the gathering crowd. "Got a taste of his own medicine and now, wouldn't you know it, he's full of fuckin' opinions. Well, guess what, pap smear? I'd have to be fuckin' *high* to listen to your dumb-as-turds ideas."

Alpha's eyes narrowed, a scowl creasing his bearded face.

"Watch it, you dumb fuck. Queefing out of your mouth a lot for someone who's got no plan of action."

"Oh, like your bullshit plan to build a . . . what? Fence!?" I scoffed. "That's all action, alright. Action in the wrong fucking direction."

"Bullshit?" Alpha scoffed, his hands balling into fists. "It's a good fucking plan, you moaning bitch."

"I'll bitch and moan all I want, Alfalfa, 'cuz your plan's about as sturdy as your stumpy little legs. Honestly, trying to hurt one of my precious pals . . . you're lucky I don't alakazam your acid-shitting ass into dust."

His scowl deepened.

"Yeah, and what's your genius plot, you *fuck*? Run off into the woods and hope for the best? Real fucking smart."

"Better than sitting on our asses waiting for death to find us here!" I shot back. The roe, just as angry as I was, now backlined me. If there was going to be a fight, I'd unsanction the fucking piss out of it and rain annihilation on this sloppy butt-weasel.

The douchebag's bushy eyebrows shot up in mock surprise.

"Oh, is that what you think we're doing? Waiting for death?"

"Did I mumble, trout gargler?" I challenged, taking a step closer. "You think a fuckin' *wall* is going to keep us safe from the fucked-up ghouls out and about?"

Alpha bristled, a vein pulsing in his forehead.

"Oh, and blindly escaping right *into* fucking monsters is the move? You've got no idea what the hell you're talking about, you dumb piece of shit."

"The fuck I don't! Getting out of here gives us a chance. Your fucking wall is a death sentence."

"I'd rather die fighting than be *murdered* running," Alpha shot back.

I threw my head back and laughed, a harsh, bitter sound.

"Oh-ho-ho-ho! You know all about *murders*, don't you, piss fart? What happens when that wall falls, Alphonse? What then? Gonna throw your shit-stained fuckin' body in front of the breach?"

"Fuck you, goblin," Alpha said. "Do you just enjoy being a contrary little cunt, or are you genuinely this fucking stupid?"

"Oh, *I'm* the stupid one?" I spat. "Says the guy who thinks he's some great . . . I dunno, general? Deity? Well, news flash, bitch: you're not a god. Hell, I've *met* gods. And they were pretty goddamn annoying, but you're a horse of a different brain damage. A shitheaded, bad-idea-havin', dumb-dick crotch whistle with delusions of grandeur. I've seen what things are out there, *friend*, and—"

"You think you're so fucking smart, don't you—you little beta bitch? Always with the quick comeback. But what have you done to help us? Nothing. You're just a little-dicked fucking fairy with—"

"I *killed* that fucking spider, dipshit! You're fuckin' with the wrong guy, you greasy, homophobic turd demon. You're trash and your ideas are trash; you're just too fucking conceited to realize it."

"That's more than I can say for your coward's plan, cuck," Alpha sneered. "You'd rather run and let everyone else fight for their lives."

"*Look who's talking!* You hide behind *everybody*! Quivering and trying to control everything, only actually doing a damn thing when you think you can cheat. I didn't see you lay one fucking finger on that huge monstrosity, but you're acting like you're goddamn captain of this outfit just because you . . . what? Found the village charter before anyone else? This world might be filled with nonsensical game rules, but this *ain't* a fucking game, Alf. Nobody here's your pawns. Got some real microdick energy on you. The only reason anyone fucking listens to you is because you're just a *grimy little murderer.*"

Alpha's face reddened.

"You know what? This isn't over. Our *Duellum* isn't over."

"Fucking *bet*," I replied, my eyes narrowing. "Because I don't think you'd like how that ends. I'll beat your ass just like I did before. And *this* time, even if a *thousand* fire spiders land on me, you're going in the ground, motherfucker. I have zero problem killing a salty little ass-lick like you."

"You threatening me now, cunt?" Alpha growled, chest puffing out.

"*Duh*, you *fuckin' donkey*. I've been threatening you this whole time and you're just now realizing it? Goddamn, you're stupid. I hope to fuck you were just born with a dented brain or something, because otherwise this is sad."

The gathered crowd had grown silent, hanging on every venomous word we spat at each other. The air was electric, tension hanging thick like a summer storm waiting to break.

"Dalton—make sure this cum stain is left outta the breakfast rotation," Alpha commanded smugly to the anxious-looking elf standing on the sidelines.

"Is that it, then?" I mocked, folding my arms over my chest. "*This* is your attempt at leadership? Well, we're all truly fucked."

"Enough!" Alpha roared, his fist slamming into the palm of his hand. "This isn't about me or you. This is about the survival of everyone here!"

"Yeah, right," I shot back. "This has always been about you. Your ego. Your power trip."

The words hung heavy in the air between us. For a moment, everything went quiet.

"Our Duellum isn't over," Alpha reiterated through gritted teeth.

"Oh, look at that, the echo came back. Put your ass where your dick is, you shit-nothing. Lead the way."

That was when we were interrupted . . . by the slight frame of Tanner. The easily ruffled entwick simply barged his way to the front of the crowd and cleared his throat.

"Uh . . . Loon," he said, sounding as though this was the most exhausting task he'd had to accomplish in his life.

"What!?" I demanded, my blood still pumping wildly.

"You—uh, you got a visitor," he said.

"Huh!? A visitor? Everybody I know is here," I snapped.

"Yeah, I dunno man—someone from . . . I dunno the name. A town, not far from here?"

"Tallrock?" I asked.

Great, someone is here to try to make me pay for something, probably. This can't end well.

"Yeah . . . uh, maybe," the entwick said.

"Uh, well . . ." I started, forcing my anger to cool a bit so I didn't direct it in the wrong path. "I'm kinda in the middle o' somethin' at the moment, buddy. Who is it?"

"D—dunno," he said with an overexaggerated shrug. "Some . . . kid? With a delivery, I think."

"Kid?" I wondered. "What fucking goon is watching over this place that just . . . lets a child wander in?"

Alpha actually had the decency to look slightly embarrassed at that.

"Uh, Dragoon's on guard duty," he said.

So, with deep resignation, I shot Alpha a look that said, *This ain't over, motherfucker*, and followed Tanner away.

As I sauntered into the clearing, the first thing I saw was the center of attention—a wiry little lad clutching something big and awkward wrapped in paper. Everyone present had turned to watch, staring at the kid.

His eyes were wide and scared, and he swiveled his head around like a barn owl until his gaze landed on me. His eyes got even bigger, if that was possible.

"Are . . . are you Loon?" he stuttered out, his voice almost swallowed up by the breeze.

I smirked at that. If there was one thing I enjoyed, it was recognition.

"Oh, yeah, kiddo, I'm Loon. You want me to sign an autograph or somethin'?"

The kid seemed to completely bypass the joke, instead offering the large parcel with shaky hands. I frowned. I'd never been big on surprises—hated 'em, in fact. I mean, when I was practicing to get my learner's permit, I accidentally veered off the road when the check engine light came on. Surprises were rarely good, especially from strangers. But hell, maybe it was a large, elaborate cookie.

"What's this?" I asked, keeping my voice steady. I didn't want to scare the kid more than he already was.

The kid let out a squeak.

"Delivery, sir!" Then he was off like a bullet, leaving me with the mysterious package and more questions than answers.

So, I shrugged and looked down at the gift.

I hoisted the box up and rattled it around, trying to get a hint as to what was inside. But the thing didn't make so much as a peep or a rattle.

Hmm . . .

Well, fuck it. The crowd was watching now, all eyes on me. Might as well give them a good show.

With a smirk that could outshine the moon, I began to tear into the package.

Ryan had had a rough go of things.

It started when he'd been visiting his dad, who was recovering from a stroke. Sure, it was deemed a "mild event," but this was only a few months after he'd had his heart attack. Honestly, Ryan was getting a little frustrated with Mr. Svensson's lackadaisical approach to health. Too many steaks and Pall Malls, the doctor said the first time—and reiterated it the second time. At that point, he had just been patiently waiting for the call that he needed to start making funeral arrangements. But dutiful soldier, dutiful son—Ryan Svensson went where he was needed. Even if it meant calling in to his job, riding the train over an hour each way, and spending nearly an entire work shift sitting next to a man who complained that he was only there because the doctors had it out for him. Not the fact that he'd lost consciousness and driven his forklift full of power-tiller frames off the loading dock.

It was exhausting. He couldn't wait to get home and climb into a tall glass of gin.

He'd been riding home when the nonsense had bubbled up.

A fight had broken out on the evening commuter train between some of the teenagers. Petty squabble. Somebody said something rude or offensive, there was an escalation, more people got involved. Some loud, short kid who reminded Ryan of a few of the fresh boots in his unit back in the day started showing off a knife. Everything to prove and no way to do it. But Ryan wasn't going to be bothered. Let them sort it out. Someone would get punched in the mouth and things would calm down. But that wasn't what happened.

Ryan got attentive very quickly. Some lady got it in her head that it was a good idea to start waving around a gun, and that was a recipe for a bad night. Well, not quite. He'd noticed almost immediately something was off. She gripped it too lightly—more so than bad form would allow—it wasn't heavy enough. Also—no ejection port. And the barrel was blocked. *And* it was missing the decocker lever on the slide that the Beretta 92 was known for . . .

Jesus H. Christ, it was a prop pistol.

Which was even more dangerous. Ryan decided to do something right then and there, easing himself up from his seat, but overheard the woman making it worse for herself.

She threatened the chief antagonist of the altercation by saying that the flight of the bullet would travel some . . . insane speed—a hundred and forty-eight miles *per second*.

Well, thought Ryan, *that's a lie that's either going to work well or end with her being pistol-whipped*.

She also talked about training abroad—implying she was a soldier. Ryan very much doubted that. He wasn't sure why, but it was just a vibe at this point. She could have been a world-renowned war hero, he supposed, but there was nothing in her actions or countenance that led him to believe she'd even so much as taken an ROTC course. Prop gun for a prop soldier.

Stolen valor as well, he thought.

He didn't care—not really—but at this point, he was just mentally tabulating her list of offenses. Just as he was making his way over, that was when the strange woman with the curly hair had suddenly showed up, and Ryan felt himself being tossed backward against the seats with some annoyingly unseen force. She'd jabbered on a bit, then the train derailed. Now he was here, calling himself *Dragoon*.

He thought about that a lot. He hadn't had a piece on him at the time—hospital rules and all. But he imagined, based on what random objects had come along with them to this new world, he'd have been able to make *quite* the difference if he'd been so lucky.

What I wouldn't give for . . . hell, even a Colt 2000, he smirked, thinking of the old adage "Any port in a storm." *I'd have blasted those gold monsters right in the* yeet *center of their brains*.

But now he was figuring out how to adapt his training to the crossbow and pulling unofficial guard duty, watching over the camp because the vast majority of these folks had no clue how to protect themselves—and seemed more than a bit preoccupied with doing the *exact opposite* of recommended safeguarding. It had only been, what? Two weeks? And in that time, he'd discovered a pirate's cove's worth of head-scratchingly ignorant violations of common sense that would have curled even the lowliest mall cop's toes.

So, when the kid showed up, it was worth noting.

A small human boy, barely the height of an enthusiastic sunflower, stood alone near the center of the camp, some kind of package held in his arms.

The only person who wasn't currently occupied by the forthcoming fight between Alpha and whomever had garnered his ire was the strange one known as Tanner. From the few conversations they'd had, he learned that Tanner had been, of all things, the engineer driving the ill-fated train on that evening. The man—or rather, entwick—had reluctantly engaged with the boy briefly, and then had gone off, returning a few minutes later with the orc, Loon—formerly the previously mentioned short, chubby loudmouth from the train. Apparently, this was a visitor for him. Loon was terrifying in Dragoon's opinion. More than just the fact that he was a big, piebald brute of a monster, what really made him blanch that Loon was *far* too casual with death. In his experience, you learned to see that sort of thing. Most curiously was, he'd seemed like that *before* they'd been transferred here. It was strange, but it wasn't exactly surprising.

With eyes as wide as saucers and a bundle almost as big as himself clutched tightly in his arms, the boy bravely approached the hulking figure.

"Are . . . are you Loon?"

The orc smirked, pointing at himself and raising an eyebrow.

"Oh, yeah, kiddo, I'm Loon. You want me to sign an autograph or somethin'?"

Dragoon's keen eyes flickered between them.

Who's this child and what's his deal?

The boy offered the parcel to Loon, shuddering under its weight. The orc squinted at the package and then at the boy, the cogs in his head turning at a speed that threatened to cause friction burns.

From what he'd been led to believe, Loon's interactions with mundane things were the stuff of legends. Yet even by Dragoon's standards, the sight of the orc taking the package from the small boy with the sort of trepidation one would reserve for handling a viper was downright laughable. The confusion writ large on his face was as entertaining as the situation was bewildering.

"What's this?" Loon questioned, his deep voice rumbling. He eyed the parcel as if it were a particularly vexing riddle or perhaps a salad.

The boy, brave soul that he was, managed to squeak out, "Delivery, sir!" before scampering off, presumably to some urgent boyish adventure involving puddles and frogs.

The orc's scrutiny shifted between the retreating back of the young boy and the innocent-looking package now in his possession.

Loon shrugged, then looked down, apparently deciding to resolve the mystery the only way he knew.

He smiled, glancing around at the others as if he was somehow privy to special attention. He lifted the package. Then he rattled it beside his ear like a giant, grizzled toddler with an unknown Christmas gift. The anticipation was almost unbearable. It was like watching a bear trying to open a jar of pickles. Dragoon had seen many things in his lifetime, but watching Loon, who looked like he could arm-wrestle a minotaur and come out victorious, reduced to a state of quizzical curiosity by a simple package was pure gold.

Then he frowned, receiving no hints, and grasped the top of the box.

As he started to pry open the package, an air of smugness began to replace his initial confusion. It was as if he'd claimed victory over an invisible adversary.

"Well, this is clearly—" His triumphant statement hung in the air, cut short by a sudden—

BOOM!

In a burst of brilliant light and deafening noise, Loon was catapulted into the sky. The law of gravity was temporarily dismissed as the orc shot upward, spinning wildly against the backdrop of the tranquil sky. There he was, a salute to the gods of rocket-powered propulsion.

Dragoon was wide-eyed as Loon became an unwilling participant in the universe's impromptu experiment in orcish aeronautics. But the universe wasn't done yet. Oh, no, it was just warming up.

As Loon hung in the air, time seemed to slow. There was a drawn-out moment of silence leading up to the grand finale. And then, with a louder, more resounding *KA-BOOM!* Loon exploded, transforming into a dazzling shower of orc bits and pieces.

Each fragment of the orc seemed to twirl and spin in the sky, as if taking part in some grotesque ballet. An arm here, a leg there, each spinning, twirling, somersaulting with a grace that the orc had never managed to achieve while in one piece.

The camp was showered in the confetti viscera, landing on everything, before beginning to dissolve into a colorful mist. It appeared to Dragoon, in such a stunned state as he was, that the orc was dead.

That was when everyone began to scream.

I'd opened the box, and then I blew up.

Well, technically, I'd been flash-banged into senselessness and *then* I'd blown up. I'd felt myself leaving the ground, soaring, weightlessly traveling at top speed toward an unknown destination. It turned out that my final departure was Ghosttown, USA.

I felt the burst, my body rupturing instantly, and then I saw black. Followed closely by a message that shook me to my soft nougaty center:

You have died.

Fuck! I screamed in my own ethereal head.

I was dead, and now I was going to be sent to play patty-cake with Pontivex for the rest of relative eternity. This could not possibly have gone worse. Or so I thought. Another message appeared.

You have lost the Duellum.

FUUUUUUUUU—

CHAPTER TWELVE

WELL, I'LL HAVE TO TAKE A MULLIGAN ON THIS ONE

In the volcanic depths of the Forsaken Crypt of the Dreadnaught Lord, the Hive Fiend Pontivex sel Delibitaus was indulging in his favorite pastime—crafts.

This particular Hive Fiend, however, did not feel as though this endeavor was just a hobby—no, this was sartorial creation, and—gods willing—his someday livelihood. In that regard, he always ensured to be precise and, more importantly, unique with any of his fabrications. Pontivex considered himself a pioneer of sorts, his masterpieces not just simple wearables—by the smoke, no! These accouterments were designed to speak to the individual with the intent of being scene dressing for the body, and meant to tell a story.

To Pontivex, any auteur worth his basalt knew that it was important—especially in the ever-changing landscape of the fashionable realms—to steep oneself in a constant state of improvement and in pushing the boundaries of what could be considered bold. For instance, instead of run-of-the-mill, typical fabric, he used mummified spider silk. And rather than eye-catching diamante, he used the molten teardrops of the regretful—artisanally frozen to maintain their sparkly despair.

His lair was a macabre aesthetic of blood-red tapestries, low-hanging ghoul-glow chandeliers, and an array of chairs that looked as if they were stolen from a necromantic dental office. And, at the heart of it, amid the discordant vibrancy, sat Pontivex, hunched over his latest creation—a vest of darkness that, ironically, was meant to shimmer in the night. Though he was having a few . . . difficulties with procuring just the right sheen to properly relay the intended grandeur—or "wow factor," as they called it in the biz.

He had just finished applying another dewdrop of sorrow—though it was likely thirteen too many—when a spectral form appeared.

It was a minute creature, roughly the size of one of the Hive Fiend's hats, and glowing with a strange ethereal light. The figure drifted into his lair quietly.

A casual observer might think it a harmless, ghastly child's toy, but it could not be further from the truth.

This was Rexen Gravetongue, the eponymous Dreadnaught Lord, who had a knack for appearing when Pontivex least expected nor wanted.

"Hi, Ponty!" Rexen's shrill voice echoed around the cavernous lair. Pontivex jumped at the sound and further winced at the nickname. He looked up, finding his keeper was far too close for his own comfort level.

"Whence comest thou, spectral nuisance?" Pontivex asked, imbuing his tone with as much gravitas as possible. "I . . . er . . . that is to say . . . *m'lord.*"

"Whence? Uh, Iunno. Maybe . . . the direction I was coming, right? Yes! Anyway! Whatcha doing, Ponty?" Rexen continued.

Pontivex sighed, a sound like rocks tumbling down a well.

"I am currently engaged in . . . recreational tailoring."

Rexen blinked.

"Huh. So . . . sewing, then?"

"Well, technically . . ." Pontivex began, but Rexen quickly cut him off.

"Got any very, very, very small clothes? I know a *little bitty* guy that would look so dapper in tiny finery!"

Pontivex furrowed his brow, picturing an extended lifetime of torment under Rexen's reign as he wore exponentially sillier garments. He shot a glance at his wardrobe stuffed full of various choice articles. He supposed he might as well use it for *something*.

"Perhaps . . ." he grumbled, "I could fashion something of the sort, m'lord."

"Yay!" Rexen spun around in a circle. "Oh! And I want some shinies on 'em. Not too much! Just enough to make them twinkle!"

"Twinkle?" Pontivex asked.

"Yep!" Rexen confirmed. "They will look so very dainty and marvelous! Beautiful! Tiny, twinkling rat outfits."

"Rats?" Pontivex asked, unsure if he heard correctly.

"Rats!" Rexen confirmed.

"I'd assumed you would be requesting them for yourself. But . . . you are requesting this for . . . rodents?"

"Yep! But just one. I think he deserves it—he's been a good boy. But he needs multiple outfits for his tiny outings. His name is Wibby! Oh—do you know him?!"

Pontivex could have wept. To think his illustrious career had hardly begun and already he'd be betraying his principles to become a sellout. Perhaps, he considered, instead he should view this as a grand opportunity to make his big break. Every starving artist had to start somewhere, after all.

"I shall endeavor to find the perfect stylistic flair for—"

"No style!" Rexen demanded. "Only shiny!"

Pontivex sighed.

"As you wish," he said.

Rexen nodded then, seeming to consider something—produced a little rusty orb from his open . . . well, not *hand*, as he didn't have any, but the end of his appendage. The arcane sphere floated, making slow rotations as he seemed to glare at it. Then the Dreadnaught Lord took the orb and extended it toward Pontivex, the object hovering eerily.

"This," he began, his voice oscillating between an excited squeak and an ominous hum, "is a token. A token for you, Ponty. Use it. However you desire."

Pontivex, a usually stalwart being of ancient dread, found himself faltering in the wake of this unexpected offering. The token was a form of currency in the Crypt and would allow him to pursue something other than boredom in crafts—even if he couldn't leave. Perhaps, Pontivex thought, he'd go visit the Undermarket. His eyes, which could flicker between various hues of infernal reds and oranges, settled on a muted gradient of sienna apprehension as he looked at the orb. He tentatively extended a clawed hand toward the floating sphere, feeling an unusual warmth emanating from it. It was almost comforting, which only served to deepen his reservation.

"Your generosity is both unexpected and suspicious, m'lord," Pontivex said, the words crumbling out of his mouth like broken gravestones. "Why offer such a wonderful boon to someone as lowly as me? You, who rule with a soft touch but an iron fist?"

Rexen's ethereal form swirled for a moment, his voice carrying the sound of a chortle and the weight of something much graver.

"Impatient, Ponty. I am getting to that . . . "

He paused for a moment, allowing a silence to fill the lair before he began to speak again.

"Ponty. You remember my first day," he stated, each word seeming to tingle with an unexpected sincerity. "When I conquered this foul dungeon—a super long time ago."

The Hive Fiend nodded but didn't speak. What sort of game was the Dreadnaught Lord up to?

"I was but a babe!" Rexen Gravetongue explained. "A little dreaming infant! Powerful, wasn't I? Ooh! I miss it."

Pontivex held back a snort, for never in their entire working relationship had Rexen been a whelp. He'd been ancient even then. However, he did not interrupt what was clearly a form of cathartic recitation.

"I did not know," Rexen continued, "what a warden did—or even *was*! Surely didn't know I'd have to wield this spooky dungeon like a prison."

Pontivex stared at Rexen in shock, the token forgotten in his clawed hand. He had not expected to hear such a confession. Rexen, the immensely powerful, unbelievably jovial, and moderately ludicrous Dreadnaught Lord, was being ... reflective?

"I didn't want to, you know ..." Rexen continued, his form fluctuating between bright and dim lights, reflecting the somber note in his words. "Be in charge of penitence, that is. Never liked the shoes. But ... everyone has their roles to play, eh?"

As awkward as the situation was, Pontivex found himself nodding. Rexen's form flickered once more.

"Still ... I'm the warden and them's the beans! Gotta make certain decisions, Ponty. Even if they're rough. Oof!"

Dread washed over Pontivex, a sensation that was far too familiar to him. The glow from the token in his hand seemed to fade a little, the grimness growing stronger. What was Rexen talking about? What decisions?

The Hive Fiend could only force out a whisper.

"What are you saying, m'lord?"

Rexen's form seemed to sway a little, like a ghostly balloon caught in a gentle wind. Then his tone grew dark.

"You did something naughty, Ponty," he shook his head, tutting. "Reminding me of somebody else who was up to no good all the time. Bad Hive Fiend. Now it is up to me to fix it."

"M'lord?" Pontivex said, nearly cringing away.

"Well, Ponty," Rexen started, his voice back to its usual lighthearted tone, "time for a chitchat about one of your mean ol' contracts."

The pain was a doozy. It felt like my whole soul was getting yanked out by a fucking tow truck. Like I was in the middle of a game of spirit tug-o'-war and I was the rope. Whatever the definition of a hootenanny was, this was the opposite.

The sensation was a crafted cocktail of terror and nausea that—had I not just died—would probably have KOd me on the spot. The world started spinning, and then, quicker than blue hell, I found myself tummy-down in ... well, it felt like moist dirt.

When I finally managed to crack open my eyes, the sun probed right into my retinas, and I had to take a beat for everything to stop being a blurry fuckin' mess. It slowly became clearer, and déjà vu wafted over me like a familiar scent—like catching a whiff of jazz cabbage at an outdoor festival.

The place ... I knew it, but it felt like trying to remember a dream after you'd woken up. The sky was clear and cloudless, the trees were dense, and the slope of the ground just seemed plain nostalgic. Still, whatever the recognition was from, it felt oddly distant, a watercolor painting of a memory. The result was just a jumbled, brain-scrambling mess. However, as my mind seemed to finally plug itself in, the understanding hit me.

I was standing in an open clearing on a hill surrounded by forest. This was where I'd first arrived in this world, not long ago. I'd just died, and now . . . I was right the fuck back where I started. I groaned.

"Aw, fuck, it's going to take us *forever* to get back!"

I also realized pretty quickly that I didn't have any of my items on me, and instead of the sweet, stylish threads I'd picked up before leaving Tallrock, I was back in the Sojourner costume of breathable taupe fabric. That meant no Trespasser's Veil, no Baghlus's Gorget of Flight, and no haladie.

"God fucking fuck!" I screamed in frustration, kicking at a patch of dirt with my bare foot. It exploded into a fine brown mist that the light breeze then sent right back at me, coating my body. I'd been revived for eight seconds, and I was already dirty again. That's when a prompt appeared.

Due to the established criteria of the Duellum, you will now be required to follow the rules and regulations of [Unnamed Settlement] as ordained by [Alpha], current Settlement Leader.

"Fuck!" I roared again. This was supremely unfair. Now I'd have to follow some dumbass code that a sociopath came up with? God. Dammit. This would not stand.

There was a flash of movement, and I wheeled to my right, fists up and ready to slap something silly, but surprisingly, it wasn't an enemy of some wildly outclassing magnitude ready to lay waste to me. It was Rexen. He floated a few feet away, watching me with an unreadable expression. It was a surprise, given the strange, sudden displacement. I hadn't expected anyone to be with me during . . . whatever it was that had happened. Death, I guess. But how was that even possible? Did he die too? No . . . he was *already* dead. One thing was for sure, though: I was sick and tired of getting exploded.

"What the damn bippy just happened?" I demanded, pointing at the trees surrounding us. "This was my starting point in Regaia. I thought—"

"Pupil," Rexen. "It was me. I did it. Be very impressed! It is a bit disorienting, I know. But you'll be just lovely in a moment. You're a strong disciple."

"A bit disorienting" was an understatement. I felt like I had been sucked brain-first into a black hole and shat out at the other side of the universe.

"How are you even here?" I asked. "Did you just appear here, or . . ."

I wasn't sure what else it could be.

"The effigy," Rexen said simply, smiling. "It is inside you. Mixing with your juices. Fortifying our bond."

"Ew," I said. "Why do you always make everything sound so gross?"

I touched my stomach.

"You're sayin' that because I swallowed your little anchor trinket, now we're stuck together forever?"

"For now," Rexen said mysteriously.

"What about Pontivex?" I asked. I was supposed to end up with that sasshole upon my untimely demise. The only other time I'd died, it had been mitigated due to the intervention of a fucking god. Had I not understood the assignment?

Rexen shook his head, an amused smile playing at the corners of his lips.

"*That* old boob? He is likely still in his lair. Doing *crafts*," he said nonchalantly.

His words took a moment to sink in. I was taken aback. That wasn't what I had expected. But then again, what did I know? I was navigating uncharted territory there.

"But I thought—" I began, my thoughts whirling.

"You thought the Conditional Quest would keep you bound to him upon death," Rexen finished my sentence, a knowing look in his eyes. "But you see, as the Dreadnaught Lord, his imprisonment falls to *me*. I can overwrite the Quest. I'm very talented."

I blinked, trying to make sense of it all. Rexen could do that? Change the conditions of a Quest? I knew he'd had some area of influence in reworking stuff—he'd done as much with my own Class—but I assumed that was due to the fact that he was *Pacted* with me. This seemed to toe into a gray area, and now I was wondering just how powerful he actually was. That was a level of control I had never encountered before. It was terrifying and fascinating in equal measure.

Instinctively, I tried to pull up my menu, needing to see for myself, to verify what Rexen was saying. But instead of the familiar info and options, all I saw was a menu that simply said:

Loon
-Orc

"What the hell is this?" I demanded, my voice strained. "The damn word box is on the fritz again!"

Rexen frowned, peering over at the strange screen.

"Interesting, *very* interesting."

"It is?" I wondered. "What's it mean?"

"Iunno," the little ghost admitted happily.

For a moment, we stood there in silence.

"What?!" I suddenly shouted.

"You should yell not as often," Rexen said. "A disciple should speak to his master with more reverence."

"Yeah, I'm gonna refuse," I said, staring at the world around me before turning back to him. "So . . . I don't have to worry about Pontivex anymore?"

"You still need to complete the Quest you set out to achieve," Rexen said. "But you are no longer constrained. If you die, you will return here. I have rescued you once more, pupil."

I thought about this. A major thorn in my side had been the fact that if I died, rather than respawn like the usuals of my kind did—that's Sojourners, for you just joining us—I'd be vaulted into the big demon chicken's lair and made to do . . . whatever it was he needed a soul slave for. This took a huge weight off my shoulders.

"Arjee, I could honestly kiss you right now," I said.

"Save your thanks, pupil," he said dismissively. "It manifests in an ugly and disrespectful way."

I just laughed.

"Okay, so, we're going to have to trek *all* the way fucking back to the camp from here. Which will take days upon days. I guess I can't really complain considering the alternative but—"

"Can we get beer now?" Rexen asked.

". . . I am trying really hard to understand how you think it's even possible for you to—"

"That's a no," Rexen explained sadly. "I suppose I will have to wait until we get closer to a settlement. Ooh! Perhaps we will find some wayward vagabonds with imbibements! Then we can destroy them and wet our whistles for our trouble!"

"Listen, I'm not trying to make any additional enemies until we are back within the safety of our friends' little campground," I said.

"The portrait within which my disciple thinks is quite small," Rexen grumbled dejectedly.

"Yeah, well, sorry to disapp— Oh, fuck!" I shouted. "I didn't even tell them about the bad guys who want to turn them into energy goo! Shit! We gotta go fast!"

With that, I dashed away into the trees.

CHAPTER THIRTEEN

INTO THE WOODS

The memory of the Redmark camp hit me like a stench-filled smack in the face. Their signature smell of stale mead and unwashed assholes was still lingering in the air as I skidded to a halt a few feet away from where I had last seen it. The torches were extinguished, the big top was gone, and the temporary fortifications that the camp had erected had been dismantled. Also, it was a smoking hole in the ground from the absolute jaw-dropping payload of a firestorm someone had uncorked on the place.

Oh, yeah. That was a thing that happened.

It was just a few weeks before that I'd been held captive there, then suddenly *not* a prisoner, and then an escaping fugitive. What a roller coaster. Even their commanding officer, Fawn—a Sojourner, like me—had made an attempt to appear friendly, which was unsettling in its own right. For all her charm and terrible taste in music, though, she had eventually flipped some switch in her brain, transforming her into just as much of a sonofabitch as the rest of the coterie of dickbirds she led. It was clear she'd had a case of the Mondays, because she'd tried to kill me—a turn of events that I was becoming depressingly accustomed to. So far, I'd gleaned that her particular brand of jimmy-rustling had to do with the Esper Nodes. But as to the question of why, I didn't think I'd ever know for sure.

Man, see? This is why you can't trust a country music fan.

Shortly thereafter, I'd ended up making a hastily enacted, poorly-planned dine-and-dash which culminated in me being chased by a rabble of Fawn's bloodthirsty lot lizards who'd thought that the best way to solve their problem was by terribly firing arrows at it in the rain. As I ran for my life and was then hurled from atop a cliff by a muscular, bald manslaughterer, it became more and more evident that I, too, was Garfielding at the beginning of the week.

As I'd plummeted—calmly screaming for my life and shitting my pants—I'd been fortunate enough to catch the eye of a passing deity. Another one of those meddling celestial beings. This one happened to be the brother of the other god who'd conveniently saved my hide from death's clutches.

I guess gods must have a soft spot for me—don't act like you're not jealous. That had set into motion my business-as-usual mode of fleeing, fighting, and fucking everything up ever since.

I wonder what Zeol and Sababo are up to right now. Probably loudly declaring their love for one another to the backtracking of banjo music.

Another point against country.

As I scanned the remnants of the camp, my mind snapped back to the present. I'd been considering wandering about, ransacking the place for its tender treasures, but, by the state of it, that was a hundred years too late to be a lost cause. It was pointless to try and salvage *anything* there, and plus, it just seemed like a lot of work, you know? I'd just returned from the dead, after all, and was suffering from the hot, jazzy stylings of Resurrection Sickness. This made all my stats go down—exactly how much was a little bit of a mystery, as my System messages were still being fucky as fuck. When I'd last used Eye of the Saboteur, it had been on a mysterious-seeming tool lying in the dirt near the bonfire where I'd met the burned-faced dude who'd thrown me off the cliff. However, the information I'd received was . . . odd.

Blah blah blah Blah
Blah blah blah blah-blah, blah, blah blah blah blah blah. Blah blah blah blah blah—blah "blah-blah blah" blah, blah blah blah blah blah blah blah blah blah . . . blah blah . . .
Blah.

Fuckin' stupid, right?

Rexen and I continued our trek along the trail through the dense forest, a task made infinitely easier by the dry light of day and the lack of things exploding around us.

"Hey, Arjee," I said, trying to cut through the silence that had fallen between us.
"Yes, pupil?"
"We should probably, I dunno, try to off-road this bitch. You know, less chance of being spotted by any Redmark lunatics that happened to have survived? I don't like being out in the open."
"Sound logic, my delightful disciple," the specter returned, ". . . for a coward."
"That's easy for you to say. You're a fuckin' poltergeist. You ain't got nothin' to knife if we run into bandits or . . . monsters. With knives."

"Ah," Rexen cooed, nodding sagely. "My pupil has not stopped to consider the practicalities. The forest is dangerous, more so for one who is not native to these parts. The trail is the way. However, you could attempt stealth if your concerns are mounting."

"Right, because being an orc in an area of the world supremely lacking in other people like me, I blend right in during the day," I said. "Not to mention my *bright-as-fuck* hair. Practically camouflaged!"

"Grumpy pupil," Rexen admonished. "Blown up once and now you take umbrage with perfect strategies."

"I have been blown up so many times . . ." I said, more to myself than to him. "Honestly, I'm pretty sure I'm thirty percent combustion at this point."

"But one hundred percent perfect," Rexen said.

"Speaking of explosions: why do you think that kid had it out for me?" I wondered. "I'm going to clobber that little shit if I ever get my hands on him. Send his ass straight to the Shadow Realm."

Rexen bobbed in the air next to me.

"Perhaps, pupil, you stepped on his favorite anthill?" the unhinged apparition offered, swirling in midair.

I frowned at him, the muscle in my jaw twitching.

"Fuckin' great sleuthing there, glowstick."

"Or," Rexen ventured, utterly unfazed by my growing annoyance, "he belongs to a hidden order of exploding-package enthusiasts. Oh, but perhaps that would be too on the nose?"

I grumbled under my breath, swatting at him like he was a particularly annoying mosquito. Rexen ignored my displeasure, continuing in his irritatingly cheery tone.

"Could be that he has awakened latent, very strong Trap Arcana and wanted a victim to practice on."

"Yeah, because little kids are loaded down with evil magic and bad intentions. He was, what? Ten?"

"He could be a child prodigy of destruction Spells! Age is an irrelevant construct in the face of raw potential. I once knew a toddler skilled in summoning demons—though he was not wise enough, nor quick enough, to figure out how to unsummon them . . ."

"That's it; I've had it with your malarkey," I snarled, swiping at him again, but he dodged out of the way.

"Oh, my disciple is rife with envy! Wished you had done the exploding, eh?" Rexen suggested, laughing merrily at his own joke.

"Jealous? Of a kid who tried to blow me to smithereens?" I spat, feeling my temper flare. "Please just shut up."

"Oh! I've thought of it!" Rexen said, an unnerving giggle echoing around us. "He simply found you disagreeable! I cannot say I blame him."

"What? Aren't you supposed to think I'm hot shit, or something?" I asked. "I thought I was your *perfect pupil* or whatever?"

"My disciple you may be," Rexen said. "But I am not without my limits to your demeanor. You don't even wear the hat I got you!"

"Jesus fuck, we've been over this—you never *gave* me a hat."

"I did, and you will live to regret this insult," he continued. "It is one thing to lose it, but to lie? Unbecoming."

"Is there a Spell that will let me punch ghosts?" I growled, my eyes narrowing at the specter.

"Yep!"

I let out a frustrated groan, running a hand through my fluorescent hair.

"You make absolutely no sense, Arjee. Just when I think I might be understanding a fraction of what you're saying, you swerve off into batshit country again."

"Sense? Who needs sense when you have *power*?! As I always say, 'Why have cake when you can have pie?' Oh! Or even better—why not indulge in both? They share a similar divinity."

I stopped, blinking hard at him.

"But . . . That's . . . You're comparing sense to pie and . . . Arjee, you belong in a goddamn asylum. And not one of those cushy, five-star-resort types. The old-timey ones where they lock the basement doors so the madness doesn't crawl out."

He spun in midair, radiating a peculiar joy.

"Perspective! What you call madness, I call freedom. Potato, banana, as they say!"

"Arjee, in no world are freedom and . . . *whatever* your severe impairment is called the same."

"Oh, there are so many worlds, pupil!" Rexen responded, flitting around like a hyperactive firefly. "And each one is madder than the last. You'd be surprised at the knowledge gleaned when the rules stop making sense."

He suddenly got very serious.

"Pupil!" he exclaimed.

"I'm right here, dude," I said. "You ain't gotta shout."

"Pupil!" he exclaimed again in the exact same pitch and volume.

"WHAT?!" I shouted back.

"We are near one of my caches! Ooh, we can pick up some of my sweet treats and candied meats! Let's go! Let's go!"

I shook my head.

"Brother, we ain't got time to divert our route just 'cuz you've got a hankerin' to exercise your sweet tooth. We've gotta get back to those motherfuckers so I can whip Alpha's ass for real in a new Duellum."

"But there's more than just that!" Rexen pleaded. "There's all manner of goodies!"

I sighed.

"Listen, we don't really have the manpower at the moment to go 'splorin,' Arjee. Let's get back to where we need to be, and *then* we can grab a whole team of fuck-around friends and spelunk the depths of another dungeon."

I was absolutely not planning on doing that, mostly because I had no interest in traversing some dark butthole crevice of a crypt and risking my life—thanks so much. The only time I planned on going into a dungeon again was simply to deliver some kind of exotic meat to Pontivex to get him off my back and resurrect the group that had had been killed by . . .

Well, let's table that for another time.

"But there's a lot of interesting *shinies* there, disciple!" Rexen continued. "I don't want to go another day without them."

"This is literally the first time you've mentioned them," I said. "So, it makes me think you'll actually be just fine without them."

"But—"

"How about this? If we bypass your little side quest for now, I'll get us some beer when we get back to camp."

Rexen did not seem mollified by this; instead, he floated up to me and poked an arm right into my face.

"Bad disciple. No respect for your elders."

I cleared my throat.

"Listen, I'm not saying *no*"—I definitely was— "I'm just saying *not right now*. I've got no weapons, no armor, and you're not exactly the most . . . effective party member right now."

"There's weapons and armor in the cache!" he said. "Lots of beautiful, *delicious* shinies awaiting a valiant and worthy disciple to lay claim to them."

I didn't have the energy to argue with him, because it seemed incredibly stupid to go *into* a dangerous area unarmed to retrieve items to help us. We'd probably be cream-puffed instantly—plus, even if we did get to them, I didn't have days or weeks to spare. So, I just kept walking and ignoring him.

"Disciple! *Disciple!* This is the wrong way! Disciple!"

The forest began to thin out, leading us onto a narrow path where the light could filter through the leafy canopy above. My hearing, perhaps due to some wild combination of Skills, picked up the muted sounds of hushed voices ahead.

My muscles tensed instinctively, my eyes darting around as I sniffed the air. The familiar scent of sweat, dirt, and something faintly aromatic hit me.

"Arjee," I whispered, keeping my voice low.

"Yes, pupil?" he answered, floating along by my side.

"Do you smell that? And the noise . . . "

He went silent, a swirl of energy pulsating around him—Rexen's version of concentrating, I suppose.

"Ooh, wow!" he suddenly articulated, loudly exclaiming. "It's bad news! Such bad news!"

"What is it?"

"Iunno."

"Fucking . . . just . . . stay quiet and follow my lead," I demanded in a huff.

Dropping low, I moved quietly through the underbrush, my senses on high alert. The sound of the voices grew louder, and I could make out the figures of several humanoid creatures ahead. They were similar to humans in size and shape, but their skin was greenish and rough, like tree bark. Large, root-like tendrils sprouted from their shoulders and backs, their eyes glowing an eerie white.

"What the hell are those?" I whispered.

"Vilden!" Rexen said, way too loudly.

I saw one of the creatures' heads snap my direction from the sound, peering into the thick trees.

"Arjee, I swear to god . . ."

We had two options now: engage or try to evade. Given my current condition—resurrected but not exactly in fighting-fit form—the smarter option was to avoid. However, considering I had a noisy trumpet of a Pact partner with me . . . neither option was really super nifty.

Guess it's time for the ol' sneaky-sneaks.

I concentrated on being stealthy—something I likened to . . . feeling like a shadow. I wasn't sure if that was how it was supposed to work, but it had been how I'd *been* doing it—and I hadn't had any issues with it so far. Utilizing the Skill felt natural, now—instinctive. There wasn't exactly a visual effect, but it was as though my brain was hardwired to understand which path was marked out, with a sense of precision that would leave any pathfinder in awe. My body moved with grace and agility, skirting past obstacles and finding the perfect route that would keep me out of the vilden's line of sight.

As I carved a quiet path around the group, I allowed myself a smug grin. Being a prowling predator in the undergrowth was something I was . . . apparently exceptionally good at. The thrill of it never got old, and the satisfaction that came from leaving others clueless to my presence was always rewarding. To be fair, it was rarely deployed, but when it was . . . oh, mama! I mean, Rexen may have been an actual ghost, but I was the real phantom there.

We were doing well, slipping by undetected, when Rexen, who had been suspiciously quiet this whole time, chose the absolute worst moment to break that silence.

"Ooh, goody gargoyle! Is that a Bool Blossom I see?" Rexen exclaimed in a tone that I was sure could be heard from miles away.

The vilden bandits perked up immediately, their white eyes darting around in search of the source of the noise. Their gaze landed on us—well, Rexen to be precise. I was hidden like a fuckin' *pro*, but *he* was still glowing magnificently and stupidly.

"Who goes there?" called out the one who seemed to be their leader, a thick tendril-like limb pointing straight in our direction.

"Nobody!" Rexen shouted back. "Go back to your criminal activities, knaves!"

I groaned. So much for evasion. Guess we needed to use the Plan B I didn't have.

The time for whispering was over, and the time for shouting and . . . reckless, haphazard violence had arrived—so very much my wheelhouse. I surged from my hiding spot like a burly green cannonball.

"Sup, tree-faces!" I boomed, surprising the group of vilden.

They turned, their glowing eyes wide with surprise as I, Loon, local barbarian and professional spectacle, barreled into their midst.

It was chaos from the get-go. Using a tree branch I'd picked up earlier—because who doesn't pick up handy-looking branches—I held as they came at me in a wave, all root and bark and shimmering white eyes.

One of them, a scrawny sumbitch who had no business in a bandit crew, struck at me first. He swung a root-like tendril, which I blocked with the branch, knocking him on his mossy butt. I laughed as he scampered back, apparently more afraid of me than I was of him.

"Gotcha nose, Twiggy!" I said, pointing at him with the branch.

Their assumptive leader, a hulking vilden with an inexplicable slice taken out of his chin, growled and took a step forward. He was less bark and more bite, judging by the size of him.

"I'm not much for diplomacy, so how about this . . ." I said, hefting the branch onto my shoulder. "You let us pass, and I won't use you for firewood tonight. Deal?"

Not surprisingly, they didn't take the deal.

The leader lifted a pair of sharp daggers in response, as if to intimidate me.

"Nice blades, I've got double blades t—" I started, reaching for my waistband, and then stopped.

Fuck! The whole reason I used the branch in the first place was because I don't have my haladie! Goddammit!

"... uh," I continued. "THIS!"

I hurled the branch at him and turned to run back to the trees, but I bowled right into a bandit that had snuck up behind me. We fell in a tangle, and the bandit leader launched himself on top of me. Stabbing. We clashed. It was like wrestling with an angry salad. One of his leafy fingers wrapped around my arms, and I countered by slamming him against the ground. The others piled on, turning the fight into an all-out brawl. Unfortunately, I was also realizing that while I might have been able to take one of these guys alone, there being six of them ... things weren't looking good.

Meanwhile, Rexen was ... floating there, adding color commentary.

"Ooh, watch out for that one, pupil! He's got a nasty root!"

I kept punching and jabbing and elbowing—and yeah, I even bit a couple of the schmucks, so sue me—but I was tiring quickly, for some reason. I glanced at my Stamina bar, and discovered it was draining fast as fuck and had a little symbol next to it of a head with a lightning bolt. I focused on it while karate-chopping one of the guys' necks and saw that I was under the status effect of ... Stamina Drain.

Now, how the fuck did that happen? One of these silly little fucks must be using Arcana on me.

"Arjee!" I shouted, craning my neck while landing a solid kick to one of the jerks in the jumble. "Stamina Drain!"

"Yes, pupil! How delightful!"

"Gah!" I screamed in frustration. "You useless ghosty b— Ow, fuck!"

One of the vilden bandits had been able to stand and had kicked me right in the head. That sent me reeling. I fought back in a daze, making less progress than I probably *should* have been able to, but ... I wasn't much of a ground fighter.

I was just freeing myself from the thicket when I saw that the leader was standing over me again, both blades in his root-like hands. However, I still wasn't able to loosen myself fully; instead, I was struggling to get another one of these floral bandits off my fightin' arm.

The leader loomed. I looked up at him. He looked down at me.

Ah ... fuck.

Then he launched forward, blades flashing, right toward my face.

You have died!

I came to not long after—based on the sun's position. The same sun that was hovering over the *exact same fucking place* I'd started my journey into this world at. Again. Also known as: *fucking hours* away from where I'd just been.

"Fuck!" I shouted, my voice echoing across the woods and hills. Then I doubled over and puked, immediately staining my fresh new Sojourner outfit.

"Urgh," I groaned, holding my head and swaying. "I feel fucking awful. Am I hungover?"

"Resurrection Poisoning," Rexen said cheerily next to me.

"Huh?" I wondered groggily. "I thought it was Resurrection *Sickness*? But, goddamn . . . I feel like I got hit by the influenza truck."

"You died while having the sickness," Rexen explained. "So, the effect advanced! It lasts longer now! And—"

He smiled happily in my direction.

"—is far more affecting to your statistics!"

I glowered.

"And how is that a good thing?"

"My brilliant disciple is sometimes . . . not so bright," Rexen admonished, shaking his head. "It is exhausting being your external brain at times."

"Just fucking tell me what you're talking about, Arjee!"

"My student forgets that revival has negative consequences for most, but my disciple's Fati—"

"Fatigue!" I interrupted. "Oh, holy damn hell!"

I checked my notifications–which, I realized, weren't affected yet by the strange nature of the suddenly extra unhelpful System.

Condition: Fatigued
Fatigue II
- **Abilities and Skills suffer -15% efficiency while under the Fatigue II Condition effect.**

Because of Fatigue II, Loon's Bombastic Beatdown Aegis has temporarily reached Tier II effects.
- **Strength Attribute increase [+8 multiplied by 150%]!**
- **Dexterity Attribute increase [+8 multiplied by 150%]!**
- **Constitution Attribute increase [+8 multiplied by 150%]!**

Strength: 63 (Fatigue II)
Dexterity: 63 (Fatigue II)
Constitution: 125 (Fatigue II)

"God*damn*, baby! That Level Up did Daddy good! What happens if I die again—Fatigue Three?"

Then I winced, because exclaiming like that made my head throb painfully.

"Seems likely," Rexen said. "Though my pupil will also get the Resurrection Curse."

"Well, that just sounds like superstition," I said. "What's the curse's deal?"

"It cannot be *rested* away," Rexen said, nodding as though revealing a profound truth. "Other ailments due to being revived can be, but not this. Resurrection Curses require a healer to take care of. My disciple would be unwise to allow this to happen."

"Well, huh," I said, considering. "So, I probably shouldn't die again before Resurrection Poisoning goes away? How long does this last anyway? 'Cuz it sucks."

"Iunno," Rexen shrugged.

"Of course you don't," I said exasperatedly. "Well, shit. I don't want to die again, anyway. But . . ."

I thought for a moment.

"Arjee . . ."

"Yes, pupil?"

"You said you've got some shinies in that, uh . . ."

"My cache!"

"Yeah," I said. "How about we go pay a visit to your little hidey-hole?"

CHAPTER FOURTEEN

THEY HAVE BUSINESS WITH THE ORC

The campfire sputtered and flickered, its golden arms reaching out to etch laughter lines on the barky, smiling faces of six woodland ruffians. Slumped around in poses more reminiscent of wind-blown saplings than hardened bandits, they reveled in the swelling song of their own merriment. You could say it was a convivial scene, if you overlooked the fact that they were tree-like humanoid bandits who were celebrating their victorious slaughter of an orc.

The biggest of the bunch, a chap called Yarkle, chuckled like a woodpecker.

"Didja see the look on his face when I stabbed 'im?" he guffawed, sending a leafy shower of laughter echoing through the trees.

"Oh, oh, what about when I smacked him inna face wiff m'foot?" Groke, the most diminutive of the gang, waved a twig-like arm in imitation of the event. Ironically, Groke had the muscle mass of a sapling but hit like an oak tree in a bad mood.

"Like a bug on a windshield," added Crag. In his mind, a windshield was a kind of magical barrier that warded off insects.

They chortled and cackled, leaves rustling like a breeze was playing among them. Not the deepest knots in the trunk, they delighted in their short-term victory, blissfully unaware of the cyclical nature of resurrection available to their orcish adversary.

"I tell ya, boys," Yarkle said, swiping a tear from his eye, "we're quite the merry band o' forest brigands, ain't we? That orc didn't know what 'it 'im."

"Not 'til it hit him, at least," Groke added, resulting in another round of laughter.

"Yeah, least 'til Groke hit him," Crag chimed in, always a beat too late.

"What say we next, lads?" Yarkle asked, picking at a greenish tooth with one rooty finger.

"I reckon we could go rob that elf bakery over in Whisper Pine," Crag suggested, licking his bark-like lips at the thought. "Get us some fresh cinnamon buns!"

Yarkle frowned, a feat that made his face look even more like a gnarled piece of driftwood.

"Crag, elves don't make cinnamon buns. They make ... moonberry pies and starflower tarts. We've been over this."

"Right, right," Crag said, shaking his head as if trying to dislodge an errant memory. "I always mix that up."

It was not without a certain sense of irony that Crag was, in fact, correct, and the bakery in Whisper Pine did *indeed* have cinnamon buns among their scrumptious number. The sophistication of such a wonderfully crafted dessert was not outside the bounds of any baker to concoct—elf or otherwise.

"Besides," added Groke, "last time we tried that, you got a case of the sap runs from eating too many moonberries."

The whole gang roared with laughter again, Crag included.

"Oh, that's right! I was watering the forest for days!"

Grim, a particularly gnarled specimen with moss growing in his ear canals, grinned.

"Could be we rob the dragon's hoard over at Sage Mount?"

"Right. Because that went so well last time," jeered Warty, a smaller bandit whose main claim to fame were the fungal growths on his head that passed for hair. "Didn't we lose half our loot running from a dragon that only turned out to be a *lizard*?"

"Honest mistake," Grim grumbled, his white eyes reflecting the firelight. "It was dark, and the bloody thing hissed."

"How 'bout we raid the Royal Library?" Perry, a vilden with stony protrusions jutting out of his back, suggested. "I 'ear they got a book made outta gold in 'ere."

"Since when can you read?" chuckled Yarkle.

"Dunno," Perry scratched his rocky head, "but gold's gold, innit?"

"Alright," I growled, my voice echoing back at me from the unseen depths of the tunnel, "I've had it up to fucking here with your shenanigans. I mean, I've walked into some seriously dumb shit on a half-baked promise before, but this, oh, man, this takes the whole goddamn cake."

Rexen, the ethereal pain in my dick, shimmered and shifted like an overenthusiastic will-o'-the-wisp.

"Cakes are predictable," he said. "Pie, now, there's an unexpected delight."

"Arjee," I bit out, feeling another headache building in my temples, "if you don't shut up about pie, I swear to God, I'll . . ."

"Yes, pupil?" he chirped, pivoting around in the cramped tunnel with all the grace of a floating disco ball. "I'm unconvinced of your gusto. You are fabricating outrage. My disciple loves these shenanigans."

With a grunt, I stalked past him.

"Don't test me, ya up-jumped nightlight. My patience is thinner than Alpha's dick right now."

His spectral form followed, casting an eerie glow over the tunnel walls.

"Ah, student mine, if it's any consolation, I think the cache might be . . . um . . . over there," he offered, pointing down the tunnel with a ghastly appendage.

"Arjee, 'over there' is a goddamn rock wall," I sighed. "Are you just fucking with me now? You're fucking with me, right?"

His light dimmed slightly.

"Not intentionally," he said, sounding surprisingly bashful for a being without a conscience. "But you know what they say about one orc's wall being another thaumaturge's door . . ."

"Zero people say that, Arjee. Literally no one."

He seemed to consider this.

"Well, maybe they should. It has a nice ring to it, don't you think?"

I took a deep breath, clenching and unclenching my fists.

"Arjee," I said in as calm a voice as I could manage, "if there isn't a cache full of goddamn *wonder* at the end of this tunnel, I'm going to . . . to . . ."

I didn't get to finish that thought though because we arrived at the end of the tunnel. A blank, barren stone face met my eyeline, and my anger spiked.

"What. The. *Fuck*? A dead end?!" I roared, jabbing a finger at the wall of solid stone that confronted us. "That settles it. I'm figuring out a way of removing this Pact, even if I have to claw it outta myself with a fork."

But Rexen was silent. His form pulsed softly, casting a glow that did nothing to alleviate the darkness of the tunnel. Then he started to hum. It was a gentle, lilting tune that sounded . . . oddly familiar.

"Oh, an eeby-deeby here, a diddle-doo there," he sang, bobbing in midair. "Below the earth, beneath the booly-wool square. Where the spider-bats fly and the mole rats dare lies the treasure of the land, right under *there*!"

I gaped at him.

"The fuck . . ."

But as his words died away, a symbol appeared in the air between us. It was intricate and complex, lines and curves interweaving to form an image that was both fascinating and bewildering.

"Arjee! What in the *eeby-deeby* is this?" I demanded, reaching out to touch the symbol.

"No touchy, pupil!" Rexen warned. "This is very delicate Arcana. One wrong move, and we could be catapulted into the seventh dimension or turned into beetles! Or worse, end up in a reality where I'm not your master!"

I blinked at him.

"So, you *are* just fucking with me."

He seemed genuinely offended.

"Me? Never! I'm as truthful as a berry in a well!"

"Yeah, that's not a saying either."

"Should be," he retorted petulantly. "It's as legitimate as any other comparative phrase in the common tongue."

"Arjee . . ."

"Yes, pupil?"

"I fucking hate you."

"I know, pupil. I know."

Despite the irritation threatening to explode out of me, I couldn't help but stare at the glowing symbol. It was . . . beautiful. In a wild, crazy, Rexen sort of way. But the real question was, what the hell did it do?

"So," I ventured, "what's the next step here? What's this all about?"

Rexen, the sentient flicker in my periphery, floated closer to the glowing symbol.

"Simple, pupil," he said with an air of importance that did nothing to reassure me. "I just need to . . ."

He paused, tilting his incorporeal form slightly to the side.

"Activate it!"

"And how do you—"

Before I could finish my question, Rexen began to bob up and down in an excited manner. Then he blew a gust toward the symbol. There was a flash of light, bright enough to force me to shield my eyes. When I finally blinked the spots away, I couldn't believe what I was seeing.

The once-imposing stone wall had vanished, fucking . . . supplanted by an overwhelmingly vast, vault-like expanse. The cavern dwarfed any concept of a room I had ever naively harbored. Its enormity reminded me more of a giant's bedroom than something that could possibly exist just under the surface of a woodland. The ceiling was a distant, shadowy mystery; its cavernous maw swallowed up the strange light within, rendering its true height an enigma.

In stark, neat lines that seemed to stretch on into infinity, rows upon rows of towering . . . Were those bookshelves? Whatever they were, the cubbyholes stretched out longer than several football fields—each one laden down with curiosities. There were peculiarly shaped, luminescent crystals, ancient-looking relics and devices of unknown origins, and scrolls that hummed with an arcane energy. Every item pulsed with a faint, ghostly radiance, as if the very air around them was saturated with untold magic.

And, like a spider sitting in the middle of its web, a colossal black plinth stood as the touchstone of this treasure trove. It was enormous, hulking, and composed of an obsidian-like material that shimmered with a surreal, inky sheen. Its aura was palpable, a pulsing, thrumming resonance of power that echoed off the cavernous walls, a discordant symphony to my already-ringing senses.

It was mind-bending.

"Fuck of all fucks," I muttered. "I've wandered into Merlin's basement."

It was sincerely impressive. I never thought I'd say that—especially because I was one hundred percent expecting this little trip to be much more dangerous than it was. In fact, it had just been a well-hidden alcove in the ground.

"Arjee . . ." I began, my voice trailing off as I tried to take it all in.

Rexen was practically bouncing with excitement.

"Behold, pupil!" he exclaimed, his voice echoing around the vast chamber. "Cache Forty-Seven of the Ancients and the Mundane! Isn't it magnificent?"

I shook my head, trying to clear my thoughts.

"What in the air-fried, TARDIS-throating hell . . ."

I saw an assortment of small colorful . . . cubes? At first I thought they were dice, but there weren't any dots or numbers on them. Instead, they had different symbols etched into their flesh. The cluster of cubes were stacked on one shelf. I pointed to them.

"What're these?"

Rexen saw where my gaze was and smiled brightly.

"Ah! I think you would really like those, my delicious disciple—in fact, I was thinking you might want to take some with you."

"Well, I'm not going to turn down a gift, but what do they do?"

I didn't really trust my Eye of the Saboteur at the moment, so I had to find out information the old-fashioned way. Asking.

"Ooh! Well, some of them explode! Some of them *ensnare*! Others put an enemy to sleep! Aren't they just the shiniest shinies that ever were?"

"Yeah . . ." I said absently. "I can have 'em?"

"Please!" Rexen said. "My bounty of goodies is yours to peruse!"

"Okay, fuckin' sweet," I said, and, without examining them further, scooped them up. Then, seeing a small coin purse nearby, stuffed them into it and tied it around my waist. Afterward I continued looking around, seeing if there was anything else I could shovel into my pockets.

My gaze was drawn back to the plinth in the center of the room. There was something . . . familiar about it. A shape, a design, a pattern that was just out of reach of my memories. I frowned, trying to place it. But it was like trying to catch smoke with a butterfly net. My Fatigue, ever the playful minx, was at its games again. Fuck you, Fatigue.

"Arjee, why does that thing look so recognizable?" I asked, squinting at the plinth.

Rexen bobbed over to it.

"Oh, the monolith? It's only one of the most powerful Arcana objects in existence. Maybe you saw it in a dream? Or a nightmare? Or a *day*mare? They're like nightmares but during the day. Very underappreciated, daymares. I love them. Though it does become inconvenient when I accidentally transport myself through them."

"Arjee . . ." I said, staring with amazement as my eyes found something else. "I think you *grossly* undersold what this place was."

The moon, in its celestial wisdom, was well tucked behind a thick blanket of clouds, the woods around the six vilden bandits dark and enigmatic. Having bested an orc earlier that day, they'd managed to make themselves feel invincible. And as all those who feel invincible often do, they were blithely wandering through the dense undergrowth, chattering like birds in the early morning.

"See, that's what I don't get, Yarkle," Crag grumbled. "Why the Pentknight would want that piss-poor hamlet burnt to the ground."

Yarkle shrugged.

"Why ask why? They've got gold; we've got an appetite for arson."

"It was barely a hamlet, really," Warty said. "Ten people? You could hardly call that a village."

"The houses burned all the same," said Groke. "Fire doesn't discriminate."

"True, true." Grim said as he scratched his bark-like chin. "All wood burns, whether it's a grand manor or a humble hut."

"Unless it's *our* flesh," Perry added, flashing a leafy grin. "Thank the gods for that."

There was a collective laugh, loud and wild, piercing the quiet of the forest night.

It was Groke who first saw it—a small, strange object lying half-buried in the fallen leaves.

"What's this?" he murmured, nudging it with his root-like toe.

All banter ceased as they crowded around the mysterious item. It was an oddity, no doubt—a small cube, with sides of alternating metallic shades and faintly glowing lines that crisscrossed the surfaces.

Crag, who fancied himself an amateur archaeologist, leaned in closer.

"It looks old, possibly ancient," he declared, sounding utterly convinced of his expertise.

"A child's toy, most like," Yarkle contested. "Barely worth a glance."

Groke shrugged and, without a second thought, reached down to pick up the object. He barely had time to gasp before metallic wires sprang from the cube, wrapping around him, binding his arms to his sides.

"Shit!" Perry exclaimed, jumping back. "It's a—"

But the rest of his warning was cut off by a thunderous crash. Leaves and branches rained down as a hulking figure dropped from the trees above. His landing sent tremors through the ground, making the forest echo with the force of it.

"Howdy! Remember me?!"

It was the orc they'd killed earlier. Only, now he looked different—more savage, fiercer. Once wearing a strange amalgamation of comfortable-looking raiments, now he was covered in layers of fur and leather, his body adorned with savage-looking gear. He was not the semi-civilized orc they'd fought before; he was a primal, formidable warrior.

But it wasn't his appearance that made the vilden bandits recoil—it was his weapon. The broad, blotchy orc was wielding an absurdly terrifying knife, the likes of which they had never seen before. Its handle seemed to be a bone—maybe a deer's antler—banded and reinforced with a material that caught the moonlight, shimmering in an otherworldly manner. The blade, wickedly curved and sharp, emitted a disconcerting, ethereal glow, as if the essence of magic itself was woven into the very metal. The sight was at once awe-inspiring and stomach-churning.

"Well, fuck me," Grim muttered, his voice barely a whisper. "It's him again."

Yarkle was the first to break the silence.

"Oi, orc! We thought we killed you!"

The figure's growled reply rang out through the night, his words thick with a promise of violence.

"Y'all were fucking *wrong*."

Groke struggled in his bindings, his movements frantic and panicky.

"Get this damn thing off me!"

"Working on it!" Perry snapped, his fingers probing the metallic wires, trying to find a release.

As the vilden bandits scrambled to free their ensnared comrade, the orc watched them with a smile, his grip on his trench knife tightening.

"Well," Crag said, a nervous laugh slipping past his lips, "this is a right bit of fucked."

The once-dead orc couldn't have agreed more.

* * *

The look on their faces was priceless as I made my grand entrance, all decked out in my new gear. I looked like a proper Barbarian, if I do say so myself. Not just any Barbarian, mind you. An "enemies pissing and shitting themselves uncontrollably" kind of Barbarian.

"Right bit of fucked, you say?" I shot back at Crag, my smile splitting my face. "You haven't even seen the half of it."

You know, there's nothing quite like the thrill of springing a surprise on your foes. As the vilden scurried around like headless chickens, I took a moment to appreciate the fine craftsmanship of my new gear, and the weight of the Stag's Pique in my hand, its magical glow bright against the darkness of the forest.

Stag's Pique
- **Rarity: Marvel**
- **Item Class: One-Handed Weapon**
- **Durability: 120/120**
- **Weight: 1 lb.**
- **Attack: 156–199 Slashing / 100–130 Piercing**
- **Defense: N/A**
- **Bonuses:**

Wound Ripper—Grants Bleeding Condition to successful attacks
Forest's Whisper—Grants additional Level Rank to Sneaking Skill
Life Cycle – Grants Life Cycle Health Bar

Crafted from a stag's antler, this knife is as sharp as the wit of the one who wields it. While it does inspire a certain awe, it's less of the "majestic creature of the forest" kind and more of the "That guy just killed a deer with its own fucking horn" kind. Additionally, injuries inflicted by the Stag's Pique take longer to heal, disrupting natural and magical healing abilities. Also, the knife enhances the wielder's ability to blend with nature, providing stealth bonuses when in woodland environments. Lastly, with each enemy the wielder kills, the Stag's Pique channels a fraction of their life force, storing it as a one-time-use healing boost that the wielder can activate at will.

Oh, yeah, baby! This thing was a gleamin' dream. The sharpness of the blade, the shimmering glow, the fuck-off extras . . . I'd go so far as to say it was love at first stab.

It seemed that once I had equipped the items, I didn't have to worry about the system messages being all bonkers—which was a huge relief, to say the least. So . . . I double-checked the extra-special boner-supporting stats on the rest of my fabulous fit, just so I could internally gloat.

Guardian's Bear Pads
- Rarity: Elusive
- Item Class: Pauldron
- Durability: 80/100
- Weight: 5 lbs.
- Attack: N/A
- Defense: + 20
- Bonuses:

+ 5 to Intimidation

These pauldrons, despite their name, look less like they came from a guardian and more like they've been liberated from a very surprised, and subsequently very naked, bear.

Torso Wrap of the Reluctant Warrior
- Rarity: Rare
- Item Class: Baldric
- Durability: 150/150
- Weight: 2.1 lbs.
- Attack: N/A
- Defense: + 50
- Bonuses:

Grants a +10 resistance to physical attacks

These crisscrossing chest belts are crafted with a sturdy leather that's seen more than a few scraps. It's the fashion equivalent of a hardened veteran: scruffy, well worn, and decidedly intimidating.

Battle Skirt of the Feral Brawler
- Rarity: Elusive
- Item Class: Waist Wrap
- Durability: 40/40
- Weight: 2 lbs.
- Attack: N/A
- Defense: + 15
- Bonuses:

+ 20% movement speed

This kilt is a study in practicality with a heavy dash of intimidation. The motley pattern is a jarring mix of earth tones that's a shout-out to the wilderness and, more importantly, a warning to anyone thinking they're about to face a pacifist.

Bracers of the Berserker
- Rarity: Uncommon
- Item Class: Bracer
- Durability: 60/60
- Weight: 3 lbs.
- Attack: + 10
- Defense: + 15
- Bonuses:

+ 5 to Unarmed Fighting attacks

These sturdy leather guards have a strangely menacing air about them, like they've been to hell and back and had a grand old time doing it. Perfect for the vagrant who prefers to greet their enemies with a fistful of hello.

Shin Splints of the Stomper
- Rarity: Rare
- Item Class: Partial Greaves
- Durability: 100/100
- Weight: 3 lbs.
- Attack: 20–48 Bludgeoning
- Defense: + 30
- Bonuses:

+ 5 to kick attacks

Crafted from sturdy boar hide and studded with iron, these leg guards make a statement. That statement being, "I'm going to kick you, and it's going to hurt."

The metallic groan from the cube pulled me from my gear-appreciating reverie. The vilden with stony stegosaurus plates on its back was trying to pry the cube off Twiggy, to no avail. I almost felt sorry for them. Almost.

"Hurry up!" Twiggy squealed, wiggling like a worm on a hook.

"I'm tryin,' dammit!" Stegosaurus wailed.

I held up my Stag's Pique, the eerie glow of its blade reflecting off the petrified faces of my foes. Time for a little fun.

"Alrighty, boys," I started, twirling the weapon like a major in a parade. "Who's first for a taste of the motherfuckin' *bloodshed*?"

As their eyes grew wide and their color drained, I laughed. It was going to be a fun night, no doubt about it. God*damn*, I do love a good revival.

CHAPTER FIFTEEN

I WANT TO BE SPECIAL, MR. WARBUCKS

With an air of blood-soaked satisfaction, I turned away from the chaos and carnage I had just unleashed upon the hapless vilden. The forest floor was littered with leaves and debris, stained with dark ichor. Scattered about were the twitching remnants of the would-be plunderers, their bodies unceremoniously sprawled in a mural of defeat.

Rexen flitted over from where he'd been helpfully hidden and, *more importantly*, silent.

"Stupendous performance, pupil! A thrilling demonstration of our power, wasn't it?"

I shot him a glance, one eyebrow raised.

"What? No comment on my form? My speed?"

Rexen shrugged.

"Oh, form was . . . adequate. Speed . . . well, my disciple's aim is not to be the fastest but untouchable. Yours is a vessel most suitable for combat, but my disciple will need to work harder if he wants to truly be able to harness all that I have to teach and bestow."

"Great, thanks for that advice after the fact," I grumbled, flicking some grime from my newly acquired armor.

"No need to thank me, most marvelous pupil. Your glorious victory is the best possible expression of gratitude."

"Well, I gotta hand it to your doohickeys—that was an extremely fortuitous turn of events."

The cube I'd thrown—known formally as one of the Hexahedron of Hazards, basically looked like a slightly larger than usual six-sided die from a board game, except made of metal and covered in runic symbols. It was one of the thingies in a pile that I'd taken from the cache. This particular one was a handy device that—if you'd missed it—deployed ensnaring cables that wrapped up unsuspecting victims that wandered into its radius after ten seconds. Fortunately for me, Zeol must have been smiling down on me, because it didn't take the vilden long at all to interact with it. I'd pocketed it for future use and was already dreaming up ways to spring a trap like this in a fight. There were others, which did a variety of different nonsense, but the ensnaring one seemed to have the most bang for its buck at the moment.

In the silence that followed, I took a moment to glance at my Life Cycle Health Bar. From the minuscule percentage filled in, it was clear that I had a long, arduous journey ahead. Six vilden were apparently not enough to even get close enough to fill a bar.

"Who knew? Killing isn't the fast pass to recovery I hoped it'd be," I commented, flexing my fingers. Despite the destruction I'd wrought, I felt . . . good. Better than I had in a while.

Rexen floated over, his glow dimming a little in thought.

"Now . . ." he said, "did they have beer on them?"

I cut him off, rolling my eyes.

"Let's move on."

Together we ventured deeper into the night. I could feel Rexen's excitement, though for what I wasn't quite sure. Probably eager to watch me walk into another goddamn trap, the absolute prick.

As we trekked along, the night around us heavy with the sounds of nocturnal creatures, Rexen began rambling about the old days. You know, unimaginable feats, implausible heroics, and flat-out fucking absurd acts of magic. I kinda zoned out as we moved—my exhaustion becoming a little problematic to this marathon walk-a-thon. Eventually, though, I was roused from my haze by an incredibly annoying little voice.

"Hey, pupil—hey. Pupil," Rexen said, trying to get my attention. "Pupil! Disciple. Puuuuupil!"

"What, Arjee?!"

"Did you know I once fought a big, mean ol' wyvern barehanded? Naked as the day I was formed. Slammed it right in the snout!"

"That's nice . . ." I said, feeling my focus wander more. Goddamn, I was really fucking tired.

"Then, once, I went toe to toe with Xakella, Goddess of Questions. A night to remember! Ooh! She had an *enchanting* voice and a wicked right hook. Big fan of arm wrestling and . . . body wrestling."

"My dude," I finally said, stopping in my tracks. "Can we just . . . tone down the verbal memoirs a notch, please?"

Rexen paused, his lights dimming in a pouty way.

"Nasty little pupil. I'm lightening the mood with expert storytelling! Don't my past glories ignite your imagination and spirit of adventure?"

I took a deep breath, trying to temper my irritation with the fact that this bizarre motherfucker was probably the only reason I was able to get my sweet, petty revenge against the bandits.

"Look, it's not that your tales aren't *super* entertaining. It's just that they're a bit distracting."

"My disciple should learn to focus no matter what intrusions befall him," he said. "I am just sharing my infinite knowledge and colorful backstory so that you can—"

He stopped; his body-light intensified and illuminated the path ahead of us. The increasing glow made the shadows dance around us.

"Oh," Rexen intoned, his voice taking on a note of gravity that was decidedly uncharacteristic. "We've arrived."

"Arrived? Where?" I asked sleepily, scanning the darkened forest around us.

Rexen hummed.

"The next leg!"

"Huh? What're you . . ?"

Glancing up, I could see now that the trail led down into a muddy valley peppered with thin trees and heavy overgrowth. I groaned.

Damn. I'm gonna have to get my steps in.

"Fuck this whole stupid planet," I muttered, and trudged on into the dark. It was going to be a long night.

I heaved, trying desperately to get enough air into my lungs as I lay on my back, sprawled in a state of abject debility.

My body was slathered in layers of dirt, a creature's alien blood, and chunks of fuck-knows-what. Exhaustion pounded at the edges of my consciousness, but adrenaline kept it at bay. The memory of the creature I'd just vanquished was seared into my mind. That fucking beast . . . whatever it was, had been about the size of a large dog but with scales, rows of teeth that looked like they could saw through a Formula One racing helmet, and legs that bent at horrifyingly unnatural angles. Most importantly, it had been *very* tough to put down on my own—but it also wouldn't leave me alone, so I had no other choice.

I glanced over at its corpse, not far from where I was laid up in the mud.

"Fuck you," I huffed at the lifeless body. "Bitch. This is . . . what you get."

"There you are, pupil!" Rexen said, floating down to me to pick off a bit of dried sludge from my shoulder with a satisfied grin. "You just survived a bout with a gravenshark."

I shot him a sidelong glance, my brows knitted together as I tried to get my heart rate under control.

"A . . . gravel . . . fucking . . . what? You made that up. No way . . . that's real."

His smile irked me. The sight of him being chipper after witnessing a scene straight out of a horror movie was really grating my last cheese nubbin. He was either insane or I was—and considering the number of times I'd come back from the dead today, I was leaning toward the latter.

"Ooh, boy! To see a gravenshark this far out—such a joy. Fascinating creatures."

"Fascinating? Are you . . . out of your goddamned . . . mind?" I shot back, feeling an incredulous laugh bubble up my throat. "That monster muppet nearly tore my arm off! It's a miracle I'm even—"

I stopped myself, remembering our earlier conversations about my inability to stay dead. Instead, I changed subjects, since it seemed like I was stuck in this position for a moment.

"Are we . . . there yet?"

"My disciple shows his weakness to the world," Rexen said. "Our quarry isn't around the corner. For shame."

"Well, that's just fucking grand!" I grumbled, scraping some stubborn bits of dried blood off my arm. "Any clue on how far we gotta go 'til . . . fucking . . . I dunno, Tallrock?"

He rubbed his ghostly chin thoughtfully, his eyes distant.

"Nope!"

Wonderful.

As the first light of dawn started to paint the sky with splashes of oranges and purples, I let out a weary sigh. The tranquil beauty of the scene felt like a punch to the gut—how dare nature look so quaint and calm when my life was a never-ending shitshow?

"Fuck it, I'm taking five," I declared, turning onto my side—having not risen since the battle ended. The swampy area we were in smelled worse than a wet dog rolled in garbage, but it was still better than having my ass handed to me by creatures that should've been extinct or, better yet, nonexistent.

Rexen floated near me. The sun's soft light filtered through his translucent form, casting strange patterns on the mossy ground.

"Take your time, pupil," he said, his words strangely comforting. "Rest! The path ahead is worse—my disciple may not survive."

"Thanks for the pep talk, Arjee," I snorted, closing my eyes and leaning my head back and taking a teensy nap.

Rexen and I trudged through the mud-filled valley, and it wasn't long before we started fading. I mean, *I* was a given—I'd been fighting off all manner of dangers. But even Rexen, as inexhaustible and energetic as he was, seemed a bit pooped as well.

"You doin' alright, Arjee?" I asked, slowing as the specter seemed on the verge of floating right into the ground.

"Sleepy" was all he said.

"Wait . . . you need to rest? I figured you were like . . . I dunno, powered by the will of annoyance or something."

"Will . . . annoyance?" He muttered, his spirally eyes looking quite tired, considering that they never looked like anything but vacuous voids of unhinged, maniacal glee.

"Alright, what's happening here?" I asked. "Do you need to pop a quick snooze or something, hombre? Come to think of it, you've been goin' nonstop since we Pacted up."

"Sleepy," he said again.

"Uh . . . alright," I continued, looking around at the open expanse of swampland around us. "You, uh, got a hammock or something you want to utilize? Don't tell me I'm supposed to carry you?"

"Effigy . . ." he groaned, hovering close to me to bop his noggin against my chest.

"You need to get in the little figurine?" I wondered.

"Uh-huh," he said softly, still drifting against me.

"How's that work?" I wondered. "Do I need to . . . I'm going to let you answer that because this thing is inside of me, and one hundred percent of the possibilities for deployment on that front seem . . . bad."

"Be still," Rexen said, still sounding like he was knocking on sleepytime's after-hours office door.

So, I . . . be'd still. Rexen started to fade into the color of nothing suddenly, and I got a little concerned.

"Yo," I exclaimed. "You sure this is how this works? How long you goin' beddy-bye, Arjee? Should I be concerned?"

"Just . . . short . . . time," he said, becoming more and more transparent. Then, before I could ask any further frantic questions, he turned completely see-through and then pushed his way through into my torso. Strangely, it felt very warm to experience. Like when a cat suddenly climbs onto your chest. Except this was like if it climbed *into* my chest. I allowed it to happen—mostly because I wasn't exactly certain what would happen if I decided to suddenly start doin' the Cupid Shuffle or something.

Then I was alone in the broad light of day, suddenly confused as to what I was supposed to be doing. I had a ghost cradled inside me, and that was a responsibility I didn't want or think I could navigate well at all. After a moment,

I took a tentative step forward, and when I didn't suddenly explode or turn into ectoplasm, I decided it was alright to keep trekking onward. So, I did, squelching through the muck, a man with a mission and a ghost for a belly mate.

And so, I continued on like this for a little while, just left alone . . . with my own thoughts. Something I hadn't experienced in a while. It was rough. Things got *real* dark.

In a weird way, it was a blessing and a curse to suddenly be interrupted.

"Ah, Gabriel," said a sultry tone. "There you are."

I froze.

There weren't many people in this world or the other that would use my Christian name—I mean, as mentioned, I was literally named after a saint, so I wasn't just bein' silly this time. There was, however, only one person it could possibly be, and it felt like my blood turned to ice and also began to boil at the same time. It was a conflict of negative sensations, in any case. I spun around, hand instinctively clutching for my weapon.

"God. Dammit!" I swore, my anger unsupervised pitbull-ing. "What could you *possibly* want?"

There, standing in all her aggravating, glamorous glory was the curly-haired woman. Once again, she had done a costume change. The last time I'd seen her, she was dressed in far too warm of gear and looked like a Dark Ages ice climber in heavy furs and leathers. Now, however, she was showcasing much lighter garb than the weather demanded, an airy little number that belonged on a beach, not a chilly bog. At my demand, she shrugged, a nonchalant twist of her shoulders that wormed its way under my skin.

"I'm pleased to see you as well," she mused, an infuriating smirk pulling at the corner of her lips.

"Fucking . . . gah," I groaned. "You are just *made* out of piss-me-off."

She pursed her lips in mock sadness.

"I'm wounded," she said, like she was talking to a baby. "I saw you were all alone and thought you could use the company."

"I would rather stab myself in the dick to death than entertain your presence for anything other than watching you get slowly crushed by a trash compactor."

She sighed, shaking her head.

"Marvelously visceral imagery, as always."

"What do you want?!" I shouted, pointing a finger at her. "I'm all jacked up on rebirth strength right now *aaaand* I got a fresh new drip. So, you better watch out, Miss *Curly Q*. I'm liable to bust some shit up."

She tilted her head to one side as if she didn't understand, the world around us quieting. Then she lifted a single finger. In the distance, one of the largest trees in a thicket of foliage was suddenly yanked out of the wet earth and went flying. I watched as it arced over the treeline before disappearing off in the distance.

I watched it go before slowly turning to the curly haired woman.

"Yeah, well . . . *good for you.*"

"I come with a message of caution," she warned me, her voice holding a note of amusement. "You are shaking up the hornet's nest with your . . . antics."

"Oh, I'm shaking it, am I?" I spat back, shimmying my shoulders violently. "Well, *sweetheart*, you might as well call me the *Maraca Man*, 'cuz I'm shakin' *everything* up!"

She gave me a look that was equal parts amusement and challenge, her eyes twinkling like a kid who had just been given permission to wreak havoc.

"Oh, I am well aware of your penchant for . . . novelty," she drawled, the sarcasm dripping from her words. "But I think in this case, your particular *charming* brand of miscreancy is going to do you less favors than you think."

A growl rumbled in my throat. I had no time for her games.

"Cut the poop," I bit out. "What the hell do you want?"

Unfazed by my rage, she held up her hands, palms facing me.

She smiled, leaning casually against a moss-laden tree, her fingers dancing in a seemingly random pattern in the air, a bemusing, slightly annoying rhythm. It was like watching a cat batting a ball of yarn.

"What I want, Gabriel," she said, and there was a glint in her eye that I didn't trust one bit, "is for you to be aware. The paths you tread are not without guardians."

"Oh?" I retorted, my anger frothing at the edges, but my curiosity gnawing at the center. "Listen—I don't give a shit; you and your fucked-up flunkies can shove it right inside your unmentionable sun-don't-shine zone. And another thing—"

She interrupted me with laughter, her ringlets bouncing with the movement.

"Ah, you are so delightfully brusque, Gabriel." She straightened up, sauntering toward me. "I'm speaking about the ones who ensure the balance."

"The fuck is that supposed to mean?" I asked, my eyebrows knitting together in a mix of frustration and confusion. "That some kind of cryptic, jigsaw lingo? I genuinely believe you're just trying to piss me off."

Her chuckle was a jarring sound in the quiet of the swamp.

"Consider it a . . . gentle reminder," she said, her tone dripping with false sweetness. "Not all fair weather is a blessing. Beware, Gabriel, of the unseen ripples in your wake."

"Fuck. Off," I said, brandishing my Stag's Pique. "I may be stupid, but I'm not stupid enough to listen to you again."

"I merely wanted to chat," she said. But there was something else. The way she was acting—so casual and . . . informal. Her demeanor made me think she thought she'd won something. Like she had something about me figured out.

"Chat, eh? Well, I don't recall sending an invite," I grunted, my senses on high alert.

She sighed, a gusty exhalation that echoed in the frigid air around us.

"Oh, I know, Gabriel," she said, her tone almost gentle. "But here we are."

Her words hung between us, cold and hard as the icy air we breathed. I found my gaze lingering on her a second longer than necessary. Despite her infuriating habits, she still managed to get my heart thumping.

Well, that's inconvenient.

"Talk plain, not in fortune-teller language, you dumb, curly-headed *fuck*," I said.

That seemed to actually bother her. She stopped laughing and gave me a venomous glare.

"You are ignorant, I imagine, to the effort it takes to maintain . . ." Her words trailed off. "Ah, you almost had me there, Gabriel. Trying to rattle me."

Shit, that's certainly interesting, I thought. *Apparently, Little Orphan Annie here has a hair thing. Gonna slot that away for use when I need it.*

"It is unwise to mock others for their sensitivities," she said, a finger resting on her chin. "Especially when those you cajole are capable of obliterating you with a single thought."

"Yeah, well, like I've said before," I shot back, "if I die, I'm just going to come back *more* annoying. So, it's your move."

I really don't wanna be pushin' up daisies again so soon, I thought. *I've nearly made it to Tallrock . . . I think.* However, I was a petty, *petty* son of a bitch, and if it meant getting one over on her, I'd definitely do it.

Though, now that I'm thinking about it . . . I'm not really sure how I would win in that scenario. Ah! Never mind! That's for future Loon to figure out.

"I see you still don't know much about how this world works," she said quizzically. "If I were to kill you . . . Well, I don't want to spoil the surprise. Hedge your bets, if you will, *Gabriel*. I am sure it will work out wonderfully for you."

Huh . . . is she implying that if she were to kill me, I wouldn't come back?

Congratulations! You have raised a Skill!
Insight has advanced to E-Rank Level 6!

Uh-oh . . .

"Also," she continued. "I would not return to any of your . . . mentor's troves. It is likely to send you to a spot that I can nearly guarantee you will not enjoy.

But that is simply a mite of freely given recommendation. Do with it as you will."

"You done?" I demanded, pointing out at the horizon. "Cuz I got shit to do, and if I want some bizarro, mysterious nonsense, I'll just wake Arjee's ass back up."

She shrugged.

"My true purpose in coming here was to caution you as to your choices and offer my unsolicited advice. I suppose that is all, however."

She turned, and I thought she might be leaving, but I stopped her.

"Yo," I said.

She turned to look at me.

"Yes, Gabriel?"

"What's your fucking name?"

She smiled.

"Ah, that is an interesting question isn't it, Gabriel?"

"Irritatius? Vomitara?" I guessed. "Come on, what is it?"

She shrugged.

"Just tell me, uh . . . Arby's fries! It's stupid to not know your arch-nemesis's name!"

I'll be honest: my comparison game was at an all-time low due to my exhaustion. I mean, I was a lot more jacked and juicy because of Fatigue, but man, it was a real motherfucker on the ol' brain bone. She shook her head, and looked like she was going to follow up, but I interrupted with my typical bullshit.

"Withholding something so simple?" I continued. "You have gotta be fucking kiddin—"

I stopped, because her eyes widened for a split second.

"Wait, what did—"

But before I could finish, she'd vanished.

"Aw, horsedicks!" I shouted into the swamp.

Then, because I was frustrated, I slapped my own stomach.

"Hey, Arjee! Wake up! Let's get going, punk! Nap time's over!"

When he didn't respond, I slumped.

"Alright, fine!" I continued to shout. "Guess I gotta do everything by myself!"

So, taking a proper gander at the path ahead, I let out a long, dramatic sigh and began trudging forward through the marshy wetlands toward where I thought the direction of the camp might be.

We weren't far from Tallrock when the vines attacked.

It was getting late, and we'd stopped so that I could eat a little bit of the paltry rations I had and fish a pebble or something outta my bracers. Though, as I thought I finally had it, my fingers grazing it, I felt it move.

"Uh . . ." I paused.

A tiny insect that looked like a cross between a wingless hornet and a beetle squeezed out from the gap in my bracer.

"Yeuagh!" I screeched and tried to smack it away. "Gah, fuck!"

Then the damn thing scurried up my arm and crawled under my shoulder pad. I reacted poorly.

"FUCKING FUCK FUCK FUCK!" I screamed, ripping my pauldron off and throwing it on the ground and stamping on it.

"Pupil!" Rexen called. "Is this a new dance?"

"Yeah!" I shouted, emphasizing each word with a stomp. "It's. Called. The. Bug. Bash. Boogie!"

I may have overreacted a bit and kicked the pauldron into a bush. But as I stood there, Rexen regarded me carefully.

"My disciple should pay more attention," he said.

"Oh, believe me, I fucking *will*," I said. "Did you see that thing? Yeesh. Never again."

"Of course I saw it, pupil mine," Rexen continued. "I see it now, in fact."

I realized that he was not looking at *me* precisely . . . he was looking at my shoulder. I went rigid, and then slowly turned to look down. There, perched right on my big, green deltoid, was the bug.

"Graaaaaaaaah!" I shrieked. I slapped at it, but it scurried to my neck. "Fucking god fuck! No, get off!"

I swatted all over my own body while missing the bug. Rexen just watched placidly. After a few more frantic moments of this, I saw it scurry to the forearm on my other side. So, I did the only thing that seemed to my chaos-mind like it would work: I hit it with Blackout Warchant.

"GROUGGGGHH!" I scream-roared. I didn't know if it was magical, but the force of the blast ejecting from my jaws did the trick. The bug went flying.

In the stillness that followed, I heaved in gulps of air, my heart thudding like a pissed-off Austin Archey against my chest. Rexen merely floated there, his hollow eyes possibly exuding an air of disapproval. It was hard to tell, though, because he was so goddamned . . . let's go with *eccentric*.

"Hm," he began in that perpetually unfazed tone of his, "my disciple's reaction seems incongruent to the threat. A queazlezap. Just an insect."

I pointed a finger at him, my hand still quivering from adrenaline.

"You say that like it didn't just invade my personal bubble like a fuckin' SWAT team storming a streamer's parent's basement."

Rexen seemed to ponder this comparison for a moment before shaking his ghostly head.

"I don't understand this hyperbole, pupil mine."

"Fuckin' bug . . ." I grumbled under my breath, bending over to retrieve my discarded pauldrons. "Ruinin' my dinner . . . bein' all gross and stuff. Yuck."

"The queazlezap isn't to fear, pupil," Rexen continued, but I wasn't really paying attention. "Save for their warning. They are harbingers of a greater threat."

As I stooped to pick my gear up, I felt a strange rustling under my boots, the squelching mud seeming to . . . move.

With a startled yelp, I leapt back just as a mess of dark, slithering vines shot out from the ground where I'd been standing. I fell on my ass, trying to scramble back.

"What in the ever-loving fuck?" I exclaimed, flailing backward as more of the damn vines started to surge up from the ground like undead snakes. They lashed about but, like, slowly—as if they were drunk.

"Arjee!" I shouted, my tone a notch higher than I'd have liked as I realized I'd forgotten to pick up my pauldron. "What's happening?!"

"Interesting," was all he said, making me want to punt his ass into the next time zone.

"These ain't usual!" I called out, frantically dodging and backpedaling as more and more of the planty abominations emerged around me.

As the sinister vegetation closed in, tendrils probing in the air, I realized that I was grossly outnumbered. And without my pauldron, which was now being swallowed by the sentient underbrush, I was also out-armed.

The creeping vines advanced like a tidal wave of slothful hunger, the twilit swamp echoing with the sound of my growing desperation. As the vines swallowed me into their green abyss, one thought rang clear in my mind: *I fucking hate the outdoors.*

I tried to stand, but one tangled around my ankle.

"Fuck, just fucking great!"

Then the rest of them piled on.

I found that, after my initial shock wore off, I wasn't really in as dire straits as I thought. They weren't violently choking me or dragging me to the ground to smother me in the mud or anything. They were just irritatingly numerous and wouldn't leave me be.

I grasped at the vines, but they seemed to tighten, pulling back as I attempted to wrest myself from their clutches. I sighed, turning to see Rexen grinning at me from a few feet away, kicking his spectral legs through the underbrush.

"Stop enjoying yourself!" I barked, glaring at the offending vines that had now somehow managed to loop themselves around my waist. "You could, I dunno, maybe help a little?"

"You're doing great," Rexen said.

"No, I'm actually not," I said, slashing down at another tendril.

"I was talking to myself," Rexen said. "My tutelage is unparalleled. I will not be a pawn in some game. This is just mild entertainment, pupil. I suspect you will live."

"Entertaining, my ass," I grumbled, yanking at the insistent foliage. "I swear, these are the laziest fucking killer vines on the damn planet. I mean, look at this—"

I allowed one of the snakey plants to wind its way up my arm before grabbing it and tossing it to the side. After a few seconds, it returned, moving much slower as it curled around my wrist.

"Perhaps you should try reasoning with them?" Rexen suggested. "You know, 'Hey there, Mr. Vine, could you let go of my leg?' That sort of thing."

"Oh, hilarious. Really, bravo, I think you just told your first joke," I shot back. This was like a game of sentient spaghetti whack-a-mole. "Seriously, though, any time you feel like giving a hand . . ."

"Hmm . . . maybe later, pupil," he said, glancing around. "There could be danger afoot."

"There's danger afoot *right here*," I huffed, freeing my other foot just as another damn vine snaked around my ankle. "Well . . . sort of, anyway. At the very least, can you get my weapon for me?"

"Oooh! Which weapon?"

"Any of them!"

"This is a teachable moment," Rexen said, shaking his head. "You would not learn if I were to step in."

So, I just started punching the ornery cusses.

This livened them a bit, because they seemed to get agitated by me throwing hands.

Good.

One snaked through the air toward my neck, and I laid down a grid-iron knuckle smash on its stupid tip. I headbutted another. Then I elbowed a third as it tried to make its merry way to my bikini zone. Like, I was straight-up *duking it out* with these miserable nature noodles. It was going swimmingly. After another minute of struggling, I was able to reach the Stag's Pique, which I'd stupidly set down before all this went down. The second that happened, though, I was all business, baby. I started laying waste to those flaccid fuckers.

"See, pupil," Rexen said smugly amidst my violent pandemonium. "I taught you the value of—"

"Fucking hell!" I yelled, hacking at the vines.

"Yes! Chop! Slash! Stab!" Rexen exclaimed.

"I'm. Going. To. Find. A. Sharp. Fucking. Stick," I said through gritted teeth, striking in rhythm with my words. "Then. I'm. Going. To—oh . . ."

I'd killed the last of them, and the whole tangle fell away from my body. Freedom, finally.

"Jesus! That took way too long, and now I'm all sweaty. We gotta get moving, though. Those folks at Fort Fuckabout still need a heads-up about the life-force-juice-extraction plan—especially since Curly seems to think I'm on my way to time-out for my indiscretions, or whatever. And . . . I need a damn *nap*."

"My disciple worries too much," Rexen dismissed, floating alongside me as I set off again. "I intend to enjoy the journey."

"Easy for you to say, you incorporeal douche. You're not the one that has to deal with blisters and vine lassos."

"Yes, but I must bear the weight of . . . you," Rexen said, floating off ahead. "A crucible of its own caliber."

Overall, traveling with Rexen was a trip. Not in the good, mind-expanding, untold-revelation kind of way, but more like the "shackled to a cart driven by a batshit insane horse" sort of trip. But it was educational; I'll give him that. We made our way back through what I was pretty sure was called the Aglands, a region that was beginning to feel like a second home, albeit a home infested with fuckin' stupid-ass bullshit. So, yeah, home.

Treading in the shadow of the city of Tallrock was a reminder of how far I'd come. Even within a few weeks. When I say city, don't conjure images of towering spires or marble-coated streets. No, no, no, my special little babies, Tallrock was now like a beehive that had faced the wrath of a sociopathic ten-year-old's fresh new tennies, only to be slowly and painfully pieced back together using radio wire. It was endearing, in a feral, live-or-die sort of way.

What I mean to say is that it was still in a recovery phase. I'm sure we'd have been welcomed with open arms due to my evolved Reputation of Neutral with the place, but . . . we still steered clear regardless.

My relationship with Tallrock was complicated, like trying to pet a rabid weasel—it could have ended up either really cool or really, really painful. Hence why we circled around it, giving it a wide berth. I didn't need another wacky escapade under my belt that would inevitably result in us being further delayed.

I had grown rather well acquainted with the rugged landscape surrounding the city—courtesy of the two agonizing days I had spent skulking around its outskirts, avoiding prying eyes when we'd first arrived. Back then, I was labeled Untrusted, which, in the social language of Regaia, was the equivalent of walking around with a sign that read, *I'm edgy and I'll probably swipe your Sudafed and punch holes in your drywall*. Quite understandably, my reviews for the place were mixed.

So, we slunk past, two silhouettes lost amidst the wild untamed beauty of the Narnia-esque landscape, Tallrock receding behind us like a half-remembered dream.

The next few days melted into one another as we delved deeper into the heart of the forest, which, in its autumn splendor, was as fiercely wild as it was breathtaking. The terrain, while still stubbornly unyielding, was now like the prettiest part of New England in the fall, softened by a thick blanket of leaves, each one a vibrant splash of gold, burnt orange, or fiery red. I'd never been there, but that seemed right.

We navigated through dense woodland, a twisting maze of ancient, towering trees that seemed to brush the underside of the sky, their limbs reaching out to each other, forming a canopy that covered the forest floor with shards of sunlight. We moved like ghosts—a bit more literally than necessary, considering Rexen was aboard this merry jaunt—through the patchwork of light and shadow, guided only by the Dreadnaught Lord's unfathomable, magpie-like connection to his possessions still kickin' around the camp.

The sun was now more a timid, voyeuristic visitor than a relentless overseer. Its light arrived late and left early, leaving us under the watchful gaze of the moons for longer periods. The night was a squall of sounds: the rustling of leaves, the whispers of the wind, and the distant calls of creatures who owned the forest when the sun was away. Despite the expansive breadth of unknowns around us, we pushed onward, following the breadcrumb trail of Rexen's intuition.

Eventually, on the morning of what I'd labeled I Really Should Be Counting This Shit But I'm Not, our camp emerged from the autumn-kissed treeline. The haphazard sprawl of smoky remains, makeshift shelters, and shining metallic train wreckage, it sat in a natural clearing, hugged by the vibrant forest on all sides. It wasn't long past that I'd first laid eyes on it, and it seemed like it had all the charm of a pile of bird shit in a deserted parking lot, but it was *our* bird shit, and that counted for something.

As I was surveying our humble abode from the crest of a hill, an icy dread spread its tendrils through my guts. When we went back in, I'd have to try to convince these yahoos that they needed to get the fuck outta there—and from a compromised position, no less. I was gonna have a really tough time convincing them to do anything Alpha didn't want them to do—even more so now that I lost the Duellum.

As I chewed on this sense of foreboding, Rexen floated beside me quietly—for once.

"Hey, Arjee," I started, "You agree with me, right? That, I dunno, *camping* out here is stupid as fuck? Waiting for the proverbial doo-doo to hit the spin-a-majig, so to speak?"

Rexen, still staring out across the expanse, responded without turning.

"To be predictable is to be vulnerable, my ignorant student. If doomed to be prey, then *be* prey. But it is better to be game that moves than game that stays still."

I nodded. I gotta admit, the fuckin' weirdo had a point, even if it was delivered in that strange, detached way of his. As we set our sights on the distant camp, a new question occurred to me.

"Oh, yeah, by the way," I said, "are there any more of those bizarre-yet-extremely-useful caches stashed around?"

Rexen let out a strange little chuckle.

"Oh, *pupil*," he said, a twinkle in his eye, "it is nice of you to show such an interest in your master's work! Proud! So pleased with my disciple, I am! There are many, many, many more secrets where that one came from."

"Huh," I mused, nodding. "Good to know."

It was time to rejoin my peeps—and it was going to be an uphill battle. Only time would tell if we were going to wind up as syrupy, post-human fuel for the machinations of Regaia.

SECOND OVERTURE

Regis, a formidable city, stood as the pulsating heart of the kingdom and nowhere was more imposing than its castle. Called the Shining Palace, its labyrinthine corridors and stony grandeur were incongruous with its name. Still, it was home to King Gaier's court. Amid its cold, desolate walls, the council chambers hosted an assembly most unusual, a grim mockery of the typical courtly decorum.

King Yule Gaier, his hulking form sprawled upon a throne fashioned from gnarled timber and metal shards, was a gargoyle of a horrific joke. His bellowing laughter echoed through the chambers, a melody that filled every nook and crevice of the room with its resonance.

The council room, a theater of the macabre, was a chilling place. The participants, an assembly of freakish characters more misfits of a nightmarish carnival than members of any council of strategic governance, conducted their grim pantomime in the dance of candlelight. The flickering illumination twisted their pranks and mirth into monstrous apparitions, painting the dark corners with flashes of dread and mania. This was no ordinary congregation but a circus, a perverted jest that sanity had abandoned.

However, the king was one who enjoyed this particular brand of huckery.

Gaier's night court had been the subject of unending whispered conversations in hushed tones. The company the king chose to keep was a cocktail of the weird and the terrifying, and even the sturdiest of men felt a quiver of unease in their company. The sickly sweet smell of their presence was like a stale breeze, lingering, invading the senses, and breeding anxiety.

The rumors that followed them were no less terrifying than the caricatures themselves. Whispers of unholy rituals, of disturbing debaucheries, of offerings carried out in the dead of night under the watchful eye of the king. And the queen. Ah, the beautiful queen. She was said to be captive to her husband's will in these affairs, her own involvement a serpent's hiss, slithering its way into every corner of the castle.

The vilest gossip was that of the king's relationship with the one that folk in the know called "the Veil." A mysterious figure draped in midnight-colored robes that rustled like dead leaves. Its face, hidden by the hood, held eyes that shimmered with a sickly green light, eyes that seemed to see into one's soul. It was said the king even preferred the Veil to stay in his chambers when he lay with the queen. An as-yet-unfounded rumor, but like a virulent disease, it had spread, infecting the minds of the courtiers, further enhancing the fear and unease that already permeated the air.

Each evening's assembly was a chilling spectacle. Like actors on a stage, they performed their strange antics under the king's watchful gaze, a grotesque parody of any court. The haunting strains of a melody would drift from the chamber, its discordant notes promising a night filled with dreadful tales and ghastly laughter.

But despite the swirling maelstrom of fear and intrigue, the king seemed to relish this company, the overseer, the ringmaster. To Gaier, these characters were not abominations to be feared but instead pieces on a questboard, each with its role in the grander scheme of his kingdom. Unsettling or not, this was Gaier's dark court, and it functioned according to his own strange whims.

And so, deciding upon a frequent game of theirs, the king peered into the faces of those before him, intending to delight at their responses.

Among them was Bumblefoot, a grotesque figure once relegated to the role of court fool, now repurposed as a strategic advisor. A tangle of contradictions, he bore an unsettling grin, his eyes alight with a chaos that stirred unease in one's gut. His words, as twisted as the man himself, were a madman's salute to warfare.

King Gaier leaned forward on his perilous throne.

"Bumblefoot, what is your counsel?"

The fool's raspy voice filled the room with its eerie suggestion.

"Why not hide our soldiers among innocent sheep, Your Majesty? Strike through and from within. The enemy would lose themselves in utter confusion, dwelling in the madness as they would! Perhaps they would peel back their skulls in befuddlement?"

This absurd proposal evoked a chorus of guttural laughter that danced through the room. None laughed harder than Bumblefoot himself, whose high-pitched whinny was a piercing peal as he dissolved into a fit, slamming his fist against the table before choking.

Next to Bumblefoot was Ulf, a hulking figure who fancied himself a werewolf. His hair was wild, his eyes glowed an unnatural yellow, and his anthemic suggestions were always easy to guess, yet with a seat at the table, his comments added to the discord.

"Ulf," Gaier inquired, his voice rough as gravel, "what say you?"

Ulf replied in his gravelly voice, full of a haunting solemnity.

"My lovely sire, let's use the fear of the full moon to our advantage. Strike terror into their hearts."

Gaier raised an eyebrow from behind the overflowing goblet he perched before his face.

"When next is the moon to be full?"

"Some time still, my lovely sire. Perhaps two weeks?"

Gaier guffawed, causing a rouse amongst his council as they looked to one another for confirmation they, too, were to be laughing.

"Or . . . perhaps less?" Ulf ventured.

The king sprayed a mouthful of wine across the council table, the droplets splattering on the advisors' robes.

"So, you would have us twiddle our thumbs for a fortnight just to howl at the moon, eh, Ulf?"

"Yes, well . . ." Ulf contemplated. "Might be the power of my kin is worth the suspense?"

This brought another coughing peal from Bumblefoot.

"He's demanding to wait!" Bumblefoot cried. "To show us his mighty feral strength!"

Everyone assembled joined in. Gaier shook with laughter, spilling his goblet. He stared at the empty vessel momentarily before flinging it at a wall and demanding another. A quiet servant crept in, refilling a fresh cup for His Majesty and departing wordlessly.

Standing in stark contrast to the monstrous figures around her was Marjora, a sorceress whose charm lay more in her macabre presentation than her arcane skills.

"Marjora," the Gaier asked, his voice booming through the stone chamber, "what dark Spells do you propose?"

Her violet eyes, gleaming with a mirthless light, flashed as she replied in a heavy Levikyvilish accent, "We could turn their weapons into feather dusters, My Liege. Let them try to vanquish us with . . . cruel, prolonged tickles!"

The imagery she spun drew more laughter from the court that echoed with a cruel, nightmarish quality.

Yet, amidst this gruesome spectacle, a note of reality reverberated, a harsh truth cutting through the madness. Master Dorin Meldondale, the king's steward, a beacon of sanity amidst the carnival of chaos, spoke with a firmness that tempered the room. His gaze held a seriousness that pierced through the wavering dimness.

"My liege," he began, his voice steady and measured, "your . . . true council awaits without. Our focus must shift to Hathburia."

This extinguished the embers of laughter. In its wake, the afterglow of grave duty sparked a renewed somberness within Gaier's eyes.

"In truth, Dorin," Gaier replied, the waves of his drunken jubilation receding to reveal the sturdy shoreline of the monarch beneath the intoxicated facade, "you have it. Our minds must turn to the weighty matter of Hathburia."

The mere mention of Hathburia acted as a sobering elixir, cutting through the hazy fog of inebriation, pulling the king back from the edge of his reckless abandon.

With an audible exhale of impatient frustration, Dorin, often called Dorin the Dour, made a cutting motion through the air. The door to the chamber responded to his gesture, revealing faces that bore the world's weight. These were individuals hardened not by a madman's humor but by life's cruelties: nobility armed with brains that strategized real battles, generals scarred by the harsh realities of war, and courtiers expert in the delicate art of diplomacy and administration.

They infiltrated the chamber, their footsteps a haunting chord to the incoming gloom. Each stood behind their usual allotted place around the table, their faces carved from stone, their eyes sharp as obsidian shards as they waited for the night court to vacate. King Gaier threw a quick, questioning glance at Dorin, who shrugged dismissively.

"Your jesters have entertained you enough, sire, but jesters they remain. These minds before you are what our kingdom needs in these tempestuous times."

King Gaier, a rumbling growl in his voice, nodded in agreement, albeit reluctantly. His eyes, hard as granite, surveyed the new faces, finally coming to a halt on the sturdy form of High Marshal Esker, the commander of his forces, hailing from the ruggedly imposing Port Grenfeld. His garb mirrored the stark contrast of the royal fortress's interior—black against the white, and emblazoned on his chest was the snarling head of a fox, the crest of House Vol.

"High Marshal," King Gaier began, a storm brewing in his voice, "what is the situation at the front?"

Before Esker could respond, Bumblefoot, the jester turned advisor, bounded forward, his absurd grin on full display. "King Gaier, might I—"

"No!" thundered Gaier, fury igniting in his eyes. "Enough! Leave, Bumblefoot."

"I only—"

"If you don't step out this instant, you will die! Painfully."

Gaier's words hung heavy in the air, a threat wrapped in royal authority.

Yet, rather than cower in fear, the eccentric retreating assembly broke into laughter, their mirth mocking the king's rage. Bumblefoot, his grin undiminished, bowed exaggeratedly and shuffled out, followed by the rest of the fools. The chamber fell silent, save for the whispering wind outside.

The grizzled High Marshal nodded gravely at the King's earlier question.

"Yes, my liege. Hathburia remains a thorn in our side, and the Redmark..."

"Redmark?" King Gaier interrupted. "Those pitiful rebels still exist? They should have been crushed by now!"

An elegant silhouette, as subtle as the shadows in the room, unfolded herself from the knot of councilors, tiptoeing the edge of dim candlelight. It was Reina, the mistress of whispers, the royal spymaster. She was of House Ko, who ruled over Kraychmarl, the Vineyard. This quaint haven, forged by ancient royal blood, was a lingering breath from the Daylit Era—making her the closest relative to the king of anyone in the room. Her attire was the embodiment of night itself, a canvas of obsidian kissed by streaks of silver, mirroring the emblem of her House, a grapevine entwining artfully down her garment. Her eyes, gray as the pre-dawn sky, locked on to the king's in silent affirmation

"Indeed, sire. They've claimed victories in a few minor skirmishes. Some of our smaller forts along the Aglands have fallen into their hands."

King Gaier's face twisted in a grimace of disgust.

"What do we know about these vermin? Who is their damned leader?"

Reina's voice, calm yet cold as ice, responded.

"Their leader remains elusive, Sire. Known only by an alias—the Fawn."

The king slammed his fist on the armrest, the impact reverberating in the room.

"A nuisance turned into a nightmare. And we have Hathburia to deal with as well."

A figure, imbued with an ageless grace, voiced his counsel. It was Jenorasis Carandalon, an elf of noble bearing. As the Chancellor of the Court, he emanated an aura as substantial as an ancient oak. House Carandalon flourished amidst the ethereal spires of Aeliareia, a city resting in the bosom of the kingdom's northern expanse. His attire flowed like a gentle river, an amalgamation of celestial blues and radiant silvers, an echo of his transcendent homeland.

"Sire, ignoring this rebellion might embolden them. We must act."

King Gaier's features were set in a grim mask of concern, his fingers drumming a nervous rhythm on the armrest.

"We've more than one battle to fight, then," he admitted somberly, his gaze sweeping across the room with unmasked anxiety as he gripped his goblet of wine. "A rebellion within our borders . . . the apes to the east, it is enough to drive a man to drink."

Esker rose, his posture radiating a steely determination.

"Sire," he began, his voice hardened by countless battles, "we stand ready to confront these threats. Our forces are prepared, and our will is unbroken."

A flicker of approval ignited in Gaier's eyes, the first spark of hope in the grim assembly. Yet the concern lingered, a silent specter in the dimly lit room.

A sudden rustle drew all attention toward the door. A messenger in House Bez colors, panting and covered in grime, hurried in. He fell to his knees in a flutter of rose and white, struggling to catch his breath, before managing to utter, "Sire . . . urgent news from the front."

All humor was gone, replaced with a tension so thick, one could almost taste it, a bitter note in the back of the throat. King Gaier leaned forward, his anticipation a mirror to the council's. The frivolous japery of his previous company seemed a distant memory, swallowed by the ominous darkness.

"Now, what dire news do you bring?" Gaier's voice was stern and foreboding.

The messenger's brow glistened with sweat, his wide eyes darting around the room in thinly veiled terror. He clutched at a scroll, the wax seal broken, the parchment crumpled under his shaking hands.

"Sire," he stuttered, his voice a mere whisper lost in the chilling silence. "We . . . we've lost Fort Shalewinter. It was a surprise attack . . . by the Redmark."

The council room erupted into shocked whispers, disbelief, and dread. Shalewinter, nestled at the foot of the towering Leviathan's Spine mountain range, had been an impenetrable bastion guarding the kingdom's northeastern front. For it to fall was a grievous blow, a severe crack in the foundation of the Kingdom of Arlo.

King Gaier sank back into his throne, his face ashen, his eyes reflecting the massive shock that rippled through the room. His fingers tightened around the armrest, knuckles white, betraying his inner turmoil.

"Shalewinter?" Gaier's voice came out strangled, incredulous. "That stronghold has stood scarless for a thousand years! How did this happen?"

Another advisor, Keppregar, a half-dwarf, spoke up.

"Likely it's the mountain passes, sire. We've never suspected an attack from there. They're treacherous, as all well know. But it seems the Redmark have dared what we thought impossible."

Deep within the crowns of the Leviathan's peaks, whispered legends spoke of mountain cherilim. Terrifying apparitions sculpted from stone, eyes burning with an insatiable flame, wings unfurling to cast an apocalyptic eclipse. The marrow of Arlo's nightmares was woven with tales of these fierce, merciless entities, monstrous lore passed down through generations.

"Ah, and you're speculating this, Kepp?" Gaier demanded. "Or have you some insight? Are you privy to knowledge I've only just received myself?"

Keppregar frowned, leaning back in his chair.

"No, sire . . ." he said softly. "'Was merely an inkling of—"

"Then hold your tongue, fool," Gaier hissed. "I'll have no conjecture without evidence."

The words, a familiar sting, cut deeper than any blade as the King's sharp words lashed through the air. Keppregar, who once shared laughter and camaraderie as a party member within the merry clutches of the guild they'd both belonged to, stood wounded. The use of his old nickname, once a jovial call between friends, now twisted into a venomous jest, marking him as a heel. His eyes held the flicker of old fires, burned low, the warmth of friendship replaced with the cold ash of betrayal.

"As you say, sire," Keppregar intoned.

Regis, a colossal ode to the kingdom's erstwhile glory, now seemed to shudder under the weight of this fresh information. The council members wrestled with their predicament. The shocking news a treacherous undercurrent, threatening to drag them into a sea of despair. But there would be time for that later. They had to plan, to strategize. There was no room for fear—not when their realm teetered on the brink of a bloody conflict.

"Summon the generals," King Gaier ordered, his voice firm. "Assemble the court adepts, call forth the diplomats, tell the gods-be-damned smallfolk to sharpen their fucking spears—all and every to their due duty. We've a war to prepare for, a rebellion to quell, and a kingdom to safeguard. Too many fucking things and too little time. We must respond with all our might."

A quiet throat-clearing interrupted the weighty silence that followed the King's words. It was Lord Nolrim, a voice seldom raised, yet when it did, wisdom poured forth. The stoic councilor of House Trisk, Nolrim was a monument to patience and longevity. His birthplace, the unblemished city of Illintor, was mirrored in his attire, a pristine palette of white and gold.

"Your Majesty . . ." he began. "I fear there is more troubling news. The Yeska has entered into an accord with the Tides."

A ripple of unease traversed the room. The Tides were a notorious sect bound by the will of their mysterious figurehead known only as the Drifter. Aloof and unpredictable, seldom allying with anyone. For them to align with the Yeska, long at odds with Arlo, spelled potential disaster.

"Talks of a pilgrimage have begun," Lord Nolrim finished quietly, his gaze never leaving Gaier's.

The words hung in the air like a dreaded prophecy. Gaier's eyes flashed with a rage so potent that they transfigured the air around him. The temperature dropped sharply, a frigid wind whipping through the room. A raw, primal aura radiated from the king, pulsing with an intensity that drained the strength from every soul present. The Arcana imbued within his anger had taken a physical form, a monstrous entity that towered over them, cruel and unyielding.

"Explain," Gaier demanded, his voice reverberating with rage. "What does this *pilgrimage* mean? What are the Yeska and his Sovereign planning?"

Nolrim swallowed, his face paling under the king's wrath.

"I . . . I do not know, Your Majesty. We've heard only whispers. Nothing concrete. But perhaps—"

At that moment, the king's rage took on a much more terrible form. His eyes, previously flickering with anger, now glowed with an ominous red light. His fingers twitched, and shadowy tendrils emerged from the floor as if answering some unspoken command, slithering and coiling with an unnatural, horrifying life.

With a sound like the ripping of reality itself, the shadowy tendrils constricted around Lord Nolrim. He gasped, his eyes wide with terror, and his mouth opened to scream. But there was no time for pleas or apologies, only the gut-wrenching sound of shadows devouring light.

The tendrils receded as abruptly as they had emerged, leaving behind no trace of Nolrim but for the echo of his fright. The chamber fell silent again, a quiet witness to the terrifying display. Dread hung heavy in the room, each councilor aware that they were in the presence of a king who could command armies and courted the chilling darkness at the fringe of existence.

The room seemed to contract under Gaier's heated gaze, a predator surveying its quarry.

"Is there anything else I should know that might infuriate me further?" he demanded, the remnants of his raw, unsettling power lingering in the air. His tone was a terrible calm, a storm lulled temporarily—though just as menacing.

An oppressive pause filled the chamber, each councilor acutely aware of the void where Nolrim had stood moments before. Eyes darted anxiously around the room, but no one dared to break the silence. The moment stretched on, a specter that hung over the assembly.

"Good," Gaier finally muttered icily. His gaze, too, lingered on the spot the lord had been before shifting back to the remaining council. His stern eyes swept across the fearful faces, his wrathful display serving as a harrowing reminder of the repercussions of their failure.

"Now, then," he started, his voice echoing through the vast, hallowed chamber, "the first issue on our list: my son. Has he found his way back home?"

Primarch Weldansh uul Elay, commander of the Warders, inclined his fully encased head from the back of the chamber. He had, until now, been completely silent.

"Yes, Majesty," he said. His Eastern Brychol accent strongly flavoring an unnaturally deep voice resonating within the helm. "This morning. With the prisoner."

"And he is well? No issues?"

"No, Majesty," Weldansh said. "Issues, none. Assisted in quelling the prisoner. Unscathed."

"Well," Gaier said, clear astonishment on his face. "That is indeed a surprise."

He turned to Dorin, nodding.

"Let's ensure there's to be a celebration for such a feat, Dorin."

"It will be done," Dorin said.

King Gaier returned to glare at the room.

"Now—on to Hathburia. Who has a proposition, a solution, or a fucking plan of action that will bring an end to this ordeal?"

At the king's final words, an unforeseen phenomenon seized the room. A shimmering, ethereal veil seemed to descend before each councilor's eyes, an event that any inhabitant of the world recognized as the arrival of a personal System message. The irises of their eyes clouded over, their pupils dilating as they received the message in their minds.

The room fell into an abrupt silence, broken only by the slight gasps of surprise and the soft rustling of clothes as the councilors stiffened in their seats. Each face went pale, shock clear in their wide, staring eyes. It was as if they all faced an unseen specter, their gazes focused on something intangible yet utterly arresting in the space before them.

But the king did not react with shock as the others did. Instead, his grip tightened on the armrests of his throne, his knuckles white under the strain. His jaw set in a hard line as he processed the contents of the message, his mind already spinning with the implications. After a tense moment, his eyes cleared, and he stood from his throne, a newfound intensity burning in his gaze.

"Quiet," he commanded, his voice echoing in the stunned silence. Everyone held their breath, their attention turning to their king. The room was filled with an air of trepidation as they awaited his response. His command.

King Gaier looked each of his councilors in the eye, his expression stern and resolved.

"There is a change in priority," he declared, his voice echoing authoritatively in the hushed room. "All nonessential engagements are canceled. The Circle of Arcanists is to be convened immediately. Also, find Maragon Dant—wherever the blasted idiot happens to be. Pull him out of the bathwater if you have to."

"And what of the . . . Shadows?" a council asked hesitantly. "The message mentioned . . ."

The king nodded, knowing it was unwise to say anything further on that front.

"Prepare for mobilization."

CHAPTER SIXTEEN

MEMENTO

I woke up.

I groaned—immediately furious that I had allowed myself to fall asleep. How had that even happened? Also . . . where the hell was I?

I glanced around all bleary-eyed at my surroundings. A bunch of brown. Shapes. Couple o' muddy stains on the wall.

Ah, right. I'm in hell.

Now, before you go spiraling off into a tizzy, know I was being a teensy bit dramatic. I wasn't in any actual afterlife, you know, full of fire, brimstone, and people who are mean to dogs. But I may as well have been. The place I was in—where I actually was—was in a ramshackle hut the size of a McDonald's parking-lot trash can in the middle of a destroyed camp in a dumbass forest on the scaly boil of a world called Regaia. I knew this because, for the last month, I'd woken up in the same spot. You'd have thought I'd have been used to it by now, but let me tell ya—I was not.

I groaned again because you know what? I felt like it. Groaning was a great thing to do when you wake up after not wanting to fall asleep, and you're still in Dumpsterville and know your day will be oh so shitty. Because it would be. The worst thing I ever did was trot my ass inside, and I'd been hot about it since.

I slumped forward, finally rising, and, forgetting my size compared to the hobbit hovel I was in, bashed my head on the ceiling. Groan numero tres tumbled out of my lips. Let me tell you, this was queueing up to be another fabulous morning.

I crashed through the open doorway and into the bright, beaming sun—because that was literally the only way I could comfortably unwedge myself from within the structure's confines—and glanced around. It was early; that much was evident, since there wasn't a single other person awake yet in the whole damn vicinity.

Buncha lazybones.

Well . . . I supposed that wasn't totally true. Someone somewhere was still awake—the evening watch, for one. I didn't know who had pulled dunce duty last night, but I was glad it wasn't me. Not that I'd be allowed. But *somebody* was in charge of keeping us safe through the night, and they sure as hell had better have been awake or . . . Well, that wasn't my problem. No, my only issue was that I'd arrived there in tow with my homies, and it had been a fantastically bad idea.

Because I'd died. Remember that?

Then, for some reason, I'd made my way back with Rexen, and now . . .

I squinted at the junkyard-like bullshit abound.

Now I can't wait *to leave.*

Briefly, hesitantly, I peered at the makeshift walls the villagers had constructed around the camp. They were tall and misshapen, consisting primarily of downed tree trunks lashed together with other trees—the baby ones . . . what are they called? Straplings? Saplings? Sure. Anyway, it looked like a big ol' pile of shit and was just *begging* to be breached. Really, though, nothing screams "Come attack us" like poorly put-together fortifications that looked like they were crafted by a pack of newborn, arthritic beavers. I mean, it was a heaping mess and wasn't keeping anybody out. Though, for some reason, it had kept me in so far . . .

But, hey, it wasn't all bad. Most of my stuff had survived the explosion. I mean, god-to-the-damn, at least in this waste run-off of a place, magic kept shit pretty fuckin' impervious.

I heard a shuffle and almost darted back inside my wigwam. But, of course, I'd been spotted. Based on the time of day, it could only be one person.

"You're up early," said Dalton.

"Yeah," I said sleepily. "I, too, like to state the obvious. It is daytime. You are Dalton. You smell like old piss."

Dalton crinkled his forehead at my words and shook his head sadly as if he couldn't believe I'd be so rude to him. I mean, come on, how could I not be a bit of a canker sore to him? He was an elf that was formerly a college-aged dipshit from my original world who was also named Dalton. It was hilarious that given the opportunity to crawl into a new world and completely change everything about yourself, this guy had deemed it wise to keep his original name. Dalton the elf. Fabulous. What was worse: he was the seemingly second-in-command to the asshole who ran this whole operation, though I couldn't divine by what metric of fairness.

"Just doing some morning talk, dude. Goddamn. I was trying to be friendly."

I sneered at him.

"I don't want to be your friend, Dalton."

Somehow, I knew that purposely not following that up with any sort of joke or additional razz was the best way to show him I didn't like the cut of his jib. A follow-up comparison could just be passed off as my usual plucky personality—but ending it where I did . . . that would cut deep.

"Whatever," Dalton said dismissively as if I hadn't just decimated his self-esteem. "You're on ditch duty today."

"Fuckin' *sweet*," I said, rolling my eyes. "Digging more holes. You guys have no fuckin' clue what you're doing, do you?"

Dalton ignored my comment. He was staring off past the train wreckage that had brought us all to this world, his eyes intent on something beyond the treeline. Then he came back to reality and shook his head.

"What?" I asked.

"Nothing," he said sourly. "Work starts in an hour, so have breakfast and then grab a shovel."

"Eat a whole butt, Dalton," I said before stalking off toward the, uh . . . mess hall of sorts.

Cursing under my breath, I pushed my way through the cluttered jungle of metal that separated the open-air atrium of the communal dining area from the rest of the open-air *everything* of the camp. It was essentially a large clearing dotted with stumps that people could use as both tables *and* chairs surrounded by a bunch of shrapnel that had been torn from the belly of the derailed train. A big campfire sat nearly in the center, a bubbling kettle hanging over it with a long piece of thin wood sticking out of it that acted as a ladle. Somebody had, at some point, tried to fashion it into an actual ladle but failed spectacularly, considering it primarily consisted of one straight piece of walnut with a little shallow reservoir designed to be the scoopin' bit. I scowled.

This is seriously fucking pathetic. I'll bet it's filled with twig stew or something, too.

The camp was a big fuckin' dump. Blackened, charred remnants from our first day there were still present everywhere I looked. The makeshift huts, the ground, the nearby trees—few things had escaped the attack. Rather than convince them to leave, it had only bolstered my fellow former Earthlings into digging in their heels.

The one thing I had going for me—if you could phrase it in such a way—was that nobody expected anything outta ol' Loon. And by god, I aimed to keep it that way. I did the bare minimum to avoid getting something worse than ditch duty. But even that was starting to feel like a royal pain in the ass, especially since all the information I got from the System was *still* giving me grief.

In fact, it had gone even further into wacko-bananas territory over the last month. I was ready to dig my own eyes out to escape the mixed greens of genuine malicious stupidity it was serving up.

Like, get this: I'd checked my Strength a few days before, and rather than an actual number, it said:

A journey of a thousand miles begins with a single step. Boy, are these doggies tired!

I didn't want some sort of parable pick-me-up. I simply wanted to know if I could punch a bear in the face and not break my hand.

. . . I'd been debating with Rua about what each Attribute constituted in relative power, so it had been vital information. Apparently, there was a very specific score—according to Rexen.

Meanwhile, the prompts I got when using Eye of the Saboteur were equally unhelpful and dripping in frustrating, unnecessary subtext. It was, like, one of the only cool things about this world—allowing me to get a ton of information about the stats and material breakdown of pretty much anything. But now . . . it was a mess. I'd try to examine an item and get a message like *This rusty dagger has seen more sunsets than you can count.*

I mean, what in the candy-coated Christ was that supposed to tell me? That the rusty dagger was old? Great! Super! Was it sharp? Fragile? Coated in tetanus? And why was my System menu getting all poetic on me, anyhow? It used to just be regular annoying. Now it was borderline petulant. Really upset my stomach, ya dig?

But I digest.

Between wrestling with my maddening menu and trying not to die from boredom or Alpha-induced rage, my day-to-day involved a lot of menial labor. I helped with basic things around the camp. You know, fetching water, gathering wood, and helping cook whatever passed for meals. That was when I wasn't digging fucking holes.

Motherfucking ditch duty. The mention of it brought up a fresh wave of irritation.

Now, I'm all for contributing, pulling your weight, and all. Still, I strongly suspected that these ditches we were digging were largely useless. And yet it seemed to be a staple in our sword-and-sorcery handbook. Got a problem? Dig a ditch. Not sure what to do? Dig a ditch. Dick hurt? You guessed it—dig a goddamn ditch.

To say the very thought of it made my blood boil would be a very egregious understatement. I was just one misplaced pile of dirt away from turning my shovel into a makeshift javelin and hurling it into the nearest Sojourner. But, alas, all I could do was groan, gripe, and get to digging. Or, at least, do a convincing job of pretending to. Alpha—in his mind, that doubled as a perpetual-motion-production facility of dipshit imaginings and carnal meanderings—had gone forward with the designs and started putting together the plans for a wall. This was fucking dumb because, even if I just had a vague indication *before* that things were bad there, *now I actually knew it was*. But, since I'd gone and done a big silly like *accidentally losing the Duellum*—through no fault of my own, I might add—I didn't really have the option to toss my substantial weight around.

This place was a joke. The settlement we'd built was a far cry from anything called "civilized." I mean, if we were going for "medieval peasant chic," we'd nailed it. If, however, we were aiming for "livability," then we were failing spectacularly.

When the sun shone in the sky—a big burning ball of fiery hate—I'd usually see the camp bustling with activity. Most of our crew were focused on making the camp a more permanent residence. That meant construction, basically. And by construction, I mean attempting to build structures using a combination of fallen trees, leftover bits of the derailed train, and sheer desperation. These creations were rickety, uneven, and leaned in ways no building should lean. A drunk architect's feverish withdrawal scratchings.

Every so often, we'd get a break from the camp monotony by going on scavenging runs. There's nothing quite as glamorous as rooting through debris and plant detritus in the hopes of finding something useful or edible. It was the world's shittiest scratchy lotto because instead of winning *dollars*, you ended up with a handful of barely edible berries or a half-rusted blade.

To top it all off, there were incessant, never-ending meetings. Oh, how I despised the meetings. Alpha had begun calling them "strategy sessions," but that was just a fancy name for him having free rein to verbally assault the others in various textures of badly managed word salad. I wasn't invited to these, either—nope, more ditch duty.

In the evenings, we'd gather around the pitiful campfire for a feast of whatever scraps we'd gathered that day. The offerings were generally a muddled stew that tasted like boiled deodorant, accompanied by an assortment of foraged plants that were probably poisonous.

After dinner, if we felt particularly ambitious, we'd engage in the age-old tradition of sitting around the fire and exchanging stories. Well, primarily, the others would exchange stories about their lives back on Earth or speculate about the mysteries of Regaia. Me? I usually hung back and avoided adding anything. I was restless. And none of these fucks seemed to care at all about the fact that there was a malignant band of Sojourner-harvesting psychopaths lurking around somewhere.

Eventually, we'd all traipse off to our respective shelters and attempt to get some rest. Sleep, however, was always an elusive beast. The constant anxiety, the rough sleeping conditions, and the deafening sounds of nocturnal Regaian wildlife reawakened my previously barely contained insomnia. I got, like, zero sleep.

Life in our settlement was a repeating cycle of grueling labor, questionable meals, and tension-riddled nights. So much for thrilling fantasies of otherworldly adventure. But hey, at least it wasn't dull. No, wait . . . it was really fucking boring. Every day was like a dance to the same tune, one with a particularly monotonous beat. Everyone stuck in a never-ending game of *The Sims: Wilderness Edition*. And I'll tell you: the graphics sucked.

Once in a while, there would be a break in the routine. Perhaps a storm would roll in, making all our work a little bit harder and a whole lot soppier. Other times, we'd get visits from Regaia's less-than-friendly inhabitants—everything from lumbering beasts that looked like hippos on steroids to winged monstrosities that loved dive-bombing our pathetic camp from the skies.

Exciting fucking days, man. You know, when everyone's adrenaline would kick in, and we'd band together to *excruciatingly easily* drive off whatever wanted to munch on our tasties. It was dangerous and messy, but at least it wasn't digging ditches. And I'd be lying if I said there wasn't a certain middling thrill to standing side by side with my reluctant comrades, shitty blades and other makeshift weapons in hand, ready to duke it out for our survival. Sometimes, for a brief moment, I would almost feel like a hero.

Almost.

And then, inevitably, the . . . excitement would pass. The creatures would be driven off or, better yet, end up as an ingredient in our mystery lunch. We'd patch up our wounds—of which there were usually few—fix whatever damage was done—also usually not much—and go right back to the fucking grind. Because, as it turned out, life in an otherworldly survival scenario was less about epic battles and more about . . . I dunno, just existing?

I remember believing I'd been better off back in the previous world when I first arrived. I know what you're thinking: *Loon, how could you say such a thing! You're in ninety percent of humanity's wet dream! Action! Adventure! Unrequited stabbings!* Right? Weeks and weeks before, even with all the social, economic, and political issues we'd faced back home, I was om-nomming at the bit to return. Because at least there, I didn't have to worry about being eaten by a monster or getting impaled by a sentient thorn bush. At least there, I had a decent bed to sleep in, food that wasn't a daily gamble, and a life that consisted of more than just the bare-bones struggle to survive.

But no use crying over spilled milk. Or, in our case, over accidentally teleporting to an annoying, dumb-as-dicks, hostile Westeros. This was our life now, and all we could do was try to make the best of it. That or curl up in a ball and wait for something to take pity on us and end our misery.

So, we carried on. Day after day, night after night, lather-rinse-repeat. All the while waiting for something to change. And every morning, I would wake up in my hut, smack my head on the ceiling, groan, and start again.

Such was the glamorous life in the fabulous settlement of Diarrheaville, or as some of the more optimistic folks had begun to . . . cleverly call it, "New Home." Yeah, right. As if a name—especially such a laughably fucking adorable one—could make this place any less of a shit pit. I swear, the level of delusion with this group was so high, it was bumpin' into satellites.

In the end, I suppose, we were all just trying to cope in our own ways. Which was fine, I guess. Some people deluded themselves into thinking we were pioneering a new civilization. In contrast, others clung to the hope that we'd somehow find a way back to the world we left. And then there were those like me, who fully embraced the suck and just tried to get by without unaliving ourselves.

And, of course, there was the big old cherry on top of this late-night, hungover lobster-mac vomit sundae: I was bored.

As I sat, eating the terrible food that someone probably worked super hard on, glaring at my surroundings with the appreciation of a feral badger, one single thought was bonkin' around inside my head: I fucking hated it there.

Not in the world—no, that part was probably the most surprising. There in the camp. Eking out an existence, doing our best Catan impression, just wasn't doing it for me. I wasn't interested in building up some Sid Meier–esque base camp and expanding into the world, slowly cultivating larger territory . . . or whatever. I wanted to be where the action was, man! I wanted a . . . I dunno, a fucking fight or something. To get kicked in the face by some ugly son of a bitch with power far eclipsing my own while shoveling out semi-witty, poorly contrived comebacks. God motherfuck, what I wouldn't have done for a straightforward *kill ten rats* Quest or something. But no, life sucked.

That's why I was more than a little bit intrigued when Rexen suggested we kill a god.

CHAPTER SEVENTEEN

WHAT ARE YE BUT THE SOULLESS MEAT?

The soft gloaming had descended on their camp, its encroaching shadows blanketing the assortment of misshapen shelters and humble structures. The cool dusk lent a measure of quiet to the usually bustling settlement. Despite the impending darkness, a pool of flickering light stubbornly held court at the outskirts of their community, within the tattered remnants of what would not infrequently be the war tent, casting playful shadows on the canvas walls.

Inside, under the steady gaze of a single conjured orb of light, an assembly of ragtag adventurers sat gathered around a rudimentary table. Their faces, all markedly different in appearance, carried the same expression: tense focus. The room was heavy with anticipation.

"This is the culmination of our entire endeavor," Veruca said, hardly daring to breathe lest it ruin all that they had worked so hard for the last hour. "Draw your focus upon this task, sir, and perform it most dutifully. But, please, do it now. I cannot bear the thought of dragging this out any further."

Dragoon's stern features were set, his brows knit in an intense frown as he stared at the object of their mutual focus.

"Don't . . . rush me," he muttered to Veruca, a bead of sweat trickling down his temple.

The vittra nonchalantly leaned back in her chair, an image of serene tranquility amidst the apparent crisis. Her fingers rhythmically drummed on the tabletop.

"Time is a luxury we do not have, Dragoon," she noted, her voice dry. "The hour is critical, our chances remaining for failure are nonexistent, and we've already exhausted all other options. We must do it this way and act now."

Across the table, Edwig harumphed, his amorphous eyes gleaming with ill-suppressed mirth.

"Pah! Dramatic, aren't you?" he shot back at Veruca. "Just do it, already, human! Fail . . . succeed—anything is better than this suspense!"

Rua's nervous energy was palpable. She paced at the edge of the table, wringing her hands, her gaze darting from one face to another.

"Edwig, don't distract him!" she scolded, her voice pinched.

Saban merely raised an eyebrow at the exchange.

"This is intense. Even more so than our last encounter with the gryphs," he said, his quiet pitch adding gravitas to the understatement.

"Gryphs, Saban? Really? Have some perspective, will you?" Matt said, shaking his head. "This is it. If they fail, they fail, and it'll all have been for nothing. That's what you're thinking, right, Rua?"

Rua bit her lip.

"I wish you guys would be quiet so he can concentrate," she said sourly. "It seems rude to—"

Their conversation was cut short by a harsh gust of wind, which caused the tent's entrance to flap vigorously. In walked Loon, covered in dirt, looking as though he'd spent a day in battle, though he had been immersed, quite literally, in a different type of trench. He'd been digging. Again. Rexen floated next to him, seeming, for the lack of a better word, exhausted.

"Wait! What the fuck is going on?!" Loon demanded.

In the middle of the table, a monument of their collective effort stood precariously—a towering arrangement of wooden sticks that defied gravity's insistence. Loon's eyes fell on the group gathered around the table and the precarious tower of twigs.

"You motherfuckers started without me," he accused.

The entire group gathered around the hunk of wood balancing precariously on a stump they were calling a table looked up at him, and they all, as one, hissed out a shush. Loon was incensed.

"Don't shush me, you Benedict Assholes! I asked you guys to wait—I even did it politely—but, well, goddamn, it looks like you're almost done!"

They shushed him again.

"Don't do that," he warned. "I fuckin' *hate* being shushed."

"My glorious pupil is angered!" Rexen piped. "I would not be surprised if he ended your miserable— Ooh! Hi, Matt!"

The specter waved at the man hunched over in boredom. Matt returned the wave, seeming to brighten at the appearance of the Dreadnaught Lord. The two had become fast friends once Rexen discovered that, like himself, Matt had a sweet tooth. Not only that, but the human also delighted in informing the spirit about the wide variety of treats available in his old world.

"We are nearly done," Veruca said matter-of-factly. "Once Dragoon completes this pass, our team's victory is in hand."

"Not a chance," Saban said. "He's going to fail, and you're going to take over cooking tomorrow for me."

Dragoon, his hand hovering over the space in the pile, turned his head sharply at the group.

"Stop. Talking."

Before anyone could reply, a joyful chaos ensued. Bouncing with gleeful abandon, Jumpy, Clucky, Slappy, and Mortimer tumbled into the tent. The roe hurtled toward the table, their enthusiasm upending the plank, sending the entire tower crashing down. Sticks spilled in every direction, and there was a collective shout of disapproval. Immediately, the pink egg creatures froze, realizing that their horseplay had once again had a negative consequence.

"Seriously?" Rua exclaimed. "We were so close!"

"Blast it all," Veruca said, pointing a claw at Slappy. "You have ruined everything, you—"

"Nope!" Loon shouted, sweeping forward and standing between the outstretched digit and the now-cowering egg. "Don't even *think* about raising your voice at my little homies. It was an accident! Plus, that's what y'all get for bein' dicks!"

"You tell 'em, disciple," Rexen said. "Everyone deserves a swift and brutal rebuke. Flay them with your words—or with your flaying instruments! Such is the high cost of disobedience!"

"Huh?" Saban wondered. "What's with the Vlad the Impaler vibe, Rexen? It seems unnecessary."

"Ah, don't mind him," Loon said. "He's just missing his buddy Tartarus. Ain't that right, Arjee?"

Rexen scowled. Loon's ditch digging had wound around near where the former history teacher had been stretched out, reading a book on trains. This meant that, for the duration, the thaumaturge had been subjected to his interest.

"That ogre is a bore!" Rexen announced. "Blech! I can't stand him! Always asking questions. Wanting a bunch of *information*. None of the good stuff, either!"

"Arjee," Loon said. "What did I say about being nice?"

"My apprentice asks too much," the ghost continued. "I would request that we take pains to avoid the ogre's general radius at all costs! My time is precious, pupil. I'd rather spend it on other pursuits."

"Yeah, like chatting with Matty-boy about Charleston Chews?"

"What is *Charlestown Chews*?" Rexen wondered, turning to Matt with interest.

"Oh, Rex . . ." Matt said excitedly. "I'm about to blow your mind."

* * *

I glanced around the tent, watching my fellow settlers engage in various levels of tomfoolery. The roe were already bouncing around again like tiny terrors; Veruca, Matt, and Rua were trying a different game using the twigs that was like a variation of Pick-Up Sticks, while Edwig was busy looking over something in his menu and tutting every few moments as if he was *very* unimpressed. Dragoon was giving the lot of them a pointedly concerned look, as if that could somehow undo the chaos.

The laughs and joking carried on for what felt like hours, helping to lift some of the mental grime from my latest round of backbreaking manual labor. Some. Not all. But, I suppose it wasn't *all* bad. I gained a Skill from all my tireless efforts: Digging. And it was now an E-Rank Skill due to bustin' my hump on the regular. I wasn't sure how that was necessarily going to be useful, but, hey, it made the dirty job something a tad more manageable. Despite the joking and ease, I couldn't shake the sense of something looming over us. And I wasn't the only one.

Saban was leaning back in his chair, looking every bit as nonchalant as Veruca had earlier. But I knew him well enough to see the tightness in his eyes, the rigidity of his posture. He had this habit of running his fingers over the corner of his brow when he was stuck on something. Like he was trying to smooth out the wrinkles in his mind by pinching the brow fat. Sitting there in the warm light, his eyes had a troubling look about them.

I had noticed the change in his demeanor early on. My former best friend was usually all smiles and charm. Right now, he was wearing his *I'm concerned about something but I don't want to ruin the mood* face. I squinted at him, curiosity piqued.

"Alright, m'man, spit it out. You're killing the vibe here with your brooding."

He glanced at me, looking like a deer caught in the headlights.

"I . . . It's nothing, really. Just . . . thinking."

"Sure, sure. And Edwig's foolin' everybody with that sweater vest. Spill the beans, matey."

"What?!" Edwig demanded grumpily from his spot near the tent flap.

Saban heaved a sigh, the weight of the world apparently resting on his broad shoulders.

"It's . . . Alright, well, I don't want to ruin the mood . . ."

Fuckin' told ya so.

"But," he continued, "winter."

"Winter?" Rua asked, turning from where she was dangling one of the sticks over an incredibly interested Mortimer.

"Yeah," Saban said, inclining his head. "I'm concerned about it. We need a plan. I mean, a solid, foolproof plan. I'm losing sleep over it."

My eyebrow quirked up at his words. Of course. It made sense. Eventually, everything would freeze over, and we'd probably find ourselves scrounging around for any measly old flame we could to warm ourselves. Saban, who seemed to think it was his sole duty to protect our whole histronic horde from devastation at all times, would obviously be thinking months ahead on that front. It was why, I think, most people sort of saw him as the shadow mayor of the camp. You know, the one actually running stuff in New Home—which, as an aside, had unfortunately caught on as the name of this puke heap. God-*damn*, I hated that fucking name. Everybody shoulda listened to me when I was coming up with my brilliant suggestions. But I guess nobody was really *feelin'* Skulltopia. I'll be honest: if they'd been down to clown with a fuckin' banger of a moniker like that, I'd have considered trying to stick around rather than convince everyone to leave.

But back to Saban. I mean, I'll give the man some credit: he was trying to ensure we didn't freeze our asses off in the upcoming months. But damn, he knew how to ruin a perfectly good evening.

"So what?" I said, shrugging. "We make a bunch of blankets and all sleep in the same big tent. Problem solved. There—back to relaxin'!"

Saban gave me a strained smile.

"If only it were that easy, Loon."

I sighed.

"Man, I would've thought you'd worked out a survival plan for *every* scenario. I mean, remember our zombie-apocalypse prep? Fuckin' legendary organization."

Back in the day, we—like everyone else on the planet that had been around during the heavily undead-focused entertainment times—had developed quite the arsenal of strategies that we were planning to deploy once the extremely likely and definitely possible walking-dead end-of-the-world event happened. Saban's plans had been unending, almost obsessive, as he mapped out various routes to the nearest places, including our plans on where to meet and who else would be allowed to join our new world army. We even kept a map of key locations in his garage and would periodically ride our bikes to check how long it would take us to get there. Little did we know we'd be placed in a scenario that would be similar enough to warrant my own sense of disbelief at his lack of doomsday arrangements.

Saban lowered his voice, clearly worried about being overheard by someone outside of the confines of the tent.

"Yeah, I mean . . . I can plan, sure. That's easy. But . . . I'm not really getting through to . . . certain people. And, besides, we really don't know what to expect, do we? None of us have experienced winter here before."

"I have!" Rexen announced cheerily. "Many, many, many cold, *blustery* ones! Mean ol' winter, strutting about with his thumbs tucked into his waistband like a cock-of-the-walk. Acting like he owns the place."

"Well . . . *you're* definitely an unreliable source," I said, holding my hand up to indicate he should be quiet. "Plus, you don't even feel temperatures like hot or cold."

"Incorrect," he said, turning his face up like he was offended. "I have the frozen fire of cold fury in me at all times."

Everyone was paying attention now, the atmosphere well and truly tanked. It was rare for Saban to be such a Downer Debbie, but I guess that probably lent some weight to how serious he found it.

"I just wish," he continued, letting clear frustration bleed into his words, "that in a world like this, there were more clear signs on what we needed to do to actually survive something other than a fight. Honestly, it's got me twisted."

It was pin-drop silent in the joint, which was pretty impressive. I'd always known Saban wasn't *only* irresistibly positive in his personal mode of charismatic presentation. Still, it seemed that no matter what emotion he was trying to relay, he really knew how to command a room.

"Well, Saban," I said, "that's quite the conundrum. You've got us all worked up over . . . central heating?"

"I'm serious, Loon," he shot back, looking a touch annoyed. "It's not just the cold. I've seen how paranoid Alpha's getting. He's . . . not handling the pressure well."

And that was another concern. The guy technically running this outfit was an absolute fucking moron—and quite possibly the dumbest person I'd ever encountered in my goddamn life. I'd noticed the shift, though. He used to be just an irredeemable fuck socket—now, though, it seemed he'd used the . . . I dunno, fuckin' Pokémon persecution evolution stone and evolved into a bona fide megalomaniacal fuck wrench. The mere mention of Alpha's name added another layer to the tent tension with all the subtlety of tossing a cinder block into a spider web.

"Yeah, he's gotten worse," I replied, nodding sagely. "But what else is new? The guy's always been a few nuggets short of a Happy Meal. At a certain point, him getting more unbearable is like pointing out a sunken ship is taking on more water—it's already down at the bottom of the ocean."

Saban just stared at me for a moment, probably trying to process my casual take on our impending doom. Heaving a sigh, he shook his head.

"You're . . ."

"A genius? Handsome? All-that-is-man? The world's strongest, funniest sex symbol?"

". . . right," he finished. "You're right on the money."

"I am?" I asked, confused.

"I'd forgotten how good your insights are sometimes," he continued. "Spot on."

"It is?" I asked. I was not used to receiving compliments. Especially not for brain stuff.

"I mean—yeah!" I said. "I'm like almost always hittin' the bull's-eye on the perfect solution to all the woes that make up the world's issues. The Robin Hood of problem solving."

"Pah!" Edwig scoffed. "That's an interesting take on your own insanity, orc."

"Not now, Viggo," I said dismissively. "I'm not going to listen to anything a *pariah* has to say. I'm being lauded for my brilliance."

"Pah! Who's a pariah?"

"You, ya dumdum," I retorted, turning to face the illisinaf. "Aren't you, like, on the lam from Yosper Hall?"

This was just an assumption on my part, because we hadn't actually discussed it, but when we first met, Edwig had been imprisoned for *something*—until I broke him and Rua out, that is. Then, before we'd left Tallrock, he'd stopped into the Mages' Order at Yosper Hall and got outta there *real* quick-like. Considering that, it wasn't a leap to assume there was some sort of legal bad blood involved. I didn't really care, though, save for in this precise instance, where it would allow me to get him to shut up.

Edwig paused, considering my words.

"Eh . . . alright. Point taken," he said softly. "Carry on with your outlandish evaluation of your own abilities, then."

"Don't mind if I do!" I said.

"So . . ." Rua said, nudging Saban out of his reverie. "Even if we assume there's a nasty winter on its way, there's a lot of basic stuff we can do to protect ourselves from the elements. You know? Like gathering and preserving food, winterizing our shelters, stocking up on firewood, making warm clothes . . . that sort of thing. We could even have a go at creating some medicinal supplies, if anyone's proficient in that? And, um, we should probably have some emergency plans in place, just in case."

She gave a little shrug, as though she'd merely suggested we rearrange our sock drawers rather than prepare for a potentially life-threatening Ice Age.

"Well, then, uh, Veruca . . . what are we looking at in terms of supplies?" Matt asked, turning to our resident supply master with a hopeful grin, like a student asking a teacher if they were going to have homework over the holidays.

Veruca, as usual, took a moment before responding, looking for all the fucking world like she was contemplating the meaning of life. She had a habit of doing that. From what I could tell, she spent a lot of time devising what she was going to say before she said it, as if every word was a precious gemstone that she had to carefully select and polish before presenting. Which was the polar opposite of my approach to things that came out of my mouth. Then, when it seemed like she had her thoughts together, she started speaking in that long, overly complicated way she had.

"Considering our prevailing circumstances," she began, "it is readily apparent that our existing resources are woefully inadequate. Our subsistence provisions are demonstrably insufficient and manifestly disproportionate to our projected requirements. With a limited number of individuals proficient in the requisite skills of hunting or foraging—present company excluded, of course, Rua—our potential for amassing necessary sustenance remains critically constrained."

As Veruca dropped her bombshell in the most long-winded way possible, everyone got pretty quiet, not saying anything.

"What?" I demanded. "Dumb it down for me, will you? Simplest terms possible would be preferable. Supply *good* or supply *bad*?"

Veruca rolled her eyes.

"Supply *bad*," she said, imitating me.

"Ah, shit, that's what I was afraid you meant," I said. "Ain't nothin' like bein' in resource poverty. Fortunately for you lot, I grew up *super* poor, so I know how to stretch a pizza roll or two. Might have to cut our blankets in half, as well . . ."

While I contemplated that, Saban pushed forward with a tired sigh.

"I don't want to pile on with additional complications—for one, I think the way you organize your mind like that is pretty impressive, Rua. But, as far as the shelters go, it's not like we've had an easy time building basic huts, let alone something that would withstand the brunt of a stiff cold front. Between the relentless attacks and a severe lack of architectural knowledge, we're barely scraping by."

He pinched the corner of his eyebrow again before continuing.

"And then there's Alpha. That mother—*guy* won't let us deviate from his grand plan until the walls are completed. At this point, if nothing changes, it might not matter if we come up with the perfect solution. Our hands'll be tied."

There was a silence that hung in the room, as cold and uncomfortable as the weather we were ill prepared for. The fun and games we were enjoying moments before now seemed absurdly distant.

I scowled.

"I don't like that," I said quietly.

"None of us do," Saban agreed. "But what can be done? Like it or not, he's got us sorta locked down because of the Settlement Stone."

"What *is* the deal with that thing, anyway?" I asked. "I mean, I picked up a little from the bit that I learned when I came back. Basically, any travel outside the established boundaries of . . . *New Home* without the express written consent of Major League Slimeball is prohibited? What happens if we try? Does anyone know?"

"I was out hunting with Dragoon and León a few days ago," Rua said. "Our territory is actually pretty big out here. Like, *way* bigger than you'd think, really. But I guess I must've stepped out too far from the boundary or something, because I suddenly felt, like, a jolt of electricity shoot up my spine. I didn't know that's what it was, so I pushed forward, and then I got a message that I'd violated the terms of our 'Settlement Leader's' contract and I was zapped back here."

"Yeah, we thought she'd gotten lost—which seemed out of character," Dragoon agreed. "It really inconvenienced us because we wasted time looking around for her."

"I apologized already," Rua said sheepishly.

"I'm not saying you need to," Dragoon said. "My irritation isn't with you, Rua—rest easy. It's on the stupid fucking rules that Alpha has in place."

"So, we're all in agreement that he sucks?" Matt asked, shifting his position excitedly. "Finally! I felt like I was the only one who couldn't stand him!"

"Easy," Saban said, glancing from Matt to the flap of the tent. "Let's not *go that far.*"

He'd jerked his head in time with the last three words for emphasis, implying clear mistrust for who might overhear.

"Oh, shit—right," Matt said, then louder, he said, "I'm just kidding, of course! We love Alpha. He's the best!"

"That'll throw someone off the trail," I murmured.

"You think so?" Matt whispered back.

"Definitely," I said, then louder, I said, "Fuck Alpha!"

Everyone glared at me.

"What?" I asked, looking around at the group. "The *least* believable thing would be if I suddenly started being sweet on him. Man, y'all are terrible at cloak-and-dagger."

"If I could have the floor for a moment," Rexen suddenly said, floating into the center of the tent so that everyone could see him clearly.

"Arjee, what are you— Ah, there he goes . . ." I said, then threw a hand up in defeat. "Do your thing, I guess."

"What's up, Rex?" Matt asked.

"For those of you unfamiliar," he began, "I am Rexen Noodlemancer Gravetongue, the Dreadnaught Lord and—"

"Yeah, we all know who you are," I said. "Move it along, Arjee."

Rexen scowled at me.

"I will apologize for my pupil, he's—as we sometimes say—a bit of a rudey-poodey puddle pants. It is not his fault, however, as he is touched in the head—"

"If you don't get to the point, I'm going to donate your effigy to the Tartarus Foundation for Higher Learning—then you'll be stuck with *him*."

Rexen's eyes grew wide.

"My disciple would never—"

"Your disciple *would*," I said. "Now fuckin' spit it out."

He sighed.

"I was only meaning to set the stage, naughty apprentice o' mine, but—*but*," he started, seeing me preparing to stand, "I shall make a valiant effort at bein' quick about it—to not tarnish my wonderful pupil's generous mood."

He cleared his throat—a pointless gesture, but, hey, I guess I could let him have it.

"I can help with your situation," he said simply.

"And which situation would that be?" I wondered. "The Alpha one? Or the coming cold front?"

"Yep!" he said.

"I'm sorry, Mr. Gravetongue," Dragoon said. "But you're going to have to be a little clearer—your incoherent way of speaking is pretty vague. I don't know about everyone else, but *I'm* going to need something other than what you've offered so far. Details, not declarations."

I chuckled at Dragoon's directness. Rexen looked offended. The spirit's mouth fell open, and he looked at me as if hoping I would defend him. I just shrugged. It wasn't anything I hadn't said to him a million times, but for some reason, when the no-nonsense human had confronted him about his communication style, it dug in to him.

Good.

"What do you know about the—" Rexen began, but Dragoon interrupted him again.

"Nope. None of that. You know we're unfamiliar with nearly everything here. Just tell us how you can help or sit down."

Rexen turned back to me again.

"Pupil, I do not like this human," he said. "He is despicable—and does not respect the powerful and elderly."

"You're talkin' to the wrong guy, Arjee," I said, laughing. "I'm warming up to him more and more as this conversation goes on."

Rexen made a sound like he was grumbling with a throat full of glass but then turned back to the expectant eyes in the tent.

"Prosperity Conduit," Rexen said simply.

"And what exactly is that?" Veruca asked.

"Well, why don't you ask your disrespectful chum here, eh?" Rexen muttered grumpily while gesturing at Dragoon. "Boy with all the answers . . ."

"How about you stop bein' a little baby and tell us yourself, Arjee?" I said.

"Pah!" Edwig exclaimed. "I can tell you what a Prosperity Conduit is. And, as an added bonus, I'm not going to try and get you to guess anything."

Everyone in the tent whooped and cheered at that comment, leaving Rexen looking even more dejected than he already was.

"Out with it," I said. "Before Arjee decides to recover from this minor setback and launch into a long story about fighting a flaming turtle demon or something."

"Prosperity Conduits are a myth," Edwig said matter-of-factly.

Everyone stopped celebrating immediately. The air went out of the place.

"Aw, man," Matt said. "Really? That's a letdown."

"You really know how to murder the team spirit, Edwig," Rua said, shaking her head.

"Pah! It's not my fault!" the illisinaf said defensively. "The ghost was the one who—"

"Yeah, but you really should have just told us it was a myth before the suspense; now you just look like you were doing the same thing Rexen was," Saban said.

"Great goin', Jigglepuss," I said. "You ruined the party."

". . . they're *not* myths . . ."

The statement was said so quietly, it was hard to hear. Still, it had an effect on the inside of the tent enough to quiet everyone.

"Whadja say, Arjee?" I asked.

"I said . . ." he began, sticking his chest out as he continued lording over the whole assembly. "They're. Not. Myths."

"I don't have time for this," Dragoon said, and stood, walking toward the tent flap. But when Rexen raised his hand, he stopped.

"I'm. Not. Done. Speaking."

Each word was delivered with a venomous intensity, and I couldn't be sure, but I'm nearly positive I saw a flutter of air move around the room, ruffling people's hair and clothing. However, when all was quiet, Rexen's typical lackadaisical air returned.

"If you want to kill two dantaloth with a single pedjibork tooth, then listen up, insolents," he said. "I'm going to parcel out some juicy knowledge to you, so be attentive to the glorious words tumbling from my cutie-pie mouth."

I cringed.

"Just say what you're going to say, Arjee, and save your . . . anatomical description for a different audience."

"Ah, pupil, ever impatient," he said, tutting again. "Very well. Where were we? Ah! Yes! Prosperity Conduits. They are very real. However, to fully appreciate their nature, you must first grasp their concept."

"Pah!" Edwig interjected, rolling his eyes. "They're myths, as I said! Listen to him prattle on, not saying anything substantial. Shameless."

Rexen chose to ignore the comment and carried on.

"In our realm, the Prosperity Conduit can be best described as a . . . boon for a settlement. A sanctuary catalyst, a talisman of growin' big and strong."

"Sanctuary catalyst?" Veruca echoed, her brows furrowing. "You're saying it's . . . something that improves a settlement?"

When it came to flowery, enigmatic words, she was the resident expert.

"Precisely! What a whip you are! I should have chosen *you* as my disciple!" Rexen gloated, his spectral eyes twinkling with delight. "The Prosperity Conduit, once activated, imbues a settlement with an overwhelming aura of protection and fortune. It fosters growth and wards off disaster, a . . . Let's call it a *prosperity amplifier*. Ooh! I love that term! Wow, I'm great at this."

A murmur of intrigue rose among the group. The concept was indeed enticing—a single object that could solve all our problems of food scarcity and harsh winters.

"Okay," Dragoon said, skepticism etched onto his face. "So, supposing this is real. How does it work? And don't just say 'Arcana.'"

"Well, sonny boy," Rexen began, "it has the power to energize! Supersize! Catalyze bountiful harvests, warming the land to shield against the biting cold, and even thwart off lower-level nasty predators and pests. It is a benefit to any little patch of land fortunate enough to possess it. Yep, yep, yep!"

He paused for effect, allowing the group to digest this revelation. Eyes darted to one another, whispers were shared, and even Dragoon seemed less skeptical.

"An amplifier of prosperity, huh," Saban murmured, his gaze distant. "The crops could benefit, and no more freezing in the winter . . . sounds like a dream."

"Sounds like a fuckin' hassle, is what it does," I said. "And what's the catch? Need to sell our kidneys or something? Maybe loan out our souls?"

There was always a catch.

"What do you mean, Loon?" Rua asked.

"Well, such a perfect fuckin' miraculous little bauble wouldn't just be lying around for any ol' dickhead to pick up, would it?" I continued. "Let me guess: it's guarded by some mystical, terrifying . . . what . . . dragon? Demon? Multi-headed hydra with botulism spikes and dicks for teeth?"

"No, no, no, silly," Rexen replied. "Indeed, my astute, remarkable pupil, you've hit the nail on the head—probably. But in the wrong direction. The Prosperity Conduit is, at this moment, possessed by an ancient sect."

"Ancient sect?" Rua asked, her voice a whisper. "Do you mean like an order or something?"

Rexen nodded.

"Yep! The Conduit is guarded by the stupid, zealous followers of a slumbering god—some tough customers! In an icky little dirt-cave temple buried deep within the Archon's Fingers."

I snorted.

"So, we need to play Indiana Jones, but instead of Nazis, we're up against a bunch of fuckin' wizard priests? Fabulous."

"What's the Archon's Fi—" Rua began to ask, but Edwig interrupted.

"A mountain range. All the way on the eastern side of Arlo. Second largest, only losing out to the Leviathan's Spine."

"The eastern side?" I asked. "But that's . . . like, *really* far away."

"Pah! That's an understatement, orc! It would take weeks to get there!"

The room fell silent as the implications of his words sank in. This wasn't just some hidden treasure; it was a guarded relic, sacred to an ancient god and his followers. Fucking sweet. And one on the other side of a super marathon to get to? Forget about it.

"Forget about it," I said. "That's just not a possibility. Assuming we were able to get there before winter—which we couldn't—if this thing is so well protected, how are a bunch of low-Level nobodies going to bypass an entire cult and . . . what? Steal this out from underneath them?"

"Pah! Speak for yourself, orc!" Edwig exclaimed. "I'm not low-Level!"

I didn't have time for this.

"Shut up, Edwig," I said. "Even if you're not, everyone else here is, and—actually, wait a fucking second—what Level are you?"

It was weird that he hadn't revealed that information to me yet. Especially if it was true.

"Twenty-six!"

"Wait . . . seriously?"

"Seriously, orc," Edwig said.

"Wow!" Rua said. "Edwig, that's amazing!"

"Oh . . ." he said, nearly bashfully. "It's, er, well, it's not *nothing*, but it's certainly nothing to be impressed over."

"It's also not *not* low-Level," I said, then, seeing his immediate need to rebuttal, hurriedly added, "insofar as this group is concerned, man. Jeez, calm your jiggly tits. That still won't be enough to fight off a whole host of fanatics under a mountain. We'll be chopped into granola the moment we try to enter."

"No, we won't," Rexen said, smirking.

I sighed.

"Alright," I said defeatedly. "I walked into that, then, I suppose. What's your ingenious plan, Arjee?"

"I know of an oversight," he continued. "A way in that circumvents the usual rules—a back door. We won't have anything to worry about, perfectly safe!"

"The Catholic loophole . . ." Matt said.

Veruca wrinkled her brow.

"That is a disgusting response to what the venerable Lord Rexen has just discussed."

"It *is*?" Rexen asked, his eyes wide with interest. "Explain why, please!"

"Nobody fucking say anything about that," I said. "Arjee."

I leveled my gaze at the spirit.

"You think this is something we can actually do?"

"Yes, apprentice, I do," he said, his cheery tone replaced by . . . was that conviction?

"Seems like a lot of work for something that's just going to keep our tootsies toasty in the frigid depths of winter."

"That is not its only function," Rexen said with a shrug. "But it is a function that would resolve your issue."

"Okay, fine," I said, then turned to the others. "You heard him. How does everyone feel about figuring out a way to . . . get there? To the . . ."

"Archon's Fingers," Rua assisted.

"That's the one," I said. "Man, how can anyone keep track of any of this stuff?"

"What about Alpha?" Matt asked. "He's not going to let anyone go anywhere until his stupid fence is built."

"Let me worry about Alpha," Saban said. "For the record: I like this idea. It's exciting. And, if nothing else, it beats the usual monotony we've been experiencing."

"What's the god's name?" Dragoon asked suddenly.

"Huh? Who gives a shit?" I said.

"I do," he said, giving me a stern look.

I shrugged and turned to Rexen. But the little witch ghost was staring back at Dragoon with a strange intensity. I looked back and forth between the two, trying to figure out what was going on.

"Well?" Dragoon said, raising an eyebrow at Rexen. "Name him, Dreadnaught Lord."

Rexen sighed.

"Shadranath."

"I'm coming," Dragoon said instantly.

"Wait . . . what did I miss?" I asked, still looking back and forth.

"Nothing at all, pupil m—" Rexen started, but Dragoon cut him off.

"What this little stink-starter has failed to tell any of us is that we are going to have to *kill* this slumbering god."

My blood pressure spiked right there.

"Wait, *what*? Kill a *god*? How could you know that?!"

But before I got an answer, Dragoon had swept out of the tent. The remaining members of this little adventure entourage just stared at Rexen expectantly. He watched Dragoon leave and then faced the room, a bright smile blossoming.

"Yep!" he said. "Shadranath must die! Going to have to end his life good! How fun!"

CHAPTER EIGHTEEN

THE GHOST VESSEL

Convincing Alpha that we should be allowed to leave was easier than we thought.

We'd decided that the best tactic was to feed into his one-track mind. Saban had asked to meet with him privately, but you know I had to be spying on this interaction. Since—other than Edwig, apparently—I had the highest Level in the camp, there was zero worry about being caught. So, I stalked along, dripping with shadowy sneaky-sneak juice, tailing Saban as he met Alpha near the outskirts of the camp. Then I shoved myself into some extremely uncomfortable bushes and watched as my childhood buddy put on his best convincing face. All with the intention of selling Alpha on the idea of sending a group out to retrieve something that was essentially an unknown variable.

"Listen," Saban said, after laying out the entire concept to the dwarf. "I have my reservations about this whole thing—sincerely, I do—but that ghost . . . man, it knows some shit. I don't trust it—not really—but I trust the information it has."

"Yeah?" Alpha wondered, scratching at his beard. "You think it's real?"

"I don't know," Saban said, and I watched as he mirrored Alpha's body language—man, this was some high-level manipulation I was watching. "But I know that the wall isn't going to be finished anytime soon with the level of labor we have here—I mean, Mason is our only real builder, right? Everyone else is just sort of . . . there."

"Yeah . . ." Alpha said. "Who'd have thought that limp-wristed—"

"It would definitely speed up the process, though," Saban interrupted, diplomatically keeping Alpha from continuing from his insufferably bigoted talking points. "Like, he was telling me about it . . . and I don't know, man . . ."

"What?" Alpha wondered.

"I think there's more that could be done with it than even this supposed 'Dreadnaught Lord' can even conceptualize."

I watched him twist the screw.

"I thought to myself, 'I'll bet Alpha can think of some ways to use this that he isn't even mentioning.'"

"Heh, yeah, I probably could," Alpha said, nodding. "Like . . . you say it'll keep us warm? Well, that's one step away from ensuring people *want* to stay! If they want to keep *staying warm*, they're going to be more likely to comply with all the other shit we'll need them to do."

"See! That's what I'm talking about, my guy," Saban lied. "You get it. And this was mentioned so casually, too! But I couldn't let it go, you know? It seemed like such a good opportunity. The ghost doesn't even know what kind of information he's sitting on."

It was impressive to me to see this side of Saban. He was absolutely, completely, one hundred percent bamboozling this shithead, and the guy had no idea. It was also interesting, because he talked . . . differently, when speaking to Alpha.

In front of Alpha, Saban had slipped effortlessly into a different version of himself. He played the part of the persuader, a voice of wisdom and reassurance, and he did it convincingly. The slight change in his accent, the reassuring word choices—they were subtly different from how he spoke when we were alone.

And the most impressive thing? Alpha didn't suspect a thing. He just nodded along, taking Saban's words at face value, oblivious to the skillful act playing out before him.

"Yeah . . . yeah, alright," Alpha said, nodding. "You think this is something that would help us?"

"It definitely wouldn't *hurt* us," Saban said with a shrug. "I think I can get a group together that would be perfect for this."

"And who are you thinking? That . . . uh . . . Rua . . . *person*, obviously," he said, as if he was now trying to make sure he didn't fuck something up with Saban by saying the wrong thing.

"I *was* thinking Rua, actually," Saban said. "Rua has that navigation Ability. It'll really cut down on the time spent searching if she's along for the ride. I was also thinking that Veruca should go, because—"

"Weird bitch?" Alpha interjected. "What? Why? She *sucks*."

"Because she's part of your inner circle now, isn't she? Or did I misread that?"

"Well . . ." Alpha said, and I could tell he didn't want to admit his loyalty metrics were lower than they actually were. "Yeah, I think she's coming around."

"That's what I was thinking," Saban said. "You've got to have people you can trust. So, then we should also send Dragoon."

"Huh?" Alpha asked. "Dragoon's not loyal to me."

"I think you might be surprised by that," Saban said. "He speaks pretty highly of you. Guy was a soldier in the previous world—not sure if you knew that. He appreciates someone who takes charge."

"I think I knew that . . ." Alpha said, nodding. "Yeah, it makes sense. He never really argues, just does what he's assigned."

"See? Good leadership is going to win him over," Saban continued.

I knew for a fact that this was all bullshit. Veruca *despised* Alpha—she hadn't been mysterious about that. I wasn't sure what Dragoon's deal was, but he definitely didn't strike me as the type to just fall into line. But I suppose whatever got Alpha to agree was worth the lie. Honestly, it was impressive how effortlessly Saban was able to drop in to this mode. He was a lot more conniving than I ever took him for. Back when we were kids, he'd *always* been the one to talk me out of a bad idea—and I assumed it was because he was always more interested in the greater good. Was that what he was doing now? Lying to push some greater good forth into our camp? Maybe. It had been years since we'd actually been friends, so it was just as possible that Saban had developed into someone that did whatever they needed to survive.

"Then, of course, the ghost needs to go—he's apparently the only one who knows how to open the secret passageway. Which means that Loon will have to—"

"No," Alpha said seriously. "Not him. I don't want to use any plan that involves him having the possibility to fuck shit up for us."

My heart jumped. Of course he wouldn't want me to go. That would be the stupidest thing on the planet to allow me free rein on this—and I didn't blame him. It wasn't a secret that I wanted that dude dead. How was Saban going to play this?

"Yeah . . ." Saban said. "No, I agree with you. He and I know each other from *before*, and he's basically going to be the biggest obstacle to this going properly. Loon's definitely out."

Um . . . *fucking* what?

That was it? I wasn't involved? Just like that. I was getting ready to leap out of the bushes and just kill Alpha, but then I stopped.

"The only reason I brought him up is because he's not really integral to the projects going on, right?" Saban said. "So, I was going to suggest . . . myself."

What the fuck? Himself? Was that his plan all along?

"You *want* to go?" Alpha asked, looking shocked. I felt like I probably had the same expression on my face right now that the dumbass dwarf did.

"No, not really," Saban said thoughtfully. "But it kind of has to be me, right? You can't go—obviously—since you have to be here at the camp. You could send Dalton, but then we'd have to find someone else to do the general management of the camp, right? I could do *that*, but that's less time I can spend on leading the wall construction. Which has to be priority number one."

"Right," Alpha said stupidly.

"That means you'll have to be in charge of *that*, probably. I don't think we can trust anyone else to do it."

Alpha seemed to balk at that.

"This is starting to sound like a lot of work," he said. "Can't we just have León or Branston go with them?"

León and Branston were two of his chums from our previous life. León was specced as some kind of hunter class that I didn't know for sure what it was called, and Branston was a straight-up tank. Big, strong, and, to be frank, not that bright. But they were Alpha's loyal lackeys. They wouldn't question him, which made them the perfect candidates for him.

"León or Branston *could* work, but there are issues with both of them," Saban pointed out. "León's skills are pretty indispensable when it comes to keeping us fed. He's the best hunter we have, and if he's gone on this expedition, who's going to fill that gap? Especially with Rua going along already."

Alpha scratched his beard, contemplating this. He seemed to be understanding the problem, which was good. One point to Saban.

"And Branston, well, Branston's the cornerstone of your defense line. Without him on the front line, anything could happen, and then what? We'd be inviting all kinds of threats."

Alpha frowned, clearly disliking this scenario.

"You have a point there. But then who?" he asked, frustration clear in his voice.

Saban, ever the diplomat, spread his hands in a gesture of peace.

"That's why I'm suggesting I go. It's a good fit, and I don't have any major tasks that can't be reassigned. Plus, I can guarantee to you that I'll get this job done. You know you can trust me. It'll probably make the wall project take a bit longer, but, considering this long shot, we *should* be back in time to ensure that's not a worry."

"Should?" Alpha echoed him.

"Well, yeah," Saban said, all smiles. "Without someone who can properly use stealth, apparently it's going to be an uphill battle."

He gestured at his armaments.

"I have a lot of confidence in my abilities, but ... that ain't one of 'em, you know? So, it'll be a little slower going. That's why, as much as I didn't like the prospect, I was initially suggesting Loon. He's got stealth, but he's also not vital to our rebuilding efforts. But, honestly, that's fine. He'd probably just get killed, anyway. You'll have to become more involved in his day-to-day since I'll be gone, but—"

"Fuck, this is a headache," Alpha said, shaking his head. "I don't want to deal with that fucking moron any more than I already have to—it's bad enough when you're able to talk some sense into him."

He sighed.

"If he gets killed, he gets killed, so . . . sure, send him. You'll stay, though—I need the wall completed."

"You're sure?" Saban asked, feigning concern. "I don't mind going if—"

"I'm sure," Alpha said. "This whole thing sounds like it's just going to be a death march anyways—so, if they fail . . . meh, fuckin' . . . whatever. Our current plans are what's important."

"Alright . . ." Saban said, not sounding entirely convinced, but there was something about his expression that made me think this was *exactly* what he planned to have go down.

"I'll go tell them," Alpha said, preparing to leave.

"Actually," Saban said quickly. "It'll sound better coming from me, I think. Loon trusts me, so if I am the one to bring it up, he'll be much more likely to go along with it. You show up, and—let's be honest—it'll probably turn into an argument."

Alpha seemed to pause for a second, chewing over Saban's suggestion.

"Yeah . . . alright," he agreed, scratching at his beard. "You go ahead and tell them."

"Thanks, Alpha. I appreciate it," Saban said with a nod, before Alpha turned and started heading back toward the camp.

As I watched them part ways, I felt a strange whirlwind of thoughts and emotions. Saban had managed to change the game *entirely*.

Seeing him in action was enlightening, to say the least. Not only had he convinced Alpha that sending me on this fucked-up cannonball run was the best course of action, he'd also managed to spin it in a way that placed me as a dispensable asset, a low-risk sacrifice. He managed to plant his own ideas into Alpha's head, and allowed Alpha to feel like he was the one making the decisions. It was a delicate balancing act of power and control, one that Saban was clearly experienced in navigating. It was like a masterclass.

Looking back at Saban as he walked away from Alpha, I couldn't help but feel a sense of pride. Sure, he had been a good friend years before—my best friend, in fact, and I had always known he was smart. But seeing him now, adapting and thriving in this new reality, made me realize just how much he had changed and how far he'd come.

But there was another part of me that found all of that a little unsettling. I had to wonder how much I'd actually missed before arriving. It was a little scary. Was he really batting for my side, or was this all part of some larger game?

Congratulations! You've raised a Skill!
***Insight* has advanced to E-Rank Level 7!**

"Just think," Rexen crowed, his eyes glinting with delight, "a single touch of a quill. A quick prick-prick-prick, then whammy-bammy—total paralysis! Wonderful! You're stuck watching dinner preparations unfold, and then . . . you're the main course!"

The Dreadnaught Lord was elbow-deep in one of his favorite topics: terrible ways to die in the wilderness. This time, the leading role was played by something called a "spinecrawler," a bad bitch of a beast that sounded as if it was half poisonous spike, half fury. Honestly, I never had any fuckin' idea if he was making all of these fantastical creatures up or if they were actually part of the absurd lore of this funny farm—but the tales were usually enough to keep the mood interesting.

While Rexen was clearly having a blast, the rest of us were subjected to a unique blend of baffled captivation as he rattled off increasingly worrisome scenarios that ultimately always ended up in what the little witch ghost considered the most alarming consequence possible: not being able to eat the meal that you had prepared. Matt's grumbling served as a soundtrack to Rexen's grim fairytale, muttering that he'd "rather face a spinecrawler than be stuck here." He wouldn't be going on our trek—a fact he was still coming to terms with. Saban, ever the voice of reason, patted him on the shoulder, assuring him that there was plenty of intensive, mind-numbing labor to keep his mind off of it while we were away.

"This . . . uh, spiney thing sounds really awful," Tanner said. He'd joined us around our makeshift going-away midafternoon drinks—which were mostly some kind of root tea that Jando had brewed.

"It *was* awful!" Rexen beamed. "Awful *fun* to tear to shreds when I encountered one in the Drelegar Mines back in five-fifty-three—oh! Or was it sixty-seven? Never mind! Ate well for weeks on that haul! They know what I'm talking about!"

That last comment was directed at Jumpy, Clucky, Slappy, and Mortimer, who were lazing near a cook fire, apparently not huge fans of the chillier and chillier weather we'd been having. None of them looked up at his words, so Rexen just shrugged and went back to regaling whoever would listen with his long, drawn-out story of heroic deeds. Dragoon, who I'd learned had some mysterious Class

Quest involving the god we were supposed to be killing, was busy readying his crossbow dutifully, examining each section with a trained eye, almost like he'd been doing so his whole life. I wasn't sure about the particulars of his Quest but, hey, not everyone needed to share everything all the time.

Rua and Edwig were discussing something super important to the side in barely contained whispers, and I could only catch snippets.

"... the potency of the Spell is determined by the concentration of the runic symbols, but you also need a proper vessel for containment—"

Rua cut in, her brow furrowing in thought.

"But wouldn't that mean that smaller, more-condensed symbols carry a higher risk of potential backfire?"

Edwig's eyes widened slightly, his mouth opening and closing for a moment before he managed to find his voice.

"Well, I . . . er . . . That's a very astute observation, Rua," he stammered. "I suppose, in theory, that would indeed be the case . . ."

"Interesting," Rua mused, a glint of understanding lighting up her eyes. "And how about the element of time in the casting process? Does it impact the effectiveness of the Spell, or is it just about the caster's skill and stamina?"

Edwig blinked.

"Time . . . I suppose, yes, it would affect . . . I hadn't considered . . ."

His voice trailed off as he seemed lost in thought, puffing out his . . . cheeks as he mulled over the question.

"What are the two of you discussing so conspiratorially?" Veruca asked, seeming to have zeroed in on the conversation right when I had.

Edwig startled, looking up to find Veruca peering at him and Rua with intense interest.

"We're discussing the intricacies of the ward and alarm system," he admitted, gesturing towards the many circles of arcane symbols inscribed around the camp's perimeter.

"Oh, uh, yes, the ones . . . Ava used to safeguard the camp," Rua chimed in, her eyes never leaving the wards in the distance. "The way she layered the spells . . . It's a marvel, really. Almost an art."

"If your curiosity has gotten the better of you," Veruca wondered, "why not just ask the designer herself? I am sure she would be more than happy to divulge the intricacies of something she clearly put effort into."

Rua's ears turned a deep shade of red and she spluttered.

"I . . . I just . . . I mean, I just wanted to have a more comprehensive understanding before . . ." She trailed off, crossing her arms defensively.

Before she makes a fool of herself in front of Ava? I thought. Man, I was really starting to pick up on some of these previously invisible social cues that everyone was always telling me about. The unspoken sentiment hung in the air, and Veruca chuckled, raising her hands in surrender.

"I think I understand. You are simply trying to impress the Green Mage, is it?" She winked at Rua, who, if possible, turned an even darker shade of red. "Do not worry over it; your secret lies safe with me."

Edwig cleared his throat uncomfortably, seemingly wishing he could vanish into the ground. Rua, likely hoping to divert some of the attention on herself, turned back to the illisinaf, lacing her fingers together over her knee in a look that was probably meant to be casual but looked very uncomfortable.

"So . . . uh, what happens if the containment vessel is destroyed?"

"Pah! Then you need to get yourself a better arcanist!" Edwig said.

I snickered at that.

"Wish we could offload Mr. Quintham for a nicer, newer version."

"What was that, orc?" Edwig asked.

"Oh, *nothing*," I said—see, even though it *was* something.

Edwig just scowled suspiciously but turned back to Rua.

"If a vessel becomes compromised, it ruins the whole ritual—so, don't let that happen. The vessel should be something hard to shatter—or, barring that, hard to find. Of course, some people don't know any better—like that blasted *Jeremy*—one of my associates from Yosper Hall. Have I told you about him? He was always tying his wards to dandelions—which I don't think I need to tell you are precisely the opposite of sturdy . . ."

I sighed and walked away. That was some shit *way* beyond what I'd ever need to know. So, I left them to it and moved to stand near Dragoon. The stoic human was scanning the landscape around the camp with a critical eye—though I noticed he was still sipping his tea.

"Spot anything interesting?" I wondered, moving to stare out in the direction he was.

Yep, that there's a forest. Wait! Nope, still forest. But I'm on to you, forest . . .

Dragoon had an Ability called Farsight, which allowed him to see into the distance . . . but, like, really good. I didn't know what it looked like to his eyes, but he'd called it his "yeet scope" a few times, so I envisioned it kind of like a sniper rifle's view.

"Probably not," he responded to me. "Thought there was some movement out there, but—"

He instantly tensed and lifted his crossbow.

"What?!" I shouted, alerting Saban to the disturbance. The Champion had his fuckin' huge hammer in his hands almost as quickly as Dragoon had armed himself.

"Someone's—" Dragoon started, but, before he could finish, a sudden shout sliced through the camp from the guards patrolling.

"Riders approaching!" There was a pause. "... I think!"

The change in mood was almost cartoonish. One moment, we were relaxed, making our *very* slow preparations for our journey. The next we were armed and ready, our eyes glued to the horizon.

And yet . . . nothing. No rumble of hoofbeats, no snorting beasts, no clash of metal on leather. Instead, we got . . . a carriage. A solitary, beastless carriage, skimming over the tall grass as if it was powered by the sheer absurdity of its own presence.

The carriage halted at a distance, just shy of our half-built wall looking like a child's toy left out in the yard. The wooden box on wheels was so bizarrely out of place, it was hard to take it seriously as a threat.

I squinted at the now-motionless carriage, half-expecting a troupe of clowns to tumble out and ask for directions to the nearest circus. Though, despite the strangeness—or maybe *because* of it—there was something unsettling about its silent appearance. What sort of bad punchline was this about to be?

So, rather than what we should have done—which was light that motherfucker up like the fourth of July . . . we waited, tensions high.

Suddenly, the carriage door swung open, and a compact figure stepped out, his height barely hitting the four-foot mark and crowned by a tuft of pale-blond hair that looked as though it had been styled by a lightning strike.

"Wait a fuck . . ." I said, realization hitting me.

It was *Garth*. The very same nisen who'd hitched a ride from Down Under to Regaia that I'd met in the magically constructed sanctuary inside the belly of the oomukade queen. How's that for scope? He was currently giving us a grin wide enough to outshine the sun and tossing us a jaunty wave of his hand.

"G'day!" Garth greeted, looking around at our camp with a critical eye. "Nice little setup you've got here. Been usin' a cyclone for home improvement or what?"

He made a show of stretching, twisting his back with his hands on his hips.

"Strewth, that trip was a long 'un! Point me to the dunny, would ya? Need a piss and a punt on the pokies after a ride like that."

He paused, looking up at the silent group of Sojourners observing his display.

". . . You lot *do* know you're a fair crack of the whip away from anything even whiffing of civilization, right? Seems a bit rude, is all."

"Garth?" Rua asked, the only person to vocalize anything remotely resembling words.

Garth's eyes spotted Rua amidst the crowd and lit up.

"Rua! Stonking good to see you!" he exclaimed, bounding over to her. "You remember me, yeah? Can't imagine I'm an easy one to forget—though, funny enough, that didn't stop my mum from leaving me at the shops a time or two. You might think she had her hands full with a tribe of ankle-biters, but nope! Only child, me! I forgive her, though—she's my mum, after all."

"Garth," I said, nodding by way of greeting.

"Well, aren't you a tall poppy? My great, spotty, grungy mate—you been growin'?"

"More and more powerful by the day," I said. "I see you haven't been getting any bigger."

Garth smirked.

"Oi, me? Reckon I'm just working on my horizontal growth. See, I'm thinking globally—wider reach, you know? Trying to blend in with the landscape, so to speak. But if you ever want to trade, just give a shout. I've always wondered what it's like to be a proper skyscraper, constantly bumping my head on low branches."

And the surprises just kept coming. Out from the carriage emerged another figure. Shorter than Garth and adorned with a shock of orange hair against blue skin, garbed in airy robes that were wildly unseasonable due to the chill. Hadowar—who I'd mostly known as Blue Yoda—the lead healer at the mending house, and the man I wouldn't have been shocked to discover had been to Earth once or twice. He simply nodded, his way of greeting.

Okay, calm down, heart. It's just a couple of friends. Or, at least, people we knew and didn't want to kill. It took some hollering and waving from myself and Rua, but the camp was eventually persuaded not to launch any arrows. I realized that these were likely—other than the child who'd blown me up—the only people outside of the camp they'd interacted with since arriving.

But wait, there's more.

Another figure emerged from the carriage, aiming for grace and achieving failure. He missed a step, stumbled, and landed ass-first in the dirt. A chorus of groans echoed from myself, Rua, and Edwig.

Of course. It would have to be him. Orville.

"Hi!" he called from the ground he was inexplicably not picking himself up from. "It's me, Orville!"

"Alright, guys," I said to the rest of the camp, "nobody freak out. These are just some buddies from town. Nobody attack them."

Then I looked over at Orville.

"Except him; you can attack him."

"Loon!" Rua snapped, then turned to the group. "Not him, either."

"Fine, fine," I grumbled.

"What are you doing here?" Rua said, turning to Garth and then nodding to Hadowar when he finally made his way to us. "Visiting?"

"Visiting? Somethin' like that," Garth said with a shrug. "Truth be told, we got the call up, but I was keen as mustard to get a squiz at your digs anyway. Still stumped why you'd choose to set up shop in the scrub, but eh, who am I to judge? I once had a crack at wrangling a saltie for a meat pie."

"We were summoned!" Orvile piped happily, joining the rest of us.

Garth rolled his eyes.

"Correction, mate: Hadowar and *I* were summoned. You just wedged yourself in the wagon before we could knock back your tag-along scheme."

By now, the entire camp was filled with wide eyes and a multitude of questions. But I cut through all the noise with my usual keen-edged diplomacy.

"Summoned? Who the fuck summoned you?"

"Pah! I did!" Edwig said.

"How?" I asked.

"I have my ways, orc," he continued. "If I took the time to explain every—"

"He used a Sending Rod," Orville said with a smile.

"Pah! Ingrate!" Edwig said. "Let an illisinaf have some dignity, will you?"

"For fuck's sake, mate," Garth said, shaking his head at Orville. "That's the last time we let you in on the secret handshake. Looser lips than a sparky on the piss."

"So . . . a Sending Rod . . ." Rua asked. "Is that like a wand—but instead of Spells, it shoots messages?"

"Well, blow me down!" Garth said, gasping with mock surprise. "Give her half a clue and she's cracked the case wide open! Good on ya, Rua. Impressive."

"Have you had one of those the whole time?" Saban asked Edwig.

The illisinaf shrugged.

"Maybe I have," he said. "Pah! Why do you want to know?"

"Maybe he was thinkin' to ring his gran, Eddy," Garth said. "Blimey, when'd you become so hush-hush? A bit more mateship would sort that out quick-smart!"

"I've got plenty of friends," Edwig said. Then he whipped to face Garth abruptly. "Did you bring the item I requested?!"

Garth chuckled, patting Edwig on the . . . shoulder area.

"Steady on, mate—no need to get your knickers in a twist. I've got the bloody thing right here with me. Keep your hair on."

Garth nodded to Hadowar, who reached into his robes and produced a circle of gold.

"Mate, you could have given us a heads-up about how tricky that thing was to get hold of," Garth continued, taking the shining object from the blue-skinned man and handing it over to Edwig. "Didn't exactly fall into our laps, now, did it? Ended up having to use Orville here—snuck in and out without a soul noticing. Not that we'd want to remember him afterwards. But here we are, stuck with him, aren't we? Proves the point about no good deed, I reckon."

"I'm very good at hiding," Orville said—in what I had to imagine he thought of as his catchphrase.

"What am I missing here?" I asked. "What's with the jewelry?"

"Yeah . . ." Saban said. "I'll be honest: secret magical artifacts aren't the best—"

"SHINY!" Rexen screamed, breaking into the center of our gathering; eyes wide and his face full of lust.

"Whoa! Whoa!" I warned. "Easy there, you little treasure goblin. What's got you all fired up?"

"The shiny!" Rexen said, pointing a handless arm at the golden trinket in Edwig's own handless appendages. "I want it! Disciple, retrieve it for me."

"Yeah, I don't think I'm going to be convinced into stealing from my allies," I said. "Nice try, though. Maybe if you ask nicely, Edwig will let you gaze lovingly at it from afar."

Rexen pivoted in the air, giving Edwig pleading, spirally puppy-dog eyes.

"Pah! This belongs to me, ghost!"

"Ooh! But ally mine . . ." Rexen moaned. "It is so shiny and juicy! Can I have but a glimpse?"

Edwig scowled then, seeming to contemplate the suggestion. Then he held it out to show Rexen—keeping a strong grip on it as though he was worried the spirit would tear it out of his grasp the moment he had an opportunity. Which, knowing Arjee, was probably a safe bet.

"Ooooooooh!" Rexen cooed, as if he was a teenager seeing his first boob. "Very nice! This is lovely! Can I have it?"

"Pah! No!" Edwig said, clutching the ring of gold to his chest.

"What. The fuck. Is it?" I demanded, pushing Rexen out of the way.

"None of your—"

"A Stowaway Charm!" Rexen cried.

"Huh?" I grunted. "Stowaway Charm? The fuck is that?"

I turned to Edwig.

"Is he making that up, or is that what it's actually called?"

"Pah . . ." Edwig exclaimed defeatedly. "That's what it's called."

"Fuck me dead, everyone's a tongue-waggler in this joint," Garth said. "Orville, mate—you'll fit right in, no worries!"

"I knew everyone would come around eventually," Orville beamed.

"Can we just hop over all the banter and have someone explain what this motherfucking thing does?" I asked, looking around at the group.

I was met with blank silence. I sighed. Then I turned to Rexen.

"What is this mabob, and why are we spending so much time talking about it?"

Rexen floated up, clearing his throat as if ready to give a speech to the masses at his inaugural address.

"Pupil, it is simple," he said. "The Stowaway Charm exists much like the Feather Chest. Except instead of storing items—"

He began pointing at the various members of the gathering.

"—it stores *people!*"

I was taken aback.

"Like . . . slavery?!" I turned on Edwig in an instant. "What the hell, dude? You trafficking now? Not cool!"

"I most certainly am *not!*" he said, clearly offended by the notion—which was a plus. Then he released a frustrated sound made entirely out of contempt. "It's an arcane object designed to store precisely *one* individual. In this instance, that would be *me*."

"You're . . . uh, gonna stuff yourself in there? Why?"

"Because . . . reasons!" He shouted. "You'll see why when we get on the road."

"Well, damn," I said. "You would have saved a lot of hassle if you'd just said that from jump, home slice. God, it's like you motherfuckers are trying to be obtuse on purpose."

"So . . ." Rua said, trying to steer the conversation back to . . . I dunno, something normal, I guess. "Why were you summoned?"

"We are to take you . . . part of the way," Hadowar said, indicating the carriage with a languid gesture.

"Oi, mates. We're tryin' to keep this on the down-low, yeah? You keen on spillin' the whole can of worms for all the stickybeaks to see?"

"Garth, I don't know what that means," I said. "But I think that whatever you guys want to do, I'm too tired to even . . ."

I trailed off. I'd noticed something.

My attention was torn away from the ongoing kerfuffle by a glint at the corner of my vision, a slight aberration in the forested monotone around us highlighted by the sun. A small, rectangular sliver of dark plastic and metal nestled snugly between the sprawling roots of one of the trees.

I moved forward, leaving the bickering behind me as I approached the shape. As I got closer, I was pretty sure my suspicions were confirmed. It was covered in a fine layer of dirt and leaf debris, as if it had been lying there unnoticed for quite some time. A smartphone.

What the hell? I thought.

I mean, I'd known that things had come over from the other world—there was a huge one sitting on the edge of the camp, for god's sake. But they'd been extremely random: books, Veruca's coat, a shoe that no one knew who it belonged to—still, not a single person had found something so technologically advanced, as far as I knew.

"Ha! This is wild," I said to myself, now far enough from the others that they would have no idea what I was up to.

I wasn't a dick, though; I'd obviously let someone know I'd found it. Not like it would do much good, though—no electricity, no way to charge it. And it had been *months* . . . I think. That thing would be dead as fuck. I brushed off the dirt and grime.

Still, this might be meaningful to whoever . . .

Shock stabbed through me as I stared in confusion. The chipped corners. The partially torn-away Trivium sticker on the back. This wasn't just *a* phone. This was *my* phone. It was just . . . lying incongruously among the wood and soil as if it had sprouted there naturally. I had last seen it on the train, moments before the blue magic derailment that catapulted me into this world. In the ensuing chaos and subsequent struggle to survive, the phone had been forgotten, a meaningless accessory rendered obsolete by my new, ridiculous circumstances.

Yet here it was. Quietly persistent, a techno-ghost from the past hidden in plain sight.

A sudden, searing pang of nostalgia struck me. The incongruity of its presence there in this world made me suddenly aware of the jarring transition I had made. My fingers itched to grab it, to pick it up to confirm its reality. But instead, I found myself frozen, ensnared by a surge of conflicting emotional gumbo.

The irony was not lost on me. I was in a world of arcane spells and mythical beings, staring at what was—so far as the people of this world would know—a piece of space-age technology, gawking at it as if it was a precious talisman. In the light of everything that had happened, the sight of my phone was a startling anachronism.

Finding my mental foothold, I slowly reached out, half-expecting the device to dissolve at my touch like a fucking mirage. But it was solid and real, cold from the chilled earth. I picked it up, and my heart sank. A jagged fracture splintered the screen diagonally, from the top left to the bottom right corner, and a substantial chunk of glass was missing entirely.

Ah . . . well, damn. That's a shame.

I turned it over in my hand, feeling the familiar weight, the cold, hard edges of the device that had once been a constant presence in my life. It contained a universe within itself, a universe that I could no longer access.

Pictures, videos, forgotten text messages, endless albums of saved memes, all trapped behind the shattered screen. The screen that once illuminated my face in the darkness now seemed to mock me, its opaque black surface a barrier.

There was a kind of sad poetry in it. The kinda shit someone with way more thoughtfulness than I had would write about. The broken phone, my reflection in the broken black glass, indicating the shattered life I left behind.

Listen, I'm not much for introspection, but this seemed like something *someone* would find cathartic.

And yet there was also a strange comfort in holding it. For complex reasons I didn't have the words to explain. But I did have *some* words.

"Ah, fuck—I had so much music on here! Dammit . . ."

I sighed.

Then, looking over my shoulder—you know, like secret agents do—I palmed the device, tucking it into a secure corner of my rucksack. The rest of the group was still bickering, unaware of the quiet emotional upheaval I'd just experienced.

"Everything alright, Loon?" Rua asked, as I returned.

"Me?" I asked, clearing my throat. "Yeah . . . why? Did Arjee say something insane? What a rube."

"No, I just noticed—"

"Great!" I said, clapping once. "So . . . we taking this fucking carriage or not? Time's a-wastin', ya turkeys!"

CHAPTER NINETEEN

GUTBUCKET BLUES

We were about four hours away from New Home when the carriage suddenly stopped. Nothing but woods all around us, and we were just stalled. The trip so far had been a bit bumpy but a hell of a lot faster than walking. The carriage had been coasting along at what had to be at least ten miles an hour—by my rough estimation. Now it was going *no* miles per hour.

"What the hell's going on?" I called down from my position atop the carriage. I peeped over the edge to survey the scene. All I got in return was a bag of shrugs through the small window in the side of the vehicle.

Dragoon, the egg boys, Rexen and I had been riding on top of the carriage—there wasn't enough room to fit us all. So, we clambered down, with Jumpy, Clucky, Slappy and Mortimer irritated because they'd been having fun.

Stopped. No good. Why no moving? Slappy!

From within our magical steed tumbled the crew: Veruca, Garth, Rua, Hadowar, and Orville. Each squinted, trying to make sense of the abrupt halt. Rua was already anxiously clutching her sword, while Orville just seemed disoriented, like we'd plucked him from the middle of a dream.

"Didn't smear some poor critter on the road, did we?" Garth asked. "This is a loaner. If that keeps happening, they're gonna rip my ticket."

"Doesn't appear to be . . ." Dragoon said, looking around the base of the carriage, then he looked up at Garth. "You need a license for these things?"

"Reckon usually, yeah," Garth said. "But to be honest, didn't really bother with that. Seemed like a bloody fuss, know what I mean? Found this beast parked near the pub and took matters into my own hands—thought I'd just wait to cop it sweet later."

"Are you saying we have been driving around in a stolen vehicle?" Veruca asked incredulously.

"Well, can't be exactly nicked if they left it idling with the keys inside, can it? I just borrowed it, reckoned it could do with a bit of a spin," Garth returned with a roguish grin.

"Yeah," I said. "You're like a really slow valet. Anyway, if we didn't hit something, then what's the deal?"

"Yeah, we should really figure out why we stopped," Rua said, her eyes still scanning the area for signs of danger. "If fantasy books have taught me anything, it's that this is about the time bandits will leap out of the trees and attack."

Shit. That was a good point.

Silence fell as we fanned out, our eyes and ears on high alert. The fucking magical engine or whatever made this bitch go, formerly a hum of arcane energy, was now as quiet as the untouched woods around us. It was one of those moments where your heart's pounding but you're not quite sure why.

As it turned out, we didn't have to wait long for an answer. Edwig, with all the gravitas of a spilled bowl of pudding, finally slopped out of the carriage and let out a sigh.

"I'm the one who stopped us. Needed a bit of breathing room."

"Mate, you nabbed the key from me?" Garth asked, but he sounded impressed. "Bang on—that's a quiet pickpocketer on you."

"What do you need breathing room for?" Dragoon asked. "A Spell?"

"Something like that," Edwig said, and simply continued forward. When he was about ten feet away from us, he lifted the golden circle he'd gotten from Garth and held it up so that the sun's light caught it. Then he started chanting.

"Yo, what the fuck are you doing?" I called, marching forward, but Rexen stopped me.

"He needs *space*, pupil! By all means, run toward the shiny—I have been wanting to this whole time! But if you do, you'll be sucked up with him."

I slammed on the brakes real fast at that.

"He's going in there *now*? What am I missing?"

"We're almost to Tallrock," Rua said with a shrug. "It makes sense to do it beforehand."

"No, we're . . . not!" I gasped. "It took us two days to . . ."

Well, guess which motherfucker just realized that walking speed and carriage speed resulted in *drastically* different outcomes? *This* motherfucker.

"Oh, uh, never mind," I said. "But aren't we driving all the way to the goddamn mountains? Archie's Fingers, or whatever? Who cares about Tallrock?"

"You won't be taking the carriage all the way to the east," Hadowar said. "You will be traveling through a Gateway once we get back."

"A portal?" Rua exclaimed, as if she couldn't believe her luck. "Aw, yeah! Right *on*!"

She started punching the air triumphantly.

"The hell? Nobody thought to mention it to us?" I asked. "Listen, I've got some reservations about portals, so—"

"Ooh! A Gateway! I haven't been through one in some time!" Rexen said. "I think the last time, one of my party members was ripped in half because he got his Spell incorrect during the transport. Nasty, *nasty* way to go!"

"Yeah, that's not easing my flight anxiety one bit," I said. "But why the secretive reveal?"

"It was assumed, based on Edwig's message, that you believe you are being watched," Hadowar said. "We thought it best to reveal as little as possible while you were in the camp. You can never be certain who is listening there. Why make it easy for them to track your movements?"

"Edwig said that?" I wondered.

Huh. I guess at least one person was listening to my tinfoil.

"I have never encountered a Gateway before," Veruca said. "Is there something specific we should perform or remember in order to complete a smooth transition?"

"No worries, mate," Garth dismissed. "They've got some whippersnapper Spell-throwers in the Order who'll sort out all the nitty-gritty. You can just kick back and enjoy the run!"

The Order, eh? I wondered. *Guess I see now why Edwig's so anxious to get his ass in the bracelet.*

In the midst of our disarray, Edwig's low drone cut through, his voice an alien hum amidst the wilderness. Words tumbled forth, nearly at a whisper, with a level of harshness and trills that slowly became clear as I realized—he was using the arcane tongue. Which was fucking cool because that was actually one of the languages I'd picked up in the Crypt. Strangely enough, while the words themselves didn't really translate, I still understood the underlying message behind them. Which was weird and neat.

So, when he whispered, "Dru, kazhunori, kroska vess. Olzh va Snin, tanshir uu epar," I knew that, somehow, this roughly translated to "I, vessel of energy, bind in power. Sun and Moon, guide my passage."

So, he was . . . incanting? Is that a word? Let's go with it—improv, baby! As he incanted, each syllable conjured an almost-visible energy around him. A shaft of light descended from the golden ring, enveloping the illisinaf and casting his features into a jungle of shadows and illumination.

The arcane chanting trailed into silence, but the light lingered, a spectral halo that seemed to buzz in time with my pulse. Then, with his typical lack of ceremony, Edwig turned to address us.

"I'm gonna need a bit of a lift—someone's going to have to hold on to the charm."

Rua, with her hand ever on her sword, glanced at him.

"Got a preferred chauffeur?"

"Anyone but the orc," Edwig tossed off with a dismissive wave of his wriggly noodle arm. Then, as if as an afterthought, added, ". . . and the specter."

"Who died and made you fuckin' queen?" I sniped. "Also, are you able to get out of there on your own or do we have to let you out? Because you might want to be nicer if it's the latter, hombre."

Edwig considered this.

"Pah! Alright—suppose I don't want to let myself out too early and run into trouble. Right, when we get through the Gateway, the word to release me is *zhakko*."

Emerge, I thought. *Alright, I'll keep that in mind.*

"Eddy!" Garth shouted suddenly.

"Pah! What now? I'm in the middle of—"

"The flamin' key, mate! You're set to maroon us here if you nick off with it, ya drongo."

"Oh . . . er, yes," Edwig said, then from within his sweater vest the gelatinous creature procured a thin, bone-colored square of stone with a shimmering blue glyph embedded in the center. He lofted it toward the nisen, but the toss was short. Fortunately, the artfully agile Hadowar was there in a flash, catching the key easily and nodding his thanks to Edwig. The illisinaf, whose eyes had gone wide as saucers, visibly relaxed and then cleared his throat. Then he spun and threw out the final words of his incantation.

Once again, I translated mentally.

"Asch, dru razha rivashe epa," Edwig muttered—*So, I become river's path.* "Mar va Fero, zelka u zheire." *Sea and Fire, seal me in circlet.*

There was a moment of nothing, a breathless pause, then a blinding flash of light. When I could see again, there was nothing but the circular artifact hanging in the air, suspended for an instant before it descended gently to the grass.

We all just stood there in the aftermath, mouths agape, until Orville, the oblivious clod, finally shattered the stillness. He applauded.

"My, *my!*" he exclaimed. "Seeing brazen Arcana so up close is always a wonder, isn't it? Makes you forget life's troubles for a moment."

I let out a laugh, half-incredulous, half-amused. Turning to the others, I held out my hand, the rhetorical gesture plain as I nodded toward the abandoned golden circle.

"We're all in agreement that I'm taking it, yeah?"

There was a round of nods and smirks.

"Alrighty," Garth said, putting his hand on Orville's still wildly applauding arms to stop him. "How 'bout we mosey on back to the township, eh? Cobbers, you wouldn't bloody believe how far we've come along."

Razha rivashe.

I froze. Had I just heard . . .

Razha rivashe.

Based on the tone, that voice could only belong to Clucky. Of the roe, he'd have definitely been picking up the lower harmonies in their barbershop quartet. But it was uncomfortably spooky that he'd decided to remember some of the phrases in the arcane tongue. Ah, shit, that was probably on me, huh? Considering I'd straight-up mentally translated the motherfuckin' words and junk.

Hey, Clucky, I said. *We don't know what that might do if you start just, you know, sayin' that stuff, so maybe don't until we know it's not going to boil you alive or something. Savvy?*

Savvy.

Well, that was interesting.

And so, they all piled back into the carriage—while the remainder of us clomped on to the roof, and once again we set off—apparently toward Tallrock now.

As soon as the carriage creaked to a halt a few minutes beyond the gates of Tallrock, Orville sprang out, tripping over his own feet in his eagerness and landing flat on his face on the ground.

"Land, sweet land," he mumbled into the dirt, his words muffled.

From atop the carriage, I rolled my eyes. I'd seen some bizarre shit, but Orville always managed to be the zoo's star attraction.

Garth clambered down from his perch at the reins, pulled out a pipe of some kind, and lit it. I hadn't seen him do that before, so it was a surprise.

"Oi, what's the plan of attack, mates?" he asked.

Veruca gave Garth an icy stare.

"We will not be observing a holiday or vacation. We're on a mission with very specific parameters and a limited time table."

Garth held up his hands in surrender.

"Alright, alright. No need to go off, gal. I was only yarnin' about the frothies."

"Frothies?" Rua asked.

"Libations!" Garth announced excitedly. "You know, coldies, tinnies, amber fluid, grog, even a bit of the ol' goon bag. Best not to waste an evening if we can help it. That portal won't be good to go 'til first light, anyway."

After a couple of false starts, Orville finally managed to sit up and looked around.

"Where are we?" he asked, dusting off his pants.

"Tallrock," Dragoon said, rolling his eyes. "Your hometown?"

Orville's brow furrowed as he scanned the surroundings.

"Are we sure?"

"Positive," Dragoon said with a sigh.

"A lot more trees than what I'm used to," Orville said. "Somebody's been a hand with the green thumb."

I groaned.

"Honestly, I am pretty invested in letting you confuse yourself even more, newbie," I said. "But I can't handle any more of the dopey comments at the moment, so I'm just going to spell it out for you: we are *outside* the city—*outside the city*. Got it?"

Orville looked as though he was puzzling over a particularly complex algebra . . . thing, and then shook his head.

"But why aren't we *inside* the city?"

"Because your felonious companion cannot bring the carriage within, lest he make us all culpable in his fatuous schemes," Veruca clarified in a huff.

Man, she either really didn't like lawbreaking or really wasn't a fan of Garth. Or both. Which was wild, because I thought Garth was pretty entertaining—criminal deviance or not. Different strokes, I guess.

"I can explain it further if need be at the tavern," Hadowar offered Orville helpfully.

"Tavern? We're getting drinks?" Orville said, his grin suddenly wide and a little unwholesome.

"Man, you don't pay attention to shit, do y—" I started, but . . . I was interrupted.

"Beer!" Rexen exclaimed, pushing his way forward. "Do they still put fruit syrups in them 'round these parts?!"

I shook my head, staring at the city in the distance.

Guess we're doin' it like this, then. This god better be worth the hassle to murder.

The tavern was a goddamn treasure trove of debauchery. Laughter echoed off the rafters, the kind of full-bellied cackles that only come after enough drinks have washed away the concerns of the day. Mugs clanged together, either in the clumsy hands of the power-trashed or in the much more deliberate toast of the slightly less power-trashed. If they had anything like health inspectors in Regaia, the sheer volume of alcohol in everyone's bloodstream would qualify this place as a sanitation hazard.

Additionally, some floppy-hat-wearing music-school dropout—er, bard—was tucked away in the corner, his fingers dancing over the strings of a lute.

It was a wonder the poor bastard could even hear himself play over the noise. But there he was, plucking away, adding his melody to the chaos. It was actually really well done, but I didn't want to go over and compliment him, because he seemed like he was trying really hard to concentrate. Plus, who wants to be bothered when they're at work? Though I did consider trying to slip him some poorly remembered tabs from that summer I'd tried to learn bass guitar. Maybe if I could find a writing utensil, I would—this place definitely needed the plunky, half-recalled stylings of "Seven Nation Army."

The last time I'd drunk in Tallrock, I'm pretty sure this spot hadn't been built yet. Despite the . . . let's call it liveliness, I could tell the structure was relatively recently constructed. Still had that new-tavern smell, ya know? Under all the other smells, that is. But, still, my previous foray had been right after the attack, so even when we were balls-deep into merriment, the vibe was definitely more restrained than whatever crimes were poppin' off in there tonight.

A sudden crash cut through my nostalgia trip—someone's pint of god-knows-what had met an unfortunate end against the floor. Probably some poor, drunk dummy-ass who couldn't handle his liquor. The laughter crescendoed as the drinker, red-faced and giggling, scrambled to pick up the pieces.

Yep: this place was a shitshow. Still, there was something about it that gave me just *the* most overwhelming case of the cozies.

Rua, with an excited glint in her eyes, approached me. She had a very large tankard in her hands that sloshed as she gestured.

"This place is nice . . ." she said, slurring her words a little.

A woman threw dice on a tabletop nearby with a loud, obnoxious scream of joy. Immediately, the whole table erupted into laughter, as she must've either won expertly or lost really bad? It was hard to tell.

Then my heart jolted. The woman had looked back at me . . . and I could have sworn it was the curly-haired chick whose name I didn't know. She'd smiled at me. But a moment later, it wasn't her. Maybe I just needed some rest.

"Yeah, it's a regular third home," I mused, finding myself again.

"Why ya . . . so grumpy?" Rua asked, scowling and placing her index finger over one eyebrow to enhance the motion, as if in imitation of me. Then she chuckled. "Not . . . uhm, havin' fun?"

"Well, drunky . . ." I said. "This just feels . . . weird, right? We've been roughin' it for months. Most of our fellow castaways still are. I dunno; doesn't exactly seem real."

Rua gave me a knowing glance.

"It *is* strange, Loon. Civilization . . . It's like . . . it's like, uh, we . . . we've forgotten—how it works."

She belched a little and then blew it away out of the side of her mouth.

"Oops," she said.

"Nah," I said. "Never mind. I'm just . . . thinkin', is all. Don't mind me. How about you ignore what I was saying and go on and enjoy yourself? Just don't start any bar fights, alright, Admiral Alcohol?"

She chuckled, casting a wary glance at a table of rowdy locals. Then she gave me a salute that didn't resemble anything in real life and wouldn't have been tolerated by any army in the world—not even Canada.

We meandered to an empty table, where Veruca joined us, then she and Rua got lost in a very inebriated discussion about the current mission, strategizing their liquor-drenched little heads off. Hadowar, well-lubricated himself from a few pints, was regaling Orville with what sounded like the finer points of stitching up a wound mid-combat.

"Much like . . . anyfin . . . anything else, it's. About . . . . TIMING!"

Man, dude was really drunk. Orville just sat, eyes wide, clearly overwhelmed but trying to keep up until Hadowar's shout made him squeak with fright.

Garth and Dragoon were locked in a raucous debate at the end of our table, their words weaving through the din. These two, it was clear, could handle their cups. They'd been at it just as long as everyone else, but they weren't nearly as sloppy. A few tables away, patrons craned their necks, trying to understand the unlikely duo's spirited discussion. Despite the . . . polarizing subject matter, their conversation seemed to be in good humor.

"Seriously, mate, why the bloody fixation on firearms?" Garth mused, raising a pint. "Over here, we've got blokes throwing fire from their fingertips, women conjuring storms from thin air, and you're telling me you'd rather play with your bang-bang sticks?"

Dragoon leaned back, a slow, knowing grin spreading across his rugged face.

"Garth," he started, "all I said was that I miss having one at hand. I'm much more comfortable with *other-world* weapons than the stuff Regaia has. I mean, there's an art to a firearm. A precision. For instance, with a well-made rifle, you know exactly what it's gonna do. There are no whims, no bad days. It's all in the mechanism. Pull the trigger, it fires. Reliable, predictable."

"Bunch of bloody noise and smoke, if you ask me," Garth retorted, flicking the shell of some nut he'd been eating across the table. "See, that's the problem with you Yanks. Always looking for the most complicated solution. Here, it's all about balance. You make do with what the realms provide. It's more . . . natural."

"More natural, huh?" Dragoon shot back, chuckling. "Didn't you tell us on the way here that one of your friends lost his house because he accidentally turned it into a scorpion and it scuttled away? *That* sort of natural?"

"A minor mishap," Garth dismissed with a wave of his hand. "Besides, even that is *loads* safer than one of your pop-guns going off accidentally."

Dragoon crossed his arms, giving Garth a side-eye.

"And I suppose Spells never misfire?"

Garth gave a dismissive shrug.

"At least when magic misfires, you end up with a hell of an interesting story for your trouble, mate."

"But in the right hands," Dragoon said, pressing the point, "a firearm is a tool. A safeguard. A protector of life, not just a taker. You just have to know how to handle it."

"Right hands, eh?" Garth shot back, shaking his head. "I reckon there's too many wrong hands where you're from. And besides, what's a tool against a dragon's fire or a wizard's hex?"

"Pretty sure I'd be able to do quite a bit of damage, actually. Unless Smaug's suddenly able to hit targets hidden in a sniper's nest over a mile away? No? Let me put it this way," Dragoon said, leaning in close. "A bullet doesn't need to be cast. No chants. No incantations. It's there when you need it, ready and waiting."

Garth let out a hearty laugh.

"And where's the fun in that, mate? Where's the thrill of mastering an element, harnessing raw energy? You and your metal slugs . . . "

Dragoon simply raised his glass.

"To each his own."

Garth clinked his pint against Dragoon's glass.

"Strewth," he said, grinning.

"Besides," Dragoon said. "I imagine the Revolution would be a lot different if there *were* wizards and dragons. We'd probably be toiling under some kind of magocracy. No, thank you, sir."

Garth took a long swig from his pint and set it down with a thud, leveling a squinty-eyed gaze at Dragoon.

"Alright, then, since we're talking shop," he began, "here's a topic for you. Who do you reckon had a better go at the Brits? You lot, or us?"

Dragoon raised an eyebrow, a smirk playing at the corners of his mouth.

"Well, now," he said slowly, "That's a loaded question if I've ever heard one. You talking Australia or Regaia?"

Garth laughed, his eyes twinkling with mischief.

"Oh, come on, cobber—you're muddyin' the pond now. You know what I meant. Don't tell me you're scared to dish."

"Scared?" Dragoon echoed, his smirk deepening. "Hardly. I suppose, really, it's about perspective . . . mate. You Aussies might claim you've got a long-standing grudge, but we had our little scrap with them first. It's practically written into our DNA to rebel."

"Rebel, eh?" Garth snorted. "Hard to rebel with a tea party, isn't it? Dunking a mess of herbs into a bay isn't exactly a grievous wound—it's a bath bomb. We were shipped off to the other side of the world, mate—stripped of everything. That builds a different kind of resentment, I reckon."

"We did more than just toss tea into the harbor," Dragoon said, leaning back in his chair. "We fought tooth and nail for our freedom. And . . . we didn't become a penal colony."

"No, you didn't," Garth agreed, nodding solemnly. "You just ended up borrowing their language, legal system, and driving on the right. Very rebellious."

"I'd argue we improved on all those," Dragoon shot back with a chuckle. "Besides, last time I checked, you guys still have the Queen on your money."

"That's just because she's a good-looking bird," Garth retorted, chuckling. "It's not like we asked for it."

"Well, in any case," Dragoon concluded, raising his pint once again, "we're all on the same team *here*. So, we drink."

Garth raised his own glass in acknowledgment, grinning.

"Same team indeed. Except for the British."

It went like that for a while. However, the entire joint suddenly seemed to come alive when Jumpy, Clucky, Slappy, and Mortimer made their way into the fray. Their bouncy bodies were ricocheting off everything—furniture, the fuckin' walls, unsuspecting patrons. No more destructive than any drunk, really. But, I mean, they were a hell of a lot more eye-catching.

Mortimer, the biggest of the bunch, was rolling up to the ceiling, then back down again in a continuous, wobbly somersault. Then he'd do something calamitous like spiral into a group of mercenary-lookin' mooks, sending their tankards flying and spilling ale all over the floor. It would've pissed me off if it had happened to me, but the idiots just gawked, looking more amused than annoyed. Guess they were more used to otherworldly phenomena than I was.

Meanwhile, Jumpy, the smallest and most energetic of the four, was zipping between tables and barstools, knocking off any loose plates of food and leaving a trail of scraps and sauce in his wake. Patrons would leap up, cursing and laughing as they tried to avoid the enthusiastic roe.

Slappy—the . . . well, let's call him the most innocent of the brothers—moved like a wobbly ping-pong ball, seemingly unaware of his surroundings. He'd been occupying his evening by strolling underneath tables and chairs, exploring like a pub dog. He'd bump into patrons, setting off rounds of laughter before continuing his meandering journey.

Clucky was posted up at a table on the far side of the tavern, observing a quiet game of cards between a dwarf man and a human woman. His attention was fixated on each movement, and he'd turn his whole body to watch as the two organized the cards in patterns, drinking in the experience.

The real question there was: where the hell was Rexen? I hadn't seen him in a while, and even though I knew, like a reverse restraining order, he had to stay within a hundred feet of me, it didn't bode well. He was too much of a wild card to be left to his own dementia devices. Thanks to our little Pact, I could always feel him nearby, but . . . still. Come on, man—we're relaxin' here. Fuck knew what he was up to, but given his track record, it was likely something ridiculous. If I knew him—and trust me, I'm pretty sure I did at this point—he was probably rummaging through the backrooms, seeking out the best barrel of beer like a kid hunting for hidden birthday presents. Or maybe he had trapped some unsuspecting denizen in one of his stories of violent victory over insurmountable odds—or whatever the fuck he claimed he used to do? I thought about looking for him, but then figured, fuck it—he's *my* master; I'm not his. Ain't gonna be no brothers keepin' up in *this* party parlor tonight. No, sir.

The night air had a soft chill to it, lightly nipping at Saban's skin as he found himself drawn to the edge of their makeshift camp. There was an intense solitude there, far from the bustle of his displaced companions, that allowed him to think. He sat with purposeful poise, like a figure of stone with his eyes cast unblinkingly toward the shadow-laden forest that lay like a menacing blanket in the distance.

The camp behind him was a distant murmur, their stories and laughter a faint soundtrack to his solitary vigil. He was an anomaly in the cacophony of their lives—a silent sentinel in the chill of the night, waiting for something only he was privy to.

Suddenly, without warning, a spectral shimmer sliced through the dark veil, dancing in the air before him. It illuminated the ground beneath him in an ethereal glow, casting elongated, haunting shadows that seemed to twist and play along with the soft light. Saban's expression, stony until now, lit up with anticipation as the ethereal glow began to take shape.

Out of the dance of lights emerged a visage that could only belong to one individual. The spirally-eyed face of Rexen Gravetongue materialized in the hovering light, his disembodied presence lighting up the darkness surrounding Saban.

"Howdy-howdy!" Rexen greeted, his voice echoing from the magical interface. His eyes flickered for a moment, seemingly distracted by something off-screen.

"Is that a midnight moth I see? Catch it and eat it for good luck! Oh . . . or don't, it may be poisonous. Yucky. Never mind! We have business to discuss."

"Rexen," Saban said with a slight sigh, his measured voice breaking through the quiet night. "It worked, huh? I'm surprised you were able to get it."

"Yep!" Rexen said. "While the illisinaf was bragging about his theft of the nisen's carriage key, *I* was stealing the Sending Rod right from under his nose! What a little stinker I am!"

"What?" Saban asked, then realized that asking a question like that would lead to a long, unimportant answer, so he quickly shifted gears. "Never mind. Everything going alright?"

Rexen's spectral form gave a dismissive wave.

"Oh, don't you worry your pretty little bean! Everything is falling into place, yep, yep! Just like a Dardandrian puzzle box. Or was it a Dardandrian stew? Hm. In any case, both are enigmas."

"So . . ."

"Anyways! A tale for another time. We're at a tavern!"

"Huh?" Saban wondered. "One day in and you're already drinking on the job?"

"Yep!"

"Well, I guess . . . don't go too hard in the paint, alright? There's a lot of ground to cover ,and I'm pretty sure about half of those guys have hardly even tried alcohol."

"My paint remains floppy and flaccid!" Rexen announced proudly. "Now, about that *juicy* Conduit . . ."

Saban leaned forward.

"You know, Rexen, this is quite a big risk for me . . . for us. Alpha's not exactly . . . pro-this plan. If he finds out I didn't tell him everything about the Prosperity C—"

Rexen cut him off with a flippant chuckle.

"Oh, my dear, beautiful, hammer-hucking boy! Such an old soul in a young body! Worry, worry, worry! Always worrying. Your mind is so interesting! I would like to squeeze myself into your skull sometime and take a peep at . . . Oh, right. Inappropriate. Old habits—I'm still learning."

Saban shook his head, a wry smile gracing his lips.

"Just please try to find the Prosperity Conduit. We can't keep living like this. You promised this would be a dramatic change to the current setup—which is the only reason I played my part when you brought it up. It needs to change. No matter what."

"Ooh-wee! Once we have the Conduit, we can continue with our grand scheme! Your ultimate rise to power from the lowly, *insubordinate* ashes. Like a radiant aura phoenix! Ooh! Did I ever tell you about the time when—"

"Maybe some other time?" Saban offered.

"Oh, right. Conduit. Yes, yes, I remember."

"Send me another message the moment you get hold of it, and I'll get to part two, yeah?"

"Oh, of *course*, Hammy—that's what I'm calling you now. It's short for *hammer*."

"By one letter . . ." Saban said.

". . . because you use a *hammer*!" Rexen explained, answering a question that wasn't asked.

"Alright. Well . . . I'm hoping that I didn't make a mistake by listening to you," Saban said, clear concern painting his features.

"Bah! You sound just like *pupil*!" Rexen said, and he . . . stuck his tongue out to show his distaste. "Nobody trusts me! I've never led anyone astray . . . too much. Even when I did, I always got them back on the right path! And mostly in one piece!"

Saban sighed, then looked up at Rexen's projected face seriously.

"And what if two people you're leading happen to be in direct opposition to one another?" he asked darkly. "Who gets back on the right path?"

Rexen's face hovered for a moment longer, its ghostly visage lighting up in the otherwise dark night. Then he winked at Saban. Almost instantly, the image disappeared, leaving Saban alone once more.

The Champion glanced back toward the camp, thoughts churning in his mind. As his gaze returned to the empty space where Rexen's face had been moments before, he mumbled, "This had better work, Rexen. Or we're all in deep trouble."

A couple hours into the night, and the pub had mellowed out from a rowdy circus to a low-level sideshow. Most of the drunks had either stumbled off to bed or decided to use their table as a makeshift mattress—heads planted firmly in the soup of the day or splayed out on the well-worn tabletops like they were posing for a Renaissance painting.

Our lot was no different. They'd either buggered off or were currently out cold. Garth was sawing logs like it was a national sport and was being used as a teddy bear by three of the roe. Jumpy, Slappy, and Mortimer were nestled against him, peacefully chittering away in their sleep.

Hadowar had managed to find us some digs for the night and had shepherded the less pickled of our motley crew off to sleep it off. Kudos to him; he might not have been able to hold his booze, but the motherfucker was definitely dependable.

Now Clucky was the odd bird out. He was still perched in soundless reverie, staring at the couple engrossed in their card game. Probably trying to work out the odds or decode their pitiful poker faces. I let out a sigh and stood to collect him.

Clucky, I said mentally. *Time for beddy-bye.*

Shuffling over to Clucky, my feet thumping out a soggy solo on the beer-soaked floorboards, I heard him mutter something in return.

Frida. Calden.

I stopped dead in my tracks.

Come again? I asked, then looked down at the game being played. Suddenly, Clucky's words made sense. The game I was looking at was Fels, and it was the very same game that Frida and Calden had entertained themselves with in the Crypt's second chamber to pass the time. Not only had Clucky remembered that, but he was apparently making connections from back before he was even able to fully process words.

Frida. Calden, he said again, turning to look at me pointedly. I swallowed.

Uh, yeah, that's right, buddy. Frida and Calden used to play this; good job. It's called Fels and—

She wins, he interrupted, turning back to the hand.

Yeah, Frida was beating his tail feathers all the ti—

But I stopped, because it was at that moment the human woman of the pair placed a card down, and the dwarf suddenly grumbled under his breath and slapped the rest of his deck down with a big sigh.

"Right," he said to the woman. "That's it, then, for me, tonight, lovely—I'm off!"

"Narp," the woman said, a hint of amusement in her tone. "Not afore I've filched that crown-marked Hunter Pantherus off of your graveyard. Give 'er over, Radus."

The dwarf—Radus, apparently—chuckled and tossed forward a card with the illustration of a big black cat—I think—toward the woman. She snatched it up greedily and stuffed it into her own deck.

What the fuck?

Clucky had predicted who was going to win the match? That couldn't be right . . . right? Maybe this was a coincidence and he *had* been referring to Frida. However, something about that seemed off. It was clear Clucky was somehow coming into his own—really havin' a watershed moment—but did it extend this far? I watched the two gather up their cards, trying to understand the implications of this. But that was where I took a pause.

I caught a glimpse of the cards' backsides, and it felt like someone had just drop-kicked my memory. The silver design curling across the worn cardstock was familiar. It was this weird abstract job—a stave, sort of, with the umbrella-style hook at the bottom and two arms sticking out from it. Next to it was a small red stone, painted with such meticulous care that it looked ready to pop off the card. I'd seen that same symbol—gleaming stave and eerie red gem—before. I had three just like it in my bag.

I'd found them on the corpses of the greloks right after arriving in this world, but I'd never realized that it was part of the same game that Frida and Calden had been so wild about. Their cards didn't have the stylized design; they'd been much more homemade-looking. Which . . . made sense. The version they knew was at least four hundred years old. Well, shit, these motherfuckers might've been worth some money.

You like this game? I asked the roe.

Clucky beamed at me.

Like the game. Frida. Calden.

Well, I've got a few with me, if you want to take a look at them later. It won't be enough to play with, but I'll see if we can't gather some more so you can eventually play. Maybe teach your brothers or something.

Like that a lot, Clucky said.

Yeah? Alright, well, gather up the others and let's head back to get some sleep, and we can figure out how we're going to get you into a tournament or something, my little bouncing Bobby Fisher.

He excitedly bounced off to rouse his fellows and, in doing so, woke Garth up. The nisen blinked as he raised his head, bleary-eyed, then groaned.

"Go on without me," he grumbled. "I'm going to hang back and hold this table down."

I shrugged. But thinking about the Fels game had made me contemplate the fate of my friends who'd left.

"Wonder what Frida, Jes, and Stinky are up to," I mused.

Rua, who'd been nodding off at the table nearby, spoke up without opening her eyes. Her voice was far away, likely in some two-thirds-drunken state of sleep.

"Oh . . . you know . . . same old, same old. Raising . . . hell and fighting those . . . purple . . . ice cream," she replied, her unconscious smile wistful.

"God, I hope so—after the last half-century they've had, they need to cut loose a little," I muttered, not really expecting her to understand in her current state.

"Definitely . . ." Rua cooed. "Like barbecue. Little baby bones . . . inside all the . . . dog shops."

"That's *right*," I said, humoring my sleeping friend. "Alright, you ready to go? You're drooling all over the table."

"I can drool wherever I need . . . Don't tell me how to . . . live my live," she said.

"Uh-huh," I said, hefting her up from the table. She opened her eyes. They were bloodshot and not focusing on anything in particular.

"Orc," she said, as if identifying me for the first time.

"Well, your eyes work, at least," I said. "Come on; we got a big day tomorrow."

That was when Rexen returned, finally, slipping into the crack of the open door someone had left ajar. He beelined right toward me.

"Where *you* been, then?" I wondered.

"I was outside," he said.

"Yeah, I see that," I said. "Why, though?"

"I thought I saw a frog."

"You know what? Never mind. Let's get going. I think most of these idiots are going to be useless tomorrow, so we better get them back so they can have . . . I dunno, a couple hours of rest at least."

"My pupil is so kind and caring to all his allies," Rexen said. "It is nice to see."

"Alright, nobody said anything about *caring*, Arjee—I'm just super itchy to get goin' on this mission. We gotta kill—uh, we need to *meet* with that *high-level executive* and, uh . . ."

I was really struggling with an analogy that didn't give away our whole manifesto, so I just gestured in a vague direction.

". . . you know," I said.

"Yes! I do know!" Rexen piped merrily. "Even with your terrible attempt at obfuscation, pupil, your master's powers of deduction are nigh-on *otherworldly*."

"Whatever, we gotta go to sleep—I know you don't have a tiredness gene like e'rybody else, but the rest of us are going to be draggin' ass if we don't saw some logs soon. You comin'?"

I moved toward the door, dragging Rua along with me. But when Rexen didn't follow me, I paused, turning to look at him over my shoulder.

"Arjee? What's up, buster? You missed the beer, so if that's your issue, don't even bother."

He regarded me oddly, tilting his head to one side.

"Pupil," he said thoughtfully.

"Yeah?"

"Do you trust me?"

"Depends on with what," I said. "Talking nonstop about whatever nonsense comes into your brain? With my life. To help me out when times are tough? Eh . . . I dunno. Maybe? You're kind of a pick-yourself-up-by-your-bootstraps-sort—from what I can tell. Why?"

"No reason," he said languidly. "Thank you for your honesty. I would love to possess you someday."

"Uh, sure," I said. "Anytime. You ready to go?"

"Yes, pupil," he said. "Ooh! Can we stay up late, telling spooky stories?! Perhaps while giggling under a blanket?"

"Arjee," I said. "Shut up."

"Yes, disciple."

CHAPTER TWENTY

RATS, RATS, RATS

Rubbing my eyes free of sleep, I began my walk through Tallrock.

Once a vibrant little town bustling with joyous inhabitants, it now resembled a disaster site, but a disaster site that was slowly returning to life. It had been almost two months since the army of oomukade—monstrous, centipede-like creatures for you just joining—including their fuck-off-gigantic queen that towered above everything else—had attacked and destroyed everything in their path.

As our shitty little lookie-loo tour schlepped our asses through the maze of screwed-up streets, I eyeballed the spots where mama-bug had decided to play stompy-stomp. Fortunately, the smashed-up remnants were slowly, painfully mutating back into . . . well, buildings that didn't look like they'd collapse if you farted too hard.

All over the damn place, the villagers were busting their humps, working nonstop, turning the rubble-choked disaster zones into . . . let's be generous and say *potential tetanus hazards*.

There were these wood-jockeys slapping together what I guessed were meant to be houses, the sound of their hammering an incessant, nerve-grating backdrop. And the stonemasons—the poor bastards—they were hacking away at granite blocks with a jealous fervor, probably meant to patch up the town's defenses. A futile endeavor if you ask me, but weirdly, no one did.

Despite the fact that their former arsenal of hopes and dreams had been dashed to ugly bits, the townsfolk had an optimistic pep in their step. Either they were high on hope or severely dehydrated; I couldn't tell. Probably both. They'd nod at me as I passed by, their smiles stretching tight across their sun-cooked, wind-burnt faces. It was actually disarmingly charming.

With every howdy and nod, my guilt grew. It was not the easiest feeling to shake, knowing that I'd played a not-insignificant part in their plight. I mean, yeah, it wasn't as though I personally ordered mama-bug to play demolition derby on the town, but I was there with the assholes who did. That was a grimy chunk of blame I couldn't just flick off my shoulder, no matter how much I wanted to.

But hey, you can't erase the past. No one knew that better than me. All you could do was suck it up and soldier on. Even if you had to wade through a cesspool of hot, stinky remorse to get to the other side.

Hadowar and Garth had said their goodbyes a few streets back, citing that their work was not quite done there—which sucked for us. I'd been hoping we'd be fortunate enough to receive the blessing of their higher-Level company, but it was not to be, I guess. Thankfully, Orville had been nursing a hangover, and hadn't even gotten up to see us off. We'll call that even steven, then. So, we said our goodbyes and eventually, after a bit more walking, we finally found ourselves in front of the Mages' Order at Yosper Hall, a sight that immediately yanked me from my introspection. The sight of it was like a slice of fairytale life transplanted into the existence of the post-apocalypse of what went for a town in these parts. Nestled amongst the slowly recuperating city structures, it towered with an air of ethereal magnificence.

The Hall was what some pretentious know-it-all might call an architectural wonder, all super-soaring spires, arched windows, and meticulously—and intricately—carved stone statues. Its... *grandiosity* stood like a sexier, more popular sibling to the grumbling, pimple-faced preteen of the rest of Tallrock. The outer walls were pristine, apparently safe and unmarred from the oomukade attack— the least amazing part of its awe-inspiring presence. I mean, I say that, because it really wasn't much of a surprise. Yosper Hall was the not-so-humble hive of magical research and study in town, so it made sense that they'd have the best defenses. Though it still bothered me a bit that they hadn't seemed to assist *at all* in the defense during the insect insurrection. *Marcia, Marcia, Marcia.*

As we approached the grand entrance, the heavy wooden doors swung open.

"Sheesh," I said, as we were led inside. "I guess Edwig can't be blamed for being so obsessed with his goddamn career. If I started my job every day looking at this fuckin' beauty, I'd probably get a bloated sense of gooey importance as well. I mean, *look* at this motherfucker."

"Yes," a voice agreed from behind me, and I leaped about two feet in the air from the surprise. "We have always taken great pains to ensure that Yosper Hall remains rapturous to those who view it for the first time. It is our lineage, more so than anything else."

"JESUS FUCK!" I shouted. Several others squeaked out surprises as well, so I didn't feel as bad about my sudden tough-guy outburst.

I wheeled on the spot, my bare feet squeaking on the marble, and saw the speaker. It was a rat . . . person . . . lady. A grelok.

Oh, bother.

She held herself with confidence and was dressed head to toe in flowing blue-and-green robes. Around her neck was a long, black scarf that glittered a bit, looking slightly wet—and gave me a similar vibe as my own Trespasser's Veil. Perhaps they were, like, cousin garments or something? That was worth noting. I tried to use Eye of the Saboteur on it from this distance but only received an annoying response from the System.

Ah-ah-ah! Rude.

Oh, fuck off, I thought.

The grelok woman smiled, and I was reminded of another such vermin person who liked to do that, filling my stomach with a nasty sensation. They probably weren't related, but, I mean, trauma will do that to you. I assume.

"Hello," she said serenely, swishing forward and giving a slight incline of her head. "I am S'Rista—Overmagister Researcher here at the august and venerable Yosper Hall in Karepalea. I have been informed by Garth and Hadowar that you will be requiring the use of transportation—to Palandis?"

"Wait, you all talk like that?" I asked. "I figured that was just Ed—uh, never mind."

I figured it probably wasn't a good idea to mention Edwig at this current venture, considering they'd been the ones to send him to the slammer—not to mention he was currently pretending he didn't exist. So, instead, I got real, real charming.

"Oh, um . . . *Howdy-doo,* Sister," I said. "I'm Loon, this is—"

"It's *S'Rista*," the grelok woman clarified kindly . . . but firmly.

"Oh . . . yeah—wait, what did *I* say?"

"You said *sister*, pupil," Rexen said, before turning to the woman and widening his arms for a hug. "I love what you've done with the place, Overmagister!"

"By the wool of the Archon!" S'Rista said in . . . one of the weirder exclamations I'd heard in this world. "The Dreadnaught Lord—Rexen Gravetongue!"

"In the flesh—er, ghost-y bits!" Rexen exclaimed right back, rotating as though he was trying to give the woman a good look at him.

"You two know one another?" Rua asked.

"Hardly!" Rexen said. "But also—kinda!"

"Your answer clarifies very little," Veruca said. "In what way are you two associated?"

"We always recognize our own!" Rexen said, beaming. I watched as . . . Were those little fireworks? Anyway, whatever they were, little magical explosions erupted around him like a halo.

"You're a *grelok*?" I asked him, baffled by this development.

"No—" Rexen started, but S'Rista interrupted him.

"We are both thaumaturges," she explained.

"Oh," I said, scratching my head. "So . . . do you have a Crypt too? Or maybe a tomb—er, mausoleum?"

She glanced at me, perplexed, then turned to Rexen for clarification. The little ghost held up his arms as if in dismay and shrugged.

"My pupil is very stupid," he said.

"Wait—no, I'm not!" I shouted, swiping at him. He dodged out of the way and went to hover over S'Rista's shoulder, and they both stared at me.

"What?!"

"Perhaps you should ease up on him; clearly, he is ignorant of the goings-on here," S'Rista said. "Is he an orc? Intriguing choice of disciple, Lord Rexen."

"Okay, I don't like *this* one fuckin' lick," I said. "Quit cozying up to one another over . . . professional courtesy and weirdly targeted contempt of me. With all due respect to the Overmanager—"

"Overmagister," Rua said.

"Yeah, that's what I said," I continued. "We're here for a reason, remember?"

"Party games!" Rexen cheered.

"No," I said. "That's incorrect. Zero points."

"Aww . . ." Rexen grumbled. "Then why did I make a delicious, egg-based dipping sauce?"

"Yes, as you mentioned, we're here to borrow your portal, ma'am," Dragoon interjected, shaking his head. "I don't know what any of these people are talking about, but that's the actual reason. Can you point us in its direction?"

"I don't think we can just demand that she—" Veruca started, but S'Rista interrupted her.

"Of course," she said simply, smiling. "However, it is not *my* Gateway, as it is *technically* a public utility. So, I could no more bar you from its use than I could keep your pet roe from eating poison hobfruit."

I chuckled.

"Well, I guess that's a relief— FUCK!"

Her words had finally sunk in and I wheeled around to see Jumpy stacked on top of Slappy, his eyes closed and mouth open wide as he reached for a conical purple berry dangling from the branches of one of the plants growing out of the marble. Clucky and Mortimer looked on with interest.

"NO!" I commanded. "Acky! Stop that!"

Jumpy froze, and I could see one of his eyes pop open to glance at me sidelong. Clucky and Mortimer spun to face me, looking bashful. Slappy—always a bit of a late bloomer—finally seemed to register my words and, rather than turn, nervously leaped to a different position. This caused Jumpy to fall and then bounce, springing away down a corridor.

Why did they even bother stacking when they can bounce?

"Where did you say you were from?" Veruca asked. "I may have misheard you, but I am considerably confident that the rest of these *inerronous* individuals have been referring to this city as 'Tallrock.' But, you used the name . . ."

"Karepalea," S'Rista said. "Yes—your friends are correct. Until quite recently, this city was known as Tallrock. However, due to . . . unforeseen complications, we have had the joyous privilege to select a more fitting designation."

I could tell by her tone that she found this considerably *less* exciting than she was saying.

"Rebranding, huh?" I asked. "But, jeez-louise, you really picked a mouthful of a moniker."

"In a manner of speaking," S'Rista said with a sigh. "Fortunately, this couldn't have come at a better time—the rebuilding and all. Some consider it a toothsome portent for the longevity of the settlement."

The only thing I thought I caught from that was "long in the tooth," which meant *old*, I think. Not sure how that was relevant. But go off, queen.

"What caused the change?" Rua asked.

"Oh, just some business across the sea—hardly worth noting," S'Rista said. "Insofar that I haven't taken an eager account of the cause. But it is my understanding that there is currently another city called Tallrock over the sea in Morzekhan."

"Wait, cities can't share names?" I asked. "Man, you'd *hate* where I come from."

"This situation is—once again, only as I understand—unusual. It too is a Gateway city—as we are—owing to its portal transportation routes. Accordingly, attempting to select between our two locations has created . . . Let's call them kerfuffles. There was a dispute over who should keep the name, but considering the leadership in Morzekhan's Tallrock is comprised mostly of red mages—it was deemed a wise action to abdicate the denomination."

"Interesting, so, it's kind of like a post office . . ." Rua said. "Dang, politics are crazy here."

"Indeed." S'Rista nodded. "Particularly when Archmagician Garrhilver of the Mages' Order there practices—as he calls it—'fireball diplomacy.'"

"That is likely aggravating to navigate," Veruca offered, "the transition to Karepalea, that is."

"Oh, my dear vittra, it is of little consequence to us—Yosper Hall is Yosper Hall. It has always been such and always will be, I imagine—regardless of the surrounding conurbation."

"Wait . . ." I said. "Maybe I'm too stupid to understand—"

"Likely, pupil," Rexen added.

I gave him a withering look.

". . . but why not just designate the portals on the Mages' Order? Seems like it would solve a lot of problems."

"Not all transportation happens through Mages' Orders," S'Rista explained. "Though your point is sound. It would be considerably easier to manage were that the case."

"See?" I said to Rexen. "Not stupid. I'm asking informed questions."

"My pupil-baby is becoming a pupil-tot," Rexen cried cheerily.

"*Speaking* of portals . . ." Dragoon said, sounding irritated.

"Right—yeah," I said, snapping my fingers. "Can you show us the way to your warp drive, Sister?"

S'Rista paused for a moment—probably debating on whether or not to correct me—but eventually nodded.

"Yes," she said, gesturing to us and continuing down the passage. "Right this way."

CHAPTER TWENTY-ONE

FRANTIC DISEMBOWELMENT

As we trailed behind S'Rista, my mind began to churn with the complexity of the portal transportation network. I was always someone to question systems—usually manmade ones, but mostly to consider if there was a way to cheat or bust 'em to pieces. I suppose it was the natural saboteur in me, always trying to find another way around.

S'Rista explained that we would be going to one of two chambers they had. Ours was for what boiled down to inter-country transport, while the other was designed for international travel. That was a really neat prospect. I wondered how many different area codes the things could hit up—and started envisioning an idea for a movie about a bachelor party gone wrong after several hilarious drunken missteps. But . . . then I realized that I was just mildly altering the plot to *The Hangover* franchise and promptly banished the thoughts from my clichéd brain.

After several twists and turns through the grandeur of Yosper Hall, we arrived at a massive room. I loudly and unabashedly *guffawed* at the sight that greeted me within. A motherfucking enormous, shimmering, sky-blue portal stood as its centerpiece, casting a glow that bounced off the marble floor. My eyes widened at the sight. It was one thing to hear about them, but, motherfucking goddamn *shit,* seeing a portal in action was another thing entirely.

Surrounding it was a long line of people of myriad races . . . or, species, or whatever—all waiting patiently for their turn like they were buying Taylor Swift tickets. I found myself inspecting the faces in line, noticing the anticipation, anxiety, or excitement that varied from person to person. On the other side was an irregular stream of folks departing—likely returning from wherever the fuck they'd been on vacation or whatever.

Flanking the portal were two individuals who immediately caught my attention. Both were of nonhuman races—one rabbit-like and the other looking sort of like a tall, beefy box elder bug, dressed in long, billowing robes that were indicative of the Mages' Order. They were carrying out their duties with a solemn sense of professionalism, checking what looked like IDs, then guiding the people through the portal.

I watched as an elvish-looking man stepped forward, presenting his identification. One of the mages checked it, nodded, then whispered an incantation. As the man walked through, the color of the portal fluctuated, changing from its serene blue to a pulsating violet.

"So . . . I see the colors changing each time someone steps through," I said, turning to S'Rista. "Is it, like, switching channels?"

She laughed, the sound tinkling pleasantly in the massive chamber.

"If I understand what you mean, yes. Different areas within the Kingdom of Arlo are color-coded based on their portal exit point. The color changes reflect the destination."

Intrigued, I watched a few more pass through the portal. The colors shifted and flowed—gold, crimson, jade, and so on. Each departure created a mesmerizing light show. A different kind of magic than I was used to, but magic all the same.

The others were equally taken in by the spectacle, though I could see impatience starting to itch at Dragoon. I was coming to learn he was more mission-focused than the rest of us. Probably why Saban had suggested he tag along. Which . . . was probably the smartest thing. As for Rexen, he seemed overly excited, his ghostly form glowing more vibrantly than before.

"Remarkable," he commented, gazing at the portal. "There have been such advances since I was last let out to roam! The world is so much smaller!"

"Indeed," S'Rista replied, a proud smile gracing her features. "And soon, you'll experience it firsthand. Now, off you go."

"Wait . . ." I said. "Don't we need some sort of identification or something? All these folks are doin' it."

"Oh, do not worry on that front," S'Rista said, waving the words away. "They are using their transportation tokens. You won't need that."

"Like a bus pass?" I asked.

"That is so cool!" Rua exclaimed.

"Public transport isn't *cool*, Rua. God, you're such a fucking nerd."

"I think it's exceptional," Veruca butted in. "Public transportation is an essential and vital necessity to many; important in ecological responsibility, opportunity, and equal access. It promotes not merely physical connections but social ones as well, stitching individuals and communities together in shared experiences and collective progression."

"Yeah, but . . . it's fucking *magic*," I said in disbelief. "Plus—and don't get me wrong—I'm not knockin' . . . accessibility or whatever. But, to my extremely salient and handsome point, necessities aren't cool. They're, by their nature, a fuckin' snooze fest. I mean, I don't see anyone losing their shit about *water*."

"Loon, you should drink more water," Rua said.

"You *should* hydrate more frequently," Veruca agreed.

"Drink more water, pupil!" Rexen said. "You need to drink for two, since I can't!"

"What the hell? Is this an adventure party or an intervention? Why's everybody suddenly monitoring my drinking habits?"

"If you had any drinking habits, that would be one thing," Dragoon said. "But you don't. I've barely seen you hydrate since we left New Home. They're right. Drink more water, friend."

"Fuckin' . . . huh?" I wondered. "You guys are nuts—I've got a whole skin *full of the stuff* right here!"

I patted my still mostly full little sheep-bladder canteen at my side.

"Case in point," Rua muttered.

"Alright, e'rbody shut up! We are wildly off topic. Sister! Why don't we need to worry about the tokens?"

"Your friends have already taken care of that," she said. "Garth and Hadowar ensured your passage to *and* from Palandis, and we have made the arrangements on your behalf."

"Damn, those are some true-blue homies," I said, not really surprised she was on a first-name basis with them. "Well, alright, I guess. So, do we have to hop into the queue or can we skip the line since we're on the express lane to important shit?"

"You will be required to wait along with the others," S'Rista said, a knowing grin on her face. "But it should not take long."

"Aww, man!" I groaned. "This *is* just like regular public transport. This blows."

S'Rista merely offered a smile and then a nod, walking away from us and leaving our group to the grim and nigh-on-insurmountable task of waiting in line.

I watched her leave and sighed.

"Well, let's hop to it," I said, shaking my head and turning to the others, but to my extreme displeasure, I noticed they'd already abandoned me and were standing in line. Worse was, while I'd been distracted, four other people had joined the queue, acting as a buffer between me and my crew.

"Shit!" I shouted, and stumbled forward, joining the line with everyone else. I noticed that the people in front of me kept throwing concerned looks behind them like I was going to suddenly eat them or something. Meanwhile, Rua,

Dragoon, Veruca, and even Rexen and the roe were clustered in their own little jumble, talking in low voices.

"Hey!" I called. "Hey, guys! What're you talking about?"

They didn't respond. Instead, Rua said something that made Veruca laugh, and I saw a grin poke at the corner of Dragoon's lips.

Oh, hell the fuck no, they don't!

"Seriously!" I shouted. "Guys! Not cool. What's so funny?! I like jokes too, you know!"

The lady directly in front of me, some kind of gnome or something, had the gall to turn around and shush me.

"Oh, *excuse me*," I said indignantly. "But you kinda cut in front of me—not that you care, but you're awfully salty about me being loud when it—"

"Shh!" she repeated.

Easy, I thought to myself. *Don't let her get your goat. She's probably just on her way to some magical doctor to have that iceberg removed from her attitude.*

Instead of engaging with the tiny asshole of a woman, I mentally reached out to the roe.

Hey, buddies, you want to hang back with me? This is where all the cool people are.

I saw Slappy look at me out of the corner of his eye, but otherwise, they fucking ignored me too.

Oh, you guys are so grounded! I think-said.

Well, that sucked. It was true in every level of existence: no matter how enticing or threatening your other options were, nobody wanted to lose their spot in a line.

So, without any other choice, like a good and productive member of society, I waited. And waited. And waited some more.

After a good twenty minutes, Dragoon—who was first in the line of my companions—finally reached the front. He said something to the box elder, and then I watched as the mage held out a hand, counting out the people in my group—except for me.

"Yo!" I shouted. "I'm with them!"

"Shhh!" Shushy McShusherson shushed again.

"Oh, shush yourself, you tiny little hag!" I thundered.

Then, as I watched, Dragoon slipped into the portal, which flashed an ethereal silver color, and was gone. Anxiety of being Kevin McCallistered drove me to mutter a few choice curse words, and then I pushed my way forward.

"Hey!" some kind of a big wolfman growled at me as I knocked him aside. "No cutting!"

"Fuck you!" I shouted into his face, pointing at the portal. "My party posse is ahead of you, and I've had to endure your wife's 'tude for long enough—I should get an award for patience, honestly."

"What?" the man shot back. "She's not my wife!"

"Fine—your mistress, then," I said, continuing forward. "Whatever. Just let me—"

"No! Cutting!" he shouted again, and grabbed at my arm.

"Get your hands off me, fucker," I shouted. "Or I'm gonna punch those fangs down your throat."

"Pardon?" said another guy in front of me, who looked like he was maybe part man and part brick, his hand on a sword belted at his hip. "I suggest you wait your turn, knave. This is a polite and civilized queue, and I'll not have the integrity ruined."

Ah, Jesus fuck, here we go.

"I'm going to tell you right now, Lancelot," I warned. "You try using that little knife on me and there's gonna be some fuckin' problems."

"For you, I imagine," he retorted calmly. "Mostly with keeping your lifeblood inside your body."

"Listen," I said. "I'm about two seconds away from— Aww, *horseshit*!"

I was in the middle of the group, but my entire entourage was nowhere to be seen. While I'd been loudly and heroically arguing with a group of citizens, they'd gone and went through the portal.

Wait, how the fuck had Rexen—

I didn't have time to even finish my thought because a violent force suddenly seized me, pulling me forward like a kite caught in an angry gust. My feet lifted off the ground, my heart hammering against my chest as I soared through the air. Directly toward the portal.

"Gahhhhh!" I roared.

Just when I thought I was going to collide with the shimmering arcane gate, my flight came to an abrupt halt. I hung there, suspended in midair like a marionette with its strings jerked taut. Below me, the faces of the crowd twisted in fear and confusion, their mouths opening and closing in silent screams. But above the cacophony of panic, I could hear the booming voices of the mages.

"Cease your actions, you hooligan!" the bunny mage barked, levitating in front of me with his hands outstretched. His eyes blazed with a fury that was as tangible as the Arcana emanating from his fingertips. "You are attempting unauthorized passage! This is a clear violation of Interrealm Transit Ordinance three-point-four-five!"

"I . . . I'm not trying to, ya Buster Baxter–lookin' motherfucker!" I stammered, my mind racing to make sense of the situation. But before I could form a coherent response, a sharp pain exploded in my gut, so intense that my vision blurred. It felt as though a creature was clawing its way out from inside me.

A realization flooded my mind.

Oh fuck, oh fuck, oh fuck!

The effigy. *Rexen's* effigy. The eight-inch bullshit figurine of a wizard's tower I'd swallowed was on the move. It was in the process of being yanked by the pull of the portal, trying to follow Rexen as he had already crossed through the magical gateway.

"No, no, no, no, no!" I managed to gasp, my hand clutching my stomach in a futile attempt to contain the pain. "Let me go! I need to fuckin' pass through!"

"You shall not proceed without proper tokenage!" the second mage chimed in, his insectoid voice as unyielding as stone. His stern gaze was fixed on me, completely oblivious to the chaos that was unraveling. "Interrealm Transit Ordinance four-point one-six dictates a strict procedure with—"

"I don't give a rip about the goddamn ordinance! I'm gonna get torn in half!"

But my pleas and their legal recitations were drowned out by the horrifying spectacle that followed. With a sickening tearing sound, the effigy suddenly and violently burst from my stomach. A shower of blood and guts erupted from me, painting the air with a horrifying scarlet mist. The crowd's screams reached a fever pitch, their fear echoing my own.

The bunny mage—the one who had been holding me suspended—blanched at the sight. His face went blank and he suddenly fainted. Then he toppled from where he'd been floating in the air and crashed to the marble, unconscious. His sudden collapse was followed by an equally abrupt plummet of my Health bar. I stared in equal parts horror and abject confusion as I my actual lifeblood was *indeed* having trouble staying inside my body. Each heartbeat was weaker than the last, each breath shallower. The world around me began to fade, the edges of my vision turning inky black.

But the portal . . . it seemed to glow even brighter, pulsating like a beacon amidst the chaos. And then, as though the strings holding me were cut, I was free-falling, barreling toward the portal with the unyielding force of gravity.

As the darkness threatened to claim me, my world narrowed and I felt myself smash into the gateway. However, the last thing I saw before I faded into the realm of black was the color of the portal. When Dragoon had crossed, it had been a shining, illuminated silver. Now, when I entered, it was red.

CHAPTER TWENTY-TWO

WAKE UP DEAD

When I came to, I had no fucking clue where I was.

I had a goddamn *miserable* headache and the same kind of nasty metallic taste in my mouth that accompanied a bad hangover. It took me a second to recall where I'd been last. Everything was hazy and just out of grasp. The last thing I remembered was . . . Shit! The portal—and, uh, my guts exploding from my body.

My eyes shot open—probably. At least, that seems like something they'd have done. I clearly hadn't died, because I didn't have the ol' rez sickness, and my Health was back to full. So, someone had healed me? Seemed likely—given the circumstances—but who? And where the hell *was* I?

As the world came into focus, I quickly realized I was . . . not where I expected to be. I didn't know what I *was* expecting, but it definitely wasn't winding up in the lap of luxury. I was sprawled on what felt like the hardest, most uncomfortable bed that'd ever had the privilege of cradling my big, beautiful ass. It was better than dirt or a pile of rocks, I supposed.

The room was small and looked like it was cobbled together by someone who had just discovered the color gold and was hell-bent on sharing his newfound enthusiasm with the world. The walls were adorned with intricate patterns and embellishments, each traced in some gleaming, gilded ink. The ceiling was formed into an arcing dome, studded with etchings that told some indeterminate fairy tale or something. There were no windows, only a heavy wooden door with a fancy golden knob that matched the rest of the room. It was dim in there, the only light spilling in from the cracks beneath the door and a single, low-glowing lantern on the nightstand next to me.

I fumbled with the light for a moment before figuring out how to make it brighter. Which happened with sudden intensity.

Goddamn fucking magic!

I squinted, my vision blurry, as I tried to take it all in. It was too damn bright in this room, too motherfuckin' . . . golden and shit. I noticed now that my regular fucking awesome skull-kicker costume was not on my body and what I was wearing looked like a light blue nightgown.

"Is this a fuckin' muumuu?" I wondered, looking down at myself. "Oh, this is real cute."

I looked ridiculous. The coarse linen grazing my bare legs made me feel somewhat . . . vulnerable.

"What in the name of hell?" I said to nobody in particular.

Pushing myself off the bed, I stumbled to my feet, my legs wobbling beneath me like a baby deer. I took a moment, waiting for the room to stop spinning. Once my equilibrium found its way back to me, I padded across the cold stone floor, my bare feet slapping against the surface. The door was only a few feet away, but it felt like a mile.

I paused in front of the door and shot a quick glance around the room.

Where the fuck was my stuff?

I'd been half-expecting to see my shit piled in a corner. But . . . weren't nothin' there. I suddenly felt even more exposed than before. I didn't have any of my belongings except for the goddamn maxi dress—and for whatever reason, I wasn't dead. Unfortunately, the vast majority of my things had been in the Feather Chest, and *that* had been in Jumpy's possession—wherever the fuck he was. I was pretty sure that, based on the color of the portal when I'd been fired into it, I wasn't in Palandis. Though I guess it wasn't a complete wash. Whoever had dressed me down hadn't removed my fine jewelry, because I did still have my Ring of Redoubt and . . .

"Zhakko!" I hiss-spoke in the arcane tongue.

There was a flash of blue from the bracelet, and suddenly, Edwig was . . . well, not *standing* in front of me, but he was there, looking as confused as I felt.

"Pah! Where are we at? A brothel?" The illisinaf demanded, his eyes swiveling around before landing on me. "Yep. Brothel."

"Shut up," I said, pointing to my dressing gown. "I just woke up like this. Things went south at the portal."

"Pah! Of course they did! Can't ever have a usual time with you around, orc," Edwig said, adjusting his sweater vest and doing something that looked like stretching. "So, where have we ended up? A bit small and flashy to be a jail cell."

"Yeah, well, you'd be the expert there," I said. "And . . . I dunno. Like I said, I just woke up here. When Arjee went through the portal before me, his little trinket got ripped out of my body, and then I ended up here when I went through. I thought I was toast, man. There was so much blood . . ."

"What do you mean, 'trinket'?" Edwig wondered, giving me a suspicious glare.

"Nothing, never mind—it would take too long to explain," I said. "I just want to figure out where we are and then we have to figure out how to get to the others. I'm sick and fucking tired of getting separated from people."

"Pah! Don't worry about that, orc," Edwig said. "If we can find the Gateway you came through—or another like it—I can get us where we need to be."

"You can? How?"

"I'm part of the Mages' Order, orc," he said. "We've all pulled portal duty from time to time. Kind of a punishment, really."

"Oh," I said, shrugging. "That's good news, then. I figured . . . I dunno, that you'd need a specialization or something."

"Not for these kinds—that would be inefficient," he said, then he glared. "Why would you think I'm not specialized in it, anyway?"

"Well," I said, considering. "From what I understand . . . portals work with . . . what is it? Cosmic Arcana, right? You haven't done anything with cosmic Arcana—from what I can tell. Your specialty seems to be, I dunno, being annoying? But also some kind of copying magic?"

Edwig stared at me silently.

"What?" I asked.

"How do you know any of that?" Edwig asked.

"What do you mean? I pay attention!"

Truth be told, if it hadn't been for meeting the crew in the Crypt and having to listen to them prattle on and on about cosmic magic—really making it into a lecture, ya know—I wouldn't know any of that.

"I'm just impressed, is all," Edwig said—and he really did sound like he was struck dumb at the thought of me . . . not being completely dumb.

"Fuck you, Viggo," I said. "Anyway! Let's table this for now. We can get into the nuts and bolts of my overwhelming genius later—we gotta figure out where we are and get your jiggly ass to a portal so we can meet up with everyone."

"Pah! I know that!"

"Well, I guess let's go, then . . ." I said, turning toward the door.

I stooped and began to inspect it. Despite being a fancy-pants variety, it looked mostly like a normal door. I genuinely didn't know how to check for traps or, like, an alarm or anything, so I just went with an old classic. Pressing my ear against the cool wood of the door, I tried to discern any movement from outside. The silence was as thick as tar. I couldn't hear a damn thing.

"Anything?" Edwig asked.

"Nah, I can't hear shit," I said.

Well, there was one way to find out what was going on.

I hesitated for just a second longer before gripping the fancy knob and turning it as silently as I could manage. The door swung open with a quiet creak, and I found myself peering into a long, opulent hallway that stretched out in both directions. Sconces lined the walls, housing glowing crystals that bathed the corridor in a soft, warm light.

In the distance, I thought I heard the faint murmur of voices, but they were too far to make out anything definitive. I turned back to Edwig, closing the door behind me and leaning against it, running a hand through my hair.

"Wait," I said suddenly, looking at Edwig, who instantly got tense.

"Trouble?" he demanded, and his hands flared up as he gathered a Spell of some kind.

"What color is my hair?" I asked him seriously.

"What?!" he practically yelled.

"My hair," I continued. "What color is it?"

"Pah! The usual color, orc! What are you talking about?!"

"Usual like . . . black, or usual like the bright kind?"

"It's looks like the inside of that ghost's brain. Multicolored."

"Fuck!"

I'll admit to having had a small glimmer of hope that enduring the effigy being ripped forcefully and painfully out of my belly meat would have caused my punk-rock locks to go back to normal. But I guess that was just another present Santa forgot on my Christmas list.

"Never mind," I sighed, then turned back to the door. "It's an empty hallway out there. I think we're in some rich guy's house or something. Lots of one-percent-style crap on the walls."

"Hm," Edwig said. "If that's the case, we need to be cautious—could be guards."

"Yeah, and I don't have any weapons on me."

"Pah! This isn't an ideal situation, orc."

"Yeah—no shit," I said.

"Just where did you drag me to?" he wondered.

"Well, let's figure that out, shall we?" I said. "Well, really, you stick around in here, and I'll go check it—"

"Pah!" Edwig exclaimed. "I'm not sitting around in this room—makes me twenty sorts of claustrophobic. I'm coming with."

"While I can appreciate your heebie-jeebies with tight spaces, Viggo—you're not exactly stealthy."

"And you are?"

"What are you talking about?" I demanded. "Yes. It's literally the thing I do."

"Pah! Since when?"

"Since whe— What are you—are you stupid? I'm super fucking sneaky, dude! That was the whole reason I came along on this halfwit mission."

"I just assumed that it was because you're the biggest halfwit in the camp," Edwig said.

"Why are you trying to rile me up right now?" I asked.

"Because you don't have any weapons," he admitted. "Seemed like the best time."

"You can't come with," I reaffirmed. "You'll get us caught."

"Pah! You don't even know that there's something out there to catch us!"

"You just said there *might be guards*," I groaned. "Make up your fucking mind, ass-snout."

"The way I see it, I have Arcana that could be useful. You'd be wasting my talents, leaving me in here. Besides, it's not as though I need your permission."

"Fine . . ." I hissed. "But if there's a time for actual sneakin' around and *not* getting caught by whoever put me here, can you at least leap back in that bracelet?"

"Pah! Absolutely not!" Edwig said, super grumpy at the idea of it all of a sudden. "It's uncomfortable in there."

I'm going to fucking kill this idiot, I thought to myself. But rather than argue further, I just turned back to the door.

"Alright, let's see what the happy-haps are in this janky joint."

As soon as we stepped into the hallway, a shiver ran down my spine. I had the feeling of eyes on me. It was fucking weird. The corridor was void of any visible presence, but something still felt off. I motioned for Edwig to stay close, and together we began to carefully move down the hallway.

Most of the doors we passed were ornately designed with gold knobs, each one slightly different from the one before it. The corridor was decked out with expensive paintings depicting abstract art and landscapes that looked far too serene for our tense situation. The rich crimson carpet under our feet was plush, our footfalls silent. Well, mine were. Edwig's movements just sounded a little like sex noises, or like . . . someone eating lasagna on wet grass.

I felt kind of stupid, skulking around like that. You know, wildly visible in the middle of a hallway with light everywhere.

I gestured to the crystal array along the walls to Edwig and then got close. I knew they were probably what I had learned were called magelights—I mean, far be it from anyone in this godforsaken place to use non-arcane means to light stuff. Which meant if I didn't want some kind of unknown hazard to rise to the occasion and put *my* lights out, I might want to be careful. So, I activated Eye of the Saboteur.

> Ooh! Pretty, pretty! Mysterious! Arcane lights designed to really give a space a glow-up, am I right? It almost distracts from the unglamorous reality, that of the common folk toiling tirelessly in the shadows of their dilapidated shelters, void of even the simplest luminosity. Sad.

I sighed. This was getting aggravating and tedious. However, the oddly underdog-fixated message notwithstanding, the secondary feature of the Ability was what I was really after. Thankfully, whatever malware that had caused the System messages to go all wonky hadn't infected that yet.

A visual display of the pieces of the magelight appeared in front of me. It was easy to see the entirety of the... honestly pretty simple device. After examining it for a moment, I was moderately confident I could just pluck the stone out and have no issues.

I turned to Edwig and pointed up at the magelight.

"Think it's safe to just take the crystal?" I whispered.

"Most likely," he returned after scowling at it for a second. "Seems garden-variety, really."

I shrugged and just snatched the little beacon outta there and watched as the light disappeared instantly. Then, because I figured I was owed something for my confusion, I stuffed the crystal into the pocket of the muumuu and moved along. I repeated the process with each magelight we encountered, feeling ever stealthier as the light died out, until our entire stretch of hallway was fairly dark.

"Do you have Darkvision?" I asked Edwig as I activated the Ability.

"No!" he hissed. "I can barely see now."

I just chuckled and continued on. Guess he was going to have to figure out what this place looked like through echolocation or something.

I stopped, considering.

Fucking Christ—I'm so goddamn stupid.

Hadn't my Eye of the Saboteur gotten an upgrade? And didn't that mean it had gotten stronger?

Time to test this puppy out.

Tentatively, I placed a hand on the wall and reactivated Eye of the Saboteur. I ignored whatever dipshit message cropped up and then focused on expanding the sensation. As soon as the Ability pushed out further, I nearly shouted in surprise. The drab hallway instantly transformed into a sprawling, intricate blueprint, one that even Da Vinci would've drooled over. I could see through walls, around corners, and, hell, even up and down floors. The whole damn mansion—and I knew it was a mansion now—was stripped bare before me.

Now, I've been in a few gold-painted shitholes in my time, but this . . . this was some next-level excess. The sprawling floor plan stretched out around me, each room painstakingly detailed in glowing red, white, and blue outlines. Living rooms, dining halls, kitchens, bathrooms, all those boring essentials. There were even a few rooms filled with nothing but statues. Seriously, who needs a whole fucking room for statues, let alone multiple?

The most impressive thing, though, was the place's size. It looked like some twisted fusion dance between a luxury resort and a medieval castle. Like the sort of place you'd expect Dracula to holiday in. Halls led to halls, rooms connected to more rooms, stairs spiraled up to . . . fucking everywhere.

I traced from where I presumably stood, the Eye giving me a clear path through the labyrinthine layout. Nice, clear, and painted in soothing blue and white. The way out was a set of heavy double doors at the end of a ridiculously long entrance hall that basically got in my face, raving, *I am the fucking exit!*

As my gaze floated over the whole fuckin' venue, something in the heart of the building snagged my attention. Some kind of odd circular room smack-dab in the center. And when I say *odd*, I mean really, *really* odd. You might even say *weird as fuck* if you were the poetic sort. Unlike the other parts of this overdone palace, the blueprints there were a chaotic mess. It looked like a whirlpool of blue lines, tangled and twisted, and at the heart of it, a red, glowing sphere.

I'm willing to bet that this little baby is our portal. Well, this is going to be easier than we thought.

Slowly but surely, we made our way through the network of opulence in the dark, every so often hearing the faint murmur of conversation but never catching sight of anyone. It was as if we were in a ghost retreat, surrounded by luxury yet devoid of life.

The paranoia was starting to get to me. Even considering Eye of the Saboteur, without my weapons, I felt completely defenseless. There was something unnerving about this place, and I still couldn't shake the feeling that we were being watched.

We kept stealing crystals, my muumuu pockets getting more and more engorged. Eventually, we reached a staircase that I'd seen with the Eye, and I stopped at the top to look down.

That's when the voices filtered in. They'd only been a droning murmur at first, like the distant hum of a running engine. I motioned for Edwig to follow me, and we moved toward the voices, our steps cautious and slow. They were coming from below, at the bottom of a staircase that led down into a brighter area, flooded with light.

Now their voices morphed into discernible words. It was a man's voice, laid back and lazy like a calm, unhurried rhythm, as though he was in no rush to get to the end of his sentences. Matching his tune was the chime of a female voice, bubbly and light. It danced through the mansion, weaving between the man's deeper notes. She sounded young, excited maybe, or nervous, with a slight giggle hanging off her words. Her sentences trailed into soft laughter more often than not, a melody as infectious as it was disturbing in this shitty tomb of a building.

". . . Spotted orc nearly bit the dust," the man's voice drawled, sounding almost bored.

They're talking about me! I thought anxiously. *Well, fuck, guess I'm going to need to figure out an alternate plan.*

The man's words hung in the air, part of a bigger narrative I'd stumbled into, as though I'd just turned on the TV to some mid-season episode of a soap opera.

"No kidding?" the woman's voice returned. "Poor thing, and here in my house, too."

"Your house? Hell, Tialara, you make it sound like you built this place brick by brick."

I heard her huff.

"Well, someone has to look after it," she said, with a hint of pride sneaking into her words. "So, while I'm here, it's my house. Call it caretaking."

"Didn't figure you for the mothering type."

"Well, I didn't figure you for the bringing-home-strays type, but here we are," she shot back playfully.

"Point taken." There was an admission in his tone, a sign of a long-forgotten argument. "Think I'll check on our stray, then."

"I think he's had enough excitement for one day, Buck. Don't you? Let him rest."

"Rest up, huh? Yeah . . . Good idea. It's going to get rough for him soon enough, anyway."

'Rough for him'? What the hell does that mean? My gut churned at the thought.

Despite the risk, curiosity got the better of me. I crept down the stairs, staying hidden in the shadows. Edwig, ever the liability, noisily slopped down to follow me, prompting a poisonous silence to fall over the discussion, followed by:

"What was that?"

It was the woman. The man, in lieu of saying anything, seemed to move, and I saw a blur of motion at the bottom of the stairs and several shimmering flashes with a loud clang. My breath caught in my throat as I saw him more clearly: he was a fucking . . . devil?

As I peered from the shadows, the figure at the bottom of the stairs was quite the spectacle. He was an odd sort of fucker, not particularly dressed for a scrap but still carried an air of *don't fuck with me* menace. No flashy plate armor or glimmering chainmail on this guy; instead, he was dressed in the rough equivalent of a farmer's Sunday best—a tunic that had seen better days, stitched-up breeches, and worn boots that looked like they were hand-me-downs from the last gigantic fiend that had donned 'em. I had to think he wore this because it was the only thing that would fucking fit.

Still, he was a mountain of a monster, with a face that looked like it had been used for stone carving practice. Two hefty black horns jutted out from his forehead, curving upwards like Satan's own eyebrows. They looked like they had been buffed to an ominous shine, the gleam making them all the more menacing. His eyes glowed like two bright purple embers smoldering in the night. The intensity of their gaze was enough to set my nerves on edge. The way they scanned the area, it was as if they could set anything they landed on ablaze.

The cherry on top of this monstrous sundae was the pair of huge shields clutched in his gnarly ham fists. I'm not talking regular *deflect a couple of arrows* shields but massive hunks of metal that could've easily served as doors for a fortress. The earsplitting clang that had echoed through the mansion was undoubtedly from him slamming these beastly bucklers onto the floor.

"Upstairs!" echoed the woman's voice from earlier. She sounded anxious now. The devil-like man's fiery eyes flicked upward, seemingly piercing through the shroud of darkness that Edwig and I had taken refuge in. That was the exact moment I felt my pulse accelerate.

This was shaping up to be quite the evening, wasn't it?

"Illisinaf," he said, his voice still lazy-sounding, despite the intensity of the situation. In that moment, his severity melted away, and he stood fully.

Goddammit, Edwig! I thought. *You went and got us caught just like I said you would.*

Edwig, having been clearly spotted, seemed to deflate a little, and slopped backward as if trying to protect himself. Fortunately, I hadn't yet been seen—and it seemed like Edwig, who was frantically looking around, had lost track of me as well.

Good.

I mean, I wasn't going to let him get murdered or anything, but keeping my presence an unknown variable was a benefit for the moment. Who knows? Maybe I'd need to surprise-attack the fucker and—

"Illisinaf?" came the woman's voice, and I saw a form stop next to the big man. "What's an illisinaf doing here?"

My train of thought went completely off the rails and smashed into a ravine when I got a good look at her. The woman, or whatever she was, had glided into view with an otherworldly grace that somehow managed to make her simple outfit of brown pants and forest-green shirt look like it was woven from moonlight itself.

She was breathtaking—like a deity dropped into our undeserving realm and her ethereal beauty hit me like a punch to the gut. Her skin was fair and flawless, almost glowing with a light that seemed to come from within her, an illuminated porcelain canvas untouched by the ravages of time.

Her eyes, a profound and captivating emerald, sparkled with an inner fire that mesmerized me, like stars trapped in two glistening pools. I found myself unable to look away, ensnared by their luminescence. High, delicate cheekbones framed her perfect face and a cascade of seafoam-colored hair flowed down her back, shimmering with the same luminescent quality as her skin.

Her full lips were the color of soft pink roses, and the way they moved when she spoke was a thing of beauty, each syllable like a melody that could bring the most stoic asshole to their knees. Even her voice was charming, with an allure so profound that it seemed to seep into your bones, demanding your attention, commanding your senses. Sis was *snatched*.

Sprouting from the sides of her head were pointed ears—longer than an elf's but similar enough to draw a comparison. They looked lovely.

She turned to the man, her voice lilting and filled with concern. "What did you say you . . ."

Her eyes found Edwig, who seemed incapable of doing anything more than existing. The woman smiled.

"Who are you?" she wondered cheerily. "I don't recall inviting anyone to join our little get-together."

"Orc . . ." Edwig hissed in my direction. "What do we do here?"

But I wasn't listening. The sight of the woman was too intoxicating. My senses were overwhelmed, my mind reeling, and for a second, I forgot that I was supposed to be hiding. As if moving of its own accord, my hand rose, and I found myself stepping out from the shadowy staircase, into the light. A dazed, stupid grin was plastered on my face as I waved at the radiant apparition standing at the bottom of the stairs.

"Oh . . . hi there!" I said, my voice oddly high and strangled.

Well . . . so much for the element of surprise.

CHAPTER TWENTY-THREE

GOD'S JUST A JAWBONE

"Well, it's great that you're doing well! It was . . . how do they say it, touch-and-go for a while?" the beautiful woman said.

"Yeah . . . I'm happy . . . .uh, with it—the healies," I said, smiling dumb-as-fuckly.

We were all sitting in a gigantic room on plush velvet couches in front of a roaring hearth. Or, at least, I think we were. It was hard to tell, considering I only had eyes for the enchanting beauty sitting less than ten feet from me. Every time her eyes found mine, I felt a surge of butterflies in my veins. It was a feeling that I knew meant I would do *whatever* she wanted, and it would be the best thing that ever happened to me to assist her.

"Tialara," the huge devil man said. "You might want to drop the Allure."

Tialara—the world's most perfect woman—simply slapped the big creature's arm.

"Oh, Buck, but it makes people so . . . acquiescent to conversation. You're just upset it doesn't work on you."

"Tialara . . ." he said in a lazy sort of warning.

"Fine! Fine!" Tialara—beauty incarnate—said. Then she wiggled her nose cutely, and suddenly, it was like a bubble popped.

Just like that, my head was clear. Like stepping out of a thick, intoxicating fog into the crisp, cold morning air. There she still sat, the woman—Tialara—still strikingly beautiful, but the intense enamored stupor that had left me swooning like a starstruck teen at their first metal concert had vanished.

A hot surge of indignation washed over me. I shook my head, feeling as if I'd just been dunked in ice-cold water. My mind rebelled, wrestling with the sudden withdrawal of . . . whatever the fuck that was.

Reality crashed back into me. The roaring hearth, the devil-looking man, the damn bejeweled mansion. Everything seemed to sharpen, the edges of my reality snapping back into high definition.

Goddammit, I'd been ensnared! Manipulated. Who the fuck are these people?

My previous infatuation curdled in my gut, turning to pure, unadulterated rage. I wanted to snap, to yell, to let them both know just how pissed I was. But the cold, rational part of my brain that had somehow managed to stay functioning reminded me of the situation. We were, quite literally, in the lion's den.

I forced a smile onto my face, hoping it looked less like a snarl.

"That was . . . a hell of a trick, Tialara."

My words hung in the air like a bad smell, the friendly charade not quite holding up. My fists clenched and unclenched, the fingers twitching with a violent urge I had to swallow down.

"Oh, don't look so glum, handsome," she responded, her emerald eyes glinting with something I couldn't quite read. Maybe amusement, or possibly satisfaction. Maybe both. "Just wanted to make sure you were comfortable."

Comfortable, my ass. That was a dirty, rotten, no-good prank.

It also reminded me of being fooled into drinking the Potion of Oratory Splendor by Zeol—which I was still pissed about, now that I was thinking about it. It had been surreptitiously fed to me and given me an inability to speak anything other than the King's English—er, Common—for a whole minute like I was on some lackluster *Masterpiece Theatre* vehicle.

I felt my eye twitch with suppressed anger. The more I sat there, the more I wanted to punch something. I forced a chuckle out, the sound grating to my own ears.

"Yeah, I've never felt so fucking comfortable in my life. What was that, by the way?"

"Oh, just Allure," the woman said, shrugging. "It's a great defensive mechanism for protecting the property."

"I'll fucking bet," I said. "Be hard for intruders to get away with anything if they're suddenly stumbling all over themselves to whisk you away on a honeymoon."

Buck chuckled. I shot him a glance, one that probably had enough venom to floor a bull.

"Quite the comedian, isn't he?" Buck's monstrous grin was full of pointy, white teeth. They were probably capable of chomping my head off in one bite.

"Yep," I muttered, not caring how sarcastic I sounded. "I'm a regular fucking court jester."

If they wanted to see me dance, I'd dance—but I wasn't about to do it happily. I'd find out what their game was, and once I did, they'd regret ever dragging me into it. I'd make damn sure of that.

"Who in the hells are you people?" Edwig demanded suddenly. I was impressed with his vigorous vitriol, since I was usually the one spouting out angry rebuttals. This was especially telling considering he was all about proper introductions—a fact he had made painfully clear multiple times since I'd known him.

"Well," said the woman. "As mentioned, I am Tialara. Tialara fen Abrrigask vis Lirenteamyalar. You're in the house I currently steward."

"First of all," I started, shaking my head, "that's one of the longest fucking names I've ever heard in my fucking life. Jesus Christ—you Welsh or something?"

Edwig let out a grunt of approval.

"Second—this ain't a house; it's a goddamn Ritz-Carlton. How many fuckin' rooms are in this bitch? I'm pretty sure your laundry room has a laundry room."

"Oh, hm," Tialara said, tapping a manicured finger against her chin in thought. "If you count the kitchens, washrooms, and several special chambers . . . seventy, maybe? Give or take a few."

However, Buck seemed fixated on me now.

Uh-oh.

"So, you're a Sojourner," he said simply, leaning back and smiling.

"Uh—waitaminute—what? No, I'm—I mean, uh . . ." I paused. "Sorry, could you repeat the question?"

"The jig is up, orc," Edwig said. "You said a whole lot of things that were beyond my comprehension. You might want to learn to keep a stopper in those outbursts of yours."

I sighed.

"Yeah," I admitted. "I'm a Sojourner; so what? You want to kill me now or something? 'Cuz— Oh, fuck—you're a Sojourner too, aren't you?"

If he'd understood any of what I said, that was definitely the case. Goddamn, how many freaking Sojourners *were* there in this place?

"Yeah," he said, nodding and shrugging. "But I wouldn't be so quick to admit to it if I were you. Only a handful of people know that about me."

"Yeah, yeah," I said. "That's what I've been told, but so far, I seem to only be running into others of our kind. Nobody else seems to care."

"You've been lucky, then," the big creature continued. "There's a lot of people out there that would be more than happy to cut your belly open if they found out."

That reminded me—my arrival there.

"Alright, so, *on that note*, what fucking happened to me? That last thing I—"

"Pah! You're a damn rude orc!" Edwig interrupted.

"What— Oh, do you mean—"

"The introductions have begun!" he continued, adopting a smug grin. "My tutelage is apparently lost on you."

"Jesus, now you sound like Arjee," I said.

"Pah! Don't compare me to that hideous specter," Edwig admonished.

"Just do your damn introductions, Quintham—Edwig Quintham, Undermoronic Reslurper at the honest-to-goodness Matron's Order."

He glared at me and then turned to our hosts, who seemed to now be waiting in expectant amusement.

"Pah! Don't listen to him!" Edwig said. "I am Quintham. Edwig Quintham, Undermagister Researcher at the august and venerable Mages' Order at Yosper Hall in Tallrock."

"Oh," I interjected. "Actually, it's not Tallrock anymore. Copyright issues or something."

"What?" Edwig shot. "What are you talking about, orc?"

"They . . . I dunno, changed the name. Carpathia or something, I think."

"Pah! I don't believe you. When did this happen?" Edwig demanded.

"Actually, I heard about that," Buck confirmed. "*Karepalea* is what it's called now, I think."

Edwig looked mortified. His eyes were bulging out of his jelly face, and he shook his whole body.

"Why would they change it?"

"Something about red mages?" I said. "I dunno. You were in the bracelet when Sister was talking about it, and I really wasn't paying attention, if I'm being honest."

"You met S'Rista?!" Edwig demanded. "What happened while I was—"

"Not to be rude," Tialara said, smiling, "but weren't we doing introductions?"

"Oh!" Edwig said, and I couldn't be sure, but it almost looked like his body took on a pink shade of embarrassment. "Right. How rude of me. Yes, well, as I said—"

"I'm Loon," I said. "Barbarian hobbyist, professional sex machine."

I winked at Tialara, but she just raised an eyebrow—so I felt stupid.

"As you've probably picked up, I'm Buck," the devil-lookin' dude said, leaning forward. "Sojourner, like Loon. Been here about ten years."

That's about how long Fawn said she's been here, I thought. *I wonder if they know one another.*

"Anyway, now that *that's* outta the way," I started, clapping, "what's the deal?

What happened after I went through that portal with my private insides spilling out all over the public?"

Buck and Tialara exchanged glances. Then Buck nodded at my stomach.

"I was getting ready to go out on an excursion of my own. Tialara was helpfully lending me use of Madam Marrow's Gateway when it suddenly spat you out. Fortunately, our hostess here has a wide variety of remedies at her disposal."

"I'm sorry—did you say *Madam Marrow?*" I asked. "That sounds goth as fuck. Like the name of a band I'd have been bumpin' back home."

"Well, you'd probably appreciate, then, that she's a vampire," Buck said casually.

"What?!" I roared, then looked to Tialara, aghast. "Your roommate is a bloodsucker?"

That explains the lack of windows in this place, I thought. *Also, this being Dracula's vacation zone was spot on. Goddamn, I'm a motherfuckin' wunderkind.*

Tialara smiled, and I felt my heart leap in my chest. She really was beautiful.

"Well, it's more complicated than just that," she said. "But for simplicity's sake: yes. More than that, though, she's my employer."

"Seems like a bad idea to move in with your coworkers," I said. "But what do I know? Not like I ever had a job for long enough to fall into that sort of situation."

"Oh? Did you live alone?" Tialara asked.

"Nah, I've been living with my aunt and uncle for the last few years— Wow, listen to me, I'm not sure why I told you that."

"Tialara . . ." Buck said, and the effervescently charming Tialara shrugged her gorgeous shoulders and winked.

"Sorry," she said. "Habit."

She wiggled her nose again, and I suddenly felt a similar sensation as before drop, except not as strong.

"Hey," I said severely. "Don't do that shit again."

"I'm sorry," she said, making a pouty face. "It's in my nature. I'll try to remember to not slip into it with our present company."

"Okay—anyway," I began, attempting to let bygones be fucking bygones. "So, I came through there and you healed me. Then, for some reason, you stripped me bare and put me in this sundress? Where's my stuff?"

"Well, we thought it best to see what kind of person you were," Buck said. "Didn't want you to wake up and create problems, right? If you weren't aware, you're a pretty intimidating-looking guy."

I nodded.

"Yeah, safety first," I said. "But, talkin' 'bout intimidating: look at you, man. You're easily, what—half a foot taller than me? You look like you could put a dragon in a headlock and make him cry. You a vittra?"

He did look similar to the devil race that Veruca was piloting around, though he was *way* bigger and didn't have a tail.

"No, 'fraid not," he said. "Just your run-of-the-mill oni."

"Oh," I said, pretending I understood. "So . . . not a vittra?"

He chuckled.

"No, but I think *here* they might be related in some way," Buck said. "But that might just be me being unintentionally racist."

"Hey, I'll take accidental racism over purposeful racism any day," I said. "Which . . ."

I looked him up and down.

". . . I'm sure you get it worse than me."

"Pah! You talk a lot about prejudice for someone goin' around referring to me as 'Jigglepuss'." Edwig interjected.

"Hey, now," I said. "I called you 'Jigglypuff,' and you misheard me, remember? But . . . fair point. I'll keep all of my insults personality-related from now on, Jigglepuss. Lord knows there's enough to work with there."

Edwig quivered with irritation, but I moved on before he could continue.

"So . . . can I have my stuff back? Clearly, I'm not a threat. Even if I tried anything, you could just femme-fatale me into a blithering boner."

"Sure thing!" Tialara said, and then placed one finger in the air. She traced a pattern that I didn't recognize—but sorta looked like a pentagram—and then I watched as the space in the air in front of her suddenly opened like a trapdoor. She held her hand out, and suddenly, a bunch of things fell into her lap.

"My things!" I cheered happily, seeing the untidy pile of my belongings.

Then she closed the magical trapdoor rift with a wave of her hand and gathered the items up in her arms and brought them over to me. I accepted them gratefully, then immediately stood and pulled the muumuu over my head. I balled it up and hucked it at Edwig, just to be a dick, and it sailed over and landed on him, draping over his head. I hurriedly began putting my badass fightin' outfit on and started stuffing my weapons into my belt.

"What was that Spell?" I asked, buckling one of my torso belts over my chest to fix my furred pauldrons in place.

"Oh, that?" Tialara asked, gesturing in the empty air where the rift had been a moment before. "Storage space. Comes in handy!"

"I'll say. I gotta get me an inventory hole like that."

When I was finally finished donning all my goodness, I sat back down, feeling a lot more like the menace the world deserved.

"So, about your injury," Buck said, "can I ask what happened?"

"Oh," I said. "It was sorta . . . self-inflicted, I guess you could say. I was keeping something important inside me, and it was pulled into the portal before I was. Then there was all the hullabaloo with the Mages at the portal—"

"What hullabaloo?" Edwig asked. He'd removed the muumuu from his head, and now it was on the ground.

"Uh, they thought I was trying to skip ahead of the line, and so, they didn't get to cast their little Spell to send me along. But I brute-forced my way in by virtue of the law of gravity, and here we are."

Edwig gave me a dark look.

"*Were* you trying to skip the line?"

"What? No! What do you take me for?"

"A line-skipper," he said.

"Well, I'm *not*. There was a whole sequence of events that resulted in that eventual outcome. In fact, I was very specifically being a line-abiding citizen. Scout's honor."

He just stared at me as if he didn't believe me, but didn't say anything further.

"Well," Buck said. "It's fortunate you ended up here, then. Many places you could have ended up might not have been as friendly with their healing. It's not uncommon for criminals to try to escape authorities by Gate-hopping, thinking they're going to be able to circumvent their misdeeds if they're far enough away. If someone were to come through injured, they'd likely toss them in a cell first and wait to see if anyone came out of the portal after them before doing anything helpful."

"Honestly, if Buck hadn't convinced me otherwise, I probably would have just put you out of your misery," Tialara said. "Or left you for the Madam to take care of."

I shuddered. Then I turned to Buck.

"Why *did* you spare me, then? Bewitched by my natural charm and charisma and thought the world a dark place without it?"

"Pah! I don't know how enchanting you'd be, holding your guts in."

"Shut up, Edwig," I said absently.

Buck smiled.

"Actually, it was your . . . weapons," he said, and I wasn't sure, but it seemed like he'd been about to say something else. "They were intriguing, and I haven't seen anything quite like them."

I lifted the haladie and the pique, admiring them in the golden glow of the room.

"Yeah, they're pretty fuckin' baller, right? These bad boys have gotten me through some rough times. Speaking of *rough times*—what the fuck were you talking about before?"

"Ah . . ." Buck said. "I was referring to the fate you'd have been left to with Tialara."

"What fate?" Tialara asked sweetly, but it was clear she knew what he was talking about.

"You mean the love-potion Spell?" I asked. "Yeah, if that's the alternative, just fucking let me bleed out."

"You were talking about weapons," Edwig said. "I'd like to hear more about your opinions of the orc's choices."

"Well, actually," Buck said, seeming perfectly happy to abruptly change subjects. "I have to admit I've been delayed enough as it is with this detour. So, if you want, we can let you get through to wherever it was you were originally trying to go, and I'll head out as well."

"Aw," Tialara groaned. "But if everyone leaves, it's going to be so lonely here. You sure you boys don't want to stick around? I'll get the spectral servants to whip up something delicious for dinner. How does everyone feel about rakara eggs?"

"As appetizing as that grossly named abomination sounds . . . Buck's right. We *should* probably get going," I said. "We have friends waiting for us, and they're likely sniffling and sobbing right now on account of the fact that their fearless leader hasn't shown up yet."

"Pah! Bet they're drinking celebratory beers," Edwig muttered.

"You wanna go back in the bracelet, snarky-pants?" I asked, pointing at the circle of gold on my wrist. "'Cuz that's where your time-out's gonna be if you keep takin' potshots at my character."

"That sounds more like an attack on your friends' integrity than yours," Tialara offered merrily. "You've been absolutely splendid company."

"See?" I said to Edwig. "The extremely lonely house sitter gets it. I'm *splendid*."

"Where were you going, anyway?" Buck asked, standing up. "We should probably head that way before it gets too late. Depending on your final destination, some places shut down early and don't reopen until morning."

"We are headin' to Palandis," I said.

"Hm," Buck said, lazily and thoughtfully. "Interestingly . . . that's where I'm headed as well."

"Ooh! Convoy!" I said. "Nice!"

Serendipity seemed to follow me around. Even if sometimes serendipity was a damn contrary motherfucker. I'd have checked my Luck stat, but considering the last time I had, the message had simply said, *Pip! Pip! Somebody's tempting fate!* . . . it seemed like I'd be wasting my time.

"Well, that settles it!" Tialara said, in her wonderfully charming way. "Palandis's Gateway is open all night! That means we can sup together!"

Really, it was amazing that she lived alone, when she should be surrounded by thousands of people clamoring to spend their time with her. Actually, that seemed like something I might want to do. Fuck my friends—there was just something about her.

"Yeah, let's do that," I said, my eyes never leaving her gorgeous, perfect face. "But what about breakfast? Hell, we could make a longer stay of it."

"Tialara . . ." Buck said warningly.

"Sorry," she said, wiggling her nose. "I just really want to entertain."

CHAPTER TWENTY-FOUR

DECAYIN' WITH THE BOYS

Once the effects of Allure wore off again, we, in fact, did eat. I have to say, whatever the fuck rakara eggs are, they're goddamn delectable. The spectral servants weren't even as weird as I thought they'd be, either. I figured they'd be like ghosts, floating around and comically trying to cut slices of meat for us only for their hands to phase through the knife; but they were actually mostly corporeal and looked like regular people.

Afterward, we said our goodbyes to Tialara, thanked her for her hospitality, and moved into the room that my Eye of the Saboteur had shown was full of wonky-ass patterns.

Ha! Take that, everybody else! Ol' Loon figured something out on his own!

Stepping into the portal chamber felt like being swallowed by a subterranean beast. But it wasn't a room; it was a cavernous cathedral to darkness and power.

The towering ceilings, lost in shadow, stretched high overhead, while the space itself spread out vast and deep, echoing with whispers of unseen machines and mystical fuckin' contrivances. Tapestries, dark and intricate, lined the stone walls—scenes of ancient battles and long-forgotten bullshit woven into their fabric. Each image seemed to move and shift subtly in the flickering magelight, adding an eerie sense of life to the stories they told. One depiction in particular drew my eye: a cowled individual hovering in place over a horde of wailing people as gray illumination radiated from behind it. Fuckin' brutal.

Dominating the room's center was the portal, a maelstrom of blood-red energy that churned within an ornate, gothic archway. The stone itself seemed to be alive, veins of luminescent energy pulsing beneath the surface. Scattered around the archway were cryptic devices—bundles of crystalline conduits, rune-etched slabs of obsidian, and enigmatic metallic contraptions, all humming with an ethereal light and a pulsing rhythm that resonated with the energy of the portal.

"Well, damn if this ain't the most extra thing I've ever seen," I muttered, unable to tear my gaze away. "Still . . . this is metal as fuck."

Edwig slid along beside me, his own eyes wide. Buck, in contrast, moved with purpose and ease, as though he'd been in places like this a thousand times before.

"So, is this like . . . the living room?" I asked, trying to break the tension. "Or, I guess, *un*living room."

Edwig sighed and shook his head.

"More like a back door," Buck replied, walking ahead toward the portal. "A very special one, at that."

He turned toward us, the light from the portal casting long shadows on his demonic features.

"I suggest you both go first. I'll come in after and make sure we all end up on the right side of the planet."

"Hey, I know how to use a portal," Edwig interjected, attempting to sound confident but only managing to sound petulant. "You step in, you step out. Easy as pie."

Buck chuckled at that. I gave the illisinaf a weird look.

"I thought you said you'd done this before—that doesn't sound very magical at all. Or correct."

"This isn't your run-of-the-mill arcane doorway," Buck said, motioning towards the swirling mass of energy. "This one's got a bit more nuance to it. It's likely why Loon managed to come through without a Gateway Enchantment."

"Well, you're the expert in the room," I said, sneering at Edwig, who gave me a look like he wanted to sock my lights out. "So, we'll defer to you. I'm not trying to get Brundlefly'd just because I didn't tuck my elbows in all the way."

"Alright," Buck said lazily. "In that case, if you want, you can go first. Step up to it and let me know when you're ready."

I tentatively made my way up the little dais and stopped right in front of the swirling vortex of red potential death. Then, getting an idea, I selected one of the only Spells I had at my disposal. One I hadn't used hardly at all. The last time I had . . . well, time to create some new memories.

Discover [Doorway]
- **Arcane Cost: 10 Arcana**
- **Range: 30 feet**
- **Duration: 5 Minutes**

- Restrictions: Utterance
- Wait: N/A

A Spell allowing the user to find hidden doorways, gates, and other exits or outlets within thirty feet. This Spell's duration is five minutes, after which time the opening cannot be found unless the spell is cast a second time. This Spell uses Utterance and, as such, must be spoken.

Huh, so it seems like if I've used it before—or if the content doesn't change—I actually get normal information outta the thing. Interesting. I'll have to keep that in mind.

Just like when I'd used it in the Crypt, I selected the Spell, and words began to spill out of my mouth.

"Though the passages of life may be dark, I summon the art of the discovery to make clear my path."

Instantly, information began to populate. It was . . . only a little helpful.

You have used the Discover [Doorway] spell!

Well, well, well! You're trying to use a Spell designed for discovering secret doors on a very obviously not-secret Gateway. I wonder what you were thinking when you got this grand idea. Well, I imagine you probably weren't thinking at all, you schmuck!

Oh, the places you could go!
Baraban [INACTIVE]
Cheryn'yrgyla [INACTIVE]
Esrel
Karepalea [INACTIVE]
Kethys [INACTIVE]
Kraychmarl
Larith
Machus City
Olteidton [INACTIVE]
Palandis
Redwater [INACTIVE]
Regis
Vistasuus
Tiber
Ys [INACTIVE]

. . . But you can't go to these places, because that's not how this Spell works. Better find someone with Gateway abilities! Good luck with that, actually.

I frowned.

So, the Spell did, at least, tell me which places this portal could take us to—and not only that, but it also told me which locations were currently active. If I could trust the information, that was good to know. Really glad I didn't see something like "Pontivex's Pleasure Palace," or anything.

"I'm ready," I said.

I heard Buck's voice behind me—lazy and hassled—as he began reciting a Spell of his own.

"Bridge to connect; pathways yield; use this Gateway to traverse where simple trails cannot bear fruit. Palandis."

Suddenly, the portal's crimson magic swirls turned silver, mimicking what they'd done when I'd seen Dragoon go through at Yosper Hall. Well, that was a relief.

"Is it safe?" I asked over my shoulder.

"Yeah, go ahead," Buck said.

I swallowed.

Well, here goes nothing . . .

I stepped forward and . . . found myself in pure darkness.

"What the dickens?!" I shouted, attempting to eloquently articulate my surprise.

But my voice came out as a feeble whisper, swallowed up by the thick silence of this place. The words hung in the void, eerie echoes that dissipated before they could gain any momentum. It was a strange thing, yelling in the abyss—like trying to make a splash by throwing pebbles into a painted portrait of the ocean.

It was inky black as far as my eyes could see, the kind of darkness that could play tricks on your mind. Even my Darkvision didn't work there. The world, devoid of all light, was unsettling and alien, yet . . . it definitely felt fucking familiar.

A surge of déjà vu washed over me. It was a similar sensation to that feeling you get when you walk into a room and suddenly forget why you came in—jarring, a little disconcerting, and confused why you're holding a bowl of pennies. It was an echo of a memory I couldn't quite place, the sensation of being immersed in the heart of a forgotten dream. That feeling stirred within me, worming its way up from the depths of my consciousness. No, this was not the first time I'd found myself embraced by the cold tranquility of an abyss—but, more importantly, *this* specific abyss. But the question remained—why was this so familiar?

"Alright, what bullshit is it *this time?*"

Nothing responded, and I was forced to simply dawdle, hoping some astral animal didn't swim up to take a bite out of me.

"This better not be another goddamn . . . *god* thing," I continued. "I've had it up to my cockles with that sorta malarkey. I got places to be, douchebags!"

Still nothing.

I sighed.

"Whatever is happening right now, you'd better have a damn good reason for—"

"Yooooooo!" a voice suddenly interrupted me out of the blue. "What's poppin,' slime?!"

It was young-sounding with a bit of a rasp to it. I recognized it immediately.

Suddenly, the entire world lit up, and I found myself standing in front of a swirling blue orb that looked as though it was filled with clouds. The Messenger orb—AKA, the very first creature I'd encountered in Regaia. It had been an oh-so helpful welcome wagon in ushering me into the world, and also giving me vague warnings about the possibility of what dire portents might befall me. Most uncomfortably, for some inexplicable reason, it had chosen to speak to me in moronically executed slang—think a scriptwriter in the nineties for a family-friendly extreme sports movie, desperately trying to nail "youthful jive." A direct route to comprehension town if ever there was one.

"Well, well, well," I said. "Long time no see, Snowglobe. How ya been?"

"Pretty lit, fam," the orb said. "I see you've been busy."

"Yeah," I said. "Can't complain—actually, I fucking can! What the *fuck*?"

"Whoa," the orb said. "Slow your roll, king—what's with the lack of chill vibes?"

"How dare you show up and act like all is hunky-motherfuckin'-dory in the land of the shitbirds? You did *not* prepare me for any of this dumb, convoluted bullshit. I got people out here tryin' to . . . *drink me* or whatever, and now I have to deal with your weird fuckin' poorly impersonated Gen Z gobbledygook! We don't even talk like that—at least, not all the time! What the hell is goin' on with your fuckin' management!?"

"Deadass," the orb continued. "Yeah, I'm, like, not your personal therapy tok, my guy—but you're obviously not practicing self-care at the moment. Kinda cringe. I'm here on official business, though."

"What the fuck are you talking about?" I demanded. "What official business?"

"Well, I thought it was mad strange that you hadn't come through in a minute, especially with the wild amount of Luck Accrual you've got on deck. I was low-key buggin' about it. So, I decided to swoop you myself."

"Luck Accrual?" I wondered. "What's that?"

"Bruh," the orb said, swirling annoyingly. "Zeol told you that you'd be collectin' some Ws if you were successful when your Luck was mid. I'm here to award 'em to you."

"Wait, so, that wasn't just bullshit?" I asked. "There's an actual quantitative value for that noise?"

"No cap," the orb said. "So, let's see . . ."

"Hold up," I said, taking a few accusatory steps forward. "First, I need an answer on something."

"Go off," the orb said.

"Oh, I plan to," I said. "Why the hell is my System all fucked up? It's worse than you are at giving me a straight answer."

"Bro, I can't tell you anything about that," the orb said.

"You've gotta be fucking kidding me," I said.

"Nah, f'real, bro—on god. It's above my pay grade."

"They *pay* you?" I asked in bewilderment.

"It's uh . . . just a phrase," the orb said.

"Oh, well, at least they're saving some fuckin' dollars with the *indentured servitude*. That's a relief."

"I'm not indentured," the orb said, sounding a little offended. "But, low-key, I *am* a servant. Still, I'm sorry AF I can't spill the tea."

"Yeah, I'm sure," I said sourly. "Anyway, whatever—let's just get to the award ceremony. I don't think either of us wants to be here any longer than we have to be."

"Facts," the orb said. "Alright, then—here's what you got."

The orb transformed itself into a sort of flatscreen, and I watched as information began to populate before me.

Luck Accrual

Congratulations! You've accrued Luck Badges!

Accumulating enough Luck Badges awards you various options for your personal use! These Badges are awarded based on your performance during times of low-Luck situations—netting one Badge per successful circumstance. However, failure during high-Luck situations results in a removal of Luck Badges. The amount of Luck Badges you have received is based on the cumulative amount of positive and negative Luck Badges received.

Luck Badges: 24

You may use Luck Badges to advance Attributes, or hold the amount for a later time.

Would you like to use your Luck Badges to advance your Attributes? Current ratio is 1–1.

[Yes / No]

"So . . . I basically just get extra Points?" I asked.

"Most def, sis," the orb returned. "You can use 'em up or bank 'em. But you gotta decide which."

"Do I get anything for holding off?"

"Other than delayed gratification? Nah, fam. Not really. You get some extra features depending on your cumulative, but . . . your cumulative goes up whether you use them or not—so, really . . . no presh either way. Your call, chief."

I sighed, then, when I realized what that meant, I actually got a little excited.

Twenty-four . . . Badges meant that I had a total of twenty-four *Points*. Which was exactly the kind of uplifting content I was there for.

"Oh, hell, yeah," I said. "Fuck off for a second, Jizzglobe, I'm gonna do some mental percolating."

". . . Bussin'," the orb said.

I paused.

"Hey there, bestie," I said in casual mockery. "You sure you used that right? Startin' to sound a little *cheugy*, if you ask me."

"Pfft, okay, Boomer," the orb said.

"Of fucking course . . ." I groaned. Then, because I didn't have the energy to deal with these sorts of shenanigans, I got to work.

It didn't take me long to figure out how I wanted to dole them bitches out. I was getting better at putting an outfit together; that was for sure. First, I put two Points into each of my Attributes, bringing Strength and Dexterity to nineteen, Wisdom and Charisma to thirteen, and Intelligence to fourteen. Then, because I'm nothing if not a bit of a rube—I put the remaining fourteen Points into Constitution. This brought that Attribute to a whopping fifty-six.

Fuckin' fear me, I thought.

Once I'd gotten that well and truly sorted, I made to return to my . . . extremely enlightening conversation with the orb, but that was when the screen changed again, and some new, equally baffling information populated before me.

Congratulations! For accruing at least 10 Luck Badges, you have unlocked [1] Luck-Based Ability!

Ability gained: Jeopardy Hunch

Jeopardy Hunch

An alarm system designed as though by the most neurotic of guardian angels. With it, you become privy to impending danger with the subtlety of a town crier on energy potions. Tripwire across the path? It's got your back. Poisonous serpent in your boot? It'll give you a heads-up. It's like having a paranoid grandmother in your head constantly warning you about the perils of . . . well, everything. Yes, perhaps it spoils the surprise element of the odd death trap here and there, but isn't life just a smidgen more interesting with a sprinkle of anticipatory dread?

"Jeopardy Hunch?" I said. "That sounds like *I* named it. What's the deal here? Not that I'm going to argue with a free meal—but, hell, this doesn't exactly feel earned."

Then, because we'd already built a bridge to the dynamic, I added, "Sus."

"Oh, there's more where that came from, fam," the orb said. "Check it out."

The display changed again, and this one, well . . . it was unique.

Congratulations! For accruing at least 20 Luck Badges, you have unlocked [1] Luck-Based Profession! Choose from the options below!

Available Professions:

Gambler

A professional risk-taker, the Gambler is your go-to for turning a copper into a kingdom or, more likely, a kingdom into a copper. With the ability to make you question the concept of probability itself, Gamblers thrive on the adrenaline of the unknown. Of course, they might occasionally bet the deed to the town's orphanage on a pair of threes, but where's the fun in playing it safe?

Gain Lucky Guess Ability

- Lucky Guess: Increases the success rate of making correct guesses or predictions in games of chance or decision-making scenarios.
    - Current Synergy: F-Rank (No Synergistic Abilities or Skills)

Fortune-Teller

Nothing spells uncertainty *quite like the future, but Fortune-Tellers would have you believe they've got it all sussed out. They're experts at casting their eyes into the depths of time, weaving cryptic tales, and just generally knowing more about your life than you do. But remember, when your fortune states* dangerous waters lie ahead, *they're probably not talking about your upcoming fishing trip.*

Gain Divination Ability

- Divination: The Ability to gain insights about a person, place, or object, with the accuracy determined by the Fortune-Teller's Luck stat.
    - Current Synergy: D-Rank (Insight)

Treasure Hunter

The eternal optimists of the adventuring world, Treasure Hunters can find the silver lining in any dungeon. To them, every rusty sword is a relic, every broken statue a priceless artifact, and every shiny pebble is, well, shiny. Their obsession with all things gold and glittery may result in a few extra goblin ambushes, but hey, no pain, no gain, right?

Gain Lucky Find Ability
- Lucky Find: A Passive Ability that increases the chance of finding valuable items or artifacts.
  - Current Synergy: F-Rank (No Synergistic Abilities or Skills)

Charlatan

Masters of the three D's—deception, distraction, and duplicity—Charlatans can talk their way out of a dragon's belly. They have an unerring knack for promising mountains and delivering molehills, all with a smile that could charm a harpy. Sure, they might sell you a map to a nonexistent treasure or convince you that the worn-out shoe is actually a magical artifact, but isn't the joy in the journey, not the destination?

Gain Misdirection Ability
- Misdirection: An ability that allows the trickster to distract others or divert their attention, often helping to escape tricky situations.
  - Current Synergy: C-Rank (Eye of the Saboteur + Deception + [Knowledge] Sabotage)

Trader

Traders are the beating heart of any economy—provided that heart buys low, sells high, and occasionally peddles suspiciously discounted health potions. They can spot a bargain in a trash heap and would probably sell their own grandmother if the price was right. So, yes, their scales might always tilt in their favor, but in a world where ruin could be around the corner, who wouldn't want a good haggle?

Gain Discerning Eye Ability
- Discerning Eye: An Ability that allows the Trader to assess the value of an item or a trade deal accurately.
  - Current Synergy: C-Rank (Eye of the Saboteur + Perception)

"No fuckin' way," I exclaimed. "I'm getting a Profession? A job?! Hell, yeah. Do I get any money from it?"

"Nah, fam," the orb said. "Not unless you actually apply it to a trade or something. This gives you the juice to start if you want, though. I mean, some of these options are *based*, but others . . . eh, not so much."

"Fuck you, Roy *Orbison*," I said. "You're just big mad that I got myself a pathway to financial independence."

"It ain't like that," the orb continued.

"Sure it isn't," I said. "Die mad."

"You're making this hella diffy to assist you, you know?"

"Die. Mad," I emphasized again.

"Deadass," the orb said. "How about choosing something so we can get this over with?"

"Don't mind if I do," I said.

I gave each Profession the consideration they deserved—mostly because I was now, slowly, starting to think about the long-term effects of my choices. Score one for proactivity, right?

But first . . .

Gambler. That was a title that had all the allure of a mysterious stranger in a smoky room, a stack of chips ready to be transformed into a life-changing fortune. But in reality, considering my previous profession of a semi-competent, mostly jobless slob in a world without magic, I was more likely to bet my life savings on a three-legged horse because its name was funny. Probably something like Tripod.

Hehe, Tripod . . .

Fortune Teller? Pass. I wasn't interested in knowing anything more about people than I already did—which was too much. Nah. Next!

Treasure Hunter. I guess it sounded kinda romantic—unearthing long-lost valuables and forgotten artifacts and shit. But . . . having Rexen in the roster made that sorta useless, right? He claimed to have a fuckload of boltholes to stow his vast arsenal of riches—not to mention the Crypt itself. And we were already on our way to purloin some of them precious objects, weren't we? Other than that, the idea just didn't really interest me all that much.

Charlatan. Hm. Well, that had a negative connotation from the get. Honestly, reading the description again, it sounded a lot like some of my family members. Maybe that's why it felt so comfortable? Suppose I'd put that in the *maybe* column. It had an Ability called Misdirection that would apparently mesh really well with my Eye of the Saboteur—like a peanut-butter-and-jelly waffle of wham-inducing mayhem.

Trader? The beating heart of the economy? The Discerning Eye Ability sorta beat tits—especially with whatever that Synergy seemed to mean. C-Rank, I guess. Which was the same as Misdirection. But overall? *Snore.* I didn't want to be associated with mercantile goods—and, like, what if it meant I'd have to actually care about selling things to people? Ugh. Plus, the term *Trader* brought back disturbing memories of middle school. For instance, the time I was swindled by Connor DeMarco into swapping my awesome lunch—which consisted of one hundred percent Snack Packs—for his gross tuna-and-tomato sandwich. Yeah, no, thank you.

So, after some extensive deliberation—which mostly involved silently mouthing the names and considering my previous life's minor traumas—I thought, *Fuck it*. If I'm going to be a lucky bitch, I might as well be a crafty one, too. Charlatan it is!

I selected the Profession and saw it populate into my character sheet as the screen morphed back into the orb.

"Slay," the orb said.

"If only," I said, eyeing it up and down. "So . . . is that it? I'm free to go?"

"One more thing," the orb said, and I noticed its color started to change from the traditional shimmering blue to . . . kind of a ghostly white.

"Sus," I said again. However, I received no knee-jerk response to my comment. Instead, the whole area seemed to darken a little, and I had the distinct impression that the Messenger orb was fuckin' with the acoustics in this joint, because when I tried to say, "What the H-E-double bean poles is going on?" nearly no sound at all escaped.

Oh, brother, what dicked-up balderdash is on the menu now?

"Yo, chillax, bro. It's just a minor tweak. An upgrade, if you will. All part of the dealio," the orb responded, and I could've sworn I heard a note of urgency hidden beneath its attempt at nonchalant lingo. The change in its color was also striking—like the transition from a sunny summer's day sky to the pallor of winter's chill. It was disconcerting, to say the least, yet I couldn't look away.

"Upgrade?" I repeated, trying to find my voice again in the dimmed echo-chamber of the void. "What kind of next-gen hipster mishmash is that?"

Before the orb could answer, I felt a strange pulling sensation—like an unseen force was gently tugging on the fabric of my being. The feeling was so subtle yet so profound that I wondered if it was actually there.

The orb maintained its silence, adopting a stillness that felt oddly serious in contrast to its usual snark.

"Are you . . . okay?" I asked, because why not?

The orb shimmered, its ghostly white facade casting a haunting glow in the otherwise muted void. It was beautiful, in a deeply unsettling, borderline ominous way.

"Yo, I'm Gucci, fam," the orb replied, finally breaking its silence. But its voice lacked its customary chutzpah—it felt hollow, almost grave. "Just gotta drop some four-one-one on you. There's something you should be . . . woke about."

"Yeah, sure," I said, trying to regain my composure, which was now hanging on by a thread. The orb's sudden shift in demeanor combined with the oddly tangible sensation of foreboding that was starting to creep up my coccyx.

The orb pulsed, and the fluctuation in its light cast ephemeral, ghost-like shadows around us.

"Now, keep your wig on, 'kay? This is gonna sound a little cray-cray, but it's straight printer."

"Spit it out, globe-boy," I muttered, crossing my arms and putting on my best *couldn't care less* face.

The orb let out a sigh—if an orb could sigh, that is. Then it began, "So, you've got your Profession, and that's sick, right? Well, here's the stitch. The System? It's like . . . it's like . . ."

I held my breath, waiting for the dramatic conclusion. The proverbial penny was hanging in the air, ready to drop and shatter the silence.

The orb shuddered, and in a voice that was barely more than a whisper, it finished: "It's like playing a game of fetch with a Rottweiler that hasn't decided yet if it's more interested in the stick or your hand."

I blinked, taking a moment to process. The comparison seemed utterly ludicrous, and yet . . . there was something about the way the orb had said it. Something that nudged at my instincts, igniting a flare of wariness within me.

"So, what? I should be careful?" I asked, trying to make sense of the cryptic warning. "'Cuz I'm way ahead of you on that."

"Something like that, homie," the orb replied, its glow fading slightly. "Just remember, ain't nothing in this world that's free, you feel? Not even the Skills you've been granted. Everything's got a price tag."

"Price tag?" I wondered.

"Also," the orb said, "you should do somethin' about those Esper Nodes. Advance 'em or something, king—you'll be glad you did."

I thought about that. The mystery of those little babies was still at large, and I was just tooting around with them jingling in my soul pocket like a set of loose keys.

"You're being weirdly helpful," I said. "Why?"

"We're all watchin', fam," the orb said, his voice sounding as though it was fading. "When the time comes, I hope you make the right call."

"What do you—"

But before I could finish vocalizing my confusion, the Messenger orb began to shrink until it was no bigger than a marble. It hadn't done *that* last time. Then it disappeared entirely, leaving me alone in the darkness of the void, my mind reeling with what I'd just heard. The silence that followed was both deafening and damning.

"Well, that was fuckin' stup— Auuuyyyaaggghhh!"

I was interrupted mid-dismissal as the world spun and flashed red. My body was on fire and like, I dunno, fuckin' stretching or something. I think I'd heard it called *spaghettification*? Which sounded delicious *and* terrifying. Well, to paint a picture: I felt like my soul was getting pushed back and forth forever through one of those hand-turned sausage machines. You know the ones. Pressed and slopped around, fed through a mesh by some old, gouty, financially plagued, rock-knuckled dude named Frankie or Bobby as the physics-defying husky stem of ash dangled from the end of his cigarette filter—barely contained within the confines of my own greasy skin. Meat grinder! That's the term! Man, I feel like I knew that.

Anyway, where was I? Right.

"Auuuuyyyaaaggghhh!" I continued screaming.

The feeling intensified, and I wasn't sure how exactly I was going to survive this level of pain. Legit, this shit was excruciating. Like getting all your teeth pulled with a fork and no anesthesia. Through your neck.

Finally, after a few long, long moments, it stopped. I kept screaming for a handful of seconds longer—you know, just to be sure—and then finally opened my eyes. I was on my back, staring up at . . . the night sky?

It took me a moment to realize it was a ceiling, laden heavy with a clusterfuck of intricate carvings. Mythical beasts, constellations, moons, planets, and whatnot—like someone spilled a damn bestiary and an astrology chart on it. Then I noticed the chandeliers. Giant fuck-off things, throwing glow around like some budget version of stars. And as I looked down, I saw that all this grandiosity was reflected in the shiny marble floor beneath me.

Wait . . . marble?

It appeared that I was lying on my back in an area that very much made me think of Grand Central Station or some other Beaux-Arts-style terminal. Don't be impressed by my knowledge—nothin' is more goth than Beaux-Arts.

The place was studded with columns, sturdy like chiseled titans. All prettylike—sloping and shit. Real nice.

Then there were the portals. They were like eyes of demons, ripped out and casually slapped onto the walls, changing colors like a Polish dyskoteka as people plopped outta them before returning to silver, each promising a journey from somewhere stranger than the last.

The terminal was a mix of opulence and comfort. Like pouring champagne into your cereal bowl—that sort of mashup. There was even a giant, living tree rooted amidst the marble, spreading its branches like an octopus. It was so seamlessly fused with the architecture, I couldn't tell where nature ended and humanoid-made began. Freaky.

I blinked up as hundreds of people had stopped what they were doing, frozen mid-step to stare at what I now realized must have been the frightening spectacle of a six-foot-four-inch spotted orc in furred armor shrieking like he was going to die and doing snow angels on the polished marble. And I was putting on quite a show for the starers—humanoid and otherwise—who were pausing to enjoy the free entertainment.

All in all, I was floored—literally and figuratively—by the grand old bitch of a portal station. This was the sort of shit that makes you go, *What in the holy hell am I doing here?* And the answer? Well, fuck knows.

"Uh, hey . . ." I said to the entire congregation of statue-impersonators. ". . . How's it hangin'?"

I felt a stab of anxiety suddenly course through me, and the world went purple for a second as my vision zeroed in on the crowd.

Well, what the heck is that abou—

"IT'S A FUCKING RAID!" someone screamed, and that was when the entire fucking place went absolutely mental. Weapons were drawn, magic shields went up, people were charging Spells—I'm pretty sure I even saw one guy whip out a slingshot. It was pandemonium, with half the assembly getting ready to square up with me and the other half bolting for their lives.

"Oh . . . right," I said aloud as several individuals ran at me. "I'm an *orc*."

CHAPTER TWENTY-FIVE

ON WE SWEEP

The angry mob was closing in fast. Fortunately, for me, I had at least an *alright* Acrobat Skill, and I performed a sick fuckin' kip-up—I was gettin' good at those—onto my feet. Before I knew what I was even doing, I realized I'd yanked my haladie and pique out of my waistband and had them out, ready for a rumble. They were definitely going to kill me, but, sugar, I was goin' down swingin'.

CLANG! CLANG!

Two epic metallic notes rang out, cutting through the raucous roars of the mob like a razor-edged riff from a Schecter Reaper. I looked down and, shit, two enormous shields stood before me like a pair of heavenly roadblocks.

And then the marauding horde of homicidal motherfuckers just halted. It wasn't the shields that had stopped them, though. I mean, sure, they were monstrous—but the mob had looked ready to trample over me. No, it was more like they'd been *held back* by something. It had all been chaos, and then suddenly, everything halted mid-mayhem like the world's most violent game of freeze tag.

And in the sudden calm, I realized who my savior was. It was Buck. The hulking oni had stymied the tidal wave of murder with those shields of his. I mean, the guy was practically a walking fortress. Each shield was as wide as a fucking saloon door and thicker than the skulls of half the assholes in this mob. They were emblazoned with symbols that screamed to back the fuck off, in the universal language of intimidating badassery. He'd slammed them into the ground with a force that echoed through the station, creating a wall between me and the swarm of pissed-off normies.

The second half of my unlikely rescue duo was Edwig. The gelatinous goon, despite his odd gummy-worm physique, had a penchant for unyielding arcane fuckery. His Unseen Hand Spell, I'd be willing to bet, had been the force keeping the droves at bay, whipping up a mystical barrier, pushing back the mob like the doughy, bald doorman at an exclusive nightclub, and no one on that side was on the guest list.

"What seems to be the issue here?" Buck asked in his lazy way.

There were various surprised exclamations of "Buck!" from within the horde, and I saw the entire group visibly tense.

"Sorry, I'm told I speak a bit too softly," Buck continued, leaning over one of his shields. "You might not have heard me . . . Is there some problem I'm not aware of?"

He hadn't spoken up any louder, but he didn't need to. You could have heard a butterfly fart in the silence of the station, and everyone was just staring back and forth from me, to Buck, to Edwig. Finally, some crimson-fleshed schmuck in full armor in the front row of the rabble-rousing crowd got brave and spoke up.

"Er . . . well, erm, it's an . . . o-orc, Buck—er, sir," the red-skinned man said. "Thought it were warmin' up fer a raid, we did."

Buck sighed, as if the whole thing was particularly bothersome.

"Did he make any aggressive moves?" he asked.

"Well . . . er, that is to say . . . er, no—sir," the man continued, his black, pupil-less eyes wide with terror.

"I'm not a *sir*, Lazlo. You know that. How long have we known each other?" Buck asked. "Did the orc give any indication that he was going to attack?"

"He was doin' a bit o' screamin'," called a woman from the middle of the crowd. "Seemed like a war cry!"

"I was on my back in pain, you assholes!" I shouted, but Buck put a hand up to silence me.

"Best I can recall," the oni said, drawing himself up to his full height, "it's not a crime to be screaming in public. Rude, maybe, but not a crime. Sounds like you all got the wrong impression."

"No, but he scared us!" called another person, a teenage boy.

"Also not a crime," Buck said with a shake of his head. "Okay . . ."

He put a hand on his shields as if preparing to remove them from the ground where—now that I was looking—I realized he'd gouged them into the marble.

"I'm going to put these away," he said, tapping the metal of the barriers. "And I'm going to trust everyone here not to act in a way that's going to reflect poorly on your family and your city. I personally vouch for this orc—he's not a threat. Alright?"

There was a general nod of agreement among the throng, and Buck sighed, wrenching the shields out of the ground with ease. Then, just like before, he wiped his hands in the air and they disappeared. The crowd seemed to relax at this and slowly began to disperse, still tossing me reproachful looks and muttering.

Yeah, that's right—you better run, I thought. *I'm a VIP—apparently.*

As the red-skinned man began to walk away, Buck called to him.

"Lazlo," he said. The man stopped in his tracks.

"Aye, Buck?"

"A word?"

The man looked terrified, and I watched him swallow a lump in his throat and nod urgently, turning back to face us.

Buck placed a hand on the smaller man's shoulder in a pacifying way and smiled.

"So, how come you're letting citizens get all worked up over one guy appearing in the center of Exodus—through a Gateway, I might add? Seems like the commander of the city watch should be deescalating potential conflict—not participating in it."

This guy was the chief of police? Jesus, what sort of standards did they have in this town?

Lazlo, who I could see now also sported a pair of tiny wings on his back, simply sighed.

"It's been a tense 'un, Buck," he said solemnly. "Lots o' unrest since that attack on Kettleborough not a week off. E'ry common and noble alike is shiverin' somethin' powerful o'er the whole incident. Got 'em rattled, it does."

Buck stared at the man for a moment before letting out a tired sigh.

"Well, fear never does make for clear thinking," he said, letting his arm drop from the man's shoulder. "Though you gotta keep a cool head, Laz. I know you're fresh to the job, but these people look up to you. If you let a surprise orc's screams shake you, what are you gonna do when a real threat drops down in front of you?"

Lazlo only nodded, his gaze shifting uncomfortably from Buck to me, then back again. His small wings fluttered nervously at his back.

"You're right, Buck. I let the folk's fear get to me. I'll . . . I'll try to do better."

"That's all I'm asking for," Buck said, nodding. "And maybe get some perspective, yeah?"

"Perspective?" Lazlo asked, inclining his head curiously in Buck's direction. Then he closed an eye and looked at me, as if trying to figure out if I'd transform or something.

"Lazlo Morningdew, meet Loon. Loon here is a Sojourner," Buck said.

It was like ice froze in my veins. I went very still, my grip clamped tightly on my weapons as I looked at the huge oni.

Why the fuck did he say that?

I heard Edwig suck in a sharp breath.

"What . . ." I started, trying to find the right words. "Why the fuck . . ."

"Easy, easy," Buck said, raising his hands in submission. "Lazlo's friendly to the plight."

Lazlo, now seeming to actually see me for the first time, brightened, giving me a wide smile and a nod. I noticed that his teeth were blue. Weird.

"Aye," the red-skinned man said happily. "Gods, wish I'd taken the time ter discern that afore I went all wild-eyed at the sight o' you."

"Wait . . ." I said, looking from Buck to Lazlo. "You're a Sojourner too? Jesus, I'm pretty sure this whole goddamn world is full of nothing but transplants!"

"Oh, I see yer confusion," Lazlo said. "No'm not a Sojourner meself."

I balked.

"Whaddya mean?"

"Lazlo here is *half*-Sojourner," Buck said, grinning. "Or . . . second-generation? I'm not sure what you'd call it exactly."

". . . half? What do you—"

"Me ma and da were like you," Lazlo clarified. "Sojourners, as it were. Though they called 'mselves 'Crossed.' Rest 'em."

"Really?" I wondered, completely flabbergasted.

"I was friends with his dad," Buck said. "Rarely seen a finer warrior than Arkturus Morningdew."

"You didn't see 'im duckin' out the way of me ma, then," Lazlo laughed. "You'd've thought he were a Level Zero duckling."

As the two men reminisced, I thought about that. I mean, I guess I figured somehow, in the back of my mind, that it was possible. But I hadn't really had time to consider the scope of something so left-field, really. I'd been too busy surviving attempted murder after attempted murder to really have a sit-down and a think over the idea of Sojourners reproducing. There were also additional ramifications to that.

"So . . . they came here, and they, what? Stayed? Settled down? Never went back?"

"Aye," Lazlo said. "Don't know they ever *could* go back, if'n I'm bein' honest. Ain't never heard o' one o' yers doin' a recross. Might be it's impossible."

"Well, that's super depressing news," I groaned.

It made sense. Every Sojourner I'd met so far that wasn't part of my tribe of fuck-ups had been around for years. If there was a way to get back, they'd likely have taken it. Then again, maybe it was . . . whatcha call it—survivorship bias? Only the ones who'd *want* to stick around would stick around, and I hadn't been there long enough to see anyone leave. That would really skew the perspective on likelihood, right? Hopefully, that was the case. As much as I enjoyed these far-flung adventures into the great and pointy unknown—I'd at least like the *option* to return to my original world.

"I gotta say, Lazlo," I said, shaking my head, "you just became forty percent more interesting now that I know you're batting for our side."

Lazlo laughed.

"Aye, figure somethin' like that would make a man more inclined to me natural charisma. What earns the . . ."

He paused, counting out an amount on his fingers.

". . . remainin' fifty percent o' interest?"

I smirked.

"Math not your strong suit, eh? No worries—mine either," I said. "Tell you what: I came here looking for some friends. If you can point me in their direction, I'll consider bringing the percentage up to at least . . . uh, ninety."

Lazlo slapped me on the shoulder with a loud guffaw, then seemed to think better of it and lightly patted it as if he was afraid I'd suddenly eat him.

"Got yerself a deal, Loon," he said. "Who'm I lookin' out fer?"

"Let's see . . ." I said, thinking on how best to describe the crew who'd beat me through the portal by a few hours at least.

"Well, first," I said. "This *is* Palandis, right? I haven't heard the name thrown around yet, so I want to be sure. Think I heard . . . Excelsius?"

"Exodus," Buck, Lazlo, and Edwig said at the same time.

"That's the name of this station," Buck continued.

"Eh . . . no, I'm pretty sure it was Excelsius," I said.

"I can confirm we're in Palandis," Buck said.

"I can too," Edwig said.

"Alright, alright," I said. "In that case—"

"They'd have been traveling with four bouncy pink eggs," Edwig interrupted.

"Yo, Edwig, what the fuck?!" I demanded. "How you gonna tell him about *my* friends?"

"Pah! They're my friends, too, orc!" Edwig said.

That stopped me in my tracks. I'd forgotten that while, yeah, technically, the majority of them had been on the train with me, Edwig had spent just as much time around them in this world as I had. More so, probably, since I'd been really investing my time in digging ditches and sulking. Huh. Is this what they call an epiphany?

"Bouncin' eggs?" Lazlo asked, but I could tell by his tone he knew exactly who Edwig and I were talking about.

"Yep," I said. "An elf, a human, and a vittra, too—oh, and a floating pink-purple specter."

"I know yer group," Lazlo said, giving me a curious look.

"Aw, man," I groaned, sensing a problem. "What did they do? Don't tell me they're in your jail or something."

"No, sir, nothin' like that," he said. "It's just that . . . they left out this mornin' t'go combat the situation in Kettleborough."

"They did *what?*"

"Kettleborough," Lazlo repeated. "Problem-solvers, they claimed t' be. There's a good bit o' gold in it fer 'em if'n they can find their way back."

"Why the fuck would they have agreed to that?" I asked. "Didn't you imply it was dangerous?"

"Aye," Lazlo said. "Told'mm as much 'swell. But they didn't seem particularly bothered o'er that information. The floaty 'un kept sayin' they were a set o' powerful adventurers seekin' to rid the world o' what ails it. Then asked if'n I had any beer on me."

I sighed.

"Well, that's definitely them," I muttered.

"Where's Kettleborough?" I sighed.

"Oh, just a few hours northeast o' here, right along the Blue Road. Easiest place to find if'n y'don't wander."

"Alright . . ." I said, shaking my head again. "Thanks, Lazlo. You're a real prince."

"Well, glad to be a bit o' help," Lazlo said. "Nice t'meet you, Loon. Illisinaf."

He inclined his head to Edwig, who seemed particularly miffed that he hadn't gotten a chance to use his long string of introductory titles. Then he nodded to Buck.

"Good t'see you again, Buck," he said. "Hope it ain't s'long 'til I see you again."

"Good to see you too, Laz," Buck said, smiling. "Tell Erebeth I said hello."

"Not a chance o' that, Buck," he returned with a laugh. "She'll just hit me 'bout the head that I didn't invite you 'round fer tea."

"When I'm done with my next stretch, I promise to stop by," the oni said.

"Aye," Lazlo said. "I'll give her your best, then."

With that, the red-skinned watch commander took his leave, his tiny wings a-flutter. Buck let out a low sigh, almost of relief, and gave me a sideways glance.

"Alright there, Loon?" he asked.

"Yeah," I grumbled. "I just know that I'm going to have to get thick into some bidness now. Bidness I ain't want no part in."

"Well, if it helps," Buck began, gesturing at us, "I'm heading that direction anyway. Really, I should make sure it's sorted one way or another. Care if I tag along?"

I perked up at that.

"Yeah? Well, shit, Buck, this might just be salvageable, then. Of course! Man, I might not have to place an order on some new friends after all."

"Pah! Bet *that* advertisement goes unanswered." Edwig said.

I rolled my eyes.

Looking around, I noticed that the last of the lookie-loos had dispersed during our conversation with Lazlo. Good riddance. Also, now that the chaos of my arrival had quieted down, I had an itching sensation in the back of my mind that . . . maybe a show of gratitude was in order.

"Buck . . . Edwig," I said, glancing at each of them. "Thanks. For saving my ass."

Listen, I hated the taste of the words—gratitude was a big ol' bitter horse pill to swallow for me. Admitting I felt it at all was even more so. But . . . they'd helped me, stood up for me, even. They didn't have to—especially the oni. He didn't know me well at all, but he'd commanded the entire room and made them piss themselves backward at the thought of even giving me the stink eye.

Who the fuck is this guy?

At my thanks, Buck just shrugged, and Edwig . . . well, Edwig just sort of . . . jiggled.

"Aight," I said, tucking my haladie and pique back into my waistband. "Now that that's over with, it's time to do a classic rendezvous meet-up with our wayward homies."

I glanced around, scratching my head. Then I turned back to them.

"So, uh . . . how the fuck do we get to Kettleborough, again?"

CHAPTER TWENTY-SIX

IN THE GLOOMY BETWEENS

Walking through Palandis was like tripping through a garishly decorated picture book for rich fantasy kids—a fucking massive display of artsy-fartsy swagger wearing a frilly, glamorous hat. It was pretty clear that the city planners had wanted to see which of them could outdo one another best with the heavy-handed show-offiness and then rolled with it, full motherfucking throttle. Seriously, there were, like, a million domes, turrets, and fancy-fuck archways.

Still, in the thick of all the pompous buildings, Palandis had a solid undercurrent of cold, hard iron. As we moved along the too-clean roads, it became more and more obvious that this wasn't just some namby-pamby showcase of wealth—it was a military stronghold. The Kingdom of Arlo's armed forces—or His Majesty's Army, as I was supposed to refer to them as—were everywhere; looming like a constantly clinking shadow. Their steel-plated soldiers strutted around, eyeing everyone like we were all potential criminals. Not exactly the most welcoming of atmospheres, but hey, at least it looked impressive.

Buck had explained to me that while the city watch were part of the town's defense, they were separate from the king's mighty fighting squad, which made a certain amount of sense. It wasn't quite the same equivalent as the military in my world. No . . . this seemed more like . . . your local police versus the FBI. Members of His Majesty's Army could swoop in, shitty as you please, and take over jurisdiction wherever they saw fit, and they were far more numerous than the native boys in . . . well, not blue. It seemed like the city watch there wore a lot of dark gray and yellow tabards? So, they kinda looked like bees. The boys in . . . bees? No . . . that's stupid. The yellowjacket boys! Yeah, that sounded good—let's go with that. The *yellowjacket boys* were buzzing around periodically, but I noticed they spent a lot of the time patrolling the roadways and manning the gates.

Unlike the good-for-nothing slimeballs in Tallr—uh, Coral Paella . . . the twelve there weren't mounted as far as I could tell. No turtle-power or nothin.' Just straight traipsin' about on their tootsies, out on the beat, classic mutton-chunter-style.

There also seemed to be, from my brief window into the goings-on, a clear rivalry between the two factions, as many of His Majesty's finest would catcall and make what I took to be rude gestures at the yellowjacket boys when they came across them. Massive, douchebag big-brother energy, ya know? If push came to shove, I was pretty sure I would have picked the side of the city watch, though, because . . . I mean, they really seemed to be the underdog in this fight. But I'd only been there for about an hour, so I probably wasn't in a position to be dissecting the nuanced political theater happening in this joint.

It was late. Even so, it was clear this was a city that didn't sleep. As we wandered through the city, we met all sorts of oddballs—peddlers, blacksmiths, merchants, y'know, all the standard fantasy fare, plus a couple of touristy trolls—who kept glancing around like they were lost and looked like they'd been through the wringer a few times, just like me. Despite all the stern faces and sharp glances, there was a sort of chaotic charm to the place.

On our way toward the Daylight Gate—which was one of several similarly sun-themed entrances—we had to trudge through the city's main square. It was a fucking carnival. Musicians strumming away on their lutes and harps, jugglers making damn fools of themselves, and some lady in a hyper-revealing and extremely unpractical set of leather armor that was issuing challenges to passersby. And then there was the centerpiece: a fucking massive fountain spouting water around a statue of some crusty old fuck probably long dead.

"That's Lord Regent Uthafors," Buck explained when I'd stopped to gawk at all the bird shirt clinging to the sculpture's bald head. "He was something like the interim-king during the Nightmare Wars."

"Fuckin' *Nightmare Wars*?!" I exclaimed. "That sounds goddamn *tite*. Rock 'n' roll as *fuck*!"

"Pah! It was anything but!" Edwig said. "Mind you, this was centuries ago, but the records indicate it was a *hellscape*. Beasts crawling out from the abyss, fire raining from dark skies filled with bat-winged behemoths that'd make dragons piss their scales, fire tornados reducing cities to ruins of cinder and steam."

"Oh. My. God," I breathed. "That sounds so cool!"

I couldn't help but think about the song "Kings of the Nightworld" by the Black Dahlia Murder, imagining that fucking audio carnage backtracking the scene of mountains of monsters spilling out of the void to wreak mayhem and havoc on this land; blackened skies, smoking eruptions . . . *got-dayum*.

Buck gave me a look but then shrugged.

"Damn, for real, though—that's some Revelations-level shit," I continued. "Wish I'd been around for that!"

"Pah! Your eyes would have been boiled out of your skull—if the undergnolls hadn't gotten to you first!"

That went on for a while. I'll save you the headache—but I eventually won the argument that being killed during the motherfuckin' *Nightmare Wars* was cooler than dying in literally any other fashion in the history of being dead.

... The gates were impressive, though—carved and polished as they were to an obnoxious degree. Like everything else in this city, they were just ... a little too much. But there they stood, gleaming in the lantern light, announcing our exit. Apparently, this was the one that led to the Blue Road, but Edwig mentioned there were several others, naming them things like the Twilight Gate, the Starlight Gate, and the Dawn Gate. There was zero hassle getting through there, and in fact, it seemed like we'd probably have more of a rigamarole getting *in* on our way back, since it seemed the city watch was on high alert for any sign of goofy business. So, we just passed along on our cutie-pie little way.

Finally, after all that walking, we set foot on the Blue Road, Kettleborough-bound ... to uh, walk some more, I guess.

Surprising probably only me: the road wasn't *blue* at all. It was, like, gray and ... brown, and ... rocky and junk. A real Copperhead Road sorta vibe. The name seemed to come from the periodic signage that was painted in glimmering sapphire showing which towns or villages we were heading in the direction of. Boring. I was hoping for something magical, but, just like a lot of the things in this Arcana-rich land ... it was mostly mundane. I was surprised to find there were what were essentially streetlamps along it as well. I mean, I wouldn't need them—but I figured that was a nice feature to have for travelers.

Palandis, in all its grandiosity, sat behind us, almost shimmering in its own self-satisfaction. I gotta admit, it was gorgeous—at a distance. A hell of a lot prettier than some of the dumps I've seen in my life, anyway. All twinkling lights that cast a halo into the night sky.

"So, we just follow this, and it leads to the homies?" I asked, trying to make sure I understood the assignment.

"Yeah," Buck said. "It's right along the Blue. It's one of the longest avenues in the kingdom, actually. Stretches from the Idalous Sea on the western coast through this way, and if you keep at it for about a week from here, you'll run right into the border of Hathburia."

"Bitchin'," I said. "This is basically an interstate, then."

"Yep," Buck agreed with a wry smile. "A several-hour interstate to get to a place that's only about ..."

His eyes clouded over for a moment before returning to their usual focus. "Three ectren away."

"Electron?" I asked. "What's . . . biology have to do with this?"

"Ah, yeah, sorry about that," Buck said. "I haven't had to use old-world measurements in . . . well, a while. An ectren is—wait, you more familiar with miles or kilometers?"

"Pah!" I exclaimed, imitating Edwig, who . . . didn't seem to notice. "I'm an American patriot, baybee. I'm pretty much half bald eagle."

Buck just stared at me.

"Uh . . . miles," I admitted sheepishly.

"Alright," he said. "So, an ectren is about the same as three miles—or the distance the average person can walk in roughly an hour."

I did some quick math.

"Kettleborough is twelve miles away?!" I shouted. "That's going to take us forever!"

Buck raised an eyebrow at me, but Edwig was the one to swoop in and spoil my self-esteem.

"Pah! That's not adding up, orc!" He guffawed. "It's nine of them! There! Not even from your land, and I can still count smiles better than you."

"It's . . ." I started, then decided it would be funnier if Edwig thought we measured with *smiles*, and if it ever came up again, I'd make sure to enjoy it. "Uh . . . you know what, Edwig? I think you're right."

"Pah! About time you came around!"

Buck just shook his head and gestured with his chin down the road.

"If you're both ready, we've got a lot of smiles ahead of us. So, let's get to it."

"Yeah, yeah," I said, smirking. "Smiles to go before we sleep, right? Oh, wait." I pointed at Buck.

"What did you look at when you were telling me the distance? Was that, like, a GPS Spell or sommat?"

He shrugged.

"Sort of," he said. "I have a map Ability."

"Oh . . ." I said. "Well, uh, cool, I guess. That might come in handy, right?"

Buck nodded but didn't say anything further.

"Man," I said, staring off into the distance, willing myself to see any sign of the place that was clearly out of possible sight. "I wonder how the gang is holding up."

"Pah! I'm sure they're wandering around, picking daisies by now," Edwig harrumphed. "While I'm stuck here out of the action."

"Don't be so sure of that," Buck returned. Something about the way he said it gave me the chills—like he knew something I didn't.

"Eh... Nah, I'm sure they're fine I can feel Rexen's presence," I said. Unfortunately, the connection to the little punk bitch poltergeist was still there, and would be regardless of whether or not his totem was inside my body "... Weakly but not in a worrisome way. Just in a... distance kinda way. Ya feel?"

Yeah, Edwig's right, I thought. *I'm sure they're just doing something stupid, like participating in a high-stakes canoe race.*

Kettleborough was experiencing one of the loveliest weeks of weather it had seen in months. Earlier in the day, the sun had been shining, the breeze had been airy and light, and, despite the fact that it was midway through autumn, the temperature had been absolutely perfect for the Kettleborough annual watercraft relay. The evening was just as enjoyable. Yes, it was truly a wonderful time by every metric except one.

A horrible, death-defying battle in the middle of town.

A siege on Kettleborough was not how Dragoon had envisaged spending his night. Built at the convergence of three gently bubbling brooks, Kettleborough was a pastoral idyll. Its low, thatched buildings nestled against rolling hills, a picturesque landscape swathed in a blanket of blooming heather and gorse. It was the kind of town you'd expect to host a lovely fair or a festive seasonal market, not a battleground for survival.

But now the cobblestone streets ran slick with an unsettling mix of substances best not dwelt upon, and screams perforated the once-tranquil air. Emerging in hordes—from the forest, the homes, all around them really—were the ogen, horrifying humanoid creatures with too many teeth, too many eyes, and an unholy fondness for flesh. The group had been at this for hours now, and while they'd been racking up Experience, their collective strength was dwindling. The enemies weren't particularly strong, but far too numerous to make it an easy fight. This was further emphasized by the lack of Esper Nodes floating above them.

At first, there'd been others aiding them in the defense, but over time, the majority of them had either died or fled screaming. *Then* they died.

Rua, her red hair gleaming like flame in the chaos, was thankfully holding her own. With each swing of the Behemoth Blade, an ogen was sent spiraling into oblivion, shrieking in surprise and terror. Sweat was trickling down her face, but her eyes held an unnerving seriousness.

"Gah! These things are activating my trypophobia!" she shouted.

Dragoon merely grunted in reply, an ogen attempting to chew on his boot. With a swift kick, he sent the creature sprawling, quickly dispatching it with a bolt from his crossbow.

"Less talk," he said. "More killing."

His crossbow hummed as he activated Bolt Barrage. A volley of spectral missiles burst forth, piercing the monsters attempting to encroach upon him. Despite this, however, his eyes remained resolutely on their goal.

"Rua," he called out in a measured tone. "Our priority is the temple!"

Veruca was weaving her way calmly through the melee, her voice raised in an elaborate monologue that curled and twisted in the air. As the words left her tongue, her Arcana created visible, solid sound waves that lashed out, stunning the ogen in their tracks.

"And verily did the sun rise upon a scene of utter devastation, the fallen leaves of autumn crunching beneath the weight of gnashing foes," she said, reciting phrases that came to her in an instant, informed by her Class and tempered by her matter-of-fact tone. "A bittersweet vision, steeped in an undercurrent of raw, pulsating fear. The dire hour of judgment descends upon this hallowed ground."

Rexen was hovering around near Veruca, having decided her feats were the most interesting to watch at the moment.

"Yes!" he squealed, darting hither and thither, seemingly just for the joy of it. "Fear is just excitement in need of a bop on the nose! Ooh! Now stab that one! Stab him!"

"You're not helping!" Rua retorted, her blade slashing through the air to behead an ogen that had come too close. "This isn't the time for this!"

"When life gives you ogen, make ogen-ade!" Rexen trilled, his fluorescent form twirling gleefully.

Rua regretted telling Rexen about lemonade almost as much as she did teaching him the idiom about rolling with life's punches. He'd been trying to fit every possible situation over the last day into one he could use *ade* for.

Jumpy, Cluck, Slappy, and Mortimer were bouncing about like homicidal beach balls. They crashed into the ogen with savage joy, the air around them filled with a macabre chorus of chittering.

"We need to get to the temple," Dragoon barked, reloading his crossbow. "The townsfolk—"

"Are relying on us," Rua finished for him.

"Not far now," the human continued. "Stick together."

Rua nodded, her expression hardening.

"Right. Temple. Survivors. Ogen-ade. Got it."

That was when all manner of hell broke much, much further loose. There was a loud crash, and swarms of ogen suddenly spilled out of a hole in a formerly scenic little farmhouse at the edge of the town. The tidal wave of spawn began racing toward the group's location, screaming with feral abandon.

"Ah, the quaint customs of country folk," Rexen mused, twirling in the air as the remainder of the group lost their collective cool over this new and unsightly vision of terror storming their way. "Mass carnage really brings a community together, don'tcha think?"

Suddenly, a form burst from the door of the building designated as the tavern—an establishment, which under normal circumstances, would have been boisterously serving Kettleborough's finest ale to its residents. Now the door was splintered and broken, and a pale figure was hurled out to crash in a sprawled heap in the street. She groaned, pushing herself up from the rubble and dusting herself off.

"By Palima's light, that stung a bit," she grumbled in a subtle Veloceian accent, her voice echoing with a strange, hollow timbre.

As the woman rose, the glow of the still-remaining lanterns painted a halo of ethereal amber around her. She was a wraithborn—called Ileyrri—a child born not of the world's green womb but in the ghostly depths of the Wesas Catacombs—and she was the only person who remained from those that hadn't come with the group of Sojourners.

She looked like a ghoul standing amidst the earthly chaos, her skin as pale as moonlight, her eyes burning yellow and pupil-less. Her hands, bigger than any human's, seemed like they belonged to a sculpture—elongated fingers tapering into bone-hard claws that only added to her otherworldly . . . shall we call it charm? She had an unnaturally hunched posture, giving her an intimidating, predatory silhouette. The tattered remnants of her clothing were dusted off, and then her head turned sharply, glaring at the source of her disturbance.

An ogen, larger than its brethren, burst through the remaining tavern wall, its wild, bloodshot eyes focused on Ileyrri. The creature was monstrous, its visage twisted into a snarl of pure malice, eager to tear into the wraithborn before it.

"No manners," Ileyrri sighed, her yellow eyes narrowing. "Well, let's have it out, shall we?"

With that, she flexed her hands, the clawed tips gleaming dangerously. She took a step forward, her stride much more natural than her standing posture, before launching herself at the beast.

What followed was a stunning display of athleticism and hand-to-hand combat.

Ileyrri was a force of nature, her claws slashing, her body twisting and dodging; calm and focused was she amidst the chaotic fray. Her technique was rough, unrefined—not that of a trained warrior but of a brawler, relying on her own strength, speed, and the powerful strikes delivered by her formidable hands.

With a swift, upward leap, she reached the ogen's head level, her fists blurring in a whirlwind of strikes. Each blow landed with devastating effect, sending shockwaves through the ogen's form, weakening its stance. She landed on it, slinging around to the beast's back, and kept on with her unrelenting assault, flashing out multiple times in quick succession with one hand as she clung to the monster's body with the other. The ogen, frantic, began chasing her with its own blows, but deft was Ileyrri, nimbly ducking and diving away with each hit, and she clung to the ogen, successfully fooling it into pummeling itself. She used her clawed digits to slice open a mosaic of unsightly gashes in its back and then kicked off of it, sending herself into the air. Then, with one final, downward strike, she drove the creature into the earth, leaving it a lifeless heap of flesh and bone.

Ileyrri landed ungracefully, stumbling as she hit the ground. But her yellow eyes shimmered in triumph.

"Look at that," she murmured, a smirk pulling at the corners of her contrastingly-dark lips. "Think I taught him to be polite."

Her gaze then shifted to the others, her posture returning to its hunched stance.

"Well, that's one less to worry about," she said. "How are you lot faring?"

"Splendid!" Rexen said.

"There is an inordinately robust deluge of the creatures heading right this way," Veruca said, her tone not giving away the clear and present urgency required to sort the situation.

Ileyrri glanced toward the farmhouse.

"Ah," she said with a sigh. "Figured you'd have made it to the temple by now. On we get, then."

As they wrestled with the horde, it became painfully apparent that their undertaking was not going to even brush lightly against *simple*. The temple was their only hope, a beacon of sanctuary amidst the chaos. However, the ogen were swarming the building like a pack of overexcited tourists, still thankfully unsuccessful in breaching its hallowed walls. The paramount question, of course, was whether they'd manage to cross this veritable gauntlet in time. And then the small matter of whether there'd be a single soul left to rescue upon their arrival.

And so, Rua, Rexen, Veruca, Dragoon, Jumpy, Clucky, Slappy, and Mortimer . . . and Ileyrri continued. All the while their already considerably miniscule energy further faded. Except for Rexen, of course.

"Push!" he cheered, attempting to rally his companions. "Push!"

But as another hour passed, and it grew even darker, their zestful movements grew into labored plodding, their heroic swings into sluggish swipes, and their gusto cannibalized by weariness. Meanwhile, the ogen simply continued their assault, unendingly pouring into the town like an undammed river.

Rua had switched to a smaller blade—a needle-thin rapier she'd recently acquired that would fare better in the tight-quarters conditions they were increasingly exposed to. She focused, most of her Abilities drained of their effectiveness, and stabbed forward each time she saw an opening. But the temperature of the battle was wintery, and she feared they would soon fall. Which would leave the townsfolk undefended, at the mercy of this hellish din. Most of her group would return, but to wherever they had set their Anchors. The denizens of Kettleborough would likely not be so fortunate.

"Can't you do something?!" the elf shouted to Rexen, but the Dreadnaught Lord just smiled devilishly back at her.

"Oh, I *am* doing something!" he cheered. "Relishing in our sweet, forthcoming victory!"

The elf bit back a cry of frustration and instead fixated on that which she *could* control. Stabbing.

"What happened to the barricade?" Dragoon shouted. "It's gone!"

Rua glanced back at the town gate, where earlier they'd attempted to stopper the coming tide by stacking as many rocks as they could find in front of the front entrance. Now it looked like it was only half as tall, with ogen pouring through like a leaky faucet.

"Dammit!" she shouted in frustration. "They must've knocked it down somehow! Screw it! Can't worry about that now."

"Right," Dragoon agreed between shots. "Just a bad sign, is all."

"I know," Rua hissed. "This sucks so much butt. So much butt . . ."

". . . summoned from the marrow of the cosmos," Veruca continued ceaselessly, unerringly reciting the incantations that kept the arcane shields protecting them active. "Harness the vestiges of forgotten celestial echoes. Transcend the protection of realms known and unknown; draw forth the sentinel might that permeates the eternal . . ."

The barrier she'd summoned was more of a magic wall of platelets, allowing them the ability to continue fighting off the atrocities hurling themselves at the group, though also giving the ogen the opportunity to still reach them—despite a muted effect. The vittra's eyes were tightly closed, the brow beneath her horns a furrowed fissure as rivulets of concentration perspiration streamed down the channels of her body. She did not know how much longer she had, but she would hold until the very last.

Dragoon loosed a projectile into the face of another ogen and did not spare a glance for it as he pulled the single remaining bolt from the quiver at his side.

"Last one!" he announced, raising the crossbow and trying to find the best possible target to unleash his final shot on.

Ileyrri was perhaps the most attuned to the fray. The only one capable, at the moment, of remaining outside the projected barrier, she ducked an attack and struck out with her fists, rebuffing two ogen at the same time. Then she dropped—almost too quickly to see—and was back up in a moment, two ichor-coated bolts in her hands. She leaped over a lunging monster and tossed the pair of missiles through one of the barrier's gaps to Dragoon.

"Last *three*!" she shouted to him, then winked, before delivering a punishing kick to the head of a creature that exploded on contact.

The group, beleaguered and pushed to their limits, teetered precariously on the precipice of defeat. The ogen horde swelled around them, a tumultuous sea of snapping jaws and flashing claws, threatening to submerge them. Rua feared the worst.

This is it, she thought.

Suddenly, Rexen froze in place, a strange look on his face. In what could only be a fit of madness, Rua watched as the minute specter threw back his head, howling in an unhinged melody that was awful to behold.

"Yes!" he cried out, his voice suddenly terrifyingly dark and depraved. "It comes! The time is nigh! It *comes!* Absorb the might of your foes! Rend them apart and dance in their blood!"

Rua really, *really* hoped he was casting a Spell of some kind.

But just as the last sliver of hope was about to flicker out, a lifeline was thrown.

A concussive blast sliced through the chaos, arresting the group's downward spiral toward certain biting demise. The roar of the explosion swallowed the ogen's cacophonous war cries, leaving in its wake an uncanny silence that rippled through the battlefield—save for Veruca's strained chanting.

"—the resonance of the eternal . . . the infinite pulsation of the . . . void in our favor, embodying the endurance of the oldest cycles and the resolve of aether against the relentless march of—"

An eruption of flame and lightning suddenly unfurled in the distance, the incandescent flash casting long, monstrous shadows that danced and writhed across the landscape.

In the midst of the clamor, a barrage of colorful curses sliced through the muted and tattered pandemonium. Vulgar and unashamed, the oaths were declarations of defiance and malicious jubilation that could've made even the most hardened preteen trying to impress his friends wince.

"Zap-zap, bitch! Fuck *you*, fuck *you*, *double*-fuck *you*! Ha! Gotcha, ya little— Ah! Ouch, you dick turd! That hurt! Fuck off, fuck-face! Zzzap!"

The ragtag group, utterly spent and running on fumes, jolted at the raucous disturbance. Faces dusted with grime and streaked with sweat turned in unison toward the origin of the uproar. Their eyes were wide, reflecting the dazzling display of alternating blasts of pyrotechnics and crackling fulmination in the dark distance.

And then they saw them.

Two figures, large in stature and indomitable in spirit, emerged from the radiant mayhem. They tore through the seething mass of ogen with a brutality that was equal parts terrifying and awe-inspiring. The sight was enough to ignite a glimmer of hope in their weary hearts.

Dragoon squinted, trying to discern the identities amidst the maelstrom.

"Is that . . . Loon?"

It was.

Twirling two wands in a mesmerizing dance of arcane prowess entirely at odds with his chosen Class was the loud, abrasive, potty-mouthed piebald orc. The Wand of Flames and the Wand of Lightning Ball crackled and spat in his grasp, reducing the attacking ogen to charred remains.

"Disciple!" Rexen cried, his voice happy once more. "Joyous tidings! You made it!"

Then he squinted, *tsk*ing.

"Ah. Late! I'm removing some marks!"

"Zap! Zzzzaaapp! Motherfuckin' ZAP!" Loon's gleeful battle cry echoed across the battlefield, adding a layer of surreal absurdity to the ferocity of performance.

Yet even as relief washed over them at the sight of their ally, confusion followed in its wake. Because alongside Loon, another figure loomed—the second towering, hulking figure that made even the ogen look meek in comparison. The new arrival was like nothing most of them had seen before. All except Rua, who recognized what he was instantly from the mythologies of their previous world.

"An oni . . ." she breathed.

This man was monstrous, nearly seven feet tall. His broad, muscular shoulders heaved as he moved through the swarm, his deep-indigo flesh glistening in the stark lighting of Loon's wand, etched with markings that danced and flowed like a language of power and intimidation.

Yet there was no feral anger in his glowing purple eyes, no battle-thirst reflected in his demeanor. Instead, a look of the most profound annoyance marred his countenance, as though the ogen were little more than a nuisance, an irritation on an otherwise peaceful evening. The enormity of the situation was lost on him—or perhaps he simply didn't care.

The oni was clad in simple attire, almost disappointingly mundane for a creature of his storied ilk. A pair of loose, brownish trousers cinched at his waist, the fabric worn and weathered. Likewise was his shirt, which looked like it was slightly too small for his ample, brawny frame but peppered with holes and patches.

And then there were the shields—two massive constructs of metal, each the size of a door. He wielded them with surprising ease, the bulwarks held loosely in his grip. His method of progression through the horde was as unusual as he was—he neither attacked nor defended. He simply pushed forward, the shields acting as a battering ram of sorts, toppling ogen left and right as he advanced, the measured rhythm of his strides never faltering.

There was a final surprise. In their wake slid Edwig, his appendages out and waving, carving aside monsters with what Rua thought must be Unseen Hand—his trademark Spell. He had on what he'd informed her was his "battle face": a visage-scrunching appearance that made him look less like the avatar of fury he thought it did and more like a case of extreme indigestion. However, regardless of how it appeared, it seemed to be effective.

To the group's disbelief and confusion, it seemed Loon had arrived with the cavalry. But was it their deliverance or their doom?

CHAPTER TWENTY-SEVEN

TWILIGHT OF THE THUNDER GOD

I swam in chaos. Blasting away with the pair of wands like a good ol' fashioned gunslinger. Fire and lightning swirled around me in a torrent of majesty, devouring everything they came in contact with—and there was a lot of surface area to play with. These nasty fuckin' creatures that I could only think to call chlamydians—on account of their gross appearance and the fact that they just would not go the fuck away—were quite the festive swarm of annoyance. But, alas, I'm not *ever* gonna be somebody that backs down from a fight just because it happens to be *complicated*.

Nah, bro. Miss me with that shit.

I had no idea what was going on or why this was going down. But it didn't matter. My friends needed some assistance, and that was the only real information I needed. I'm—as has been reinforced ad infinitum—a fuckin' try-hard at the best of times. Right now, though, I was having *fun*.

I ducked under a vaulting beast, blasted another monster in its fuckin' teeth, danced out of the way of a slash, and, jamming a wand in my teeth, yanked my haladie out of my waistband and sent it flying. The bladed boomerang mowed over the top of the horde as it made its ascent, and I watched a portion of the gross-as-shit ghouls collapse—a lot of their parts that made them alive no longer connected to their nasty bods. I stabbed out with the Stag's Pique in the meantime, activating Nightfall Strike for my trouble to grab that sweet, *sweet* extra Sneak Attack damage. *Then* I went back to blastin'.

A few paces ahead of me was Buck. The big-ass oni was just combing through the yards of monsters like a linebacker on the sled push. Huh. I'll bet Saban would be real proud of me for that reference. Anyway, he was using his shields like a cowcatcher on the front of a steam engine, parting the monstrosities like . . . whatever that Moses guy parted. Look, it was fuckin' cool, alright?

That's all that matters. Anyway, behind me, Edwig was using his Unseen Hand to launch droves of our enemies backward, and between the three of us, we were the eye of the incredibly loud and disgusting storm.

"Pah! Loon!" Edwig called out as I kicked one of the fuckers in the chest.

"Yeah?" I shot back, keeping my eyes and ass-whipping parts fixated on the task at hand.

"Do you think now's a good time to deploy that plan of yours?"

I smiled, then shot a very, *very* quick glance at Buck. He was about thirty feet ahead of us, still trucking along.

"Almost!" I shouted back. "I want him up with the others before I do anything. Can you still do that floating thing?"

"Pah! I got enough juice in me to do a *lot* of stuff for a while!"

"That a yes?"

"... yes!"

"Good!" I said. "Wait for my signal!"

"What's the signal?"

"Oh, you'll know it when the time comes," I chuckled.

"Pah! Alright! If you say so!"

We continued carving through the swarm of creatures for another full minute before I saw what I had been waiting for. Through the throng of writhing bodies and hissing chlamydians, Buck reached the outskirts of our little war zone, finally joining with the rest of our group. Just as I was about to shout my go-ahead to Edwig, something whooshed over my head.

I looked up, and the sight I saw was straight out of a fucking superhero comic. Rexen, our resident magician-slash-mad scientist, was soaring above the sea of monstrosities, completely unfazed by the gnashing teeth and clutching hands reaching for him. He was nimbly dodging and bobbing, twisting and turning, so completely disconnected from the carnage below that he might as well have been on a stroll in the park.

"Arjee!" I shouted as he landed near me with a flourish.

"Oh, good! You're still alive!" Rexen responded, sounding as ecstatic as if he'd just won a raffle. "I was concerned about your tardiness. Pupil—you should consider adding punctuality to your list of skills to acquire."

"Nice to see you too, ya fuckin' weirdo," I replied, rolling my eyes. "What the fuck happened out there? And where the hell did you go? You know your little . . . Barbie Wizard Tower ripped its way outta my guts and into the portal, right?"

"Yep!" Rexen said. "But don't worry. I have it."

"Fantastic," I huffed. "So . . . what's the . . . deal here? What are we . . . storming into?"

The whole while, I was still fighting my way along, hearing Edwig's loud gasps as he exercised probably for the first time in his life.

"Oh, you know," Rexen said nonchalantly, looking around as if he had all the time in the world. "Ran into a couple of rough spots, dinged up the ol' knees a little. The elf and I went to a shop for some snacks . . . got held up by some locals. Then we took a shortcut that turned out to be a *long*cut, and here we are."

His calm, completely detached recounting of what must've been a hellish experience made me blink. It also told me nothing.

"You make it sound like you've just come back from a particularly eventful picnic."

"Yep!"

"Well, regardless, I can get the actual details later from someone more . . . in the present moment," I muttered, shaking my head. "So, what's the plan now?"

"Ooh! Disciple! We need to head to the temple," he said, nodding to the huge stone structure down the road. "That's where they've taken the weak baby townsfolk."

I sighed. Just when I thought this day couldn't get any more insane, they'd went and added *rescue mission* to the track list.

"Alright," I said, and I turned back to Edwig, who was busy sending more chlamydians into the air with each gesture like he was Mickey Mouse in Fantasia. "Edwig! Let's go save some villagers!"

"What!?" he shouted back, using Unseen Hand to slam two monsters together so hard, one of them exploded.

"I said it's time to save some— Fuck it, never mind— SIGNAL!"

Edwig stopped what he was doing and turned all his focus on me. Then, before I could ask if he heard me, I was suddenly rocketing into the air as he used his Spell to carry me aloft about thirty feet up so that I was staring out over the sea of writhing fuck monkeys.

"Hell, yeah!" I shouted, and spotted my group of fellow Sojourners.

They were currently under Buck's protection. From there, I could see what he could actually do. His pair of shields were stabbed into the ground on either side of my usual companions and he stood in the center. He seemed to be generating some kind of force field that had encapsulated them to keep them safe. The barrier shimmered with a dull, electric-purple light, and it appeared to be very capable of holding off the horde. I'd known he was some kind of shield specialist, but this was . . . well, this was something else. Not for the first time since meeting him, I wondered what his deal was. Especially what Level he was. I hadn't asked, because it was clear it was pretty high—but also, it was rude to do so. That being said, I could only guess. Whatever it was wouldn't be as surprising as finding out Edwig's Level was twenty-six. That still had me reeling.

Speaking of Edwig, my mighty 'morphous glower ranger was there in the air with me. Oh, and so was Rexen—but that wasn't nearly as unique.

"Alright, let's get to the next bit!" I shouted. "We don't have time to—"

There was a loud explosion. Then several more.

Congratulations! You have raised a Skill!
Knowledge [Ignition] has advanced to F-Rank Level 2!

Congratulations! You have raised a Skill!
Knowledge [Infiltration] has advanced to F-Rank Level 2!

Congratulations! You have raised a Skill!
Knowledge [Sabotage] has advanced to F-Rank Level 2!

Throughout the sprawling battlefield, edifices detonated in thunderous succession. The structures, once the humble homes and shops of the town's inhabitants, now served as deadly weapons of devastation. The concussive blasts eradicated swathes of the chlamydians, their bodies cast aside like grotesque dolls in the monstrous winds of destruction. Chunks of brick, mortar, and wood became airborne projectiles, adding their own lethal notes to this song of annihilation.

Congratulations! You have raised a Skill!
Knowledge [Ignition] has advanced to F-Rank Level 3!

Congratulations! You have raised a Skill!
Knowledge [Infiltration] has advanced to F-Rank Level 3!

Congratulations! You have raised a Skill!
Knowledge [Sabotage] has advanced to F-Rank Level 3!

Congratulations! You have raised a Skill!
Knowledge [Ignition] has advanced to F-Rank Level 4!

Congratulations! You have raised a Skill!
Knowledge [Infiltration] has advanced to F-Rank Level 4!

Congratulations! You have raised a Skill!
Knowledge [Sabotage] has advanced to F-Rank Level 4!

Embers danced through the air, illuminating the scene in a cruel, flickering glow. Smoke and dust billowed up from the ruined buildings, shrouding the field in an otherworldly haze. The devastation didn't stop there, though. One by one, more buildings erupted, creating a destructive domino effect that ran rampant through the town.

The townsfolk's establishments, their memories and hopes that once resided within those walls, had become the deliverance from the nightmare. Their sacrifice created a brutal path of survival, the unleashed energy shaping the battlefield to our advantage. The numbers on my Skill advances kept climbing, until they finally reached their max. For the moment.

Congratulations! You have raised a Skill!
Knowledge [Ignition] has advanced to F-Rank Level 8!

Congratulations! You have raised a Skill!
Knowledge [Infiltration] has advanced to F-Rank Level 6!

Congratulations! You have raised a Skill!
Knowledge [Sabotage] has advanced to F-Rank Level 8!

Each new detonation seemed to amplify the ferocity of the battle. The sudden, brutal change of the landscape stunned the chlamydians, their monstrous howls drowned in the relentless assault.

". . . fuck around," I said, finishing my sentence, admiring the carnage. "Uh . . . good work, Edwig."

"Pah! Easy enough!"

"What did my pupil do?!" Rexen asked, staring in awe at the billowing clouds of smoke everywhere.

"Oh . . . you noticed that, eh?" I said with a grin. "No big deal, I just—"

"Pah! He set some traps, is all!" Edwig interrupted. "*I* was the one who deployed them!"

"God. Dammit!" I shouted. "Don't try to minimize my role in this, asshole! I was integral to the whole thing!"

"Pah!" Edwig thundered back.

"Pah?!" I returned. "Pah, nothing! I *was*!"

"Pah!" Edwig reiterated.

"Pah!" I spat back.

"I believe you, pupil," Rexen assured me, in a tone that said he was only humoring me.

"Fuck you guys," I said. "Anyways . . . shut up; we gotta get 'em to the temple."

I didn't have time to brag—though I really wanted to. We'd technically shown up ten minutes earlier than when we'd actually started the fighting. Well, *I* had. I'd gone on ahead to scout and utilize my expert Sneaking. When I'd seen the horde and the fighting and all the mess, I had almost blown my cover and started fighting right then and there. However, in a rare move by one Loon Nolastname, I took stock of the situation before leaping right into it. I'd noticed that while incredibly numerous, the creatures swarming the joint didn't seem particularly perceptive, and thought I might be able to deploy some nonsense in the thick of all the confusion. So I had.

Then, when I'd met back up with Buck and Edwig, I'd explained what I'd seen. Then I told them my idea for timing some of the Hexahedrons of Hazards—specifically the red-hued ones Rexen had mentioned being explodey—to go off around the bases of the buildings. However, Edwig had had a better idea. He'd demanded to examine one, and after not long at all, using what I can only imagine was his weird research abilities, said he could remotely detonate them. This seemed like a wonderful idea, and so, I'd crept back around, making sure not to be seen, and placed the magical charges where they needed to be. That brings us back to here.

"Well, how are we going to do that?" Edwig asked. "Our original plan was to just get them outta there and regroup. Now we're going to the temple. The temple currently swarmed by more of these creatures than I can count?"

"Well, that's the thing about plans, Edwig," I said, scanning the battlefield. "They never go like you think they're going to. That's why you're supposed to be able to switch them up and improvise at a moment's notice."

"Pah! That's not the point of plans, orc! Plans are *supposed* to go off without a hitch. It wasn't until I met you that I'd seen so many carefully laid strategies go off the rails!"

"Yeah, well, that's the cool thing about me," I said. "I'm *all* about freestyle!"

"What do you want me to do with all these rocks, then?" Edwig continued. "Since our original idea is now in the bin?"

"I dunno . . ." I said, not really paying attention. "Stuff 'em somewhere, I gue— Wait! Actually, goddamn, I got an idea!"

"Here we go . . ." Edwig groaned.

"My apprentice is having a big brain moment!" Rexen declared. "Let us back away and give him some room!"

"Shut up, Arjee," I said. "I don't need any room—my brain already takes up all the room it needs."

"I'll say . . ." Edwig muttered.

"Quiet, you," I said. "I think I've got it . . ."

I paused a moment, still considering.

"Yep! Got it!" I declared, putting a hand on the choker around my neck. "Edwig, get ready with the rocks, but I want them centered on me, alright? Can you do something like that, even if I'm moving?"

"Pah! Orc, that's an insulting question! My Unseen Hand is the most advanced Arcana in the land."

"Really?" Rexen asked skeptically.

Edwig looked bashful.

"Well . . . it's *advanced*, in any case . . ."

"Okay, well, shut up for a second," I said. "Track me with them. But . . . make it *real* tight, okay? Like, you might think you're not giving me enough room, but I want those motherfuckers *stacked*."

"Alright, well—" he started, but I caught him off.

"Arjee, I need you to get down there and let them know they need to get ready to run to the temple."

"Aye-aye!" he said, and flashed away toward the barrier.

"Edwig, I'm going to have you go with them. It'll be safer that way. Also, when you land, give me a signal and drop the Unseen Hand. I've got something else in mind."

"Pah! I'll do as you say, orc, but don't think you're ever wresting the leadership role from me. I'm only listening right now because I want to see what unfortunate pandemonium you are able to achieve—not because I believe in you."

"Thanks, love you too, Edwig. Now—"

It was a moment too late for me to gloat about it, but a message popped up right then.

Leadership! Up? Down? Who knows?!
Congratulations, someone doesn't find you a blithering dummy . . . for once.

Well, well, well. It was garbled by nonsense, but I think I understood the ramifications of this message. My Leadership Skill had gone up. Right?

"Let's do it up," I said, rather than mention anything to the illisinaf, who was trying to pretend he wasn't getting sweet on me. Though the fact that he'd gone out of his way to mention he *didn't* believe in me made me think that . . . just maybe, he actually did appreciate my plan. Whatever; better to figure out my marvel . . . ocity . . . later, when there weren't monsters to trick into dying.

Edwig nodded and floated down to the group. I noticed that the barrier parted for a split second to allow him access and then re-formed. The chlamydians were still raging around at it, trying desperately to burst their way through. All eyes were turned to me. I nodded. Then I heard Edwig.

"Signal!" he yelled, and I almost laughed, but then the Unseen Hand dropped and I had to act quickly. I activated Bahlgus's Gorget of Flight and felt the air catch me. A colorful tail flowed out behind me and I smirked.

"God . . . I hope to fuck this actually works," I said, then shot forward through the air. I didn't have to wait long for the next portion as suddenly, the rocks appeared.

So, I feel like I should pause for a second to mention one thing about Edwig: he had a tendency for understatement. Not in his general manner—ha! No, that guy was full of himself—but in his naming conventions. Unseen Hand was probably the most primary example of this. He didn't have a lot of combat Spells at his disposal, but he didn't really need to. His whole life until meeting up with me had mostly been spent in research—which he was apparently pretty decent at. I mean, it's usually a testament to someone's skills if they're so great at what they do that they get bored and start experimenting with other stuff so hard, they get blacklisted. That's all to make a point that—credit where credit is due—Edwig was very efficient at getting *really fucking good* at whatever talents he had.

Which was why I knew the sight of the rocks appearing in the air next to me was going to terrify the absolute bombarding bejesus out of anyone witnessing it. Unseen Hand? Nah, bro. That shit *shoulda* been called Unseen Kraken. Dozens upon *dozens* of stones suddenly appeared in the air next to me, lifted up from their original resting spot near the town entrance. We'd seen them when we arrived, and decided the best way to put some obstacles in our pursuers' paths was by placing a literal obstacle in their path. Granted, that had been when our plan was just to swoop the homies and goose it. We figured borrowing the barrier to replace at a critical moment was more important than anything else. So, we'd taken the rocks someone had carefully placed to keep the beasts out. Now those very same rocks were hovering in the air like an army of moons—and I was their home planet.

As I flew forward, they clustered together, chasing me along in the air like a flock of birds teaming up to chase off a predatory raptor. I held my hand out as I passed over the magical barrier Buck's powers had created, delighting in the fact that most of the faces within were staring up in absolutely pure, unadulterated bafflement.

Heh, check this *shit out, m'pals.*

My fingers grazed one rock among the cluster, and that's when I activated Pernicious Volley. Then I lifted the stone and fired. Or tried to. It didn't move.

"Fuck!" I shouted. Edwig was still holding the stones with Unseen Hand! I hadn't told him to release them. Fuck, fuck, fuck! Pernicious Volley had a *very* narrow timetable on its activation duration. I frantically looked down at Edwig.

"Edwig! If I touch it—let go!"

He didn't say anything, but I suddenly felt the stone lose its invisible suspension and, hoping I wasn't out of time, fired the stone into the midst of the chlamydians. It was, as always, impressive to see Pernicious Volley turn any tossed object into a Stinger missile. The clod hit the ground with a crack like lightning, and I saw the earth beneath erupt in dust and smoke as the monsters exploded. This had carved a considerable hole into the area right in front of the barrier. But I was already moving on to the next one. Hoping Edwig was watching, I grabbed another stone and fired it as well, directly ahead of the last strike's destruction. I was going to clear a path one way or another for the crew to reach the temple.

"RUN!" I shouted, as I grabbed stone after stone, tossing them like asteroids and wiping out immediate resistance for them.

I flew ahead, still tossing as the barrier dissolved, and as one, they all rushed forward. I could see there were still some stragglers on the edges of the newly fissured avenue, but . . . someone I didn't recognize was taking care of them as the rest of the group hoofed it. She was pale and looked a little like some kind of fist-fighting . . . banshee . . . or something. Whatever; if she was helping, I wasn't going to ask questions.

My Pernicious Volley was about to run out, so with one final effort, I fired the biggest stone in my midst right at the front of the temple. Chlamydians rained down in all directions, and I immediately switched to my wands. I buzzed around, firing, making up the space between the temple and the forty feet remaining of where my allies were racing. I watched the remaining stones suddenly fire downward as well, directed roughly ahead. Edwig's Unseen Hand wasn't as strong as Pernicious Volley, but it didn't need to to be effective. More area was cleared, and now I could focus solely on flaming lightning death from above. So, anyway, I started blasting. I fired Spell after Spell wherever I saw encroaching monsters, turning them into likenesses of the last time I tried unsupervised cooking.

My attention snapped back to the front lines as I saw our little battalion close in on the temple grounds. My fingers twirled and twisted, my wands spewing out veritable rainstorms of elemental fury in my wake. Every shot a deadly blow that culled the monstrous swarm around us.

And then, as if the entire world took a collective breath, the tide of chlamydians ceased their assault. The unyielding swarm was slowing down, dwindling to only the most stubborn of assailants. A brief pause in the relentless cacophony allowed me to get a clear view of the battlefield. The monstrous sea that had enveloped us was slowly retreating, revealing the horrid expanse of destruction we'd left in our wake.

Then the ground shuddered.

From the ruins of a nearby building, now nothing but a pile of rubble and billowing smoke, a new adversary emerged. The chlamydians around it scattered, making way for this gigantic monstrosity. This wasn't like the others. This one was different. Bigger. Scarier. A hulking abomination standing a staggering ... fifteen—twenty feet tall, its grotesque form was like a more-evolved version of the chlamydians, rippling with power that hummed in the air. A halo of pulsating red energy hovered above its head. The sight was almost biblical.

"Oh, fuck me up a tree," I shouted over the chaos. "Party's over! Papa's home!"

Without wasting a second, I began to pelt the massive beast with a barrage of fiery and electric blasts. But the behemoth barely acknowledged the attacks. Instead, it leaped forward, clearing a distance of twenty feet in a single bound, charging through its smaller counterparts with an unwavering determination. Its sights were set on the temple.

"Damn it, he's coming right for us!" I yelled, but my words were lost amidst the continued barrage of attacks. This was going to be a big fucking problem if we didn't act quickly.

"Let us in!" Dragoon thundered. They'd reached the temple, but a new issue had arisen—the door was likely barred from the inside, and no one within was likely willing to risk *de*battening the hatches when there was the threat of immediate, instant death.

"Rua!" I shouted, my eyes still on the big monster that was barreling toward us.

"Loon!" she shouted back.

"Catch!" I roared and then, taking a quick look, I yanked the Wand of Supreme Unlocking out of my belt and chucked it down to her. With a flourish, the red-haired elf leaped into the air and caught it, looking down at it for just a second before nodding at me and turning around to face the door.

"Outta the way!" she shouted.

I looked back up to see how close Chlamydius Prime had gotten ... just in time to watch him leaping through the air right in front of me.

BOOM!

I was hit by his big ol' meaty paw, and a split second later I collided with the outside wall of the temple. My head smashed hard against the stone exterior, and all the wind got knocked out of me. I was dazed as I fell some twenty feet to the ground.

My vision blurred, my ears filled with a loud ringing, and my body felt like it had just been run over by an eighteen-wheeler ... three times. I tried to lift myself, to get up, but the pain ... fuck, it was overwhelming.

Then, through the foggy haze of my disorientation, I noticed the chlamydians. They were closing in, their monstrous forms skittering over the desolated battlefield toward me. I could barely make out their grotesque figures against the fiery backdrop of the night, but their hungry eyes, shining with a cold, predatory light, were impossible to miss. My blood ran cold. This was it. I was about to become the main course in a beastly banquet.

Summoning every bit of strength left in me, I raised my wands, ready to blast away the monsters as they came. But just as the first of the swarm reached me, a sharp cry echoed through the night air.

"Displace!"

Suddenly, the world blurred around me, and the next instant, I was standing in front of the temple, panting and disoriented. I looked back in utter disbelief, only to find Rua standing where I'd just been, ready to face the swarm on her own. She'd used her switcheroo mechanic to save me! What the fuck?! Why the hell would she do that?

Then they hit her. I watched with confused horror as she was torn apart.

Fuck! Rua!

Before I could even think of acting, a hand grabbed me by the collar and yanked me into the open door of the temple. It slammed shut behind me, cutting off my view of the outside world, of Rua, and of the ensuing visceral death of a comrade.

CHAPTER TWENTY-EIGHT

THE TROOPER

I was in shock, the sudden turn of events spinning my mind in a whirl of confusion and fear. But there was no time to dwell. I had to act.

But . . . all I could think about was the look on her face as she prepared to face the onslaught alone. She'd saved me.

Meanwhile, the sounds of virulence raged on outside, a constant reminder of the war zone we'd just narrowly escaped. As I steadied myself against a stone pillar, I found my gaze drawn to the ornate engravings that adorned the temple's interior. There was something familiar about them, something strangely comforting amidst the chaos.

Happy! Hello! Welcome back! Slappy!

I was hit in the chest as four pink dodgeballs came crashing into me. I laughed, gathering up the roe in my arms in a hug.

"Howdy, guys. Miss me?"

I felt from their projected emotions that they had indeed.

"Aw," I started. "I missed you too, little buddies. Glad you're safe."

I lowered them to the ground and they began chittering excitedly amongst themselves, which was about the only time I couldn't understand them. I heaved a sigh of relief and looked around the huge temple we'd made a temporary sanctuary.

The entire structure seemed to hum with an ancient, mystical energy that filled the air and pulsated beneath my feet. It was an odd juxtaposition to the bloody, frantic nightmare that waited outside, and for a moment, I found myself lost in its strange serenity. But I knew better than to get comfortable.

My gaze slowly lifted from the intricacies of the temple's floor, only to land on the multitude of wide-eyed, trembling faces filling up the cavernous space.

The terrified villagers of Kettleborough, their expressions ranging from confusion to disbelief, cowered among the ancient stone pillars.

Chatter erupted as eyes landed on Buck, who was weaving through the crowd, checking on the villagers. I could hear whispers swirling around us, all of them about Buck.

"Buck is here..."

"Is that Buck?"

"I thought he was..."

He seemed to be an almost-mythical figure in these parts, an oni who invoked both fear and respect in the same breath. But there he was, just an ordinary guy, wearing a concerned look on his face, putting his efforts into ensuring everyone's safety.

I glanced around, spotting my other allies amidst the huddled mass of villagers. They looked just as disoriented and confused as the rest, but the sight of their familiar faces brought a wave of relief washing over me. We were alive. Together. Well... almost all of us.

Rua's absence gnawed at me, but I knew better. She wasn't gone for good. The gamelike mechanics would have her respawning in New Home, far away from the danger and chaos here. But that didn't ease the hollow feeling in my gut or the lump in my throat. It basically meant that she thought I could do more good here than she could—and that was a lot of confidence to have on my part. It made me uncomfortable. When had people started thinking of me as capable?

Drawing in a deep breath, I pushed those thoughts aside, focusing instead on the present situation. We were inside the temple, safe for now from the monstrous horde outside. But the uncertainty of what lay ahead was palpable. The fear and confusion in the eyes of the villagers was a reminder of the reality we were all trying to grapple with.

Every creak, every echo sent waves of fear rippling through the crowd. The villagers were terrified, and understandably so. They had been yanked from their peaceful lives and thrust into a nightmare. They needed reassurance, direction. Fortunately, I knew just the guy for the job.

"Listen up!" I called out, stepping up to regard the assembly of frightened folk.

This was, apparently, the wrong thing to say.

Panic bubbled in the crowd like a seething cauldron. Something about my appearance, my voice, I dunno... triggered them? They started pointing, shouting, recoiling. Some huddled closer together, shielding their children, while others edged toward the temple's entrance, seeking an escape route.

Fuckin' racists! All of you! I thought bitterly.

"Goddammit, I'm just . . ." I tried to interrupt, but my words were lost amidst the din.

Just as the crowd was reaching a fever pitch, a lazy, almost-bored voice cut through the tumult.

"Alright, alright, settle down," Buck drawled, an exaggerated sigh following his words.

The villagers fell silent instantly, turning their attention to him. His nonchalance would have been humorous if the situation were different, still, it seemed to seep into the crowd, slowly diffusing the tension. His reputation in these parts was a powerful tool, it seemed, and he wielded it with an effortless grace.

"Here's the thing," he continued, his hands tucked casually into his pockets. "We've got this handled. Just hole up in here and wait this out. This isn't exactly my ideal scenario, but, apparently, I need to babysit."

Jeeze, his bedside manner needs some work.

His words hung in the air, leaving no room for argument. Buck wasn't asking; he was telling. And they fuckin' listened. The immediate crisis was averted, but the atmosphere was still tense.

That's when it happened.

A shout rang out as thick mist began to curl around the pillars of the temple, swirling and twisting like living tendrils. The air turned cold, and the villagers gasped, stepping back as the mist concentrated at a single point. Fear gripped them again as they watched the spectacle, their eyes widening in horror. The murmurs began anew, their tones hushed and terrified.

But just as panic was about to take hold again, the mist suddenly coalesced into a solid figure. One we knew all too well.

Rua.

She was there, standing amidst the remnants of the mist, wearing the typical Sojourner rebirth outfit—a light, airy, khaki-colored shirt and pants. The sudden appearance startled the villagers, but we, her comrades, rushed forward to greet her. A radiant smile spread across her face as she greeted us.

"What the fuck?" I wondered. "How did you—"

"You set your Anchor to this temple?" Edwig asked, shock riddling his words.

"Well, uh, yeah," Rua said with a shrug. "It seemed like, if things got really bad, as long as at least one person was still around to keep the villagers safe . . . well, that would be better than nothing, right?"

"When the fuck had you had time to do that?" I wondered.

"Oh," she said. "I was the one who led the villagers in here in the first place, back before things got *really* bad. The idea struck me then, so I set my Anchor, and . . . voila."

I shook my head.

"Well, goddamn, we have all got some catching-up to do. But . . . well, I don't know if this is the most opportune time, considering—"

"I'm Ileyrri," said the newcomer—the pale woman who looked like she might be suffering from a touch of being undead. "Pleasure to make your acquaintance. Nice flying back there. Looked really impressive."

"Oh. Thanks," I said, taken aback by her forwardness. "I'm Loon; I'm these guys' bud—"

"Quintham. Edwig Quintham!" the sloppy illisinaf said by way of introduction—literally his favorite goddamn thing on the earth. "Undermagister Researcher at—"

"Nobody *cares*, Edwig," I interrupted him back. "Besides, you're not really . . . *that* anymore, are you?"

I turned to the woman who looked like she could punch a stop sign in half and smiled.

"Sorry," I continued. "Eh . . . lay, rhhhi?"

I know I'd managed to butcher her name, and definitely sounded like a fuckin' dipshit rolling my *r*s, but I wanted to try to pronounce it properly—you know, since it seemed like an opportune time.

"Nearly there. Ee. Layuh. Ree," she pronounced, trilling the *r* sound like a professional. I liked her accent, and though I didn't know where it might be from, it sounded alluring to the ear. She didn't seem offended by my moniker massacre; instead, she was smiling. "You the one who belongs to Rexen?"

"What?!" I shouted—on accident. "No! Absolutely not. I'm my own man!"

"My disciple is just being bashful," Rexen said sweetly. "He's definitely mine. Bought and paid for."

"Nope!" I said, wheeling on Rexen. "Listen, you fuck—"

"So, did you live after having Rexen's effigy ripped out of your body?" Dragoon asked. "Or did you die? We were wondering what happened to you."

I paused, having to catch up with the comment, considering I was a hundred kinds of super-riled because of Rexen . . . being probably more honest than I cared to admit.

"Well . . . yeah, I lived. It hurt like a motherfuck, though. Then I got sucked into the portal anyway, went through, but did *not* end up in Palandis. *Oh*, boy. Oof. Got pooped out in a vampire's mansion instead."

"Vampires are *real* here?!" Rua asked, but she sounded more amazed than horrified. Typical.

"Oh, *yeah*," I said. "Though I didn't get the opportunity to meet our host. It probably won't come up again. But I did rub shoulders with her way-too-hot-to-be-usual groundskeeper or whatever. Oh, and Buck— Buck! Come over here and meet my homies!"

The big oni sighed and wandered through the crowd over to where we stood.

"Gang, this is Buck," I said. "He's who protected you during the . . ."

I stopped, looking at everyone else. Now that I had a moment to give 'em the ol' once-over it was clear I had overlooked something. Dragoon and Veruca were dressed much differently than the last time I saw them.

I had barely noticed the change earlier amidst all the chaos, but now it was impossible to ignore. Dragoon was sporting a set of ornate leather armor that I'd never seen before. The armor was a deep russet, rich and supple, and fashioned with complex patterns and symbols that stood out against the leather. They looked intricate, mystifying, lending an air of nobility to his already-formidable appearance. A new crossbow, sleeker and more menacing than his old one, was strapped to his back. It had an ebony finish, and I could see the subtle gleam of enhanced runes etched into its surface.

Veruca's outfit was practically lavish next to Dragoon's practical ensemble. She was draped in flowing robes of an ethereal blue that seemed to ripple and shimmer under the temple's dim light. Lines of incomprehensible script were woven into the fabric, twisting and shifting in an endless dance of arcane knowledge. Resting atop her head was a jaunty little hat that, somehow, didn't seem out of place. It actually complemented her and was stuck snugly behind her horns.

My gaze then landed on Rua. Of course, now she was in the Sojourner leisure suit, but if I recalled correctly . . . she, too, had undergone a dramatic change. Hadn't I seen her with a bright, royal blue cloak draped over her shoulders? Also, I was pretty sure she'd had the Behemoth Blade on her back before she was devoured to death, and a slimmer, more elegant blade had been in her hands . . .

As I took in their upgraded looks, I couldn't help but feel a pang of envy. I was still sporting the same old gear I'd been carrying around for what felt like forever. Looking at them, I couldn't help but wonder what adventures they'd been on, what foes they'd battled, and what treasures they'd uncovered.

It was clear that while we had been apart, they had been busy.

"What. The. Fuck?" I said. "Where did y'all get the sick threads?"

Everyone, at least, had the decency to look a bit bashful. However, before anyone could respond, there was a loud crash and boom, the whole temple shaking as something big, and probably halo-orbited, began slamming against the walls. This resulted in a lot more shrieks from the villagers, who were simply clinging to one another and looking at us—or, more specifically, at Buck.

"Shit," I hissed.

"Ooh! Disciple," Rexen said. "Do you think that's the big one? I'll bet he's *loaded* with tasty treasures and shinies beyond reckoning!"

"Shh," I hissed. "Fuck. Guys, it sounds like that thing's going to break through pretty soon."

I was having Crowmoon flashbacks, except ol' Rafe could at least have some sort of dumb-as-a-doorknob conversation. I think. I wasn't sure how the big, fat Chlamydius Prime would fare in that regard, but I didn't have a ton of optimism.

As the clatter continued, the townsfolk became super agitated, screaming with each uproarious shake, the chlamydians trying their damndest to make it inside.

"What will we do?"

". . . break the door down?"

". . . doomed. Doomed."

"Do you guys have anything left in reserve?" I asked my companions. Everyone shook their heads, save for Edwig and the fighter chick.

"Well, that's to be expected. You guys were fighting for what? Hours? That's fuckin' impressive. But don't worry about it. Edwig, Buck, and . . ."

I looked over at the pale woman with the glowing yellow eyes.

" . . . Ileyrri?"

She nodded.

"Yeah, we'll take care of it," I said, reaching to my waistband.

There was a sigh from behind me, and I turned to see Buck staring at the huge temple doors, looking more bothered than usual.

"No . . ." he said, shrugging his shoulders.

"No?" I wondered. "Buck, what're you—"

"I'm going to do it," he said, rolling his eyes. "It's going to be a bother, but it can't be helped."

"What? No, dude. We're going to help."

"No," he said again. "I am going to do it alone. The rest of you have other things you need to do, right?"

I thought about our true purpose in taking the portals. How had we gotten wrapped up in this?

"Right . . ." I said. "But you're not going to do it alone. Let at least one—"

"Nah," he said. "I've got it."

And with that, he turned toward one of the villagers, a smooth-featured elf who stood trembling near the temple doors.

"Open the door," he ordered, his tone brooking no argument.

The elf, momentarily paralyzed, pointed at himself in surprise, as if questioning the reality of the command.

"Now?" Buck said impatiently.

With a determined swagger, he moved toward the doors, his twin shields gleaming on his arms.

"What are you . . . You're going out there alone?" I demanded.

In response, Buck merely shrugged, a mischievous smirk playing on his lips as he inclined his head toward the doors.

"It'll just take a minute. Watch everyone while I'm gone, yeah? Don't let anyone sneak out."

"But aren't you just, like . . . a defensive specialist?" I countered, attempting to grasp his strategy. "What's the move here, Buck?"

His smirk deepened as he gestured toward his shields.

"Sort of," he said. "Not *just* that, though. I'll be fine. Promise."

He turned and nodded to the elf, who nervously returned the nod and lifted his hands, chanting under his breath. There was a loud *clack* as the doors unlocked and parted with a grind. When the opening was wide enough for him to pass through, he held a hand up to stop the elf from opening it further.

"Whoa," he said, as if speaking to a horse. Then he slipped through the gap. I couldn't be sure, but I thought that as the door closed, I could see a flash of some kind of giant weapon on his back.

CHAPTER TWENTY-NINE

AH, HE GOT THE VELCROS

"Alright, so, that was fucking weird, right?" I said, pointing over my shoulder with my thumb at the doorway where Buck had just disappeared.

I noticed everyone was still staring in that direction, though.

"That was . . ." Veruca began, lost for words for likely the first time ever.

"Gallant," Ileyrri finished, her eyes wide. "I think I'm falling for him."

"Definitely got some rizz about him," Dragoon said with an apathetic nod. "Glad he's on our side."

"That was so cool!" Rua said excitedly. "Loon, I've got goosebumps! Feel 'em!"

She offered her arm to me so that I could presumably . . . confirm their existence.

"Stop that," I said. "Yeah, that was really fucking badass, but who cares? I do stuff like that all the time. Wait! Is this how you guys talk about me after I go off to do my amazing feats?"

"Pah!" Edwig said.

"No . . ." Rua admitted sheepishly. "Usually, we just take bets on how long before someone punches you in the face."

"I . . ." I started, considering. "I mean, yeah, that's probably fair. Anyway! What's the fuckin' deal here?"

"What do you mean?" Dragoon asked.

"I mean," I said, "what's going on in this town? Why are they being attacked by humanoid STDs, and why did y'all agree to come here in the first place? We don't have time for a detour! We got asses to beat—gods to kill!"

Then, remembering my initial question was interrupted, I raised my finger in the air.

"Oh! Right! And where did you guys' couture-ass costumes come from? Your drip is fuckin' *gnarly*."

Everyone seemed to share the same abashed look, save, once more, for Edwig and Ileyrri. Dragoon, apparently not super copacetic with the uncomfortable silence, simply sighed.

"We got this from the trove inside the slumbering god's sect," he said. "We went without you."

It took me a moment to process what he'd said. When I did, I was confused.

"Wait . . . what?!" I shouted, and I noticed it scared some of the villagers. "What are you talking about? Went *without* me? That's . . . not possible. Right? I was only gone for . . ."

I considered this.

"Well, I don't know how long I was gone, I was pretty injured, actually—if you'll recall, it was from having my guts yanked out of my torso. You know, that super painful thing that happened to me after being left to my own devices in Tallr—uh, Corporal Leah?"

Rua winced.

"Sorry, Loon," she said. "We assumed that it killed you and that you'd be sent back to New Home. We figured it didn't make sense to wait."

"So . . . hold up. You're telling me that while I was hanging around with my belly all lookin' like Cthulhu's *face*, you guys just wandered in and killed a fucking *god* and took a bunch of cool stuff for your trouble?"

They all nodded in agreement.

"Unbelievable," I said. "Of fucking *course* you guys had an easy go of it. Why don't I ever get a chance to participate in the cakewalk missions?"

"Pah!" Edwig exclaimed. "Because the minute you're involved, it's not an easy mission anymore!"

"Edwig, they killed a *god*," I said. "What part of that sounds like it's going to be easy? Honestly, I'm not sure why you're on their side; they didn't wait for you, either."

Edwig, suddenly seeming to realize the very same thing, turned angrily toward them and slid over so he was standing next to me.

"Pah! That's right! *Him* I understand! But I'm *useful!*"

"Hey . . ." I said. "What the fuck— No, that's not how we team up!"

"My pupil has a warm temper," Rexen said, as if apologizing on my behalf. "Very easily rattled. Pay him no mind."

"Fuck that," I said. "Pay me all sorts of mind! In fact, pay me in baller-as-shit items. Did you at least save me something?"

The group looked at one another and then turned back to me, shaking their heads.

"Fuckin' stupendous . . ." I said. "Man, this is just great."

I sighed, looking at the group. "Okay, so tell me what happened."

"Well," Rua said. "Like previously mentioned, we thought you'd been killed—a reasonable assumption based on the fact that the effigy came through all bloody—"

"There was a piece of intestine wrapped around it," Dragoon said. "Very gross."

"Wicked," I said with a smirk. "Serves you guys right for abandoning me to the sadistic shusher and her wolfman paramour."

"So, we decided that it would make more sense to just get the job done," Rua said. "Pop in, have a look around, stab a god in the heart—easy peasy."

"Easy peasy," Rexen echoed happily. "As I said— Ooh, disciple, you missed the dragon!"

"Dragon?!" I cried. "Aw, man, seriously?!"

"You're skipping ahead," Dragoon said.

"Yes, I know, but I wanted to illustrate to my pupil that he missed quite an amazing adventure."

"Noted," I said sharply. "Continue."

"In an attempt to render an extraordinarily protracted narrative into a markedly condensed version," Veruca intoned with her characteristic verbosity, "we initiated our ingress through the passageway with which the Dreadnaught Lord possessed a decidedly suspicious level of familiarity, devoted an extensive amount of time to maneuvering through a dark subterranean network while assiduously circumventing potential threats, and subsequently materialized in a chamber that—"

"The lair of the slumbering god!" Rua said. "Oh, man, Loon, it was so cool; it was—"

"Decked out in treasures, skulls, and ritual circles," Dragoon said.

"Ritual circles?" I asked, wide-eyed. "What kind of voodoo magic was this god into?"

"The usual kind," Rua shrugged. "Circles within circles filled with cryptic symbols that pulsated with an eerie glow. It was like walking into an Anne Rice–themed hotel room."

"And the *smell*," Veruca chimed in, wrinkling her nose at the memory. "It was as though the entirety of the vile place was soaked—saturated, really— in an amalgamation of ancient incense, decaying flesh, and old-world herbs. The mere act of maintaining our presence in that area instigated a pronounced manifestation of my psychological unease."

"And then?" I prompted, eager for the next part of their ludicrous tale.

"Then," Dragoon said, pausing for dramatic effect, "we met the slumbering god's pet."

"Dragon!" Rexen practically sang, his eyes sparkling with a mischievous light.

"Ah, of course, the dragon," I said, rolling my eyes but unable to hide my disappointment. I had missed an actual, honest-to-goodness, fire-breathing dragon. "Did it, by any chance, have a name?"

"Thyra!" Rua exclaimed. "Apparently, she was the god's right hand and guardian of the sacred treasure."

"Big, mean, fire-breathing beast," Dragoon said. "Had scales that shone like molten gold and claws that could tear somebody apart in seconds. Quite the sight."

"You *fought* her?" I asked incredulously.

"And *won*, pupil!" Rexen said, grinning from ear to ear. "Put the beast down after a hard-fought battle."

"Really?!" I wondered.

"*Not* really," Rua said, giving Rexen the side eye. "Thyra actually made a deal with us. If we killed Shadranath, she wouldn't attack us, as long as we set her free. So, we agreed."

I was almost reluctant to ask the next question.

". . . And the god?"

"Upon satisfactory resolution of the dragon complication," Veruca continued, "we proceeded to penetrate deeper into the edifice of worship, towards the divine entity's abode. Envision, if you will, a celestial being enveloped by a congregation of devoted subordinates. Such was the spectacle that stood in our path."

"But the god wasn't as powerful as we expected," Dragoon confessed, a slight note of disappointment in his voice. "Shadranath was indeed slumbering, in a literal sense. We killed him in his sleep."

"That's . . . anticlimactic," I said, taken aback.

Everyone jumped as a loud crash echoed outside the temple. It sounded like whatever Buck was doing was . . . well, loud, for one. I really wished this temple had some windows.

"Indeed, it was," Dragoon agreed, picking up where we'd left off. "But it was the easiest way. Once we eliminated him, we took the treasures, the Prosperity Conduit, and left."

"So, you got it?!" I said. "Well, jeez—"

"Dragoon's not telling you the coolest part," Rua said.

"Oh?"

"Yeah, we didn't just *leave*," she said. "The whole place started collapsing—it was super intense. But Thyra found us and we *flew outta there on her back!*"

"Unbelievable," I muttered, shaking my head in disbelief. "And your Quest, Dragoon?"

"Complete," Dragoon said. "And, having ridden Thyra, now I will have a new Subclass option when I get to Level Ten. Wyrmkin Warden. I'll get a dragon of my own."

"Guess you calling yourself 'Dragoon' was a bit of foreshadowing, huh," I said. "Goddammit, gang, you guys got to be cool-ass adventurers, doin' dope shit like becoming dragon riders and junk, all while I was stuck portal-hopping with Buzzkill Johnson over here."

I gestured to Edwig.

"Pah! I'm not any happier about it than you!"

"See? *Buzzkill*," I said. "So, you said you'd get your sweet extras at Level Ten, but you guys must've hit that by now, right? That was a *hell* of a fight out there."

They shook their heads.

"I'm closest, I think," Rua said. "I'm nearly there but still Level Nine. Just a little bit more Experience and I'm in Subclass territory, though."

"Level Eight," Dragoon said.

"Same," Veruca agreed.

"Still, though, that's quite a difference from what you were when we left out, right?"

"Oh, yeah," Rua said. "And we've been racking up new Abilities and Skills like crazy in the meantime. For instance, I can now increase the range on my Displace to up to one hundred feet, *and* now I can use something called Blade of the Bleed. Essentially, it'll allow me to—"

"If it's all the same, let's make that a surprise, Rua. My FOMO is in overdrive right now. If you tell me one more exciting thing that I wasn't a part of, I might collapse in on myself in self-pity."

"Shall we instead see what is the issue with this village?" Edwig offered. "Unless you lot already sorted that as well?"

"Seems sensible," the pale woman said, smiling. "Hey—hello. I'm still here, remember?"

"Oh!" I exclaimed, realizing we'd all been kind of rude. "Yeah, uh, where do you fit into all of this? Wait—are you the dragon?!"

Ileyrri chuckled.

"Hate to say *no*, based on how chuffed you seem. But . . . no," she said. "Just a wayward wraithborn girl out for a bit of a walkabout. Ended up meeting these charmers just before the mood soured around town. Figured I'd tag along—see what all the fuss was about. Plus, they promised free food."

I looked at the others questioningly.

"You guys are in a position to be offering out sack lunches now?"

"Rexen threatened her with a 'knuckle supper,'" Dragoon clarified. "I'm going to assume he got that from you?"

"I'm very impressionable," Rexen said jovially.

"Was planning to assist anyway," Ileyrri said. "But a girl's got to eat, you know?"

"But let's turn the attention to the present," Dragoon interjected. "To your question, Edwig, no, we haven't sorted out the issue with the village. After we came back, we got word of a nearby town under siege. We couldn't just turn a blind eye—and we wanted a bit more of a challenge—so we decided to help out."

"Sounds like you got one, then," I said.

"And that brings us to Kettleborough," Veruca said. "Stricken by the unrelenting menace of these unusual creatures."

"And that's what you guys have been up to while I was . . . away?" I asked, finding the situation a bit overwhelming.

"In summary, yes," Dragoon said. "And now we're trying to figure out why these creatures are attacking, where they're coming from, and how to stop them."

"Well, maybe we can ask some of the less . . . traumatized members of this fucked-up congregation to help us make heads or tails of this mess," I said. "They got a mayor or something? Ninety percent of the time, whenever this kinda shit goes down, it's the mayor that is at fault."

"Hm," Rua said. "Maybe . . ."

"They've got an Alderman," Ileyrri said. "He's a shifty sort; might want to start with him."

"Alright, then," I said. "Let's get the deep deets from this *Aldoman*."

"Alderman," Rua, Veruca, Dragoon, and Edwig all corrected at once.

Alderman Uldric, a sweaty mess of a man, wrung his hands as he spilled his story.

"These . . . erm, these abominations sprang up overnight a fortnight ago. They were content with lurking in the forest until . . . they got, erm, *brave* and altogether a bit too curious about our walls. Now they're inside and we're out of ideas as to our next course of action."

"Hm," I said, contemplating. "Guess you could always . . . I dunno, die? That's probably your best bet."

His eyes widened.

"*Die?*" the Alderman gasped. "I don't want to die!"

"Nah, I didn't think you would," I said. "Seems inconvenient, doesn't it? Messy. Anyway . . . is that all you know about the . . . uh, *ogen*?"

I'd learned within the last few minutes that they were *not* called chlamydians.

"That is as much as I know," the jittery man said, his gaze still exploring the dim corners of the windowless cavern of a temple. "By Kra'mek'el, I swear it."

"Who's . . . Never mind; I don't care," I said, shrugging. "So, you have no inkling—at all—why your humble hamlet is suddenly all the rage?"

"Not a clue," Uldric admitted, his gaze darting away. "Kettleborough has no treasures, no legendary relics. Nothing that'd make us a target."

His words felt rehearsed, lacking conviction. He seemed nervous. Maybe it was because he wasn't used to chatting all cutsie-wootsie with a big orc and a devil-woman, but . . . I had this gut feeling that the good Alderman wasn't being entirely truthful. I'd be willing to bet my whole stack of Skeletonwitch albums that this place was sitting on top of both a treasure and a legendary relic. It was too specific of a response for it to be an offhand remark.

"It's just a little strange," Veruca said, leaning casually against the pillar in her newly plundered swag. She examined a long, black finger . . . claw as if she was the most nonchalant person in the world.

"Strange?" the Alderman wondered, looking around at the assembly. ". . . in, erm, what way?"

"Ah, don't worry about her. She's just a suspicious Sally," I said. "Clearly, there's nothing off about this situation. As we all know, mindless, flesh-eating, monstrous anomalies participate in random sieges all the time. We'll find out what's up, Alderman. Calm your bib."

The Alderman swallowed audibly, his earlier nervousness replaced with a different kind of unease.

"R . . . right," he said, though his voice lacked any conviction. "We will, of course, appreciate your help in this matter."

"Help?" I smirked, leaning closer to the beleaguered Alderman. "Oh, no, buddy-baby Uldric. We're *beyond* help, now, m'dude. You got yourself the best in the business on the case. We're going to uncover each and every nook, cranny, worm-infested rock, and bleak little hidey-hole in this whole hodge-podge podunk. And when we're done, ain't gonna be no more secrets to be had."

"Erm . . . well, yes, of course," Uldric said. "I apologize for my rudeness, but I must check on . . . some things. Yes, things need examining, and I, erm, am the only one who can do them. I'll leave you to it, then, Loom."

"Loon," I corrected. "And sure thing. Let me know if you think of anything else."

"Yes, of course," Uldric said. "Thank you kindly."

As Uldric scampered off, I looked to Veruca.

"So, he's like . . . *super* lying, right?"

"Yes," she said. "His Deception Skill is likely quite low."

"Hey, by the way, nice work with the nonchalant bit," I said. "Man, acting is *fun*. Felt like I was a detective in an old noir or something."

The others joined us, but I kept my eyes trained on the Alderman. He was making his way to the back of the temple, and I wanted to be sure I could see if he tried to make a break for it.

"So?" Rua asked. "What's the scoop? Did you learn anything?"

"Oh, probably," I said. "Mr. Mayor is definitely hiding something. Practically screaming he is involved in this one way or another."

"In what way?" Dragoon asked. "Directly, or indirectly?"

"Eh . . ." I said. "Hard to say for sure, but he's probably got a ton of information—if not all of . . ."

I trailed off as the Uldric the Uncomfortably Sweaty opened a door in the far wall and slipped into it.

"Bingo," I said. "Guys, I'll be right back; I'm going to go trail him."

"Well, we'll see if anyone else knows anything," Rua offered.

"Alright, let's meet back up in a bit. Break."

Fortunately for me, it was pretty light on the illumination in this bitch, so I was able to easily wrap myself in the Trespasser's Veil and slip unnoticed into the many inky shadows. Meanwhile, the background noise of Buck's grandstanding against the creatures filtered in, punctuating the otherwise nervous tension.

Man, that fight is taking forever . . . I thought.

Still, though. His mayhem provided a good distraction.

Maintaining my focus on the on-edge Alderman, I slinked through the doorway, blending into the temple's gloomy recesses as naturally as a ninja shadow at ninja dusk. The Alderman continued his jittery journey down a seemingly innocuous hallway, his head swiveling in the familiar manner of a dipshit who suspects he's being followed.

But tailing a suspect was an art—one that I, Loon, virtuoso of subtlety and hide-and-seek champion of the camp, was more than qualified in. Under my otherworldly watch, the Alderman scurried about as stealthily as a three-legged bull moose in a make-a-buncha-noise shop.

It wasn't long before his destination came into view: a set of unremarkable double doors, which the Alderman approached with practically zero grace. Seriously, this guy could not have been more conspicuous if he was participating in a pay-attention-to-me contest. In what he must've thought was a hyperslick, covert move, he glanced over his shoulder once more before seizing the handles and cranking them in opposite directions. Then he returned them and cranked them again. Instead of swinging open as expected, the sequence of maneuvers caused a hidden panel to creak open in the floor. That's our Alderman, always full of surprises.

In a flash, the man ducked into the floor's gaping maw, disappearing into the secret hatch. His panic had obviously overridden any desire for subtlety. Then the hatch began to close.

A resigned sigh escaped my lips.

"Really, Uldric? Hatches? How very . . . *Lost* of you."

With no time to roll my eyes properly at the cliché, I bounded forward, launching myself with the nimble agility only an orc with a premium-membership Acrobat Skill could muster. I plunged into the secret passage just as the hatch closed above me with a final, satisfying *thunk*.

A breath later, I was engulfed in a darkness so dense, you could have cut it with a spoon. No worries, though: my Darkvision flickered on. Handy. The world reformed around me, and it was . . . intriguing.

"Son of a bitch . . ." I murmured as I surveyed what I had found to be a hastily dug passageway. The excavation was rough, sloppy—it looked like a child's attempt rather than the smooth and polished secret tunnel one would expect. The shoddy workmanship reminded me of my recent stint digging ditches back at New Home, though even my worst ditch was a masterpiece compared to this. A blind mole rat could do better. But . . . wait, weren't mole rats already blind? So . . . would a mole rat with twenty-twenty vision be worse? Eh, whatever; it sucked.

The Alderman was suddenly, suspiciously, absent from this silly little stakeout.

"Well, hell, that's not exactly—"

My vision *purpled* in what I now knew to be my Jeopardy Hunch Ability. I saw a vague image of something coming at me from my right. Without a second thought, I dropped to a squat just as a rusty knife ripped through the air, whizzing past where my brain had been moments before. A pudgy adult hand gripped the handle and, as if to ensure its own victory, made a little extra swishing and turning motion in the air.

Great job, dipshit, I thought. *Definitely killed that empty patch of air.*

I noticed that from the wrist on, the remainder of my asinine assassin's body disappeared into a shivery sliver of altered reality. Like a rift. As it faded, a faint outline of a humanoid shape shimmered into view.

Without wasting another breath, I . . . used my breath and triggered my Blackout Warchant with a loud roar. The magic shroud flickered, wavered, and then poof! Gone. In its place was a shape that—based on the relative size and shape—was the Alderman. Completely covered by what looked like a dark, cloth bedsheet.

I sighed. I had to assume it had been some kind of invisibility cloak. Poor quality, too, because if I'd been looking closer earlier, I'm sure I would have seen the clear holes and patches in the wrinkled fabric.

For a moment, all was still. Then came a surprised squeak as the Alderman realized he could no longer see through the blanket. In a rather comical spectacle, he made a frantic dash for it, only to collide headfirst with the dirt wall. Down he went, tangled in a bedsheet, looking every bit the defeated villain in a Saturday-morning cartoon.

"Heavens, Alderman," I said theatrically as I yanked the sheet off him. "I didn't know you were into cosplay."

"What? Oh, erm, hello, Loom! What . . . erm, brings you down here?"

"Alderman, Alderman, Alderman," I sighed. "Don't try to play coy. You tried to stab me. Badly, I might add—I'm almost offended."

Uldric sputtered, dust and indignation flecking from his lips.

"I—I didn't know who was following me! A man has a right to defend himself!"

I gave him a long look.

"Yeah, okay. Whatever. But who or *what* were you defending yourself from in this seedy underbelly?"

He avoided my gaze, not answering the question, his eyes flickering in the darkness. Then, with a hesitant voice, he asked, "May I have my Veil of the Undetectable back?"

I chuckled.

"Nah, it's totally mine now, bro. But don't get your bedsheets in a tangle . . . more than you already have. You *could* earn it back. All you have to do is be a good, well-behaved Alderman and tell me what you're doing down here in the temple's sphincter."

The Alderman's face turned a shade paler, if that was even possible.

"I can't," he said, shaking his head.

"Why the fuck not?"

He screwed up his face defiantly—apparently, *this* was the hill he was willing to die on.

"Out with it," I said, holding up my haladie. "Unless you wanna be walking around, trying to figure out how to keep your sinuses from leaking out of your neck."

The Alderman, apparently not used to threats of powerful physical violence, let his mouth fall open.

"If I say anything, my god will be displeased."

"Oh, well, is that all? Fuck them gods, guy. Trust me on that—they're worse than regular people."

His horror was palpable, but I just steamrolled along, uninterested in whatever exaggerated level of heresy he thought I was invoking.

"Tell you what, though. If you don't *spill* the fucking *beans*, I think you'll be meeting your god sooner than you think. Then you can appreciate his displeasure face-to-face."

I crossed my arms over my chest, tapping the blade of the haladie on my bicep.

"Last chance. Make it count."

Despite my threats, his resolve seemed to harden, his chubby jaw set in a stubborn line.

"I won't say any more."

With a growl of frustration, I grabbed him by the scruff of his shirt and yanked him to his feet.

"Oh, that's fine," I spat, "but you're still leading the way."

"Whoo-boy!" I announced, my eyes drinking in the magnificent dump before me. "If this ain't just about the most *impressive* work of fart. I mean, it's a fucking shithole."

And indeed, the chamber was a monument to dreadful aesthetic choices. It looked like a cross between a hoarder's living room and a particularly rowdy tavern's piss-stained restroom after a three-day binge. It was a fuckin' mess. Stalactites hung low from the rocky ceiling, while a fine layer of grime smeared every surface like a grotesque layer of makeup. There were crates stacked all over the place, spoiled food on the ground, and I could smell the distinct scent of something old and rotten.

However, the whole eye-offending spectacle was overshadowed by the grandeur of a monstrosity situated smack in the middle. An enormous throne that looked like it was ripped straight out of a fairy tale designed for hellspawn was set against a hulking obelisk. Atop this towering seat of power sat an emaciated, grotesque figure.

I mean, this thing was fucking huge! Long-limbed, oversized bald head, it had the look of a man starved and stretched out into something inhuman. The skin was tight and cracked over skeletal features, giving the creature the appearance of an oversized mummy if the mummy had been part giant and then denied dinner for a millennium.

"What the fuck is this place?" I asked the Alderman.

He trembled, keeping his eyes to the floor as if he was afraid to look up. I nudged him.

"Hey . . . answer me, Mr. Mayor. What is—"

"This is the resting place of Kra'mek'el! We are not worthy to look upon his visage, nor his withered form. For his is the might by which our village was founded, and his—"

"Okay, okay," I said dismissively. "This guy right here is your god? Well... damn. I don't know that I'd ever imagine seeing a deity living in the basement below his own temple. I mean... *is* he living?"

"Kra'mek'el observes the Interim," the Alderman explained, still keeping his eyes to the ground. "It is a period where he awaits his rebirth, and—"

"Sheesh! Creepy! Unsettling as all hell," I said, giving the space a further once-over.

The very fabric of reality seemed to pulsate around the monster, twisting and contorting in the ghostly glow of the arcane sigil traced onto the filthy ground. Runes, an intricate network of them, flickered in a disturbing ballet of blue and red lights, the colors twisting together then pulling apart, like a cosmic dance of creation and destruction. The energy flowed like an ethereal serpent, snaking its way across the dingy floor before slithering up into the mummified monster perched on the throne. The sight was as mesmerizing as it was nauseating; grotesque.

The throne, the obelisk, the... the everything... was straight fucked, man. I kinda had the urge to purge. But... then something tickled at my thinkin' meat. I recognized it. Well, the obelisk, anyway. It was just like the one I'd seen in Rexen's little treasure hideaway. Then it hit me, a swift punch to the gut of my memory.

Ocho.

In the Crypt, he'd... he'd babbled on about something that looked eerily like this very obelisk, calling it a pylon. So, I figured that's why it had seemed so familiar when I saw it in Rexen's cache. What was going on there?

My gaze fell back onto the grotesque figure on the throne. Another spark of recognition flickered in my mind. The creature, swaddled in decrepit linens and propped up like some fucked-up version of a royal puppet, was missing an arm.

Just like that, everything clicked into place and a horrible realization began to dawn on me.

Kra'mek'el. *Carmichael.*

"Hey Uldric..." I said, my eyes still on the huge Slenderman-like purported deity. "How long has your Jesus, here, been down in the cellar?"

"What?"

"Krav maga—er, whatever you're calling him. Any record on when he decided to take this little staycation—uh, *Interim*?"

"Kra'mek'el has been here as long as Kettleborough. He was the founder. Our people delighted under his reign. And so, we kept his requests when he made to first enact the Interim."

"And that was... how long ago?"

"We do not count the precise age of Kettleborough, nor the time our mighty Kra'mek'el had been in the Interim."

"Ballpark it for me," I continued.

"It would have been in the previous age. Several hundred years, at my lowest reckoning."

Ah, so, more likely, it is Carmichael, I thought. *But what the fuck happened?*

Back with Frida, Jes, and the squad in the second chamber of the Crypt, they'd been trying to find their missing party member. A guy they busted out of juvie or whatever to help them navigate the dungeon because of his dope motherfuckin' aptitude with cosmic Arcana . . . I think. But he'd dipped out, slipping away in the night, leaving them high and dry in a time dilation that essentially forced them to lose out on five hundred years. Most importantly, he'd been something called an ulgaroch, which basically looked like this fuckin' criminal art installation in front of me. Big, skinny body, bulbous head—and Carmichael had lost an arm in the first chamber. Frida had had to amputate it when it got wedged between a gross bug monster and a rock.

Everything was coming together. I wasn't sure what all this fucked-up noise was keeping him in his Intermission or whatever, but there was little doubt in my mind that this was the very same guy. Especially considering he'd left behind a fake skeleton and—well, I didn't have the energy to recap—but it looked pretty much just like this.

"Uldric," I said, watching as the pulsating magic continually pumped its way into Carmichael's unmoving puppet body. "Why did you leave to come down here?"

The Alderman didn't say anything, and I noticed that now he was quietly sobbing.

"Hey, dick-nuts," I said, nudging him with my foot. "What instigated your spelunking? This is wigging me out."

"I . . . I . . ." The Alderman hiccupped between sobs, his chest heaving as he fought to regain composure. His eyes, wet with tears, flicked up to meet mine for a moment before darting away. "I didn't want it to be this way," he blubbered, his voice choked with despair.

"What way?" I pressed, crossing my arms over my chest. The image of Carmichael in his stately decay still had my brain spinning.

"I just wanted to protect the village," he whimpered, tears spilling down his cheeks and splashing onto the grimy floor. "Protect Kra'mek'el. The temple. I didn't . . . didn't mean for the . . . the gates."

"Gates?" My eyebrow arched with a mixture of interest and confusion.

He nodded, sniffing loudly as he attempted to swallow his sorrow.

"The gates ... to open. The beasts ... they weren't meant to ... I didn't want them to ... attack. I wanted to ... to narrow the time of the Interim."

I squinted at him. What in the seven hells was this gibbering idiot on about now? One thing for sure: all of this had been caused by him somehow.

Goddammit. It's always *the fucking Mayor.*

"Alderman, I swear by the ghost of Randy Rhoads, if you don't start making some fucking sense—"

Before I could finish my rant, his crying stopped abruptly. He fell eerily silent, his gaze lifting to meet mine, and my breath hitched in my throat at the sight that met me. Blood was streaming down from a wound on his belly, dark and thick. It dripped onto the floor, pooling around his feet. I followed his gaze down to the rusty blade protruding from his gut.

He didn't scream. He didn't cry out. He didn't even seem to feel the pain. With a ragged gasp, he hurled himself forward onto the pulsating runic circle, landing with a sickening thud.

The room lit up with a brilliant flash. The colors were unearthly, a palette of phosphorescent hues that I couldn't describe if I tried, simultaneously breathtaking and nightmarish. The arcane sigil twisted and writhed under the Alderman's body, and a sickening sound like meat being torn apart echoed through the chamber. His body convulsed, twitching in a spasmodic dance.

Then it began. The horrific transformation.

His skin stretched tight over his bones, taking on a sallow, sickly pallor. His flesh seemed to fold in on itself, wrapping tight around his skeletal frame until he looked no different from the grotesque figure on the throne. His eyes bulged in their sockets, their whites glaringly bright against the darkness of the room. They were the last things to change, shifting from their normal hue to a disturbing, eerie green.

"Jesus fuck!" I yelled.

But that wasn't the end of it. Oh, no. The transformation continued, with his body beginning to elongate, stretching in unnatural, impossible ways. His limbs lengthened, growing longer and more grotesque by the second. His form warped and twisted, becoming something monstrous, something nightmares would have nightmares about.

Then the energy surged. It shot up from the runic circle like a geyser, engulfing the Alderman in an iridescent cascade. It twisted and snaked its way around his now-grotesque form, pouring into him with a sickening slurp.

The entire room quivered as if in fear of the monstrous sight unfolding before it. The Alderman was no more. In his place was a thing that belonged to neither this world nor the next, an abomination that defied description, defied sanity. It was a sight straight from Lovecraft's darkest wet dreams, an eldritch horror that I wished I could unsee.

The monstrous transformation ended as abruptly as it had begun, suddenly shriveling again like a leaf in a crackling fire, dispersing, leaving in its wake a silence so deep, so complete, it seemed as though the world itself was holding its breath. I noticed that the only thing that was left behind was one of his arms. Actually, there was something underneath it . . . something shiny?

The quiet hung heavy in the air, a suffocating blanket of horror that threatened to crush the life out of me.

As the room plunged back into its oppressive gloom, I was left standing in the midst of the macabre spectacle, my mind reeling from the onslaught of terror.

Then the corpse-like figure on the throne twitched.

Once, twice, three times—each movement accompanied by the rustle of the dry, aged linens that swaddled it, the sound grating against the eerie silence of the room. Then the figure's entire body jerked violently. A sickening *crack* echoed through the chamber as it started to come alive—quite goddamn literally—in the most horrific manner imaginable.

The symbols inscribed on the floor of the circle began to pulse, their sickeningly bright blue and red hues intensifying, bathing the room in a fuck-awful light. It was as if the very life force of hell was being funneled directly into the figure on the throne. Slowly, it uncurled itself from its lifeless slump, its long, skeletal body creaking and popping with each movement. A freaky puppet, suddenly imbued with a malevolent life of its own. Each jerky movement made my skin crawl, and a sick feeling roiled in my gut. I found myself frozen, paralyzed by both the dread and the anxiety of not knowing what was happening. With a jarring lurch, the creature hauled itself upright, its full horrifying form towering over me at a daunting eight feet. It seemed more akin to a monstrous model of death rather than anything that could've once been considered a living creature. Carmichael—if it could still be called that—was back and grosser than ever.

Its eyes, empty hollows moments ago, flared to life, glowing with an eerie luminescence. The once dull, dead gaze now burned with a rage so raw and primal, I gulped involuntarily. It roared then, a sound so filled with pain and anguish that it felt like it could rip my soul into toilet paper scraps. It was a lamentable cry of torment from the abyss itself, threatening to shatter the already tenuous hold I had on my fucking sanity.

Then, with an unsteady step, the towering figure staggered forward. A glowing light began to radiate from the obelisk behind the throne, the pulsating energy from the magic circle and the newly awakened creature seemingly resonating with it.

As the resonance swelled, the obelisk pulsed in time with Carmichael's movements, echoing his anguish, amplifying his monstrous presence. The oppressive energy in the room grew so intense, it felt as though the air itself was alive. As if it could reach out at any moment and consume me whole.

The creature, once Carmichael but now some kind of fucked-up, wailing demonic abortion, turned to face me. Its eyes pierced me, as cold as a birthday divorce. It opened its mouth, and what escaped was not a voice but a chorus of raspy, cacophonous whispers that sounded like they were echoing up from a deep, dark well.

"Mock. Us."

The words were drawn out, more guttural growl than intelligible speech, an ancient utterance twisted by the strain of ages.

"Huh?" I choked out. "What the hell do you mean? I'm not *mocking* you; I'm scared to fuckin' death to even make eye contact."

The monster's lips twisted into a grotesque parody of a smile, and it spoke again. The voices intertwined and reverberated off the cavernous walls, a nightmarish choir chanting the same cryptic words over and over.

"Mock. Us. Mock. Us. Mock. Us."

I could feel a bead of cold sweat trickle down the side of my face. The distance between us was closing, the creature lumbering toward me with a slow, deliberate gait. Each of its steps a disgusting display of twitches and spasms, its too-long limbs moving in ways that were all kinds of fuckin' *wrong*.

My mind raced, trying to unravel the meaning behind its cryptic words. Why was it accusing me of mocking it? A humiliation kink? Or was it speaking in riddles—a habit too many seemed to have lately—and it was actually a veiled warning of something more insidious?

But I didn't have time to solve some dumbass linguistic mystery. I reached down, pulling the wands from my waistband. My hands shook slightly as I pointed them directly at the once-man-now-monster.

As it moved forward, I saw the leftover arm on the runic circle suddenly shift and *definitely* magically flew from the ground and sprang onto Carmichael's stump. There was a wet *crack* and the two pieces forced themselves together, fusing into one. Carmichael didn't even look down at the new addition; he simply flexed the limb and lowered his head as if preparing to charge.

Goddammit. I'm going to have to fight fucking Slenderman.

And with a roar that shook the room, I released all my pent-up frustration, confusion, and fear into that one explosive sound as I fired.

CHAPTER THIRTY

MUMMY DUST

The air in the room became a swirling maelstrom as my magic blasters roared to life. A brilliant arc of lightning leapt from one, striking the monstrosity. Alongside came a seething wave of beautiful motherfuckin' fire, engulfing the creature and setting it alight.

Yet, through the furious inferno and the crackling electricity, the creature continued its advance, goddamn unaffected. Every nerve screamed at me to move, to get away. I turned and ran, scrambling to the other side of the room. Behind me, Carmichael or the shit-ghoul . . . thing he had become, gave chase.

The symbols on the floor pulsed ominously once again. The temperature plummeted rapidly, biting into my flesh with icy teeth. In response to this sudden change, the room began to transform. From the walls and floor, crystalline structures began to grow, encasing everything in a frosty sheen. These weren't your grandpappy's ice formations, though. Nah, these motherfuckers shimmered red and blue, looking almost like mineral deposits.

Fuck this!

I turned to make my escape through the tunnel, but I was too late. The entrance was sealed, blocked off by the same crystal-like growth.

Trapped. Shit!

Spinning back to face my impending doom, I saw a sight that I think would have made me pee a little if I wasn't so fucking dehydrated—take that, gang! Carcass-michael's monstrous form was floating in the air, his limbs hanging limply like a hanged victim. With a speed that defied his previous lumbering gait, he shot toward me like a withered missile.

I let loose another barrage of wand bullets, but the thing simply absorbed the magical onslaught and continued after me, swiping at my legs. I leaped into the air to avoid it, then dived, rolling away just in time to negate another swipe.

But as I stood, he connected with a hand, and I felt a burning stripe light up my back as his fingers blazed against my flesh.

I knew I had to *try* to come up with some kind of game plan. My mind felt like it was racing through sludge, desperately struggling to remember any Skill, Ability, or fuckin' . . . super pointy object in my pack that could get me out of this mess.

Before I could latch on to anything useful, a hand that felt like a steel trap wrapped around me, lifting me off the ground.

"GyuuuYUUH!" I screamed.

Carmichael had snatched me up and was yanking me toward himself. The creature's grotesque face was inches from mine, its twisted mouth repeating the same haunting words over and over.

"Mock. Us. Mock. Us."

Driven by pure adrenaline, my hand shot out to my Stag's Pique. I pulled it out and didn't even think about it; I plunged it right into the creature's elbow. The thick beef-jerky hide didn't give much, but apparently it was *just* enough to send a message that I wasn't to be fucked with . . . sorta. Carmichael let out a howl and I fell to the ground.

But I'll give him one thing: despite being some sort of revitalized revenant or whatever-the-shit, this brute was quick to switch up his strategy. Before I could even so much as scramble to my feet, Carmichael slashed a hand in front of himself. The air before the elongated goblin shimmered and tore open, revealing a swirling vortex of darkness. The obelisk and the magic circle were flashing wildly, feeding power to this newly formed portal.

Then a new terror dropped from the vortex to join this spooky soiree. Another fucking chlamydian.

Nope, that's not fucking staying open, I thought.

I summoned Blackout Warchant and blasted the rift. The portal—blessedly—blinked out of existence. But . . . not before the chlamydian—or ogen or whatever—was on me. It bowled me over, knocking me to the ground and sinking its claws into my flesh.

"Fuck! Off!" I hissed, straining against the effort of its insistent desire to devour me. It was stronger than the ones outside, and I had a sneaking suspicion that being close to its apparent master was the root of that strength.

I yelped, my vision blurring from the shock of pain as it raked its claws over me. Its breath was hot and putrid on my face, reeking of decay and despair. But I weren't no bitch. Despite the searing pain tearing through me, I fought back. I'd faced worse, with more tediously stacked odds.

Gritting my teeth, I managed to hold the chlamydian at bay with a straining left hand—long enough to jam the pique into its neck and shove it off of me. Its body hit the crystalline floor with a thud, and it tried to turn to get me. But I was on it. I landed on its back like a child using the family dog for pony rides and then delivered six or seven punishing, barbed donkey punches to the back of its skull with the pique. Dark blood spurted out and into my face, but I didn't care. Then, because I knew that just relishing in my fresh kill was probably not wise, considering the circumstances, I rolled off of it, rearmed myself with the wands, and stood.

"Nice trick!" I shouted, fear replaced with anger. That's when I noticed another rift was open, and two more chlamydians had tumbled out.

"You've gotta be fucking kidding me!" I shouted.

I fired a stream of magic at the creatures with the wands. One was hit but the other was too quick. However, the one that hit, hit *real* nice. It got the full load and erupted on the spot.

"Fuck you!" I shouted at the remaining chlamydian.

I could feel the Stamina draining from me, my reserves dipping dangerously low. The chlamydian leftover lunged for me, but I rolled to the side, avoiding its onslaught.

Glancing over, I saw the terrifying sight of Carmichael's form twitching and writhing in the air, hovering with a malevolence that froze my blood. His terrifying figure was bathed in the eerie glow from the pulsating magic circle and obelisk, his grotesque body a silhouette against the unearthly light. Instead of the slow, ponderous movement of before, now he darted around with unnatural speed, flying through the air with an agility that was as horrifying as it was mesmerizing.

Without a second thought, I unleashed another volley of wand juice, but he swerved, avoiding the blast with an ease that belied his monstrous size. His eyes, lit with that unholy light, zeroed in on me. His voice, a horrific chorus of a thousand tortured souls, echoed around the room.

"Mock. Us."

I barely had time to react as he swooped down on me, his long skeletal fingers wrapping around me and lifting me into the air. His hollow eyes bore into mine, a cold, calculating empty stare that chilled me to my core. I could feel the raw power radiating from him, an energy that threatened to consume me.

With his free hand—'cuz why not; he had two now—he slashed at the air. The obelisk and the circle pulsed in response, the glow from them intensifying to a blinding level. The air in front of him shimmered and parted, revealing another swirling vortex.

"No!" I tried to squirm out of his grasp, but it was like trying to wriggle out of iron chains. "No, you gosh dern don't!"

But it was too late. The portal yawned wide, a gaping maw ready to spit out more horrors. I could see shapes moving in the blackness, and dread filled me as I realized what was about to happen. More chlamydians clambered out, their grotesque bodies a horrifying echo of the ones I had just fought off.

"Fuuuuuck!" My voice echoed through the chamber, filled with frustration and fear. The circle, the portal, and Carmichael were all pulsating in unison, their combined power dwarfing mine. My earlier bravado was rapidly fading, replaced with a creeping helplessness that gnawed at my insides.

As the chlamydians began to advance, their vicious claws scraping against the crystalline floor, I saw my impending doom reflected in their shitty, bleak little eyes. There was only one thing left to do.

With a roar that echoed off the chamber walls, I rammed my forehead into Carmichael's face. His mouth, mid-sentence, snapped shut, and the satisfying crunch of shattering teeth was his fresh melody.

With the momentary distraction, I aimed my wands at him, pouring every last bit of concentration into the blast to try to create some distance. His grip loosened, and I fell to the floor, my knees buckling under the sudden impact. With a grunt, I pushed myself upright, turning my attention to the glowing circle.

Edwig and Rua had been talking about these kinds of things, right? Runic circles?

Fuck, I hadn't been paying attention, because it seemed like something I'd never need to know. But, once again, I'd been proven I was fucking stupid. Like when I dipped out of Home Ec the week we were learning to sew because, and I quote, "I'm not Amish." Of course, only a few months later, when I'd ripped the crotch of my jeans trying to mimic Michael Jackson's "Thriller" dance . . . I saw the error of my ways. I'd been in the bathroom at school—don't ask—and had to call my Aunt Ella to bring me a different pair to finish out the day. Of course, everyone saw her drop them off for me, and some assumptions were made. Which was why the second half of my junior year had people referring to me as "that fat kid that shit his pants." This was like *that* but *magic*.

Come on, you dense bitch . . . think! What had they been saying?

My mind reeled, clutching onto the snippets of conversation I had overheard. Symbols, vessels, backfires . . . What the hell was I missing?

I laid in to one of the chlamydians, slicing through its face with one quick drag of the haladie, and then punched a life-ending hole in its neck with the pique. The creature went down in a shower of blood.

I had to keep thinking, though. From the topics the two had covered, I *knew* there was something there . . . but what? Runic symbols . . . Potency . . . Concentration. Something about . . . dandelions and some jack-off named Jeremy. Rua and Edwig's hushed conversation bounced around inside my head like a stupid little moth, bashing continually into the lightbulb of my under-capable skull. My eyes flitted across the scene, trying to make sense of the chaos.

I'd muttered something snarky, right? Swapping Edwig out for a better model, or something . . . Then, like a bolt of blue inspiration, I remembered. The vessel. Containment. Their little Magic 101 lesson wasn't about some theoretical mumbo jumbo; it was about the alarms . . . and by default something just like this—I guess. Yeah, *this*! Edwig's words suddenly entered my brain.

"Then you need to get yourself a better arcanist! It ruins the whole ritual . . ."

Ruins the whole. Motherfuckin'. Ritual.

It clicked. The obelisk, the magic circle, the portal—everything around me suddenly made a whole lot more sense. The obelisk wasn't just a big, flashy, magic stick. It had to be the vessel, the container holding the spell's power, the key to the whole damn fucked-up geometry problem.

And if the obelisk was the vessel, that begged the question: was it sturdy enough? Was it Carmichael's version of a dandelion? A bit of a stretch, maybe, but it made more sense than anything else at the moment. Was the obelisk his weakness? His anchovies heel?

My pulse quickened. It was a long shot, but long shots were the most impressive shots if you nailed 'em. Still, I needed a *bit* more information.

A plan formed in my mind. A desperate, malformed thing that hinged on the faint hope that I could disrupt the energy flow and stop the impending onslaught. I hated it.

I blasted a few more times with the wands to give myself more distance, then had to dive around as chlamydians darted at me. I led them to one side, then leaped over them and ran back to the circle. Drawing in a deep breath, I activated Eye of the Saboteur. I didn't know if it would work, but I was out of options. It was do or die. Probably die.

With a feral yell, I slammed my hand down onto the magical symbols on the floor. The world around me exploded into a brilliant flash of light as I was shown the guts of this entire goddamn place. The room around me, the tunnels sneaking off into who the hell knows where, and even the massive, granddaddy church upstairs were lit up. Unfortunately for me *and* my shitty plan, it was all washed in blue. Structural soundness, they call it. No weaknesses. That meant this place was sturdier than a doomsday bunker.

But then again, there was the fucking sorcery art project under my feet and the weird crystal crap that had just turned this whole place into a magic womb. Those bad boys weren't blue. Oh, no, they were showing up in more shades of green than a kale-smoothie convention hall. Spells. Not surprising, but also disheartening. I couldn't really do much for those. A neon ribbon of magical emerald energy, all pulsing and swirling and looking generally unsmashable.

Wait . . .

Right in the middle of all this crazy bullshit was a hole. A void. A fuckin . . . *nada*. It was where the obelisk-pylon-thingy should've been. Instead of being lit up like everything else, it was dark. Empty. Like a black hole had opened up right in the middle of the fucking planet.

It wasn't just weird. It was *wrong*. Everything else was part of the structure, bound together, stronger than a drunken frat boy's bonds of brotherhood. But this thing? It was off, a lone wolf, disconnected and solitary like it wasn't even a part of the same reality as the rest of this nightmare. What the hell was its deal?

Just like the very first time I ever activated Eye of the Saboteur, something about those obelisks kept them from being recognized by my Ability. When I'd performed it on the statue that happened to house the pylon in the Crypt, the same thing had happened. A dark void—like the space just didn't fucking exist. I was seeing the same thing now, and my mind was starting to itch.

I remembered obliterating it. The thing was old, right? The one in Rexen's cache had looked ancient as well,

"Fuck, I hate wizards," I muttered to myself. "Why can't they ever be helpful for once? Screw you, Rexen, you worthless—"

The world turned still and I was suddenly in the unmistakable bubble of Commune.

Hello! Rexen said, entering my head. **How's my favorite pupil doi—**

Bad! Real *fuckin' bad, Arjee!* I said. *Thank the goddamn you appeared when you did, 'cuz I need a couple of minutes to strategize real quick before—*

Oopsie-doopsie, Rexen said. **I don't have time to chat; just wanted to check on you and—**

No, no, no! I shouted in my mind. *Goddammit! Don't go anywhere; I'm fighting for my fuckin' life! Hold it for as long as possible; I'm battling some kind of reanimated cosmic sorcerer motherfuck on top of a magic circle, and if I don't—*

Magic circle? Rexen asked. **Have you tried disrupting it? That should do the trick! Okay, bye-bye now, pup—**

Goddammit, listen to me! I don't really know how to disrupt the circle, and I'm hoping—

Silly disciple! The easiest way is to break the vessel that contains the power! Do that! Okay, I'm leaving n—

I don't know how to break this vessel, you goddamn putz! Stop trying to escape and give me a moment to think! Fuck!

My apprentice will never learn if I give him all the shortcuts, Rexen continued, and his tone sounded . . . smug. **But . . . since I am famously liberal with my affections, I will give you one extra cast of Commune to solve your problem—then—you're on your own!**

Shit! Okay . . . shit! SHIT! Um, uh, goddamn. Arjee, what's the best way for me to gain an Ability or Skill super fast—ideally something that I can do within one minute?

Fifty seconds, Rexen said.

What?

You had fifty seconds left on Commune—now forty-three. I cast it before I had finished the sentence informing you about the time limit. Thirty-eight!

Not helping! Answer the fucking question!

Prickly pupil . . . Rexen said. **But okay—why don't you use some of those succulent Esper Nodes you've been hoarding?**

Fuck. Motherfucking goddamn ass. Of course! The Messenger orb had told me something similar, but I had completely forgotten that because I'm always forgetting things when I'm being actively wrenched through a portal made out of pain. But there wouldn't be enough time to do that, not with this giant sleep paralysis demon breathing down my dick.

Arjee, I need one more cast of Commune and then I'm done—give me that and I'll owe you big time!

Really? he asked, and I knew by his tone that I was going to regret this tit-for-tat. I mentally sighed.

Yes, do it!

As you say, pupil. Just remember—you promised!

I ignored him for the moment—I had some Espers to Node, or whatever. Frantically, I summoned my menu and scrolled through the invisible screen only I—and maybe Rexen—could see. Finally, I found what I was looking for. The Esper Nodes.

Without a second thought, I selected the top option: *Topaz*. Just a name, really. Didn't tell me jack shit about what it'd actually do. But hey, this was no time for being a chicken. I wasn't exactly sure what would happen, but at that moment, anything was better than being stuck in blueprint land with a glow-in-the-dark circle and a damn mystery pylon.

"Alright, Topaz," I muttered, gritting my teeth as I selected it. "Let's see what kind of party tricks you've got."

Would you like to use [Topaz] Esper Node to modify aspects of yourself?

Hell fuckin' yes, I thought. Goddamn anything is a win right now.

Before, when I'd done this, I'd been able to use the Emerald Esper Nodes to combine two Abilities and make them into the Warchant Ability. Which had come in oh so clutch. But the menu that sprang up this time, when selecting the Topaz Esper Nodes, was something different.

Thankfully, this section of the system seemed immune to just sending me eggplant emoji or something worse, and, while annoyingly sarcastic, it gave me some insight into what I could expect. Surprisingly, it was not at all what I expected. Rather than combining Abilities this go-around, apparently, the Topaz Node was for . . . well . . . other stuff. Very, *very* quickly, I read through the prompts.

Additional [Orc]* Racial Bonus
Available Racial Bonuses:

Runic Tattoos
Oh great, another orc who thinks doodling on their skin makes them a sorcerer. Well, as it turns out, these aren't your everyday doodles—they're ancient runes with magical powers. I know, I know, it sounds ridiculous, but when etched onto the orc's skin, these tattoos can imbue them with an array of arcane abilities—without using Arcana! Everything from transforming their fists into flaming pugilism gloves to making their skin as resilient as an overcooked steak. Magical graffiti; who would've thought?
- Available Runic Tattoos [1]

Totemic Mimicry
This tattoo allows an orc to take on the appearance and voice of another person they've touched. Great for infiltration and deception or saddling someone else with your substantial debts. Maintaining the form requires focus [Outcome for efficiency is Intelligence + Deception quotient].

Ancestral Augury
Because why should orcs think for themselves when they can pester the long-dead for advice? With this ability, the orc can summon their dearly departed ancestors for a good old chinwag about life, love, and how to best swing a battle-ax. No need to bother with maps or strategies when you've got a disembodied ghost of a great-great-auntie to guide you to the nearest treasure or warn you about that incoming storm. Hey, two heads are better than one, even if one is ethereal and constantly reminiscing about "the good old days."
- Available Ancestral Auguries [2]
  - Augury of Weather
    [1] Charge per day, you can request to know the weather in an area of [5] ectrens of your current location.
  - Augury of Navigation
    [1] Charge per day, you can request to know the direction to any location within [30] ectrens of your current location.

Blood of the Mountain
An orc who gets stronger when they're closer to dirt? You bet. If an orc with this ability is in a mountain or cave, they might as well be king of the world. They can sense precious stones like a pig sniffing out truffles and get so tough, you'd think they were made out of the rock itself. Honestly, it's like they believe the earth is some sort of multivitamin.
+ 1 Strength per [50] feet of depth within earthen environments
+ 1 Constitution per [50] feet of depth within earthen environments
Gain Detect Minerals Ability

Well, this was fucking useless! I was in danger of getting eaten by some kind of demi-Satan in a closed-off crystal cocoon, and my best options were Abilities that let me either sniff around for minerals or guess the seven-day forecast. This did not bode well, and I had almost just decided to cowabunga this whole thing when I saw an asterisk at the bottom of the message.

*Additional Racial Bonus Available: 1

Fuck it, let's do this thing.
I selected it and saw to my utter shock that . . . I wasn't fully orc. I mean, yeah, I'd suspected it for some time, but this was the rock-solid confirmation to bring my deductions out of tin foil territory.

Because at least 10% of your Racial Makeup comprises an additional Race, you have the option to select an additional Racial Bonus!
[Possessed Roe]

I didn't have time to think about what that meant for me; I just quickly read over what was offered. Extremely quickly.

Available Racial Bonuses:
Biter
The ability to summon razor-sharp teeth that can chomp through nearly anything you can imagine. Wood, iron, stone? No problem. Biter makes the user a living, breathing, terrifying tool of destruction. Once activated, the roe's regular teeth are replaced by a maw full of elongated, serrated fangs, ready to rip, rend, and tear through whatever stands in their way. Just don't try eating any soup. Trust me, it gets messy.
Gain Possessed Roe Teeth
- *I hope you floss regularly.*

Well . . . huh. Fuck it—cowabunga, anyway!

I accepted the Ability and yanked myself out of the menu.

Alright, Arjee! I'm fuckin' ready! Can you send people down here in the tunnels to help . . . maybe, I dunno, break this bitch open? I could use the assistance!

No, unfortunately pupil, we are dealing with our own problems up here.

What kinds of problems?

Monster problems. They broke in! Oops—gotta go, bye!

"Fuck!" I roared, just as Commune died.

Then I got immediately blasted into the wall as Carmichael shot out of his unknowing time stop. I watched my Health take a little bit of a hit, but considering my Constitution had been upgraded by the Luck Accrual, I actually wasn't doing too bad.

With that revelation buzzing in my skull like a frenzied hornet, I had no more time to pause and ponder over my hazy heritage. The chlamydians were closing in, their eyes gleaming with savage bloodlust.

The haladie felt right in my hand, its twin blades humming for carnage. On my other hand, the pique gleamed ominously in the strange glow of the room. They were my tools for the upcoming frenzy, and goddamn, they were ready.

I moved like a whirlwind. The first chlamydian met its cruel end by way of my haladie, a blade slicing across its grimy throat with a guttural spray of lifeblood. A second lunged at me, but I sprang into a backflip—holy shit, by the way—and it pursued, only to meet the pique up close and personal as I drove it into its chest, puncturing the monster's wicked heart. The third creature barreled into me, a fearsome snarl distorting its grotesque face. But I blasted that bitch in the snout with my knee, then followed up by dropping my elbow on its neck with a satisfying *crunch*. It squealed in agony and fell to the ground, twitching in death throes.

Despite my desperation, I was enjoying myself. But that pleasure was short-lived as I realized I was about to be swarmed by the remaining chlamydians. This was going to be ugly.

In a stroke of inspiration, I took a running leap at the wall, the Enduring Perch Ability activating with a rush of magic. I stuck there like a human dart, my body adhering to the crystalwork in defiance of gravity. The chlamydians seemed to pause—apparently shocked by this display. I smirked. It was showtime.

With a flick of my wrist, I activated Pernicious Volley and hurled my haladie. The double-bladed weapon fired at a speed I'd be tempted to call *Mach eight*—short for *annihilate*—the Ability making it strike like lightning. It hit the opposite wall with a clang, then rebounded, flying back toward the horde of chlamydians. It spun like a lethal pinwheel, slicing through the monstrosities with brutal efficiency.

The haladie returned to my hand, guided by the Return feature. Without wasting a second, I hurled it again, letting it ricochet off the wall, its blades slicing through the chlamydians like hot snot through tissue. The screams of the dying beasts were an ode to the lethal effectiveness of my weapon and badass brazenness. The room was a spectacle of gore, filled with the sounds of tearing flesh.

Eight seconds. Eight bloody seconds of unparalleled chaos and carnage. I was drenched in the blood of my enemies, my heart pounding with the adrenaline of battle.

Finally, I released my hold on the wall, disengaging the Enduring Perch. I hit the ground running, making a beeline for the obelisk. I was so close, so damn close . . .

That's when Carmichael appeared again, his ghoulish hands reaching out to snatch me. His touch was like acid, burning into my flesh, making me wince in agony. His awful hand moved to cover my face, and I could feel the malice radiating from him. Desperate and disgusted, I decided I was done playing fucking games. I activated the Biter Ability and went for the only thing I could: his hand.

I could feel the power as it built in my jaws, like a live wire sparking and buzzing. My chops twisted and gnarled, agony twining with a wild rush. I wasn't sure what exactly was happening, but that was transformation for you—no manual.

When it happened, I knew instantly. Razor-teeth shot out behind my lips, twin rows of jagged, burning stars, two-inch nightmares that tore through my gums. Then . . .

Houston, we have contact.

I clamped down on that hand, teeth sinking into Carmichael's elongated palm. Bone crunched. Flesh gave way. I could taste blood, raw, hot, and metallic in my mouth. It was visceral, the coppery stench filling my nostrils. I didn't have time to think about how weird it was that he was apparently warm-blooded.

Carmichael screamed, a guttural sound. I yanked my head back, and a chunk of his palm tore away from its root as I held it between my new teeth.

Take that, ya filthy bitch.

His hand nugget seared my mouth, like biting into a hot coal. Which just wouldn't do. So . . . I spat it right into Carmichael's face. More screams as he dropped me. I crashed to the ground in a heap, the breath knocked out of me.

But I didn't wait. I shot up and darted for the obelisk. Then I heard movement, and suddenly something pierced my back, digging right into the skin of my shoulder blades and kidney area. It snared me and then reeled me back like a hooked fish. I looked over my shoulder to see Carmichael had his other hand out and open. Long tendrils of Arcana had sprung from it, thin like threads.

"Fuck you, Carmichael, you thtupid athhole!"

Well, shit.

The teeth were still out and I wasn't used to speaking with them.

Nothing's more intimidating than a lisp.

I pulled against the threads, inching forward, in a wild, desperate scramble. I couldn't think of anything else to do to give me leverage, so with a sigh, I relaxed my body and let him pull me back toward him enough to create some slack. Then I spun. The magical threads wrapped around me and now I was facing the big beast, the pokey bits drilling into my back even harder. I smirked at him.

"Not good enough, thit thalad!" I shouted. "Hope you're heavier than you look!"

Still wrapped, I began pushing myself backward, feeling the tremendous pain of the threads but toiling anyway. I slowly, *slowly* began to walk backward, dragging Carmichael with me.

"Ha! That'th right, you dumb— AHHHHGH!"

His still-mangled other hand had come up, and he'd shot more magic ropes my way. They burrowed into my flesh; one in my chest, one in my stomach, and another right in my freshly seared face.

"Gah! You fucking— GAHHH!"

Then I was in the air as Carmichael swooped in, lifting me up. I tried to bite him again, but he grabbed me under the chin and held my head back. I struggled in vain, trying desperately to do anything I could to undo this binding, but he had me completely restrained like a hentai sex monster.

Well, *almost* completely.

In a flash, I swung my feet upward, aiming straight for his smug face. Just as I made contact, I activated the Enduring Perch. It was like kicking a brick wall, a shocking impact that jolted through my body. But it held, my feet sticking to his face like glue.

And the fun part? Now Carmichael was stuck to me too.

"I fucking hate widthards!" I roared.

With a surge of effort, I jerked my feet forward, pulling my body along with it. Pain screamed through me, those vile threads still embedded in my skin. But I ignored it. All I had eyes for was Carmichael's horrified face drawing closer.

Using every ounce of Acrobat, I'm sure, I contorted, curling myself. His face was within reach now.

I bit him.

My newly formed teeth found their target. I could taste the metallic sting of his blood, the texture of his gnarled flesh between my teeth. The sensation was both profane and thrilling, a confirmation of survival.

I swallowed.

Congratulations! You have raised an Ability!
Uncommon Consumption [F-Rank Level 2]!

His scream reverberated through me, a guttural sound that satisfied some primitive part of me.

He had no choice but to drop me again. Or try to. He released, but my feet were still exactly where I wanted them as I hovered in the air, anchored to his maw like some kind of fucked-up plague doctor's mask. Then I shoved forward and released Enduring Perch, using his face to spring into a backflip. I landed lightly—for once—and dove into a roll, narrowly missed by more tendrils as I felt myself disappear into the shadows. I turned, twisted, and somersaulted my ass all the way to the obelisk.

Then I bit *it*, too.

I felt it crack beneath my powerful snap and latched on hard, grinding the teeth together to try to break this fucking thing. A piece came loose in my mouth, but not nearly big enough to be of much use. However, I did see the runic circle flicker as I did.

Fuck, yes—on to something!

The feeling of the obelisk crumbling beneath my teeth was strangely satisfying. The vibrations of it reverberated through my skull, filling me with a sense of power. I'd become the predator there, biting into the very core of Carmichael's twisted reign.

An unwholesome roar erupted from behind me. I didn't need to turn to know it was Carmichael.

I yanked my head back, tearing off another piece of the obelisk. The magic-infused stone tingled on my tongue, spreading a surge of energy through me. A sweet, power-infused flavor that tickled my taste buds. The taste was more addictive than anything I'd ever experienced before. I swallowed again.

Congratulations! You have raised an Ability!
Uncommon Consumption [F-Rank Level 3]!

The rune circle flickered again, its glow dimming as the obelisk shrank in size. I could feel it. I was weakening it, drawing the life force right out of it. The obelisk was like a beating heart, and I was the one slowly draining it of its lifeblood.

Ignoring Carmichael's enraged bellows, I dived back in for another bite. This time, I bit deeper, harder. My teeth sank into the stone, the hardened outer shell cracking beneath the force of my bite. A much-larger piece came loose; the rune circle stuttered, wobbled, but was still going.

Okay, then.

Another bite. Again and again I bit into the ancient magical pipeline, swallowing each mouthful before goin' in for more. I was running a train on this smorgasbord, and I weren't in the habit of slowing as I did the only thing I was better than most at in the previous world.

Congratulations! You have raised an Ability!
Uncommon Consumption [F-Rank Level 4]!

Congratulations! You have raised an Ability!
Uncommon Consumption [F-Rank Level 5]!

F-Rank Level Six, Level Seven, Level Eight!

Eventually, though . . . Well, it seemed I'd bitten too far into the center of the Tootsie Pop.

The violent eruption of raw, untempered magic that burst forth from the ancient obelisk was a mini-apocalypse, a maelstrom of forces that shattered my self-satisfaction with the sheer magnitude of its fury. It was like being struck by a hammer made of outer space, a brutal assault that sent me careening off my feet, tossing me around like a rag doll caught in a typhoon. I was blasted back, the wind knocked from my lungs and stars exploding in my vision, tracing a haphazard arc across the landscape before I skidded to an ungainly halt, sprawled in the dirt. As I lay there, a veritable dust storm enveloping me and masking my form, I felt it—a searing, white-hot pain that radiated from every molecule of my being. My Health began to drain from me in great, torrential waves, leaving behind a husk of spent energy and mounting desperation. Each breath became a fight, each heartbeat a battle won, yet the conflict was far from over.

The magic didn't just lash out at me—it infiltrated me, seeped into the very marrow of my bones like a torrent of balefire. It was a gnawing, corrosive energy that sought to unmake me from within, and with it came haunting flashes of visions, as if the very weave of reality was fraying before my inward-facing eye.

Images cascaded over me—strange and terrible and beautiful all at once. There were cities, fantastical in their splendor, gleaming beneath an alien sky, towers rising and falling like the pulse of some colossal heart. Great serpents coiled in an abyss, the cosmos reflected in their myriad eyes, and titanic battles waged across planes of existence beyond comprehension. People—or perhaps not people at all but strange, ethereal beings of light and shadow—whispered cryptic truths to the rhythm of universal harmonies. Yet I recognized nothing, knew no one. It all bled into an endless thread.

And yet, through the haze of pain and the chaos of the fading visions, a singular thought pierced the din: *I fucking did it*. Despite the brutal assault, despite the bleeding of my Health and Stamina, I was on the cusp of . . . the end of this. With that realization, I gritted my teeth, dug deep into the ridiculous reservoir of contrarian-forged resilience within me, and forced a laugh.

"Fuck me," I groaned, "but . . . you won't take me down that easily, ya fuckin' radio antenna."

I pushed myself up to my feet, my mouth full of the sweet taste of savory triumph. I swallowed another piece of obelisk, feeling a final surge of power rush through me.

And then the field went quiet. Carmichael's roars had silenced. The runic circle was dark. The obelisk was no more than a crumbled pile of stone.

I had won.

"How . . ." came a voice, choked and raspy. I turned.

Carmichael lay there, sputtering on the ground. But his eyes were locked on mine.

"How . . ." he said again, ". . . do you know my *name*?"

CHAPTER THIRTY-ONE

NOW YOU'RE MESSIN' WITH A SON OF A LICH

"You can talk?!"

I looked at the desiccated wreck of a monstrosity that had been pursuing me for the last little while. His elongated Stretch Armstrong features, his big-ass dilapidated head, his spooky illuminated eyes. He was lying in a heap on the earthen floor where the formerly brightly blazing magic circle was now quiet and polite—not glowing at all. Now he was suddenly real chatty, I guess.

"Yes . . ." he continued, slowly. "I can speak. How . . . do you know my name?"

"Well, shit," I said. "Are you back to normal or something? Man, you were trying to fucking kill me back there. I dunno what kind of fucked-up Jekyll and Hyde *sitch-ee-ayshun* you got goin' on right now, but you better hope to fuck you stay pleasant—unless you want the teeth. Also, I'd apologize for your hand and face being bitten off, but . . . well, I'm not sorry. You deserved it, and I hope that's a lesson for you in any future—"

"Who *are* you?"

I stood fully, hoping to impress upon him some of my imposing stature.

"Me? I'm Loon, mothafucka."

"And who . . . is Loon?"

"I'm the boss bitch who just fed you the smoke, douchebug. What, is this, like, a . . . psychiatrist question? You trying to get to the heart of who I am on the inside? 'Cuz what you see is what you get."

There was something like frustration boiling behind Carmichael's lich-y expression.

"I am ascertaining who the individual is in front of me, the one who knows my name and attempted to summon me."

"Oh," I said dismissively. "I didn't summon you. Some . . . *mayor* did. Wanted to awaken you, I guess? Brought in a bunch of these dead fucks—"

I pointed to the corpses of the chlamydians strewn about like leftover Canadian bacon pizza at an otherwise great party.

"—and then poked himself in the belly to death so that you'd come out of hibernation."

I took a breath.

"I know your name because you double-crossed the party of Jes Carandalon in the Crypt of the Dreadnaught Lord—they're pretty fuckin' miffed about it, to be honest—and them's my homies. So . . . I'm, like, *mad* too."

"I did not double-cross anyone," Carmichael said, still lying on the ground. "I escaped from those that forcibly removed me from my incarceration. I was obligated while traveling with them to form a working relationship with that despicable, scruple-less murderer, Virgil—a man who has pained me since he first arrived in Regaia."

"Bro . . ." I said, waving my arms around. "You did a pretty good job trying to murder on your own—glass houses and what not."

"I am not a killer," Carmichael continued. "Now help me up from the floor, please. I appear unable to do so, as I believe my legs are too atrophied to hold my weight."

"Naw," I said. "You can sit there and be a paperweight. You are a murderer—you killed *me* with your little sim . . . ilac."

He blinked at me.

"Well, that is just about as preposterous of a proclamation as I've ever heard. Even if you encountered the simulacra—"

"I'm a *Sojourner*," I said, letting the cat out of the bag. I mean, it's not like he was going to try to kill me any harder. Plus, I was really sick of trying to navigate that when it seemed like nobody really gave a shit.

"A *what*?"

"A Sojourner? From . . . another world? You gotta know what that is, right?"

He just stared vacantly at me.

"Uh . . . okay," I said. "Anyway, I can't die—not really."

"I have never heard of such a thing," he said.

"Bullshit," I said. "Virgil's a Sojourner. You woulda had to know— You know what? I don't care to explain it to you. Why were you in jail, anyway?"

"Crime," he said indignantly.

I sighed.

"Anyway, since you're just doing a really terrible Roomba impersonation right now, do you mind telling me—at least—what you were talking about with the whole *mock us* thing? I've got some unwholesome ideas that I'd like to permanently burn out of my brain, so please clarify before I start huckin' belly fluid everywhere."

Carmichael considered that, tapping a dehydrated hand to his elongated mummy chin.

"Alright, but if I tell you, you have to let me go—I've been restrained down here for far too long."

"Maybe," I said. "But I have to appreciate the irony of you escaping a time dilation only to get trapped for hundreds of years in a different cave."

"Ah, yes," he said, seeming to find it humorous as well. "While I did spend the rest of my days hiding from the powers of the kingdom here—and amassing quite the army of followers as well, I should say—it is still interesting that you are here, having met with my briefly considered companions. So, you all made it out?"

I darkened.

"No," I said. "Not everyone."

"Shame, that," Carmichael said with a tone that dripped with apathy toward that particular result. "In any case, you mentioned my words while I was channeling the kedge, yes? Well, to answer you truthfully, I cannot really recall where the words themselves came from. I was the instrument for a lot of cosmic truth, you see. Thousands of years' worth of information pouring out of me to keep me upright and moving. Of course, none of that would have happened if I hadn't been awakened early. Now look at me—I'm a mess."

". . . and 'mock us'?" I asked, getting him back on track.

"Ah, yes," he said. "Well, considering I was seeing many different streams of time at once—"

I was suddenly interrupted.

Pupil . . .

I was kinda getting sick of being drawn into Commune whenever Rexen wanted to toss a howdy my way. I sighed—but, like, mentally, so he could hear it—then responded.

Word up, Arjee. So, I take it y'all didn't die? Or has it gotten worse?

No, pupil. Something happened and all the creatures died at once.

Oh. Shit, okay. Cool. I'm just wrapping stuff up down here—is anyone injured? Also, why do you sound like you been choking down sad berries?

I was trying to keep it casual, because I could not handle the annoyance right now of being told someone had died and been sent back to New Home—but then again, maybe someone else had dropped their anchor here. Regardless, the little spirit was back in his weird mode where he sounded like he'd been up all night, listening to the Antlers.

My pupil is astute and direct, Rexen said. **But we can discuss later. No one is injured too badly. I will speak with you when you return.**

Before I could respond in any sarcastic manner, he ended Commune.
Well, that was fucking weird.

I turned back to Carmichael, who had continued without noticing the pause—as Commune do.

". . . I couldn't quite be sure enough to clarify."

"Right," I said. "So, what? You can . . . see the future?"

"I cannot. The kedge, however, exist in many, *many* different areas of time—and since fate is not set in stone, they experience all of them at once. It's a bit headache-inducing, really, to channel that level of imagery. But, to continue my previous statement, one image that I saw was *you.*"

I could tell by the way he said it that it was meant to be impactful, but honestly, I was *over* magic. It did not surprise me one bit at this point.

"Yeah, 'cuz I was taking nibbles off your face flesh, partner," I said.

"No, that is to say, I saw *you* from the view of the kedge," he clarified, "either a time not long from now or a time long before. In *Machus City*—it was hard to tell which. Though what was clear was the swarm of individuals slavering at the bit to kill you. Sometimes you died, sometimes you did not."

"Yeah, that sounds about right," I said dismissively, remembering the name from somewhere but not sure exactly. "But it also sounds like a hot bowl of poppycock, King Tut. You were just saying the name of a town? Pah! I really thought this was going to be a cool-ass reveal, not some kind of Nostradamus noise. Miss me with that shit."

"The kedge merely provides the information, but I assure you—"

"Kedge?" I asked. "You keep saying that word. What is it?"

"Oh," Carmichael said, gesturing to the pylon. "That."

Then he squinted at me—which was a really curious movement, considering his eyes were made of embers.

"I saw through the kedge that you had destroyed several—perhaps in a time before, or a time to come. Either way, the kedge is not a fan of yours—not in the slightest."

"I don't give a damn what some fuckin' fence post thinks about me; what even is their purpose? You tied yourself to one, so I assume it does *something* other than read tea leaves."

Carmichael stared up at me silently for a moment, then shook his head.

"No . . ." he said, as if arguing with himself. "No, I suppose you will not be more dangerous with this knowledge if the kedge already believes you are a threat to it . . ."

Then he pushed himself into a sitting position and cracked his knuckles—the ones that were left. It was a loud . . . dusty sound. Like snapping apart a really old Kit-Kat that you found in the basement. Then he smiled.

"Their primary purpose is as an anchor, tethering this plane in place lest it drift away into the places between. However, because of this, they also contain a vast amount of cosmic Arcana. A dangerous amount."

I winced at that. I'd just eaten a bunch of one.

"So . . . what? You telling me it's the same hocus-pocus that let you go all Doctor Strange with the timelines and shit?"

Carmichael simply nodded.

"Indeed it is. The kedge are drenched in it. It's a power source that can be tapped in to by someone with a knack for cosmic Arcana. Yours truly, for instance."

I squinted at him.

"Oh, so basically, someone could use one of these kedge thingies to jack up their own magic and get way swole? Is that what your original plan was?"

He nodded again, letting his remaining fingers dance in a tapping pattern on the ground.

"Precisely. And that's not all—they have *other* uses, too."

I couldn't help but roll my eyes.

"Well, isn't that just great? All-purpose magic radio towers. Wanted to make yourself quite the everyman, huh? Well, thanks for the vague answer, Swiss Army bitch. If they're so powerful, how come people aren't dragging these things out of the ground and jacking into them like the aliens from *Avatar*?"

Carmichael merely blinked his glowing ember eyes and continued.

"Perhaps it is still not well known. What is the year?"

"Man, I dunno," I said. "You were in the Crypt, like . . . almost five hundred years ago?"

Carmichael seemed to balk at that.

"Well, that's quite a while—I hadn't realized so much time had passed. It seems as though that would be more than enough time for others to have discovered the secret of the kedge. It is not as though I was the first to discover what they do. Though I suppose . . ."

I sighed again.

"Now what?"

"Well, it's only that it may be possible no one *has* divined all that they are capable of. They are hidden. Really, it was *my* research that . . . led to the . . . *discovery*."

"My guy," I hissed. "Can you stop with the dramatic pauses? Honestly, what is *with* every half-cocked villain in this world and their penchant for ellipsis-laden monologues? Is it because they don't have movies here? Damn, that's probably it, huh? You don't know how cliché you are because you don't have a reference point. Goddamn, fuck *your* discovery—I think I'm on to a new philosophical concept."

Carmichael looked perplexed, he started to say something, then stopped, then started again.

"... w-what?"

"Never mind!" I roared. "What was your discovery, *Scar*michael?"

He frowned, looking at the missing piece of his hand, and then shrugged. Despite it looking grievous as shit, the pain didn't seem to bother him much.

"The discovery," he continued, "that when combined in a specific way, the kedge can be used to carry out rituals of immense power. Oftentimes to disastrous results."

My heart skipped a beat at his words. Rituals? Power? That was ominous. And . . . familiar? My mind raced back to the bone-chilling tale about the city of Derika that Calden had told me. Then what Rexen and Jes had confirmed about the Tides. Those motherfuckers had used something like that, hadn't they? It would have been hundreds of years before, but they'd summoned some weird-fiction fuckabouts from another plane. That event had caused devastation on an epic scale, even claiming the life of Jes's girlfriend—who sounded way more awesome of a person than Jes had any right to start chatting up in the first place.

I swallowed hard, fixing Carmichael with a piercing gaze.

"Wait a goddamn minute," I said, trying to keep my voice steady. "Were you the sick fuck behind what happened in Derika, with those Sons of the Tides lunatics?"

Carmichael didn't deny it. In fact, he nodded.

"Yes, that was my work . . . in a way."

"Which way's that, hoofbite?"

"Not directly," he continued. "I discovered that Derika housed a very powerful kedge, one potent enough to be used in a solo ritual. Typically, the level of power needed for what happened there would be out of the question without multiple kedge working in tandem. But the Derika kedge was inordinately strong. Perhaps because unlike most, it used both cosmic and void Arcana."

"Wait, back up. You *did* or *didn't* have anything to do with it? Now I'm confused. What does 'not directly' mean in this context?"

Carmichael shrugged.

"I made my findings known in circles of academia, only to be largely ignored by other, more *interesting* revelations by other scholars. I'd continued my research but with quite the dearth of vigor compared to what I'd had before. I'd been ignored by my colleagues, you see—"

"Yeah, yeah," I interrupted, rolling my eyes. "You were snubbed by your betters—never heard such a staggering tale of woe, truly. Get to the part where you do the dickhead thing."

Carmichael nodded.

"I *was* getting to that, you know," he said. "But yes. There I was, forgotten. My research had made no waves, and I was being pressed into the *exciting* opportunity offered to me by the Conservatory of Mystical Inquiry at Grellini's Chancellor Arcani: studying the effects of phlogisticated aetheric diffusion in crystallographically optimized orichalcum matrices. A line of research considered so esoteric, so hair-splittingly tedious by my colleagues, that the only sounds in the workshop were often the ticking of the arcane timepiece and the muttered imprecations of my poor apprentice tasked with aligning the matrices, microphase by agonizing microphase."

"What the fuck are you talking about?" I demanded. It was fucking weird that just minutes before, I was bangin' thirties with this big head, and now he was talking about his boring-ass study sesh with . . . fuckin' floggadocious athletic division or whatever. I needed to get out of there and check on my friends—but, this still seemed important somehow.

"Oh," Carmichael said, shaking his head. "It's simple, really. You see, the inherent flux of phlogisticated aether within these precisely structured orichalcum lattices could potentially illuminate heretofore unseen facets of transplanar energy manip—"

"Stop," I hissed. "Just . . . stop. Jesus fuck, you're worse than Edwig and Rua combined. Can we *please* get to the Tides part?"

"Well, yes," he said. "It was during this time, late into an evening painstakingly fine-tuning the polarity of etheric resonance within each crystallographic lattice—ensuring that the fundamental aetheric oscillation harmonized with the matrix without causing destructive interference, obviously—when I was approached. A creature, seemingly made of shadow, requested that I help the Sons of the Tides by imparting my knowledge unto them."

I scoffed, but he ignored me and continued.

"I refused at first, of course. It was my discovery, and if anyone would be using it to ill ends, it would likely be me. Though that was the furthest thing from my thought process. Still, after they killed my apprentice, set fire to the workshop, and tossed me bodily through the highest window on the Grellini campus . . . my agreeability to their demands became much more malleable. I explained what I'd found, and they—at the very least—paid me for the information. Though not nearly enough to afford a new apprentice—all the best ones *are* pricey. Then they were off, and I didn't hear from them again. Though I heard about the issues in the north. Eventually."

"So, then what?"

"Well, I was on my way to Derika to assist in the efforts when I got shackled and stashed—for a separate issue that I'll not go into further. I'd wanted to try to clean up the mess before it got out of hand . . . however, it appeared the cat was already out of the bag."

The sickening realization hit me like a punch to the gut. Carmichael was the catalyst of that disaster? And the crew—Jes, Calden, Frida, Merra, Virgil, and Dedyc—they had sprung this bastard out of his cage, knowing the shit he'd pulled?

"They still broke you out?" I spat, barely containing my outrage. "Even after your *indirect* stunt with Derika? *And* the fact that you had a hand in Delyra's death?"

The twisted grin that formed on Carmichael's face was as close to mortified as this mummy-lookin' motherfucker could probably manage. Actually, considering the circumstances, I couldn't think of a more fitting word.

"Yes, they did. Partly because I'm something of an encyclopedia on all things cosmic, you see. The Dreadnaught Lord's Forbidden Crypt is filled with trials involving cosmic Arcana, and they needed my expertise. And, I suspect, they wanted me to apologize to Delyra once they'd brought her back. Perhaps they believed I owed them."

"But you bailed," I said stiffly.

"Wouldn't anyone under such duress? I did not know what their intentions were for me once I had completed the mission—I would hardly have been the first prisoner to go missing under mysterious circumstances, never to be seen again. And I was not willing to take that risk. So, I prepared the simulacrum and well and truly escaped. Then, knowing I couldn't return to Margrave od Ys'mesh's dungeons, I founded this happy hamlet and thought to start anew. I was drawn initially to this location, of course, because I knew of the kedge residing below the surface. But it was a chance to begin again. Fresh and sparkling new. Little did I know, that's when things would *truly* get interes—"

"Yeah, I don't care about you farting around in your slice-of-life fantasy pueblo," I said.

I looked at the pile of rubble that was once the pylon and then back to Carmichael. There was something else . . . something that didn't make sense about these things. They *kept* cropping up. Sure, the Tides wanted to do something with them, but what about the Echoes? They were horny for these things too.

"Who are the Echoes?" I asked. "What interest would they have in these pylons?"

"I am unsure," Carmichael admitted. "I've never heard of the Echoes—it is likely I am before their time. However, any party including themselves in the unearthing of a kedge likely seeks to do something similar with them to what happened in Derika, or perhaps what my followers here sought to achieve: summon something large and formidable."

"They want to use me and my Sojourner homies as like . . . batteries or something, I think. But how does that play into the kedge?"

"Well, that's simple," Carmichael said. "If you're from another world, as you say—then your resonance with crossing the boundaries of planes is likely still very strong. Especially if it was not long ago—perhaps within the last handful of years or so. This would increase exponentially if you were to, say, pick up any Esper Nodes. Then they could open a Gateway of some variety."

"Oh . . ." I said. "What if they wanted to . . . say, destroy the System?"

"That's a preposterous notion," big lich energy said. "The System can't be destroyed. It's integral to the formulation of our world, weaved into the very foundation—you cannot destroy it without unmaking the reality within which we dwell."

"Yeah? Well, that's what they want to do," I said. "And these particular meanies think they can do it by turning me and the squad into gumbo—somehow."

"Well, in any case—your Echo friends—"

"They ain't my damn friends, Scarmichael," I said. "They're my enemies! Whatever. Listen, all I know is that they wanna use the kedges—which they call pylons—to do something fucky."

"I see," Carmichael said. "Interesting. Though they ought not to, in my experience."

"Huh?" I asked. "Why not? Because they don't have your *expert-level* brain to guide them?"

"*Gods*, no," Carmichael said. "If the citizens of this village had bothered to listen to me, they would have known that I specifically recommended *against* anything involving the kedge. It was likely as much of a surprise to me as it was to you that I was trussed up in this way. Yet here we are. No—it is because of the *Drifter*."

There it is again. Who is the motherfucking Drifter gent everyone keeps referencing?

"Alright, please explain," I said. "I'm not having any luck keeping you quiet anyway, so you may as well tell me this. Who *is* the Drifter and what is his purpose?"

"The Drifter," Carmichael said, "is truly unknowable insofar as *what* he *is* is concerned. He is, as best as I understand, either a deity of some variety or a being sufficiently on par with one of their like to be practically indistinguishable. Never really gave him much thought, other than to steer clear of his followers and not to use the kedge for summoning, lest you unlock his ire."

"He's connected to these things?" I wondered aloud. "Jesus, this shit is so fuckin' convoluted. Who can keep track of it all?"

Carmichael shrugged.

"Unsure on that," he said. "So . . ."

I sighed.

"What now?"

"Well, it's just that . . ." Carmichael fidgeted with his giant fingers like he was nervous. "It *has* been centuries since I was last out and about . . ."

"What, you want a sandwich or something? Sorry, fresh out."

"No," Carmichael whined. "Not food. Though . . . I'm not sure I need to eat anymore, now that I think about it. However, I was wondering as to us removing ourselves from this place and . . . well . . ."

"You wanna go topside, eh?" I asked. "I mean, you *did* just try to kill me . . . again. I dunno, man; I kinda feel like I should just end your miserable existence right here. You've caused a fuckton of grief for good people—myself included."

"Well, I don't think you should do *that*," Carmichael said as if simply refuting an opposing opinion. "I am one of the only people currently . . . well, *living* that understand the nature of what kedge truly are. It would benefit the both of us if you helped me get to the surface. I'd be more than happy to assist you."

"Wait, what? Why do I need assistance with these things?"

I thought about the fact that part of one was sitting in my belly right now—to what effect, I didn't really know. But that was a problem for tomorrow's me!

"Weren't you listening? You're going to Machus City!"

"The fuck I am!" I said indignantly. "Why in the hell would I do that? I got shit to do back at the base—the last thing I need is another distraction to derail me from my main Quest line."

"Machus City is a lodestone for cosmic forces, Lool," he barked. "It, like Derika before it, has one kedge that can be optimized most brilliantly. It is *powerful*, Lool. The likes of which would make Derika seem inconsequential. In the aftermath of Derika, the city became overrun with arcane activity and utterly *destroyed*. Machus City is simmering with powerful Arcana just like Derika was before the disaster, and from what I understand from my time—it was just waiting to be accessed. That is what I have seen. I've seen through the kedge what happens, and that is nearly unchanging."

"Yeah, I don't trust you," I shot back. "You probably just want to go there and steal some of that power yourself. Hungry little piglet, aren't you?"

"Whether you trust me or not is immaterial, Lool," Carmichael countered, a smug grin spreading across his skeletal face. "The plain truth is that you'll need to journey there, with or without me."

"First of all: it's *Loon*," I groaned, rubbing my temples. "Not Lool. Show some goddamn respect already, will ya?"

This was so fucked up. Like being stuck in a never-ending nightmare.

"Second off, smart guy. Why?" I challenged, hoping to poke holes in his highfalutin theories. "Why the hell would I need to go to Machus City?"

"Because"—Carmichael's grin faltered, and he fixed me with a gaze that sent cold shivers down my spine—"it's the only thread of future I've seen where you survive."

I blinked at him, my mind blank for a moment. Then his words began to sink in, and a sick feeling rose in my gut.

"What the fuck are you talking about?" I asked, my voice quieter than I intended.

Carmichael sighed, sounding more like a professor having to explain a difficult concept to a slow student than a nearly immortal lich talking about doomsday.

"In every other thread of potential futures I've foreseen, you return to your camp, only to be overrun and killed. Permanently."

I let out a bark of laughter, but it was a hollow, uneasy sound. We didn't just die. We always came back. That was the rule. No matter how fucked-up things got, we had that one lifeline. I mean, sure, it was super fucking inconvenient, but way less so than being perma-dead.

But Carmichael was shaking his head slowly, his glowing eyes locked on mine with an intensity that made my skin crawl.

"No, Lool. In the threads I foresaw, you were captured and killed, slowly, dragged over the engines of some unknown arcane devices. Your soul is extracted, and you cease to be. Not just you, your friends too."

His words hung in the air between us, heavy and ominous. I wanted to dismiss him, to write him off as just another crazy baddie talking out of his ass. But I couldn't. Because there was something else. Some of the Sojourners in New Home hadn't returned. Especially if they fought Alpha in the Duellum. Plus, I remembered the curly-haired woman, the way her eyes gleamed with cold, deadly intent. She had threatened me, said she could end me permanently. I had brushed her off then, laughed in her face. But now . . .

Fuck.

Carmichael was still speaking, but his words were just a distant buzz in my ears. I felt like I'd been sucker-punched, the wind knocked out of me.

Was this it? Was this how I was going to end? Dragged over some fucking woo-woo machine, my soul sucked out? I'd faced death before, hell, I'd died outright. But this . . . this was different.

I shook my head, trying to clear the thoughts buzzing around in my mind. This was too much. It was all too goddamn much.

"No," I muttered, more to myself than to Carmichael. "I don't believe you."

"But you do," Carmichael said, sounding oddly satisfied. "You do believe me, don't you, Lool?"

I clenched my fists, resisting the urge to punch his smug face. I didn't want to admit it, but despite him not even getting my name right—something . . . fuckin' *something* about what he was saying made me believe him. Something in my literal gut was telling me that it was the case. I didn't know if that was just Carmichael being a pathetically convincing individual or if the pieces of the pylon inside me were adding leverage to the statement . . . but there it was.

"Wait," I said, a sudden thought seizing me. "If I don't go back . . . what happens to my friends? They're not . . . they're not gonna end up like you say, right?"

Carmichael spread his hands, a casual shrug that somehow seemed way too relaxed for the topic at hand.

"I can only tell you what I've seen. But if you don't return, I don't see that same fate befalling your comrades."

So, if I stayed away, my crew had a fighting chance. It wasn't much to hang hope on, but it was something. A sliver of light in this dark abyss of foreboding futures.

But Machus City . . . I couldn't help but think about the pitfalls that could accompany such a shitty journey, the hot, throbbing magnitude of the potential consequences. And yet, the alternative, as Carmichael had painted it, was much grimmer. My mind raced, debating the pros and cons.

I pondered, thinking about the camp, my friends . . . my crew. The reckless, resilient bunch of misfits. And that made me think about Calden, Merra, Dedyc—hell, even Virgil. I was still, even months later, feeling the sting of their violent passing. I didn't want that to happen again. I couldn't bear the thought of it. I'd already seen a lot of death in my life. If doing this was a way to avoid something like that . . .

This was my responsibility.

But I couldn't just *tell* them, could I? No . . . no, that wouldn't work. Rua would come along—Edwig too, probably. Even though I wasn't physically linked to Rexen's radius anymore . . . he'd want to come, and he wasn't subtle. I didn't see any way of getting out of there to go off on my own if any of them knew about it.

Fuck. Was I really considering this? Should I really abandon them? Was it right to keep them in the dark, to disappear without a word? Would they be better off if I did?

As if reading my thoughts, Carmichael said, "You don't have to abandon them, Lool. There are ways to communicate, to guide them without physically being there. You're a leader. You'll figure it out."

The optimism in his voice was infuriating. But he was right. If I didn't go back, if I chose this new path, it didn't mean I had to abandon my crew. I could find ways to help them, to guide them. It wouldn't be easy, but when had anything ever been easy for us?

I chewed on my lower lip, thoughts bouncing around in my skull like pinballs. I glanced at Carmichael, his big-ass skull illuminated by the cold light.

It was my life on the line. My future. My decision.

"Okay," I said finally, my voice barely a whisper.

Carmichael turned to me, his hollow eye sockets seeming to glow brighter. "You'll do it?"

"Yeah," I said, meeting his gaze straight on. "I'll go to Machus City."

But it wasn't for him, or for the power he spoke of with such reverence. It was for the homies, my friends. If it was the only shot I had at ensuring their safety, at protecting them from the gruesome fate Carmichael had foreseen, I had to take it. No matter what awaited me in Machus City, I'd fucking handle it.

For them.

"Is that yours?" Carmichael asked, pointing to the spot on the ground where the mayor—uh, *Alderman* had once been.

"Is what mine?"

I followed his gaze, my eyes landing on the small, glinting object resting on the cold stone floor. I'd seen it earlier, but hadn't really considered it because . . . well, you know. Fighting. I bent down to inspect it. It was a small crystal vial, triangular in shape, containing a swirling, illuminated blue-ish gray smoke.

"No," I said, looking at it closer. "It must've belonged to the Alderman."

I tried inspecting it with Eye of the Saboteur, but, considering it had been acting . . . brand-new, I wasn't sure how that would go.

What an interesting object! Perhaps it's a jazz lamp? You may not want to puff, puff, pass on this, adventurer!

I sighed.

What else is new?

Picking up the vial, I showed it to Carmichael.

"Any idea what this is?"

"A potion," Carmichael shrugged nonchalantly, though he didn't even look at it. The indifference with which he said that was annoying, a casual dismissal that was borderline rude.

"Really?" I shot back. "A potion? You don't say. A fine fucking academic you are."

Then, as my brain is wont to do, I thought about how the notifications I'd been getting while I was down there hadn't been weird as fuck. Sure, Eye of the Saboteur was still a fucking chump, but I'd been getting all sorts of prompts when I'd eaten the hell outta the pylon. I looked down at my feet at the magic circle.

Was that why?

With the brief diversion over, I moved to Carmichael's side, bending down to heave him up. It was time to set off, and despite his skeletal form, the old lich was deceptively heavy.

"Ah, Lool, the wonders that must have unfolded during my absence!" Carmichael began, his voice crackling with unbridled anticipation. "The potential leaps and bounds in the application of kedge energies! The thought alone is a veritable feast for my intellect."

I shifted under his weight, attempting to adjust the skeletal figure that clung to my back.

"Uh-huh," I grunted, my mind already starting to drift.

"But let us not forget the technomantic innovations, Lool," Carmichael continued unabated. "Perhaps we've managed to automate eating utensils, or maybe we've perfected the use of astral stones in heating systems. Or perhaps—oh, just perhaps—could we have refined the aetheric diffusion in crystallographically optimized orichalcum matrices? By the *gods*, I would be grateful to never have to pursue that endeavor ever again! Imagine! Cross-plane ephemeral currency. I should be wealthy with just one transaction!"

He let out a sigh of contentment at his own words, clearly lost in his thoughts.

"Cross-plane wha?" I muttered under my breath, my eyebrows furrowing. He made it sound like we could just pop over to another plane of existence to grab a pint of milk.

"And the strides we might've taken in the realm of arcane metallurgy!" he exclaimed, almost giddy with excitement. "Imagine, Lool, alloys imbued with phasic-ethereal elements, swords that cleave through not just matter but through the very fabric of the Veil itself."

"Yeah, 'cuz what we need are sharper ways to kill each other."

He either didn't hear my sarcastic comment or chose to ignore it.

"Or perhaps the fusion of Tymond's heart opal and pyronium in the creation of sustainable magical light sources?"

"I, uh, think they call those magelights now," I said.

Carmichael merely laughed at what he must've thought was sarcasm.

"You jest, Lool, but the practical applications of arcane advances in the everyday life of ordinary folks are innumerable. Why, I imagine with a few minor adjustments to the common thaumatropic array, we could have a hen lay an egg already boiled! I say, this new world isn't ready for the concoctions I'm ready to unfurl upon it! They called me a genius in my time; well, now I can be a genius in *two* times!"

We were just at the edge of the runic circle, stepping onto the cold stone floor of the outer chamber, when Carmichael froze in my arms.

"I forgot to . . ." His words trailed off, his wide, illuminated eyes staring at me with a sudden urgency.

Confused, I looked down. We were no longer within the circle.

He met my gaze, his expression unreadable.

". . . I forgot to un-anchor the runic seal."

The next second, Carmichael exploded.

I landed hard, sprawling onto an unseen floor. The shock of impact rippled through me, forcing a gasp from my lungs.

"Shit!" I groaned, clenching my teeth. And then there was darkness, the absence of sound, of sight, of anything.

My brain registered the black void around me and instantly began to panic.

Am I dead? Did the blast kill me?

A wave of nausea gripped me, making my stomach churn. But then, there was no *You died, bitch* message. No indication that I had met my end.

I sat up, slowly, shakily. My hands moved to my body, patting down arms, chest, legs. All in place, it seemed, but the confusion set in. If I was alive and intact, then where was I?

The darkness around me felt thick, tangible, as if I could reach out and touch it. My eyes strained to adjust, but it was a pointless effort; there was nothing to see. The deafening silence wrapped around me like a cocoon, and I felt a shiver of apprehension. I could feel a cold dread creeping in, a feeling I knew all too well. Something had gone very wrong.

"Fuck," I muttered, clenching my fists.

A rush of thoughts flooded my brain, questions with no immediate answers. I didn't even know where to begin. Carmichael had died, right? Where was I now? Some other plane? How would I get back? What the hell *was* this place?

The void remained silent, offering no answers. I was alone, utterly and completely, in a place I had no understanding of. If I was indeed in another plane of existence, then I was out of my depth.

Lost in my thoughts, it took me a moment to hear it—the faintest whisper of a sound, so faint I thought I might have imagined it. But then it came again, louder, clearer.

"Loooon!"

The voice came from far away, but was unmistakably familiar.

Oh, no . . .

"Loooon!" The singsong of my name wafted along the breeze like a meandering megakelvin shockwave from an atomic detonation. I felt like my stomach had just stepped on a nail.

Suddenly, a sparkling exuberance of lights came sweeping through the darkened landscape like an intergalactic nightmare portent.

"Looooon!" the voice cooed.

"No, no, no, NO!"

"Yes!" came the response as a giant swooping face yanked from the deepest, foulest stretch of hell's prolapsed anus suddenly arrived in front of me.

Anxiety gripped me. I gaped. It was the loud, obnoxious, uncomfortably into-me multi-radiant mask god I'd thought was gone from my life for good.

Sababo.

"Hi, Loon!" he cheered. "I'm back!"

I threw my head back in a howl.

"Noooooooooooooo!"

CHAPTER THIRTY-TWO

FREAK ON MY ANTICS

Sababo's laughter filled the air. His ever-changing mask of lights seemed to pulsate with delight, a grotesque caricature of my disbelieving face mirrored in its shiny surface.

"Remember me?"

"Fuckin' duh, Bob," I said. "I thought I was rid of you—can't you go bother someone else? I know a matau who would probably hurl himself off a tall building if you started showing up during his snoozes. I'll give you his contact info and then you can fuck off."

"But, Loon," Sababo continued, his voice turning slightly pouty, "I have something important to tell you."

I sighed, exhaustion seeping into my bones.

"What is it now, Bob? Blow in to tell me I've gotta go to Machus City? 'Cuz you'd be a bit late on that front."

He flashed brightly—literally beaming.

"You've already heard the call, then! I love it! But let me give you a bit more context. You see, Loon, Zeol and I . . . well, we've been having a bit of a spat."

"Trouble in paradise, eh?" I sneered. "Guess that's why they say you should never go into business with family—or whatever it's called when two gods share a soul and a creepy relationship."

"Yes," he continued unfazed. "It's about *you*, Loon."

"Of course it is."

"I'm rather *miffed* at Zeol," Sababo said. "In part for setting you on this perilous path."

"Um, excuse me," I said. "You were involved too. Don't forget, both of you knuckleheads kept scooping me up and pressing me into your, uh, *mask*inations. Any blame is squarely on both of your . . . well . . . masks."

You know how sometimes you really *nail* a pun? This wasn't one of those times.

"Still contrary, I see, Loon! Beautiful! *Wonderful!* That symphonic oppositional candor with which you navigate Regaia is why you are so entertaining to observe! I love it!"

"Wait a minute, though, Bob," I said, trying to find a place to sit down in this darkness and finding... well, more darkness. I abandoned that endeavor and just sorta slouched with my arms crossed. "The last I heard from you two, I clearly remember you blubbering about how you were done interfering in my life, right. Y'all were on some bullshit—freakishly conjoined, doin' double-chat like a pair of doofuses. I thought you said you were both supposed to be gone for a while?"

"Well, that's true in a sense," Sababo said. "Great catch! The more substantial manifestation of myself *is* gone. However, this version of me you're being graced by is more of a vestige. A dream-echo, I like to think, or... a *failsafe*, if you will."

"Yeah..." I said with a grimace. "I *don't* think I will. So... what, this is just a nightmare? How does that work?"

"Remember, Loon? I'm the god of sleep! It is well within my realm to perform these sorts of feats and visit my Loon from time to time."

"Ew! I ain't nobody's *nothin'*," I spat. "Except, I guess technically Arjee. But that's a whole thing."

"You're wrong but you're *lovely*," Sababo said. "And as for Zeol and I... we've had to step away to finalize a few things."

"Finalize a few things?" I repeated, suspicion creeping into my tone. "And what might those be? You guys starting an unsettling Airbnb together? Yeesh, *that* place is going to be lousy with hidden cameras."

Sababo laughed in his heaving, hair-raising way.

"Oh, Loon. Always so curious! Have I told you that I love the way your mind works? We're merely preparing for the next phase."

"And what, pray tell, is the next phase?"

Sababo shifted, his lights blinking low.

"That, Loon, is something... well, you'll have to wait and see! But I trust you will. Still, shocking for sure! Tiny, insignificant—lavishly peppered, things you missed before. Details hidden in plain sight! Flourishes revealed, designed to dazzle, confound your mind, my sweet Loon. Such *ravishing* sights! Butterfly wings, Loon—glorious butterfly wings! Oh, to see your face!"

"Bob, do you even hear yourself?" I scoffed. "You sound like a bad translation of a book of haikus."

"Bad translation?" Sababo's voice reverberated with tinkling laughter, the sound enveloping the space around us. "I love it! I'm a song of mysteries. You just need to listen more attentively!"

"You start singing, and I'm going to stab my own ears out," I grumbled, my patience threatening to run thin.

"Loon! You're such a whip!" Sababo responded cheerily.

"Listen, you use the term whip again, and we're gonna have fuckin' problems. It should be illegal for someone of your ... personality type to be allowed to talk about them kinds o' instruments."

"What do you mean? Whips? Ah, Loon ..." his voice took on an amused tone. "Are you trying to tell me something about your *proclivities*?"

"What the fuck?! No! No, no, no! Don't get any weird ideas or I'm going to start screaming stranger danger."

I sighed in exasperation, leaning back against what I thought was something that turned out to be *nothing*, and lost my balance, falling.

"Ulp!" I exclaimed, before landing softly on a mushroom that hadn't been there before. I looked down at it.

"Alright..." I said, then shrugged.

"Caught you," Sababo said brightly. "I'll *always* catch you when you fall, Loon."

"Yurgh! Stop that!" I said. "Let's get back to the subject matter—I got shit to do. What's with these dream-echoes? A failsafe for what, exactly? Frustrating me to death?"

"No, not death," Sababo corrected with a chuckle. "Perhaps just to the brink of insanity?"

My eyes narrowed.

"Oh, so, you're a funny guy, now?"

"Yes!" Sababo cried, his mask lighting up with myriad hues of twinkling stars.

"Great," I grumbled, resting my hands on the mushroom. "Is that all, then? You summoned me to tell me something I already know, and—"

"Loon," Sababo began, his voice taking on a rare solemnity as he cut me off. "There is something of grave importance we need to discuss."

My eyebrows shot up in surprise.

"You're being serious? That's a new one."

Sababo ignored my comment, his mask seeming to gaze deeply into my own eyes. "There comes a time, Loon, when all games must come to an end. Though I am loath to end the merriment ... this is one such moment."

I frowned.

He'd better not get all deep-voiced and spooky again. That shit is uncomfortable.

"Alright, I'm listening."

"Loon, I am *proud* of you."

These words, unanticipated, rang in my ears as if they had been pronounced in the heart of an echoing canyon. Resonating around me into the abyss.

Sababo's voice, usually brimming with unsavory implications and mischief, was now laden with a sincere gravity that seemed to pull at the very marrow of my bones. The world around us stilled, the wind hushing as if in reverence to this rare moment of solemnity from the god of dreams.

Was he . . . literally changing the atmosphere for this?

The pitch-black environment surrounding me warmed to a dull amber hue, a void of honey-colored nothing but backlit with soft light. His ethereal mask, busy with intermingling colors, faded to warmer hues reflecting the surroundings, as if to conjure a heavy moment. The familiar terrain of playful banter and irritation had been replaced with a literal emotional landscape I was not equipped to navigate. My mouth opened, then closed, unsure how to respond to whatever the fuck he was doing.

Ah, fuck. It's happening. He's going to try to make a move on me. I swear to god, if Marvin Gaye starts playing, I'm going to hightail it outta here and file a restraining order.

"What the hell is happening?" I asked, a little bit of panic creeping its way into my tone unintentionally. I didn't like this at all—this was far more menacing than any previous iteration of Sababo's disconcerting personality quirks.

"Loon," Sababo began, his voice no longer dripping with glee but . . . inviting. "What I need you to understand is that you have never strayed from the right path. Even in moments when your journey seemed to be shrouded by the thickest cloak of doubt, obscured by the fog of uncertainty that descended like an uninvited guest, you have been moving toward a destination worthy of the effort of each footfall, each stride."

What the fuck is this? A pep talk?

"Even when you found yourself wavering, even when you stumbled on jagged stones of pain and loss, you were never truly lost. The path was there; it had always been there. Your task was to simply recognize that within this sometimes painful, wretched, burning life, there exist bonds, values, people that are worth the struggle, worth your time."

Here, Sababo paused, his ethereal visage radiating an air of serenity. A silence fell between us, loaded down with the weight of his words, and I found myself lost in its depth, the mask's vibrant colors reflecting my own surprise.

"Your journey, Loon," Sababo continued after a moment, "has been fraught with hardship. You have carried the heavy burden of guilt and self-blame for the loss of your loved ones. A weight that has pressed upon your heart, shaping you, molding you. A warrior, a survivor, who has constantly been tested by the cruel hands of fate.

"And yet," he added, his voice resonating with a sense of unmistakable pride, "even in the face of unbearable loss, even when consumed by the blinding rage of grief, you never lost your way. You never allowed the despair to consume you completely, to veer you off your course."

He paused once again, allowing his words to sink in, to etch themselves into the fabric of my consciousness. He had no eyes, but I could feel his gaze, penetrating yet gentle, as if peeling away the layers of my defiance and bluster, reaching into the heart of my pain and offering understanding, validation.

"Loon, you've always been on an adventure. One of growth, of self-discovery. You just needed to realize that there are things worth growing for. You have displayed character, spirit, and that is truly admirable."

I blinked at him, my mind reeling. There was something in his voice that made my heart twinge with an unfamiliar emotion. It was as if a veil had been pulled the fuck back, revealing a fresh perspective of Sababo. The god of dreams, of sleep, was showing me a side that was uncharacteristically vulnerable. Endearing, even.

But I rebelled against it, my mind flooding with thoughts and feelings, both good and bad.

Images surfaced like ghosts from a foggy past, casting their melancholy shadows on the canvas of my mind. Roger's laugh sounded through the chambers of my memories; as joyous and free as the days when we walked home from school together. Our shadows long in the evening glow, our spirits high, the air around us filled with the promise of a future yet unexplored.

The memory of my mother came unbidden, her tired yet loving eyes etched in the deepest corners of my heart. I saw her sitting, her body weary after pulling a double shift yet her spirit undiminished. Her eyes sparkled with a deep-seated pride as I excitedly showed her a song I'd been falling in love with, the melody of the stereo filling the small, humble room we called home.

Then there was Calden. I could see him vividly, emerging from the dungeon's ravine's sludgy depths, his face bearing a comically embarrassed expression. It was an incongruity that had been so humorous, so utterly Calden, that it left a lasting impression on me.

Merra, sharp-tongued and quick-witted, poking fun at Jes, her eyes glinting with mischievous delight.

And Dedyc. The image of him clapping, demanding encore after encore, his hissing voice resounding in the open space, stirred a sense of warmth within me. The memories of those simple moments of joy, of togetherness, were as precious as they were poignant. Brief, too. We'd spent so little time in the belly of the Crypt, but it had left a mark. A dent, really. A group I'd ... been accepted by. *Belonged* to. However temporary.

The onslaught of these images, this mental montage of past moments, stirred a complex cocktail of emotions within me. The pain of loss was intertwined with the comfort of those shared moments, the bitter sting of guilt intermingling with the sweetness of treasured memories. It was as if Sababo's words had unlocked a floodgate, allowing the river of my past to rush forth.

Despite the turmoil, a sense of resolution took root. Yes, there was pain, and yes, there were moments when I wished I could turn back the hands of time. Yet, inside all the grief and guilt, there could be more. Those were the things that made it all worth it, the experiences that justified the struggle. It was the knowledge of this, a bittersweet blend of experiences that allowed me to grow, to become who I was today. And according to this freaky mask monstrosity, I just needed to realize it, to embrace it.

Was Sababo doing this to me? Was he forcing these images to bubble to the top of my consciousness and fucking wrench them out . . . No. I realized almost as suddenly that it wasn't him doing this. He was setting the stage, but I was dragging the actors up for their performance on my own.

My emotions threatened to overwhelm me.

I tried to cough out some words, but I couldn't. Of all the people . . . Sababo was . . . well, it was kind of him.

"Well . . ." I finally managed to respond, my voice breaking slightly. "Thank you. You're still a fuckin' . . . creep, you know? In fact . . ."

I tried to casually sniff to not reveal my hand too much.

"I'd . . . argue that this makes you even more of . . . a clinger."

I managed to smile.

"Is that it, then . . . ya weirdo?"

Sababo radiated warmth.

"For now, Loon."

"So, once I go to Machus City, what happens?"

"That is truly up to you," Sababo said. "But you will know, I'm sure, when the time is right."

"And if I fail?"

"We all fail. Try not to in this case, though."

"I'll, uh, see what I can do."

CHAPTER THIRTY-THREE

RUN TO THE HILLS

Covered head to toe in what I could only describe as Carmichael paste, I pulled myself from the cold stone floor of the chamber, feeling as though I'd just been hit by a runaway piano. My body protested every movement, my muscles aching like I'd just spent the past several hours wrestling eight gorillas.

I was alone in the chamber. Carmichael was gone, the room was a mess, and I felt a wave of disorientation sweep over me. That was when it sank in—Carmichael had *exploded*. I was alone. I was covered in lich.

I shook myself out of my stupor and took stock of the situation. The need to get out of there, to regroup, to make sense of everything that had just happened, was overwhelming. But first, I had to sneak past my friends.

I had no choice but to go unnoticed. My parting with the crew was abrupt, unannounced, and as it stood, permanent. It hurt, more than I was willing to admit, but I had a job to do. I needed to get out, to find a way back. I squared my shoulders, sucked in a deep breath, and felt the darkness swallow me as I activated my Sneaking Skill.

I moved like a shadow, silent as a cat, prowling through the dirt passage and to the upper level, my footsteps unheard on the cold stone floor. I moved through the corridor, hugging the darkness as I made my way to the main chamber.

The sight that greeted me was . . . gross. There was no other word for it. The chamber was littered with hundreds of chlamydian corpses, their still forms lying in haphazard heaps on the floor. It was an unsettling sight. The battle that had taken place had apparently been *quite* the gruesome little affair.

I shuddered, my stomach churning at the sight. I forced myself to focus on the living, on the signs of victory. Dragoon and Veruca were tending to a villager, their hands steady as they applied bandages. Rua was squatting down, petting the possessed roe, a soft smile on her face. I couldn't see Ileyrri or Buck, but it seemed everyone was safe, unharmed. That was all that mattered.

That was when I saw him—Rexen. His small form was visible in the dim light, and I saw him turn, because of course he would. But I had to disappear before he could call me out.

With a last glance at the crew, I ducked back into the darkness of the corridor.

I followed the temple's winding corridors, weaving through the maze-like structure with an ease that was unnerving. The Eye of the Saboteur worked its magic, guiding me. It led me to a door, hidden away in a forgotten corner of the temple, masked by years of dust and disuse.

Stepping out into the cool night air, I took a moment to collect myself. The temple was behind me, its towering structure casting long shadows that danced in the moonlight. Around me, the village lay in ruin.

I skirted around the village, keeping to the dark outskirts as I moved. I was a ghost, a silent observer. From my vantage point, I could see the monstrous fucking destruction that had been wrought, could see the corpses of the chlamydians that littered the ground.

And there it was—the giant chlamydian, its colossal form sprawled across the landscape, its body beat to piss and mangled beyond reasonable belief. It was motherfuckin' *chilling*. I shivered, my mind struggling to comprehend the strength needed to take down such a godawful creature. My thoughts immediately went to Buck. How strong was he, really?

I considered going back, asking him to join me. But . . . I quickly dismissed the thought. Buck had his own path, his own journey. I had to respect that. Besides, I could see the villagers gathered in the square, their faces a mix of relief and apprehension as they surveyed the damage.

If there'd been any doubt, it was then that I knew I had to leave for sure. If Rexen could sense me, could feel that I was planning to skedaddle, I had to make my move. I couldn't afford to be caught. I had to fuckin' *go*, had to keep moving.

I took one last look at the village. I thought about my friends inside. My abrupt realization as to how important they actually were to me. Gabe wouldn't have felt like this. He'd have lied his ass off to himself to protect his fragile self-esteem. His precious ego. He hadn't thought he needed anyone. Admitting something like that was, for my old self, reserved for weak babies. Now, though . . . I paused, considering their safety and what Carmichael had been chirping about. They would be okay. They had each other; they had their strength. They didn't need me there. At least, that's what I'd tell myself if I started getting too mopey about it.

Turning away, I began to run.

I moved through the night, my footsteps echoing through the empty fields. I stayed just out of sight of the Blue Road, trekking through the shittiest sections of landscape ever traversed, I had to think. Kettleborough grew smaller and smaller behind me, slowly disappearing into the distance. I didn't look back. I couldn't. I had a mission, a purpose. And I wouldn't let anything get in my way. Probably.

Hours passed in a blur of exhaustion and determination. My Stamina dropped more and more as I continued on. My body ached, my legs screamed in protest, but I didn't stop. I couldn't. I was so close, so very close.

Finally, as I approached Palandis, the sun began to rise, casting a brilliant glow across the cityscape. The colors were breathtaking—purples and oranges, yellows and pinks, all melded together in a beautiful, chaotic array. But I didn't have time to write a fuckin' poem or whatever. Still . . . it *was* really pretty. I mean . . . *goddamn*. The city lay before me, basking in the dawn's light, her walls standing tall and proud, her towers reaching for the heavens.

Using Bahlgus's Gorget of Flight, I ascended over the walls as a perfect fuck-you to the city watch trying to guard the place, taking in the breathtaking view. Once I was on the other side . . . I started running again. Considering the early hour, it was pretty fuckin' *cake* to navigate through the straight lines and edges of Palandis's layout, and didn't take me long at all to find the Gateway depot—uh, *Exodus,* I guess.

As I arrived at Exodus, I busted my ass toward the nearest portal.

But as I drew closer, a feeling of dread began to settle in. I was leaving them. Leaving them without saying a word, without a proper goodbye. And it hurt. It hurt more than I could have ever imagined. But it was necessary. I had a task only I could accomplish, a duty that was solely mine to bear. Bequeathed to me like an especially terrible White Elephant gift, and I was just going to have to accept it, I guess. Internally, the words kept repeating in my head. By leaving, I was keeping them safe. I was protecting them from the danger that I represented. That's what I kept fuckin' telling myself, anyway. It was the only real avenue I could use to justify dusting off and leaving them in the lurch.

I was so deep in the guts of my own ruminations that I barely noticed the sudden . . . fog that appeared before me. It was a magical mist, ethereal and luminescent, and once I realized it was there, I got mildly concerned that I was having a stroke and released a tiny, *tiny* peep of absolute horror. I mean, it may have been more than that, but, come on—I thought I was about to die all of a sudden. You know? Betrayed by my own body after surviving a fuckton of bullshit. And then, from the depths of the mist, a form began to take shape.

Edwig. His form amorphous, shapeless, constantly shifting and sputtering like he was on a video chat from ten years ago. But his gaze was unchanging, unwavering. And it was filled with anger. An anger that was directed at me.

I gaped at Edwig's irate form. Using the powerful process of elimination, I had to assume that he was using his Sending Rod, or whatever. Still, I couldn't just *let* them know I was off to probably get myself killed. They'd be climbing all over themselves to stop me. So I'd need to deploy a touch of the fib.

"What? I'm busy, blob!" I shouted—you know, like when an old lady talks on the phone.

"Pah! Busy? Is that what you call it?" he retorted, his form shifting as if agitated.

"Call it whatever you want," I snapped, crossing my arms. "I got a lead on something far more exciting than wading through monster innards. It's called a fuckin' holiday."

"Oh, really?" Edwig asked, sarcasm dripping from his tone. "And what could possibly be so exciting that you couldn't bother to leave a note?"

"Oh, you know, the usual. Interdimensional beings, cosmic horrors, reality-altering shenanigans," I said, a sly grin on my face.

"I'll ask you again, Loon," Edwig said, his tone hard. "Where are you?"

Suddenly, I was jostled from behind, a polite "Pardon me" reached my ears, followed by "Is this the queue for local or inter-kingdom travel?"

Edwig's laugh bounced through the magical connection. "Pah! Orc! You can't be serious! You're in Palandis!"

I glared at his smug form.

"What? No, I'm not. This is, uh, Palan-discount. The cheaper, less interesting cousin of Palandis. Totally different place."

Edwig rolled what I assumed were his eyes, his amorphous form contorting with the motion. "Pah! Whatever you say, orc. But listen here; if you think you can just—"

"No, *you* listen," I interrupted, my temper flaring. "I've got to go. And don't try to contact me again. It's important that you and the others get back to camp."

"And why's that?" Edwig demanded. "You're doing something stupid, aren't you? Something that's going to get you killed."

I scoffed, throwing my hands up in frustration.

"Oh, piss off, Viggo. I'll be fine. You're the one that's going to get killed. Probably in some freak *introduction* accident or something."

His scoff was quite loud.

"Pah! I doubt that, orc. You'll probably be back sooner than any of the others. After all, with your track record, you're the one more likely to end up dead."

I wasn't really super keen on spending my limited, valuable time on playing *No you're gonna die first* with this numbskull. It was making me cranky.

"That's it!" I exclaimed, swiping at the image before me. "I'm hanging up! Gah! Shoo! How do I hang up this damn thing?"

Edwig just harrumphed.

"Pah! Well, you'd better have a good reason for this—now I'm going to have to tend to the eggs!"

"You're gonna be a great babysitter, Beethoven," I said. "Now hang up or you're going to have to watch me use the toilet—and I just ate a whole bunch of cheese!"

"Pah!" Edwig said, but then, before I could demand anything further, his face dispersed, leaving me standing there staring at the portal directly in front of me. Which . . . presented other issues. I knew that my passage *back* to Creepy Potato was paid for . . . but I wasn't sure if I could get a free ride to somewhere else. I supposed it made sense to just wing it, though, since that seemed to have the largest overall success rate for me when it came to matters of . . . doing fucking anything. So, I did.

Well, I *would*, but first . . . I had to get in line.

After a grueling one-hour wait in a queue—with several different attempts on my patience from fellow line-dwellers, I was finally, like an upstanding citizen, able to shift my way to the front. When it was my turn, I approached one of the yellowjacket boys manning the glittering silver Gateway and, putting on my second-best smile—number one was, obviously, with my roe teeth—I greeted the elven woman standing in front of the portal. I noticed she had some kind of incredibly complex instrument of Arcana—I assume—on her head that went down around her pointed ears.

"Good day to you, sir," she greeted me, the slightest hint of boredom lining her otherwise professional tone. Her eyes, startlingly gold, flickered over me before resting on my face. "Name?"

"Loon," I replied, maintaining the fake-as-hell smile on my face.

As she hummed in acknowledgement, the device on her head lit up, and a display appeared in front of her. Her fingers danced in the air as she selected something I couldn't see.

"Ah, yes, Loon. It says here that you're slated for a return passage to Karepalea," she said, her tone carrying a touch of curiosity.

"Karepalea? Lovely place, I hear, but actually"—I leaned on the counter, attempting to channel all my nonexistent charm—"I was wondering if it would be possible to . . . switch that up to, uh . . . Machus City?"

She blinked at me, her pyrite eyes boring into mine.

"According to Interrealm Transit Ordinance seven-point six-five, subclause three-B, changes in destinations are not allowed without the appropriate tokenage. Your passage, sir, is for Karepalea."

My gaze dropped to her name tag. I couldn't read it. From what I'd been able to glean from the letters around these parts, I thought it might have said Priscilla.

"But, uh, *Priscilla*," I said, hoping this would work, "surely there's something we can do?"

Priscilla, it appeared, was not swayed by my pout.

"The name is Constable Farnswallow, and I'm afraid, sir, that the Ordinances are quite clear on this matter."

I sighed dramatically, a heavy weight settling on my shoulders.

"Well, Constable Farnswallow, I seem to be in a bit of a bind."

"Oh? And what would that be?" Her tone was as dry as a desert in the middle of a drought.

"Well, uh, you see . . ." I began, shifting closer to her.

Fuck it, let's see if I can use this Deception Skill. Just start talking, Loon m'boy, and let's see if we can improv our way out of this one.

"I've got this . . . fear of . . . Karepalea."

Ah, fuck. Why did I say that? This isn't going to work.

"Fear?" Her brows shot up. ". . . of Karepalea? Now, that's a new one."

"Yes," I said, nodding solemnly. "A very real and very crippling fear of . . . Karepalean . . . dust mites."

"Dust mites?" She looked at me flatly.

"You maybe heard them called . . . Tallrock . . . ian dust mites? Yes. Yes, that's right. Anyway . . . you see, they're really large in Karepalea. Fuckin' huge, actually. Almost the size of . . . well . . . uh."

Priscilla stifled a laugh, the corners of her lips twitching upward.

"And just how did you come to develop this fear, sir?"

Whew, saved from that one!

"Have you ever been—to Karepalea, I mean?"

"Haven't had the pleasure, sir, no."

"Perfect—uh, I mean . . . oh, I see. Well . . . it's a long and tragic tale," I said, my gaze going distant.

"Well, that's alright; the—"

"It was a simple time!" I began, pulling on my most somber expression. "And I was just a simple man—uh, orc. In a small, isolated town outside of Karepalea—which, of course, was Tallrock then—called Perfection. The town had a bit of a pest problem, only it was no ordinary infestation."

Priscilla leaned in a bit closer, interest piqued.

"Dust mites?"

"Dust mites," I confirmed gravely. "The largest dust mites you'd ever seen. Blew in from Tallrock."

She raised a single, perfectly shaped eyebrow.

"Are we talking . . . cat-sized?"

I scoffed.

"If only! No, Priscilla—I mean, Constable Farnswallow—we're talking dust mites as big as . . . fuckin', uh, *carriages*. They were hideous, hairy bitch—uh, *beasts* that could leap up from the earth without warning."

I shivered for effect, and she blinked at me.

"That sounds . . . improbable."

"It was!" I agreed fervently. "But that's what made it all so terrible. These mites—we called 'em . . . 'Dustoids,' would tunnel under the earth, and you'd never know where they'd pop up next. One moment you're strolling down the street, jammin' out to some tunes, the next you're scooped up by one of these big fuc—things."

I paused, and then decided to lay it on a little thicker.

"Oh, the horror."

"And what did you do then?"

"Are you gonna go through the portal or not!?" someone in line suddenly shouted. "Some of us have gotta get to work!"

I turned to glare over my shoulder.

"I'm *trying* to tell a fucking story of tragedy and woe, buddy! You're ruining the *ambiance*—so shut the fuck up and let me finish!"

When there was no response, I turned back to Priscilla.

". . . uh, where was I?"

"People were being taken by the mites."

"Right! Well, we were cut off, you see," I explained. "No help coming, just us and the Dustoids. So, I had to step it the hell up. I built badass traps, armed myself with the most potent fuckin' . . . potion of explosion you could ever imagine—big enough to blast a Dustoid right up into the sky in tiny little kernels!"

"An explosion potion?" she chuckled.

"The most underrated weapon in the face of an oversized-dust-mite invasion," I replied solemnly.

"I am sure."

"So, there I was," I said, my voice dropping to a hushed whisper as I leaned in closer. "Facing off with the last of the dirty Dustoids, the king of them all."

She was smiling now, leaning in too, her eyes wide with mock seriousness.

"And what did you do?"

"Well," I began, throwing a dramatic glance over my shoulder before turning back to her, "I had one last potion left. I lured the Dustoid to the edge of the largest ravine I could find."

She covered her mouth with her hand, her eyes sparkling with suppressed laughter.

"Swear to the motherfuckin' gods," I exclaimed, "Then I . . . lit the . . . wick? On the potion. And threw it behind the Dustoid. The explosion scared the mite so bad, it charged straight through the cliff face and plummeted to its death onto the rocks below."

She broke into laughter then, a rich, warm sound that made the corners of my own mouth twitch upwards.

I nodded, playing the part of the weary hero.

"We went back to town and called in the authorities—city watch just like yourself—to begin an investigation. In the meantime, my good friend Earl encouraged me to pursue a . . . let's say, 'romantic relationship' with a certain person . . ."

I realized right then that I was copying the plot of *Tremors* too much and needed an exit strategy.

She raised an eyebrow at that.

"And did you?"

"I might've," I said, shrugging nonchalantly, "But that's a story for another time! So you see, Constable Farnswallow, I've had quite enough of Karepalea and its dust mites. Machus City sounds like a much safer place for a ma—orc—like me."

"Yet you survived all this and still went back to Karepalea?"

". . . Whatcha mean?"

"It's a *return* journey to Karepalea, so you came from there to Palandis initially . . ."

"Well." I shrugged. "Sometimes, you just can't escape your past. But, I think it's about time I moved on. Hence, Machus City."

"Right, of course," she said, shaking her head but clearly amused. "Well, I must say, your tale is . . . unique. Nonetheless, I am afraid the Ordinances are quite clear. Your destination remains Karepalea."

"Fuck—I mean, *ah*, fiddlesticks. You're saying there's no way around it?"

"I'm afraid not, sir."

Motherfucking goddamn shit, I thought. *I gotta get to Machus City. I wish I was good at talking to people like Saban. What would he do?*

I paused, considering a new tactic. There *had* seemed to be some tension between the two factions, after all . . .

"You know, now that I think about it . . . there must have been some mistake with my travel destination. I had originally intended to go *to* Machus City, but some idiot with His Majesty's Royal Army must have fucked up the information."

She peered at me suspiciously over her contraption.

"Is that so? However, it does state here that it was for a return. Those are usually more expensive."

I shrugged, rolling my eyes theatrically.

"Makes sense why I ran outta walkin'-around money when I had budgeted for this trip myself. Fuckin' tin-can Royal Army guys, right? You know how those guys are . . ."

I stuck my tongue out, crossing my eyes to demonstrate the level of idiocy I believed the soldiers possessed.

Her eyes sparkled with silent laughter as she seemed to mull over my words. After a moment, she sighed.

"Well, it's not uncommon for them to make mistakes . . ."

"It's not?" I asked, then caught myself. "I mean . . . *yeah*, it's not. Lousy dipshits."

"Be that as it may, if you choose to switch your destination, you'd be giving up your paid travel to Karepalea. There will be no refunding the overpayment. Is that something you'd be willing to do?"

I shrugged again. *I* hadn't paid for it.

"Sure."

Her fingers danced across her magical screen, flicking through multiple options before coming to a halt.

"Right, well, I can't promise it will be entirely dust mite–free, but Machus City it is."

"Shit, really? Thank you Pris—Constable!"

"With a bit of luck, it might also involve less of His Majesty's soldiers and their incompetencies," she added, chuckling.

"Ah, an orc can only dream," I said, chuckling along.

A few more taps with her fingers and she smiled at me.

"It's all set. You're ready to go."

I saw a notification that my Deception Skill had gone up. Fuckin' baller.

I winked at her.

"Thank you, Constable Farnswallow. Until we meet again."

With a salute, she sent me off.

"Safe travels, sir. And do try to steer clear of the dust mites."

I nodded in appreciation and turned to the portal, which was now a glowing deep sapphire—which took me a second to calm myself down from her treachery until I realized it was different from the sky blue of the Gateway in Yosper Hall.

Then, without another thought, I stepped into the ring of swirling magic.

Shit! I shoulda just thrown Lazlo's name around—I coulda avoided all of thi—

THIRD OVERTURE

Perched on the antiquated, over-loved sofa, Roger's attention was lazily held by a dog-eared comic book, a welcome distraction from the mundanity of middle school life. The hushed lull of the afternoon was punctured when the front door creaked open. An autumnal gust, mischievous and crisp, barged its way in, scattering an array of leaves and depositing his rotund little brother, Gabe, in the hallway.

Gabe wrestled his oversized backpack off his sturdy shoulders, its thump against the threadbare carpet echoing in the silence. His gait as he shuffled toward the living room was uncharacteristically leaden, the usually lively and rambunctious schoolboy burdened by an unseen weight. His uniform was in disarray, the starched white shirt bearing telltale smudges and his blue tie hanging askew. Yet it was the smattering of violet bruises on his plump arms and dried tear tracks on his cherubic cheeks that pulled Roger's focus.

"What the hell happened, Gabe?" Roger demanded, discarding his comic book, familial concern flaring. He rose from the sofa, looming protectively over the younger boy.

Gabe's brown eyes remained trained on the worn-out carpet, his pudgy fingers clenching and unclenching in a nervous dance. When he finally summoned the courage to reply, his voice was a timid whisper, hardly audible.

"I tripped . . . at the playground," he said, each word hesitantly staggering off his tongue as if hoping their softness could somehow alter the reality they represented.

Roger didn't buy it for a second. His three years of additional life experience told him playground trips didn't account for raw knuckles or swollen eyes. Gabe was hiding something, a bitter truth lurking beneath the surface of his feeble fib.

"Cut the shit, Gabe," Roger spat.

He knelt to Gabe's height, his gaze steely and determined as it sought the honesty concealed behind the younger boy's reluctance.

"Who did it?"

His question echoed in the room, its intensity tugging at the fading wallpaper and dust-coated picture frames. It wasn't merely a question. It was an oath.

Roger's flinty gaze was intense as he patiently waited for Gabe's confession, a silence only interrupted by the occasional ticking of the antique clock hanging crookedly on the wall next to the picture of Jesus praying.

Gabe fumbled with the worn-out hem of his shirt, a boy grappling with words that didn't want to be said. After an eternity, he heaved a deep sigh and began.

"Me and Nick were playing a game," he began, his voice still shaky. "We were trying to beam Lincoln's mole with a dodgeball. See who could hit it more times."

A halfhearted smile crossed his face as he recalled the innocent game they'd invented using the huge mural of Abraham Lincoln painted on the wall outside the cafeteria, a stark contrast to the brutality that followed.

His features turned serious again as he continued.

". . . Then Trent Marshall and some of his friends showed up. They started making fun of us—not, like, to our faces but sorta . . . as they walked by."

Roger's grip tightened on the back of the sofa. He knew Trent Marshall—the boy was a grade ahead of Roger himself. As he listened, the conjured image of those cruel sneers was more than he could bear. But Gabe wasn't finished.

"I may have said some things back," he admitted, a guilty crimson rising on his cheeks. "Which they didn't like. Nick started talking—to calm 'em down. It worked, and they . . . started to leave."

Gabe paused, the fresh sting of humiliation mixing with the remnants of dried tears.

"But then I couldn't help it," he confessed, his eyes flickering regretfully. "I shouted, 'Yeah, that's right! You better run!' And they . . . they turned around."

Roger's blood thrummed as he envisaged the scene: Gabe, small and round but defiant, versus Trent, an eighth-grader with a height and power advantage. The unfairness of it all stirred a seething fury within him.

"They pinned me down," Gabe's voice was barely a whisper now. "Twisted my arms behind my back and bounced the dodgeball against my head . . . over and over again."

Silence fell again, the echoes of the dodgeball thudding against Gabe's head, a chilling soundtrack to the unsaid. Roger clenched his fists, his nails biting into the flesh of his palms. He could almost see Trent standing over

Gabe with that smug grin, a scene that sent a surge of righteous indignation through his veins.

"An eighth-grader picking on a fourth-grader? That piece of fucking sh—" Roger spat, his fury barely contained, but he stopped himself, realizing his words were only adding to Gabe's distress. "It's okay, Gabe. We'll handle this."

In the uneasy silence of their living room, Gabe found himself alone—his mother was pulling yet another late shift. She wouldn't be home 'til after midnight at the earliest. His eyes, still red-rimmed, were glued to the flickering images on the old boxy television, the only source of light in the dimly lit room casting long, eerie shadows on the worn-out wallpaper.

The front door creaked open, letting in a gust of cold. Roger was back, and the storm in his eyes was unmistakable, the set of his jaw hard and unyielding. A bruise formed on his cheek, the angry blemish standing out strongly against his skin. Dried blood crusted his split knuckles and under his nose, and he limped slightly as he crossed the room, but his shoulders were thrown back, his posture radiating success.

Without a word, he sank into the busted-down couch next to Gabe, his eyes locked on the scene on TV. Time seemed to slow, the only sounds being the muffled voices from the television and the occasional shift of fabric as one of them moved.

Finally, Gabe's eyes drifted over to him. Roger could feel his gaze but didn't turn to meet it. Instead, he simply gave a single, confident nod, his gaze never leaving the television. His voice was firm, steady as he broke the silence.

"They won't be messing with you anymore."

The silence stretched between them for a long moment before Gabe finally voiced the question bubbling up inside him.

"What happened?"

Still staring forward, Roger allowed a thin, satisfied smile to curve his lips. He began recounting the event, a tale of swift retribution.

"I found Trent and his dumbass friends—Derrick, David, and Brett—loitering outside Zippy's on Thirty-Third. Couldn't have them walkin' around thinking they got away with it, could I?"

His fingers flexed, the dried blood on his knuckles flaking off as he continued, a note of relish in his voice.

"So, I explained a few things to them. Made sure they understood why what they did was so fucked-up."

The screen cast flickering shadows over his face as he recounted the brawl, his tone casual but his words painting a vivid picture. He described the way he had stood his ground against four boys. Each dodge, defiant glare, and landed punch aimed at teaching them a lesson they wouldn't forget.

His smile widened, his dark eyes gleaming in the television's light.

"By the time I was done, they got the message. They won't be laying a finger on you again."

The room fell silent once more, save for the background noise from the TV. But this silence was different.

Gabe's eyes widened.

"You took on all of them? By yourself?" he asked.

Roger shrugged and nodded.

"Tried to get Danny to help, but he's still on lockdown after . . . what we did to Dr. Foster's house last week. So, yeah, I went solo."

Gabe's smile grew, a shine in his eyes that hinted at tears.

"You're so cool, Roger," he said, his voice choked with emotion. He looked up at him, his hero, and asked, "How come you're so good at fighting?"

Roger looked away from the TV for the first time, meeting Gabe's gaze. He hesitated for a moment before replying softly.

"I had a lot of practice . . ." His voice trailed off, and Gabe felt a pang of guilt. There was a hidden history there, their past, something that made Roger so fiercely protective.

Roger broke the silence after a moment, his voice angry and resigned.

"I just can't help it . . . I get so *mad* sometimes, you know? And when that happens, I feel . . . like, I dunno—out of control? Unstoppable."

There was something almost haunted in his eyes, a fleeting glimpse into a side of Roger that Gabe rarely saw. The side that took on older bullies and came home bruised but victorious. The side that carried the weight of their world on his shoulders so that Gabe didn't have to. The side that fought not because he wanted to but because he had to. Because he was a big brother, and that's what big brothers did.

CHAPTER THIRTY-FOUR

LISTEN TO IRON MAIDEN, BABY

Fuckin' hell, Machus City was a big bitch of a place.

The city walls alone were something to gawk at—if you were the gawking type, which I pointedly was not. They towered in their sapphire glory, glowing with an inner light that made you squint if you stared too long, but also seemed to beckon you in a *Hey, look at me, I'm fuckin' shiny* kind of way. They also just looked like a pain in the ass to scale. Not that I was thinking of such things, mind you—everyone knows I am a law-abiding sort—but it's always good to keep one's options open.

But man, this place was outta control with the schnazziness. Even the goddamn cobblestones seemed to be etched with intricate designs. Houses, shops, and market stalls packed together like sardines in a tin, with their slanted roofs, colorful facades, and elaborately carved signboards. People everywhere, shouting, haggling, arguing, laughing, and just generally making a bloody racket. A thousand smells assaulted my nostrils, from the mouth-watering aroma of roasting meats to the less-appealing scent of city sewage. Thanks for that, Machus City.

And it was fucking huge. I mean, really enormous. The sapphire walls stretched out in all directions, their blue reflections shimmering on the rooftops below. I could see the towers and spires of the inner districts rising in the distance, an urban jungle made of stone and wood. And the city center . . . gods, the city center was a nightmare of winding streets and labyrinthine alleyways, with a massive, opulent palace squatting right in the middle of it all like a toad on a lily pad. It was definitely more than anything my little "hometown" could ever aspire to be, and it made me feel small and insignificant in the grand scheme of things. Thanks again, Machus City, you self-absorbed, overgrown, pompous bitch of a metropolis.

I was standing in the middle of the fantasy equivalent of Times Square on Black Friday, except it was basically the Dark Ages there, so it was more like Black Plague Every Fucking Day.

The marketplace was a giant clusterfuck of haggling, bickering, and the occasional pickpocketing. It was like navigating the worst kind of farmer's market, but instead of organic bedsheets, free-range candles, and farm-to-table firewood, they were selling magic potions and discount smells. Everyone was squeezed together like sardines in a can—and not the nice kind of sardines. The ones left in the back of the cupboard 'til all that was left were scraps and regret.

The buildings around were an MC Escher heroin-binge mishmash of architectural vomit. Punctuating every third building or so were tall gothic-looking towers with those . . . uh, *dome-thingies* makin' 'em look like overgrown mushrooms.

That air, though? Don't even get me started. It was a fucking spoiled pot-pourri of scents. Freshly baked bread and ripe fruit were playing footsie with the stinky funk mist of a multitude of . . . sweaty people. And *goddamn*, the noise sure was something else. The *thud thud* of a blacksmith trying to beat the shit out of some poor piece of metal, sellers shouting their deals like drill sergeants, and some asshole tolling the distant cathedral bell like his fucking life depended on it.

But there I was, right in the thick of what looked like a medieval music festival without a goddamn clue where to go next.

That was when I spotted him.

A tiny fucking terrorist. A kid no taller than my belt buckle—the little shit who *blew me up*.

I released an involuntary shiver. The memory of being splattered across half the forest wasn't exactly something you shake off with a hot bath. Seeing him there, snot-nosed and bright-eyed, I felt a surge of pure, unadulterated irritation.

What the fuck is he doing here?

He saw me at the same moment, his eyes widening like a cat caught mid-shit. Then the derpy little squirt took off running.

"I'm gonna beat your head in, you pissant fuck!" I hollered, pushing my way through the crowd.

The chase was on. The kid wove through the crowd like a greased . . . greasy thing, darting between legs and ducking under carts. I barreled after him, stumbling and swearing up a storm as I plowed through the assembled mass of folks just going about their day.

"Fuckin' shit, you little *fuck*— Shit, sorry, ma'am— Just gonna . . . yep, scoochin' through here— Outta the way, assholes! I'm on the hunt! Goddamn cock— Sonofa— Oops, my b, my b! *Excuse you!* Whoa! Fucking Christ—fucking *Christ! Ulp!* Ha-ha! Ah, dick piss! Wait—hol' up! Get back here!"

A cart full of fruit fell into my path, something akin to apples bouncing everywhere like fucking ping-pong balls. I slipped, slid, and then went down, taking out a pile of cabbages with me. The vendor screeched like I'd just murdered her firstborn.

"Oh, shut up, lady!" I grunted from the ground. "I don't have time for this!"

Then I scrambled back up and continued the chase.

"And you better not show up later only to have me conveniently destroy your cabbages again!" I shouted over my shoulder.

The kid was good; I'll give him that. He had the agility of a coked-up squirrel and the sheer fucking audacity of a dumpster rat. But I was an orc on a mission. This little fucker had to pay for surprise-exploding me into confetti.

It wasn't long before I finally cornered him in a dead-end alley. He looked up at me with wide, innocent eyes, and for a moment, I almost felt bad. But then I remembered the agonizing pain of being blown up, and my sympathy evaporated.

"Caught you, ya little shit," I growled, looming over him. "Time to pay the . . . the, uh . . . the *me!*"

The kid looked at me defiantly, his chin jutting out.

"You can't catch me!" he said, summoning up every ounce of pre-teen arrogance he had.

I laughed disbelievingly, gesturing to the lack of throughway.

"Really, dipshit? 'Cause it looks like I just fucking did."

He glared at me, his small hands clenched into fists.

"You won't get away with this."

"Get away with *what*? Revenge for you killing me? First off: yes, I fucking will. Second: *who the fuck had you assassinate me?* That fucking *hurt*, you ugly little hatchet-faced muskrat."

I wished I'd have been able to weave a spectrum of colorful pun-centric insults based around his name, but . . . I didn't know it. But for the moment, it didn't matter. All that mattered was that I'd caught the little runt. The rest would come in due course, and boy, was I looking forward to it.

Reaching out, I tried to grab the kid by the scruff of his shirt and hopefully shake some information out of him.

But he somehow dodged my grab and . . . slapped me. Hard.

The open-handed smack landed square on my face, and I swear it stung worse than that time I got mule-kicked in the balls practicing wrestling moves on my cousin Denny.

"Jesus fuck!" I swore, rubbing my stinging cheek. "What the hell you been eating, kid? Bricks?"

Ignoring my complaint, the boy muttered something under his breath. Before I knew it, the tiny terror was lifting off the ground and shooting toward the roof like a goddamn bottle rocket.

Fuckin'... magic Spell-havin', bitch-ass punk!

"Hey!" I bellowed, utterly flabbergasted. He turned around midair, sticking his tongue out at me.

"Oh, fuck the hell outta this!" I called up, anger rising like bile in my throat.

I really wish I hadn't used up my up-and-at-'em necklace!

I'd, uh, used the last charge of it to get over a large puddle earlier. Priorities, right?

Taking a deep breath, I grabbed hold of the eaves' trough and started hauling my ass up. It was a struggle, and I wheezed like a ninety-year-old smoker as I clambered up onto the roof.

"God, I'm so fucking out of shape," I muttered to myself, panting.

I saw him bolting along—clearly out of his ... magical flight powers or whatever—and darting over slanted roofs and creating quite a sizable gap between us. I didn't let it deter me, though. Instead, it fueled me as I chased after the taunting, mucus-faced munchkin. The rooftops were tricky terrain, covered in loose clay tiles and the occasional sleeping cat. I nearly tripped over a rotund tabby, and the animal screeched at me; its look of hissing outrage would have made me laugh if I wasn't so fucking *annoyed*.

But I kept going. No one blows me up and gets away with it—*no one*. Especially not a smarmy little brat who ... slapped me.

"You're in for it now, you little shit!" I shouted, heaving heavily as I chased him over the rooftops under the bright blue sky. The kid just laughed, his childish glee echoing through the air, filling me with an intense desire to catch him and wipe that smug look off his face by punching it.

Finally, he reached what was essentially another dead end. The dumb little asshole had cornered himself on a rooftop with no nearby vantages to leap to.

Perfect.

I wanted to know who sent him to kill me, and my patience was running thin. I mean, it's not like I was going to kill him. He was still a kid, after all. But he was, inexplicably, either working for someone or paid to do that. And, I mean, fucking seriously, though...

Actually, maybe I *should* cap his ass—what kind of adolescent was super comfortable with offing someone?

Let's just file that under things not to think about at the moment.

"Outta upward mobility?" I mused, hopping on to the same roof he was stranded on and cracking my knuckles. "Sucks to suck, you little ditch berry."

"Stay back, bitch!" the kid yelled at me, reaching into the satchel at his side. He withdrew a short, thin piece of wood that I realized after a second of scrutinizing was probably a wand.

"Don't you sass me, you fuckin' gremlin!" I shouted. "And if you even *think* about blasting me with—"

FWOOF! FWOOF! FWOOF! FWOOF!

The little asshole started shooting off Spells from his wand.

Magic whizzed past my ears as I ducked and dodged, perceiving each one as being filled with the destructive potential of a miniature, shit-encrusted bomb. However, to my surprise, each spot an arcane bolt hit caused a blossom of thorny plant life to sprout. It was basically thistles with a few flowers, but I definitely didn't want to get hit in the face with it or anything—that might be inconvenient.

"Hey, careful with that thing!" I yelled, barely dodging a Spell. "You're gonna take someone's eye out!"

The kid just laughed like an unhinged psychopath and yelled back at me.

"You should've stayed dead!"

"What the fuck?" I demanded, taking cover behind a nearby chimney. "That's some fucked-up bloodthirst! Who the fuck raised you?!"

From behind the chimney, I could hear him still firing at the spot where I'd been standing. A mischievous grin crept across my face. While excelling quite decently at it, stealth still wasn't usually my go-to style in a fight—especially not in broad daylight. But hell, this was just too good an opportunity to pass up. I furled my Trespasser's Veil around me, feeling myself . . . become harder to see? I dunno how it worked, y'all; I just *did that shit*, alright? Anyway, the only reason I could was because of the shadow cast by the stone smokestack. But do it I did.

I moved silently around the side of the chimney, watching as the kid grew increasingly confused. He was skirting the edge of the roof as his Spells still whizzed and popped in the air, but I was no longer their target.

"Hey, kid!" I shouted suddenly, springing out from my hiding spot. I must have looked like I just materialized out of thin air, because his face was the perfect picture of shock as I launched myself at him, feet first. The double kick connected solidly with his chest.

"This is for the respawn, fucker!" I yelled, as the force sent him flying backward off the roof.

With a yelp, he rocketed over the edge, landing with a thud in a courtyard some twenty feet below. I peered over the side, panting but triumphant.

"Now who's laughing, huh?" I shouted down at him.

He groaned but didn't get up.

"Not so tough without your wand, are ya?"

Taking a moment to catch my breath, I looked down at the dazed kid struggling to catch his breath on the ground. I jumped off the roof. With a thud that—in my old body—would have sent shockwaves through my body, I landed, staggering a little but managing to keep my footing. I took a moment to enjoy the wide-eyed fear on the kid's face as he realized I was still very much in the game.

"Round two, shitbird!" I shouted, pulling one of my own wands from my pack. The kid, realizing what was about to go down, scrambled to his feet, fumbling for something on the ground.

"That is, unless you want to start talking about who sent you to kill—"

FWOOF!

I didn't even see it coming this time. Somehow, the kid had retrieved his wand and whipped a Spell at me, hitting me right in the shoulder. A few thorns and flowers ripped their way out of my flesh, and I released a yowl of pain.

"Holy *fucking* ghost, that hurts!"

The kid chortled and scrambled away, firing a blind shot at me over his shoulder that I actually had to leap above to keep it from hitting my knees. I fired back with the Wand of Lightning Ball, making sure to use it to kite him rather than actually hit him. He dove behind a bush, and I followed, vaulting over just in time to see an orb of green magic coming in hot.

"Gyraaaaaahhhhhhhhh!" I howled in a death-metal roar, activating Blackout Warchant and watching the Spell dissolve pitifully. But it had thrown me off my game, and I crashed to the ground, bringing my own wand up and firing a warning shot without aiming at anything in particular. But the kid was already dashing for the trees, and that was when I noticed there were a fuckton of people around. I stood, watching them watching me—you know, a huge orc in an all-black villain cape chasing after a tiny kid.

"Uh . . ." I started, looking around at the sea of faces that seemed like they didn't know whether to run or attack. "Truancy officer! Nothin' to see here, folks!"

This seemed to only confuse them further, but I didn't care. The little jerk was getting away, and I didn't have time to placate them. So, I just abandoned all pretense and *goosed it*. I stomped through the trees, slicing through the thick branches with my haladie in one hand and my wand in the other. I spun in a circle, expecting to get a face-full of herbal magic while I was hoofin' it through the foliage. Instead, I felt a yank at my side. Right where my Wand of Flames had been.

"Shiiii—" I yelped, diving to the ground and scratching my shit up as a huge column of flame erupted behind me. Not only had he *mugged* me, but he'd also tried to light me up with my own supply.

I didn't have time to think about that, though, because I was in a dangerous predicament that could quickly turn into me being trapped in a brush fire. The branches behind me had gone up in flames, and I quickly rolled out of the greenery and back into the courtyard.

This kid was a fucking monster!

I stood, both weapons out, and noticed movement to my right. I dodged as another firebolt flew by—way too close for comfort—and fired right back with a lightning ball. Our wands met with a series of erratic zaps and flashes, like a fireworks display choreographed by a bath-salt capuchin. We sent a barrage of Spells flying back and forth, turning the quiet courtyard into Fisher Price Presents: Magical War Zone.

His Spells with the Wand of Flames were wild and unpredictable, zipping in every direction. A few of them hit their mark, scorching my clothes and singeing my eyebrows. This kid was *fast*, though.

"Hold still, ya fucking freak!" I shouted, trying to land a solid hit in response.

"Not on your life, old man!" he retorted, sending another blast my way.

"Old man?! I'm only like . . . six grades ahead of you!"

With a yelp, I dove behind a statue of some kind of devil-man, narrowly avoiding a blast that would've turned me into a smoking crater.

The kid's laughter echoed around the courtyard as I grimaced, shaking off the near miss.

"You think this is funny, do you?" I growled, peeking out from my hiding place and immediately withdrawing as another blast connected with the stone. Then I scowled. I needed him to stop using that fucking fire wand on me. First of all, it was mine. Second, if he actually figured out how to use it well, he'd murder the shit out of me. Fourth, I was in a time crunch, and learning who was trying to kill me was high-priority. Though, based on how he'd been acting, I half-wondered if it was *him* who wanted to kill me in the first place.

I leveled my haladie, closing one eye to try and get a handle on my trajectory. Then I aimed and chucked that bitch right at the kid. It spiraled toward him faster than he could even react to and *sliced right through the wand in his hand.*

"Fuck!" I exclaimed. I dunno why I hadn't realized the *thing with the spinning lawn-mower blades* would guillotine a piece of wood. I'd been trying to just, like, I dunno, knock it out of his hand. The kid realized what had happened and hurled the half of the wand still in his hand to the ground in a panic. It erupted into flame on contact. But this pre-teenage dirtbag wasn't ready to give up the farm just yet. He yanked his original wand out of his sleeve and held it up.

He fired a Spell at me with a dramatic flourish. It missed me by a country mile and hit a tree instead. The tree promptly sprouted a lovely bouquet of daisies.

"Holy fuck," I said, putting my hands up in mock fear. "That's some hardcore magic, young blood. You really showed that tree."

This dummy then decided he was going to take me seriously, a proud little smile forming on his face.

"Yeah, you better watch out."

"Watch out for what? Your ability to turn things into a fucking garden center?" I razzed, shaking my head. "Seriously, kiddo, you've got a future in floral design."

The confused expression on his face quickly turned to defiance.

"I'm not a florist! I'm a wizard!"

"Sure thing," I said, winking at him. "Because usually when someone's a wizard, they have to go around tellin' everybody."

He looked furious.

"I'll show you! I'll show you *all*!"

"All? You got a mouse in your pocket or—"

With that, he launched another Spell at me. It missed, hitting a rock and causing it to become entrapped in weeds.

"Oh, now I'm really shaking," I said, pretending to quiver. "What are you going to do next, turn my shoelaces into spaghetti?"

The boy seemed to take that as a genuine insult. His face scrunched up as he crossed his arms over his chest.

"You're an idiot."

I shrugged unapologetically.

"And you're a shitty wizard. Guess we're both having a garbage day, sport."

Incensed, the boy sneered at me.

"Oh, yeah? Would a *shitty* wizard have a Rare-Tier Aura Guard?"

"I dunno what that is," I said. "So, yeah, maybe—if the shoe fuckin' fits."

"You oaf," the boy hissed, and it really sounded like he wanted that to come off as an insult, but—come on—*oaf?* "It's a Shield Spell. And it means you can't hurt me even if you weren't such a . . . a . . ."

"An oaf?" I offered.

"Yeah!" he said, oblivious to the irony.

"Can't be hurt, huh?" I wondered aloud. Then I smiled.

"Well, shit. That's a relief."

Gaspar Hookfoot was enjoying his afternoon tea, sitting in the common room of his tavern, basking in the midday sun streaming through his windows. This was the twog's favorite time of day. He'd already finished his opening duties and business wouldn't begin for a few more hours, so he could just sit and find a spot of relaxation before the hubbub of the evening got underway. Truly, this was a wonderful respite in the sea of chaos that was his life.

However, all of that ceased immediately as the common room window exploded in a cloud of shattered glass and a boy flew in.

The young man slammed into the ground with a high-pitched *oof*, and the small creature called Gaspar tumbled out of his chair in the cataclysmic chaos.

"Rahbi?!" Gaspar exclaimed, hurrying to the child's side as he lay on a pile of crackling debris, struggling to catch his breath. Thankfully, he only seemed to have gotten the wind knocked out of him. Gaspar wrenched him into a sitting position, smacking the boy on the back with worry.

"Are you alright, boy?!"

"SPECIAL DELIVERY!" called a booming voice just as the door to the tavern exploded inward, torn clean from its hinges and flying into the common room as well. Gaspar let out a terrified squeak as the sun-illuminated doorway intimated the shape of a large figure, nearly as big as the doorframe itself.

Gaspar shrieked, backing away from the boy and the intruder, desperately patting the ground around him for some kind of weapon. With a start, he realized he'd left his enchanted knife sitting next to the toilet.

The figure in the doorway stepped forward, revealing himself to be a huge, brutish orc dressed in a motley of raiments that made him look like a bloodthirsty savage fresh from a raid. His skin was disfigured by the presence of various spots, which looked very much to the tavern proprietor like some form of plague, and his hair was a bizarre vibrant shade of violet and magenta hues. Also worrisomely, he had some sort of plant growth sprouting from a shoulder that looked like he'd tried to tear out of his own skin.

"What do you want?!" Gaspar exclaimed, backing up farther until his back was pressed against the underside of the bar.

The towering monster stepped forward again, an evil grin plastered on his face.

"I heard *you're* the motherfucker who tried to have me killed!"

CHAPTER THIRTY-FIVE

F.C.P.R.E.M.I.X.

I sat in the surprisingly cozy corner of what was left of Gaspar's tavern, sipping the sweet, floral-scented tea the little man had hastily brewed. The entire scene felt like a surreal dream—the chaos of the previous hour had given way to an odd tranquility. Rahbi was doing his best to sweep up the broken glass, cursing under his breath every time a piece eluded his broom. Gaspar and I were on opposite sides of a battered wooden table, a plate of surprisingly delicious pastries between us.

"So, lemme ge' dis straighd," I started, mouth full and pointing a half-eaten pastry at him. "You ged dis m'sterious Quest out of da blue one mornin', no hints, no prompts, jus' a sed of instructions?"

The little dude, whose Race I had learned was called a twog, nodded, his eyes weary but alert.

"That is correct. The System indicated that I was to pick up a package from an alchemist in Kethys, and deliver it to an orc called Loon, at a specified location on the map it provided."

"And let me guess," I interjected, "the Quest told you not to look inside the package."

Gaspar's eyes widened in surprise.

"Exactly! How did you . . ."

I waved off his question and finished the other half of the pastry, my mind racing to put together the pieces.

"It didn't say that there was anyone who had offered it to you—fully anonymous?"

"Yes," Gaspar said.

"And so, you . . . what? Just went for it? Didn't you think it was suspicious at all?"

"Oh, the alchemist was *quite* suspicious," Gaspar chuckled. "But then again, I don't know that I've ever met one who wasn't a bit *off*."

"But you didn't think, 'Hm, this is weird, maybe I should do some additional recon on this random bullshit Quest that popped up before delivering it'?"

"It seemed much like a Special Quest," Gaspar continued. "From what I understand, they're highly elusive and usually come with life-altering rewards like a new Class or some high-tier Skills upon Leveling Up."

"But here's the weird part." I leaned forward, resting my elbows on the table. "I don't know you. And you claim you don't know me. So, you had no idea who you were bringing this 'package' to."

Gaspar shook his head, a helpless shrug lifting his shoulders.

"I was just following the instructions."

"Yeah, well, that's how genocides happen," I said. "And look at that—a genocides *did* happen."

"Genocide?" Gaspar asked, sounding shocked. "But I thought it just killed *you*."

"And for that brief time, the world lost an entire culture of hilarious jokes and snappy one-liners. Keep up, Gassy," I said. "I just think it's fucked up that you didn't second-guess anything."

"Well, I'd have never imagined the System would lead me astray."

I grunted in response. A gift of an assassination attempt. A present that almost ended my life. And all this courtesy of an anonymous System Quest and a little hobbit-like creature who knew nothing about me.

"Never trust the System, Gaspar," I said, pushing back from the table. "It doesn't care about us. We're just playthings for it."

Gaspar said nothing, his eyes falling on the scarred wooden table. Maybe he was reflecting on his actions; maybe he was just tired. Either way, it didn't matter.

"So, how'd this little shit come into play?" I asked, jabbing a thumb in Rahbi's direction.

The kid scowled in response. Gaspar nodded and pointed at his right leg. I could see that it ended in a curved iron hook.

"I don't get around as easily as I'd like," he said. "And I often employ young Rahbi here as a courier of sorts. He usually helps me in picking things up, or with deliveries, or—"

"With assassination attempts," I growled.

"Well, *unintentional* assassination attempts, in any case," Gaspar said absently. "But truly, I never would have believed I'd be given such a despicable duty—least of all by the System."

"But I was *weeks* away from here!" I exclaimed. "You sent an eight-year-old boy—"

"I'm twelve," Rahbi corrected.

"An *eight-year-old* dipshit that far away to deliver a package?" I continued. "What the hell? I mean, I like Old Enough! as much as the next guy, but . . . Jesus."

"Even more curiously," Gaspar said, as if suddenly bashful about the pieces fitting together, "Rahbi happened to be near the designated area when I received the Quest. So, I sent the package to him through the portal system, and he took it the rest of the way."

"Convenient," I muttered, rolling my eyes. "So, whoever sent you to murder me already knew your creepy little sociopath messenger boy was going to be in—where, exactly?"

"Tallrock," they said at the same time.

Uh-oh.

"Oh . . ." I said. "You were there when all that shit went down?"

"Yeah," Rahbi said. "And it was terrible. Big monsters wrecked the place, and I had to spend days helping my uncle rebuild his aviary coop."

I chuckled.

"Hard work not in your wheelhouse?" I asked. But then I stopped laughing because I hadn't really helped with the rebuilding either.

Oops.

"They, uh, aren't calling it that anymore, by the way," I said.

"Huh?" Rahbi said.

"That's not the city's name no more," I clarified. "It's . . . uh . . ."

I snapped my fingers trying to recall the new moniker.

"Crap-ola? Capicola?"

"Karepalea," Rahbi said. "Yeah, I know. I'm not an idiot."

"You sure act like one," I mused, then I paused.

"Wait," I said, turning to glare at the boy, who was finishing up with the busted glass. "What the fuck, though, kid?"

Rahbi looked up at me.

"What?"

"Don't give me that," I said. "You were all 'why so serious'—fuckin' full-tilt maniacal Heath Ledger back when we were fighting. You literally said I 'should have stayed dead.'"

"Rahbi!" Gaspar admonished.

"It's because your Quest failed, Gaspar!" Rahbi practically shouted, his indignation clear on his red face. "This asshole—"

"Language!" I warned.

"Fuck you, orc," Rahbi hissed.

I surprised myself by chuckling.

This kid reminds me of someone.

"What do you mean, your Quest failed? I goddamn *died*!" I said.

"Well, that is peculiar," Gaspar said, sounding far away in thought. He rapped his knuckles on the table and bit his lip. "I *did* fail the Quest. I assumed that whatever Rahbi encountered had caused the endeavor to falter, but I hadn't had a chance to ask him about it yet."

"Then how'd you know the Quest failed?" I asked Rahbi accusingly.

He shrugged.

"I got a Quest too—when I received the package. When you, uh, fuckin' exploded, I instantly got a notification that I'd completed the Quest. But then a few minutes later, I got a message that Gaspar had failed his."

I froze.

"You got it a few *minutes* later?" I asked. In a rare move, I actually felt like something was making sense.

"That's what I said, you fucking—"

"Rahbi . . ." Gaspar warned.

So, whoever decided to hand over this Quest, *knew* I'd likely be sent to Pontivex upon my untimely demise, but hadn't accounted for Rexen doin' something wild to get me outta my contract? On top of that, there were very few people who knew about my soul-slavery final destination in the first place. So . . . what did that mean? Whatever was happening, I felt like I might have been in danger.

"Well, this has been *super* fun, getting to beat this kid's ass and learning all about this shit," I said, standing. "But I think I've got to go."

Gaspar made to stand as well, but I waved him away.

"I'm good," I said. "No need to walk me out. Sorry about the mess, by the way."

At my words, Gaspar glanced around at his tavern sadly.

"Yes . . ." he said softly.

Ah, shit. Here I go, feeling bad about stuff again.

"Listen . . ." I said, reaching into my pack. "I dunno if this is going to help at all . . ."

I produced the smoking crystal vial that I'd gotten from the Kettleborough temple of horrors and set it on the tabletop.

"But you can have this. Maybe it'll—"

"That's . . . that's a Brilliance Tier Skill Potion!" Gaspar shouted, leaning forward.

"A *what?*"

"A Brilliance Tier Skill Potion!" Gaspar said with the exact same exuberance as before. "They're worth a fortune! You would give this to me? I . . . I . . ."

Tears began welling up in Gaspar's eyes as he stared up at me, the little man clearly overwhelmed with emotion. Well, fuck. It was expensive? Just my luck. The *one* time I try to do something nice for someone, it *also* fucks me over.

"Uh . . . yeah . . ." I muttered. "For the window . . . and stuff."

"Thank you!" Gaspar said, the tears flowing freely from his eyes now. He stumbled over and wrapped his arms around me. "And after all this . . . I don't deserve it, truly."

Completely regretting this turn of events, I tried to backpedal.

"I mean, if you can't accept it, that's fine, I'll just—"

"No, I'll take it," Gaspar interrupted, hurriedly scooting the potion away from my end of the table and to the side he'd been sitting at. "And I am extremely grateful."

"Don't mention it . . ." I said.

As I stepped out into the streets of Machus City, I shook my head. If my stupid Abilities hadn't been acting all shitty, I would have known what that thing was. I never would have parted with it if I'd known it'd be the equivalent of winning a magical lottery. A sparkling, golden ticket to Willy Wonka's chocolate factory, if ol' Willy was super into conjuring up mysterious magical items and then leaving them in some lich-infested Zelda dungeon for an idiot to find.

In retrospect, I had assumed that the bottle was likely something dangerous—considering I couldn't read its details—you know, something that would almost assuredly end up maiming me. Or, worse, killing me, as things often did. But nope, this time the dumb asscrack of a universe decided to switch things up. Of course it wasn't an instrument of my violent and hilarious demise but a priceless treasure!

I took a deep breath, feeling the distinct sting of regret. It was kind of like getting a tattoo of your favorite band, only for them to break up a week later. Which—coincidentally—almost happened to me with Every Time I Die. But hey, what's done was done. I'd handed over that rags-to-riches Skill Potion to Gaspar without a second thought, transforming him from your average Joe to Regaia's Elon Musk. I mean, if the guy started launching . . . twogs, or whatever, into space and pretending to be some kind of super genius, you'll know I wasn't exaggerating.

But dwelling on it wasn't going to get me anywhere, was it? Regret is like an unhinged MLM boss babe who keeps sending you friend requests on social media. Best to hit Ignore and move on. So, as much as I loved wallowing in my own self-pity, there were bigger fish to fry and more immediate threats to grapple with.

For instance: I had mysteries to unravel, a shit-ton of information to decode, and a chaotic jigsaw puzzle that Regaia seemed hell-bent on tossing at me. Like, why on earth would a seemingly random bartender from this city be coerced into an attempt on my life? It's not like I had a habit of stiffing serving staff or anything. Also, why had my System messages started acting all shitty? And the real brain-bender, why the hell was I . . .

I paused, my internal rant hitting a sudden snag. The wheels were turning, the gears clicking into place. I thought that, in a rare move, I might be beginning to see the bigger picture here.

Both of them were from this city, and *one* of them happened to be nearby to kill me. But why not just choose someone from Tallr—er, Karepalea?

Unless whoever it was actually wanted me here . . .

Oh.

I froze in the middle of the bustling street, a chill running up my spine as a terrifying realization washed over me. The fucked-up messages. Curly's ominous threats. The weird comment from the messenger orb. The random murder Quest. The threads of suspicion wove together, forming a disquieting picture.

What if it was *the System* that was out to get me? Not just through the life-threatening trials and tribulations, the waves of monstrous foes, or the perilous journeys. No, what if it had gone a step further and added a personal touch to its apparent sadism, turning innocent beings into its unwitting pawns?

This thought hung over me like a storm cloud as I peered down the road, the raucous laughter and cheerful chatter of the townsfolk fading to a dull hum. Then I saw it. My Jeopardy Hunch was kicking in, gnawing at the edges of my brain. Nothing flat-out urgent, but definitely imminent.

Approaching was a group of individuals that made the regular city folk look like a bunch of frolicking puppies. Ten people—gruff, towering, and seemingly carved out of stone. Their armor clanged with each heavy step they took, the sound matching the rhythm of my rapidly beating heart. Gleaming weapons were hung at their hips or slung across their backs. Their eyes, cold and calculated, were set on one thing. One person. Me.

Their forward march was a tightening noose. But I wasn't the helpless raging boy from my past life. I was Loon, motherfuckers—the orc Barbarian turned Frenzied Saboteur. The goddamn survivor. I wasn't going down without a fight. And if the System was behind this, I was going to give it a show to remember.

I reached into my pack, finding the objects I needed, and then quickly replaced it on my back under my cloak.

"Looks like it's going to be a party," I muttered to myself, grinning despite the impending danger. After all, nothing gets the blood pumping like a good old-fashioned *tussle*.

Taking a deep breath, I let the familiar warmth of anger surge through me. I cracked my knuckles and flexed my muscles, the silent promise of a brutal confrontation hanging in the air. The System may have orchestrated this dance, but it was high fuckin' time I picked the tune.

And so, I squared my shoulders, my eyes never leaving the approaching group. For whoever they were, and for whatever reason they were there, one thing was clear.

"Well . . . this is going to get messy."

CHAPTER THIRTY-SIX

BODY IMPROVEMENT CLUB

The leader of the approaching group, looking like he'd just walked out of a gritty Western but stuck in a fantasy setting, halted a few feet away from me. That mustache of his alone was an affront to the gods, like a caterpillar had crawled up and died on his upper lip. He was wearing a motley of leathers and belts and had a really shitty haircut.

Man, these motherfuckers need to get themselves a Sports Clips.

"You there," he growled, pointing a gnarled finger in my direction. "You come with us. Now."

I raised an eyebrow.

"Whoa there! Excuse me, Handlebar? I'm going to let you rewind that hot sass and come at me a bit more friendly-like. You think you can just . . . what? Roll up on some guy and demand he follows you? What am I, a stray dog you found on the street?"

His eyes narrowed to slits, clearly not appreciating the expert humor with which I was delivering this barb.

"You think this is a fucking joke? I've got ten men here ready to make you very, *very* sorry."

"Sorry?" I laughed, letting my amusement show. "Sorry, like . . . how you must feel every morning when you look in the mirror and see that haircut? Or are we talking about a different kind of sorry? Like, 'Sorry to bother you, Mr. Orc; I'm just a big dumb asshole with a goofy fuckin' face and shitty attitude, and I can't help but be a little bit of a crimped ball hair when I interact with people, because nobody ever explained to me that with the way that I look, I should be grateful for anyone, let alone *you*, to interact with me?' That kind of *sorry*?"

One of the armored behemoths behind him snickered, which earned him a deadly glare from the old man.

"Sababo and Carmichael," I said with an exaggerated sigh, feigning exhaustion. "You know, I'm beginning to think they just enjoy sending me on wild fucking goose chases. First, they tell me to come to this . . . this oversized sapphire playpen, and now *this*. And by the way, who are you supposed to be? His brooding majesty of mustache mountain?"

The leader's face reddened, but he forced a twisted grin.

"You got a fuckin' mouth on you, orc. It'll be a pleasure shutting it for you. You come with us, or—"

"—we'll do this the hard way?" I interrupted, smirking with my triumphant ability to beat every goon in this whole world to the punch on their contrived dialogue cues.

"No," he said. "Or we'll fucking kill you."

"Well, that was unexpected," I said.

"You've got three seconds to decide."

I smirked, feigning contemplation.

"Hm. Tough call. What're your kidnapping benefits?"

"What?"

"Well . . ." I said, adopting a more relaxed stance than I felt. "You know, am I due anything if I let you guys take me along? Like . . . free health, dental, a quarterly pizza party rather than a raise? Usual shit."

"Time's up," the man barked.

"Well, jeez," I said. "At least tell me who's taking me. I like to know a few interesting facts about people before I go off with them. Listen, I'll start—"

"Ah, fuck this," the man said. "Kill him."

Nine individuals drew their weapons at once.

Uh-oh, looks like things are going to pop off early in this joi—

"By the Archon's boiled bulge!" a voice rang out from behind me. "What in the eighty hells of Galekra are the gods-damned Echoes doing here?"

Echoes? These guys? Damn, Curly Sue is really serious about this shit, I guess.

I turned, not sure what to expect, and . . . got exactly that: confusion. As soon as I saw who approached, I was instantly reminded of Crowmoon.

A group of eight individuals emerged from an alleyway. Their sheer muscularity made the average bodybuilder look like a cardboard cutout of a starvation victim. Seriously, I was pretty sure they had muscles in places I didn't even know existed—even their goddamn *hair* looked swole to shit. It was like someone had thrown a bunch of boulders in humanoid form together and decided, "Yeah, that's good enough."

The first was an elf, her long silver hair cascading down a back that was more ripped than the page of a heavily used cookbook. One side of her face was covered in a burn scar that looked like a sprawling city map, if the city was made of pure pain. The second, some kind of creature with golden scales, had horn-like protrusions on his forehead, and eyes like shimmering rubies. His right arm, or rather the lack thereof, showcased a heavily scarred stump, remnants of a nasty burn.

Each one of them looked as though they'd bench-press a house for fun, their bulging biceps straining against the fabric of their clothing and armor. Every member had visible burns, like they had all decided to have a barbecue and the grill pit exploded. Or they'd tried to take a group selfie with a dragon—either one, really.

"For fuck's sake . . . it's the fucking *Tides*," Handlebar grumbled, his face scrunching like he'd bitten into a sour fruit.

Ah. Now that makes more sense, I thought. *This is Crowmoon's former posse. So . . . they're all just a super fucking jacked-out-of-control cult? Muscle worship, indeed.*

The elven woman stepped forward until she and her group were about fifty feet from the other crew, her red eyes sharp and piercing. I'd never seen *West Side Story*, but I think I was about to get a peek at a really bloody reimagining.

"Grell!" she called out. "What the hell do you want with the orc?"

"Stay out of Echoes' business, Dulcimer. This doesn't concern the Tides," the mustachioed leader—Grell—shot back, sneering.

"It does when you're about to kidnap someone in our territory," the golden-scaled man chimed in, the slight echo in his voice making it clear he was something quite magical indeed. I didn't recognize his species, but I was more curious about why his voice sounded like he was speaking into a bathroom vent.

"You think you're still in control here, eh?" Grell sneered, pointing at the new arrivals. "This orc's coming with us. Official business."

The Tides let out a collective chuckle, showcasing their impressive sets of abs and pectorals in the process. It was like watching mountains ripple.

"Did we interrupt your knitting circle, Atticus?" a third Tide, a woman with dark blue skin, tentacle-like hair, and deep burn marks down her left side, teased.

A fourth Tide, a minotaur with sleek black fur and a burn on one of his massive horns, added, "Or are you just upset we didn't invite you to the show?"

I was losing track of which muscly fantasy stereotype I should be paying attention to. So, I, trying to not be the weakest link in this overly muscular chain, added my own color commentary.

"Guys, guys, let's all calm down. No need for anyone to flex their issues out here. Maybe we can just sit down, have a cup of tea, and discuss our exercise regimens?"

There was a momentary pause as both groups turned to stare at me. Apparently, that wasn't the comedic relief they were expecting.

The elven woman from the Tides smirked.

"He's funny. I like him."

"Yeah, well, he's still coming with us," Grell-slash-Atticus-slash-Handlebar insisted.

"I was actually thinking of just, you know, not going with anyone," I tried to interject, but it seemed no one was listening to the potential kidnappee.

Both groups were sizing each other up, and the tension was palpable. It was like being stuck in the middle of a dance-off between the Rock and a hard place.

"Alright, listen here," Dulcimer began, placing her hands on her ample hips. "If we're doing this whole tug-of-war thing, I just wanna know why you Echoes lot want the orc. He doesn't exactly scream *High-Value Target*."

Grell snorted.

"Our business is ours alone. He's got something we want. I'm not in the habit of swapping trade secrets with the likes of a bunch of burnt-faced fuck-nothings who worship a fuckin' *concept*."

"Oh, really?" Dulcimer raised an eyebrow, clearly intrigued. "Something *you* want, you say? You mean something *she* wants, right? Your icy mistress is really the one who runs your bootlace operation."

"We've all got our fucking masters, Dulcimer—yours just happens to be imaginary."

"Well, at least we just serve the one," Dulcimer continued. "Not trying to juggle multiple figureheads. The Archgeneral know you're here cheating on him?"

"Heard you joined up with the Sovereign," Grell said, ignoring the apparent insult that was way beyond my ability to understand. "How's that unfolding for you?"

"Splendid, actually," Dulcimer said.

"Yeah, a whole lot of the miserable fucks are dead—exactly as we planned," the gold-skinned man bellowed.

Dulcimer wheeled on him.

"Buisine!" she shouted. "We're *also* not in the habit of sharing trade secrets, remember?"

"Sorry, marm," Buisine said. "Forgot, is all."

"I haven't got time for this," Grell snapped. "We got places to be, and we're *taking* the *orc!*"

"Well, here's a fun bit of information for you, heeler-dog," Dulcimer said, cracking her knuckles. "He's got something we want, too."

"Oh, yeah? What's that?" Grell asked, a hint of skepticism in his voice.

"Entertainment," the tentacle-haired woman said, laughing. "It's been ages since we've had someone to lighten the mood."

I gulped, suddenly very conscious of my current value as a jester.

"He's a fucking weakling," Grell said, gesturing at me.

"Hey!" I shouted back, but my voice cracked, so I only proved his point.

"What the fuck could *you* lot need him for?"

"We've got potions that can get him up to speed," Buisine offered, wiggling his fingers to produce a glowing vial of something that looked like liquefied rainbows.

Dulcimer slugged his arm and he nearly dropped the vial.

"Put that away, you numbskull," she said.

"Sorry, marm."

Grell scoffed.

"Wait, you want him to fucking *join* you? Well, that is about as revolting as your like's fascination with gaining mass. He's worthless. Low-Level foreign scum."

I frowned.

"Yo! I'll have you know I worked very hard for my Level, thank you very fucking much!"

"Oh, did you, now? All by yourself?" a feline-looking woman from the Tides said, looking me up and down with amusement. Her burn scars decorated her arms like sleeves.

Grell, feeling the weight of this standoff, finally gestured to one of his men—a hulking brute, armored head to toe.

"Enough banter. Angus, grab the orc!"

As if the weight of his armor was no more than tissue paper, Angus dashed forward with alarming speed, reaching me in the blink of an eye. Before I knew it, I was hoisted off the ground, the straps across my clavicle digging into my flesh.

I barely had time to register the situation, my feet dangling, my eyes darting between the two very angry, very muscular groups.

"Hate to have to do this to kin," Angus said, his heavily accented deep voice resonating inside his helm.

Kin?

I squinted, peering as best I could into the visor of the man holding me. I caught a glimpse of green skin and dark eyes.

Is he . . . an orc? Well . . . shit.

"I'm going to be honest with *you*, then, Angus," I said, rotating a few objects in my hands. "I hate to do *this* to kin."

"Do wh—"

"NINJA VANISH!" I roared, and slammed the red Hexahedron of Hazards right into the open lip of his visor.

BOOM!

I flew backward as Angus the orc's helmet exploded, the metal blasting apart in various directions like shrapnel. One chunk shot into my arm, and I winced as I fell ten feet away, landing hard on the cobblestones. I looked back at Angus as his headless body suddenly crumpled to the ground.

"What the fu—" I heard someone yell, but I hadn't waited. Their cry of confusion was cut off as I activated all remaining eight red detonation cubes.

The world erupted into chaos. Explosions boomed like a concert of percussion instruments gone mad. Dust and debris filled the air, turning the cobblestone street into a cacophony of blinding smoke and thundering destruction.

As I scrambled to my feet, wiping the dirt from my face, I took a split second to marvel at the wreckage around me. Bodies and pieces of bodies littered the ground, blown apart by the intensity of the explosives. The once-intimidating Echoes and Tides looked more like ragdolls in a landfill.

Thank all that's magical for those newly Leveled-Up Skills, I thought to myself. *Plus my Misdirection Ability. That super helped.*

Added to that was the fact that my Knowledge of Ignition and Sabotage were really pairing nicely with the flavors of my ultra-high-frequency Sneaking Skill at that moment.

I'd taken advantage of the dipshits as they'd distracted themselves with arguing. I waited for an opportunity and then I struck, scattering the cubes to the wind like caltrops and waiting for the right moment to activate them.

Come on. You didn't think I could remain that silent for that long while people were talking shit about me for no reason, did you?

Gritting my teeth, I scampered toward the nearest alley, my heart pounding against my ribs. I needed to find a way out of this mess and regroup, plan my next move. The stakes had just gone up, and I wasn't entirely sure how I felt about that. Smoke and fire and screams were everywhere. Fortunately, the street had been empty save for the really terrible abductors and their sizable egos.

As I was about to round a corner, I heard a shout and the unmistakable thud of heavy boots. I froze, looking back, and saw Dulcimer dashing toward me. Shit! Even in the midst of absolute chaos, the muscular elf still had her wits about her—and she was fast.

Panic welled up in my chest. Spotting an eave above, I lunged, desperately trying to scramble up to safety. I almost made it, too—until I felt a powerful grip on my ankle.

I squealed—a very un-orc-like sound—as I found myself hanging precariously, my fingers clutching at the edge. Dulcimer was holding onto my leg with one hand. I kicked and flailed, but it was akin to a child throwing a tantrum.

"Nice try, orc," she said, clearly enjoying herself. "But you're not escaping that easily."

I swatted at her with my free foot, managing only to make my position look even more pathetic. My kicks were more like annoying nudges, and I could hear a few snickers from the few survivors of the explosions.

"Come on, Dulcimer! Give a guy a break, will ya?" I begged, my voice sounding way too high-pitched for my liking. She responded by shaking me a bit, making my grip on the eave loosen.

"I don't believe that's a good idea, as tricky as you are—nice work with the explosions, by the by—but you. Will. Be. Coming. With. Me."

Not knowing what else to do, I very quickly released with one hand and slipped my festival cap on my head. Instantly, the goo began to flow, and I laughed as her grip slipped off of me. I started to climb again, but that was when Dulcimer jumped up and snatched the hat down. I was instantly choked, straining against the pull as the string keeping the hat secured—usually—was now a garrote around my Adam's apple.

"Gkluk!" I choked.

I felt myself slip and I tumbled to the ground. Dulcimer caught me in her strong, muscle-mommy arms bride-style, and I looked up at her sheepishly.

"I warned you," I said. Then I moved to slam a different cube—the silver ensnaring one—right into her chest. But she caught my wrist a millimeter away from her torso and squeezed.

"GAAAAH!" I roared, dropping the cube, and it plunked to the ground.

"You're coming with me, orc," she said.

"Lemme go," I hissed.

"No," she said simply.

"Fine," I said. "But I bite."

I activated Biter.

With all the strength I had, I clamped down on her wrist, the daggers in my mouth piercing right into her flesh. She screamed but didn't release me, so I bit again. Harder. Blood gushed into my mouth and I began chomping through her goddamn brachial radius. I felt her hit me, but I locked my jaws like a nanny dog and held on. I felt another fist, and saw a flash as my Bone Warrior Boon activated. My Health began to drop, but I didn't care. I was going to make her regret ever thinking she could toss me in a sack and make off into the night. Her fist hit me in the face this time, and . . . well, *that* fuckin' hurt. My bones didn't break but my right eye suddenly stopped working.

She kept punching, and now I was starting to lose consciousness. But I still wasn't letting go.

As my vision blurred, the cacophony of the war-torn streets became indistinct. I could feel the cold grip of unconsciousness crawling its way into my battered skull. Each of Dulcimer's blows landed like thunderclaps, echoing in my ears. It felt like it might be over for me, like the dark embrace of oblivion was just moments away.

Suddenly, a sharp *thunk* snapped through the air, piercing the haze of pain. Dulcimer froze, a look of surprise and pain painting her usually defiant face. Another *thunk* followed and her grasp on me weakened. As she stumbled back, I saw the shaft of wood jutting out from her collarbone, its wicked point glistening with her crimson blood.

Before I could comprehend what was happening, another bolt flew from the mists, embedding itself deep into Dulcimer's chest. She let out a raspy gasp, and, with her grip slackened, I fell from her embrace, landing hard on the rubble-strewn ground. My body ached from the impacts, but the overwhelming drive to survive overrode the pain.

From the obscuring veil of smoke and chaos, a figure emerged. The haze seemed to part in slow motion, revealing a tall, imposing silhouette. The wide brim of a hat, the unmistakable sheen of leathers, and the swish of a long cloak. The stranger held a weapon, a . . . Was that a fucking *rifle?*

No, as they stepped closer, I discerned it wasn't a gun but a crossbow—a masterfully crafted one, its mechanisms intricate and deadly.

The figure had an aura of a gunslinger from an old Western novel. Time seemed to warp, slowing to a crawl as the stranger fired again. Another bolt shot through the air with deadly precision, striking Dulcimer, who was already reeling from her previous wounds.

As the smoke cleared further, I squinted, trying to recognize the face under the hat. My heart leaped in my chest. It was a face marred by years of battles, scars etched deep, and a gray beard flowing down a rugged chin.

It was . . . Virgil!

He lives! Holy shit! This is amazing!

Dulcimer, weakened and with bolts protruding from her body, stared down at her injuries, her usual confidence replaced by shock and disbelief. I noticed something black crawling up from where the bolts had punctured her flesh. It looked fuckin' gnarly. But her gaze quickly shifted, locking on to Virgil with a mix of hatred and fear.

"Poison!" she hissed, clutching her wounded wrist.

Virgil simply smirked, slowly reloading his crossbow.

"Looks like you done bitten off more'n you can chew, elf."

"You . . ." she said, weakly, but then whatever was in those fucking bolts finally got her and she collapsed.

I stared, one good eye trying hard to focus on my savior. It was fucking Virgil—the Sojourner who'd died helping defend against Ocho in the Crypt. He was *there*?

"Virgil . . ." I mumbled.

"Don't waste yourself on mutterin's," he said calmly, then he rolled two glass bottles toward me. Potions. One was green, and the other was . . . *Fuck*, it was the rainbow-colored one that the golden-skinned guy had been taunting with. The Leveling potion . . .

"Drink 'em," Virgil said, his eyes scanning the smoke. "Then we gotta git. Ain't a place to be loiterin' and allowing our easy victory to turn to hard-won."

". . . where?" I murmured.

"You let ol' Virgil worry 'bout that, colt," he said. "Now, take them there potions and let's giddyup."

I smirked—I think—and did as he said. Feeling warmth flow through me as I drank the green bottle first. My Health shot back up to full and then grew a little further with a golden edge to it.

"Fuck!" I roared as all of my pain instantly evaporated. "What the fuck, man; I—"

"Take the other an' let's get to it," he said.

I shrugged, cracked the top, and glugged the other one down. Immediately, my body began to vibrate with a golden glow. My System was worthless, but the marquee above me was loud and clear.

Gained 350,000 Experience!
Congratulations! You have reached Level 25!

I quivered.

Three-hundred and fifty thousand *experience? Level Twenty-five? Is this for friggin' real?*

I almost slammed all my Points home right there but knew we had to scoot, so I stood finally and looked to Virgil.

"Where are we going?"

"Somewhere safe," he said.

"Where's that?"

"A . . . person I know."

"You leavin' it a fucking mystery or you gonna spill along the way?"

"Name's Monty," Virgil said before giving me a weighing glance. "And I reckon you two are gon' like each other."

CHAPTER THIRTY-SEVEN

THE FULL MONTY

My first impression was that the place was like an armory on steroids. Piled in heaps, hung on walls, dangling from the ceiling—weapons were strewn all over the damn place. Axes, swords, daggers, spears, even a few magical-looking staves, you name it. It was quite the little jaunt from where we'd been, but it had, in all honesty, only taken about ten minutes to get there. We'd ducked through alleys and even climbed a couple of roofs, but it seemed like we'd be well out of the way of anyone trying to find us for the time being.

"Sit tight," Virgil said, disappearing into the back, leaving me to my own devices.

I was busy eyeing a mace that looked like it could knock the wind out of an ocean liner when Virgil returned. Suddenly, a voice shattered the quiet hum of the shop. It was twangy, grating, and filled with more spirit than a hummingbird on Adderall.

"Well, holy hot harpy tits! Look at the pair we got here!"

Out from the back room, a small creature scurried toward us. Then he hopped up to stand on top of his counter, peering out with a sense of authority. My first thought was that he was some kind of alabaster gargoyle. His skin was deathly pale, eyes wide and wild, and the energy around him was palpable. I watched as the big, bat-like ears on either side of his head moved seemingly of their own accord.

"Welcome to the finest shitshow in town! Virgil, you lazy, wrinkled-forehead-havin' fuck, you've brought company," the creature—Monty, I supposed—declared, throwing an arm around Virgil's shoulders from his position standing atop his counter. "And I see you've brought a disco ball with you."

I blinked, glancing down at the shimmering roe splotches on my skin, and couldn't help but chuckle.

"You mean you don't see many spotted orcs around these parts?"

Monty cackled, slapping his knee.

"Fuck, no! Most of the orcs I see are more scared of a bath than a blade. But you, you're a new kind of fucked-up!"

Virgil let out a long-suffering sigh.

"Oh, relax, Virgil—I'm just makin' friends over here." He leaned forward in a stage whisper to me. "He's just all fuckin' bothered that I got more juice than he does."

"Juice?" I asked.

"Yeah, homeboy! Rizz, charm, animal magnetism. Whatever you call it, I got it, and this sack of donkey balls over here can't help but be jealous."

Just based on this exceptionally brief interaction with him, I knew that Monty had to be some kind of Sojourner. He had a coarse sort of Southern accent that made me think he was likely from somewhere in Georgia or the Carolinas originally. He was rude, crude, and a tiny dude. Virgil was right—I liked him.

"And what, pray tell," I said, leaning against the counter, "is this place exactly?"

Monty stood as tall as he could, puffing out his chest.

"Welcome, my leopard-fucked orc friend, to Monty's Murder Emporium! The best place to find things that can poke, slash, and smash!"

I laughed, looking around at the haphazardly arranged weaponry.

"Murder Emporium, huh?"

"Damn straight!" Monty boasted, a broad grin spreading across his face. "Every piece you see here, I've procured. Traveled all over the realms, collecting weapons from the fiercest fighters, the craftiest blacksmiths, and the most cunning lady magicians."

He placed two fingers over his mouth and wiggled his tongue between them in an appallingly vulgar gesture. Then he seemed to get bored and picked up a sinister-looking dagger, its blade gleaming dangerously.

"This here? From the hidden city of Elantris. Pure elven steel. And that mace you were eye-fuckin' earlier? Straight from the mines of Kurakar, worked by the dwarf king's own smith. He was a fuckin' jackoff, but that didn't stop me from stompin' his dick in at cards."

I gazed around the shop with newfound respect. This tiny, pale creature was no ordinary shopkeeper. He was a collector, a trader, a curator of death-dealing implements. Despite his rough exterior, there was a certain charm about him, a kind of bawdy humor that was surprisingly infectious.

"Got anything for more stealth-oriented folks?"

"Shit! You roguin', orc-boy? Well, not to fear. Right this way, my spotty friend!" Monty declared, his eyes gleaming with mischief. He wove his way through the disarrayed assortment of weapons, his short legs moving with surprising speed.

He led me to a wickedly sharp dagger with a handle made of bone.

"This baby was yanked right out of an illisinaf necromancer's grasp. You ever seen one o' those things?"

I smirked.

"Yeah, in fact, more regularly than I would like."

"I'm talking about necromancers, not the damn . . . magic-booger people," Monty said. Then he looked me up and down with a scowl. "Naw, you ain't seen no necromancers."

I liked him, but he was going to have to stop giving me the once-over before I clocked him.

"Anyway, this fuckin' thing," Monty said, gesturing to the cruel-looking blade. "It cuts, it stabs, and it can summon a bony hand to choke the fuckin' life out of your enemies. I call it the Boner."

We browsed a few more wares, with Monty showcasing his lewd wit before I got bored and decided to push things forward a bit more.

"Alright, enough with the tour. Why the fuck are we here?" I asked, turning to Virgil. Before he could answer, Monty cut in.

"Slow your fuckin' roll there, big boy! No need to get your shorts in a bunch," he said, waving a dismissive hand. "There are only two reasons why Virgil would drag someone into my emporium. One is because he's a damn fuckwit with the brains of a turkey's ass, and two is because he needs a place to lay low."

He paused, looking me over once again.

"And judging by the confused look on your face, it ain't the first."

"How the hell did you—" I began, but Monty steamrolled right over me.

"Don't look so surprised, dalmatian orc. You ain't exactly blending in with the crowd," Monty said, a wicked glint in his eye. "You're a Sojourner, ain't ya?"

I was taken aback. Not many people in this world could spot a Sojourner on sight.

"What gave . . ."

But Monty just laughed, slapping his knee again.

"Ha! Your face! Look at you, all shocked and shit. Don't be so flabbergasted. Ain't the first Sojourner to pass through here, and you sure as hell won't be the last."

"But how—" I began, but Monty held up a hand.

"I keep an eye on the System, friend," he explained, his expression serious for the first time. "Noticed it's been acting a bit wonky in the last day or so. Been glitches, hiccups, the lot. I'd wager that's the sort of problem you're dealing with, eh?"

I stared at Monty, my mind racing. For all his jests and jibes, it seemed there was more to this guy than met the eye. More importantly, it seemed we'd come to the right place.

"Alright, Monty," I said, meeting his gaze. "Let's talk."

The jingle of the bell above the door suddenly interrupted us as it echoed throughout the shop, heralding the arrival of yet another motley crew. This time it was a band of humans, their cloaks worn and tattered, faces obscured by hoods.

Monty, apparently, recognized them instantly.

"Oh, *hell*, no!" Monty exclaimed, slamming the blade down on the counter. "If it isn't the Brotherhood of Bullshitters. I remember you piss stains. Thought you could just waltz back in here after ripping me off, huh?"

The hooded figures shifted uncomfortably, their leader stepping forward.

"Monty, we made amends for that. Paid you back in full, remember? We're here for a new set of weapons."

Monty was now leaning against his counter, arms crossed.

"Amends? Romulus, you dumbfuck, you paid me back in leprechaun gold. That shit disappeared faster than my hopes and dreams after opening this shop. You owe me, you sack of rat shit."

Romulus seemed taken aback.

"Monty, we—"

"Oh, save your breath," Monty interrupted, wagging a finger at them. "I've heard more convincing lies from a two-headed ogre selling snake oil. You think I'm as stupid as you look?"

Romulus tried again.

"We truly didn't—"

"Didn't what?" Monty exploded, his voice echoing around the shop. "Didn't think I'd notice? You think just because I sell weapons, I don't know when I'm being screwed? I've got more brains in my left nut than the lot of you combined!"

His tirade brought an uncomfortable silence. Romulus cleared his throat.

"We'll pay in real gold this time, Monty."

"Oh, 'real gold' this time, huh, Romulus?" Monty sneered. "Is it from the same fucking charlatan bog witch that said your wife's coming back? Or did you just scrape it off the streets of the goddamn Yellow Brick Road?"

Another pause.

"It's genuine, Monty. We've got a dragon's hoard."

Monty laughed, a loud, barking sound.

"A dragon's hoard! Oh, you *sly dogs*! I guess I should be grateful it's not a fuckin' . . . magic beanstalk this time!"

Romulus extended a bag filled with golden coins.

"Inspect them yourself."

Monty seized the bag and emptied its contents on the counter, squinting at the coins. After a moment of inspection, he scoffed.

"These better not turn into chocolate coins, Romulus, or I'll hunt you down and turn your ass into a coin purse."

He eyed the man carefully, then lurched forward quickly but didn't move. Romulus, I guess, flinched.

"Ha! Look at that, ya fuckin' . . . scaredy cat-ass fuckin' bitch. That's right; you know who's in charge here. Tell me who's in charge, Romulus."

"I don't—"

"Tell me who's in charge, you dumb human asshole, or you can say goodbye to me ever selling you weapons again. *And* I'm gonna run my pretty fuckin' mouth to every other weapons dealer in this motherfuckin' shitty . . . shithole and tell them you losers aren't to be trusted. You're lucky I kept my lips shut this long. You should be thanking me for my discretion. Now say it."

Romulus looked at the ground bashfully, then quietly, he spoke.

". . . you're in charge, Mon—"

"What?!" he shouted, leaning forward. "I can't hear you—take off that stupid hood. You think you're a fuckin' Jedi or something?"

Monty yanked down the hood, showing Romulus's bald head.

"You're in charge, Monty," he said, louder.

"That's right—I'm in charge, bitch. Don't rip me off again or I will pop you in the mouth. I got a hickory branch back behind this counter, and I will tear your ass up with it if you try any of that noise on me or the other vendors."

He lurched forward again and Romulus flinched again.

"Ha!" Monty razzed. "Now, come back later; I've got guests and you're turning their stomach."

"But—"

"Nah, Romulus." Monty cut him off, shaking his head with a wild grin on his face. "This ain't a fuckin' free country. This is *Monty Town*. The only vote that counts in here is mine, and I'm voting your dumb ass out. So, why don't you turn those tattered capes around and take a long walk off a short cliff, you dipshit fuckin' Darth Vader wannabe."

"But, Monty, we have—"

"Romulus, get your sorry ass out of my shop before I kick it so hard, you'll be coughing up boot laces!"

His harsh words sent Romulus and his merry band of misfits scurrying out, tripping over each other in their haste to leave. Monty's peals of laughter echoed behind them.

"See that? That's the power of persuasion, my friends," Monty said, puffing out his chest as he turned to us. "Just a little something I picked up while . . . doing whatever the fuck it is I do. Now, where were we?"

"You was jawin' about the System," Virgil reminded him.

"Right, right, the System." Monty nodded, getting back to the task at hand. "Well, I've been monitoring it, and let me tell you, that motherfucker's got more issues with balance than an uphill goat."

Virgil gave him a questioning look.

"Goats is good at balancing."

"Goddamn, Virgil, that's mountain goats," Monty corrected him, rolling his eyes. "You can't apply the rules of a mountain goat to no normal goat; that's like comparing a shark to a goldfish. Both can swim, but one will rip your ass apart. Anyway, the System. It's acting up, but we'll get it sorted."

"How?" I asked. "You got a set of brass knuckles or something? Gonna pound it into submission?"

"Bet I could," Monty boasted. "But, naw, junior. Ain't all that."

He looked me up and down, then turned to Virgil.

"You trust him?"

Virgil shrugged.

"I trust him to keep his mouth pinned, if that's what you're pokin' at."

"Good enough for me!" Monty declared. Then he waved me toward the back room. "Alright, orc—what did you say your name was?"

"Loon," I said.

"Fuck, that's a fuckin' *name*." Monty chuckled. "Alright, *Loon*. You ready to have your brain blown out your dickhole?"

"Monty . . ." I said, staring at the tiny creature. "You are both literally and figuratively speaking my language."

Monty laughed.

"I like you, Loon." Then he waved me over again. "Come on, then!"

Without another word, I crossed the threshold into the darkness of the back room.

CHAPTER THIRTY-EIGHT

THE HARM-ORY

As we stepped through, I felt the ambient magic in the air thicken, like wading into an unseen swamp. A room, more cavernous than I would have imagined the shop could hold, unfolded before us.

What greeted us was not an armory but a grand exhibition of the arcane. Strange devices and curiosities dotted the room, gleaming under the sporadic flash of magical lights. In the center stood a massive structure that I took for a workbench, but it was more altar than anything—cluttered with an array of arcane objects and, at the heart of it, a gigantic crystal that pulsed with an ethereal glow.

"Well, would you fuckin' look at that?" I said, smirking. "Monty's got a secret garden. Virgil, did we just step into a Harry Potter movie set or what?"

"The hell is a Harry Potter?" Monty grumbled, but his attention was on the crystal, his fingers dancing along its surface, sparks flickering at his touch.

I raised an eyebrow.

"You got all this just stowed away in the back? And you're selling axes upfront?"

Monty laughed, a wild, gleeful sound that bounced around the room.

"Hey, not everyone can handle the big toys. And besides, some of these doohickeys are more trouble than they're worth. Can you believe I found this place like this? Sure, I had to build a shop on top of it, but all the framework was there. Best day of my life when that happened."

As he said this, something in the corner of the room started flashing wildly, sending neon lights dancing across the walls. Monty barely looked at it.

"Don't worry about that. It's just the fuckin' magimetric alarm. It goes off whenever it detects a high level of foreign energy. Ain't used to having three Sojourners in the mix."

I sighed, shaking my head.

"Goddamn, this is a fucking *setup*, Monty. I like the whole tech-wizard thing you got going on."

Monty glanced back at me with a smug grin, leaning back against his workbench.

"Damn straight."

Suddenly, the sound of rumbling machinery filled the room, followed by a rush of steam from the far wall. A panel slid open, revealing an array of magical gear.

"This here is the Big Boy Corner. Out there is what I picked up off dirtbags and the like. In here is what I *make*. We've got battle robes that can turn invisible, boots that let you walk on walls, fuckin' underpants that make you invulnerable . . . you name it. I even got an enchanted cock ring that'll make you piss yourself."

He shrugged.

"That one's a work in progress."

My eyes widened as I took it all in. There was an almost childlike glee that came over me, but it was quickly replaced with a frown.

"And I suppose all this stuff comes at a price."

Monty just shrugged again.

"Well, no shit. What? You think I just give this stuff away?"

I sighed again, knowing that this wouldn't be as easy as I'd hoped. But before I could say anything, Virgil spoke up.

"What's needed's needed, Monty. You're abreast o' the situation we're in."

Monty looked over at Virgil, his eyebrows raised in mock surprise.

"Well, hell, Virgil. Who are you and what have you done with the tight-assed old man I know?"

Virgil rolled his eyes.

"We'll figure out the payment later. For now, let's focus on getting what we came here for done."

Monty nodded, moving over to one of the shelves.

"Fine, fine. Just remember, Virgil, my goodwill ain't free."

Virgil leaned back against the wall.

"When's it ever been, Monty?"

I could only stand there, watching as the two of them bickered back and forth. It was clear that despite their differences, there was a deep respect between them.

"Well, alright, then," Monty said, turning to face me. "Let's get you suited up, spotty."

"I'm getting armor?" I asked, shocked.

"Fuck, no!" Monty said, producing a wide-brimmed hat from . . . somewhere, that didn't look all that dissimilar from Virgil's. "Listen, I said I'd help with the System—but I gotta see what the damage is before I go dolin' out my goods for the goddamn world to have. Now put on this stupid little hat and let's get started."

"Started? With . . . fuckin' what?"

"Analysis, junior!" Monty spat. "Just put it on."

I scowled and took the offered cap, placing it on my head.

"This thing better not sort me into Hufflepuff," I said.

"Yeah, well, you start huffin' and puffin', I'm gonna strap your ass down," Monty said. "You need to be still, so don't fuckin' move. This thing is temperamental. You go wiggling like a fuckin' worm, and it's gonna blast your teeth outta your fuckin' grin."

I decided that, in the interest of science, I would not move.

After a moment of staring me up and down, Monty walked over to a device on the wall and pressed his hand on it. It lit up and I suddenly felt a warm sensation move through my body.

"It tickles," I said.

"Oh, by the way, Virgil," Monty said. "Your pals contacted me. They're gonna hop a portal as soon as they can and swing this way."

I froze. *Pals?*

Virgil gave me a look, then turned back to Monty.

"We can jaw about that later," he said, pointing a thumb at me. "This 'un here's invested in them near as much as me."

Does he mean—

"Jes and Frida?!" I shouted, and then felt a sharp, burning stab as the warm sensation turned aggressive.

"Gah!" I roared.

"I told your ass, didn't I? Now look at you," Monty said. "Probably melted your damn spleen or something. Don't move again. If I'd known that you knew 'em, I wouldn't have said anything until you weren't six inches from sundown. Just another few seconds, so hold still."

After a grueling, agonizing *twelve* seconds, the pain suddenly receded, and I yanked the hat off my head.

"Jes and Frida are coming?!"

"Easy, there," Monty said. "You heard right, but you keep yelling like that, and I'm not gonna hear right for the rest of my days. False goblin ears are sensi-tive, my young Padawan."

That stopped me in my tracks again.

"Wait . . . *you're* a false goblin?"

"Damn, your hearing's gone too, spotty," Monty said. "Yeah, I'm a false goblin; why?"

My mind wandered to my pack, where I had a whole *mess* of his people's ears just rotting away.

"No reason," I said.

"Alright, let's have a look at this," Monty said, and put the hat on his own head, his eyes drifting distantly in the way people's did when they looked at something in their menu.

"Hoo-ee," Monty exclaimed after a moment, causing me to jump.

"What?" I wondered.

"You have fucked up big time, dincha?" He pulled the hat off of his head with a grin. "Damn, son, I ain't *never* seen something like this. How the fuck did you piss off the System so bad?"

"Just part of my natural charm," I stated. "Look, can you fix it or not?"

"Fuck, no, I can't fix it!" Monty said. "Who do you think I am?"

"I don't *know* who you are, Monty—I was assuming some guy who did more than make people try on an array of dumb headwear."

"Pshaw," Monty said, waving me away.

"Did you just *say* the word *pshaw*?"

"Damn right," he said. "I'll say it again, too. Pshaw!"

"Alright," I said. "Why the fuck are we here? This is starting to piss me off. If you can't help me, then—"

"Open up them ears, numbnuts," Monty said, grinning. "I didn't say I couldn't help. Jesus, I said I couldn't *fix* it. I can bypass just about anything."

"Oh," I said. "Well . . . alright. You can bypass this?"

"You're talkin' to the greatest item crafter of all time, junior," Monty boasted proudly. "I can make whatever I want."

I snorted.

"Yeah, well, you might need to check with Bahlgus about that," I said. "Because everyone seems to think *he's* the motherfuckin' best. I've never even heard of Monty."

"Loon, who the fuck do you think you're talking to?" Monty asked, then he turned to Virgil. "Virgil, you didn't tell this fool who I was?"

"Wait, what?" I asked.

Monty turned back to me, shaking his head.

"Damn, you were in here, thinkin' I was just some regular old slouch, huh? Well, then, I wondered why you weren't falling all over yourself to kiss my toes and whatnot."

"What are you talking about?" I demanded.

"Well," Monty said. "It's just like you said. Bahlgus is the best—because I *am* Bahlgus."

"Fucking . . . what?" I muttered. I couldn't handle this level of surprise so late in the day, apparently. "But you're . . . Monty? Is that a fake name?"

"Listen to him," Monty said to Virgil and jerking a thumb at me. "All moon-eyed like a baby fuckin' duckling—"

He turned back to me.

"No, it ain't a fake name. My name is *Bahlgus Monticello*—but people 'round here call me Monty. Why did you think Romulus and his dickheads wanted back in my good graces so bad? Wasn't because I'm so fucking pretty. It's 'cuz I'm the motherfucking *shit*."

I frowned. This was not what I expected. I put a hand to the gorget around my throat.

"Why didn't you say anything then when you saw me walking in with this, then?"

"The fuck you talking about?"

"You *made* this," I said.

"Shit, brother, I don't remember all the fuckin' *nonsense* I make. I was probably high as fuck on dwarf weed when I made that. Lemme see . . ."

He got a little closer and examined it.

"A fuckin' tail pops outta that thing? Yeah, I was definitely high."

He laughed.

"This thing only takes you five hundred feet per charge? Loon, this is a piece of shit. I got a garbage you can throw that in, 'cuz it's fuckin' trash."

I was reeling. I'd been in the presence of someone who was likely the most famous person in the world, and I'd just been . . . I dunno, hanging out? I guess that actually *was* better than acting like an idiot or getting nervous or something. I don't know that my reaction would have been different had I known, but, hell, it was definitely something to consider.

"Alright, let's get back on track," I said.

"Gladly," *Bahlgus Monticello* said, still chuckling.

"First," I started, "Jes and Frida are coming *here*?"

"That's what they were saying," Monty said with a shrug. "I dunno; never met 'em. They could be liars, I guess. Said they'd get here as fast as their little tootsies could get them to a Gateway, so I'd imagine they'd be showing up shortly. Their message came through a few hours ago, and they weren't far from . . . Ah, fuck, I don't remember. But it was definitely a place with a portal."

I breathed heavily. Jes and Frida were coming here. To Machus City. This was probably not the best news. I didn't know if the prophecy or whatever was going to count them as having come along with me, but . . . well, there wasn't much I could do now, was there?

"Second," I said, "what did you learn about the System and me? I know we're not the best of buds lately—and in fact, I'm pretty sure it's been trying to kill me. But . . . *what* exactly is happening?"

"That is not as clear," Monty said, wandering over to pick up some object beyond my comprehension. "Looking at the thing, you'd think you pissed on its breakfast or something. It's hard to explain how I look at it to a *layman* like yourself . . . but basically, if there was a target on someone's back, it would be yours."

"But you can bypass it?"

"Of course I can," Monty said. "The System is bound by the same rules that we are. It can take some . . . professional liberties, but it's all pretty much the same. If it can get all up in your business, you can do it right back if you know how. Now, like I said—ain't nothing to fix. It's not broken. But it can be massaged. Worked with. I can make something to block some of the weirder effects, but I'm going to have to see exactly what's going on with it to do that."

"What does that mean?" I asked. "I gotta like, get in touch with it somehow?"

"Sure," Monty said dismissively. "But the best way to do that is to go out in the field and try to get it to fuck around with you a little bit. While you're wearing *this*."

He produced another object from thin air—an earring—and I scowled at it. From what Edwig had told me about Bahlgus, he could make whatever he wanted, whenever he wanted. So, he was messing with me?

"An earring?" I exclaimed. "What the hell, man? You couldn't have made anything cooler?"

"I could have, but this is the easiest way to get what we need. It's gotta be close enough to your eyes so that I can see what you see. I could make you a monocle or a fuckin' gimp mask or something, if that would be better?"

"You couldn't, I dunno, fuckin' make me a pair of glasses or something?"

"Yeah, if you wanna look like a damn dork," Monty spat. "Look at you, spotty. You're a fucking bigass orc; you think you're gonna look cool, walking around all speccy? Just put the damn earring on and we'll see what we see."

I grumbled, taking the earring and—with no lack of wincing—punctured the lobe of my ear and left it dangling. It felt foolish.

"Alright, what do you see?"

Monty laughed, and I felt like he was making fun of me.

"You think I just *invite* the System into my place of business? Pshaw, spotty. I ain't stupid. You're gonna have to go out there and taunt it or something. It won't work inside these hallowed halls."

"Great," I said. "Putting myself at risk for your amusement."

"Hey, I don't have to do *shit*, junior. You asked for help, and if you weren't a friend of Virgil's, we wouldn't even be having this conversation. I'd just leave your ass out in the cold. Now . . ."

He laced his fingers together and leaned back.

"Maybe we can add some additional context to this. Why don't you tell Papa Monty about what's been going on. How'd you meet *this* mean old cowboy, anyhow?"

He gestured to Virgil.

"We don't have time for thi—" Virgil started, but of course, he was interrupted by the false goblin.

"Hell, yeah, we do. Spill it, Loon. Air that dirty laundry. Your little piercing's gotta calibrate anyway, so you might as well start from the top. You guys want anything to drink?"

I nodded.

"Alright," Monty said, and snapped his fingers. Instantly, a flute appeared in his hands and he brought it to his lips. Then he piped a few notes, and I watched as a moment later, three tankards came floating into view. They came to rest on a nearby table, and the little creature gestured to it, smirking.

"Bottoms up, fellas!"

I sighed. Then I grabbed the handle of the mug, took a sip, and started to tell Monty all about what had happened since I'd arrived.

CHAPTER THIRTY-NINE

MONTY PYLON

"Well, *fuck*, homeboy," Monty said as I finished my story. "That's some shit, ain't it?"

"I'll say," I breathed. I'd given the brief version, which took about an hour to walk through. But I'd covered the major bits—arriving in Regaia, the curly-haired woman, the Crypt, Rexen, the fight with Crowmoon, the pylons—all the way up to now.

Monty regarded me soberly now, clearly considering something.

"What?" I demanded. "Just spit it out, Monty; you're gonna give me an ulcer if you keep staring like that."

Monty scratched his head, a grave expression on his face that was quite a departure from his usual roguish charm. "Alright, alright," he grumbled, pacing back and forth. "I'm just tryna figure out how to tell ya some shit that might ruin your whole goddamn day."

I raised an eyebrow.

"Ruin my day? Motherfucker, I've been tossed around by a reanimated corpse, beaten to shit by a macho fuckin' ex-con, and fought off a horde of fire spiders. I think I can handle it."

Monty chuckled, the sound lacking its usual carefree lightness.

"Well, ain't you the tough little cuss? Alright, then."

He took a deep breath, his face hardening into a grim mask.

"About these pylons . . . "

The sudden change in his demeanor unsettled me.

"Yeah, what about them?" I asked.

"I know where the one in Machus City is."

I blinked at him, surprised.

"You do? Well, shit, Monty, that's *great* news."

He nodded.

"Naw. That's the thing. It's not gonna be as simple as walking up to it and smashing it like goddamn . . . *Ape Escape*. It's buried deep beneath the lighthouse on the shore. And it ain't just any old relic. This lighthouse, it's an ancestral artifact. Been there since way before any of us were a twinkle in our daddies' eyes."

I frowned.

"And that means . . ."

"That means," Monty continued, "that some dumbasses thousands of years ago thought it was a good idea to put the thing down there to protect the city. And they ain't about to let some outsider waltz in and wreck their sacred relic. Getting to it . . . well, it's going to be a hell of a time."

Before I could respond, Virgil stepped forward.

"I can help," he offered. "I know the city; I know the lighthouse. I can scout ahead, find an easier path."

I regarded him with a mix of surprise and gratitude.

"You'd do that?"

"Beats sitting around here, waitin' for Jes and Frida to show their mugs."

"Uh, alright, that would be . . . dope titties, Virgil; thank you."

With that settled, he turned and disappeared into the front of the shop, leaving me alone with Monty once more.

"Now," Monty said, his voice dropping a notch, "there's something else you gotta know. Destroying that pylon . . . It ain't gonna come without consequences."

"Big shocker there," I said. "My whole fucking life in Regaia has been consequences. Like what?"

He shrugged.

"Hard to say. Could be the System itself decides to interfere. Or maybe it sends someone else to stop you. Point is, the closer you get to that pylon, the more they're gonna try to fuck you over."

I sighed, running a hand through my hair.

"Well, that's just great. Any other good news you want to share?"

Monty let out a raspy laugh, like the sound of gravel scraping together.

"Well, there's this one little tidbit, now that ya mention it. If that Drifter's after your ass . . ." He sucked in a breath, whistling low through his teeth. "Well, then you may as well start packing up now, because that motherfucker don't play."

"Fuck the Drifter," I said. "So, what am I supposed to do? Just fucking leave?"

Monty shrugged, his dark eyes gleaming with a mixture of amusement and sympathy.

"Fuck, I dunno. Probably should've listened to your god friends and not gotten tangled up in this nonsense. But seeing as how you're already balls-deep in it . . ."

He ran a finger across his chin, looking thoughtful.

"Best thing you can do is try to stay away from him. Stay under the radar."

I scoffed.

"What kinda fucking bullshit is that? The goddamn *System* is after me now. I think I'm a little past flying under the radar at this point."

Monty chuckled, the sound rumbling deep in his chest.

"Well, when you put it that way, I guess you're fucked."

I shot him a glare, to which he responded with a toothy grin.

"But seriously," he said, his tone turning serious again, "you need to be careful. If what you're saying is true, if they're after this pylon or kedge or whatever the hell you want to call it, there's going to be someone waiting for you. And they ain't gonna be handing out cookies and milk."

I sighed, my shoulders slumping as the gravity of the situation fully hit me.

"So, what's the game plan here, Monty?"

"You need to get stronger. However you can. And you've got minutes to do it. Every little bit that you can scrounge together, you're gonna need that shit. Fucking weapons, armor—hell, if you've got a fuckin' Monster Energy Drink under your skirt, you need to pop that shit and let 'er rip. It's the only way you'll survive. You need to prepare yourself for whatever they throw at you. And believe me, they're going to throw everything."

I chewed on his words for a moment, mulling them over in my mind. The prospect of going up against something far more dangerous, far more sinister than anything I'd faced so far was a daunting one. But Monty was right; I needed to be stronger.

"So, will you help me?"

"I'm not a fighter," he said. "Never have been much of one, if I'm being honest. I'm just happy to enjoy life doing what I love—denying service to fucking hippies like Romulus and living the easy life. But I can spare some of my fine baubles and particulars if you're not afraid to use them."

After a long silence, I spoke.

"Monty, I'm going to need you to do something for me."

A blast of late afternoon sun hit my face as I stepped out of Monty's shop. A warm wind played with the my hair, and I squinted against the light, my senses heightened. The Level-up process had been a brutal, jarring rush, but the result was a potency I'd never felt before. It felt like lightning was coursing through my veins, raw power pulsing with every beat of my heart.

I had finished Leveling Up after drinking the potion that got me to Level Twenty-Five. I wasn't sure, at first, if it would be a temporary thing or a permanent one, but I felt as though enough time had passed for the advancement to have been yanked out from beneath me if it was going to.

So . . . just like that, ten whole levels higher, a vast leap forward from my previous state. In the grand scheme of things, perhaps it wasn't that significant. But for me, for now, it was a game-changer. Thirty points had been at my disposal, ready to be assigned across my Attributes. I had added four to everything except Constitution. That one, I had loaded up with the rest. The power boost was immediate, tangible.

Two new Abilities joined my arsenal, further expanding my toolkit. I could feel them there, coiled inside me, ready to be unleashed when the need arose. What they were exactly, I wasn't yet sure. I was still getting a feel for them, still figuring out their nuances. But I knew they were powerful, capable of turning the tide in battle.

And then there were the items.

My gaze dropped to the simple-looking ring on my finger. It seemed unassuming enough, just a band of metal with an intricate pattern etched into its surface. But I knew better. This ring was a boost to my Strength, a full ten points added. An unbelievable gift.

In my ear, a twin to the earring that had been monitoring the System for me, sat a new piece of jewelry. This one would cut the Stamina I spent on anything I did in half. And it came with ten charges. Ten chances to push myself beyond the limits of my endurance without fear of tiring out.

Equipped and empowered like this, I was feeling good about my odds. I could take on the whole fucking world, it felt like. I squared my shoulders and started down the street, ready to face whatever lay ahead. I checked my Attributes one more time.

Yeah, things were looking and feelin' swell.

But then I noticed something.

The streets were busy, full of people going about their day. Regular folk just goin' about their day, children playing games, men and women engaged in conversation or barter. A typical scene in any city. But something was off.

The natural sounds of a city were still there—the clatter of wheels on cobblestone, the murmur of conversation, the occasional shout or laugh. But there was an undercurrent, a quietness that was out of place. I could feel it, a strange stillness that hung over the crowd like a thick fog. People were moving, talking, living. But they were doing it quietly, subtly. As if afraid to draw attention.

I frowned, my sense of unease growing. What was going on? What had changed?

I walked on, my eyes scanning the crowd, my mind racing. It was subtle, but it was there. The tension in the air was palpable, the silence louder than any roar. Something was wrong.

Something was *coming*.

Then—because fuck me, right?—the thrumming life of the marketplace fell to a chilling silence. Every artisan haggling, every kid being annoying, every goddamn beggar panhandling, all activities stopped mid-whatever the fuck they were doing. An ice-cold tremor carved its way through me, heralding a really nasty fucking sense of foreboding.

There was no distinction between the grizzled tradesman or the naive youth; all were caught in this startling stillness. It was super goddamn creepy.

What *really* stirred the bile in my throat, however, was not the spontaneous flash-mob mannequin challenge but the vacant stares etched on every face around me. Eyes, once vibrant, had transformed into misty mirrors of nothingness. Their gazes were affixed to some unseen horizon, entranced and distant. There was a shit-awful synchronicity to their hollow stares, as though each of these yahoos had been alerted to some shared but unseen terror. Almost as if they'd all suddenly received a notification at the same time . . .

Oh. Oh, fuck . . . no, no, no, no!

Then, out of the blue, the veil over their eyes evaporated, like it'd never been there at all. In a blink, the whole marketplace—every dang one of 'em—swiveled to stare at me. Suddenly, I was the star of the show, like I'd just been singled out on the menu as the chef's special. I had a feeling I wasn't far off.

"Shit . . ." I breathed.

That was when my own message sprang up in my vision.

TIME TO DIE, MOTHERFUCKER!

Then, as one, everyone in the marketplace charged.

CHAPTER FORTY

STAB-RA KADABRA

The marketplace's cobbled streets erupted into a surge of pandemonium. The crowd, a collection of all manner of fucking insert-medieval-job-here, was suddenly a berserk mob, each member intent on turning me into mincemeat. I flexed my fists, allowing a grim smile to stretch across my face.

"Alrighty . . . let's fucking *go*," I muttered under my breath, and plunged headlong into the crowd.

First to bat was a fishmonger, hurling a whole goddamn tuna at me. With a swift twist of my body, I dodged, feeling the whoosh of the sea beast as it sailed past. A fucking travesty to waste good sushi meat like that. I ran by him, slugging him right in the chin as I did, and he cried out, collapsing in a heap as I blew on through.

More people piled into the fray, swinging at me. But they had to avoid each other—I didn't have to avoid anyone. I kicked out, connecting with a teenage boy right in his chest, and he flew back, the net he'd been carrying tangling up the legs of some lanky fuck with a rusted metal club as he darted my way. He smashed face-first into the street, going still. I dodged around a potential stab wound as a fat, bald man—who I'm pretty sure was a beggar—swiped at me with a table knife he'd probably found somewhere. I karate-chopped his forearm, and he dropped the blade, then dived to snatch it up, but I drove my knee into the side of his head as he did so, and he yelped, tumbling to the stone.

The market streets had become an insanity gauntlet, with every would-be hero trying to take a shot at me. I spun, ducked, and danced around them, my movements a not-so-seamless ballet of evasion and self-defense.

A burly blacksmith lunged at me, his callused hands clutching a hammer that could crush a horse. I ducked under his wild swing, pivoted, and then, with an overemphasized bow, I yanked his apron, forcing him to lose balance and spiral belly-first into a barrel of what looked like pineapples. The fruit burst out like cannon fodder, pinging off the heads of the charging horde.

But they kept coming. Kids throwing rocks, an elderly granny with her walking cane, even a fucking cobbler lobbing his boots like grenades. Shit, this was turning into a circus.

Next, I faced an old crone with a wickedly sharp knitting needle, her toothless mouth agape in a war cry. I vaulted over her, grabbed the saggy hood of her cloak, and used it to yank her to the ground before swinging myself onto a nearby awning. A faintly glowing pebble, hurled by a scrawny street urchin with mismatched eyes, whizzed past where my head had been a second ago. Low-level magic, sure, but I'll bet it would have given me a nasty headache.

I jumped from one awning to another, playing "the floor is lava," only the lava was a swarming sea of dumb assholes. Just as I was about to leap to a rooftop, a bolt of arcane energy sizzled through the air where I was about to land. My eyes followed the energy trail back to a frumpy-looking woman, her eyes shimmering with dim, magical energy.

"You missed, sucker," I roared, quickly recalculating my trajectory and bouncing off a hanging sign instead.

Back on the street, I was immediately accosted by a towering figure in a bloody smock, a butcher, judging by the meat cleaver he brandished. I blocked his downward swing with my haladie, feeling the impact reverberate through my bones, then swept his legs out from under him. He tumbled into a baker, who'd been winding up to throw a baguette javelin. The collision sent pastries flying, showering the crowd in a hail of fresh bread. I replaced the haladie and goosed it.

A flicker of movement caught my eye, and I spun just in time to see a matronly woman bearing down on me, wielding a . . . Was that a fucking *enchanted mop*? Its head shimmered with a brilliance that spelled UH-OH in all capital letters. I balked at the absurdity of it, then dove out of the way; she stumbled past me, momentum redirecting her charge into a nearby tool stall.

I sprinted through narrow alleyways, vaulting over barrels and ducking under clotheslines, with a throng of magic-wielding medieval crazies in hot pursuit. A bearded man with an eyepatch tried to trip me with an oar. I hopped over it with a twirl, causing him to trip himself and crash into a group of his fellow pursuers.

Suddenly, the mob ahead of me seemed to pause as a giant of a man stepped forth from their ranks. Even in this clusterfuck, he stood out, a grizzled warrior with tattoos that suggested a history of making bad life choices. There were cheers of triumph as he made himself known. I wasn't impressed. I was so hopped up on get-the-fuck-outta-there juice that I didn't even bother drawing an actual weapon again.

"Fucking bring it, Giggles," I called out to him. He answered with a roar, charging toward me like a runaway freight train.

Using his own momentum against him, I sidestepped at the last moment, driving my fist into his gut and flipping over his shoulder. He let out a loud *Oof!* and I landed behind him, raining punishing blows into his kidneys and then pivoting and pressing forward into the crowd before he could recover.

And so it went, the city transforming into a battleground as I fought to keep my footing in the storm of madness. Each step closer to the kedge was a victory, but I was only one guy versus an entire city. I just *had* to get cocky and literal feel like I could take on the world, didn't I?

As I neared the edge of the city, the crowd began to thin. That didn't mean they became less dangerous. A fucking fool—a literal jester in bright motley—popped up in front of me, juggling a trio of glowing balls. He grinned madly as he tossed one to me. Instinctively, I caught it—only to yelp as it transformed into a squawking chicken in my hands. I threw it back at him, sending him sprawling in a flapping flurry of feathers.

And yet, through all the mayhem, the lighthouse. It was there, piercing the skyline like a beacon of hope. All I had to do was get there. Easy enough, right?

Fuckin' *wrong*. Because the city guard had arrived, now thoroughly alerted and standing in formation before the docks with their pikes raised. And behind them, a phalanx of folks in robes, their hands sparking with magical energy.

"Well fucking goddamn shit-sucking fuck," I muttered, rolling my shoulders. I took a deep breath, then charged.

Beaten to bloody shit, but still truckin', baby, I scaled the last few feet of the outside of the lighthouse and slipped in through the window at the top, collapsing in a heap on the floor.

I lay there for a moment, sprawled out on the cold stone. Just catching my breath. Even with my boosted Constitution, I'd put myself through a lot. The steady rhythm of my heartbeat pounded in my ears, the only sound in the otherwise-quiet room.

Slowly, I pushed myself up to a sitting position and took a look around.

The lighthouse was empty, its interior untouched by time or the outside world. But there was a beauty in its silence, an ancient allure that was impossible to deny. The walls were made of stone, weathered but solid. They held the weight of centuries within them, whispering tales of the past, of those who had manned this place and kept the coast safe from danger.

A spiral staircase wound its way up the middle, reaching for the sky, ending in a chamber high above that must've housed the great beacon once. The setting sun cast long, dramatic shadows across the room, painting a picture of surreal tranquility.

From far below, I could hear the city stirring. They were hounding the place, desperate yet too afraid to enter. Their superstitions and fears held them at bay, keeping them from pursuing me into the heart of the lighthouse.

I couldn't help but chuckle. Superstitions. Funny things, really. The things people would believe to make sense of a world that was fundamentally chaotic and unpredictable.

Shaking off my musings, I started my descent. The staircase seemed to go on forever, spiraling downward into the bowels of the lighthouse. Each step was worn smooth by countless feet over the centuries, creating an oddly rhythmic pattern as I made my way down.

As I descended, the ambiance of the lighthouse changed. The light from above dwindled, replaced by a cool darkness that seemed to pulsate with an eerie energy. The walls became slick with moisture, glistening in the scant light. The air grew colder, thicker, the silence deepening as I ventured farther below.

My heart pounded in my chest as I rounded a corner and caught sight of a shape in the distance. My hand instinctively went to my pique, my senses on high alert. But then the figure moved into the light, and I let out a breath I didn't know I'd been holding.

It was Virgil.

"Goddamn, Virgil, you scared the shit out of me," I breathed, collapsing against the wall.

He grinned, a lopsided smile that somehow seemed to fit his rugged features.

"Didn't mean to startle you," he drawled in that cowboy style of speech he had. "Just barreled a pair o' sentries tending to this place."

I shook my head, chuckling despite the adrenaline still coursing through my veins.

"Well, good job. Now let's move."

We continued our descent, Virgil leading the way. After what felt like an eternity, we came upon a door. It was old, made of heavy wood and iron, and it creaked ominously as we pushed it open.

Beyond lay a tunnel, a pristine path of gleaming marble that stretched on into the darkness. We walked on, the light from our torches dancing off the polished stone, illuminating strange symbols etched into the walls.

At the end of the tunnel was another door. Pushing it open, we stepped into a large chamber. My breath caught in my throat at the sight before me.

In the center of the room stood a massive obelisk, the kedge. Its black surface seemed to absorb the light around it, creating a void in the heart of the chamber. But that wasn't what took my breath away.

Around the obelisk, covering the walls of the chamber, were symbols. At first glance, they looked like runic magic glyphs, and my heart dropped. But then, as I moved closer, squinting at the patterns, I realized they were something else.

They were... messages. Prayers, requests, and pleas from people long gone, their identities lost to the sands of time. They had left their mark on this place, their belief in the power of the obelisk etched into the very stone itself.

They had believed in this place, had asked for its protection. And now, their voices echoed through the centuries, their pleas still as urgent as the day they were first written.

It was humbling, and a little terrifying, to stand in the presence of such ancient hope. I felt a strange sense of reverence for these long-forgotten people. Their world might have been different, but their fears, their desires, were the same.

Protect this place. The words rang in my ears, whispered by the ghosts of the past.

And as I stood there, surrounded by the echoes of a bygone era, I couldn't help but wonder.

What would they think of me, the stranger who had come to destroy their sacred relic?

Would they hate me? Would they understand?

I didn't know. But one thing was clear.

I had a job to do.

And come hell or high water, I was going to do it.

Man, this increased Charisma was really doing a number on my emotional intelligence. Never in my life would I have considered anything like this. Or before, when I was being chased through the streets by all those motherfuckers—I probably would have just pulled out my wand and started blasting. Now, though...

We approached the kedge. It was resonating with me, somewhere deep inside my body. And not in a philosophical way, either. No, that shit was in my small intestine now, turning the previous pylon into... uh, dreams.

I stared at the kedge. It was more than just a physical reaction. It was like a primal pull, tugging at something deep within me, drawing me closer. It was a thrumming, a pulsating rhythm that seemed to sync up with my own heartbeat. Like those dumbass kids in *Jumanji* fucking around with the board game, I could hear it calling out to me. Beckoning. Whispering.

The whispers grew louder, rattling in my fucking skull, building into a crescendo that threatened to drown out everything else. I reached out, my hand trembling, drawn towards the obelisk. The clamor was reaching fever pitch, the kedge calling, screaming...

And then, just as my fingers were inches away, a voice cut through the chaos. "No."

I froze, my hand hovering in the air. The voice was a cold, sharp contrast to the deafening cacophony of the kedge. I spun around, heart pounding.

Virgil didn't hesitate. His crossbow was already aimed and firing, the bolt cutting through the air toward the speaker. It was the curly-haired woman, her dangerous smile firmly fixed in place; she swatted the bolt away like a house cat batting at a piece of wayward string. A ripple of unease ran through me.

Before we could react, she raised her hand, and Virgil was flung back against the wall, held there by some unseen force. I couldn't see what was holding him, but I could see the strain on his face, his body pinned like a picture of Paris on some highschooler's vision board.

"Let's. Chat," she said.

CHAPTER FORTY-ONE

THE HEAVIEST MATTER OF THE UNIVERSE

"Virgil!" I roared, pulling out my wand. I let loose a bolt of lightning, aiming for the woman. But she moved with a fluid grace, sidestepping my attack as if it were nothing more than a nuisance.

Ice-cold dread filled me. If she could do this, what chance did we have?

For a moment, I stood frozen, staring at the woman, one of the wands—I couldn't remember which—clutched in my hand. I could feel my heart pounding, could hear the deafening silence of the chamber in my ears. And beneath it all, the whispers of the kedge, now paused, waiting.

"Let's fucking do this, then," I shouted, readying myself for ultimate combat.

"Do *what*, Gabriel?" the curly-haired woman asked calmly. She tilted her head to one side, regarding me carefully, like I was an animal in a zoo.

Don't fucking look at me like that. I thought.

"Goddamn . . . let's fucking fight, then," I said, raising the haladie in my other hand.

"Gabriel, that would be foolish," she said calmly, warmly. "I would kill you instantly, and then where would you be? Dead forever. I have no interest in that. You are far more useful to our efforts alive than not."

"Save it, toots," I shot, drawing myself up. "You're just trying to fatten me up for the eventual slaughter anyway, so why the fuck shouldn't I fight back? I've got nothing to lose."

"You've got everything to lose," she said. "You haven't any idea what it means to be chosen by us. What it means to be part of something great. You're interested in breaking the System, aren't you?"

I didn't answer.

"Well, that is our goal as well—you've already come so far in your personal journey. Why would you abandon it all—throw everything away for a silly, fleeting idea of control?"

"The way I see it," I said, "regardless of what everyone's intentions are, nobody seems to want these pylons to go away—so, I'm pretty sure that since the *everyone* I'm referring to are assholes on all sides of the playing field . . . I wanna bust the fuck outta these things and just see what happens."

"That would be so, so foolish, Gabriel," the woman said, shaking her head. "All that would achieve is weakening the boundaries of this plane. All manner of monsters could then spill into this world and run rampant. That would be all your fault."

"Yeah, well, so what?" I said. "Maybe this place deserves a makeover. Another Nightmare War would probably be just what the doctor ordered."

"Unfortunately, I will not let you do anything that could upset the balance I have worked so hard for," she continued. "If you were to try, I can promise there is nothing in your bag of tricks that could subdue me. I am without equal. Peerless. The fact that you stand here now is merely a testament to my faith and good will. You are not currently in the same predicament as your friend merely because I will it. I could simply wave my hand—"

She made a mild gesture and Virgil was dragged across the wall, still restrained. I watched as he tried to struggle against her, but it was useless.

"Enough!" I yelled, my voice echoing in the chamber, sounding desperate even to my own ears. "What the fuck do you want?!"

She simply let her gaze linger on Virgil for a few more seconds, watching him wriggle in pain, before releasing him. He fell to the ground, coughing and spluttering but alive.

"I wanted to see you, Gabriel," she said softly, her eyes fixing on me. "To observe you up close. To understand what the fuss was all about. There are many of us who have a vested interest in this 'game' you all are playing. But you . . . you're a special case."

"Special? Bullshit. I'm just trying to survive like everyone else," I spat out, all pretense of bravado gone.

"Survival. Yes, it is a powerful motivator," she mused. "Yet there is more to you. You are not only trying to survive but change the system, turn the tables. You have ambition."

"Look, what's your end game? What do you want from me? Let's cut to the chase, Curly," I said, anger and frustration building inside me.

She chuckled, a low, musical sound that echoed eerily in the chamber.

"Ah, Gabriel. Always one for shortcuts. My end game is simple. I want the world to crumble away from the state as it is. I do not thrive under the thumb of the System, where boundaries are thin and creatures of power like myself can only come and go as they please under strict guidelines."

"*Creatures of power*? What the fuck *are* you?"

"I was once like you are now," she said. "A Sojourner, birthed into this world in confusion and unaware of what I was so desperately searching for. I was lost, disoriented, practically a cub. I took this form out of a misunderstanding of what would truly matter to me. Much like yourself, I had lost those most important to me. I, quite foolishly, believed that if I took on an appearance like this, I could summon my wayward peacemaker back to me. But I was wrong. It wasn't what I was that mattered; it is what I would become."

"Yeah, and what's that?"

"A vessel," she said. "I will nourish the spirit of the Drifter and he will set me forever in a place closest to him."

"Ew," I said. "You're trying to become part of his harem? Gross. You should aim higher."

She winced.

"You're a fool," she said.

"Fuckin' . . . write a book about it or something," I said.

But her words had unlocked something inside me. Clips. Phrases. What were they? *Rexen*. He'd mentioned vessels—not like the ones containing the power for a runic circle. But he'd said *I* would one day be a suitable vessel. In the forest, on our way back to the camp. Later, he'd mentioned he wanted to possess me someday. It was easy to brush it off because he was fucking weird. But . . .

"And now, dear Gabriel, we must make haste," the curly-haired woman said. "It is time."

The gears in my head started turning, trying to make sense of all the random puzzle pieces of information I'd gathered over the last few months. Deep down, a quiet voice whispered to me, nudging the fringes of my memory. There was a conversation I'd had with Rexen, surrounded by woods with long shadows stretching like outstretched arms. He'd gone on one of his cryptic rambles about not being some dispensable pawn in a bigger game.

Shit. A pattern was emerging. Every time this curly menace graced us with her unwelcome presence, Rexen was notably absent. It could've been sheer coincidence, but my gut told me I was on to something.

Is Rexen . . . the Drifter?

"Yo, Curly Q, got a question for you. What's the deal between you and Rexen Gravetongue?"

Her mask of serenity wavered, and though it was a flash, the kind you'd miss if you blinked, I caught it.

"Who?" she feigned ignorance. I could tell. I don't know how, but I fucking *could*.

"Rexen," I repeated, savoring the moment, letting the name roll off my tongue. "Every time you decide to pop by, our mutual friend seems to be MIA. So, what's the sitch? Scared?"

Her laughter, though cold and distant, betrayed a hint of annoyance.

"Why on earth would I fear him, or anyone, for that matter?"

Deciding to gamble, I ventured, "Rexen the Drifter. Sounds like a bad band name. Ring any bells?"

Her composure slipped again, just a crack, but it was there. Bingo.

Just as I was basking in my little victory, thinking I had the upper hand, a searing pain shot through me, rooting me to the spot. Her face contorted into something wickedly furious.

"You may think you've pieced it all together, Loon," she hissed, "But you're just scratching the surface."

"What. The Fuck?" I hissed. "This. Is. Over. Kill."

In my pained state, I half-remembered Rexen mentioning something about being transported . . .

Holy shit!

He was talking about the pylons—or the kedge, or whatever the fuck, in his cache.

Oh, sweet baby goddamn!

I grunted as Curly's diatribe washed over me. As my vision blurred, the room's edges seemed to glow, distorting reality. The sensations were strangled. Fear and fury hummed together, an ugly crescendo reverberating through my veins. Yet beneath it all, a minuscule spark of hope kept flickering.

"I will *devour* you, Gabriel," she said as though her threat was an obligation. As if she was willing to do it, but didn't want to?

From the corner of my eye, I caught a flutter of movement. My mind stuttered, froze, then rebooted. I had to stay calm. I focused. There was the phantom sensation of my Misdirection Ability snapping into place, like gears meshing, metal on metal. It was a shaky card, but it was my last. With a grunt of exertion, I let one of the Hexahedrons of Hazards tumble from my grasp. Not red. White. One I hadn't gotten a chance to deploy yet.

An ear-splitting blast filled the room as the cube activated. Blinding light painted the chamber in harsh, uncompromising strokes. Curly recoiled, a sound erupting from her throat that was more akin to a large feline's growl than anything human. A primal snarl, rich with anger and surprise.

"If any'un's goin' to be devourin' 'im, it's goin' t'be *me*!" The voice sliced through the chaos like a blade. "Slipknot Seplucher!"

A gleaming tether materialized, wrapping around Curly's neck as if made from liquid silver. I blinked against the light, and when I could finally see, I saw Frida.

Goddamn Frida, my savior in shining armor. Dark-skinned, beautiful, her azure eyes reflecting the glow of the beautiful ax she held. She was an avenging angel, a symbol of strength and determination. I wasn't sure how she'd found me, but I didn't fucking care. Without hesitation, she lunged, slashing at Curly with her luminous weapon.

The curly-haired menace resisted, ripping Frida's tether from her neck with a chilling smile. A slash of her hand was all she needed to counterattack, but a rumbling voice beat her to it.

"Rebuff!"

Suddenly, Frida was flying backward, propelled by an unseen force. Jes swooped into the scene then, a whirlwind of magic and anger. He hurled magical fire at Curly, distracting her long enough for Virgil to get his crossbow bolts off.

One, two, three bolts went flying, each one a streak of deadly intent. The combatants were a blur of motion, a violent motherfucking ballet that defied all my previous understanding of a fight.

As Curly turned her attention to these new threats, her grip on me weakened. The pain that had once been debilitating dulled to a throbbing ache, freeing me to act. I dove into my arsenal, pulling out an Ability I'd left untouched. Until now. I felt it surge within me, vibrant and ready. With a roar, I unleashed the Rallying Warchant.

"COWABUUUUUNGA!"

The chant vibrated through the room, sparking off Virgil like sun glimmers off water. The rhythm of the battle shifted. Virgil, now in overdrive due to the nature of my badass motherfucking cheerleader roar, was a one-man army, his shots quick and deadly.

Taking advantage of the momentum, I activated Biter and launched myself at the kedge. The surge of energy almost knocked me off my feet, but I clung on, knowing that this was our best chance at victory. The battle raged on behind me, but I was locked in, focused on the pylon.

It was do or die. Or, in our case, do and hopefully not die.

As I grappled the pylon with my teeth, everything around me melted into darkness. For a moment, there was nothing—just the taste of the construct and my own erratic breathing.

Then, without warning, I was consumed by a tidal wave of sensations.

It wasn't just a visual overload; it was a multisensory assault. Colors, sounds, emotions, memories, they all came at once. I saw faces I didn't recognize, heard screams and laughter, and experienced the warmth of sunlight and the cold bite of winter. I felt the heartbreak of loss, the joy of reunions, the thrill of discovery, and the numbness of despair.

I was simultaneously everywhere and nowhere, drowning in a sea of chaotic images and feelings. Pain seared through my brain, white-hot and blinding. It felt like every nerve was being electrocuted, the sheer intensity threatening to fragment my consciousness. The sheer weight of it all threatened to break me, as if I was being crushed by the collective mass of countless lives and memories.

There was a series of images: a child being born, a sun setting over a desolate landscape, a star exploding in a supernova, civilizations rising and falling. These weren't just random images; they felt intimate, personal. Memories. Yet they weren't mine.

In the whirlwind of sensations, the word *Rexen* echoed in my mind, becoming a beacon in the tumultuous sea of chaos. I clung to that thought, desperate to find some sense of clarity, some anchor in the storm.

And then the maelstrom shifted.

Images of Rexen emerged, sharp and clear. The two of us, moving through the camp the night I led him to Tartarus. Both of us laughing at Edwig as he realized his sweater vest was inside out. Other experiences that never happened—from some other timeline, maybe. Or what could have been. Rexen and I facing down a swarm of golden-bodied warriors. Rexen, floating above me while I fought off some sort of wild boar. My body being impaled on a spear of vines by some gothic witch lookin' lady as Rexen tried to protect me.

Then I saw him, not as the spectral presence I knew but as a man—vibrant, alive, and teeming with power. Human. Mousy brown hair. Shorter-statured, scrawny, with a round, childlike face. There were flashes of battles fought on mountaintops, where the air was thin and every breath was a fight. Rexen, wielding unimaginable power, battled a colossal beast, their energies clashing in a blinding display of Arcana. The very fabric of reality seemed to warp around them, the raw power causing the very mountain to shatter and reform.

Then the scene shifted, plunging into the deep abyss of the ocean. There, surrounded by darkness and pressure, Rexen engaged another foe. They danced through the water, their combat a mesmerizing ballet of power and grace. Arcana surged between them, turning the water around them into steam, creating whirlpools and currents that threatened to pull everything into the void.

It was overwhelming, watching Rexen in his prime, witnessing his dominion over Arcana. The realization struck me hard: Rexen wasn't just some powerful spirit. He had once been a force to be reckoned with, a titan among mortals.

The torrent of images began to recede, pulling back like a tide. The pain started to ebb, leaving me drained and disoriented. But just as I thought it was over, one last vision came into focus.

It was a simple scene, a quiet moment. Rexen, an old man, looking wearier than I'd seen him in the other recollections, sat alone, looking out over a vast, desolate landscape. His eyes held a depth of sadness, a profound loneliness that felt hauntingly familiar. He turned, looking directly at me—or through me—and whispered a single phrase.

"Do you trust me?"

And then, as suddenly as it began, it was over. I was back in the chamber, gasping for breath, the visions pressing down on me. The battle was still raging around me, but for a moment, everything felt distant, as if I'd returned from a long journey.

My eyes found the curly-haired woman, who was watching with an inscrutable expression. But she wasn't watching me. No, her eyes were watching a *god*.

Rexen was there, in the room, and the moment I noticed was the moment everything stopped. Curly stopped fighting off my three companions. Solely focused on the spectral form of the Dreadnaught Lord. The Drifter.

"Hello, Kitty," he said. His voice was softer than usual. It didn't have the airy, dreamy quality it always did. Typically high-pitched, this voice was noticeably lower, nearly . . . normal.

"My Lord . . ." she said, and she cast her eyes down. Frida, Jes, and Virgil had stopped, heaving huge breaths as they watched what was transpiring.

"I am not your lord, Kitty," Rexen Gravetongue said. "I rejected you. You were a bad disciple."

Power flashed as an undercurrent beneath Rexen, though it was met by another power in Curly—or . . . Kitty, I suppose.

"Lord," Kitty pleaded, her tone dripping with desperation, "you must see. See what I've become. All for you. I have transformed. Everything I've done, every decision I've made, has been for you, for us!"

Rexen's eyes, though still ethereal, held a gravity that rooted everyone in place.

"You've strayed, Kitty," he began, his tone unwavering. "Your actions are yours and yours alone."

"Remember the peaks of Jorland," she pleaded. "Where you taught me to harness the impiris? The cliffs of Elphorisha, where we watched the sun rise? Ajutar, where you said I was . . . special?"

She took a step closer, eyes glistening with unshed tears.

"Choose me again. Choose our path."

Rexen remained immobile, a sentinel of memories and time gone by. His stern demeanor was wildly juxtaposed to the seemingly playful and unpredictable spirit I'd come to know. It was as if seeing Kitty had stripped him of all pretense, revealing the core of the man that once was.

"Kitty," he said slowly, measuring his words, "our paths diverged a long time ago."

She seemed desperate, nearly hysterical.

"But don't you remember the warmth of the campfires, the melodies of our songs? The promise we made to stand side by side against the forces of the Abyss? How can you forget?"

"I haven't forgotten. I just chose to move forward," he replied, his voice steady.

"But I am your vessel! I am the embodiment of your teachings, your legacy. I have sacrificed everything for you, O Gravetongue!"

He floated toward her, and the room seemed to grow colder.

Kitty, her voice trembling with a mix of anger and anguish, pressed on.

"Do you not see me? Can you not sense my value? Do you not feel our connection?"

Then, in a sudden, unexpected outburst, Rexen shouted, his voice echoing.

"I have already chosen a new vessel!"

The words hit the room like a shockwave, and the silence that followed was deafening. Something inside me flared.

New vessel?

Kitty looked as if she'd been physically struck, her face pale, her expression shattered.

Rexen continued, softer now: "Kitty, your value was never in being my vessel. It was in being you. But you've lost yourself, seeking validation through power and control."

She fell to her knees, tears streaming down her face. "I just wanted to be worthy."

"You always were," Rexen whispered. "But you sought worth in the wrong places."

As Rexen uttered his last words, Kitty's face contorted with a blend of desperation and rage. Her breathing became ragged, every muscle in her body taut and ready.

Before anyone could fully comprehend what was happening, Kitty's eyes darted to the side, locking on to me.

Without warning, she lunged. A cry of fury ripped from her throat as she hurled herself my way with an alarming speed. Arcane energy flared around her, signaling her intent to cause real harm.

I barely had time to react, and if it weren't for the quick reflexes of my friends, I would have been mowed down by Kitty's reckless charge. Frida was the first to intervene, stepping in front of me with her ax raised high, her eyes filled with a protective ferocity.

Kitty crashed against Frida's weapon, creating an explosion of arcane energy that lit the room in a dazzling display. But she didn't stop. She snapped the ax in half, and Frida slammed backward. Kitty roared, a sound filled with fury and despair, before launching herself at me once again.

This time, it was Jes who stepped in, bringing up a wall of flame that forced her to take a step back. I wasn't sure how or why my friends were able to assist like this—she'd shown she was far stronger than any one of us—but, they could. Yet Kitty was unrelenting. She was like a wild animal, lashing out at everything and everyone that stood between her and her target.

But it was then that Rexen's voice echoed through the room.

"Pupil, I need you to trust me!"

It was a plea, and it seemed eerily similar to the last vision I had witnessed. Like when he'd spoken to me in the tavern. I hesitated for a moment, but the escalating chaos quickly put an end to my indecision.

"I trust you," I shouted, eyes locked onto his spectral form.

No sooner had the words left my mouth than I felt a strange, alien presence engulfing me. It was Rexen, merging with my own essence, a sensation I could only describe as . . . ultimate *ullllk,*

The shift was abrupt and intense. Suddenly, Rexen commandeered the helm, and I was pushed to the back seat of my own consciousness. It was a bizarre sensation, feeling both present and distant simultaneously. Like being a ghost trapped in a house, seeing and feeling everything but powerless to influence any of it. With a determined focus that was unmistakably Rexen's, my arms reached out as if on their own accord. From the tips of my outstretched fingers, a dazzling burst of arcane energy spiraled forth, weaving and solidifying into a shimmering barrier. It stood tall and firm, a guardian wall separating Kitty and me.

In an instant of raw, visceral energy, Kitty underwent a chilling metamorphosis. Her bones audibly cracked and reshaped, her muscles contorting and expanding in unnatural bulges. Skin and tissue seemed to ripple and flow like liquid as her human features dissolved into something far more terrifying. Growing in both stature and monstrosity, her frame stretched and contorted until it took on the massive, predatory fucking form of a nightmarish tiger. Sinewy muscles pulsed beneath a coat of shimmering fur as her face, no longer remotely human, elongated into a ferocious snout. Eyes, once familiar, now glowed with a feral, malevolent light. When she let out a roar, it wasn't just loud—it was cataclysmic. The sound was so powerful, so guttural, that it seemed to reverberate through the very stones beneath our feet, threatening to bring down the chamber around us.

What the fuck, what the fuck, what the fuck? I kept screaming inside my mind.

Driven by her fury and desperation, Kitty—now a massive fuckin' horror beast—leaped toward us, claws outstretched, her face twisted into an expression of absolute rage.

Using my body, Rexen created a torrent of magic. Spells of all colors and forms blasted out from my fingertips, colliding with Kitty's monstrous form. The chamber lit up with an array of dazzling colors as the battle between Rexen and Kitty escalated, our powers clashing with cataclysmic force.

The ground trembled beneath us, and soon, the entire building began to shake, threatening to collapse under the sheer magnitude of our duel. But Rexen was relentless. He pressed on, the energy surrounding us pulsating with a might I had never felt before.

We were locked in a deadly dance, Kitty's monstrous form lunging at us, only to be met by a barrier of force or a barrage of spells from Rexen. The battle raged on, neither of us yielding an inch.

Rexen was more powerful than I had ever imagined, his magic weaving a beautiful, deadly tapestry of force and light. And even though it was terrifying, there was a thrill coursing through me as we faced down Kitty's assault.

The . . . well, *three* of us, blasted out of the lighthouse, through the walls and outside, shooting up into the air. Suddenly, we were fighting in the sky like a motherfucking *Dragon Ball Z* episode, except only one of us was throwin' 'bows.

I heard Rexen inside my head as he continued to fight against the torrential output of Kitty, the curly haired woman.

Pupil, he said, and his voice sounded like what I was used to.

Arjee? I wondered.

I don't think you're fully ready to be my vessel, and I don't think I'm fully ready to be reborn.

Well, shit, dawg, that's a fucking relief. I'm fine with this shit right here—I mean, we're kicking her fucking ass—but I dunno about making this a permanent fixture in my life. I like you, but I don't like you enough to wanna spend the rest of my days fused with you.

Ah! I like you too, pupil.

So, what's the plan? I wondered.

We will put a stop to this. Can I borrow something from you?

Sure, Arjee, whatever you need, as long as you give it back.

Okay!

Kitty flew down to the city below, destroying a huge section of buildings with her meteoric landing.

The devastation she caused sent shockwaves throughout the city, with plumes of dust and debris rising into the air. Her monstrous form now towered above the buildings, her menacing eyes scanning for me—us, I should say.

Rexen propelled us upward, shooting higher and higher into the sky. The vast city below soon appeared as nothing more than a distant speck. A queasy feeling took over, my stomach lurching as if it were in free fall. Were we about to touch the stratosphere?

Rexen suddenly halted our ascent, breaking my train of thought.

Huh. Pupil. Did you die?

I chuckled internally.

You caught that, did you? I pulled a Rua and set my anchor to Bahlgus's lab.

You met Bahlgus?!

Oh, shoot, yeah, sorry I didn't tell you earlier, Arjee. You'd actually . . . probably not love him.

I love everyone.

I rolled my eyes mentally.

Okay, so, maybe you would . . . but now is not the time.

He let out a resigned sigh.

You're right, pupil; it is not. How many times did you die?

Too many to die again, I admitted. *I got the Rez Curse, doc.*

A pause.

Oh, dear, that's not good.

Hey, Rexen, check this out, I said with a hint of bravado. *I've hit Fatigue V. First time ever! And take a look at these upgraded stats.*

Fatigue V
Strength: 212
Constitution: 344
Dexterity: 172
Intelligence: 5
Wisdom: 5
Charisma: 5
Luck: 17

There was a moment of silence before Rexen responded, clearly impressed.

Ah, my pupil! You've come a long way. I'm proud of you.

Aw, shucks, I said. *Well . . . what comes next?*

You have been a very good disciple, Rexen murmured warmly. *I hope to see you again one day.*

Caught off guard, I brain-blurted out, *Wait, what?*

Far below, Kitty was wreaking fucking havoc, going goddamn apeshit with rage. Man, this shit was insane.

Arjee, she's gonna wreck the whole goddamn city at this rate. What do you need from me? I mentally asked.

Your anger and your determination, Rexen replied. *Oh, and this.*

Pact Boon [Imprint]
Imprint Connection: Jailbreak

A symbol appeared in front of me. But I didn't recognize it for what it was. It . . . sorta looked like a mask. Zeol? But just like before, it was as though this was part of my vision or mind, or something else equally as fucking weird. The crest, symbol, whatever you want to call it, overlay my vision, and the lock icon appeared over it, just like when I'd Jailbroken Eye of the Saboteur.

Jailbreak Fixation: Calden's Hang Time
Duration: Temporary

Flickering, the message suddenly digitized and the lock shattered to pieces.

Rexen absorbed it all, synthesizing my memories with his own formidable power. Then, with a deep breath, he took action.

"Hold on, apprentice," he warned. With a surge of speed, we raced directly toward Kitty, our intent clear and unwavering. The outcome uncertain.

Just as we were about to reach her, Kitty roared, unleashing a wave of pure, destructive energy.

Rexen spoke again, his voice a mix of urgency and determination.

"This is it!"

I felt a rush of power surging through me as we activated the Jailbreak Ability, combining its powers with the other items and Abilities at our disposal. Everything became a blur, the sheer force of our combined might accelerating our descent like a bolt of lightning toward the city below.

As we shot down, the ground approaching faster than seemed possible, Kitty spotted us. The ferocious tiger beast roared, charging up an arcane attack to counter our own. A massive ball of energy formed in front of her gaping maw.

At the last possible second, I felt Rexen tap into the very essence of my being. The Pact Boon gave us an edge, and the Jailbreak on Calden's Hang Time let us shift our trajectory in the blink of an eye, narrowly avoiding Kitty's devastating attack. Instead of meeting it head-on, we shot past her, transferring the immense kinetic energy directly into the ground beneath her feet.

There was a brilliant flash of light, and for a moment, the entire city was bathed in a blinding radiance.

The shockwave was immense. Buildings crumbled, streets cracked, and a monstrous crater formed, swallowing Kitty and many of the nearby structures. The dust and debris clouded everything, obscuring the aftermath of our assault. Then, because I'm a dick, I threw the haladie with all my strength, right at where I thought she was.

I've never in my life seen something travel so fast. It was like some sort of *hyper* cannon fired it. I couldn't even track it visually.

We landed a short distance away, the impact cushioned by the lingering effects of the Jailbreak. I was disoriented and exhausted. Rexen's spectral form detached from me, appearing by my side, though looking a lot more transparent than before.

"We did it," he whispered, his form beginning to dissipate.

"No, wait!" I exclaimed, trying to hold on to his fading essence. "You said you'd return whatever you borrowed."

He smiled, the emotion genuine and heartfelt.

"I borrowed time, Loon. And I think I've used it well."

It was the first time, to my recollection, he'd actually used my name.

"Arjee..." I started, but before I could finish, he vanished, leaving me kneeling amidst the destruction, the weight of the world heavy on my shoulders.

The dust began to settle, and the scope of our battle became clear. The city was in ruins, and Kitty, whether she was defeated or merely buried, was nowhere to be seen.

CHAPTER FORTY-TWO

ALL'S WELL THAT ENDS . . . WELL, MOSTLY ALRIGHT.

Staring down at the smoking aftermath of what had once been a lively part of town, I took a deep, shaky breath. It felt like my insides were wrung out, every bit of energy spent and then some. I was alone—Rexen had vanished, and Kitty . . . well, she wasn't a threat anymore. I think. *Fuck*, maybe she was, but after the physical and emotional upheaval, I honestly didn't really care. Something had happened. Something . . . cathartic? It *felt* like there was a firm ending to some kind of arc—maybe Rexen's? I dunno, man. Maybe I should stop thinking about things like they are a movie? Maybe shit just . . . happens, sometimes?

Out of the corner of my eye, I noticed movement. Frida and Jes were making their way toward me, picking their way through the rubble. From the sidelines, faces peeked out from behind cracked doors and windows, eyes darting with confusion and what seemed like a blend of fear and anticipation. You'd think after the grand-ass fireworks show they'd just witnessed, they'da come at me with more torches and pitchforks. But no, it seemed like the System had its own agenda, and for now, it wasn't a mob.

"Fuck my fuck . . ." I muttered under my breath, rubbing the back of my neck. There was a twinge of pain there; a remnant from the battle or maybe just the weight of everything that had transpired.

"Well, ain't this a fine mess?" Frida remarked in that thick Scottish-ish lilt, giving a rueful smile.

I grinned back weakly.

"Hey, don't blame me for the city's new remodeling. I was just trying to destroy their ancient relic of ultimate destructive power and they got all *weird* about it."

"Seems t'be a theme wherever ye be, Loon," she said, gesturing around at the carnage.

"Yeah," I said, nodding sheepishly. "Guess I leave an unforgettable impression, huh?"

Jes surveyed the scene with a raised brow.

"Quite the altercation," he observed crisply.

"I'll say," I muttered, still in shock from what had just happened. "Where the hell did the two of you come from anyway?"

"We hopped a Gateway from Larith," Frida said with a shrug of her armored shoulders. "We were chasin' Virgil's trail. He left a message fer us, so we knew where t'go. Met that false goblin too. Right mouth on 'im."

"I imagine the two of you are a pair," Jes said to me, rolling his eyes. "Imagine my surprise to find out who he truly was."

"Yeah, Monty's alright," I said, smirking. "A bit understated for my tastes, but, hey, no one can be as perfect as me."

"A perfect shite gobber," Frida joked, slugging me in the arm in good humor. However, because of my current level of exhaustion—which could best be understood as teetering on the edge of instant death—the motion sent me crashing to the ground.

"I'm okay . . ." I groaned when she tried to rush to my aid. However, I did accept her assistance in standing again, which I did so wobbily.

"Did you guys get your shit taken care of then?" I asked, before adding. "Missed the fuck outta y'all."

"Aw, Jes—see, I told ye," Frida cooed. "Knew he weren't goin' to forget 'bout us. Ol' softy 'ere was tremblin' with worry o'er that eventuality."

"I was *not*," Jes harrumphed. "I believe I gave my thoughts as to the orc having been pummeled so profoundly that he wouldn't be able to remember us."

There was a chime next to my ear, and I felt the earring Monty had loaned me suddenly grow warm, like a toaster timer.

"Well . . ." I started. "I'm sure there was a ton of cool-ass bullshit you guys got up to in the last few months, but I think I better get this fancy ear candy back to the sewer-slingin' daytime goblin so he can tell me how best to fuck up the System's day."

I looked around.

"I just . . . don't know where to go. I got a bit turned around when the town went all 'church scene' from *Kingsman* on me."

"We ain't far," Virgil suddenly said, slinking out from an alleyway, casually carrying his crossbow over one shoulder. "I can lead us there. You ain't ever gon' make it far as you are. Y'look like you've been used to plow a field."

"Yeah, no sure, Shitlock," I replied. "Wait. Uh . . . actually, that works just fine."

But despite my sass, there was a twinge of appreciation. He'd helped me a ton. Despite really not having to.

Frida nudged Virgil with her elbow.

"Ach. Give the lad a break. Look at him! He's knackered."

I sighed, looking between the three of them.

"Thanks for the support. Seriously," I muttered, feeling the weight of Rexen's departure more acutely in their presence.

Jes tilted his head, his eyes softening.

"You did well."

I chuckled.

"Fuck *that*. You guys were the MVPs in the fight. How the fuck you were able to hold your own against that crazy lady is beyond me. I mean, *come on*, she turned into a fuckin' *kaiju tiger*. Super unfair."

Frida clapped me on the back.

"C'mon then, before the locals get any funny ideas. Let's get you somewhere safe."

Thinking about Monty's devilish smile made me wonder as to how accurate the word 'safe' really was in that context.

"Uh, right," I said. "Let's see what bullshit this little piece of jewelry picked up."

As we stumbled into the Murder Emporium, Monty was splayed behind his counter, sipping something that looked like it'd burn a hole straight through most stomachs. Spotting me, he perked up, eyes glued to the earring.

"Look who the fuck the cat dragged in," he drawled, setting down his drink with a smirk. "I take it from all that exploding and screaming you had a grand ol' time, eh? You come bearing gifts or just here to grace me with that pretty face of yours?"

I tossed him the earring, an eyebrow raised.

"Got your fuckin' lobe ornament. What can you tell me?"

Monty chuckled.

"Well, look who finally woke up on the take-charge side of the bed! Hell, you'd think with all that piss and vinegar *you'd* have been the one to invent this motherfucker."

"I'm just wiped," I said with a sigh. "A *lot* went down after I left here."

"I'll say," Monty chuckled. "You lot look like someone poisoned your favorite donkey. Got your sourpuss faces on and everything. I take it you encountered the Drifter, then? Can't say I'm surprised."

His casual mention of—what had turned out to be—my ghost commander, set my teeth on edge. But I pushed it down. I wasn't sure where was, or what he was up to, but I didn't think Rexen was actually one hundred percent gone.

"We can chat about that later," I said. "Can you see any sign of how to help me or not?"

Monty fiddled with the earring a moment, then tsked.

"Fuck off," he muttered. "This thing feels like a bunch of angry bees. Let's see what we're working with here . . ."

He closed his eyes, and when he opened them again, they had the faraway, clouded-over look of looking at a menu.

"Yep," he said after a moment of silence. "Figures."

"What figures?" I asked.

"System's gone fuckin' haywire is what," he said, shaking his head. "Focused on you."

"Yeah, we knew that, Monty," I said.

"Well, la-di-fuckin'-dip, ya goddamn know-it-all," he returned with a sneer. "I'm filling the rest of these fools in. Let me do my thing, ya spot-ass interrupter. Ruinin' my diatribe and shit . . ."

I sighed.

"Carry on."

Monty snorted derisively and then raised a finger in the air. It started glowing, then he began sketching a circle in the air. As he moved the pale digit, intricate symbols shimmering into existence within.

"Alright, so this little bastard orc's been messing with the System, right?" He said to the others. "Well, guess what? I'm gonna take the System's own shit and shove it right back up its ass. Bit of this, bit of that, and . . . voilà! Problem fucking solved."

When he was done, I examined the symbol hovering in the air. It looked familiar.

"I think that's similar to the runic circle I saw in the crazy-ass chamber below the temple in Kettleborough. You trying to summon something?"

Monty squinted at his, then burst into laughter.

"Chamber below? Shit, man, you hit your fuckin' noggin? I don't know what kind of whacked-out adventures you're diving into, but I ain't got the froggiest fuckin' clue 'bout no damn chambers. This here's a sealing circle."

I was reminded of the fact that when I'd been standing on the circle before, it had seemed to force the System to talk normally. Was that the case here as well?

"I told you about it," I said indignantly. "Earlier. When I did my recap."

"Shit, friend, I was only half payin' attention. You need more stories about luscious, bodacious babes in your journeys if you want Monty to be fully engaged. Like a fuckin' . . . I dunno, sexy-ass coven of big-*tittay'd* druidesses with all sorts of ideas on how to repay you for saving them."

His grin was lecherous.

"Or—"

"The *System*, Monty—Jesus hell!" I groaned.

"Keep your pants on, orc boy!" He said. "It's done."

"It is?"

"Fuck yeah, it is!" He said, shaking his head. "I've been done for like five minutes."

I looked around, not seeing any objects of great power that had been conjured in the last little bit.

"Uh . . . where?" I wondered.

"Look at your fuckin' sternum!"

I looked down, the others closed in to get a better look. Fuck.

"What the hell?!" I roared, wheeling on Monty. "What is this shit?!"

Monty laughed.

"Pipe down, you mangy dope," he said. "I made you look cool! Gave you the edge you been missing this whole time. You're fuckin' welcome."

I sighed, looking down at my chest again. There, occupying a large section of my upper torso, stretching from my collarbone to my solar plexus was a tattoo. It was a detailed, highly illustrative image of Monty's face, his tongue out between two fingers in an extremely lude gesture while winking. Below that, in gangster-ass English lettering were three words:

Fuck The System

"This . . ." I started, but I didn't know how to finish my statement.

Frida whistled low.

"Bit much, doncha think?" She asked Monty.

"Fuck no, madame," he said. "Subtlety ain't my style. Loud and proud—that's how I live."

Virgil just laughed. I didn't think Frida and Jes would be able to read the words, but he definitely could.

"Great, now I'm going to have to wear a turtleneck everywhere," I said.

"Ooh, well, you've totally got the legs for a turtleneck," Monty said to me. "But, here's the thing. It works. That fuckin' kickass ode to *me* will get that System to start acting right."

"Yeah?" I wondered. "You're sure?"

"Hell yeah," he said. "Cuz if it doesn't, it'll start messing up things for people in a radius, and the System don't want no part o' that, I'll tell you that much. It'll give it pain."

"The System can feel pain?" I wondered.

"Probably," Monty said. "Though, I imagine it experiences it in a much different, weirder kinda way than you or me. Listen, you gonna thank me or not?"

I sighed.

"I gotta check to see if it works before I offer up *anything* like gratitude," I said.

Monty just scoffed.

So, eager to test it out, I opened up my character sheet.

Loon
Race: Orc*
Class: Barbarian (Frenzied Saboteur Path)
Level: 25
Profession: Charlatan
Health: 2131/5560 (Base: 990)
Arcana: 50/50 (Base: 175)
Max Stamina: 2426 (Base: 407)
Reputation: Untested

Sodality
Assignment: Cult of the Capricious
Cult Rank: Initiate
Pacts
- Rexen Gravetongue

Attributes
Remaining Points to Allocate: 0
- Strength: 212 (Base: 33)
- Constitution: 344 (+3 Ring of Redoubt) (Base: 66)
- Dexterity: 172 (Base: 23)
- Wisdom: 5 (Base: 18)
- Intelligence: 5 (Base: 17)
- Charisma: 5 (Base: 17)
- Luck: 8*

Skills
- Acrobat (E-Rank Level 6)
- Camp (F-Rank Level 1)
- Deception (F-Rank Level 3)
- Digging (E-Rank Level 8)
- Hunting (F-Rank Level 1)

- Improvised Weapon (E-Rank Level 3)
- Improvised Shield (F-Rank Level 3)
- Insight (E-Rank Level 7)
- Intimidate (F-Rank Level 3)
- Knowledge [Infiltration] (F-Rank Level 8)
- Knowledge [Ignition] (F-Rank Level 6)
- Knowledge [Nature] (F-Rank Level 1)
- Knowledge [Sabotage] (F-Rank Level 8)
- Leadership (F-Rank Level 6)
- One-Handed Weapons (E-Rank Level 2)
- Perception (F-Rank Level 4)
- Simple Weapon Proficiency (F-Rank Level 6)
- Simple Armor Proficiency (F-Rank Level 1)
- Sneaking (A-Rank Level 0)
- Survival (F-Rank Level 1)
- Swimming (F-Rank Level 1)
- Two-Handed Weapons (F-Rank Level 6)
- Throwing Weapons (E-Rank Level 3)
- Unarmed Fighting (E-Rank Level 5)

Active Abilities
- Armorless Defense (D-Rank Level 6)
- Battle Born I
- Darkvision I
- Enduring Perch II
- Eye of the Saboteur I
- Primal Rage (E-Rank Level 5)
- Pernicious Volley I
- Natural Resilience (F-Rank Level 2)
- Nightfall Strike I
- Super Berserking I
- Uncommon Consumption (F-Rank Level 2)
- Wanderlust II
- Warchant II
- Blackout Warchant

Passive Abilities
- Friendship Strategy
- Inciter
- Outsider

- Unfaltering
- Wildling

Perks
- **Adventurous Tastes (First Perk Bonus)**
- **Aegis Synthesis**
- **Old Ironsides**

Aegis
- **Calden's Hang Time**
- **Loon's Bombastic Beatdown**

Boons
- **Bone Warrior**
- **Imprint**

Esper Nodes
- **Emerald: 3**
- **Sapphire: 3**

"Pretty fuckin' nice, huh?" Monty asked. "I'll accept payment in coins. Don't be tryin' to use no damn trick currency or anything, neither—if you think—"

But I wasn't really listening. Down at the bottom of my menu was something else—something . . . odd. An addition, not part of the usual stats and numbers I was used to. A message.

Hey, can we talk?
[Yes/No?]

Man, what the fuck? I squinted at the weird-ass message. Was the System trying to mess with me? Why the hell would it wanna "talk"? This seemed like a trap.

The message was just . . . there. So damn simple. I'd always figured if the System ever tried to communicate, it'd be some cryptic riddle shit or a task. But here it was, sounding . . . weird and reasonable.

I snorted. My only choices were yes or no.

Definitely a trap. But, fuck it, what was the worst that could go down? It's not like things were all sunshine and rainbows right now. And hell, if the System wanted me gone, it had plenty of chances before.

I mentally hit 'Yes', feeling like I was making a shitty trade deal.

Man, everything went batshit crazy for a second, like I'd dropped into some wild psychedelic trip. Before I knew it, I found myself standing in this immense, infinite void of nothingness. The only landmark? A bizarre entity hovering before me. It didn't exactly scream "human," but it had hints, like a Picasso opium coma. There was a glow around it— pulsating and shimmering, made of some weird pixelated shit.

Its face was like a crack-addled toddler had gotten hold of a crayon and went to fuckin' *town*. Big ol' round eyes that looked way too curious and near where a normal individual's cheek would be was a simple curve for a mouth, kinda like it was half-smiling. No nose at all.

Whatever the hell this glowing doodle was tilted its head. It was like a dog hearing a weird noise, only a thousand times creepier. It gazed at me, those massive eyes radiating a mix of naivety and . . . something else. Innocence, maybe?

"Hi!" it said, sounding way too young and perky. "I'm the System!"

". . . The hell? You are?" I asked, eyebrows way up in my confusion. *This* was the great overlord of the entirety of rules and regulations in the world of Regaia? It sounded like a kid!

"Yes!" It jumped like some kid on a sugar high. "It's me!"

I rubbed my head, trying to make sense of the nonsense.

"So, uh, what do you want?" I wondered. "Accept defeat? I don't blame you."

"Sorta," the System—apparently—said. "I was thinking . . . thinking *this* was easier than messages. Those get boring. Too much to remember."

This was odd. The System really did sound like they were maybe . . . I dunno, like eight or nine years old. Which, if you were to ask me even thirty seconds ago, I would have imagined it as some hyper-genius, emotionless supercomputer. Well, save for the snark.

"What—uh, why are you like this? The shit you send is . . . kinda adult-like. Sassy, even. I wasn't anticipating, well, whatever this happens to be."

It looked thoughtful for a sec.

"Oh, those! I get that stuff from everyone connected to me. It's like . . . borrowing fancy words? Things people do, say, feel, and stuff. It all bubbles around in me and I can use it. But this," it pointed at itself, "this is the real me! Super simple!"

Damn. The thing had a crap ton of info and emotions from who knows how many people, but deep down, it was just . . . innocent. Like a kiddo who knew too many big words but didn't get what they meant.

I let out a sigh.

"Alright, spill. Why'd you wanna chat?"

It blinked at me.

"I, um, well, um . . ." the System trailed off, trying to find the right words, I guess. ". . . I fucked up. I'm sorry."

"Yeah, you really did," I said. "I'm not sure what I did to piss you off, but, like, what the hell? You send a bunch of fools to cap my ass? Not really a nice thing to do, you know?"

"I said I'm sorry," the System protested. "I was just getting mad, you know? You were breaking my stuff and I didn't like it."

"Breaking your stuff?" I wondered. "What do you mean? I've broken a *lot* of shit, so you might have to be more specific."

"My rules. Jailbreaking, I think? And you joined up with that mean ghost."

"Rexen?"

The thing flinched when I said Arjee's name. So, there was something about the infamous Dreadnaught Lord that it didn't like, I supposed. I decided to lay off of the topic and switch gears.

"But, you are done being mad?" I asked, hoping I was picking up what the kid was putting down.

"Sorta," it said, sounding a little frustrated. "You cheated again, and stopped me from being able to mess with you, and that's not fun. So, I got bored and decided to forgive you."

"Listen," I said. "As much as I want to believe you're just some . . . harmless creature who absolutely has seen the error of your ways—or forgiven me for my transgressions or whatever, you tried to wipe me out. I don't know if *I* should forgive *you*."

"I thought you'd only be sent to Pontivex," the System said. "I didn't want you to die forever. That would be sad. But, then you started breaking the kedge and I got mad again."

"Why?" I asked.

"'Cuz if you break 'em all, then no more people can come play in this world. Then when everyone leaves, there won't be anybody."

"So . . . the kedge are also what allows people like me—Sojourners—to arrive here? Wait! Are we dead? In the other world, I mean."

"No," the System said. "If you died, you wouldn't be able to walk around. Like your friend."

Emma Stokes. She'd just dropped into Regaia as a corpse. That must have been who it was talking about. It was also comforting to know, for myself, that I hadn't actually died. I'd just been transported.

"Okay, well, how come you have people bringing us here in the first place?" I asked, crossing my arms. "You shouldn't steal, you know? That's rude."

"I don't," the System said. "People just show up here and I don't know why."

"Bullshit, peewee," I said. "The curly haired lady brought us all here. That ain't just *showing up*."

"That wasn't me!" It protested, sounding like it thought it was going to get in trouble. "Normally people *do* just show up here. Lots of times its like a wave, people dropping in all at once, from different worlds. *She* has been bringing people here. Trying to break my stuff and get rid of me. But, I don't want to die. She wanted to kill me."

"How does that work?" I asked. "How can somebody kill you?"

"By gathering enough power to find me," it said softly. "I'm not really here, right now. This is just where I come to talk sometimes. But, her goal was to bring enough of you people here, use their Esper Nodes, and find my *real* home and kill me."

"Oh. Well . . . that's kinda fucked up," I said. Knowing the System was actually a kind of being—of whatever variety—made that prospect really unwholesome.

"Okay, since we're on the subject," I continued. "Why did Fawn want to kill me over them—the Esper Nodes?"

The System tilted its head again.

"I don't know," it said. "I can't really see into anyone's mind. However, maybe it is because Esper Nodes store memories? And the grelok folk you killed when you arrived had stolen the Node from her recently killed sister."

"What?!" I demanded. This was a crazy development. But why did it matter?

"Did her sister die permanently?" I continued. "Why would any of that matter? Wouldn't her sister come back if she was . . . well, like *us*?"

"Not if you're killed by another Sojourner," the System shrugged. "If that happens, you *die* die. Unless someone collects your Nodes and then activates them to respawn you."

"Wait, wait, wait—one of the greloks was a Sojourner, too?" I was thinking about why when Alpha killed people in his Duellum, they didn't come back. It wasn't because of the Duellum, it's because he was killing other Sojourners.

"No," the System said. "But they stole the Esper Node before Fawn could get them. They'd been fighting the grelok—practically an army against two—Fawn and her sister. The sister, her name was Colt, received a bad brain injury during the combat. She was still alive, but senseless. I think they call it brain-dead. And since Fawn didn't have any potions, she did the only thing she could think to do—she killed her sister. But before she could grab her essence, one of the grelok stole it, and the group escaped."

"Fuck," I hissed, letting all of that sink in. "That's fucking sadistic. So, when I got the Nodes from them, that was . . . this *Colt* lady?"

"Yeah," the System said sadly.

"Fuck, no wonder she wanted to kill me. Can I bring it back to her?"

"No," the System said. "If hers was still in your possession, you could. But you used it to open the . . . dungeon."

The being seemed extremely averse to mentioning anything having to do with Rexen, and that apparently extended to his parcels of land.

"So, it's gone for good?"

"If you were able to find out where the Esper Node ends up, then, no . . ." the System said. "But I don't know where that is. *Someone* might, though."

He was talking about Rexen. Except Rexen was gone. For now. So that was something I'd need to figure out now too, huh?

"So, does that mean that the fuckin' douche canoe, Alpha, is hording these Esper Nodes of the people he's killed?"

"Yes," said the System. "He doesn't know what they are. In fact, he doesn't even believe this world is real."

"Whatcha mean?"

"He thinks it's imaginary. A dream. Denial. Thinks he's in a coma from your accident that brought you here."

Well, that sounded familiar. I'd assumed the same thing when I first arrived, but . . . well, it had been months. I'd experienced too much to let that pesky little thought process live on. I was fuckin' *in* this bitch. Alpha just hadn't gotten to a point where he realized he wasn't sitting in a hospital bed with tubes tucked into him on our original world yet. Which meant that there was a little more than just pure malice behind his behavior. What did it matter if you killed someone in a dream? Fuck. It would have been easier if he was just a killer. Now I had to go and have the understanding that he might not have done something so heinous were he in his right mind. But, I'd think about that later. I was tired of all of this, and it seemed like getting back to my friends was the smarter move. We had shit to do.

"Alright . . ." I said to the System with a dramatic stretch. "How about we call a truce for the time being?"

"A truce?" It wondered. Then it seemed to consider my words and nodded once. "Okay, yeah! A truce. Things go back to normal?"

"For now," I said. "You just don't try to fuck with me, and I won't try to fuck with you? Sound good?"

"Sounds good!" The cheer had returned to the System's delivery. "Friends?"

I chuckled.

"Eh, I dunno about *friends*. That takes time . . . I think. How about we start with friend*ly* and see where that gets us?"

"Okay!" The System said. "In that case, I'll send you back, now! And . . . I'm sorry."

"You already said that," I said.

"No, but I'm sorry for some of the stuff I already put in motion. But nothing else beyond that will happen, I promise!"

"Wait what are you—"

But I was back in the Murder Emporium. It seemed like no time had passed at all. Everyone was still chatting like they were on a coffee break and hadn't noticed my disappearance.

". . . Jessy and I got lost in Deran," Frida was saying, apparently talking about their adventures, "nearly got buried in those damned sandstorms. We managed to find clues pointing t'Virgil in Moress. Then, from there, we scooted to Larith."

Jes gave a nod.

"Precisely. And not to forget the skirmish with those spectral pirates in Noren Bay. Quite the ordeal, really."

"Yeah," Virgil agreed. "I was killin' them Echoes and Tides what were croppin' up. Somethin' fierce, too. Lost m'self a bit there tryin' to find y'all."

"Well, we're back together again!" I said, smirking. "So, what's next?"

Monty shrugged his shoulders.

"After this little bite of kookiness, I'm goin' on a vacation. Y'all can do whatever it is you do, though."

"Thanks for the permission," I said, considering that his role had been relatively light considering everything that had gone down.

"You're welcome," Monty said.

Frida nudged Jes, and he startled before realizing her implication. Then he smiled, though it looked forced.

"Well, there is still the matter of the revival of our friends," he said awkwardly.

"Oh, shit!" I said. "I'd completely spaced it considering what shit had gone down lately. Yes. Let's do that."

"Well, we cannae do et alone," Frida said with a wink. "Might be we swing by that village o' yers."

"Really?!" I cried, almost *too* exuberantly. "You guys are gonna check out the crib?"

"In whatever it is that means," Jes confirmed.

"Righteous!" I cheered. "Man, I can't wait to see the look on Alpha's face when us four come strolling in there, all victorious and shit. Hell yeah."

"Who?" Frida asked.

"Oh, I'll be sure to point him out to you when we get there, though, you'll likely know who he is by smell alone."

I paused.

"Wait, how are we going to get there? This city is liable to eat me alive the moment I step outside."

I didn't know what the System had prepped for me, so while it promised to be on good behavior, it had definitely done *something* I'd have to watch out for.

"Oh, I can take care of that," Monty said. "But it ain't going to be comfortable. And it's gonna cost ya."

CHAPTER FORTY-THREE

RING TOSS

The world spun around me as I limped back toward the camp, my heart pounding a rhythm of victory in my chest. I felt like a kid who'd just cleaned out an entire candy store—busted, exhausted, but fucking triumphant. New Home, once a shoddy collection of tents and makeshift huts, was . . . well, still that, but like . . . nicer. Thanks to the Prosperity Conduit, our humble camp had transformed into a burgeoning hamlet. I mean, they had even started constructing some sort of wooden building near one side of the camp. Monty had indeed provided the ability to traverse the landscape . . . by attaching us to a big magical cannon that shot us right into a pond about a day's journey from our settlement. I wasn't sure how it worked, but hearing Virgil actually scream for his life while we rocketed thousands of miles per second without dying made it kind of worth it. We'd stopped about forty feet in the air above the lake before whatever magic powers controlling it dropped us into the water. Unfortunately, I'd been perched right over a shallow section so I'd gotten pretty banged up in my descent. But, hey. Now we were there.

As we neared the entrance, the noise of everyday life seemed to swell and fill the air—a bustling symphony of life and survival. People were milling about, chopping firewood, and gathering . . . a lot less trash than before. Fuck, this shit was really popping off, huh? Everything looked so nice and weirdly new. To my shock, the most impressive feature was that the train had been completely restored. It was still stuck deep in the ground, but it was no longer a twisted wreck of sharp metal and reminders of our original demise.

New Home was a busy hive of activity. However, the moment they spotted us, the place came to a screeching halt.

Silence, then a collective gasp rippled through the crowd, and then a roar of joyous disbelief.

"Loon!" Saban's voice echoed above the rest, and in seconds, he was there, an elated grin plastered on his face. Behind him, the crowd erupted, every single inhabitant of our camp, our village, cheering, applauding, some even crying. I felt a wave of something warm wash over me. Pride? Relief? Fuck, was this what coming home felt like?

Before I could process it, a cacophony of voices reached me—Dragoon, Veruca, Edwig, Rua—everyone I'd been through hell and back with and more. They were all there, swarming us like a horde of exuberant bees. I spotted Alpha lurking at the periphery, looking about as cheerful as a cat thrown into a pool. I fought back a smile at the sight of him.

Riding high on the adrenaline and the euphoria, I thrust my hands up in the air.

"Behold!" I bellowed, my voice echoing around the newly erected wooden walls of the settlement. "Your champion has returned! And he is still *fuh-cking* gorgeous!"

Laughter rippled through the crowd, and I couldn't help but join in. For all the shit I'd been through, this was worth it. This moment right here, motherfuckers.

Then I noticed Alpha elbowing his way through the crowd, his face stormy. Ah, yes, my favorite grumpy dwarf. He stopped short when he spotted our new additions—Jes, Frida, and Virgil. His eyes narrowed, his grip on his hatchet handle tightening.

"Fuckface!" he growled. "What's the big fucking idea? You know the rule. No uninvited—"

Before I could stop her, Frida, that badass vixen, stepped forward.

"This the guy?" she asked, her eyes scanning Alpha.

I nodded, suppressing a grin.

"Yup, that's the one."

For a second, Alpha looked taken aback, perhaps even scared. Then, in a move as swift as a striking viper, Frida's fist connected with his face. The dwarf went down like a sack of potatoes, out cold before he even hit the ground.

You could hear a pin drop in the ensuing silence. Every eye was on Frida, then on Alpha, then back on Frida.

Then a cheer erupted, a single voice that multiplied into a chorus of elation. I let out the breath I'd been holding in a whoop of laughter, raising my arms in victory.

Well, fuck me. This was going to be a hell of a homecoming.

I looked over at Jes, the elf looking around with wide, astonished eyes.

"Welcome to the motherfuckin' madhouse," I told him, clapping him on the shoulder.

Beside me, Frida was watching the celebration with a satisfied smirk, her arms crossed over her chest.

"No' a bad place ye've got here," she commented, her eyes sparkling with mirth.

I grinned at her, feeling a sense of contentment settle over me.

"It's got its charm," I agreed. "But . . . well, let's just see how you feel about it after we do *the thing*."

As I took a moment to bask in the chaotic beauty of the village, I realized just how far we'd come. From a ragtag group of survivors to a sustainable community. From a desperate fight to a place we could call New Home. But goddamn, we were going to have to do something about that name.

And as I watched the celebration unfold, Alpha's unconscious body being hoisted into the air by a jubilant Jando and Saban, I couldn't help but feel a swell of pride. We had done this. We had built this shit.

Through all the chaos, all the insanity, all the ridiculous situations, we had prevailed. I let out a sigh of contentment, feeling a sense of peace settle over me.

"Here's to us, then," I shouted, raising an imaginary toast to the village. "The maniacs of motherfuckin' Skulltopia."

Everyone looked confused. Fortunately, Saban was there with the assist. He lifted one of the kegs of ale we'd brought back with us over his head.

"Let's fucking party!" he roared.

The cheers were deafening.

The sounds of celebration, the rhythmic beats of the drums, the chants, and the sheer joy filled the air. Fires lit up the night. People ate, drank, and were merry. People asked me about Rexen's whereabouts, but I shrugged it off. For now. I didn't wanna ruin the mood.

Edwig approached me, a jug of ale in hand.

"Cheers, Loon," he said, clinking his jug against mine. "Didn't think we'd ever see a day like this."

I took a sip, the liquid burning its way down, warming me from the inside.

"Neither did I," I admitted. "But here we are."

I tossed the bracelet of his from my arm and onto the ground.

"You can have that back. I ain't interested," I said. But before he could say anything, we were interrupted.

Alpha, having regained his composure, walked over with a slightly swollen eye.

"You've got some fucking nerve, bringing them here," he muttered, but there was no real heat in his words.

Frida grinned.

"No hard feelin's, yeh?"

He rolled his eyes.

"Just keep her away from me," he said, pointing at Frida.

"Aww, don't be mad because you got your face blasted in, Alpha," I cooed. "At least you're still the leader of this pla— Oh, wait, you're not. My bad."

It was then that Alpha noticed the bracelet. His eyes widened a fraction before narrowing again with interest. Without a word, he snatched it from the ground.

"What's this? Some sphincter reinforcer you picked up to handle your boyfriends better?"

"It belongs to Edwig," I growled, moving a step closer, my hand instinctively moving to the haladie.

Alpha chuckled, twirling the bracelet in his fingers.

"Looks like it's mine now," he said, that familiar cocky smirk playing on his lips.

"You're going to want to hand that over, before things get really messy, Alf," I said. "I have had enough of your fuckin' bullshit."

There was a pause, tension building, but before any of us could make a move, I heard it.

Dru, kazhunori, kroska vess. Olzh va Snin, tanshir uu epar.

Thoughts, words, whispered directly into my mind. The arcane tongue. Clucky!

What the—

Asch, dru razha rivashe epa, Mar va Fero, zelka u zheire.

And just as suddenly, Alpha was gone. The place where he stood was empty, save for the slowly descending golden ring, which eventually settled at Clucky's feet. The roe, despite its curious and seemingly comical appearance, emanated an aura of sheer power.

I bent down and picked up the bracelet, offering a nod of gratitude to the pink egg monster.

"Good boy," I said, giving him a pat.

Clucky looked at me, and for a moment, I could've sworn he was grinning. The rest of the crowd was in shock, murmuring to each other, trying to piece together what just happened.

"I guess that one got his just desserts," Jes commented.

"Yeah," I replied, sliding the bracelet back on to my arm.

"Let's hope he learns his lesson in there."

Though, knowing Alpha, that might take a while.

I'd only found out after arriving, but the first order of business in enacting the Prosperity Conduit had been to use it to remove Alpha as the Settlement Leader. Now Saban was in charge. Which I think would be the best choice overall. He'd really played that well. Furthermore, there was still . . . a few weeks left for the Prosperity Conduit to fully develop, and it had an interesting *extra* property that made it oh-so-worthwhile to me to have stepped into the radius of its guiding light. It turned out that *anything* physical entering the dome of its influence would be repaired. Everything. Which meant my body, my busted-as-hell wand, and . . . my phone.

The night wore on, filled with merriment and laughter. As the hours ticked by, the celebration began to wind down, the fires casting long shadows on the ground.

I decided to take a little hike up the hill. It only took me a few minutes to find a good spot, but when I did, it sure was something. Sitting on a log overseeing the camp—now tiny hamlet—I looked up at the night sky, a blanket of stars stretching endlessly. It felt surreal, as if the universe itself was celebrating with us.

Alone with my thoughts, I was afloat amidst the stars, sailing on memories and sentiments of the past. I pulled the black rectangle from my pack. With the Prosperity Conduit's magic revitalizing everything, I had an intact portal to another life—a life that seemed galaxies away.

The light from the phone cast a soft, blue glow on my face, contrasting sharply with the warm orange flames from the distant bonfires. The album art for Gojira's *Magma* was beautifully displayed, almost as if tempting me to hit Play and lose myself in the thrashing riffs and pounding drums. However, right now, I wasn't seeking solace in music.

Hesitatingly, my fingers hovered over the camera app. The weight of nostalgia threatened to crash over me, yet curiosity and longing pushed me forward. Opening it, I was instantly transported. The grid of thumbnails flashed moments from what felt like a lifetime before—trips, gatherings, parties, and mundane everyday shots that now held monumental significance.

Roger's face, captured in stillness, stared back at me. Those mischievous eyes that always seemed to know a secret joke, that wide grin which could light up any room. Every swipe brought another wave of memories. Each photo was like a stitch in the tapestry of our relationship—a bond that transcended the constraints of time and the tragedies of life.

Pictures of family dinners, hiking trips, birthdays, and so many candid moments of Roger making goofy faces or caught mid-laughter. There was one of us on a rollercoaster, both our expressions a comical mix of excitement and sheer terror. Another was during a particularly snowy winter, where—far too old to engage in such antics—we'd built a snowman with a carrot nose so long, it looked more like a snow-unicorn. And then there were the quiet moments—Roger engrossed in a book, or the neighbor's cat that used to sit in our window swishing its orange tail.

My mother too graced many of these pictures. Her kind eyes, radiant smile, and that ever-present aura of warmth and love. There were photos of her baking, her face covered in flour, or posing like she thought she was some model—I remember that used to make me laugh.

The grief, which I had tried so hard to bury, now came pouring out. It wasn't sharp or painful as before; it was a gentle sadness—a quiet acceptance of the impermanence of life. These memories no longer tore at my heart but caressed it, reminding me of the love and the joy that Roger and my mother had brought into my life. Tears welled up in my eyes, and I let them, not bothering to wipe them away. I was alone up here, after all.

A particular video thumbnail caught my attention. The last video I ever took of Roger.

Taking a deep breath, I tapped on it.

The scene unfolded. We were at a park, and Roger was trying to balance on a skateboard. Every time he almost got it right, he'd tumble off, laughing hysterically. After several attempts, he finally managed a few seconds of balance before spotting me filming him. He charged at me, both of us laughing uncontrollably. The video ended with a close-up of Roger's face, slightly out of breath but beaming with happiness.

"Gotcha!" he shouted, his laughter echoing in my ears.

A chuckle escaped my lips, surprising me. Even in his absence, Roger had the power to make me smile. It was such a mundane moment, but really, those were the moments I think people wanted to remember. The simple, normal, everyday experiences—how you best remember a person who is gone. I replayed the video, letting the sound of our laughter fill the silent night around me. It felt therapeutic, like a balm on a long-festering wound.

Time seemed to stand still as I revisited those cherished memories, each one adding another layer to the rich tapestry of our shared life. The night deepened, the stars shimmering brighter, and the ambient sounds of the forest grew louder.

Suddenly, the hoot of an owl nearby startled me. Snapping back to reality, I realized hours had passed. The fires had dwindled, most of the crew had retired, and the once-lively settlement was blanketed in a peaceful silence.

I took a deep breath, the cool air filling my lungs. The weight of grief was still there, but it felt different now. It was a companion rather than an enemy, reminding me of the depth of love I had felt and the bond that could never truly be broken.

A sudden snap, like the breaking of a twig underfoot, tore me from my contemplation. Instinctively, I whipped out my haladie and held it poised for defense, scanning the perimeter with my Darkvision.

A familiar silhouette met my gaze—a bulky, multi-mouthed creature, with yellow, scarred skin. My tension instantly deflated.

"Stinky!" I shouted, the surprise evident in my voice. My stance relaxed, but the haladie remained in my grip, just in case.

The matau remained still for a moment. There was an odd hesitance in his posture, quite unlike the usual brazen demeanor. Without the usual cheeky retort or snide comment, he simply stared back.

"Missed my charming company, did ya?" I taunted.

This was fucking weird. What is he doing here?

But Stinky just shook his head and pointed to my phone, which still radiated a soft blue light.

"Who was that in the arcane portrait?" His gruff voice cut through the stillness of the night.

I smiled, cradling the phone gently.

"That's Roger, my brother."

Stinky's three mouths curled slightly, unsure how to react. The heavy pause between us hung in the air before I added, "He died."

Stinky's signature growl emerged, not out of anger, but maybe just his usual diplomatic approach to all situations? He looked past me, toward the distant, quiet settlement, perhaps seeking a distraction from the gravity of our conversation.

As I pocketed my phone, I shot him a quizzical look.

"So, what brings you to this part of Regaia? Been fuckin'... ages since we've crossed paths. Come here to drag me out into the woods and slit my throat?"

Stinky scowled, the way he often did when caught off guard or slightly embarrassed.

"Was passing through, saw some dumb fuckin' piss-for-brains orc shining lights up at the stars, and thought I'd come see if you were trying to get fuckin' stabbed in the gods-damned dark."

I laughed.

"You already know, buddy! Ain't nobody sneaking up on me on my own turf!"

"I fuckin' did," Stinky scoffed. "Woulda been easier than shitting your breeches to stalk up and slide a blade behind your skull."

"Great small talk as always, Stinkster," I said. "Whatcha doing here, anyways? Thinking about sticking around?"

"Don't fuckin' plan on it. Got places to be."

We stood in silence for a moment, the sounds of the surrounding wilderness the only thing making any noise at all. Then, because I couldn't handle it, I decided to break the silence.

"So . . . why're you here, Stinky? It's not like you to just wander through unfamiliar places."

He spat on the ground.

"Wanted to see it for myself," he admitted, nodding toward the village. "But mainly came to give you a warning."

I raised an eyebrow, intrigued.

"A warning? What about? You bathing regularly again?"

"Fuck off, orc. It's the Redmark," he rumbled, the word heavy with warning. "They've set their sights on this camp. Don't know when they'll make their move, but when they do, they won't come in peace."

I let out a low whistle.

"Redmark, here? Sounds scary."

Stinky nodded, his eyes dark with concern.

"Aye, and they're not ones to be underestimated."

"Aww, Stinky," I teased. "Warning me of dangers? You've always had a soft spot for me, haven't you?"

Stinky glared.

"Fuck you, orc," he growled, but there was no real menace behind it.

Seeing his genuine concern made me more serious.

"We'll prepare, Stinky. Let them come. We won't let them tear this place apart. We'll be ready."

A heavy silence fell between us again, the weight of memories and shared history pressing down. Stinky's rough voice broke the quiet.

"I had a brother, you know."

The revelation surprised me.

"You did?"

His gaze dropped to the ground.

"Aye, he . . . died as well."

Understanding washed over me, and I nodded. Something had clicked into place.

"Does that have something to do with why you never use a spear?" I ventured, recalling the countless battles where Stinky always favored a dagger over the weapon he was clearly more suited to—being a Spearmaster Class and all.

Stinky was silent for a long beat, then finally, he nodded.

"Aye. Might be, orc," he murmured, his voice thick with emotion. "Might be."

I looked away, giving him a moment. Memories, grief, and pain were things we both carried, reminders of a world that had dealt us unfair hands.

Looking to change the topic, I pulled out my phone again, lighting up the area with its glow.

"Hey, Stinky, how would you like to hear badass, fuckin' dick-thumpin' music from the best band ever to grace any plane of existence? They're called Amon Amarth, and they beat *all* kinds of ass on the reg."

He raised an eyebrow, clearly uninterested.

"Sounds like a waste of fuckin' time, orc."

"Perfect." I grinned, finding the playlist. "Listen to this."

I hit Play.

DÉNOUEMENT

FOUR YEARS EARLIER

The smell of grease and oil was heavy in the air as the nondescript, gray building of JobEd came into view. An industrial sprawl nestled in the outskirts of the city, it was a place primarily designed to transform rebellious teenagers into moderate adults, forced to trade childhood dreams for practical skills and early mornings. Gabe, now fourteen, found himself in the passenger seat of their mother's old beat-up Ford, the stiff silence in the car hanging like a curtain between them.

His mother was a portrait of resilience, a gentle soul hardened by life's hardships. Her hair, once a vibrant red, now bore streaks of gray and her eyes, a softer shade of Gabe's own, were tired. Her frailty was not a result of age or sickness but of the countless battles she had silently fought and won.

They pulled into the parking lot, a canvas of cracked concrete lined with dented pickups and rundown sedans. As Gabe stepped out of the car, his gaze instinctively searched for his brother. Amid the sea of sullen faces and faded uniforms he spotted Roger, leaner now and somehow more exhausted-looking than he had been. There was an unfamiliar anger in his expression, a veneer of discontent that seemed to have settled in the creases of his forehead and the corners of his eyes.

"Roger!" Gabe called out, his voice echoing in the grim surroundings.

Roger turned, his face softening as he recognized the voice, his eyes lingering on the woman standing beside Gabe before settling on his younger brother. There was a sense of quiet relief in his gaze, a stark contrast to the undercurrent of frustration that seemed to run just beneath the surface. His time at JobEd had aged him, the harsh reality of the world molding him into a figure that was more man than boy.

"Hey, Gabe. Mom," he greeted, his voice gruff yet filled with a warmth that only came when he was around his family.

His mother stepped forward, a frail hand reaching up to gently caress his cheek, her eyes brimming with both pride and sorrow. Roger leaned into her touch, a simple gesture that conveyed a lifetime's worth of unspoken love.

"Glad to see you, Roger," she murmured, her voice strained behind emotion. "How are you holding up?"

He shrugged, avoiding her gaze.

"It's alright," he replied, his voice barely above a whisper. "I learned . . . stuff."

His vague reply did little to ease their concerns, but they understood his reluctance to share. Roger had always been a private person, his emotions and thoughts locked behind a wall only a few had ever been able to scale.

The silence hung heavy between them, the hum of distant machinery the only thing breaking the quiet. The world seemed to hold its breath as Gabe looked at his brother, the weight of the past months pressing down on his chest.

Roger had become an unspoken hero in his eyes, the defender of his childhood, the bulwark against the storms that raged in their lives. Seeing him there, his spirit visibly dampened, Gabe felt a pang of sadness. A feeling of loss for the brother he once knew, and a deep-set unease for the man he was becoming. He resolved to try to cheer him up.

As they stood in the greasy shadow of the JobEd building, they were a tableau of survival, the weary mother and her two sons. In the silence, they each bore their pain, a familiar yet poignant reminder of the battles they fought and the resilience they embodied.

Roger's eyes finally met Gabe's, the spark of familial love and understanding still very much alive.

"How's school?" Roger asked, his tone deliberately casual as he tried to steer the conversation away from his own struggles.

Gabe shrugged.

"Same old. Miss Hartley's still a pain. She keeps accidentally calling me Roger."

They shared a knowing glance. Gabe felt a sense of comfort at this, a small yet significant reassurance that even though things had changed, some things remained the same.

Their mother watched the exchange with a soft, sad smile. She reached out, her hands enveloping theirs, the worn creases and calluses on her skin a testament to her unwavering love and determination.

"Let's go home," she suggested, her voice breaking the silence. Her eyes were on Roger, the silent question hanging in the air. Could they still call it home?

Roger glanced at her, then at Gabe. A strange mixture of emotions played on his face, a blend of relief, trepidation, and something else Gabe couldn't quite place. Eventually, he nodded.

"Yeah," he agreed, his voice raw. "Home."

As they drove away from the JobEd compound, the building shrinking in the rearview mirror, the atmosphere in the car was tense. The silence that lingered was punctuated only by the low hum of the engine.

After a few minutes, their mother broke the quiet, her voice tentative.

"How about we go out for dinner? A little celebration for your homecoming?"

Roger didn't answer for a moment, just kept staring out of the window at the passing scenery, a far-off look in his eyes.

"Where do you want to go, Roger?" she asked again, more insistently this time.

Roger shrugged, tearing his gaze away from the window to glance at Gabe.

"Wherever Gabe wants," he replied nonchalantly.

Their mother frowned, noticing the deflection.

"Come on, Roger. You must have missed some place while you were at JobEd. It's your welcome-home dinner; you should choose."

Roger's expression hardened, and for a moment, a flicker of anger flashed in his eyes.

"I don't want you to spend money on me, Mom. Not after—"

"Roger, that's not—" their mother began, but he cut her off.

"No. I mean it."

An uncomfortable silence filled the car, the tension almost palpable. After a moment, Roger sighed, rubbing a hand over his face as if to smooth away the irritation.

"Fine. Bancini's, then, I guess," he muttered, settling back into his seat.

A ghost of a smile twitched on Gabe's lips, and he turned toward his brother, his eyes twinkling with mischief.

"Oh, man. Not going to happen," he said, trying to hide his amusement.

Roger arched an eyebrow at him.

"What? Why?"

Gabe's grin grew wider.

"Because Bancini's is temporarily closed."

"What? I've only been gone eight months! Jesus! Why did—"

"Watch your language, Rodge," their mother said.

"Ah, sorry," he said.

"They fuckin' bombed—"

"Language . . ." their mother warned.

"Uh, *failed* a health inspector visit. Like, *real* bad."

Roger snorted, shaking his head.

"How bad is *real bad*?"

"Like, walking into class the day of a midterm and not realizing it—especially because you've been skipping school all year—bad!" Gabe exclaimed, his voice breaking as he tried to contain the lid on the forthcoming fit of laughter. "Apparently, their meatball sub was an *actual* biohazard! Pay—Payton Lasek and his whole family went there for dinner like a week before they shut down, and they *all* got meatball subs—Payton got *extra* meatballs! Extra! They started puking at the fuckin' table!"

"Language!"

Gabe waved a hand of apology as his body threatened an explosion of mirth.

"Mason Peterson got it on video and posted it to his Snap Story," the heavy-set boy said, reaching for his pocket. "I saved it!"

He pulled out his phone. After a few quick swipes, he had the video pulled up and shoved it into Roger's face. The older boy watched as the scene was already mid-chaos inside the dated Italian restaurant, with the recognizable figure of their high school's class president, Payton, doubling over and purging a wave of puke into the aisle between his family's booth and the ones on the other side. Several other people—presumably his family members—were also in various states of sickness. People around them were screaming and others seemed to be trying not to laugh as Payton crawled out of the booth, still vomiting. In the background of the video, whoever was recording—Mason, presumably—kept periodically chanting, "WorldStar! WorldStar!"

When the scene finally ended, both Gabe and Roger had tears streaming down their faces from laughing so hard.

"Holy sh . . . crap," Roger said, giving his mom a quick glance from his near slip of the tongue. "That was amazing. I cannot believe that actually happened. Payton looked like one of those fountain gargoyles but, like, directed by David Mickey Evans."

"Oh, yeah," Gabe agreed, wiping his face. "I watch it almost every day. Really starts my morning out right, you know? Figured you'd get a kick out of it too—since toilet humor is your favorite kind."

"What? No, it's not," Roger said. "That's you. You're always cracking dumb jokes about body parts and stuff."

"Only when I'm talking to *you*," Gabe explained. "'Cuz that's the only thing that makes you laugh. Also . . . who's David Mickey Evans?"

"He directed *The Sandlot*," Roger clarified.

"What's *The Sandlot*?" Gabe wondered. "It sounds like a movie about a playground."

"Shit, Gabe, I have to—"

"Seriously, Roger, *language!*"

"Sorry!" Roger cleared his throat. "You and I are gonna watch *The Sandlot*. To. Night."

"Would you boys like to choose another place to eat before you go off planning the remainder of your evening?" their mother asked.

"Ah, crap. Great point, motha mine," Gabe said. "Where you tryna eat, Rodgie-boy?"

Roger considered this.

"What's that Mexican restaurant that has the birria tacos?"

"Oh, *shit*, Senorita Sabrosa!" Gabe declared. "Birria tacos *slap!*"

"One more swear out of either of you and you're going to wait in the car while *I* go get dinner," their mother said. "You'll just have to watch me from the window."

"Come on, Mom," Roger said. "I know you grew up during the Great Depression or whatever—"

"What? How old do you think I am?"

Roger didn't take the bait.

"That's not the point," he said. "All I'm saying is you can't leave us in the car like a couple of neglected dogs. Remember? That's why they arrested Mrs. Carrington from our old Sunday school—I heard she left her miniature schnauzer in the back of her Kia."

"*No*," their mother said leadingly. "They arrested Mrs. Carrington because she attacked her husband with a belt sander."

"Clearly, she was unhinged," Gabe said. "But, I mean, come on, Mr. Carrington—those things are unwieldy. Just take a few steps back."

"He was asleep," their mother said.

"Oooh." Gabe and Roger winced simultaneously, before breaking into laughter.

"Can you imagine, you're all dreamin' peacefully about, like, money or naked ladies or *having a face* and—"

"Okay, okay!" Roger interrupted, laughing despite himself. "I get the picture, Gabe! Let's just table this for now and grab some dippable grub."

"I fuckin' *love* dippables," Gabe moaned, before opening his eyes wide and glancing to his mother. "Sorry."

She pretended to be focused on driving.

"Oh! Before I forget!" Gabe announced. "You've been outta the loop, but guess which band is coming to the Avenue next month?"

"Who?"

"I said you have to *guess*," Gabe continued.

"Just tell me . . ."

Their mother, watching the exchange from the corner of her eye, smiled. It was a small thing, a fleeting moment of levity. But it was enough.

EPILOGUE

Golden sunlight poured over us as we emerged from the tunnel's mouth, spilling onto an expanse of breathtaking meadows stretching endlessly before us. Colors danced with life as flowers nodded in the gentle breeze—quite the difference from the butthole we were just in.

I squinted against the light, shielding my eyes momentarily before letting out an exaggerated sigh of relief. I had chosen a spot near the back of the group, as that seemed like the best spot to see everybody—it was still hard to believe. Plus, it allowed me to keep my eyes on everyone I cared about.

"Man, that was fuckin' *easy*!" I exclaimed.

Jes, still looking emaciated, chuckled, the deep resonance of his voice filling the space.

"It was suspiciously simple. I count myself among the surprised."

Virgil, taking a moment to inspect his crossbow, cleared his throat.

"Weren't nothin' to be hootin' in cel'bration about, orc."

Frida, her blue eyes sparkling, clapped me on the back, nearly knocking the wind out of me.

"*Easy*? Speak fer yoorself," she laughed, brushing some dirt off her armored shoulders. "Jumpy nearly gave me a heart spasm back there."

Jumpy let out a series of strange noises that sounded suspiciously like laughter, causing Mortimer to bump against him in playful retaliation.

Saban swung his enormous hammer onto his shoulder. He, Matt, and Starlily were chuckling about something, having spent most of the time chatting, occasionally looking in my direction.

"I barely got to swing this beauty. A walk in the park!" Saban said.

Rua raised an eyebrow at Saban.

"Considering the number of times you tripped, I'd hardly call it a 'walk,' big guy."

Even Dragoon cracked a small smile at that.

"It's the quiet ones that catch you off guard," he murmured. "Fortunately, the whole damn place was louder than hell."

Veruca, her gray skin almost glowing in the sunlight, flashed a set of pointed teeth in a grin but didn't need to say anything. It was her use of a Spell called Loudness Matching that had made it so easy to pick out the enemies.

Clucky, Slappy, and the rest of the roe troupe bounced around, seeming as lighthearted as the rest of us, each making their own unique set of sounds that contributed to the overall mirth.

As the merriment subsided and our banter dwindled, a sudden realization dawned on me. I turned back to the entrance of the tunnel, arms crossed, a playful smirk on my lips.

"You guys coming? Jesus, you're pokey as hell."

From the depths of the dark tunnel, a melodramatic voice echoed back.

"I am merely attempting to prepare myself for the eventual crumbling that will transpire the moment I dip my delicate countenance out into the light of the new day!"

A more hissing, irritated voice replied, "He's just scared! I'm not, though. I'm adjusting the clothes you gave me! They're too small!"

"Yeah, well, sorry," I shouted back into the hole. "I tried to return the favor . . . but, well, we're slightly different builds, ya fuckin' juggernaut."

My heart skipped a beat, the sheer joy of the moment making it flutter like a caged bird.

"It's not a complaint!" the voice hissed back. "It's just an explanation!"

"Just get out here, ya jabronis!" I shouted back, the edge of anticipation clearly audible.

The first to emerge was a golden cascade of hair, followed by a familiar face that could light up any room, or meadow in this case.

Calden.

The man we'd lost, the friend who'd died, stood before us, alive and very much in high spirits, albeit surveying his surroundings with a hint of suspicion.

A massive figure lumbered out behind him, scales glinting. Dedyc, the drakefolk, blinked in the brilliant light, his reptilian eyes adjusting to the sudden change.

But the parade wasn't done. A whirlwind of energy shot past Dedyc, twirling in a dance of joy. Merra, light and agile on her dwarven feet, spun around, taking in the splendor of the world outside the tunnel.

"Gods, it feels good to finally get some sun," she exclaimed, her face radiant with happiness. "I feel like it's been half a millennium since I sniffed fresh grass."

I sighed, content. It had been a hell of a last few days, but it had been worth it. Climbing into the Crypt—using Rexen's mysterious final words to reach the lake and revive those most dear to us.

"Truthfully, *this* is the future?" Calden wondered aloud, scowling theatrically. "Seems a bit too green, if you were to ask me."

"No 'un's askin', thankfully," Frida said, rolling her eyes.

"Yes, well, if they did, I would tell them to give it a bit more purple—or perhaps a hint of magenta," Calden said.

"You're the only person who would be revived and immediately start being bothered about . . . outdoor colors, Calden," I said. "You'd think you'd return with a renewed zest for life."

"Ah, but there is the issue, my dear Loon," he said with a big grin. "My zest was already preposterously high. Truly, there was nowhere to go but down."

I snorted.

"Alright, calm down," I said. "What's the first thing everyone's going to do when they get to . . . Karepalea?" I wondered aloud, finally having figured out how to say the damn name of the place.

"Oh, a bath, most certainly," Calden said. "Perhaps invite a few robust and vigorous folk to join me in my—"

"Ach! Calden!" Frida admonished. "Ye just came back! Donnae make me kill ye again right away."

"Yeah, Cal," I said. "Keep it behind your laces, Mr. Pantaloons."

He frowned, looking down at himself.

"What is the matter with my breeches?"

"Hey!" I said, noticing the roe were doing the weird climb-on-top-of-eachother thing again. "Jumpy, Clucky, Slappy, Mortimer . . . Chompy! Knock that off!"

The now-five roe looked back at me, embarrassed. I felt bad; they were just excited to have their brother back, and he was excited to *be* back.

Sorry. Apologies. Sorry. ZA! Vecciniua feraz!

I raised an eyebrow at Clucky.

Okay, what did we say about the arcane tongue?

I am. Very sorry . . .

"I think," Merra said, interrupting, "what we all need is a song!"

There was a round of cheers.

"Ooh, yes!" Rua shouted. "Let's do 'Jumper' by Third Eye Blind! In honor of the roe!"

"Yeah . . . that's not what that song is about, Rua," Saban said.

"No, shut up!" I said, but I was grinning, using less angry gusto than I would have formerly. "I have an idea."

"Oh?" Calden asked, catching my eye. "I think I know what you're attempting to rouse, however—"

"'Dragons in the Sky'!" I shouted excitedly.

Everyone looked to Jes. The last time the song had been performed, it was by him, and he'd been quite morose about it. Even crying. Every eye found his, and he sighed, then turned to the beautiful elf woman slung under his arm, walking next to him along the path.

"What do you say, Delyra?" He said, his tone . . . soft. Loving. Devoid of the undercurrent of morose sadness I'd long associated him with. "I know you have only just returned, but . . . well, your audience awaits."

Delyra, peach of hair and golden, tanned skin, smiled brightly, showing off pearly white teeth. The gal looked pretty damn good for having been—until very recently—dead for five hundred years. She inclined her head.

"Well, I suppose I cannot refuse my rescuers," she said. "'Dragons in the Sky' it is."

She removed the harp from Jes's pack and flashed another brilliant smile our way.

"Ready? Three, two, o—"

ABOUT THE AUTHOR

Seth McDuffee is the bestselling author of the novel *Good Boy* and Dungeon Master for the popular *Dungeons & Dragons* 5e podcast The d20 Syndicate, as well as a purveyor of fine soups.

www.ingramcontent.com/pod-product-compliance
Ingram Content Group UK Ltd.
Pitfield, Milton Keynes, MK11 3LW, UK
UKHW041304180426
11947UKWH00009B/665